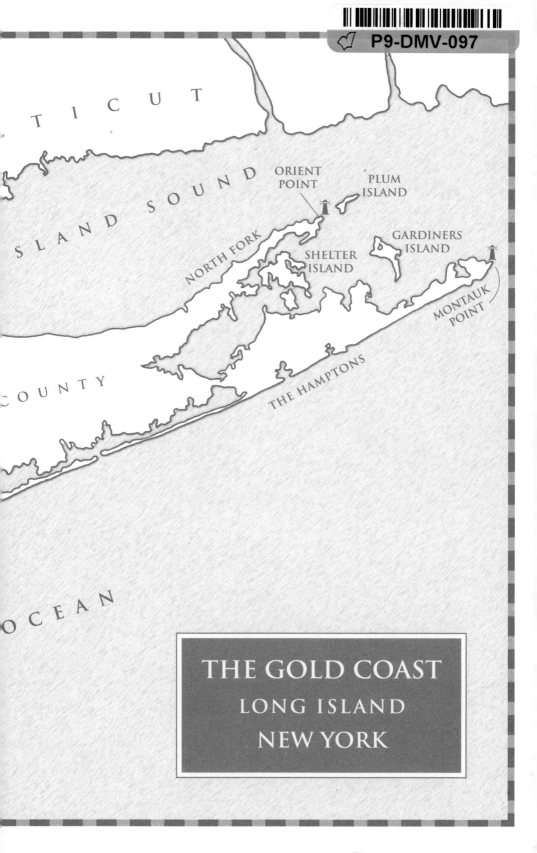

T I C U T

I S L A N D   S O U N D

ORIENT
POINT

PLUM
ISLAND

NORTH FORK

SHELTER
ISLAND

GARDINERS
ISLAND

MONTAUK
POINT

COUNTY

THE HAMPTONS

OCEAN

THE GOLD COAST
LONG ISLAND
NEW YORK

The
Gate House

Nelson DeMille

The Gate House

GRAND CENTRAL
PUBLISHING

NEW YORK   BOSTON

Grand Central Publishing
Hachette Book Group
237 Park Avenue
New York, NY 10017
Visit our Web site at www.HachetteBookGroup.com.

Printed in the United States of America

First Edition: October 2008
10 9 8 7 6 5 4 3 2 1

Grand Central Publishing is a division of Hachette Book Group, Inc.
The Grand Central Publishing name and logo is a trademark of Hachette Book Group, Inc.

Library of Congress Cataloging-in-Publication Data

DeMille, Nelson.
    The gate house / Nelson DeMille.
        p.   cm.
      ISBN-13: 978-0-446-50540-6 (large print edition)
      ISBN-13: 978-0-446-53342-3 (regular edition)
      1. Large type books.   I. Title.

PS3554.E472G38   2008
813'.54—dc22   2008026065

This book is for
James Nelson DeMille,
a new chapter in my life.

── P R O L O G U E ──

*How beauteous is this garden; where the flowers of
the earth vie with the stars of heaven.
What can compare with the vase of yon alabaster
fountain filled with crystal water?
Nothing but the moon in her fulness, shining in the
midst of an unclouded sky!*

—Inscription on a wall of Alhambra Castle,
Granada, Spain
From Washington Irving, *The Alhambra*

It is a warm summer evening, and by the light of a full white moon, I, John Whitman Sutter, am watching my wife, Susan Stanhope Sutter, as she rides her horse Zanzibar across the quiet acres of Stanhope Hall, her ancestral estate.

The rising moon is eerily bright, and it illuminates the landscape with an unearthly glow, which transforms all color into silvery shades of blue and white.

Susan passes through a line of tall pines and enters a neighboring estate called Alhambra, and I wonder why she has trespassed on this property, and I hope she has gotten permission from Alhambra's new owner, a Mafia don named Frank Bellarosa.

Majestic trees cast long moon shadows over the grassy fields, and in the distance I can see the huge stucco villa, which is dark except for a light from the closed glass doors of a second-story balcony. That balcony, I know, leads to the library where Frank Bellarosa sits in his leather armchair.

Susan draws near to the house, then dismounts and tethers Zanzibar to a tree. She walks to the edge of a long marble reflecting pool set in a classical garden of mock Roman ruins.

At the far end of the pool is a statue of Neptune, holding aloft his trident, and at his feet, stone fish spout water from their gaping mouths into a large alabaster seashell, which overflows into the pool.

At the opposite end of the pool, closest to me, is a statue of the Virgin Mary, which is new, and which I know was put there by Bellarosa's wife as a counterbalance to the half-naked pagan god.

A soft, balmy breeze moves the cypress trees, and night birds begin their song. It is a beautiful evening, and Susan seems entranced by the moonlight and the enchanted garden. I, too, am mesmerized by this magical evening.

As I turn my attention back to Susan, she begins to take off her clothes, and she drapes each piece over the statue of the Virgin, which surprises and bothers me.

Susan moves to the edge of the pool, her red hair billowing in the breeze, and she is gazing down at her naked reflection in the water.

I want to take off my clothes and join her, but I notice that the light from the library has gone out, and the doors of the balcony are now open, though no one is there, and this gives me an uneasy feeling, so I stay where I am in the shadows.

Then I see a man silhouetted against the white walls of Alhambra, and he is moving in long, powerful strides toward the pool. As he comes closer, I see that it is Bellarosa, and he is wearing a black robe. He is now standing beside Neptune, and his face looks unnatural in the moonlight. I want to call out to Susan, but I can't.

Susan does not seem to see him, and she continues to stare down at her reflection, but Bellarosa's stare is fixed on Susan. I am incensed that this man is looking at my wife's naked body.

This scene stays frozen, Susan and Frank as motionless as the statues beside them, and I, too, am frozen, powerless to intervene, though I need to protect Susan.

Then I see that she has become aware of Bellarosa's presence, but she does not react. I don't understand this; she should not be standing naked in front of this man. I'm angry at her, and at him, and a stream of rage races through my mind, but I can't put this rage into words or sounds.

As I stare at Susan, she turns her back to the pool, and to Bellarosa, and I think she is going to leave. Then she turns her head in my direction, as though she's heard a sound. I make a move toward her, but suddenly she lifts her arms and springs backward into the pool, and in long, powerful strides, she moves naked through the moonlit water toward Frank Bellarosa. I look at him, and I see that he is now naked, standing with his arms folded across his chest. He is a large, powerfully built man, and in the moonlight he appears as imposing and menacing as the naked stone god beside him.

I want to shout out to Susan, to warn her to come back, but something tells me to stay silent—to see what happens.

Susan reaches the far end of the pool and lifts herself into the water-filled seashell, where she stands near the towering statue of Neptune. She is looking up at Bellarosa, who has not moved from the edge of the pool, except to turn his face toward her.

They stare at each other, unnaturally motionless, then Bellarosa steps into the shallow water of the seashell where he stands in front of Susan.

They are speaking, but all I can hear is the rushing sound of the spouting water. I am enraged at this scene, but I still can't believe that Susan wants to be there, and I wait for her to dive back into the pool and swim away from him. Yet the longer she remains standing naked in front of him, the more I realize that she has come here to meet him.

As I let go of any hope that Susan will dive back into the pool and swim away, she kneels into the shallow water, then moves her face into Bellarosa's groin and takes him into her mouth. Her hands grasp his buttocks and pull him closer to her face.

I close my eyes, and when I open them again, Susan is lying on her back in the scalloped seashell, her legs are spread wide and they dangle over the edge of the waterfall, and Bellarosa is now standing in the re-flecting pool, and he buries his face between her thighs. Then, suddenly, he pulls Susan's legs up so they rest on his shoulders, and he seems to rise out of the water as he enters her with a powerful thrust that forces a deep cry from her lips. He continues his rough thrusts into her until she screams so loudly it startles me.

"Mr. Sutter! Mr. Sutter! Sir, we are descending. Please fasten your seatbelt."

"What . . . ?"

"We're descending," a female voice said. "You need to fasten your seatbelt and put your seat in the full upright position."

"Oh . . ." I adjusted my seat and fastened my seatbelt, noticing that Little John was also in the full upright position. My goodness. That's embarrassing. What brought that on . . . ? Then, I remembered my dream . . .

I never asked Susan how, when, and where she began her affair with Frank Bellarosa—this is not the sort of information one needs to hear in any detail—but it was something that remained missing from what I did know. My shrink, if I had one, would say that my dream was an unconscious attempt to fill in this lacuna—the missing piece of the affair. Not that it mattered a decade after I divorced her. In legal terms, I charged adultery, and she admitted to it. The state did not require any juicy details or explicit testimony, so neither should I.

The British Airways flight from London to New York crossed over the Long Island Sound, descending toward John F. Kennedy International Airport. It was a sunny day, a little after 4:00 P.M., Monday, May 27, and I remembered that today was Memorial Day in America. Below, on the North Shore of Long Island, I could see a place called the Gold Coast, where I used to live, ten years ago. Probably, if I looked hard enough, I could see the large neighboring estates called Stanhope Hall, and what was once Alhambra.

I now live in London, and the purpose of my return to America is to see an old lady who is dying, or who may well have died during my seven-hour flight. If so, I'd be in time for the funeral, where I'd see Susan Stanhope Sutter.

The presence of death in the coffin should compel us into some profound thoughts about the shortness of life, and make us rethink our many disappointments, resentments, and betrayals that we can't seem to let go of. Unfortunately, however, we usually take these things to the grave with us, or to the grave of the person we couldn't forgive in life.

Susan.

But now and then, we do find it in our hearts to forgive, and it costs nothing to do that, except some loss of pride. And maybe that was the problem.

I was sitting on the starboard side of the business class cabin, and all heads were turned toward the windows, focused on the skyline of Manhattan. It's truly an awesome sight from three or four thousand feet, but as of about nine months ago, the main attraction for people who knew the city was the missing part of the skyline. The last time I'd flown into New York, a few weeks after 9/11, the smoke was still rising from the rubble. This time, I didn't want to look, but the man next to me said, "That's where the Towers were. To the left." He pointed in front of my face. "There."

I replied, "I know," and picked up a magazine. Most of the people I still knew here in New York have told me that 9/11 made them rethink their lives and put things into perspective. That's a good plan for the future, but it doesn't change the past.

The British Airways flight began its final descent into Kennedy, and a few minutes later we touched down.

The man next to me said, "It's good to be home." He asked, "Is this home for you?"

"No."

Soon I'd be in a rental car on my way back to the place I once called home, but which was now a place that time had partly eroded from my mind, washing away too many of the good memories and leaving behind the hard, jagged edges of the aforementioned disappointments, resentments, and betrayals.

The aircraft decelerated, then rolled out onto the taxiway toward the terminal.

Now that I was here, and would remain here until the funeral, perhaps I should use the time to try to reconcile the past with the present—then maybe I'd have better dreams on my return flight.

━ PART I ━

So we beat on, boats against the current,
borne back ceaselessly into the past.

—F. Scott Fitzgerald
The Great Gatsby

CHAPTER ONE

A week had passed since my return from London, and I was sitting at the table in the dining room of the small gatehouse of Stanhope Hall, my ex-wife's former estate, wading through old files, family photos, and letters that I'd stored here for the last decade.

After my divorce from Susan, I'd fulfilled an old dream by taking my sailboat, a forty-six-foot Morgan ketch named the *Paumanok II*, on a sail around the world, which lasted three years. Paumanok, incidentally, is the indigenous Indian word for Long Island, and my illustrious ancestor, Walt Whitman, a native Long Islander, sometimes used this word in his poetry—and if Uncle Walt had owned a forty-six-foot yacht, I'm sure he'd have christened it the *Paumanok*, not "I Hear America Singing," which is too long to put on the stern, or *Leaves of Grass*, which doesn't sound seaworthy.

Anyway, my last port of call was Bournemouth, England, from which my other distant ancestors, the Sutters, had set sail for America three centuries before.

With winter coming on, and sea fatigue in my bones, a dwindling bank account, and my wanderlust satisfied, I sold the boat for about half what it was worth and moved up to London to look for a job, eventually signing on with a British law firm that needed an American tax lawyer, which is what I was in New York before I became captain of the *Paumanok II*.

I spread out some photos of Susan on the table and looked at them under the light of the chandelier. Susan was, and probably still is, a beautiful woman with long red hair, arresting green eyes, pouty lips, and the perfect body of a lifelong equestrian.

I picked up a photo that showed Susan on my first sailboat, the original *Paumanok*, a thirty-six-foot Morgan, which I loved, but which I'd scuttled in Oyster Bay Harbor rather than let the government seize it for back taxes. This photo was taken, I think, in the summer of 1990 somewhere on the Long Island Sound. The photograph showed a bright summer day, and Susan was standing on the aft deck, stark naked, with one hand covering her burning bush, and the other covering one breast. Her face shows an expression of mock surprise and embarrassment.

The occasion was one of Susan's acted-out sexual fantasies, and I think I was supposed to have climbed aboard from a kayak, and I'd discovered her alone and naked and made her my sex slave.

The woman had not only a great body, but also a great imagination and a wonderful libido to go with it. As for the sexual playacting, its purpose, of course, was to keep the marital fires burning, and it worked well for almost two decades because all our infidelities were with each other. At least that was the understanding, until a new actor, don Frank Bellarosa, moved in next door.

I picked up a bottle of old cognac that I'd found in the sideboard and topped off my coffee cup.

The reason I've returned to America has to do with the former residents of this gatehouse, George and Ethel Allard, who had been old Stanhope family retainers. George, a good man, had died a decade ago, and his wife, Ethel, who is not so nice, is in hospice care and about to join her husband, unless George has already had a word with St. Peter, the ultimate gatekeeper. "Wasn't I promised eternal rest and peace? Can't she go someplace else? She always liked hot weather." In any case, I am the attorney for Ethel's estate and so I needed to take care of that and attend her funeral.

The other reason I've returned is that this gatehouse is my legal U.S. address, but unfortunately, this house is about to pass into the hands of Amir Nasim, an Iranian gentleman who now owns the main house, Stanhope Hall, and much of the original acreage, including this gatehouse. As of now, however, Ethel Allard has what is called a life estate in the gatehouse, meaning she has a rent-free tenancy until she dies. This rent-free house was given to her by Susan's grandfather, Augustus Stanhope (because Ethel was screwing Augustus way back when), and Ethel has been kind enough to allow me to store my things here and share her digs whenever I'm in New York. Ethel hates me, but that's another story. In any case, Ethel's tenancy in this house and on this planet is about to end, and thus I had returned from London not only to say goodbye to Ethel, but also to find a new home for my possessions, and find another legal U.S. address, which seems to be a requirement for citizenship and creditors.

This is the first time I'd been to New York since last September, coming in from London as soon as the airplanes were flying again. I'd stayed for three days at the Yale Club, where I'd maintained my membership for my infrequent New York business trips, and I was shocked at how quiet, empty, and somber the great city had become.

I'd made no phone calls and saw no one. I would have seen my daughter, Carolyn, but she had fled her apartment in Brooklyn right after 9/11 to stay with her mother in Hilton Head, South Carolina. My son, Edward, lives in Los Angeles. So for three days, I walked the quiet streets of the city, watching the smoke rising from what came to be known as Ground Zero.

Heartsick and drained, I got on a plane and returned to London, feeling that I'd done the right thing, the way people do who come home for a death in the family.

Over the next few months, I learned that I knew eleven people who'd died in the Twin Towers; mostly former neighbors and business associates, but also a close friend who left a wife and three young children.

And now, nine months after 9/11, I was back again. Things seemed to have returned to normal, but not really.

I sipped my coffee and cognac and looked around at the piles of paper. There was a lot to go through, and I hoped that Ethel would hold on a while longer, and that Mr. Nasim wasn't planning on getting his encumbered gatehouse into his possession the minute Ethel's life tenancy expired. I needed to speak to Mr. Nasim about that; speaking to Ethel about hanging on until I tidied up my papers might seem insensitive and selfish.

Because the night was cool, and because I didn't have a paper shredder, I had a fire going in the dining room fireplace. Now and then, I'd feed the fire with some letter or photo that I wouldn't want my children to see if I suddenly croaked.

In that category were these photos of their mother whose nakedness revealed a lot more about her head than about her body. Susan was, and I'm sure still is, a bit nutty. But to be honest, I didn't mind that at all, and that wasn't the source of our marital problems. Our problem, obviously, was Susan's affair with the Mafia don next door. And then to complicate things further, she shot and killed him. Three shots. One in the groin. *Ouch.*

I gathered the photos and turned in my chair toward the fireplace. We all have trouble parting with things like this, but I can tell you, as a lawyer and as a man, no good can come of saving anything you wouldn't want your family or your enemies to see. Or your next significant other, for that matter.

I stared into the fire and watched the flames dancing against the soot-blackened brick, but I held on to the photos.

So, she shot her lover, Frank "the Bishop" Bellarosa, *capo di tutti capi*, boss of all bosses, and got away with it—legally, at least—due to some circumstances that the Justice Department found mitigating and extenuating.

Fact is, the Justice Department took a dive on the case because they'd made the mistake of allowing Mrs. Sutter unobstructed access to don Bellarosa, who was under house arrest in his villa down the road, and who was also singing his black heart out to them, and thus needed to be kept happy with another man's wife.

I'm still a little pissed off at the whole thing, as you might guess, but basically I'm over it.

Meanwhile, I needed to decide if this trip was a death vigil, or perhaps something more permanent. I had kept up with my CLE—continuing legal education—and I was still a member of the New York State Bar, so I hadn't burned *all* my bridges, and theoretically I was employable here. In my last life, I had been a partner in my father's old firm of Perkins, Perkins, Sutter and Reynolds, still located at 23 Wall Street, a historic building that was once bombed by Anarchists at the turn of the last century, which seems almost quaint in light of 9/11.

For the last seven years in London, I'd worked for the aforementioned British law firm, and I was their American tax guy who explained that screwing the Internal Revenue Service was an American tradition. This was payback for me because the IRS had screwed up my life, while my wife was screwing the Mafia don. These two seemingly disparate problems were actually related, as I had found out the hard way.

I guess I'd hit a patch of rough road back then, a little adversity in an otherwise charmed and privileged life. But adversity builds character, and to be honest, it wasn't all Susan's fault, or Frank Bellarosa's fault, or the fault of the IRS, or my stuffed-shirt law partners; it was partly my own fault because I, too, was involved with Frank Bellarosa. A little legal work. Like representing him on a murder charge. Not the kind of thing I normally did as a Wall Street lawyer, and certainly not the kind of case that Perkins, Perkins, Sutter and Reynolds would approve of. Therefore, I'd handled this case out of my Locust Valley, Long Island, office, but that wasn't much cover when the newspapers got hold of it.

Thinking back on this, I couldn't help but know I was committing professional and social suicide when I took a Mafia don as a client. But it was a challenge, and I was bored, and Susan, who approved of and encouraged my association with Frank Bellarosa, said I needed a challenge. I guess Susan was bored, too, and as I found out, she had her own agenda regarding Frank Bellarosa.

And speaking of Susan, I had discovered through my son, Edward, that, quote, "Mom has bought our house back."

Bad grammar aside—I sent this kid to great schools—what Edward meant was that Susan had reacquired the large guest cottage on the Stanhope estate. This so-called cottage—it has six bedrooms—had been our marital residence for nearly twenty years, and is located about a quarter mile up the main drive of the estate. In other words, Susan and I were now neighbors.

The guest cottage and ten acres of property had been carved out of the two hundred sixty acres of the Stanhope estate by Susan's father, William, who's an insufferable prick, and deeded to Susan as a wedding gift. Since I was the groom, I always wondered why my name wasn't on the deed. But you need to understand old money to answer that. You also need to understand pricks like William. Not to mention his ditsy wife, Susan's mother, Charlotte. These two characters are unfortunately still alive and well, living and golfing in Hilton Head, South Carolina, where Susan had been living since the unfortunate gun mishap that took her lover's life ten years ago.

Before Susan left for South Carolina, she'd sold the guest cottage to a yuppie corporate transfer couple from someplace west of the Hudson. You know your marriage is in trouble when your wife sells the house and moves to another state. In truth, however, it was I who ended the marriage. Susan wanted us to stay together, making the obvious point that her lover was dead, and thus we needn't worry about bumping into him at a party. In fact, she claimed that was why she'd killed him; so we could be together.

That wasn't quite it, but it sounded nice. In retrospect, we probably could have stayed together, but I was too angry at being cuckolded, and my male ego had taken a major hit. I mean, not only did our friends, family, and children know that Susan was fucking a Mafia don, but the whole damned country knew when it hit the tabloids: "Dead Don Diddled Lawyer's Heiress Wife." Or something like that.

It may have worked out for us if, as Susan had suggested, I'd killed her lover myself. But I wouldn't have gotten off as easily as she had. Even if I'd somehow beaten the murder rap—crime of passion—I'd have some explaining to do to don Bellarosa's friends and family.

So she sold the house, leaving me homeless, except, of course, for the Yale Club in Manhattan, where I am always welcome. But Susan, in a rare display of thoughtfulness, suggested to me that Ethel Allard, recently widowed, could use some company in the gatehouse. That actually wasn't a bad idea, and since Ethel could also use a few bucks in rent, and a handyman to replace her recently deceased husband, I'd moved into the extra bedroom and stored my belongings in the basement, where they'd sat for this past decade.

By spring of the following year, I'd made a financial settlement with my partners and used the money to buy the forty-six-foot Morgan, which I christened *Paumanok II*. By that time, my membership in the Seawanhaka Corinthian Yacht Club had been terminated by mutual consent, so I sailed from the public marina where I'd bought the boat and began my three-year odyssey at sea.

Odysseus was trying to get home; I was trying to get away from home. Odysseus wanted to see his wife; maybe I did, too, but it didn't happen. I'd told Susan I would put in at Hilton Head, and I almost did, but within sight of land, I headed back to sea with just a glance over my shoulder. Clean break. No regrets.

I threw the nude photos of Susan on the table, instead of in the fireplace. Maybe she wanted them.

I poured more cognac into the dregs of the coffee and took a swallow.

I looked up at a large, ornately framed, hand-colored photo portrait of Ethel and George Allard, which hung over the mantel.

It was a wedding picture, taken during World War II, and George is dressed in his Navy whites, and Ethel is wearing a white wedding dress of the period. Ethel was quite a looker in her day, and I could see how Susan's grandfather, Augustus, who was then lord of Stanhope Hall, could cross the class line and fiddle with one of his female servants. It was inexcusable, of course, on every level, especially since George, a Stanhope employee, was off to war, protecting America from the Yellow Peril in the Pacific. But, as I found out as a young man during the Vietnam War, and as I'm discovering with this new war, war tears apart the social fabric of a nation, and you get a lot more diddling and fiddling going on.

I stared at Ethel's angelic face in the photograph. She really *was* beautiful. And lonely. And George was out of town for a while. And Augustus was rich and powerful. He was not, however, according to family accounts, a conniving and controlling prick like his son, my ex-father-in-law, William. I think Augustus was just horny (it runs in the Stanhope family), and if you look at a picture of Augustus' wife, Susan's grandmother, you can see why Augustus strayed. Susan, I guess, got her good looks from her mother, Charlotte, who is still attractive, though brainless.

And on the subject of brains and beauty, my children have both, and show no signs of the Stanhope tendency to be off their rockers. I'd like to say my children take after my side of the family, but my parents aren't good examples of mental health either. I think I was adopted. I hope and pray I was.

Actually, my father, Joseph, passed away while I was at sea, and I missed the funeral. Mother hasn't forgiven me. But that's nothing new.

And on the subject of children, paternity, and genetics, Ethel and George had one child, a daughter, Elizabeth, who's a nice woman and who lives in the area. Elizabeth gets her beauty from her mother, but looks enough like George to put my mind at ease about any more Stanhope heirs.

I'm taking the long view of this in terms of my children inheriting some of the Stanhope fortune. They deserve some money for putting up with Grandma and Grandpa all their lives. So do I, but a probate court might find my claim on the Stanhope estate—to reimburse me for years of putting up with William's bullshit—to be frivolous.

In any case, there is a history here—my own family goes back three hundred years on Long Island—and this history is entwined like the English ivy that covers the gatehouse and the guest cottage; interesting to look at from a distance, but obscuring the form and substance of the structure, eventually eating into the brick and mortar.

F. Scott Fitzgerald, sitting not too far from where I was now, had it right when he concluded *The Great Gatsby* with, "So we beat on, boats against the current, borne back ceaselessly into the past." Amen.

As I reached for the cognac, I noticed a stack of old greeting cards held together by a rubber band, and I slid a card out at random. It was a standard Hallmark anniversary card, and under the pre-printed words of love, joy, and devotion, Susan had written, "John, you don't know how many times I wake up in the morning and just stare at you lying beside me. And I will do this for the rest of my life."

I gathered the stack of cards and threw them in the fireplace.

I got up, went into the kitchen, and poured another coffee, then went out the back door and stood on the patio. I could see the lights of the guest cottage, where I used to live with my wife and children. I stood there a long time, then went back inside and sat again at the dining room table. I didn't think this would be easy, but I certainly didn't think it would be so hard.

CHAPTER TWO

I stared at the fire for some time, sipping coffee and cognac, my mind drifting between past and present.

So, I thought, I'm here in the gatehouse of the Stanhope estate, partly because Ethel Allard had an affair with Augustus Stanhope during World War II, and partly because my wife had an affair with a Mafia don. As Mr. Bellarosa himself would say, if he were alive, "Go figure."

And now, according to Edward—and confirmed by my daughter, Carolyn—Susan, a.k.a. Mom, had shown up on the doorstep of the yuppie couple and made them an unsolicited and probably spectacular offer for their home, convincing them, I'm sure, that they'd be happier elsewhere and that she, Susan Stanhope Sutter, needed to return to her ancestral roots.

Knowing Susan, I'm certain this couple felt as though they were being evicted for using the wrong decorator. Or maybe they knew that Mrs. Sutter had killed a Mafia don, and they thought this was an offer they shouldn't refuse. In any case, it was a done deal, and my former wife was now back in our former house, within the walls of the former Stanhope estate, and a five-minute walk up the drive from my temporary lodgings. It was as though someone had turned back the clock a decade and captured that brief moment in time when Susan and I were still living within walking distance of each other, and all it might have taken for us to be together was a phone call, a knock on the door, or a note. But that time had passed, and we'd both written new chapters in our histories.

Susan, for instance, had remarried. The lucky man was, according to Edward, "an old guy," and with age comes patience, which one would need to be married to Susan Sutter.

Edward had also described the gentleman as "a friend of Grandpa's, and really boring." The boring old guy's name was Dan Hannon, and he had lived down in Hilton Head, and as per Edward, played golf all day, and had some money, but not a lot, and as per Carolyn, "Mom likes him, but doesn't love him." Carolyn added, "She kept our last name."

My children apparently thought I needed to know all of this, just in case I wanted to go down to Hilton Head, smack Dan on the head with a golf club, and carry Susan off to an island.

Well, before I could do that, Dan Hannon played his last round of golf and dropped dead, literally on the eighteenth hole while unsuccessfully attempting an eight-foot putt. Edward said that Mr. Hannon's golf partners gave him the shot, finished the hole, then called an ambulance. I think Edward is making up some of this.

In any case, Susan has been widowed for almost a year now, and according to Carolyn, Susan and her hubby had very tight prenuptial agreements, so Susan got only about half a million, which is actually not that bad for five years of marriage, boring or not. My own prenup with Susan Stanhope gave me the wedding album. The Stanhopes are tough negotiators.

And so here we are again, and we can see the lights from each other's house, and the smoke from our chimneys. And I've seen Susan's car pass by the gatehouse and out the big wrought-iron gates. She drives an SUV (these things seem to have multiplied like locusts in my absence); I think it's a Lexus. Whatever, it still has South Carolina plates, and I know that Susan has kept her Hilton Head house. So maybe she intends to split the year between here and there. Hopefully, more there than here. Though, on second thought, what difference does it make to me? I'm only passing through.

My car is a rented Taurus that I park beside the gatehouse, so she knows when I'm home, but she hasn't stopped by with home-baked brownies.

I don't actually follow her movements, and it's rare that I've seen her car passing by in the last week. The only other car I've noticed is a Mercedes that belongs to Mr. Nasim, the owner of the mansion. What I'm getting at is that I don't think Susan has a boyfriend. But if she did, I wouldn't be surprised, and I wouldn't care.

As for *my* love life, I'd been totally abstinent during my three-year cruise around the world. Except, of course, when I was in port, or when I had a female crew member aboard. In fact, I was a piggy.

I suppose there are all sorts of complex psychological reasons for my overindulgence, having to do with Susan's adultery and all that. Plus, the salt air makes me horny.

But I had calmed down considerably in London, partly as a result of my job, which required a suit and a bit of decorum, and partly as a result of having gotten rid of the sailboat, and not being able to use clever lines like, "Do you want to sail with me on my yacht to Monte Carlo?"

Anyway, for my last year or so in London, I've had a lady friend. More on that later.

I stoked the fire, then freshened my coffee with cognac.

Regarding the former Mrs. Sutter, as it stands now, neither of us has called on the other, nor have we bumped into each other on the property or in the village, but I know we'll meet at Ethel's funeral. To be honest, I'd half expected that she'd come by to say hello. Probably she had the same expectation.

This place is heavy on etiquette and protocol, and I wondered how Emily Post would address this situation. "Dear Ms. Post, My wife was fucking a Mafia don, then she shot and killed him, and we got divorced, and we both moved out of the state and met other people whom we didn't kill. Now we find ourselves as neighbors, and we're both alone, so should I bake brownies and welcome her to the neighborhood? Or should she do that? (Signed) Confused on Long Island."

And Ms. Post might reply, "Dear COLI, A gentleman should always call on the lady, but always phone or write ahead—and make sure she's gotten rid of that gun! Keep the conversation light, such as favorite movies (but not *The Godfather*) or sports or hobbies (but not target shooting), and don't overstay your visit unless you have sex. (Signed) Emily Post."

Well, I think I'm being silly. In any case, my children are bugging me about calling her. "Have you seen Mom yet?" I'm sure they ask her the same question.

I'd actually seen Susan a few times over the last decade since we'd both left Long Island—at our children's college graduations, for instance, and at the funeral of my aunt Cornelia, who was fond of Susan. And on these occasions, Susan and I had always been polite and cordial to each other. In fact, she had been friendlier to me than I to her, and I had the impression she had gotten over me and moved on. I, on the other hand . . . well, I don't know. And I had no intention of finding out.

On the subject of funerals, I'd attended Frank Bellarosa's funeral because . . . Well, I actually liked the guy, despite the fact that he was a criminal, a manipulator, a sociopathic liar, and my wife's lover. Other than that, he wasn't a bad guy. In fact, he was charming and charismatic. Ask Susan.

Also on the subject of funerals, the one I was really excited about attending was the one for William Stanhope. But last I heard from Edward, "Grandpa's feeling pretty good." That's too bad.

I picked up the stack of photos again and flipped through them. She really was beautiful and sexy. Smart and funny, too. And, as I said, delightfully nutty.

As I stared at a particularly sexy photo of Susan mounted naked on her stupid horse, Zanzibar, the doorbell rang.

Like most gatehouses, this one is built inside the estate wall, so no one can come to my door unless they pass through the iron gates that face the road. The gates remain closed at night, and they are automated, so you need a code or a remote control to open them, and I can usually hear them or see the headlights at night, which I hadn't. Therefore, whoever was at my door had come on foot from the estate grounds, and the only current residents of the estate were Amir Nasim, his wife, their live-in help, Susan, and me.

So it could be Mr. Nasim at my door, perhaps to pay a social call, or to inform me that Ethel died two minutes ago, and I had ten minutes to move out. Or possibly it was Susan.

I slipped the photos back into the envelope and walked into the small front foyer as the bell rang again.

I checked myself out in the hallway mirror, straightened my polo shirt and finger-combed my hair. Then, without looking through the peephole or turning on the outside light, I unbolted the door and swung it open.

Standing there, staring at me, was the ghost of Frank Bellarosa.

CHAPTER THREE

He said, "Do you remember me?"

It was not, of course, the ghost of Frank Bellarosa. It was Frank's son Tony, whom I had last seen at his father's funeral, ten years ago.

I get annoyed when people ask, "Do you remember me?" instead of having the common courtesy to introduce themselves. But this, I suspected, was not Tony Bellarosa's most irritating social flaw, nor his only one. I replied, "Yes, I remember you." I added, in case he thought I was winging it, "Tony Bellarosa."

He smiled, and I saw Frank again. "Anthony. It's Anthony now." He inquired, "You got a minute?"

I had several replies, none of which contained the word "Yes." I asked him, "What can I do for you?"

He seemed a little put off, then asked, "Can I come in? Oh . . ." He seemed suddenly to have thought of the only logical explanation for my slow response to the doorbell and my not being thrilled to see him, and he asked, "You got somebody in there?"

A nod and a wink would have sent him on his way, but I didn't reply.

"Mr. Sutter?"

Well, you're not supposed to invite a vampire to cross your threshold, and I think the same rule applies for sons of dead Mafia dons. But for reasons that are too complex and too stupid to go into, I said, "Come in."

I stepped aside, and Anthony Bellarosa entered the gatehouse and my life. I closed the door and led young Anthony into the small sitting room.

I indicated a rocking chair—Ethel's chair—near the ash-heaped fireplace, and I took George's threadbare wingback chair facing my guest. I did not offer him a drink.

Anthony did a quick eye-recon of the room, noting, I'm sure, the shabby furnishings, the faded wallpaper, and the worn carpet.

Also, he may have been evaluating some personal security issues. His father used to do this, more out of habit than paranoia. Frank Bellarosa also had an unconscious habit of checking out every female in the room while he was checking to see if anyone might want to kill him. I admire people who can multitask.

In the case of Susan Sutter, however, Frank had missed some crucial clues and signs of trouble. If I could speculate about those last few minutes of Frank Bellarosa's life, I'd guess that the blood in Frank's big brain had flowed south into his little brain at a critical moment. It happens. And when it does, the rest of your blood can wind up splattered around the room, as happened to poor Frank.

Anthony said, "Nice little place here."

"Thank you." In fact, these old estate gatehouses looked quaint and charming on the outside, but most of them were claustrophobic. I don't know how I managed to share this cottage with Ethel, even for the short time I was here. I recall going out a lot.

Anthony asked me, "You lived here for a while. Right?"

"Right."

"And you're back from London. Right?"

I wondered how he knew that.

"But this Arab who owns the mansion owns this place, too. Right?"

"Right." I further informed him, "He's an Iranian."

"Right. A fucking Arab."

"The Iranians are not Arabs."

"What are they?"

"Persians."

This seemed to confuse him, so he changed the subject and asked, "So, you're . . . what? Buying it? Renting it?"

"I'm a houseguest of Mrs. Allard."

"Yeah? So, how's the old lady?"

"Dying."

"Right. No change there."

Obviously, he'd been making inquiries. But why?

"So what happens after she dies?"

I informed him, "She goes to heaven."

He smiled. "Yeah? And where do you go?"

"Wherever I want." I suppose I should find out what plans Mr. Nasim had for this house. Maybe he wanted to rent it by the month. But rental prices and sale prices were astronomical on the Gold Coast of Long Island, and they'd actually been going up since 9/11 as thousands of people were quietly abandoning the city out of . . . well, fear.

"Mr. Sutter? I said, how long are you staying?"

"Until she dies." I looked at him in the dim light of the floor lamp. I suppose you'd say Anthony Bellarosa was handsome in a way that women, but not men, would think is handsome. Like his father, his features were a little heavy—the women would say sensual—with full lips and dark liquidy eyes. His complexion, also like his father's, was olive— his mother, Anna, was very fair—and his well-coiffed hair, like Frank's, was dark and wavy, but probably longer than Pop would have liked. No doubt Anthony—also like his father—did well with the ladies.

He was dressed more casually than his father had dressed. Frank always wore a sports jacket with dress slacks and custom-made shirts. All in bad taste, of course, but at least you knew that don Bellarosa dressed for his image. In the city, he wore custom-made silk suits, and his nickname in the tabloids had been "Dandy Don," before it became "Dead Don."

"So, when she dies, then you leave?"

"Probably." Anthony was wearing scrotum-tight jeans, an awful Hawaiian shirt that looked like a gag gift, and black running shoes. He also wore a black windbreaker, maybe because it was a chilly night, or maybe because it hid his gun. The dress code in America had certainly gone to hell in my absence.

He said, "But you don't know where you're going. So maybe you'll stay."

"Maybe." Anthony's accent, like his father's, was not pure low-class, but I heard the streets of Brooklyn in his voice. Anthony had spent, I guess, about six years at La Salle Military Academy, a Catholic prep school on Long Island, whose alumni included some famous men, and some infamous men, such as don Bellarosa. No one would mistake the Bellarosa prep school accents for St. Paul's, where I went, but the six years at boarding school had softened Anthony's "dese, dose, and dems."

"So, you and the old lady are, like, friends?"

I was getting a little annoyed at these personal questions, but as a lawyer I know questions are more revealing than answers. I replied, "Yes, we're old friends." In fact, as I said, she hated me, but here, in this old vanished world of gentry and servants, of ancient family ties and family retainers, of class structure and noblesse oblige, it didn't matter much at the end of the day who was master and who was servant, or who liked or disliked whom; we were all bound together by a common history and, I suppose, a profound nostalgia for a time that, like Ethel herself, was dying but not yet quite dead. I wondered if I should explain all this to Anthony Bellarosa, but I wouldn't know where to begin.

"So, you're taking care of the place for her?"

"Correct."

Anthony nodded toward the opening to the dining room, and apropos of the stacks of paper, said, "Looks like you got a lot of work there." He smiled and asked, "Is that the old lady's will?"

In fact, I had found her will, so I said, "Right."

"She got millions?"

I didn't reply.

"She leave you anything?"

"Yes, a lot of work."

He laughed.

As I said, I am Ethel's attorney for her estate, such as it is, and her worldly possessions are to pass to her only child, the aforementioned Elizabeth. Ethel's will, which I drew up, left me nothing, which I know is exactly what Ethel wanted for me.

"Mr. Sutter? What were you doing in London?"

He was rocking in the chair, and I leaned toward him and inquired, "Why are you asking me all these questions?"

"Oh . . . just making conversation."

"Okay, then let me ask you a few conversational questions. How did you know that Mrs. Allard was dying?"

"Somebody told me."

"And how did you know I was living in London, and that I was back?"

"I hear things."

"Could you be more specific, Mr. Bellarosa?"

"Anthony. Call me Anthony."

That seemed to be as specific as he was going to get.

I looked at his face in the dim light. Anthony had been about seventeen or eighteen—a junior or senior at La Salle—when my wife murdered his father. So, he was not yet thirty, but I could see in his eyes and his manner that unlike most American males, who take a long time to grow up, Anthony Bellarosa was a man, or at least close to it. I recalled, too, that he used to be Tony, but that diminutive lacked gravitas, so now he was Anthony.

More importantly, I wondered if he'd taken over his father's business.

The most fundamental principle of American criminal law is that a person is innocent until proven guilty. But in this case, I recalled quite clearly what Frank Bellarosa had said about his three sons. "My oldest guy, Frankie, he's got no head for the family business, so I sent him to college, then set him up in a little thing of his own in Jersey. Tommy is the one in Cornell. He wants to run a big hotel in Atlantic City or Vegas. I'll set him up with Frankie in Atlantic City. Tony, the one at La Salle, is another case. He wants in."

I looked at Anthony, formerly known as Tony, and recalled Frank's pride in his youngest son when he concluded, "The little punk wants my job. You know what? If he wants it bad enough, he'll have it."

I suspected that Tony did get the job and became don Anthony Bellarosa. But I didn't know that for sure.

Anthony asked me, "Is it okay if I call you John?"

"I'm Tony now." It's probably not a good idea to make fun of a possible Mafia don, but I did it with his father, who appreciated my lack of ring-kissing. In any case, I needed to establish the pecking order.

Anthony forced a smile and said, "I remember calling you Mr. Sutter."

I didn't reply to that and asked him, "What can I do for you, Anthony?"

"Yeah, well, I'm sorry to just drop in, but I was driving by, and I saw the lights on here, and like I said, I heard you were back, so the gate was closed and I came in through the . . . what do you call it? The people gate."

"The postern gate."

"Yeah. It was unlocked. You should lock that."

"I'm not the gatekeeper."

"Right. Anyway, so I got this idea to stop and say hello."

I think it was a little more premeditated than that. I said to him, "I hope you're not blocking the gate."

"No. My driver took the car up the road. Hey, do you remember Tony? My father's driver."

"I remember that *he* used to be Anthony."

He smiled. "Yeah. We made a deal. Less confusing."

"Right." I didn't think the dead don's driver had much to say about that deal. Regarding the family business, the surviving employees, and the rules of succession, I recalled quite clearly that there was another member of the family who wanted Frank Bellarosa's job, so, to see how Anthony reacted, I asked, "How is your uncle Sal?"

Anthony Bellarosa stared at me and did not reply. I stared back.

The last time I'd seen Salvatore D'Alessio, a.k.a. Sally Da-da, was at Frank's funeral. Prior to my wife clipping Frank Bellarosa, someone else had attempted the same thing, and the prime suspect was Uncle Sal. This had occurred at a restaurant in Little Italy, at which I was unfortunately present and close enough to Dandy Don Bellarosa and Vinnie, his bodyguard, to get splattered with Vinnie's blood. Not one of my better nights out.

In any case, Uncle Sal was not present at the failed hit, of course, but his signature was most probably on the contract. I hate it when families squabble, and though I'm personally familiar with the problem, none of the Sutters or Stanhopes, to the best of my knowledge, have ever taken out a contract on a family member . . . though it's not a bad idea. In fact, I think I just found some use for Anthony Bellarosa. Just kidding. Really.

Anthony finally replied, "He's okay."

"Good. Give your uncle Sal my regards when you see him."

"Yeah."

There are some things in life that you never forget, and those months during the spring and summer leading up to Frank's death in October and my leaving Susan are filled with sights and sounds that are truly burned into my mind forever. In addition to seeing Vinnie's head blown off with a shotgun right in front of my face, another sight that I will never forget is of young Anthony Bellarosa at his father's graveside. The boy held up extremely well—better than his mother, Anna, who was wailing and fainting every few minutes—and in Anthony's eyes I could see something beyond grief, and I saw him staring at his uncle Sal with such intensity that the older man could not hold eye contact with his young nephew. It was obvious to me, and to everyone, that the boy knew that his uncle had tried to kill his father. It was also obvious that Anthony Bellarosa would someday settle the score. So I was surprised to discover that Uncle Sal was still alive and well—and that Uncle Sal hadn't killed Anthony yet.

These gentlemen, however, as I'd learned in my brief association with don Bellarosa and his extended family, were extremely patient and prudent when considering who needed to be whacked, and when.

On that subject, I wondered how Anthony felt about Susan Sutter, who'd succeeded where Uncle Sal had failed. Now that Susan was back—about four hundred yards from here, actually—I wondered . . . but maybe that was a subject best left alone, so I stuck to family chatter and asked Anthony, "How is your mother?"

"She's good. Back in Brooklyn." He added, "I'll tell her I saw you."

"Please pass on my regards."

"Yeah. She liked you."

"The feeling was mutual." Hanging over this conversation, of course, was the awkward fact that my then-wife had made Anna Bellarosa a widow, and made Anthony and his two brothers fatherless. I asked, "And your brothers? Frankie and Tommy, right?"

"Right. They're doing good." He asked me, "How about your kids?"

"They're doing fine," I replied.

"Good. I remember them. Smart kids."

"Thank you."

The road that passes by Stanhope Hall and Alhambra, Grace Lane, is private and dead ends at the Long Island Sound, so Anthony Bellarosa was not just passing through, and I had the thought that he still lived in this area, which was not a good thought, but I wanted to know, so I asked him, "Where are you living?"

He replied, "On my father's old estate." He added, "There's some houses built there now, and I bought one of them." He explained, "They're called Alhambra Estates. Five-acre zoning."

I didn't reply, but I recalled that as part of Frank's stay-out-of-jail deal with the government, he'd had to forfeit Alhambra for unpaid taxes on illegal earnings and/or for criminal penalties. The last time I was on the property after Frank's death, the magnificent villa had been bulldozed, and the acreage had been subdivided into building plots to maximize the income to the government, and also for spite.

I'd actually driven past the former estate a few times since I'd been back, and I'd caught a glimpse of the new houses through the wrought-iron gates, and what I saw were mini-Alhambras with red-tiled roofs and stucco walls, as though the rubble of the main mansion had regenerated into small copies of itself. I wondered if the reflecting pool and the statue of Neptune had survived.

Anyway, I now discovered that Anthony Bellarosa had purchased one of these tract villas. I wasn't sure if this was ironic, symbolic, or maybe Anthony had simply gotten a good deal from the builder, Dominic, who was a *paesano* of Frank's.

Anthony seemed to be brooding about his lost patrimony and informed me, "The fucking Feds stole the property."

It annoys me when people (like my ex-wife) rewrite history, especially if I was present at the historical moment in question. Anthony, however, may not have actually known the circumstances surrounding his lost birthright, but he could certainly guess if he had half a brain and a willingness to face the facts.

Apparently, he had neither of these things, and he continued, "The fucking Feds stole the property and put my family out on the street."

Against my better judgment, I informed Anthony, "Your father *gave* Alhambra to the government."

"Yeah. They put a gun to his head, and he gave it to them."

I should have just ended his unannounced visit, but he had a few more points to make, and I was . . . well, maybe worried about Susan. I mean, she was still the mother of my children. I looked closely at Anthony. He didn't *look* like a killer, but neither did his father. Neither did Susan for that matter. I'll bet Frank was surprised when she pulled the gun and popped off three rounds.

Anthony was expanding on his subject and said, "They used the fucking RICO law and grabbed everything they could get their hands on after he . . . died." Anthony then gave me a historical parallel. "Like the Roman emperors did when a nobleman died. They accused him of something and grabbed his land."

I never actually thought of Frank Bellarosa as a Roman nobleman, but I could see the Justice Department and the IRS in the role of a greedy and powerful emperor. Nevertheless, I lost my patience and informed him, "The Racketeer Influenced and Corrupt Organizations Act is tough, and not always fairly applied, but—"

"It sucks. What happened to due process?"

"Do you have a law degree, Mr. Bellarosa?"

"No. But—"

"Well, I do. But let's forget the law here. I happen to know, firsthand, that your father agreed to hand over certain assets to the Justice Department in exchange for . . ." I could see that Anthony Bellarosa knew where this was going, and he did not want to hear that his father had broken the only law that counted—the law of *omertà*—silence.

So, under the category of speaking only well of the dead, I said to Anthony, "Your father owed some back taxes . . . I was his tax advisor . . . and he settled for turning over some assets to the Treasury Department, including, unfortunately, Alhambra." Frank had also forfeited this property, Stanhope Hall, which he'd purchased, I think at Susan's urging, from my idiot father-in-law William. But I wasn't sure Anthony knew about that, and I didn't want to get him more worked up, so I just said, "It wasn't a bad deal."

"It was robbery."

In fact, it was surrender and survival. I recalled what Frank Bellarosa had told me when he was under house arrest, trying to justify his cooperation with the Feds. "The old code of silence is dead. There're no real men left anymore, no heroes, no stand-up guys, not on either side of the law. We're all middle-class paper guys, the cops and the crooks, and we make deals when we got to, to protect our asses, our money, and our lives. We rat out everybody, and we're happy we got the chance to do it."

Frank Bellarosa had concluded his unsolicited explanation to me by saying, "I was in jail once, Counselor, and it's not a place for people like us. It's for the new bad guys, the darker people, the tough guys."

Anthony glanced at me, hesitated, then said, "Some guys said . . . you know, my father had enemies . . . and some guys said he was . . . selling information to the government." He glanced at me again, and when I didn't respond, he said, "Now I see that it was only tax problems. They got him on that once before."

"Right."

He smiled. "Like Al Capone. They couldn't get Capone on bootlegging, so they got him for taxes."

"Correct."

"So, bottom line, Counselor, it was you that told him to pay up."

"Right. That's better than facing a criminal tax charge." In fact, it was Frank Bellarosa who had helped *me* beat a criminal tax charge. Frank had actually engineered the tax charge against me, as I later found out, so the least he could do was get me off the hook. Then I owed him a favor, which I repaid by helping him with his murder charge. Not surprisingly, Frank's role model was Niccolò Machiavelli, and he could quote whole passages of *The Prince*, and probably write the sequel.

Anthony asked me, "So, the Feds taking his property had nothing to do with the murder charge against him?"

"No." And that was partly true. Ironically, Frank the Bishop Bellarosa, probably the biggest non-government criminal in America, hadn't committed the murder he was charged with. There was undoubtedly little else he hadn't done in twenty or thirty years of organized criminal activities, but this charge of murdering a Colombian drug lord had been a setup by the U.S. Attorney, Mr. Alphonse Ferragamo, who had a personal vendetta against Mr. Frank Bellarosa.

Anthony said to me, "You were one of his lawyers on that murder rap. Right?"

"Right." I was actually his only lawyer. The so-called mob lawyers stayed out of sight while John Whitman Sutter of Perkins, Perkins, Sutter and Reynolds stood in Federal criminal court in the unaccustomed role of trying to figure out how to get a Mafia don sprung on bail. Frank *really* didn't like jail.

Anthony asked me, "Do you know that the FBI found the guys who clipped the Colombian?"

"I know that." I'd actually heard this a few years ago from my daughter, who's an assistant district attorney in Brooklyn, and she was happy to tell me that I'd defended an innocent man. The words "innocent" and "Frank Bellarosa" are not usually used in the same sentence, but within the narrow limits of this case, I'd done the right thing, and so I was redeemed. Sort of.

Anthony informed me, "That scumbag, Ferragamo, had a hard-on for my father."

"True." Fact was, Mr. Ferragamo, the U.S. Attorney for the Southern District of New York, wanted to bag the biggest trophy in his jungle—Frank Bellarosa. And he didn't care how he did it. The murder indictment was bogus, but eventually Alphonse Ferragamo, like a jackal nipping away at a great cape buffalo, had brought down his prey.

Anthony continued his eulogy. "Nothing that scumbag charged ever stuck. It was all bullshit. It was *personal*. It was *vendetta*."

"Right." But it was business, too. Frank's business and Alphonse's business. Don Bellarosa was an embarrassment to the U.S. Attorney. Some of it—maybe more than I understood—was the Italian thing. But professionally, Alphonse Ferragamo couldn't allow the biggest

Mafia don in the nation to walk around free, living in a mansion, riding in expensive cars, and eating in restaurants that Alphonse Ferragamo couldn't afford. Actually, I guess that's personal.

So Ferragamo, through various means, legal and not so, finally got his teeth on the big buffalo's balls, and Frank Bellarosa went down and screamed for mercy.

It's part of our culture to romanticize the outlaw—Billy the Kid, Jesse James, the aforementioned Al Capone, and so forth—and we feel some ambivalence when the outlaw is brought down by the sanctimonious forces of law and order. Dandy Don Bellarosa, a.k.a. the Bishop, was a media darling, a source of endless public entertainment, and a celebrity. So when the word got out that he was under "protective custody" in his Long Island mansion, and cooperating with the Justice Department, many people either didn't believe it, or felt somehow betrayed. Certainly his close associates felt betrayed and very nervous.

But before Frank Bellarosa could be paraded into a courtroom as a government witness, his reputation had been saved by Susan Sutter, who killed him. And his death at the hands of his married girlfriend, a beautiful red-haired society lady, only added to his posthumous legend and his bad-boy reputation.

The husband of the Mafia don's girlfriend (me) got pretty good press, too. But not good enough to make it all worthwhile.

Oddly, Susan didn't come off too well in the tabloids, and there was a public outcry for justice when the State of New York and the U.S. Attorney dropped any contemplated charges against her, which would have been premeditated murder and murdering a Federal witness, and whatever.

I missed a lot of this media fun by sailing off, and Susan missed some of it by moving to Hilton Head. The New York press quickly loses interest in people who are not in the contiguous boroughs or the surrounding suburban counties.

Anyway, to be honest, objective, and fair, the people who suffered the most in this affair—aside from Frank—were the Bellarosa family. They were all innocent civilians at the time of this crime of passion.

Anthony may have made his bones since then, but when he lost his father he was a young student in prep school.

So I said to him, "I knew your father well enough to know that he did what he had to . . . to get the Feds off his back so that he'd be around for his wife and sons."

Anthony did not reply, and I used that silence to change the subject. He was wearing a wedding ring, so I said, "You're married."

"Yeah. Two kids."

"Good. A man should be married. Keeps him out of trouble."

He thought that was funny for some reason.

Rather than beat around the bush, I asked him, "What business are you in?"

He replied without hesitation, "I took over my father's company. Bell Enterprises. We do moving and storage, trash carting, limo service, security service . . . like that."

"And who took over your father's other businesses?"

"There was no other businesses, Mr. Sutter."

"Right." I glanced at my watch.

Anthony seemed in no hurry to get up and leave, and he informed me, "My father once said to me that you had the best combination of brains and balls he'd ever seen." He added, "For a non-Italian."

I didn't reply to that, and I wasn't sure how I felt about hearing it. Aside from the fact that it was a qualified compliment (non-Italian), I needed to consider the source.

Anthony's visit obviously had a purpose beyond reminiscing about the past and welcoming me to the neighborhood. In fact, I smelled a job offer. The last time I'd worked for a Bellarosa, it had ruined my life, so I wasn't anxious to try it again.

I started to rise, and Anthony said, "I just need a few more minutes of your time."

I sat back in the wingback chair and said to him, "Please get to the point of your visit."

Anthony Bellarosa seemed lost in thought, and I watched him. He had none of the commanding presence of his father, but neither was he a weenie trying to fill Pop's handmade shoes; Anthony was the real thing, but not yet a finished product of his environment. Also, I had the impression he was toning down his inner thugishness for my benefit. And that meant he wanted something.

Finally, he said, "I ask around a lot about my father, from his friends and the family, and they all have these great things to say about him, but I thought since he really respected you . . . maybe you could give me some . . . like, something about him that his paesanos didn't understand. You know?"

I know that people want to hear good things about their dearly departed from those who knew them, and clearly the boy idolized his father, so the alleged purpose of Anthony's visit was to hear John Whitman Sutter—Ivy League WASP—say something nice and grammatical for the record. Then why did I think I was on a job interview? I replied, "I knew him for only about . . . oh, six months."

"Yeah, but—"

"I'll think about it."

"Okay. And maybe think about how I can repay you for what you did."

"What did I do?"

"You saved his life."

I didn't reply.

"The night at Giulio's. When someone shot him. You stopped the bleeding."

What in the world was I thinking when I did that? I mean, by that time, I was sure that he was screwing my wife. Not only that, it's not a good idea to interfere with a Mafia hit. I mean, someone—in this case Salvatore D'Alessio—paid good money to have Frank Bellarosa clipped, and I screwed it up. So under the category of "no good deed goes unpunished," Frank, after he recovered, hinted to me that his brother-in-law, Mr. D'Alessio, was not happy with me. I wondered if Uncle Sal was still annoyed. Or maybe, since my wife killed Frank afterwards, all was forgiven. Maybe I should ask Anthony to ask his uncle about that. Maybe not.

"Mr. Sutter? You saved his life."

I replied, "I did what anyone who was trained in first aid would have done." I added, "You don't owe me anything."

"It would make me feel good if I could return that favor."

I clearly recalled Frank's favors to me, which were not helpful, and I was certain that Anthony's favors also came with a few strings attached. So, to nip this in the bud, and make myself perfectly clear, I said, "As it turned out, all I did was save your father's life so my wife could kill him later."

This sort of caught Anthony by surprise; he probably thought I wasn't going to bring up the actual cause of his father's death. I mean, Frank Bellarosa did not die from natural causes, unless getting shot by a pissed-off girlfriend was a natural cause in his universe.

To make my point more clear, I said, "Your father was fucking my wife. But I guess you know that."

He didn't reply for a few seconds, then said, "Yeah . . . I mean, it was in the papers."

"And do you know that she's back?"

"Yeah. I know."

"How do you feel about that?"

He looked me right in the eye and replied, "I think she should have stayed away."

"Me, too. But she didn't." We locked eyeballs and I said to him, "I assume there will not be a problem, Anthony."

He held eye contact and said, "If we were going to have that kind of problem, Mr. Sutter, it wouldn't matter if she was living on the moon. Capisce?"

I was sure now that I was speaking to the young don, and I said, "*That* is the favor you can do for me."

He thought a moment, then said, "I don't know what happened between them, but it was personal. So, when it's personal between a man and a woman, then . . . we let it go." He added, "There's no problem."

I recalled that when Frank Bellarosa said there was no problem, there was a problem. But I let it go for now, making a mental note to follow up with Anthony Bellarosa on the subject of not whacking my ex-wife. I mean, she hadn't done *me* any favors lately, but as I said, she's the mother of my children. I would point this out to Anthony, but then he'd remind me that Susan had left him without a father. It's incredible, if you think about it, how much trouble is caused by putting Tab A into Slot B.

In any case, I'd really had enough strolling down memory lane, and I'd made my point, so I stood and said, "Thanks for stopping by."

He stood also, and we moved into the foyer. I put my hand on the doorknob, but he stood away from the door. He asked me, "You seen your wife yet?"

"My ex-wife. No, I have not."

"Well, you will. You can tell her everything's okay."

I didn't reply, but I thought that Susan Stanhope Sutter had probably not given a single thought to the fact that she'd moved back into the neighborhood where she murdered a Mafia don. And by now, she must have heard that Anthony lived on the old Alhambra estate. Maybe she planned to pay a belated condolence call on Anthony since she hadn't attended her lover's funeral. I'm not being entirely facetious; Susan has this upper-class belief that just because you shoot a man, it doesn't mean you shouldn't be polite to his friends and family.

Anthony suggested, "Maybe we can go to dinner some night."

"Who?"

"Us."

"Why?"

"Like, just to talk."

"About?"

"My father. He really respected you."

I wasn't sure I felt the same about don Bellarosa. I mean, he wasn't pure evil. In fact, he was a good husband and good father, except for the extramarital affairs and getting his youngest son into organized crime. And he could be a good friend, except for the lying and manipulating, not to mention fucking my wife. He also had a sense of humor, and he laughed at my jokes, which showed good intellect. But did I respect him? No. But I liked him.

Anthony said, "My father trusted you."

I'm sure Anthony really did want to know about his father; but he also wanted to know more about me, and why his father thought so highly of me. And then . . . well, like his father, he'd make me an offer

I should refuse. Or was I being egotistical, or overly suspicious of Anthony's neighborly visit?

Anthony saw that I was vacillating, so he said, "I'd consider it a favor."

I recalled that these people put a high value on favors, whether they were offered or received, so I should not take the word lightly. On the other hand, one favor needed to be repaid with another, as I found out the hard way ten years ago. Therefore, absolutely no good could come of me having anything further to do with Anthony Bellarosa.

But . . . to blow him off might not be a good idea in regard to my concern about Susan. And if I was very paranoid, I'd also consider my own concern about Salvatore D'Alessio. As Frank once explained to me, "Italian Alzheimer's is when you forget everything except who pissed you off."

Anyway, there were still some blasts from the past that perhaps needed discussion, and with those thoughts in mind I made my second mistake of the evening and said, "All right. Dinner."

"Good." He smiled and asked, "How about Giulio's?"

I really didn't want to return to the restaurant in Little Italy where Frank took three shotgun blasts. Bad memories aside, I didn't think the owner or staff would be happy to see me show up with Junior. I said, "Let's try Chinese."

"Okay. How about tomorrow night?"

It was Monday, and I needed about forty-eight hours to come to my senses, so I said, "Wednesday. There's a place in Glen Cove called Wong Lee. Let's say eight."

"I can pick you up."

"I'll meet you there."

"Okay. It'll just be us." Anthony reminded me, "You don't want to mention the time and place to anybody."

I looked at him, and our eyes met. I nodded, and he said, "Good."

I started to open the door, but Anthony said, "Just a sec." He pulled out his cell phone, speed-dialed, and said, "Yeah. Ready." He hung up and asked me, "You want to come out and say hello to Tony?"

I wouldn't have minded some fresh air, but as I learned at Giulio's, it's a good rule not to stand too close to anyone who needs a body-guard, so I said, "Perhaps another time."

He apparently needed a minute to be sure he wouldn't be standing alone on a dark road, so to pass the time, he asked me, "How come you haven't seen her?"

"I'm busy."

"Yeah? Is she busy? She got a boyfriend?"

"I have no idea."

He looked at me and surprised me with a deep philosophical in-sight by saying, "This is all pretty fucked up, isn't it?"

I didn't reply.

His cell phone rang, and he glanced at the display but did not an-swer. He said to me, "Thanks for your time."

I opened the door and said, "Thank you for stopping by."

He smiled and said, "Hey, you looked like you saw a ghost."

"You have your father's eyes."

"Yeah?" He put out his hand, and we shook. He said, "See you Wednesday."

He walked out into the chill air, and I watched him go through the small postern gate and out to the road where Tony stood beside a big black SUV of some sort. What happened to the Cadillacs? The SUV was running, but its headlights were off, and Tony had his left hand on the door handle and his right hand under his jacket.

Some of this was a little melodramatic, I thought, but you might as well follow the drill. You just never know. Then, I thought, maybe there's an open contract out on Anthony Bellarosa. And I'm having dinner with this guy?

Before the boys completed the drill, I closed the door and went back into the dining room, where I poured myself a cup of cognac.

"Right. Pretty fucked up."

CHAPTER FOUR

The following day, I drove my Taurus along Skunks Misery Road, one of a number of roads around here with less than appealing names, which you'd think the residents or realtors might want to change—but these are historic names, some going back to the 1600s, plus people who are worth a zillion bucks wouldn't care if their estate was on a road called Chicken Shit Lane. It actually adds to the charm.

The Gold Coast is a collection of colonial-era villages and hamlets on the North Shore of Long Island's Nassau County, about twenty-five to thirty miles east of Manhattan. Some of these villages have quaint downtowns, and some, like Lattingtown, where Stanhope Hall is located, are exclusively residential, a quiltwork of grand estates, smaller estates with pretensions, and new McMansion subdivisions built on former estates.

In its day—between the Gilded Age and the Roaring Twenties, which ended on Black Tuesday, October 29, 1929—the Gold Coast of Long Island held the largest concentration of power and wealth in the world. You couldn't throw a stone without hitting a billionaire. Since then, the Depression, the war, income tax, and the spreading suburbs had delivered what should have been mortal blows to this Garden of Eden of old money, old families, and old customs; but it's hung on, a shadow of its former self, though now, with all this new Wall Street wealth, I sense a resurrection of the form, though not the substance, of this vanished world.

The Village of Locust Valley is the quintessential Gold Coast village, and that was my destination. My modest goal was a sandwich; specifically, Black Forest ham with Muenster cheese and mustard on pumpernickel bread. I'd been thinking about that for a week or so, and now the time had come. This sandwich could be obtained at Rolf's German Delicatessen, which I hoped had not succumbed to gentrification, food fads, or healthy eating habits.

It was a perfect June day, mid-seventies, mostly sunny with a few fair-weather clouds in a light blue sky. The flowers were in bloom, and the big old trees were fully leafed and fluttering in a soft breeze. Outside the car, the birds were singing and bees were pollinating exquisite flowers while butterflies alighted on the little pug noses of perfect children, causing them to giggle to their nannies, "Oh, Maria, isn't it wonderful to be rich?"

Being back here had sharpened my memories of why I was still teed off after a decade. I mean, I'd gotten on with my life, and my three-year sail, complete with a few life-threatening episodes, had been sufficiently cathartic and distracting so that I didn't dwell on the past. And the seven years in London never seemed like an exile, or a place where I'd gone to escape the past. But now that I've returned, I feel that the past has been waiting patiently for me.

On a more positive note, most of these familiar sights brought back some good memories. I mean, I was born here, and grew up here, and got married and raised children here, and I still had family and friends here. And then I left. Maybe that's why I'm still angry; it shouldn't have turned out this way—and wouldn't have if Frank Bellarosa hadn't been screwing my wife, or vice versa.

I continued my drive down memory lane, which was now called Horse Hollow Road, and passed my former country club, The Creek. This brought back a lot of memories, too, such as the time Susan and I took don Bellarosa and his gaudily dressed wife, Anna, to the club for dinner. The members were not pleased, and looking back on it, I was not displaying good judgment. But it *was* pretty funny.

Anyway, it was Tuesday, near noon, and the day after Anthony Bellarosa had dropped by for what I knew had been an exploratory visit. I couldn't believe I'd actually made a dinner date with this guy. As one of *my* own *paesanos* once said, "If you are going to sup with the devil, bring a long spoon." Or, in this case, long chopsticks. Better yet, cancel that dinner.

This was my first trip to the village since I'd returned, and as I approached I noted the familiar landmarks. This area was settled in 1667 by the English, including my ancestors, and the residents have been resisting change ever since, so there wasn't too much new in the quaint hamlet. It's all about the zoning.

I turned onto Birch Hill Road, the old main street, and cruised through Station Plaza, where I used to take the Long Island Railroad for my fifty-minute commute into Manhattan. In the plaza was McGlade's Pub, where Susan would sometimes meet me when I got off the train. Thinking back, I now wondered how many times she'd had afternoon sex with Frank Bellarosa before having drinks with me.

I slowed down as I approached my former law offices, where I used to put in a day or two each week to break up the commute into the city. The Locust Valley branch of Perkins, Perkins, Sutter and Reynolds had been housed in a Victorian mansion at the edge of town. The mansion was still there, and it was still a law office, but the ornate sign on the front lawn now read: JOSEPH P. BITET & JUSTIN W. GREEN, ATTORNEYS-AT-LAW.

I didn't recognize those names, and not seeing my name on the sign was a bit of a shock, though it shouldn't have been.

If this was a *Twilight Zone* episode, I'd now enter the building and see that the furniture was different, and I'd say to the receptionist, "Where's Kathy?" and the lady would look at me, puzzled, and reply, "Who?"

"My receptionist."

"Sir? How can I help you?"

"I'm John Sutter. This is my office. Why is my name not on the sign?"

And the lady would say, "Just a moment, sir," then disappear and call the police, who would come and take me away as I was ranting about this being my office, and demanding they find my secretary, or call my wife to straighten this all out. Then Rod Serling's voice-over would say, "John Whitman Sutter thought he'd just returned to his office after lunch—but he'd been gone longer than that . . . in the Twi-light Zone."

I doubled back toward the center of the village. Anyone from west of the Hudson who was dropped into this little town would not mistake Birch Hill Road for Main Street USA. For one thing, there are an inordinate number of imported luxury cars on the street, and the stores, I noticed, were still mostly antiques and boutiques, art galleries, and restaurants, with not a Starbucks to be seen.

I'd been avoiding Locust Valley, where I probably still knew a lot of people, but now that I was here, I could imagine a chance encounter with a former friend or neighbor. "Hello, John. Where have you been, old boy?"

"Around the world on my boat, then London. I left about ten years ago."

"Has it been that long? How is Susan?"

"We got divorced after she shot her Mafia lover."

"That's right. Damned shame. I mean, the divorce. Why don't we have lunch at the club?"

"I'm never allowed to set foot in The Creek or Seawanhaka for the rest of my life."

"You don't say? Well, you look wonderful, John. Let me know when you're free."

"I'll send my man around with some dates. Ciao."

Anyway, I turned onto Forest Avenue and found a parking space near Rolf's German Delicatessen, which I used to frequent whenever I got tired of Susan's organic compost.

I was glad to see that the deli was still there, but inside, I discovered that there had been a Mexican invasion, and the English language was not on the menu.

Nevertheless, I ordered in my usual brusque New York manner, "Black Forest ham, Muenster, mustard, on pumpernickel."

"Mister?"

"No, *Muenster.*"

"Muster."

"No. Good Lord, man, I'm ordering a *sandwich.* What part of that order couldn't you understand?"

"Blaforesam. Yes?"

I could hear the soundtrack from *The Twilight Zone* in my head, and I whispered, "Where's Rolf? What have you done with Rolf?"

He made a joke and said, "He go, amigo."

"Right." Anyway, I didn't want a German sandwich made in Mexico, so I said, "Just give me a coffee with leche. Milko. Okay?"

"Okay."

I got my coffee and left.

A few doors down was a new gourmet food shop, and as I sipped my coffee, I moved toward the shop window to look at the menu. Suddenly, the door opened and out walked Susan Stanhope Sutter. I stopped dead in my tracks, and I felt a thump in my chest.

She would have seen me, not twenty feet away, if she hadn't been talking on her cell phone.

I hesitated. But having thought about this already, I decided to go up to her and say hello.

Susan sat at a small café table in front of the shop and, still talking on the phone, unpacked her lunch bag. Lady Stanhope laid out her paper napkin, plastic utensils, imported water, and salad exactly as it belonged at a well-set table.

It had been four years since I'd seen her, at my aunt Cornelia's funeral, and her red hair was a little shorter than I remembered, and her tan was browner than I'd ever seen it. She wore a frosty pink gloss on her pouty lips, and those catlike green eyes still looked like emeralds in the sunlight. I found myself thinking of those photographs of her nude on the boat.

I got rid of that image and noticed that she was wearing one of the standard Locust Valley outfits—tan slacks and a green polo shirt in which was hooked a pair of sunglasses. She had on a sports watch, but no other jewelry, not even a widow's wedding ring, and on the table was what I think was a Coach handbag to complete the look; simple and not too chic for an afternoon in the village. Most of all, it signaled that she was gentry, not townie.

Anyway, I drew a deep breath and took a step toward her, but before I could get into full gear, the shop door opened and another woman came out, glanced at me, then turned to Susan and sat down opposite her.

Susan got rid of her phone call, and she and her lunch companion began to chat.

I didn't know the lady, but I knew the type. She was somewhat older than Susan, but still dressed preppie, and her name was probably Buffy or Suki or Taffy, and she firmly believed that you can never be too rich or too thin.

I couldn't hear what they were saying, but I could tell that Taffy (or whatever her name was) spoke in the local dialect known as Locust Valley Lockjaw. Okay, I'll tell you. This is an affliction of women, mostly, but men are sometimes stricken with it, and it occurs usually in social situations when the speaker's teeth are clenched, and enunciation is accomplished by moving only the lips. This produces a nasal tone that's surprisingly audible and distinct, unless the speaker has a deviated septum.

Anyway, Taffy's lunch consisted of bottled water and yogurt with five grapes that she plucked from a thousand-dollar handbag. She and Susan seemed at ease with each other, and I couldn't tell if they were talking about something light, like men, or something important, like shopping.

I had this sudden urge to walk over to them and say something uncouth to Taffy, like, "Hi, I'm John Sutter, Susan's ex-husband. I divorced her because she was fucking a Mafia greaseball, who she then shot and killed."

But Taffy probably already knew that, since this was not the kind of local gossip one could hide or forget. This place thrived on scandal and gossip, and if everyone who had done something scandalous was ostracized, then the country clubs would be empty, and the house parties would be poorly attended.

There were, however, limits to bad behavior, and the Sutters taking the Bellarosas to dinner at The Creek was one such example. On the other hand, Mrs. Sutter having an affair with Mr. Bellarosa was not likely to get her stricken from the A-List. In fact, her presence at charity events, cocktail parties, and ladies' luncheons would be most desirable.

As for shooting your lover, well, it was not completely unheard of, and with a little spin, a tawdry crime of passion could be repackaged as a matter of honor. Bottom line on this was that Susan Sutter was a Stanhope, a name permanently entered into the Blue Book. Substitute any other local family name—Vanderbilt, Roosevelt, Pratt, Whitney, Grace, Post, Hutton, Morgan, or whatever—and you begin to understand the unwritten rules and privileges.

I watched Susan and Taffy lunching and talking, and I took a last look at Susan. Then I turned and walked to my car.

CHAPTER FIVE

The next day, Wednesday, was overcast, so I didn't mind spending the day in the dining room of the gatehouse, my mind sometimes focused on the paperwork at hand, sometimes wandering into the past that was spread before me.

I still hadn't burned the nude photos of Susan, and I thought again about actually giving them to her; they weren't exclusively mine, and she might want them. What would Emily Post say? "Dear Confused on Long Island, Nude photographs of a former spouse or lover should be returned, discreetly, via registered mail, and clearly marked, 'Nude Photographs—Do Not Bend.' An enclosed explanation is not usually necessary or appropriate, though in recent years the sender often indicates in a short note that the photographs have not been posted on the Internet. The recipient should send a thank-you note within ten days. (Signed) Emily Post."

On the subject of communication between ex-spouses, in my phone calls to and from Edward and Carolyn, they'd both given me their mother's new home phone number and told me that she had kept her South Carolina cell phone number. Plus, I had her e-mail address, though I didn't have a computer. Susan, of course, knew Ethel's phone number here, which hadn't changed since FDR was President. So . . . someone should call someone.

I went back to my paperwork. I found my marriage license and I also found my divorce decree, so I stapled them together. What came in between was another whole story.

Regarding my divorce decree, I'd need this in the unlikely event I decided to remarry. In fact, the lady in London, Samantha, had said to me, "Why don't we get married?" to which I'd replied, "Great idea. But who would have us?"

I'd spoken to Samantha a few times since I'd left London, and she wanted to fly to New York, but since the relationship was up in the air, Samantha wasn't up in the air.

I pulled a manila envelope toward me that was marked, in Susan's handwriting, "Photos for Album." They hadn't made it into any album and were not likely to do so. I spilled out the photos and saw that they were mostly of the Sutters, the Stanhopes, and the Allards, taken over a period of many years, primarily on holiday occasions—Christmas, Easter, Thanksgiving, birthdays, and all that.

The whole cast was there—William and Charlotte Stanhope and their wastrel son, Susan's brother, Peter, as well as Susan herself, looking always twenty-five years old.

Then there was me, of course, with Edward and Carolyn, and my parents, Joseph and Harriet, and in one of the photos was my sister Emily with her ex-husband, Keith. There was a nice shot of my aunt Cornelia and her husband, Arthur, now both deceased.

It was hard to believe that there was a time when everyone was alive and happy. Well, maybe not that happy, but at least encouraged to smile for the camera, helped along by a few cocktails.

As I looked at the photos, I couldn't believe that so many of these people were dead, divorced, or, worse, living in Florida.

I noticed an old photo of Elizabeth Allard, and I remembered the occasion, which was Elizabeth's college graduation party, held on the great lawn of Stanhope Hall, another example of noblesse oblige, which is French for, "Sure you can use our mansion, and it's not at all awkward for any of us." Elizabeth, I noticed, was a lot prettier than I remembered her. Actually, I needed to call her because she was the executrix of her mother's estate.

I pushed the photos aside, except for one of George and Ethel. Longtime family retainers often become more than employees, and the

Allards were the last of what had once been a large staff, which reminded me that I needed to go see Ethel. I needed to do this because I was her attorney, and because, despite our differences, we'd shared some life together, and she was part of my history as I was of hers, and we'd all been cast in the same drama—the Allards, the Sutters, and the Stanhopes—played on the stage of a semi-derelict estate in a world of perpetual twilight.

Tonight, I decided, was as good a time as any to say goodbye; in fact, there probably wasn't much time left.

But that reminded me that I had another date with destiny this evening: Mr. Anthony Bellarosa. I'd thought about canceling that dinner, but I didn't know how to reach him, and standing him up wouldn't make him go away.

On the subject of calling people, Ethel's pink 1970s princess phone was my only form of communication, and I used it sparingly, mostly to call Samantha, Edward, and Carolyn, and my sister Emily in Texas, whom I loved very much, and my mother who . . . well, she's my mother. As for incoming calls, a few of Ethel's elderly friends had called, and I told them the bad news of Ethel being in hospice. At that age, this news is neither shocking nor particularly upsetting. One elderly lady had actually called from the same hospice house, and she was delighted to hear that her friend was right upstairs, perched on the same slippery slope.

Ethel had no Caller ID, so each time the phone rang, I had to wonder if it was hospice, Mr. Nasim, Susan, or Samantha telling me she was at JFK. Ethel did have an answering machine, but it didn't seem to work, so I never knew if I'd missed any calls when I was out.

The idiotic cuckoo clock in the kitchen chimed four, and I took that as a signal to stretch and walk outside through the back kitchen door for some air.

The sky was still overcast, and I could smell rain. I stood on the slate patio and surveyed this corner of the old estate.

Amir Nasim had gardeners who cared for the diminished grounds, including the trees and grass around the gatehouse. Along the estate wall, the three crabapple trees had been pruned, but there would be no crabapple jelly from Ethel this year, or ever.

Beyond the patio was a small kitchen garden, and Ethel had done her spring planting of vegetables before she became ill. The garden was overgrown now with weeds and wildflowers.

And in the center of the neglected garden was a hand-painted wooden sign that was so old and faded that you couldn't read it any longer. But when it was a fresh, new sign, some sixty years ago, it had read VICTORY GARDEN.

I needed to remember to give that to Ethel's daughter, Elizabeth.

I could hear the wall phone ringing in the kitchen. I really hate incoming calls; it's rarely someone offering me sex, money, or a free vacation. And when it is, there are always strings attached.

It continued to ring, and without an answering machine, it kept ringing, as though someone knew I was home. Susan?

Finally, it stopped.

I took a last look around, turned, and went inside to get ready to see an old woman who was going to her final reward, and a young man who, if he wasn't careful, was going to follow in his father's footsteps to an early grave.

CHAPTER SIX

At 5:00 P.M., I drove through the magnificent wrought-iron gates of my grand estate and headed south on Grace Lane in my Lamborghini. Reality check: not my estate, and not a Lamborghini.

Grace Lane—named not for a woman, or for the spiritual state in which the residents believed they lived, but for the Grace family of ocean liner fame—was, and may still be, a private road, which means the residents own it and are supposed to maintain it. The last time I was here, my neighbors were trying to unload this expense on various local governments, who didn't seem anxious to bail out the rich sons of bitches of Grace Lane, some of whom were no longer so rich, but who nonetheless remained sons of bitches. The issue seems to have been resolved in my absence because Grace Lane was now well paved.

I continued south toward the village of Locust Valley, where I needed to stop to buy something for Ethel. One should never arrive empty-handed when paying a visit, of course, but I never know what to bring except for wine, and that wouldn't be appropriate for this occasion; likewise, flowers might seem premature.

Ethel enjoyed reading, so I could stop at the bookstore, but I shouldn't buy anything too long, like *War and Peace*. She also liked fruit, but I shouldn't buy green bananas. All right, I'm not being very nice, but when faced with the hovering presence of the Grim Reaper, a little humor (even bad humor) helps the living and the dying to deal with it. Right? So maybe she'd get a kick out of a gift certificate to Weight Watchers.

"Dear Ms. Post, I need to visit an elderly lady in hospice, whose time left on earth could be measured with a stopwatch. Why should I bother to bring her anything? (Signed) COLI. P.S. I don't like her."

"Dear COLI, Good manners don't stop at death's door. An appropriate gift would be a box of chocolates; if she can't eat them, her visitors can. If she dies before you get there, leave the chocolates and your calling card with the receptionist. It's the thought that counts. (Signed) Emily Post. P.S. Try to make amends if she's conscious."

I turned onto Skunks Misery Road, and within a few minutes found myself again in the village of Locust Valley. I hate shopping for anything, including cards and trivial gifts, so my mood darkened as I cruised Forest Avenue and Birch Hill Road, looking for some place that sold chocolates. I saw at least a dozen white SUVs that could have been Susan's, and it occurred to me that she was good at this sort of thing, so if I ran into her—figuratively, not literally—I'd ask her for some advice. The last gift advice I'd gotten from her—at Carolyn's graduation from Harvard Law—was that the T-shirt I'd bought for Carolyn in London, which, in Shakespeare's words, said, "The first thing we do, let's kill all the lawyers," was not a good law school graduation gift. She may have been right.

Anyway, I gave up on the chocolates, parked, and went into a florist shop.

A nice-looking young lady behind the counter asked how she could help me, and I replied without preamble, "I need something for an elderly lady who's in hospice and doesn't have much time left." I glanced at my watch to emphasize that point.

"I see . . . so—"

"I am not particularly fond of her."

"All right . . . then—"

"I mean, cactus would be appropriate, but she'll have other visitors, so I need something that looks nice. It doesn't have to last long."

"I understand. So perhaps—"

"It can't look like a funeral arrangement. Right?"

"Right. You don't want to . . . Why don't we avoid flowers and do a nice living plant?"

"How about hemlock?"

"No, I was thinking of that small Norfolk pine over there." She explained, "Evergreens are the symbol of eternal life."

"Really?"

"Yes, like, well, a Christmas tree."

"Christmas trees turn brown."

"That's because they're cut." She informed me, "We deliver a lot of living evergreens to hospice."

"Really?"

"Yes. They smell good. And the family can take them home as a memento afterwards."

"After what?"

"After . . . the . . . person . . ." She changed the subject and asked, "Which hospice is the lady residing at?"

"Fair Haven."

"We can deliver that for you."

"Actually, I'm on my way there now and that's too big to carry, so . . ." I looked around, and in the corner of the shop was a shelf lined with stuffed animals, including a few Teddy bears, which are big around here because the man who inspired the bear, Teddy Roosevelt, lived in nearby Oyster Bay. I took the best-looking Teddy bear from the shelf, put it on the counter, and said, "I'll take this."

"That's very nice." She put a pink ribbon around the bear's neck and stuck a sprig of lavender in the ribbon.

I paid in cash, and the young lady said to me, "She'll like that. Good luck."

Back in the car, I headed west toward the hospice house in Glen Cove. I glanced at the fluffy bear sitting beside me, and suddenly I felt a rush of emotion pass over me. It hit me that Ethel Allard was dying, and that so many of the people I once knew were dead, and in an instant I remembered all of them and saw their faces from long ago, smiling, usually in some social setting or holiday occasion, a drink close by, like in the photos I'd just seen.

Where, I wondered, had the years gone? And why hadn't I appreciated those moments when my world was safe, familiar, and intact?

Well, you can't go back, and even if I could, I'm not sure if I could have or would have changed anything that led to the end of my life as I knew it, or the end of Frank Bellarosa's life as he knew it.

Frank Bellarosa, on a cold winter day a decade ago, was driving from Brooklyn and heading to a restaurant in Glen Cove with some business associates for a meeting. They got off the Long Island Expressway, became lost, and somehow wound up on Grace Lane.

They spotted the abandoned estate called Alhambra, and, as Frank told me later, the Lombardy poplars that lined the driveway, and the red-tiled stucco villa, reminded him of his Italian roots. He made inquiries, and bought the estate. Then he moved in. Then I met him. Then Susan and I accepted his invitation to come by for coffee. Then a lot of things happened, ending with my wife murdering her new neighbor and lover.

And now, ten years later, the original cast of this tragedy—including the dead and the dying—has reassembled for the last and final act.

CHAPTER SEVEN

I headed west on Duck Pond Road, passing Friends Academy, a prep school founded by the local Quakers. Susan had gone to Friends, driven to class, she told me, in a big Lincoln by George Allard, who, as one of the last of the Stanhope servants, wore many hats, including a chauffeur cap.

The Gold Coast of the 1950s and early '60s, as I recalled, was in a state of transition between the old, pre-war world of Social Register families with dwindling fortunes, and the social upheavals that would sweep away most of what remained of the old order.

Many of these changes were for the better. George, for instance, ceased being a servant and became an employee. That didn't improve his driving, I'm sure, but it did give him weekends off.

As for Ethel the Red, as I secretly called her because she was a socialist, she never considered herself a servant (especially after she slept with Augustus Stanhope), and she's lived long enough to see many of her idealistic dreams realized.

A sign informed me that I had entered the Incorporated City of Glen Cove, which is actually a medium-sized town of about twenty thousand people—or more, if you count the newly arrived immigrants who did not bother with the citizenship requirements.

Glen Cove is located on Hempstead Harbor and the Long Island Sound, and like many north shore Long Island communities, it was founded by English settlers in the 1600s, including my distant ancestors, who, when they arrived, did not bother asking the local Matinecock Indians for citizenship applications or work visa permits.

Anyway, the white skins and the red skins lived in relative peace and harmony for a century, mostly as a result of the Indians dying from European diseases. The British occupied Long Island for much of the Revolution, and many of the local inhabitants remained loyal to the Crown, including, I confess, the Sutters, who still have this conservative streak in them—except for my late father, who was a liberal Democrat and who used to get into political arguments at Republican-dominated family gatherings. My crazy mother, Harriet, is also a progressive, and she and Ethel were always allies against the majority of unenlightened, repressive male pigs who once dominated the society of the Gold Coast.

But even that had been changing, and when I left here ten years ago, if you had a friend or neighbor who was a Democrat, you could talk about it openly without worrying about real estate values plummeting.

On the subject of war and politics, I was half listening to a conservative radio talk show, and I turned up the volume to listen to a caller saying, "We need to nuke them before they nuke us."

The host, trying to sound a bit rational, replied, "Okay, but *who* do we nuke?"

The caller answered, "All of them. Nuke Baghdad first so we don't have to send our boys there to get killed."

"Okay, but maybe we should just nuke the Al Qaeda training camps first. They'll all get the message."

"Yeah. Nuke the camps, too."

The host cut away for a commercial break that was preceded by the rousing patriotic music of John Philip Sousa, a former Long Island resident who seemed to be making a comeback.

There had been an amazing transformation in the political and social culture since 9/11, and it was sort of jarring if you hadn't been here to see it developing. Virtually every house had an American flag flying, including the shops and houses here in Glen Cove, not usually a bastion of conservatism. And nearly every vehicle had a flag on its antenna, or a decal on a window, or bumper stickers that said things like "9/11—Never Forget," or "Bin Laden—You Can Run, But You Can't

Hide," and so forth. Also, nearly everyone I'd seen in Locust Valley wore an American flag pin. Thinking about this, I had the distinct feeling that people had been checking out my car for signs that I was a loyal American.

Anyway, back to the last century, when Glen Cove became home to a large immigrant Italian population, who found work building and maintaining the grand mansions and estate grounds. This manual labor for the rich eventually morphed over the generations into successful Italian-American-owned construction companies, landscaping enterprises, and related endeavors.

This was a great American success story, but unfortunately, a side effect of the large Italian population of Glen Cove is the existence of a small but persistent group of gentlemen whose business is not landscaping. Thus it was that Mr. Frank Bellarosa from Brooklyn was on his way to Glen Cove, Long Island, a decade ago to meet some business associates at an Italian restaurant. Ironically, today, with GPS, he and his driver—was it Anthony, now known as Tony?—would not have gotten lost and wound up on Grace Lane, and Fate would have been sidetracked by satellite technology. Go figure.

I headed north on Dosoris Lane, a seventeenth-century road that led toward the Sound, and on which some Sutters had lived in centuries past.

I've never had occasion to visit the Fair Haven Hospice House, but the nice lady on the phone had given me good directions, and assured me that Mrs. Allard could have visitors—though she also cautioned that this situation could change by the time I arrived.

Dosoris Lane passed through what had once been eight great estates, all belonging to the Pratt family, and built by Mr. Charles Pratt of Standard Oil for himself and seven of his eight children. Why number eight didn't get an estate is a mystery to me, but I'm sure Charles Pratt had his reasons, just as William Peckerhead of Hilton Head had his reasons for deeding the Stanhope guest cottage and ten acres to Susan, as sole owner. Susan, of course, could have changed the deed, but that would have angered William, and we don't want to get Daddy angry.

On the subject of real estate, I always wondered what William Stanhope thought about Ethel Allard's life tenancy in the gatehouse. I never knew if William was aware that his father, Augustus, had been popping the chambermaid, or whatever Ethel's position was at the time. But he must have known if Susan, who told me the story, knew. And yet William never shared that family secret with me. Probably he was embarrassed—not by the sexual indiscretion of his father, but by the fact that the little servant girl got a good real estate deal from a Stanhope. As I said, Tab A does *not* go into Slot B—follow directions.

I passed one of the former Pratt estates, Killenworth, which was used as a weekend retreat for the Russian Mission to the United Nations. When the bad old Commies were around, there were KGB-type guards with guns and mean dogs at the iron gates. Now it looked peaceful and unguarded.

The ultimate rite of passage for boys—and even girls—when I was a kid growing up in Locust Valley, was to "cross the border" into the Soviet estate and play a dangerous game of hide-and-seek with the Russian guards and their dogs. The secret, incidentally, was raw ground beef—the dogs loved it.

We were more crazy than brave, I think, and we all had a story about some kid who had disappeared forever behind the Iron Curtain. I don't think any of those stories were true, and most kids who vanished from the neighborhood were later discovered to have moved away with their families on a corporate transfer or gone to boarding school.

The Russian guards, I'm sure, thought we were incredibly daring, resourceful, and courageous, and I'm certain this was reported back to Moscow and led directly to the collapse of the Soviet Empire and the end of the Cold War. Like most Cold War heroes, however, I and my idiot friends remain anonymous and unsung. Maybe someday the world will know what we did here, but until then, the Glen Cove Police will continue to carry us on their incident reports as unknown trespassers, vandals, and juvenile delinquents. That's okay. *We* know.

Up the road was the J. P. Morgan estate and the F. W. Woolworth estate, now both abandoned and partly developed, and as per directions, I turned left onto a private lane, which passed through some woods. Up ahead, I saw a big old white stone mansion with a slate roof. A sign directed me to VISITOR PARKING.

I pulled into the nearly empty lot, retrieved the Teddy bear, and got out of the car.

The sky had cleared and wispy white clouds scudded north toward the Sound, and big gulls glided low on the horizon. After three years at sea, I'd developed a sense for the weather and nature, and I felt that the Sound must be close by. In fact, I could smell a whiff of salt air, which made me nostalgic for the open ocean.

I walked toward the mansion, thinking, "Not a bad place to spend your last days on earth, Ethel, before the pearly gates swing open to welcome you to the Big Estate in the Sky. Rent-free for eternity and you don't have to sleep with the boss."

CHAPTER EIGHT

I entered the white building, which I could see had once been a private home. It's a good thing when these old estate houses can be recycled for another use, like a school, or museum, or, in this case, a nursing home and hospice house. That's better than the wrecker's ball and another upscale subdivision to house what seemed like an endless supply of Wall Street whiz kids whose mortgage credit rating somehow exceeded their IQs.

A nice lady at the desk greeted me, and in reply to my inquiry, she informed me that Ethel Allard was "doing as well as can be expected," which was probably as good as it got here. The only other likely responses were "not well, no visitors" and "passed away." I didn't think that "in the gym" was one of the likely status reports at Fair Haven.

The lady directed me to a small elevator in the lobby. "Second floor, room six."

I was alone in the elevator, which took a long time to ascend one flight, during which I listened to a piped-in minute of Vivaldi's *Four Seasons*—"Summer," if you're interested. I imagined the doors opening to a celestial landscape of white clouds and blue skies with pearly gates in the distance. I really needed a drink.

The doors, in fact, opened to a floral wallpapered corridor, in which stood a Lady in White. She greeted me by name, and introduced herself as Mrs. Knight, then said, "Call me Diane."

"Hello, Diane."

"Follow me, please."

I followed her down the long corridor. Mrs. Knight seemed like one of those health care professionals who was both stern and gentle, a result, no doubt, of having to deal with every conceivable human emotion in the House of the Dying.

She said to me as we walked, "Mrs. Allard is medicated for pain, so you may not find her as alert as you remember her."

"I understand."

"She is, however, lucid now, and all her mental faculties are intact."

"Good."

"Her pain is tolerable and manageable."

"That's good." I had the feeling I was supposed to be asking questions to elicit these statements, so I asked, "How are her spirits?"

"Remarkably good."

"Many visitors?"

"A few. Including your mother and your wife."

"My ex-wife." I inquired, "They're not here now, are they?"

"No." She glanced at my gift and said, "She's going to love that Teddy bear."

Mrs. Knight stopped at a door and said to me, "I'll go inside and tell her you're here." She added, "It's very good of you to come all the way from London to see her."

"Yes, well . . . she's a wonderful lady."

"Indeed, she is."

I wondered if there was another Ethel Allard here.

Mrs. Knight was about to open the door, but I asked, "How long . . . ? I mean—"

"Oh, I'd say about half an hour at most."

"Half an hour?"

"Yes, then she gets tired."

"Oh. No, I meant—"

"I'll stick my head in every ten minutes."

"Right. What I meant . . . I'll be in town for only a few more weeks, and I wondered if I'd have the opportunity to see her again." Mrs. Knight was either not following me, or didn't want to address the subject, so I asked bluntly, "How long does she have left to live?"

"Oh . . . well, we never speculate on that, but I'd say the end is near."

"How near? Two weeks?"

"Maybe longer." She informed me, "Ethel is a fighter."

"Three?"

"Mr. Sutter. I can't—"

"Right. I had an aunt once who—"

"You have no idea what I've seen here. Death is the great mystery of life, and so much depends on attitude and prayer."

"Right. I believe that. I've been praying for her." I need her house.

Mrs. Knight looked at me and delivered what I guessed was a well-rehearsed piece of wisdom, saying, "It's natural for us to want to hold on to our loved ones as long as possible. But that's selfish. Ethel has made peace with her condition, and she's ready to let go."

That sounded like one week, and I might need two more weeks in the gatehouse. I'd been encouraged by Mrs. Knight's assertion that Ethel was a fighter, which seemed now to contradict this report that Ethel was ready to let go. Rather than ask for a clarification, I tried a new tack and said, "I'm also her attorney—in addition to being her friend—and there is some paperwork to be drawn up and signed, so perhaps I should speak to her doctor about her . . . remaining time."

She nodded and said, "Her attending physician here is Dr. Jake Watral."

"Thank you." Maybe the key to my continued stay in the gatehouse was less in the hands of God or Dr. Watral and more in the hands of Amir Nasim, whom I should have called when I got here. Which prompted me to ask Mrs. Knight, "Has a Mr. Amir Nasim called on Mrs. Allard? Or phoned?"

She shook her head and replied, "I'm not familiar with that name." Mrs. Knight seemed anxious to move on, so she said, "I'll let her know you're here."

"Thank you."

She disappeared inside room six long enough for me to have a little guilt pang about my motives in wanting Ethel to keep fighting. I mean, putting aside my housing problem, Ethel's pain was under control, she was lucid, she had visitors, and she *did* have some paperwork to sign—so why shouldn't she hang in there? That's what her daughter, Elizabeth, would want her to do.

Mrs. Knight reappeared and said to me, "She's waiting for you."

I moved toward the door, then turned back to Diane Knight and said to her, "You are a saint to work here."

A sweet, embarrassed smile passed quickly over her stern lips, and she turned and walked away.

I entered Ethel's room and gently pulled the door closed behind me.

God, how I hate deathbeds.

CHAPTER NINE

I t was a west-facing room, and the sun came in through the single window, casting a shaft of light across the white sheets of Ethel's bed.

The room was small, probably once a guest room or a servant's room, and it was furnished with two institutional nightstands, on one of which sat a monitor, and on the other a Bible. There were two faux-leather armchairs and a rolling tray near the bed. From an I.V. stand hung three plastic bags connected by tubes to Ethel.

On the sky blue wall facing the bed was a television, and sitting on the tile floor, near the window, were a few floral arrangements and a small potted Norfolk pine.

All in all, not a bad anteroom to the Great Beyond.

Ethel was sitting up in bed, staring at the opposite wall, and didn't seem to notice me. I moved to her bedside and said, "Hello, Ethel."

She turned her head toward me and, without a smile, replied, "Hello, Mr. Sutter." I recalled that Ethel reserved her smiles for when she had the opportunity to correct you on something.

I said to her, "Please call me John."

She didn't respond to that, and said, in a clear voice, "Thank you for coming," then asked, "Are you looking after my house?"

"I am." I asked her, "How are you feeling?"

"All right today."

"Good . . . you look good." In fact, in the full sunlight streaming over her, she looked ashen and emaciated, but there was still some life in her eyes. I noticed, too, a touch of rouge on her gray cheeks.

I hadn't seen her in years, but we'd communicated by letter when necessary, and she'd been good at forwarding my occasional mail to me every few months. And, of course, we exchanged Christmas cards.

She asked me, "Have you tended to my garden?"

"Of course," I lied.

"I never let you or George in my garden," she reminded me. "Neither of you knew what you were doing."

"Right. But I've learned to garden in England."

"Nonsense."

"Well . . . right."

She said to me, "You've been back for over a week."

"Right . . ." I explained, "I would have come sooner, but I thought you might be coming home."

"I'm not going home."

"Don't—"

"Why don't you sit? You're making me nervous standing there."

I sat in the armchair beside her bed and handed her the Teddy bear. "I brought this for you."

She took it, looked at it, made a face, then set it beside her. I guess she didn't love it after all.

I was batting about zero for three or something, so I picked another subject and asked her, "How are they treating you here?"

"All right."

"Is there anything I can see to?"

"No."

"Well, if you think of anything—"

"What is the purpose of your return from London, Mr. Sutter?"

"John."

"Mr. Sutter. Why have you returned?"

Well, Ethel, I need to get my things out of your house before you die and the Iranian guy changes the locks.

"Mr. Sutter?"

"Well, I came to see you, of course." This sounded a bit insincere, so I added, "Also, I have some business in New York, and I thought this might be a good time to recover some of my personal effects from the gatehouse."

"You'd better hurry. That Iranian man won't let you stay. Have you seen him?"

"No."

"You should speak to him. My life tenancy allows for a reasonable amount of time to have my property removed." She asked, rhetorically, "But who knows what he considers reasonable."

"Let me worry about that, if the time comes."

"Augustus should have been more specific."

Well, not *too* specific, Ethel. I'd actually seen the document in question, and it names both George and Ethel, of course, and mentions their loyal and faithful service over the years. George was certainly loyal and faithful, and Ethel was . . . well, apparently a good lay. I often wondered if George understood the reason for Augustus' generosity. Anyway, I said to Ethel, "It's premature to—"

She interrupted, "Have you seen your wife?"

"My ex-wife. No, I have not. Have you?"

"She stopped by yesterday."

"Then you know I haven't seen her."

"She's a wonderful woman."

I rolled my eyes.

"She looks so beautiful."

I was getting a little annoyed, so I replied, "Many men seem to think so."

She ignored that and said, "I think she would like to see you."

I didn't inquire as to why Ethel thought that. I changed the subject and said to her, "I opened a jar of your crabapple jelly, and it was wonderful. Would you like me to bring you a jar?"

"No, thank you. But see that Elizabeth gets them."

"You'll want some when you go home."

"And give her all the vegetables I canned last fall."

I nodded, but she was staring straight ahead, the way dying people do who suddenly catch a brief glimpse into eternity. She then said, as if to herself, "What will become of my harvest?"

I let a few seconds pass, then asked her, "How is Elizabeth?"

Ethel came back to earth and replied, "She's fine."

"Good." I'd also heard she was divorced, but ladies of Mrs. Allard's generation would not mention that. I said, "I need to call her." I was about to explain that Elizabeth needed to do an inventory of personal property and look over the paperwork, but that might confirm to Ethel that she had one foot in the grave and the other on a banana peel, so I recovered nicely and said, "I need to arrange with her for your home health care."

She was getting annoyed with my pretense that she was going home, and quite frankly, so was I. She said, "I am *dying*, Mr. Sutter. Didn't they tell you?"

"Well, I'm—"

"That's why I'm in hospice, and not the hospital."

"Right."

"What I need you to do is to take care of my affairs after I'm gone."

"That's what I'm here for."

"Thank you." She added, "I won't keep you here very long."

I wanted to say, "Take your time," but instead I said, "I'll be here as long as necessary." I added, "And thank you for your hospitality."

She reminded me, "You were, and I assume still are, a paying guest. A boarder."

"Right." Check's in the mail, Ethel. I mean, talk about the world turning upside down. Upward mobility in America can be fast, but downward mobility is always a free fall.

Anyway, to put her mind at ease, I said, "If you'll let me know how much the rent is, I'll deposit the amount in your account."

She replied, "The same rent as you were paying ten years ago."

"That's very generous of you."

"You may deduct that amount from your bill."

"There's no charge for any legal work I may need to perform on your behalf."

"Thank you." She asked me, "How long are you staying here, Mr. Sutter?"

Even if I knew the answer to that, I wouldn't tell anyone who was in contact with Susan.

"Mr. Sutter? Are you going back to London? Or are you home?"

"I'm not certain."

"Does that mean you may stay?"

"It means I'm not certain."

She detected a note of annoyance in my tone, so she changed the subject and asked me, "Is my will in order?"

"I believe it is." I added, "I'll need to bring you a few documents to review and update, and perhaps a few papers to sign."

"Don't wait a week."

"I'll come Saturday or Sunday."

"Sunday is the Sabbath."

"Right. Saturday or Monday."

I never quite understood these old Christian socialists. I mean, it wasn't a pure contradiction of terms, and socialists could certainly be religious—social justice through Jesus—but Ethel was, in some ways, among the last of a dying breed.

I noticed a few magazines on her tray table and saw that none of them were the old lefty magazines she used to read; they were mostly house and garden monthlies and a few local, upscale Gold Coast publications that, as I recalled, chronicled the activities of the rich and famous, the charity balls, grand house restorations, and some goings-on in Manhattan. Maybe Ethel was collecting the names of millionaires for re-education camps when the Revolution came.

Or maybe, by now, in the clarity of approaching death, she'd realized, like everyone else, that in America all change is superficial; the structure remains the same.

Mrs. Knight, as promised, stuck her head in and inquired, "How are we doing?"

Why do hospital people use the first person plural? I wanted to say, "I'm doing fine. Your patient is still dying." But before I could say that, Ethel replied, "We're doing fine, Diane. Thank you."

"Ring if you need anything."

I needed a Dewar's and soda. *Ring!*

Ethel got back to business and informed me, "I have given Elizabeth written instructions for my funeral. See that she follows them."

"I'm sure she will."

"See to it."

"Right."

"She's strong-willed, and wants everything her way."

I wonder who she got that from?

"I've picked out my dress. Have her find it."

"Right." Apparently, there's a lot to think about when you're dying, and I'm not sure I'd be as cool or organized as Ethel was being. Hopefully, I'd drop dead of a heart attack, or get run over by a bus, and let other people worry about the details.

"Also, be sure that Elizabeth speaks to Father Hunnings."

"I will." The Right Reverend James Hunnings was, and I guess still is, our parish priest at St. Mark's Episcopal Church. I thoroughly disliked him, and if he were honest, he would say the same about me. I'd driven past St. Mark's in Locust Valley and noticed that Hunnings still had top billing on the signboard, which didn't surprise me; this was a good gig in a wealthy parish, and though Episcopalians should be on the endangered species list, there were still enough of us around here to keep Father Hunnings in the style to which he'd become accustomed.

I asked Ethel, "Have you spoken to Father Hunnings?"

She replied, "Of course. He comes almost every day." She added, "He's a wonderful man."

He wouldn't be saying the same about Ethel after I told him that Mrs. Allard had left the church only five hundred dollars. Maybe I'm being cynical, but I was looking forward to that phone call. Better yet, I'd invite him to the reading of the will. *And to St. Mark's Episcopal Church, I leave* . . . pause for effect, smile, continue—*five hundred dollars.* Don't spend it all in one place, Jim.

"Mr. Sutter? What is making you smile?"

"Oh . . . I was . . . So, how is Mrs. Hunnings? Delightful woman."

"She's well. Have you gone to church?"

"I'm afraid not."

"You should go. Your wife goes."

"My ex-wife."

"I've discussed my service with Father Hunnings."

"Good. He does a good job."

"I didn't like George's service."

Neither did I, but to be fair to Hunnings, George didn't give him much notice and left no instructions.

Ethel said, "I've picked the scripture and the hymns."

I wondered if she'd also picked the day. If so, I'd like to know about it.

She informed me, "I'm being buried in the Stanhope cemetery."

I nodded. The Stanhopes, who, as I once said, needed so much land in life, were now all packed neatly into a few acres of a private family cemetery. And, in Pharaonic fashion, they'd made arrangements for their staff to join them. I mean, they didn't kill them, but just offered the plots as a perk, and it's free, so why not? In fact, many of the old family servants had been planted in what I called "The Stanhope Bone Orchard," including George Allard. I think I actually had a plot there, too, but maybe I lost that in the divorce.

Ethel said, "I'll be next to George."

"Of course." Poor George.

I remembered George's funeral ten years ago, and I recalled that Ethel had disappeared after the graveside service, so I had gone to find her, and I discovered Ethel Allard at the grave of Augustus Stanhope, her long departed employer and lover. She was crying. She had turned to me and said, "I loved him very much . . . but it could never be. Not in those days." She'd added, "I still miss him."

I looked at Ethel now, lying there, her life ebbing from her wasted body, and then I thought of her as I'd seen her in the old photos—a young, pretty girl born into a world where lots of things could never be.

Now all things were possible—or seemed to be—but the happiness quotient hadn't risen much despite, or maybe because of, our freedom to do pretty much what we wanted.

Ethel was looking at me and said, "I'm going to see him again."

I wasn't sure if that masculine pronoun referred to George or Augustus, and I also wondered how they handled love triangles in heaven. I said, "Yes, you will."

Ethel said to me, or to herself, "I'm looking forward to seeing all my friends and family who went before me."

I didn't reply.

On the subject of reunions, Ethel informed me, "Mrs. Sutter would like to see you."

I feigned confusion and replied, "My mother and I are barely speaking, Mrs. Allard."

"I'm speaking of your wife."

"Ex-wife."

"She's very disappointed that you haven't called her."

This came as a surprise, and I didn't know how I felt about that. Actually, I felt pretty lousy, but I informed Ethel, "The phone works both ways."

"Mr. Sutter, if I may be personal, I think you should forgive and forget."

I slipped into my old master/servant tone of voice and said, "Mrs. Allard, I have forgiven and forgotten, and I have no wish to continue on this subject."

But Ethel did, and since she was in a unique position to say whatever she wanted without consequence, she said to me, "You're hurting her, and yourself."

My goodness. Crotchety old Ethel Allard was seeing some sort of celestial light, and was determined to do something good before she got grilled by St. Peter.

Also, on a more earthly level, Ethel knew a thing or two about adultery and the weakness of the flesh, so she gave Susan a free pass on that. In other words, Ethel and Susan had something in common; to wit, they'd both crossed the Do Not Diddle line. These were two very different cases, of course, with far different results, but the bottom line was a pair of men's shoes under their beds that didn't belong there.

I was a little annoyed and said to her, hypothetically, "Would George have forgiven you if you—?"

"He did."

"Oh . . ." I never thought that George knew about Augustus. Well, George was a forgiving soul, and I'm not. Plus, George got the free housing. I reminded her, "This subject is finished." I looked at my watch and said, "Perhaps I'd better be going."

"As you wish."

I stood, but didn't leave. Instead, I walked to the window and stared out toward the sinking sun. From here, I could see a glimpse of the Sound between the trees, and the sunlight sparkled on the water.

"What do you see?"

I glanced back at Ethel.

"Tell me what you see."

I took a deep breath and said, "I see sunlight sparkling on the water. I see trees, and the leaves are glistening from the rain. I see the sky clearing, and white clouds blowing across the horizon. I can see the head of Hempstead Harbor, and boats, and I see land across the Sound, and there are flights of gulls circling over the water."

"It's very beautiful, isn't it?"

"It is."

"I should have noticed it more."

"We all should."

Neither of us spoke for a full minute, then I moved to her bedside.

She was clutching the stuffed bear, and I saw tears in her eyes.

I took a tissue from the box and patted her cheeks. She took my hand and said, "Thank you for coming, John."

Her hand was very cold and dry, and this, more than her appearance, made me aware that she was closer to death than to life.

She squeezed my hand and said, "I never liked you, you know."

I smiled and replied, "I know."

"But I respected you."

Deathbed confessions are admissible as evidence, and deemed to be truthful, so I said, "Thank you."

She further confessed, "You're a good man. There are not many left."

I agreed with that, and said, "You are a lady."

"You're lost, John. Find your way home."

"I'm trying."

"Call her. And call your mother. And call your children. Reach out to those you love, or once loved."

"I will."

004500-134882

OFF!® Deep Woods®
Product

on any

75¢

Save

| MANUFACTURER'S COUPON | EXPIRES JULY 27, 2013 |

She squeezed my hand again, and said, "Goodbye."

I returned the grasp, then let go of her hand and moved away from the bed. Then I turned back, bent over, and kissed her on the cheek.

I left the room quickly and headed to the elevator.

CHAPTER TEN

I exited Fair Haven Hospice House into the bright sunlight, and took a deep breath of fresh air, glad I was out of there, but happy I went.

Though Ethel and I never cared for each other, she'd been one of my last links to a long-ago past, and a link to George, whom I liked very much. So, to be honest, I was feeling a little sad.

Also disturbing were Ethel's mentions of Susan. I was perfectly happy carrying around a grudge, and I didn't want to hear that Susan was . . . well, whatever.

On that subject, it occurred to me that Susan could be coming here for a visit, and I didn't want to bump into her, so I kept an eye out as I made my way to the parking area.

Also, I could imagine my mother coming to see her old socialist buddy. In America, politics crosses all lines—class, race, ethnicity, and levels of intelligence.

And regarding Harriet Sutter, I should explain, in my defense, that I'm not a bad son; she was a bad mother, more interested in saving the world than in raising her two children. My father was a decent if distant man, but his wife ran his life, and Harriet made little time for me, Emily, or my children. Oddly, though, Harriet was and remains close to crazy Susan, and Susan's betrayal of me did not cause Harriet to change her favorable opinion of Susan; in fact, my mother suggested to me that I try to understand why Susan "strayed," as she called it (I call it fucking another guy), and she also suggested counseling so that I could better comprehend my own failings, which may have led to Susan's unfulfilled whatever.

I mean, pure bullshit. I could almost hear Ethel Allard and Harriet Sutter chatting over tea, wondering why silly John had his shorts in a knot over an unfortunate lapse of judgment by poor, sweet Susan. Ethel, I can forgive. My mother, never.

Anyway, the other person I didn't want to run into was the Reverend James Hunnings, who was annoyingly cordial to me, and to everyone who disliked him. Hunnings always spoke as though he was on stage, and there wasn't an ounce of sincerity in his voice or heart. But if I *did* see him, I'd drop a little hint that Ethel had put St. Mark's in her will. Then I'd wink and nod.

I made it to the parking area without running into anyone, and I was about to get into my car when I heard a car door close, and a female voice said, "John Sutter."

That's me, so I turned and saw Elizabeth Allard coming toward me, carrying a small pastry box.

I walked toward her and said, "Elizabeth. How are you?"

We shook hands, then, by mutual consent, engaged in a clumsy hug.

She said to me, "You look great, John."

"So do you." In fact, she was, as I said, an attractive woman, and when she was younger, she'd looked like her mother in that wedding picture above the fireplace. As I also said, she looked enough like George so that I didn't have to worry that she was my . . . what? Ex-wife's grandfather's illegitimate daughter, making her my children's blood relative of some sort—and a possible Stanhope heir.

Actually, I realized that Elizabeth's age would not comport with her mother's World War II affair. But what if Augustus got in a post-war pop? *Is that a Stanhope nose?*

"Are you coming or going?" she asked.

"Huh? Oh . . . well, I never know."

She smiled.

Stanhope mouth?

I said, "I've just come from your mother's room. She looks well."

"It's very nice of you to visit."

"Well . . . I've known your mother for a very long time." I smiled and added, "We lived together once."

Elizabeth returned the smile, then said, "John, I'm sorry about your father. I should have sent you a card."

I replied, "I was at sea."

"I know . . . that must have been very difficult for you."

"It was." And my mother made it more difficult. I wonder if she ever understood the irony of her calling me a son of a bitch.

Elizabeth said, "I meant to write to you when you got to London. I got your address from your mother."

"Did you?" I wondered if Elizabeth asked for my address, or if it was offered. Probably the former, knowing Harriet. In any case, Elizabeth hadn't written that condolence note, but if she had, what would she have said? *Dear John, Sorry you couldn't make your father's funeral. Everyone was asking about you.*

I was still feeling a little guilty after eight years, so I said, "I learned of my father's death a month after it happened."

She nodded.

I continued, "I'm going to visit his grave before I return."

Again, she nodded and changed the subject by asking, "So, how is London?"

"Good."

"How long are you staying?"

"I'm not sure." I also wasn't sure of my relationship with Elizabeth. Were we family friends as a result of me knowing her father and mother for decades? Or were we acquaintances because I'd hardly ever seen her, except now and then in the village and at a few social and family functions? I said, "Sorry to hear about your divorce."

She shrugged and replied, "It was for the best."

Elizabeth Allard, daughter of estate workers, had married well. His name was Tom Corbet, and he came from what's called a "good family." He's a Yalie, like I am, and he worked on Wall Street, as I did, and in my past life I'd see him on the train now and then. Elizabeth, I recalled, used her maiden name for business, but socially she was Mrs. Corbet. Mr. and Mrs. Corbet had two children, a girl and a boy, both of whom must be in college now or graduated. Tom Corbet, by the way, was a crashing bore, and the only interesting thing about him was that he'd gone gay some years ago, so, yes, the divorce was probably for the best.

Elizabeth added, in case I didn't know, "Tom has a boyfriend."

"Right. Well . . ." That must have been very difficult for her when Tom sat her down and told her there was another man. I mean, that should have been *her* line.

She changed the subject and said to me, "Sorry about you and Susan."

"Oh, did you hear about that?"

She suppressed a laugh and reminded me, "It was national news."

"That's right. It's been so long." Elizabeth owned three or four upscale clothing boutiques in the nearby villages, so I asked her, "How's business?"

She replied, "Not too bad, considering the stock market has gone to hell, and people have been putting their money into hazmat suits and freeze-dried rations since 9/11 and the anthrax thing." She smiled and continued, "Maybe I should carry designer gas masks."

I smiled in return. I don't usually notice women's clothing, unless it's really outrageous, but I recalled that Elizabeth used to dress conservatively, despite some of the weird stuff I'd seen in her shops years ago when Susan had dragged me into them. Today, however, Elizabeth had left her severely tailored business suits in the closet—or perhaps Tom took them—and she was wearing a frilly pink blouse that accentuated her tan, and a black silk skirt that didn't reach her knees. Maybe she felt that her formerly mannish attire had been the reason that Tom . . . well, I shouldn't speculate on that, but—

She interrupted my train of thought and said, apropos of her statement about hazmat suits and gas masks, "People are such wimps." She asked, "What's wrong with this country?"

"I don't know. I just got here."

I should also mention that Elizabeth was a local Republican activist, to the extent that Republicans around here engaged in *any* activity other than golf and drinking.

In any case, her politics, like her membership in The Creek Country

Club and the Locust Valley Chamber of Commerce, may have been driven more by business than conviction. Nevertheless, Elizabeth's affiliations had caused Ethel no end of grief and bewilderment, and I could imagine Ethel crying to George, "How could a child of mine be a *Republican*?" Adding, "It's *your* fault, George!"

Elizabeth asked me, "What are they saying in London?"

"They're saying they're next."

She nodded.

Elizabeth Allard Corbet, by the way, had wavy chestnut hair that she wore shoulder length, nice big brown eyes, a nose with slightly flared nostrils (like George's), and lush lips that, now and then, flashed a slightly amused smile. Bottom line, she was a good-looking woman with a cultured voice and manner—the result of being an estate brat.

Men, of course, found her attractive, though she never rang my bell (and apparently not Tom's), and women, too, seemed to like her. Susan, I remembered, liked her.

On that subject, against my better judgment, I said, "I assume you know that Susan is back."

She replied, without any silly pretense of ignorance, "Yes. I've seen her here a few times. We actually had lunch once." She asked me, "Have you seen her?"

"No."

"Do you plan to?"

"I don't—but I probably will."

There was a lot more to talk about on that subject, if I cared to, and I was sure Elizabeth, like her mother, had things to tell me about Susan. But the last thing I wanted was for people to be carrying messages and information back and forth between the estranged parties. So I dropped the subject and asked, "How are your children?"

"Fine. Tom Junior is a senior at Brown, and Betsy graduated Smith and is in an MFA program at Penn."

"You must be very proud of them."

"I am." She smiled. "Except for their politics. I think bleeding-heart liberalism skips a generation. Mom, however, is delighted."

I smiled in return.

She informed me, "Susan has filled me in on Edward and Carolyn."

"Good."

On the subject of genes versus environment, Elizabeth could be a little severe and strong-willed at times, like her mother, but mostly she was quietly pleasant and straightforward, like her father, with her father's strong work ethic. And did I mention that she'd gone to Bryn Mawr, all expenses paid by her secret and perhaps reluctant godfather, Augustus Stanhope? Augustus' rolls in the hay barn with Ethel had cost him a few more bucks than he'd figured, and possibly a few sleepless nights.

Things were different then, of course, in regard to social and sexual rules of behavior; but even today adultery isn't acceptable, and carries a high price tag. Ask Susan Sutter. Or John. Or Frank Bellarosa . . . Well, he's not talking.

Elizabeth said to me, "Now that Mom is . . . at the end . . . I'm thinking more about Dad. I really miss him."

"I do, too."

George Allard and I could have been considered friends, except for the artificial and anachronistic class barrier, which was enforced more by George than by me. George, like many old-school servants, had been more royal than the King, and he truly believed that the local gentry were his social superiors; however, whenever they slacked off or behaved badly (which was often), George respectfully reminded them of their obligations as gentlemen, and he would gently but firmly suggest corrections to their behavior and manners. I think I was a challenge to him, and we didn't become close until he gave up on me.

Elizabeth suggested, "If you have time, why don't you come up with me—or wait for me? I'm staying only fifteen minutes tonight. Then, if you'd like, we can go for a drink." She added, in case I was misinterpreting the offer, "I'd like to speak to you about Mom's will, and whatever else I need to speak to you about."

I replied, "I do need to speak to you. You are, as you know, the executrix of her estate, and her sole heir, aside from a few minor bequests. But unfortunately, I have plans this evening."

"Oh . . . well . . ."

Actually, I had time to at least walk her to the front door, but I kept thinking that Susan, my mother, or Father Hunnings might pull up.

On the other hand, that might not be a bad thing. I could imagine some interesting reactions from my ex-wife, ex-mother, and ex-priest if they saw me talking to the attractive divorcée.

To get another rumor mill going, I should have said, "I'm having dinner with a Mafia don," but, in a Freudian slip, I said, "I'm having dinner with a business prospect."

"Oh. Does that mean you're staying?"

"I'm not sure." I suggested, "How about tomorrow night? Are you free?"

"No . . . I'm having dinner with friends." She smiled. "Thursday is ladies' night out. But you're welcome to join us for a drink."

"Uh . . . perhaps not." I considered asking her to dinner Friday night, but that would sound like a weekend date instead of a weekday business dinner, so I said, "I'd like you to do a quick inventory of the personal property—Mom and Dad's—and look over some paperwork. Also, your mother asked that you . . . find the dress she wants to wear . . . so, why don't you come to the house on Saturday or Sunday?"

"Saturday afternoon would be good. Would four o'clock work?"

"Yes. I'll be sure my estate gate is open."

She smiled and said, "I have the code." She informed me, "You are sleeping in my room."

"I know."

"I'd like to see it, one last time. Is that all right?"

"Do I need to clean it?"

"No. If it was clean, I wouldn't recognize it."

I smiled. She smiled.

I suggested, "If you have a van or station wagon, we can get some personal things moved out."

She replied, "I have that." She nodded toward a big SUV of some sort. Maybe these things ate the other cars. She asked, "Will that do?"

"It should. Or we can make a few trips." I added, "You should arrange for a mover for the furniture."

"All right." She suddenly asked me, "John, do you think I should buy the gatehouse? Is it for sale?"

"I don't know. I'll ask Mr. Nasim. Why would you want to buy it?"

She shrugged. "Nostalgia. Maybe I'd live there. I don't need the big house in Mill Neck. The kids are gone. I got the house in the divorce. Tom got my shoes and purses." She smiled and said, "Or I could rent the gatehouse to you, if you stayed."

I smiled in return.

She looked at her watch and said, "I should go. So, I'll see you Saturday, about four."

"Right. If there is any change, you know the number."

"Do you have a cell?"

"Not in the U.S."

"Okay . . ." She handed me the pastry box, then fished around in her purse, found a business card, and wrote on the card, saying, "My home number and my cell."

I exchanged the card for the pastry box and said, "See you Saturday."

"Thanks, John, for all you're doing for Mom."

"It's nothing."

"And what you did for Dad. I never properly thanked you."

"He was a good man."

"He thought the world of you." She added, "And your father was a good man, and he . . . he understood what you were going through."

I didn't reply, and we did a quick hug and air kiss. She turned, took a few steps, then looked back and said, "Oh, I have a letter for you from Mom. I'll bring it Saturday."

"Okay."

I watched her walking quickly toward the hospice house, then I turned and got into my rental car.

As I drove down the lane toward the road, I replayed the conversation, as people do who are trying to extract some meaning beyond the words spoken. I also analyzed her body language and demeanor, but Elizabeth was not easy to read; or, maybe, as several women have told me, I miss the subtleties. If a woman says, "Let's have a drink and talk business," I actually think it's about business. It's a wonder I ever got laid.

Anyway, on to my next adventure: dinner with don Anthony Bellarosa.

Ethel, Elizabeth, Anthony. And, eventually, *Susan.*

An individual life passes through a continuum of time and space, but now and then you enter a warp that sucks you back into the past. You understand what's going on because you've been there before; but that's no guarantee that you're going to get it right this time. In fact, experience is just another word for baggage. And memory carries the bags.

More importantly—egg drop or wonton? Chopsticks or fork?

I pulled into a diagonal parking space in front of Wong Lee's Chinese restaurant.

CHAPTER ELEVEN

I noticed a big American flag decal displayed in the front window of Wong Lee's, next to the credit card decals. I also noticed Tony (formerly known as Anthony) sitting in the driver's seat of the big black SUV I'd seen a few nights earlier on Grace Lane. The windows were tinted, but the driver's window was down, and I didn't see Anthony Bellarosa (formerly known as Tony) inside the vehicle.

Tony spotted me and shouted, "Hey! Mistah Sutta! Hey! It's me! Tony. How ya doin'?"

It would have been difficult for me—or anyone within half a mile—to ignore him, so I walked toward the SUV and said, in my best St. Paul's accent, "I'm doing very well. Thank you for asking."

"Hey, you look great." He reached through the window, we shook hands, then he opened the door and jumped out. He wanted to shake again, so we did, and he said, "The boss is inside, waitin' for ya."

I glanced at my watch and saw I was fifteen minutes early. Frank Bellarosa, a graduate of La Salle Military Academy, once advised me, apropos of meetings and battles, "Like General Nathan Bedford Forrest said, Counselor, 'Get there firstest with the mostest.'" Probably Frank had passed that on to his son, and that made me wonder how much Anthony had learned at the knee of his father before Frank's life and Anthony's education had been cut short. And, I wondered, how much was in the blood?

Tony inquired, "So whaddaya been up to?"

"Same old shit."

"Yeah? You look great."

I think we covered that, and I wished I could say the same about Tony, but he'd aged in ten years, a result, possibly, of job stress. Nevertheless, I said, "You're looking good, Anthony. Well—"

"Tony."

"Right."

He took a pack of cigarettes from his black sweatsuit warmup jacket and offered me one, which I declined.

He lit up and said, "The boss says no smokin' in the car."

"Good rule." The SUV, I now noticed, had the Cadillac logo on the hubs, and the word "Escalade" on the front door. There was an American flag decal on the side window. If I could see the rear bumper, I'm sure the bumper stickers would say, "Suburban Mafia," and "My kid can kill your honor student."

Tony took a drag, then returned to his subject, saying, "You can't fuckin' smoke no place no more."

It's been a while since I've heard compound double negatives interspersed with the F-word, and I actually smiled.

Tony, by the way, was dressed in running shoes and the aforementioned black sweatsuit ensemble. Frank Bellarosa would have fired him on the spot. Or fired at him.

Interestingly, Tony sported an American flag pin on his warmup jacket, which at first surprised me, then did not. The Mafia always considered themselves loyal and patriotic Americans.

"So," Tony inquired, "how's Mrs. Sutta?"

"I have no idea."

I should mention that Susan was a favorite with the late don's goons, and she in turn found them exotic or something, including their totally whorish girlfriends. I didn't share her fascination with these characters, and she called me a snob. I'm quite certain that Tony had changed his opinion of Mrs. Sutter after she capped the don.

"You ain't seen her?"

I didn't like him asking about her, and I replied, "No. All right, good seeing you—"

"Hey. Those were the days. Right?"

"Right."

"You, me, the don, God rest his soul, that scumbag Lenny, may he rot in hell, and Vinnie, God rest his soul."

A scorecard would show three dead and two living. The don, God rest his soul, had been killed by you-know-who, and Vinnie, God rest his soul, had his head blown off with a shotgun, and scumbag Lenny, may he rot in hell, was Frank's driver, and also the guy who dropped a dime on Frank, resulting in the Saturday night shoot-out at Giulio's in Little Italy. Lenny had sped off with the two hit men in Frank's stretch Caddy, but he was later found by the police in the car's trunk at Newark Airport with a garrote around his neck—which reminded me, if I needed reminding, that these people played for keeps, and could not be trusted.

I said to Tony, "Those were the days."

"Yeah. Hey, remember that morning when the Feds came for the boss? That little wop, Mancuso. Remember that?"

The gentleman in question was FBI Special Agent Felix Mancuso, with whom I'd had some prior conversations about me working for Frank Bellarosa, and who, despite that fact, liked me. Mr. Mancuso had shown up at Alhambra to arrest don Frank Bellarosa for the murder of the Colombian drug lord, and Frank knew this was coming, so I was there as his attorney, and Lenny and Vinnie were there to look tough, and Tony, I recalled, was in the Alhambra gatehouse. Felix Mancuso had come alone, without an army of agents, to show Frank Bellarosa that his balls were at least as big as Frank's. But before Mancuso put the cuffs on Frank, he took me aside and tried to save my soul, telling me to get my life together and get away from Bellarosa before it was too late. Good advice, but it was already too late.

And here I stood now, at the threshold of perhaps another great folly, and I realized I could choose not to walk into Wong Lee's Chinese restaurant.

Tony said, "Hey, I'm keepin' ya. Go 'head. Third booth on the right."

I turned and walked toward the restaurant.

CHAPTER TWELVE

T hird booth on the right.

Wong Lee's hadn't changed much in ten years, or in thirty years, for that matter, and the décor could best be described as 1970s Chinese restaurant.

Anthony was sitting facing the door, as is customary for men in his profession. He had good lines of sight and fields of fire, except for his rear, which seemed unsecured, unless there was another goombah back there somewhere.

He was talking on his cell phone, holding it in his left hand, so that his right hand was free to nibble fried wontons or pull his gun.

Well, maybe I'm overanalyzing his choice of seating; I mean, it's a Chinese restaurant in a suburban town, for goodness' sake. Did you ever see a headline saying, MAFIA BOSS HIT IN CHINESE RESTAURANT?

On the other hand, based on Anthony's cautious behavior in front of the gatehouse, it was very possible that he knew he was on some-body's clip list. And I'm having dinner with this guy? You would think I should have learned my lesson at Giulio's.

Anthony had seen me as soon as I opened the door, and he was smiling and waving his free gun hand as he kept talking. He was wear-ing another version of the awful shirt he'd had on the other night, but this time he wore an electric blue sports jacket over it.

The hostess noticed we were *paesanos*, and escorted me to the booth saying, "You sit with your friend."

Then why am I being seated *here*?

Anthony was still chatting, but he stuck out his hand and we shook. He said into the phone, "Okay . . . okay . . . I'm sorry . . . yeah . . . okay . . ."

Wife or mother.

He continued, "Yeah . . . he's here, Ma. He wants to say hello . . . yeah . . . here . . . Ma . . . Ma . . ." He covered the mouthpiece and said to me, "You know why Italian mothers make great parole officers? They never let anyone finish a sentence." He handed me the phone and said, "My mother wants to say hello."

I hate when people hand me a phone to say hello to someone I don't want to say hello to, but I liked Anna Bellarosa, so I put the phone to my ear and heard her say, "All the Italian restaurants in Glen Cove, and you take him to the Chinks? You don't *think*, Tony. Your father knew how to *think*. You—"

"Anna, hi, this is—"

"Who's this?"

"John Sutter. How are you?"

"John! Oh my God. I can't believe it's you. Oh my God. John, how are you?"

"I'm—"

"Tony says you look great."

"Anthony."

"Who?"

"Your son—"

"*Tony*. Tony says he saw you the other night. He says you're living here now."

"Well, I—"

"Why don't you go to Stanco's? Why are you eating at the Chinks?"

"Chinese was *my* idea. So, you're back in Brooklyn?"

"Yeah. In the old neighborhood. Williamsburg. Since Frank . . . oh my God, John. Do you believe he's dead?"

Actually, yes.

"It's ten years, John, ten years since my Frank . . ." She let out a sigh, followed by a little sob, caught her breath, then continued, "Nothing is the same without Frank."

That's good news.

She went into a brief eulogy of her deceased husband, which sounded well-practiced, emphasizing his qualities as a father, and said, "The boys miss him. In a few weeks is Father's Day, John. The boys take me to the cemetery every Father's Day. They cry at his grave."

"It must be very sad for them."

She let me know how sad it was. She didn't say anything specific about Frank as a perfect husband, but neither did she say anything negative, of course, nor would she ever.

The last time I'd seen her was at Frank's funeral, and she hadn't looked good in black with mascara running down her face. In fact, though, she'd been an attractive woman in a fertility goddess sort of way—full-bodied, big-busted, good skin under the makeup, big eyes, and a Cupid's bow mouth. I wondered what ten years and widowhood had done to her.

As Anna prattled on, I glanced at Anthony, who seemed to have tuned out and was absently stirring his beverage, which looked and smelled like a Scotch on the rocks. I got his attention and motioned to his drink. He nodded and summoned the waitress.

Anna Bellarosa was going on about life without her sainted husband, avoiding any mention of my then-wife putting three .38 caliber slugs into dear Frank.

It happened, incidentally, on the mezzanine that overlooked the palm court atrium at Alhambra. Frank had been wearing a bathrobe, and when he went over the railing and hit the red-tiled floor below, his bathrobe flew open, and when I saw him, he wasn't wearing anything under his black silk robe, and it occurred to me now that this image of him had somehow transferred itself to my dream in another form.

Anna was saying, "He loved you, John. He really did."

Then why was he fucking my wife?

"He always told me how smart you were. How you helped him when they tried to make up charges against him."

Ironically, Frank Bellarosa would have been safer in jail. "Well, I was just doing what he paid me to do." And he still owes me fifty thousand dollars.

"No. You did it because you loved him."

"Right." Or did I write off the fifty thousand and chalk it up to experience? I seem to remember that the Feds had seized all his assets and his checkbooks.

Anna was rambling on. The waitress came, a very young Chinese lady, and I tapped Anthony's glass and pointed to myself, so she pushed Anthony's glass in front of me.

Anthony seemed not amused and snatched his glass back, then barked an order for two Dewar's, and mumbled in Italian, "Stonata," which I recalled means something like "bubble brain."

Out of nowhere, Anna asked, "Why did she do it, John?"

"Uh . . ."

"John. *Why?*"

"Uh . . . well . . ." Well, because they were having a lover's quarrel. But I didn't think Anna wanted to hear that. I mean, she had to know— it was in all the newspapers, as I recall, not to mention radio and television, and supermarket tabloids—so it was a silly question.

"She didn't *have* to do it, John."

"I know." But Frank had made promises to her, then broke those promises, and Susan, not used to being scorned, shot him.

By the time I saw him, the blood around his three bullet holes had coagulated like red custard, and the wound in his groin was in his pubic hair, and his genitals were covered with clotted blood. His skull had hit the hard floor with such force that a splatter of blood radiated out from his head like a halo. His eyes were still open, so I closed them, which ticked off the CSI people and the crime scene photographers.

"John? Did she tell you why?"

"No." Actually, she did, but she was lying.

Anna asked me, "Why is she back?"

"I don't know."

"Did you see her?"

"No."

"She should burn in hell for what she did."

I was getting a little annoyed at Anna's suggestion that her sainted husband, Frank the Bishop Bellarosa, was the innocent victim of an evil, cold-blooded murderess. I mean, come on, Anna. Your husband was a notorious Mafia don, probably himself a murderer, and for sure an adulterer who screwed more women than he'd had spaghetti dinners at home. So, to use a phrase she'd understand, I should have said, "What goes around, comes around." And furthermore, Anna, if anyone is burning in hell, it's your husband. But instead, I said, "Okay, Anna—Tony wants to speak—"

"You shouldn't eat there. You don't know what they put in the food."

"Right. Okay—"

"Next time you're in Brooklyn, you stop by for coffee or come to Tony's house for dinner. Next Sunday. I'll cook."

"Thank you. Take care." I added, "Ciao," and handed the cell phone back to Anthony, who will always be Tony to Momma.

He said into the phone, "Yeah, Ma. I gotta—okay, okay. Stanco's." He listened, then said, "I'll tell her to call you. She's busy with the kids, Ma. You can call her—"

Poor Tony. Harriet Sutter was starting to look good.

He finally hung up, slammed the phone on the table, downed the rest of his Scotch, and said, "What's the difference between an Italian mother and a Rottweiler?"

"What?"

"Eventually, the Rottweiler lets go."

I smiled.

Anthony lit a cigarette and stayed silent awhile, then asked me, "What was she saying?"

"Your father."

He nodded, and we dropped that subject, or, I was certain, tabled it for later.

The waitress brought the two Scotches and correctly put one glass in front of each of us, then inquired, "You want order now?"

Anthony informed her, "We don't have a friggin' *menu*." He added, "Cretina."

Maybe I should have suggested Stanco's.

Anthony raised his glass and I raised mine. We clinked, and he said, "Salute," and I said, "Cheers."

He said, apropos of Mom, "She and Megan—that's my wife—they don't get along."

"That can be difficult."

"Yeah. Difficult. Megan, you know, she's Irish, and they have different . . . what do you call it . . . ?"

"Ethnic traditions? Cultural practices?"

"Yeah. Anyway, it's not like I married a melanzana or something."

"Right." That means eggplant, which one would not normally marry, but it's also Italian slang for a black person. It was all coming back to me. Check, please.

On the subject of marital bliss in the 'burbs, and because I was curious, I asked him, "How do you like living in Alhambra Estates?"

He shrugged. "It's okay . . . but I'd like to move back to the city." He delivered a hot piece of news by saying, "There's a million good-looking broads in New York."

"That shouldn't interest a married man."

He thought that was funny. He said, "I almost got her to move into the city, but after 9/11, forget it."

I said, "This is a good place to raise children."

"Yeah. I got two. A boy, Frank, five years old, and a girl, Kelly Ann—Ann for my mother. Kelly is Megan's mother's maiden name." He continued, "My mother—you know how they are"—he did a bad impersonation of Mom's voice—"'Tony, what's this Kelly name? The only Kellys I know in Williamsburg are drunks.'" He laughed, then realizing he'd broken the rule on revealing anything negative about *la famiglia*, he said, "Forget that."

Returning to the subject of life in the country, he said to me, "Do you know that the road that runs by the estates is private? Grace Lane is private."

"I do know that."

"Yeah, well, it was falling apart, and those cheap bastards along the road didn't want to repave it. So I got one of my companies to do it as a favor to everybody."

That was interesting, and it revealed something about Anthony. His father didn't care what anyone thought about him, as long as they respected him and feared him. Anthony seemed to be looking for acceptance. But it's really hard for narrow-minded suburbanites to accept a Mafia don as a neighbor. I mean, I had a problem with that myself. I said to him, "That was very nice of you."

"Yeah. Do you think I got a thank-you? Not one fucking thank-you."

"Well, I thank you. The road looks good."

"Fuck them. I should tear it up."

"Hold up on that. Maybe they're planning a surprise party for you."

"Yeah? Maybe I got a surprise for them."

Don't whack your neighbors, Anthony. Your kids have enough problems with Dad being a Mafia guy. I hesitated, then asked him, "Did the developer save the reflecting pool and the statue of Neptune?"

"Huh . . . ? Oh, yeah, I remember that when I was a kid. There was, like, make-believe Roman ruins, and gardens and stuff. That was some place. You remember that?"

"I do. Is it still there?"

"Nah. It's all gone. Just houses. Why do you ask?"

"Just wondering."

"Yeah. I loved that place." He informed me, "I went skinny-dipping once in the pool." He smiled. "With the college girl who my father hired to be my tutor."

"What subject?"

He laughed, then seemed lost in that memory, so I took the opportunity to think about how to get the hell out of here. I also looked around to see if there was anyone in Wong Lee's whom I knew. Or anyone who looked like the FBI.

The restaurant was mostly empty, except for a few families with kids, and people waiting for takeout orders. Then I noticed a guy sitting by himself in a booth on the other side, facing toward the back of the restaurant.

Anthony noticed my interest in the gentleman and said, "He's with me."

"Good." So we had interlocking fields of fire if a situation developed. That made me feel much better. More to the point, Mr. Bellarosa was definitely in full security mode. I looked back at him, and it appeared to me now that under his loose-fitting Hawaiian shirt was quite possibly a Kevlar vest. This is what had saved his father's life at Giulio's. Maybe I should ask if he had an extra vest.

If I wanted to speculate on what or who was making Anthony jumpy, I'd guess it was Sally Da-da. Though why this should be happening now, after ten years, was a mystery. So maybe it was someone else. The only way I'd know for sure is if the same two guys with shotguns who were at Giulio's suddenly appeared at the table and blew Anthony's head off. Maybe I should order takeout.

The waitress brought the menus, and we looked at them. He asked me, "You like Chinese?"

"Sometimes."

"I dated a Chinese girl once, and an hour after I ate her, I was hungry again." He laughed. "Get it?"

"Got it." I studied the menu more intensely and took a long swig of Scotch.

He continued, "So I was dating this Chinese girl, and one night, we're making out hot and heavy, and I said to her, 'I want sixty-nine,' and she says, 'Oh, you want beef and broccoli *now*?'" He laughed again. "Get it?"

"Got it."

"You got one?"

"Not one that comes to mind."

"I once heard my father say to somebody that you were a funny guy."

In fact, Frank appreciated my sarcasm, irony, and humor, even when he was the butt of it. I wasn't sure that his son was as thick-skinned or as bright, but the jury was still out on Anthony's brain power. I said, "Your father brought out the best of my wit."

The waitress returned, and I ordered wonton soup and beef and broccoli, which made Anthony laugh. He ordered sixty-nine, which was not on the menu, and settled for what I was having. He also ordered another round of Scotch, and a clean ashtray, and I asked for chopsticks.

He said to me, "You know why wives like Chinese food?"

"No. Why?"

"Because wonton spelled backwards is not now."

I hoped that exhausted his repertoire.

I noticed that Anthony, like Tony, had a flag pin on the lapel of his sports jacket, and my recollection of Frank and his friends was that they exhibited a sort of primitive, jingoistic patriotism, based for the most part on xenophobia, racism, and a lingering immigrant culture that said, "America is a great country."

Indeed it is, and despite some serious problems, I was seeing it more clearly now after three years of wandering the globe, and seven years in London. I mean, England was a good place for self-exiled Americans, but it wasn't home, and I suddenly realized that I was home. So maybe I should stop playing the part of the ex-pat on a brief visit to the States.

As though reading my mind, Anthony asked me, "So, how long you staying?"

This, I guess, was the threshold question whose answer would determine if we had any business to discuss. So I needed to carefully consider my answer.

He asked me, "You still up in the air on that?"

"I'm . . . leaning toward staying."

"Good. No reason to go back." He added, "This is where the action is."

Actually, that was a good reason to return to London.

Anthony suddenly reached into his pocket, and I thought he was pulling his gun, but instead he produced a flag pin and set it down in front of me. He said, "If you're staying, you want to wear this."

I left it lying on the table and said, "Thank you."

Anthony instructed, "Put it on your lapel." He tapped the flag on his lapel, but when I didn't follow instructions, he leaned forward and stuck the flag on the left lapel of my blue blazer. He said, "There you go. Now you're an American again."

I informed him, "My family has been in America for over three hundred years."

"No shit?" He inquired, "Why'd they wait so long after Columbus discovered America?"

Further on the subject of history, Anthony informed me, "I majored in history." He added, "I went to college for a year. NYU. I fucked my brains out."

I could see that.

"I read a lot about the Romans. That shit interests me. How about you?"

I informed him, "I took eight years of Latin, and I could read Cicero, Seneca, and Ovid in classical Latin."

"No shit?"

"Then, in my senior year of college, I got hit in the head with a baseball, and now I can read only Italian."

He thought that was funny, then got serious and said, "What I'm getting at is I see this country like Rome, when the Empire was in serious trouble. Understand?"

I didn't reply.

"Like, the days of the Republic are over. Now we're like an imperial power, so every asshole out there wants to take a shot at us. Right? Like those fucks on 9/11. Plus, we can't control our borders, like the Romans couldn't, so we got ten million illegals who can't even speak the fucking language and don't give a shit about the country. They just want a piece of the action. And the assholes in Washington sit around and argue, like the Roman Senate, and the fucking country is going to hell with weirdos screaming about their rights, and the fucking barbarians are at the border."

"What book was that in?"

He ignored me and continued his riff. "The fucking bureaucrats are up our asses, the men in this country act like women, and the women act like men, and all anyone cares about is bread and circuses. You see what I'm saying?"

"I know the argument, Anthony." I gave him some good news and said, "At least organized crime is almost eradicated."

He stubbed out his cigarette, then said, "You think?"

Anthony was a perfect example of a little knowledge being a dangerous thing. Regarding the purpose of this dinner, I asked him, "So, what would you like to know about your father?"

He lit another cigarette, sat back, then said, "I just want you to tell me . . . like, how you met. Why you decided to do business. I mean . . . why would a guy like you . . . you know, get involved in a criminal case?"

"You mean organized crime?"

He wasn't about to go there. I mean, like, you know, there is no Mafia. No Cosa Nostra. Whaddaya talkin' about?

Anthony reminded me, "You defended him on a murder charge, which, as you know, Counselor, was bullshit." He asked me again, "So, how did you and my father get together and wind up doing business?"

I replied, "It was mostly a personal relationship." I added, "We clicked, and he needed some help."

"Yeah? But why did you stick your neck out?"

Anthony was testing the water to see what motivated me—*why* I hooked up with the mob, so to speak, and what it would take for me to do it again. In his world, the answer was money and power, but maybe he understood that in my world, it was more complex.

I replied, "I told you the other night—he did me a favor and I was repaying the favor." Also, the whole truth was that Frank Bellarosa, in cahoots with my wife, played the macho card, i.e., Frank had a gun and a set of balls, and nice guy John had a pen and a good intellect. They were very subtle about that, of course, but this challenge to my manhood worked well. Plus, I was bored, and Susan knew that. What she didn't know was that Frank Bellarosa also appealed to my darker side; evil is very seductive, which Susan discovered too late.

I said to Anthony, "Your father was a very charismatic man, and very persuasive." Plus, he was screwing my wife so he could get to me through her, though I didn't know that at the time.

And I don't think Susan knew that, either. She probably thought that Frank was interested only in her. In fact, Frank was partly motivated by the convenience of pillow talk with his attorney's wife, not to mention the thrill of screwing an uppity society bitch. But on another level, probably against his will, Frank felt something for Susan Sutter.

Anthony said, with some insight, "My father had a way of picking the right people. Like, he knew what *they* wanted, and he showed them how they could get it."

I recalled learning about a guy like that in Sunday school, named Lucifer.

As per the supposed reason for this dinner, Anthony asked me a few questions regarding my personal memories of his father.

I answered by relating a few anecdotes that I thought would give him some nice snapshots of Pop.

I then recounted my and Susan's first visit to Alhambra, at Frank's invitation for coffee, and how I enjoyed Anna's hospitality and warmth. I didn't share with Anthony that I was royally ticked off at Susan for accepting the invitation, or that my impressions of the Bellarosas as my new Gold Coast next-door-mansion neighbors were not entirely favorable. In fact, I was horrified. But also a little intrigued, as was Susan.

In any case, I kept it light and positive, skipping over my subsequent seduction by Frank Bellarosa, and Frank's seduction of my wife (or vice versa), and our final descent into hell. That might be a little complicated for Anthony, and none of his business.

This all took about fifteen minutes, during which my wonton soup came and sat there, while I sipped Scotch and Anthony smoked, flipped ashes on the floor, and said very little.

When I'd finished, I said, "So, that's about it." I added, "I was sorry for what happened, and I want you to know that I share your grief, and that of your mother, brothers, and your whole family."

Anthony nodded.

I announced, "I'm not really hungry, and I have a lot of work to do at home, so thanks for the drinks." I reached for my wallet and said, "Let me split the bill."

He seemed surprised that I'd actually want to forgo his company, and asked, "What's your rush?"

"I just told you."

"Have another drink." He called out to the waitress, "Two more!" then asked me, "You want a cigarette?"

"No, thank you."

That settled, he returned to a prior subject and asked, "Hey, how did you let the Feds grab Alhambra? I mean, you do this for a living. Right?"

"Right. You win some, you lose some." I added, "Even Jesus said to give unto Caesar that which is Caesar's."

"Yeah, but Jesus was a nice guy, and he didn't have a tax lawyer. Or a criminal attorney." Anthony smiled and continued, "That's why he got nailed."

I reminded him, "I was on my way to beating the murder charge."

"Yeah, okay, but if my father didn't do anything criminal, then how did they get his property?"

"I told you. Tax evasion."

"That's bullshit."

"No, it's *criminal.*" The truth was, as I said, and as Anthony surely knew, the Justice Department and the IRS had enough real and manufactured evidence on Frank Bellarosa to make his life a living hell. Plus, Frank's own brother-in-law, Sally Da-da—Anna's sister's husband—had tried to whack Frank, and Frank's aura of power and strength was waning. So he took the easy way out and accepted the government's deal. To wit: Tell us about every crime you ever committed, Frank, and give us the names of your hoodlum friends. Then you abdicate your title, give us all your money, and you can go into exile a free man. Not a bad deal, and better than prison. Plus, the exile to Italy fit in nicely with Frank and Susan's plans to run off together, but I didn't think Anthony wanted to know all of that. In fact, he *wanted* the bullshit.

"And there was nothing you could do to hold on to Alhambra?"

"No."

"Okay . . . hey, I heard that my father also owned your place. He bought that, too."

"He bought Stanhope Hall from my father-in-law." I was tempted to say, "I think he needed more room to bury bodies," but I said, "He wanted to control the land development around his estate." In fact, as I said, Susan had most probably talked her lover into that purchase. My father-in-law, William the Skinflint, wanted to dump this expensive white elephant, and for the right price he would have sold it to the devil. Actually, he did.

Susan had been upset at the thought of the family home passing into the hands of some stranger or a developer, and I believe she saw don Bellarosa as her white knight who could save the estate for her. I have no idea what the deal was between her and her lover, but I suspected that she at least had thoughts of living there with Frank. But then Frank sold out to the Feds and went into the Witness Protection Program, and Italy, I think, became Plan B.

I really should have insisted that I had to go, but Anthony seemed obsessed with the Federal government seizing a sizable fortune in property and cash from his father, going so far as to ask me, "Hey, do you think I have a shot at getting that back?"

"You have about as much chance of recovering assets seized under the RICO Act as I have of getting the Man of the Year Award from the Sons of Italy."

He persisted. "How about those millions in bond money that you posted for my father? Right? He died before the trial, and he didn't commit the murder. So why can't you get that back?"

I saw where this was going, of course, and I definitely didn't want to go there. I said, "As I understand it, those assets, including Stanhope Hall, were returned to your father's estate, then seized as part of his tax settlement with the IRS."

"Yeah, but—"

"There are no buts, Anthony. I did what I could at the time. Your father was satisfied with my representation, and there are no do-overs."

Bottom line, his obsession with the lost fortune was mostly smoke. What he was after was me, and thus his veiled criticism of how I handled this case a decade ago, and now he was going to give me the opportunity to get it right; to see that justice was done. Next stop after that was the slippery slope into his underworld. Thanks, but no thanks. Been there, Anthony. The pay is good, but the price is too high.

He said to me, "If you took this on, I'd give you two hundred up front, and a third of what you got back from the Feds." He added, in case I didn't get the math, "That could be three, four, maybe five million for you."

He wasn't actually as dim as I thought, and he also figured out that I probably needed the dough, which would make most men vulnerable to the temptations of the devil. I replied, "Actually, it's about zero."

"No, you at least get two hundred up front and it's yours."

"No, it's *yours*."

He seemed a little exasperated and tried a new approach. "Hey, Counselor, I think you owe me and my family something on this."

"Anthony, I don't owe you a thing." In fact, Junior, your father owes me fifty large. I continued, "At the end, I wasn't working for your father when he cut his own deal with the government. The only representation he had, as far as I know, was his personal attorney, Jack Weinstein"—who was actually a mob attorney—"so you should speak to him if you haven't already."

"Jack is retired."

"So am I."

As far as I was concerned, this meeting was over. We'd covered the walk down memory lane, and I'd squashed the clumsy recruiting pitch, so unless Junior wanted to hear that his father had actually been a government stool pigeon, or wanted to hear about my feelings on the subject of his father pulling some strings to get my tax returns examined, or seducing my wife, then there was little else to talk about—unless he wanted to talk about the night his father was murdered. On that subject, I reminded him, "Don't forget what we discussed regarding my ex-wife."

He nodded, then asked me, "I mean, do you give a shit?"

"My children do."

He nodded again, and said, "Don't worry about it."

"Good." I was about to reannounce my early departure, but then he said, "I never understood how she got off on that."

"She had good lawyers."

"Yeah? I guess that wasn't you."

"Anthony, go fuck yourself."

Like his father, who rarely, if ever, heard a personal insult, he didn't know how to react to that. He seemed to be wavering between explosive rage or sloughing it off as a joke. He picked the latter, and forced a laugh, saying, "You got to learn to curse in Italian. You say, vaffanculo. That means, like, Go fuck your ass. In English, we say, Go fuck *yourself.* Same thing."

"Interesting. Well—"

"But, I mean, do you think it's fair that she walked on a premeditated murder? She got a different kind of justice because of who she is. Right? I mean, what is this? Open season on Italians?"

"This subject is closed. Or take it up with the Justice Department."

"Yeah, right."

"And don't even *think* about what you're thinking about."

He stared at me, but said nothing.

I started to slide out of the booth, but the waitress appeared with two covered serving dishes, and the sweet but obviously inexperienced young lady asked us, "You want to share?"

Anthony, whose mood had darkened somewhat, reminded her, "We got the same fucking thing." He looked at me and asked, "You believe this moron?" He turned to her and inquired, "You jerking us around? We look stupid to you?"

The waitress seemed not to understand and asked, "You no like soup?"

Anthony snapped at her, "Get the soup out of here and bring a couple of beers. Chop, chop."

She took the soup and left.

Frank Bellarosa had hid his thugishness well, though I'd seen it a few times, and heard about it from FBI agent Mancuso. His son, however, apparently hadn't learned that a good sociopath understood how and when to be polite and charming. Anthony had been okay in the gatehouse—in fact, I'd thought he was a bit of a lightweight—but if you watch how powerful men treat the little people, you know how they will treat you when you don't have anything they want.

Anthony said, "She forgot the fucking chopsticks. Didn't you ask for chopsticks?" He raised his hand and was about to shout across the room, but I said, "Forget it."

"No. I'll get—"

"I said, *forget* it." I leaned toward him, and he looked at me. I said to him, "When she returns, you will apologize to her for your bad behavior."

"What?"

"You heard me, Anthony. And here's another etiquette tip for you—if I want chopsticks, *I'll* ask for them—not you. And if I want a beer, *I'll* order the beer. Understand?"

He understood, but he wasn't happy with the lesson. Interestingly, he said nothing.

I slid out of the booth.

He asked, "Where you going?"

"Home."

He got up, followed me, and said, "Hey, Counselor, don't run off. We're not done yet."

I turned toward him, and we were almost face-to-face. I said to him, "We have nothing more to talk about on any subject."

"You know that's not true. We both got some things to work out."

"Maybe. But not together, Anthony."

We were attracting a little attention, so he said, "I'll walk you out."

"No. You'll go back to your seat, apologize to the waitress, then do whatever the hell you want with the rest of your life."

A sudden thought seemed to strike him, and he said, "Yeah, I see the balls, but I don't see the brains, Counselor."

I noticed out of the corner of my eye that Anthony's goon had stood and moved a few feet toward us. The restaurant was very quiet now, and I said to Frank Bellarosa's son, "You have your father's eyes, but not much else."

I turned and walked toward the door, not knowing what to expect.

I went out into the cool night air. Tony was on a smoke break, leaning against the Cadillac SUV, and called out to me, "Hey, you done already?"

I ignored him, got into my car, and started the engine. I saw the goon coming out of the restaurant, and as I backed out of the parking space, I saw him speaking to Tony, and both men looked at me as I drove, without haste, into the street.

I didn't *need* to provoke a confrontation, but he was starting to annoy me, and I thought he was being a little condescending. Well, maybe I was reading him wrong. Or maybe I was seeing Frank across the table, and maybe I had a flashback or a mental image of Frank Bellarosa having sex with Susan—that damned dream—or Frank scamming me into working for him, or Frank screwing up my life with a smile on his face.

In any case, whatever it was that set me off, it felt good, and it had the added result of getting Junior out of my life.

I glanced in my rearview mirror, but didn't see the Cadillac SUV. I left Glen Cove and headed back toward Lattingtown along a dark country road.

Also, I'd put Anthony on notice again about staying away from Susan. Of course, if I was working for him, then Susan had nothing to worry about, assuming she was worried, which I was sure she was not. Worrying used to be my job, and apparently still is.

The other thing for me to keep in mind was that Anthony, who hadn't inherited his father's wealth, had most probably inherited his father's enemies; those within his immediate circle of friends and family, such as Uncle Sal, and those outside his family, such as some of the goombahs I'd met at a gathering at the Plaza Hotel one night, and finally, those, such as Alphonse Ferragamo, whose job it was to put young Anthony in prison for a long time. Therefore, Anthony's tenure as don might be short, and being around him might be dangerous.

And somehow, Anthony thought I might be able to help him with these problems, as I'd helped his father. Was I supposed to be flattered?

History can definitely repeat itself if everyone concentrates very hard on making the same stupid mistakes.

And yet, something draws us back to the familiar, because even if the familiar is not so good, it *is* familiar.

Within fifteen minutes, I was on Grace Lane—Anthony Bellarosa's gift to his neighbors—and my headlights illuminated the shiny new blacktop stretching out before me. A verse from Matthew popped into my head: *Wide is the gate, and broad is the road, that leadeth to destruction.*

CHAPTER THIRTEEN

The following day, Thursday, brought thunderstorms, which were good background for sorting and burning files, and by late afternoon I'd made a large dent in this task, which was onerous and, now and then, sad.

At 6:00 P.M., I rewarded myself with a bottle of Banfi Brunello di Montalcino and Panini Bolognese (baloney sandwich), then sat in George's armchair and read the *New York Times*. John Gotti, the former head of the Gambino crime family, was near death in the hospital of the Federal maximum security penitentiary in Springfield, Missouri, where he was serving a life sentence without parole.

I wondered how, or if, this would affect Mr. Anthony Bellarosa, then I wondered why I was even wondering about that.

And yet, aside from Anthony's professional gain or loss after Mr. Gotti's death, I couldn't help but think about why young men still got into that business, knowing that the careers of nearly all their extended *famiglia* ended in early death or imprisonment. Well, maybe that was better than a retirement community in Florida. In any case, it wasn't my problem.

I did think, briefly, about Anthony's offer of two hundred thousand for doing a little legal work, and I thought, too, about my cut if I could recover some of the Bellarosa assets seized by the Feds. As Anthony said, the two hundred large was in my pocket, but as I knew, that was the shiny lure to attract me—the fish—to the potential millions—the bait—which actually hid a sharp hook.

There was nothing illegal or even unethical about this; fish and lawyers need to eat. The problem was the sharp hook. One needed to be careful.

In fact, one needed to stop thinking about this.

Friday was also rainy, and by noon I'd nearly finished getting my paperwork organized and boxed, ready to be shipped someplace after Ethel was boxed and shipped. My next task was to gather and pack my personal effects—old Army uniforms, sailing trophies, books, desk items, and so forth. How did I ever live for ten years without this stuff?

Anyway, I'd found some documents and papers pertaining or belonging to Susan, as well as some photographs of her family, and since I didn't want to be reminded of the Stanhopes—especially William, Charlotte, and their useless son, Peter—I put these photos in a large envelope with Susan's papers; delivery method to be determined.

The weather cleared in the afternoon, and I took the opportunity to go for a run up to the Long Island Sound. There was a large gaff-rigged sloop out on the water, and I stood on a rock on Fox Point and watched it glide east, its white sails full and its bow cutting effortlessly through the whitecaps.

I could see the skipper at the helm, and though I couldn't see his face clearly at this distance, I knew he was smiling.

I doubted I'd ever go back to sea, though the sea did beckon now and then, as it does to every sailor. But as every sailor knows who has ever loved the sea, its embrace is too often deadly.

At about 4:00 P.M., back in the gatehouse, I happened to notice a gray Mercedes coming through the gates, driven by a man who looked like he could fit the description of someone named Amir Nasim.

Living in London had brought me into close proximity to men and women who practiced the Islamic faith, including a few co-workers, and I assumed that Mr. Nasim, an Iranian, was a Muslim, and thus his Sabbath would begin at sundown with the call to prayer.

Mr. Nasim, and probably his whole household, would get themselves to a mosque, or they'd simply roll out the prayer rugs in the former chapel of Stanhope Hall, take off their shoes, face Mecca—which from this part of the world was east toward the Hamptons—and pray.

I didn't want to intrude on this religious devotion, but I did need to speak to Mr. Nasim before too long, so I might as well do it now. Figuring I had a few hours before the prayer rugs were unrolled, I changed into tan slacks, blue blazer, golf shirt, and penny loafers, with clean socks, just in case he rolled out another rug and asked me to stay.

I'd found a box of my engraved calling cards that said, simply, *John Whitman Sutter, Stanhope Hall*, and I slipped a few of these in my pocket.

Susan had given me these useless and anachronistic cards, and I probably hadn't used six of them in the dozen years I owned them, the last one being sent—to amuse myself—to don Frank Bellarosa, via his building contractor, with instructions that Mr. Bellarosa should call Mr. Sutter regarding Mrs. Sutter's horse stable project, which our new neighbor had offered to help us with. Insisted, actually.

Normally, I'd walk the half mile up the main drive to Stanhope Hall, but I didn't want to pass Susan's guest cottage—our former marital residence—on foot. So I took the Ford Taurus and headed toward the mansion.

I passed the turnoff to her cottage, which I could see a few hundred feet to my left, and which I noticed had lights on in the front room, which used to be my den. Susan's SUV was in the forecourt.

Some distance from the guest cottage I saw Susan's stable—a handsome brick structure that once sat closer to the main house, but which Susan had moved, brick by brick, from her father's property to her property in anticipation of Stanhope Hall being sold. This was a formidable and expensive project, but as I said, and as good luck would have it, Mr. Bellarosa was happy and eager to have his contractor, Dominic, do the job immediately, and for peanuts. I refused; Susan accepted. The lesson here is that if something looks too good to be true, it is. But I already knew that. What I didn't know was that Frank Bellarosa had been as interested in Susan as he was in me.

Anyway, up ahead, I saw Stanhope Hall, set on a rise amidst terraced gardens.

To envision this place, think of the White House in Washington, or any neo-classical palace you've ever seen, then imagine a world with no income tax (and thus no tax lawyers like myself) and think of cheap immigrant labor, sixty-hour workweeks with no benefits, and the riches of a new continent pouring into the pockets of a few hundred men in New York. This Gilded Age was followed by the Roaring Twenties, when things got even better, and the mansions continued to grow bigger and more numerous, like golden mushrooms sprouting along Fifth Avenue, and in Bar Harbor, Newport, the Hamptons, and here on the Gold Coast. And then came Black Tuesday, and it all crashed in a single day. Shit happens.

I should mention that the back sixty acres of the Stanhope estate, where Susan had done most of her horseback riding, had been subdivided like Alhambra, as part of the Federal land grab, to build about a dozen horrible phony Beaux-Arts mini-mansions on the required five-acre lots. Thankfully, a stockade fence and a ditch had been constructed to separate these monstrosities from the front acreage, and a new access road led out to another main road so that no one on this end of the former estate had to see or hear the residents of this nouveau riche ghetto. Well, that may have sounded a bit snobby, and in any case it's not my problem.

Still remaining on the original Stanhope acreage was a classical, rotunda-shaped, X-rated love temple, which housed a nude statue of Venus, the Roman goddess of love, and a nude statue of Priapus, the Roman god of boners. Susan and I had played out a few classical themes in this temple, and on one occasion, I recalled, she was a virgin who'd come to the temple to ask Venus for a suitable husband, and I was a centurion with erectile dysfunction who'd come to pray to Priapus for a woody. As with all of our fantasies, this one had a happy ending. The real marriage, unfortunately, did not.

As I approached the mansion, I wondered what Amir Nasim thought of his pagan temple, and wondered if he'd draped the statues, or had them removed or destroyed. Talk about a clash of cultures.

I parked the Taurus under the huge, columned portico of Stanhope Hall, and there I sat, thinking that in the nearly vanished world of established custom and protocol—now called the pecking order—John Whitman Sutter would not be going from the gatehouse to the mansion to call on Amir Nasim. And maybe that's why I'd put this off.

I sat in the car, thinking I should leave. But I took some comfort in the fact that my visit was unannounced, and thus I was asserting my status and privilege, or what was left of it.

On the subject of maintaining one's dignity while asking a favor of the recently arrived barbarians now living in the villa, I recalled Susan's favorite line from St. Jerome: *The Roman world is falling, yet we hold our heads erect . . .*

I got out of the car, climbed the granite steps between the classical columns, and rang the bell.

CHAPTER FOURTEEN

A young woman—possibly Iranian—in a black dress opened the door, and I announced myself by stating, "Mr. John Sutter to see Mr. Amir Nasim."

At this point, the house servant would usually inquire, "Is he expecting you, sir?"

And I would reply, "No, but if it's not inconvenient, I would like to see him on a personal matter." Then I'd hand her my calling card, she'd show me into the foyer, disappear, and within a few minutes she'd return with the verdict.

In this case, however, the young woman seemed to have limited English as well as limited training, and she replied, "You wait," and closed the door on me. So I rang again, she opened the door, and I handed her my card, saying sharply, "Give this to him. Understand?"

She closed the door again, and I stood there. That was my third encounter with an English-challenged person in as many days, and I was becoming annoyed. In fact, I could almost understand Anthony losing his cool with the young Chinese waitress, and his rap on the decline and fall of the Roman Empire. I mean, the Goths, Huns, and Vandals probably learned Latin as they overran the Empire. *Veni, vidi, vici.* It's not that difficult.

I waited about five minutes, the door opened again, and a tall, thin gentleman with dark features and a gray suit, holding my card in his hand, said, "Ah, Mr. Sutter. How nice of you to visit." He extended his hand, we shook, and he asked me to come in.

He said to me, "I was just about to have tea. Will you join me?"

I didn't want tea, but I needed some of his time, so I guess it was teatime. I replied, "Thank you, I will."

"Excellent."

I followed him into the huge granite lower vestibule, which was designed as a sort of transit area for arriving guests. Here the house servants would take the guests' hats, coats, walking sticks, or whatever, and the guests would be led up one of the great sweeping staircases that rose into the upper foyer. This was a bit more formal than the way we greet houseguests today, such as, "Hey, John, how the hell are you? Throw your coat anywhere. Ready for a beer?"

In any case, Mr. Nasim led me up the right-hand staircase, which was still lit by the original painted cast-iron statues of blackamoors in turbans holding electric torches. I wondered if Mr. Nasim was offended by the statues, which obviously represented his co-religionists as dark-skinned people in a servile capacity.

Thanks to Anthony, the fall of the Roman Empire was still on my mind, and I recalled something I'd read at St. Paul's—where Roman history was big—about Attila the Hun, who, upon capturing the Roman city of Mediolanum, entered the royal palace and spotted a large fresco depicting an enthroned Roman emperor with defeated Sycthians prostrate at his feet. Unfortunately, Attila mistook the groveling Scythians as Huns, and he was so teed off that he made the Roman governor crawl to him on his hands and knees.

I guess I was concerned about a similar cultural misunderstanding here regarding the blackamoors, and I thought I should say something like, "The Stanhopes were insensitive racists and religious bigots, and these statues always offended me."

Well, maybe that was a silly thought, and quite frankly, I didn't give a damn what Amir Nasim thought; he'd had ample time to get rid of the statues if he'd wanted to.

Anyway, we chatted about the weather until we reached the top of the stairs and passed into the upper foyer, where in days gone by the master and his wife would greet their now coatless, hatless, and probably winded guests.

From the upper foyer, I followed Mr. Nasim to the right, down a long, wide gallery, which I knew led to the library.

Mr. Nasim inquired, "How long has it been since you have been here?"

Obviously, he knew something of my personal history. I replied, "Ten years."

"Ah, yes, it is nine years since I purchased this home."

I recalled that the government, which had seized the property from Frank Bellarosa, had sold Stanhope Hall and most of the acreage to a Japanese corporation, for use as a retreat for strung-out Nipponese executives, but the deal had fallen through, and I'd heard from Edward that an Iranian had purchased the property a year after I'd left. I should tell Mr. Nasim that Anthony Bellarosa wanted his father's property back.

He asked me, "You have good memories here?"

Not really. But I replied, "Yes." In fact, Susan and I had been married in Stanhope Hall, while William and Charlotte were still living here, and Cheap Willie had given us—or his daughter—an outdoor reception, to which he'd invited about three hundred of his closest and dearest friends, family, and business associates, as well as a few people I knew. Of course, with William footing the bill, the food and booze ran out early, and the orchestra packed it in at 10:00 P.M. sharp, and by 10:30 the remaining guests were scavenging for wine dregs and cheese rinds.

That was not my first clue that my new father-in-law was a master of the bargain-basement grand gesture, nor was it the last. In the end, he'd gotten back the only thing he ever gave me: his daughter.

Mr. Nasim informed me, "We are still in the process of decorating."

"It takes a while."

"Yes." He added, "My wife . . . the women take their time with decisions."

"Really?" I mean, nine years isn't *that* long, Amir. You're married. Learn to be patient.

In fact, the wide gallery and the adjoining rooms were almost devoid of furniture and totally devoid of paintings or decorations. There were, however, a scattering of carpets on the floor—undoubtedly Persian—and ironically, this is what covered most of the floors of Stanhope Hall when William and Charlotte lived here.

The last time I'd seen this place, it was unfurnished, except for a few odds and ends here and there, plus there were a few rooms that Susan and I used to store sporting equipment, awful gifts, and Susan's childhood furniture. Also, I recalled there had been steamer trunks filled with clothing belonging to long-dead Stanhopes of both sexes. These outfits spanned the decades of the twentieth century, and Susan and I would sometimes dress in period costume—we both preferred the Roaring Twenties—and act silly.

Mr. Nasim said to me, "I suppose you know the history of this house."

His English was good, learned from someone who spoke with a British accent. I replied, "I do."

"Good. You must tell me the history."

"If you wish."

We reached the library, and Mr. Nasim stood aside and ushered me through the double doors.

The paneling and bookshelves were as I remembered, a rich pecan wood, but the new furniture was, unfortunately, a really bad French style, white and gold, the sort of thing you'd see in the Sunday magazine ads for a hundred dollars down and low monthly payments.

Mr. Nasim indicated two chairs covered in baby blue satin near the fireplace, between which was a white coffee table with bowed legs. I sat in one of the uncomfortable chairs, and Mr. Nasim sat facing me. I noticed that the bookshelves were nearly empty, and what was there were mostly oversized art books of the type that decorators sold by the foot.

I noticed, too, that Mr. Nasim hadn't invested in air-conditioning, and a floor fan moved the warm, humid air around the big library.

On the table was a silver tray piled high with sticky-looking pastry. My host said to me, "I enjoy the English tea, but I prefer Persian sweets to cucumber sandwiches."

I noted his use of the word "Persian" as opposed to "Iranian," which had some negative connotations since the Islamic Revolution, the '79 hostage crisis, and subsequent misunderstandings between our countries.

Mr. Nasim whipped out his cell phone, speed-dialed, said a few words in Farsi, then hung up and said to me with a smile, "The high-tech version of the servant call button." He informed me, "Tea will arrive shortly," just in case I thought he'd called the Revolutionary Guards to take me hostage.

He sat back in his satin chair and asked me, "To what do I owe the pleasure of this visit, Mr. Sutter?"

I replied, without apologizing for my unannounced house call, "First, I wanted to let you know—personally and officially—that I'm staying in the gatehouse."

"Thank you." He added politely, "Perhaps I should have called on you."

My limited experience with Arabs, Pakistanis, and Iranians in London was that they fell into two categories: those who tried to emulate the British, and those who went out of their way not to. Mr. Nasim, so far, seemed to fall into the former category of, "See how Western I am? Am I getting it right?"

I informed him, "It is I who am living on your property, so I should call on you. Which brings me to the other point of my visit. I saw Mrs. Allard a few days ago in the hospice house, and I believe she doesn't have much time left."

He seemed genuinely surprised and replied, "Yes? I didn't know that. I thought . . . well, I am sorry to hear that news."

"When she dies, as you know, her life tenancy expires with her."

"Yes, I know that."

He didn't seem outwardly thrilled to learn that he was about to get his property back, but he knew, of course, this day would come, and he'd already made plans for it, and I'm sure those plans didn't include me. Nevertheless, I said, "Therefore, I'd like to ask you if I could rent—or buy—the gatehouse."

"Yes? You want to live there?"

"It's an option."

He nodded, thought a moment, then said, "I see . . ."

"If I rented, it would be only for a month or two."

"I see. So you need a place to stay while you are not in London."

"How did you know I lived in London?"

"I was told by Mrs. Sutter."

"I assume you mean my ex-wife."

"That is correct."

"And what else did she tell you? So I don't take your time by repeating what you already know."

He shrugged and replied, "When she purchased the house—the former guest cottage—she paid a courtesy call. It was a Sunday, and I was here with my wife, and we had tea and she spoke generally of her situation."

"I see. And since then, she's informed you that her ex-husband has returned from London."

"Correct." He added, "Not me, actually. Soheila. My wife. They speak."

I wanted to warn him that Mrs. Sutter was an adulteress and not good company for Soheila. But why cause trouble? I returned to my subject and said, "So, if you have no objection, I'd like to rent the gate-house for a month or two—with an option to buy."

"It is not for sale, but—"

Before he could continue, the woman who'd answered the door appeared carrying a tea tray, which she set down on the table with a bow of her head.

Mr. Nasim dismissed her, and she literally backed out of the room and pulled the doors closed. Well, maybe her training wasn't all that bad; she just needed a lesson in front door etiquette. Or, more likely, Amir Nasim scared the hell out of her. Maybe I could pick up a few pointers from him on gender relations.

Anyway, Mr. Nasim did the honors and opened a wooden box that contained tins of teas and said to me, "Do you have a preference?"

I did, and it was called Scotch whisky, but I said, "Earl Grey would be fine."

"Excellent." He spooned the loose tea into two china pots and poured in hot water from a thermal carafe, all the while making tea talk, such as, "I generally let it steep for four minutes . . ." He covered both pots, then flipped over a sand timer and said, ". . . but you can time yours as you wish."

I glanced at my watch, which he could interpret as me timing my tea or me getting a little impatient. In any case, I guess tea is what people of Mr. Nasim's religion did in lieu of six o'clock cocktails.

As we waited for the sands of time to run out, he made conversation and said, "I lived in London for ten years. Wonderful city."

"It is."

"You have lived there, I believe, seven years."

"That's right."

"And before that, you sailed around the world."

"Correct."

"So, you are an adventurous man. A man who likes danger, perhaps."

"I went sailing. I didn't attack any warships."

He smiled, then said, "But it is dangerous out there, Mr. Sutter. Aside from the weather, there are pirates and explosive mines. Did you sail into the Persian Gulf?"

"I did."

"That is very dangerous. Did you visit Iran?"

"I did. Bushehr."

"And how were you received there?"

"Quite well."

"Good. I have this theory that people who live in seaports are happier and kinder to strangers than those who live inland. What do you think?"

"I think that's true until you get to New York."

He smiled again, then changed the subject and said, "So, you will return to London in a month or two."

"Perhaps."

"And where do you live there?"

I told him my street in Knightsbridge, without giving him my house number, flat number, or telephone number.

He nodded and said, "A very nice neighborhood." He informed me, "I lived in Mayfair."

"Nice neighborhood."

"Too many Arabs."

I let that alone and watched the sand run. I'm aware that other cultures make lots of small talk before they get down to business, and I know this is not simply politeness; the other guy is trying to get a measure of you that he will use later. In this case, however, the business was fairly simple and should have taken less time than a three-minute egg. Well, maybe Amir Nasim was simply being polite to a now landless former aristocrat.

He said to me, "So, you are an attorney."

"That's right."

"And this is what you did in London."

"American tax law for British and foreign clients."

"Ah. Interesting. Yes, there is a need for that. In fact, I have a company in London, so perhaps we can meet there one day and—" Time was up, and he took hold of his teapot and poured through a strainer into a dainty cup, saying to me, "Please go ahead, unless you like it stronger."

I poured my tea as Mr. Nasim heaped several spoons of sugar into his cup. He asked me, "Sugar? Cream? Lemon?"

"I drink it straight."

"Good. That is the correct way. But I like my sugar." He sipped and said, "Very good. I use filtered water."

"Me, too." I said to him, "About the gatehouse—"

"Try a sweet. May I recommend that one?" He pointed to a gooey heap of something and said, "That is called Rangeenak." He then named the other five desserts for me.

My Farsi, never good to begin with, was a bit rusty, so I said, "I'll try number one."

"Yes. Excellent." He plucked up a wad of what looked liked dates with a silver tong and put them on my plate. "If you find it too sweet, I would recommend this one, which is made of sesame paste."

"Okay. So, as to the purpose of my visit, it would be convenient for me, and I hope not an inconvenience for you, if I stayed for a month or two in the gatehouse."

He put one of each pastry on his plate and replied offhandedly, "Yes, of course."

This took me by surprise, and I said, "Well . . . that's very good of you." I added, "I can draw up a short-term lease for one month, beginning on Mrs. Allard's death, with another month's option. So, assuming we can agree on a rent—"

"There is no charge, Mr. Sutter."

This, too, took me by surprise, and I said, "I insist—"

"No charge." He joked, "Do you want to complicate my American taxes?"

Actually, that's how I made my living, but I said, "Well . . . that's very kind of you, but—"

"Not at all. I ask only that you be out by September the first." He added, "Of course, if Mrs. Allard is still living at that time, then you are still her guest. But otherwise, September the first."

"That won't be a problem."

"Good."

"But why don't I draw up an agreement to that effect?" I explained, "Legally, it would be good for both of us to have this in writing."

"We have a gentleman's agreement, Mr. Sutter."

"As you wish." Now, of course, I was supposed to offer my hand— or did we cut open our veins, exchange blood, then dance around the table? After a few awkward seconds, I extended my hand and we shook.

Mr. Nasim poured more tea for himself, and I took a sip of mine.

He said to me, "I just had a thought."

My antennae went up.

He continued, "I'd like to ask a favor of you."

I suddenly had this flashback to the evening when Frank Bellarosa invited Susan and me to Alhambra for coffee and Italian pastry, and afterwards don Bellarosa and I retired to his library for grappa and cigars, at which time he asked me for a favor that wound up ruining my life. Mr. Nasim did not indulge in alcohol or tobacco, but otherwise I was certain he and the dead don had a lot in common.

Mr. Nasim inquired, "May I ask a favor?"

"You may ask."

"Good." He popped a rather large pastry in his mouth, then plunged his fingers in his finger bowl and wiped them on a linen napkin. He chewed thoughtfully, swallowed, then said, "With Mrs. Allard in the gatehouse and Mrs. Sutter in the guest cottage, I have felt a lack of privacy. You understand?"

I reminded him, "You have nearly two hundred walled acres of land here, Mr. Nasim. How much privacy do you need?"

"I enjoy my privacy." He further informed me, "Also, I could make use of the gatehouse for my own staff, and I would like to have the guest cottage for my own use as well."

I didn't respond.

He continued, "I was about to make an offer to the owners of the guest cottage for their house and the ten acres when, suddenly, I discovered that Mrs. Sutter had purchased the property. And so I made her a very substantial offer for the property, but she refused. Very nicely, I should say, but refused nonetheless."

"Make her a better offer."

"I would, but I take her at her word that the property is not for sale at any price." He added, "Of course, there is a price, but . . ." He looked at me and said, "She told me that this is her home, with many memories, a place where your children grew up, and where they can visit, and . . . well, a place that she associates with a good time in her life . . ." He continued, "And, of course, it is a part of this estate—Stanhope Hall, where she grew up. And so she intends to stay here, she said, until she dies."

I didn't respond, but I thought that made at least two people in the neighborhood who wouldn't mind if Susan were dead. Finally, I said, "That sounds like a pretty definite no."

Mr. Nasim sort of shrugged and said, "People, as they get older— Not that Mrs. Sutter is old. She seems quite young. But people become more nostalgic as the years pass, and thus they have an urge to revisit the places of their youth, or they become attached to an object or a place. You understand. And this can lead to a degree of stubbornness and perhaps the irrational making of decisions."

"What is your point, Mr. Nasim?"

"Well, I was wondering if you could reason with her."

I informed him, "I couldn't reason with her when we were married."

He smiled politely.

I continued, "We don't speak. And I have no intention of speaking to her on this subject."

He seemed disappointed, but said, "Well, I thought this was a good idea of mine, but I see that it was not such a good idea."

"Can't hurt to ask."

"No." He switched to a more important subject and said, "You haven't eaten your Rangeenak."

To be polite, I popped one of the date-things in my mouth, then rinsed my fingers in the rose petal water, dried them and said, "Well, I won't hold you to the free rent, but I do need the place for that time."

He waved his hand and said, "I am good to my word. No strings attached."

That's what Frank used to say.

My business was finished, and I didn't want to be asked to take off my shoes to stay and pray, so I was about to take my leave, but he said, "My offer to Mrs. Sutter was four million dollars. Far more than the property is worth, and more than double what she paid for it only a few months ago. I would be willing to pay someone a ten percent commission if that person could facilitate the purchase."

I stood and said, "I am not that person. Thank you—"

He stood, too, and replied, "Well, but you don't know that. If you do speak to her, keep this conversation in mind."

I was getting a little annoyed and said brusquely, "Mr. Nasim, what in the world makes you think I have any influence over my ex-wife?"

He hesitated, then replied, "She spoke well of you, and so I assumed . . ." He changed the subject and said, "I will walk you to the door."

"I can let myself out. I know the place well."

"Yes. And you were going to tell me the history of the house."

"Perhaps another time. Or," I suggested, "Mrs. Sutter can give you a more detailed history." I extended my hand and said, "Thank you for tea, and for the use of the gatehouse." I added, "If you change your mind, I understand."

He took my hand, then put his other hand on my shoulder and turned me toward the doors, saying, "I insist on walking you out."

Maybe he thought I was going to roll up a Persian carpet and take it with me, so I said, "As you wish."

As we walked down the gallery, he handed me his card. "This is my personal card with my private number. Call me if I can be of any assistance."

I thought about asking him to help me load up Elizabeth's SUV tomorrow, but I didn't think that was what he meant.

He pulled my calling card from his pocket, looked at it, and read, "Stanhope Hall. I assume this is an old card." He made a joke and continued, "Or did you just have these printed in expectation of my agreeing to your request?"

I replied, "These are old cards. But rather than throw them out, I'll make you an offer for the whole estate."

He laughed. "Make your best offer. Everything has a price."

Indeed, it does.

He asked me, "Do you have a cell phone?"

"Not yet." I got nosy and asked him, "What sort of business are you in, Mr. Nasim?"

"Import and export."

"Right."

He said, "Please feel free to make use of the grounds." He added, "Mrs. Sutter runs or takes long walks on the property."

Good reason not to make use of the grounds.

He added, "I have maintained the English hedge maze." He smiled and said, "One can become lost in there."

"That's the purpose."

"Yes." He asked, "Did your children play there?"

"They did." He'd opened the subject of the estate grounds, so I asked him, bluntly, "Did you remove the statues from the love temple?"

"I'm afraid I did, Mr. Sutter."

He didn't offer any further information, and I didn't want to be too provocative by asking what became of the statues.

He did say, however, "I, myself, didn't find them offensive—they are simply examples of Western classical art of that pagan time. But I have guests here of my faith, and those statues might be offensive to them."

I could have suggested bathrobes for the statues, or locking the temple door, but I let it drop.

He, however, did not let it drop, and informed me, "Mrs. Sutter understood."

Apparently she'd become more sensitive to other cultures in the last decade. I said to him, "It's your property."

"Yes. In any case, as I said, feel free to use the grounds, including the tennis courts. I ask only that you dress somewhat modestly on my property. You can dress as you wish on your own property, of course."

"Thank you."

This subject brought back a memory of Mr. Frank Bellarosa and Mrs. Sutter, when Bellarosa made his first, unannounced visit to Stanhope Hall, while Susan and I were playing a game of mixed doubles on the estate's tennis court with Jim and Sally Roosevelt. Our new neighbor brought us a gift of vegetable seedlings, and aside from interrupting our match, which was annoying enough, Bellarosa kept glancing at Susan's bare legs.

Well, if only Mr. Nasim had owned the estate then, Susan would have been playing tennis in a full-length chador and veil, and Frank Bellarosa would have just dropped off the seedlings and left without a thought about screwing Susan. So maybe Amir Nasim had a point there about modest dress.

Anyway, I certainly didn't want to run into Susan on the Stanhope acreage—though she and Mr. Nasim may have wanted that—but to be polite I said, "Thank you for your offer." We reached the stairs, and I said, "I can find my way from here."

"I need the exercise."

We descended the wide, curving staircase together, and he said, apropos of the stair lighting, "I've seen these blackamoors in paintings, and as statues in museums and palaces all over Europe. But I'm not certain of their significance."

"I have no idea."

"I suppose there was a time in Europe when these people were slaves or servants."

"Well, they don't look like they own the place."

"No, they do not." He stopped abruptly about midway down the staircase, so I, too, stopped. He said to me, "Mr. Sutter, I quite understand."

"Understand what, Mr. Nasim?"

"Your feelings, sir."

I didn't reply.

He continued, "Your feelings about me, about me being in this house, and about my culture, my money, my religion, and my country. And about your position in relation to all of that."

I ran through several replies in my mind, then picked the best one and said, "Then we completely understand one another."

"And I must say I don't really blame you for how you feel."

"I don't care if you do or you don't."

"Of course. I understand that as well. But I want to tell you that the reason I'm here, and the reason I was in England, is that I am an exile, Mr. Sutter. Not a voluntary exile, as you were. But a political exile who would be arrested and executed if I returned to my country, which is now in the hands of the mullahs and the radicals. I was a very ardent and public supporter of the late Shah, and so I am a marked man. I have no country, Mr. Sutter, so unlike you, who can come home, I cannot go home. Unlike your wife, who has come home, I cannot simply fly to Iran and buy back my old house. In fact, I will probably never see my country again. So, Mr. Sutter, you and I have something in common—we both want me back where I came from, but that will not happen in my lifetime, nor yours."

I had the feeling that this speech was rehearsed and given on the appropriate occasions, but I also thought it was probably true. Or partly true. I suppose I was now feeling a little less unkind toward Mr. Amir Nasim, but that didn't change my situation or his.

I said to him, "Thank you for your time."

I continued alone down the stairs, but I sensed he was still there.

I walked across the stone floor, and my footsteps echoed in the cavernous foyer. The front door was bolted, so I unbolted it.

He called out to me, "Mr. Sutter."

I turned and looked at him on the staircase.

He said to me, "I should tell you that there are some security issues here which have recently arisen and of which you should be aware."

I didn't reply.

He continued, "This is why I need the gatehouse and the guest cottage—to put *my* people in them. You understand?"

I understood that this was quite possibly a convenient lie—a ruse to make me tell Susan that Stanhope Hall was under imminent threat of attack by an Islamic hit squad. Actually, I didn't think Susan would care as long as the assassins didn't trample the flowerbeds.

Mr. Nasim, not getting any reaction from me, continued, "If you see anything suspicious or odd, please call me."

"I certainly will. And you do the same. Good day."

I left and closed the door behind me.

I descended the steps under the portico, got into my car, and drove off.

As I moved slowly down the tree-covered lane toward the gatehouse, I processed what Amir Nasim said about his security issues. I mean, really, how many political exiles get whacked around here? None, the last time I counted. Surely there were local ordinances prohibiting political assassination.

On the other hand, the world had changed since September 11 of last year. For one thing, there had been dozens of local residents killed in the Twin Towers, and there were people like Mr. Amir Nasim who were feeling some heat from their countries of origin, or from an irate and increasingly xenophobic population—or from the authorities. Or they were just feeling paranoid, which might be the case with Amir Nasim.

And then there was Mr. Anthony Bellarosa down the road. How odd, I thought, that Messrs. Bellarosa and Nasim, from opposite ends of the universe, had a similar problem, to wit: Old enemies were out to kill them. But maybe that was not coincidence; it was an occupational hazard when your occupation is living dangerously and pissing off the wrong people.

Enter John Sutter, who just dropped into town to take care of some business, and gets two offers for some fast money. I mean, this was really my lucky week—unless I got caught in the crossfire.

I approached the guest cottage, and I thought about stopping and ringing her bell. "Hello, Susan, I just stopped by to tell you that if you see a group of armed men in black ski masks running across your lawn, don't be alarmed. They're just here to kill Mr. Nasim." And I should add, "If a Mr. Anthony Bellarosa comes by, don't forget that you killed his father. And, oh, by the way, I have some nude photos of you, and photos of your dysfunctional family."

I slowed down as I came abreast of her house, and I could actually see her through the front window of what was once my den. She was sitting where my desk used to be, and it looked as though she was multitasking on the phone and the computer, and probably eating yogurt and doing her nails at the same time.

I considered seizing the moment and stopping. I did need to speak to her about what Nasim said, and about Anthony, and a few less urgent matters. But I could do that by phone . . . I continued on to the gatehouse.

It was a dreary day, weather-wise and otherwise, but I could see some breaks in the clouds, and tomorrow was supposed to be sunny. Plus, I'd gotten my housing situation straightened out—if I didn't mind Islamic commandos scaling the walls—and I'd completed my desk work, made my peace with Ethel, made a sort of date with Elizabeth, and turned down an offer from Anthony Bellarosa, which is what I should have done with his father ten years ago.

All in all, things were on the right track, and quite possibly I had a wonderful, bright future ahead of me.

And yet I had this sense of foreboding, this feeling that there were forces at work that I comprehended on one level, but dismissed on another, like black storm clouds at sea that circled the horizon around my boat as I sat becalmed under a sunny patch of sky.

I went into the gatehouse, got myself a beer, then went out through the kitchen and sat on a bench in Ethel's Victory Garden.

I thought about the changes she had seen in her long life—her spring, her summer, her autumn, and now her cold, dark winter.

I knew she had many regrets, including a lost love, and this made me think of Susan.

As my late father once said to me, "It's too late to change the past, but never too late to change the future."

What I didn't want at the end of the day were any old regrets; what I really needed now were some new regrets.

CHAPTER FIFTEEN

Saturday morning was sunny and cool. Good running weather.

I got into my sweats and began a jog along Grace Lane, heading south toward Bailey Arboretum, forty forested acres of a former estate, now a park, which I remembered was a good place to run.

I do some of my best thinking while running, and today's first subject was my meeting with Elizabeth. I needed to tidy up the gatehouse, then drive into the village for some wine and whatever. Then I considered an agenda for my afternoon with her: legal matters first, followed by an inventory of everything in the house. After that, maybe a glass of wine. Maybe several glasses of wine. Maybe I should stop thinking about this.

I switched mental gears and gave some thought to my long-term plans. As I was going through an abundance of bad options, a black Cadillac Escalade passed me from behind. The vehicle slowed, made a tight U-turn, then headed toward me. As it got closer, I could see Tony behind the wheel.

I slowed my pace as the Cadillac drew abreast of me, then we both stopped, and the tinted rear window slid down. One of my bad options, Anthony Bellarosa, inquired, "Can I give you a lift?"

I walked across the road to the open window and saw that Anthony was alone in the back seat. He was dressed in black slacks and a tasteful tan sports jacket, and I didn't see a violin case, so I concluded he was on some sort of legitimate errand. He asked again, "You want a lift?"

I replied, "No. I'm running."

Tony was out of the car, and he reached past me and opened the door as Anthony slid over. Tony said, "Go 'head."

I think I've seen this in the movies, and I always wondered why the idiot got into the car instead of making a scene, running and screaming for the police.

I glanced up and down Grace Lane, which was, as usual, nearly deserted.

Anthony patted the leather seat beside him and repeated his invitation. "Come on. I want to talk to you."

I thought I'd made it clear that we had nothing to discuss, but I didn't want him to think I was frightened, which I was not, or rude, which I do well with my peers, but not that well with the socially inept, like Anthony. And then there was the Susan problem, which I might be making too much of, but I wouldn't want to make a mistake on that. So I slid into the back seat, and Tony shut the door, then got behind the wheel, did another U-turn, and off we drove.

Anthony said to me, "Hey, no hard feelings about the other night. Right?"

"What happened the other night?"

"Look, I understand where you're coming from. Okay? But what happened in the past should stay in the past."

"Since when?"

"I mean, it had nothing to do with me. So—"

"Your father screwing my wife has nothing to do with you. My wife murdering your father has something to do with you and her."

"Maybe. But I'm talking about you and me."

"There is no you and me."

"There could be."

"There can't be."

"Did you think about my offer?"

"What offer?"

"I'll make it a hundred and fifty."

"It was two."

"See? You thought about it."

"You got me," I admitted. "And now you see I'm not that smart."

"You're plenty smart."

"Make it a hundred, and we can talk."

He laughed.

Were we having fun, or what?

Anthony nodded toward Tony, then said to me, "Let's save this for later." He asked me, "So, what do you think of my paving job?"

"I miss the potholes."

"Yeah? I'll rip it up."

We left Grace Lane and were passing Bailey Arboretum, so I said, "You can let me off here."

"I want to show you something first. In Oyster Bay. This might interest you. I was going to bring it up the other night, but you ran off." He added, "I'll drop you off here on the way back."

End of discussion. I should have been royally pissed off about what amounted to a kidnapping, but it was a friendly kidnapping, and if I was honest with myself, I'd say I was an accomplice.

And on the subject of my prior voluntary involvement with the mob, Anthony was starting to remind me of his father. Frank never took no for an answer, especially when he thought he was doing you a great favor that you were too stupid to understand. Frank, of course, never failed to do himself a favor at the same time. Or, at the very least, he'd remind you of the favor he did for you and ask for a payback. I've been down this road, literally and figuratively, so Anthony was not tempting a virgin. In fact, the tricks and lessons I'd learned from the father were not doing the son any good.

We turned east toward Oyster Bay. Tony, being a good wheelman and bodyguard, was paying a lot of attention to his rearview mirror. I couldn't help thinking about the tollbooth hit scene in *The Godfather*—which actually took place not too far from here—and I thought, *It's the car in* front *of you that you need to watch, stupid.*

Anyway, Anthony, wanting to keep the conversation away from business and from me thinking I was being taken for a one-way ride, said, "Hey, I spoke to my mother this morning. She wants to see you."

"Next time I'm in Brooklyn."

"Better yet, she's coming for Sunday dinner. You're invited."

"Thank you, but—"

"She comes early—like, after church. I send a car for her."

"That's nice."

"Then she cooks all day. She brings her own food from Brooklyn, and she takes over the kitchen, and Megan is like, 'Do I need this shit?' Madonna. What's with these women?"

"If you find out Sunday, let me know."

"Yeah. Right. But if we have other company, then it's usually okay. Hey, one time Megan wants to cook an Irish meal, and my mother comes in and says to me, 'It smells like she's boiling a goat in there.'" He laughed at the happy family memory, then continued, "And Megan drinks too much vino and hardly eats, and the kids aren't used to real Italian food—they think canned spaghetti and pizza bagels are Italian food. But she cooks a hell of a meal. My mother. The smells remind me of Sundays when I was a kid in Brooklyn . . . it's like I'm home again."

I had no idea why he was telling me this, except, I suppose, to show me he was a regular guy, with regular problems, and that he had a mother.

Apropos of that, he asked me, "Did you ever eat at the house?"

I replied, "I did not." But Susan did. I added, "Your mother always sent food over."

Tony, eavesdropping, said, "Yeah. Me and Lenny or Vinnie was always taking food over to your place."

I didn't reply, but this would have been a good time to remind Tony that his departed boss could not have been screwing my wife without the knowledge, assistance, and cover stories of him and the aforementioned two goombahs. Well, I couldn't blame them, and two of them were dead anyway. Three, if you count Frank. Four, if Susan got whacked, and five if I leaned forward and snapped Tony's neck.

I looked out the side window. We were passing through a stretch of remaining estates, most of which were hidden behind old walls or thick trees, but now and then I could see a familiar mansion or a treed allée behind a set of wrought-iron gates.

The local gentry were tooling around in vintage sports cars, which they liked to do on weekends, and we also passed a group on horseback. If you squinted your eyes and excluded some modern realities, you could imagine yourself in the Gilded Age, or the Roaring Twenties, or even in the English countryside.

Anthony, a modern reality, intruded into my thoughts and inquired, "Hey, did you see that piece of ass on that horse?"

I assumed he wasn't admiring the horse's ass, but rather than ask for a grammatical clarification, I ignored him; kidnap victims are not required to make conversation.

I retreated into my ruminations and wondered if Susan had found what she was looking for when she returned here. Based on what Amir Nasim had told me, maybe she had. And I wondered what she thought about me returning. Quite possibly, she saw, or imagined, this circumstance as an opportunity to resume our lives together.

But it's not easy to pick up where you left off, especially if a decade has passed. People change, new lovers have come and gone, or not gone, and each of the parties has processed the past in different ways.

Anthony asked me, "What are you thinking about?"

"Your mother's lasagna."

He laughed. "Yeah? You got it."

Dinner at the Bellarosas' was not high on my social calendar, so I said, "I'm busy Sunday. But thank you."

"Try to stop by. We eat at four." He added instructions, saying, "I'll give the guy at the guard booth your name and he'll give you directions."

I didn't reply.

We drove along the shore, then entered the quaint village of Oyster Bay, and Tony headed into the center of town, which was crowded with Saturday people on various missions.

Saturdays, when I was younger and the kids were younger, were hectic. Carolyn and Edward always had sporting events, or golf and tennis lessons, or birthday parties, or whatever else Susan and the other mothers had cooked up for them, and they needed to be driven, usually with friends, on a tight schedule that rivaled the split-second timing of the Flying Wallendas.

This was all before cell phones, of course, and I recalled losing a few kids, missing a few pick-ups, and once dropping off Edward and his friends at the wrong soccer game.

"What's so funny?"

I glanced at Anthony and replied, "This is exciting. I've never been kidnapped before."

He chuckled and replied, "Hey, you're not kidnapped. You're doing me a favor. And you get a ride home."

"Even if I don't do you the favor?"

"Well, then we see." He thought that was funny and so did Tony. I did not.

Tony found an illegal parking space near the center of the village, and he stayed with the car while Anthony and I got out.

Anthony walked along Main Street and I walked with him. It occurred to me that I wouldn't want anyone I knew to see me walking with a Mafia don, but then I realized it didn't matter. Better yet, it could be fun.

Anthony stopped near the corner where Main Street crossed another shopping street, and he pointed to a three-story brick building on the opposite corner and informed me, "That's a historic building."

"Really?" I knew the building, of course, since I've lived around here most of my life, but Anthony, like his father, couldn't imagine that anyone knew anything until you heard it from him.

Anthony further informed me, "That was Teddy Roosevelt's summer office." He glanced at me to see if I fully appreciated his amazing knowledge. He pointed and said, "On the second floor."

"No kidding?"

He asked me, "Can you believe that the President of the United States ran the country from that dump?"

"Hard to believe." It wasn't actually a dump; it was, in fact, a rather nice turn-of-the-century structure, with a mansard roof, housing a combination bookstore and café on the ground floor, and apartments on the upper floors, accessible through a door to the right of the bookstore.

Anthony continued, "You got to picture this—the President drives into town from his place on Sagamore Hill"—he pointed east to where Teddy Roosevelt's summer White House still stood, about three miles away—"and he's got maybe one Secret Service guy with him and a driver. And he just gets out of the car, and, like, tips his straw hat to some people, and goes in that door and walks up the stairs. Right?"

To enhance this image, I suggested, "But maybe he stops first for coffee and bagels."

"Yeah . . . no—no bagels. Anyway, there was offices up there then, and he's got a secretary—a guy—and maybe another guy who sends telegraph messages and goes to the post office to get the mail. And there's, like, one telephone in the drugstore down the block." He looked at me and asked, "Can you believe that?"

I thought I'd already said it was hard to believe, but to answer his question I replied, again, "Hard to believe." In fact, Roosevelt did most of his work at Sagamore Hill, and rarely came to this office, but Anthony seemed enthused, and he had some point to make, so I let him go on.

He continued, "And it's summer, and there's no air-conditioning, and these guys all wore suits and ties, and wool underwear or something. Right?"

"Right."

"Maybe they had an icebox up there."

"Maybe."

He inquired, "Did they have electric fans then?"

"Good question," which reminded me of another good question, and I asked, "What's the point?"

"Well, there are two points. Maybe three."

"Can I have one?"

"Yeah. The first point is the building is for sale. Three million. Whaddaya think?"

"Buy it."

"Yeah? Why?"

"Because you want it."

"Right. And it's a piece of history."

"Priceless." I glanced at my watch and said to him, "I need to get going. I'll call a cab."

"You're always running off. First you show up, then you run off."

This was true and astute. I guess I had an approach/avoidance response with the Bellarosas. I said, "I didn't exactly show up this time. I was kidnapped. But I'll give you ten minutes."

"Make it twelve. So, what I'm thinking is, I'll get rid of that bookstore on the ground floor and put in a high-end moneymaker—some kind of Triple A chain boutique, or maybe like a food franchise place. Baskin-Robbins ice cream or a Starbucks. Right?"

"You need to speak to the village fathers about that."

"Yeah. I know that." He added, "That's where you come in."

"This is where I leave."

"Come on, John. It's no big deal. I buy the building, you handle the closing, then you see what the old shits are going to allow." He motioned up and down the crowded street and said, "Look at this place. Money. I could get five times the rent if I push it as an historic location. Right?"

"Well—"

"Same with the upstairs spaces. Maybe a law firm. Like, rent Teddy Roosevelt's office. The clients would love it. I get a decorator in and make it look like it did a hundred years ago. Except for the toilet and the air-conditioning." He asked me, "Am I off base on this?"

"Anthony, I've been gone ten years. Get someone to work out the numbers for you."

"Fuck the numbers. I'm buying history."

"Right. Good luck."

"And here's my second point. And this has nothing to do with business. And here's the question—what the fuck has happened to this country?"

Well, for one thing, the Mafia is still around. But people who are part of the problem never see themselves as part of the problem; the problem is always someone else. I replied, "The problem, as I see it, is fast-food chains and lawyers. Too many of both."

"Yeah, but it's a lot more than that. Do you think a President could walk down this street today with one bodyguard?"

"You do. And he's in the car."

"I'm not the fucking President, John."

I noticed he didn't say, "No one is trying to kill me, John," which was what most people would have said.

He continued, "Julius Caesar walked out of the Senate building, with no bodyguards, no Praetorian guards, because that's how it was then. But they stabbed him to death. And that was the end of the Republic, and the beginning of the emperors thinking they were like gods. Understand?"

"I get your point. But there's no turning back to a simpler time. Or a safer time."

"Right . . . but, standing here, I think . . . I don't know. Maybe . . . like, we lost something."

He didn't finish whatever thoughts had been forming in his mind, and quite frankly, I was surprised that he even had thoughts like this. I recalled, though, that his father also harbored some half-expressed worldviews that made him unhappy. And, I suppose, after 9/11, Anthony, like a lot of people, had come to the understanding that there was more to his self-absorbed life than a difficult wife, a complex family history, a clinging mother, and a stressful occupation. Quite possibly, he was thinking, too, about his own mortality.

Anthony lit a cigarette and continued to look at the building across the road. Finally, he said, "When I was a kid at La Salle, one of the brothers said to us, 'Anyone in this room can be President of the United States.'" Anthony took a drag on his cigarette and concluded, "He was full of shit."

Funny, they told us the same thing in my prep school, but at St. Paul's, it was a possibility. I said to him, "We shape our own destiny, Anthony. We have dreams and ambitions, and we make choices. I, for instance, have chosen to go home."

He actually thought that was funny, but he didn't think that was one of my choices. He said, "Here's my other point—my thought—" The traffic light changed and he took my arm and we crossed the busy street. I would have given anything just then to run into the Reverend James Hunnings. "Father, may I introduce my friend and business partner, don Anthony Bellarosa? You remember his father, Frank. Oh, and here's my mother. Harriet, this is Frank Bellarosa's little boy, Tony, all grown up and now called Anthony. And, oh my goodness, there's Susan. Susan, come here and meet the son of the man you whacked. Doesn't he look like his father?"

All right, enough of that. We reached the opposite sidewalk without meeting anyone I knew, or having to stop so don Bellarosa could sign autographs.

Anthony said to me, "My father once said, 'There's only two kinds of men in this world. Men who work for other people, and men who work for themselves.'"

I didn't reply, because I knew where this was going.

He continued, "So, like, I work for myself. You work for other people."

Again, I didn't reply.

He continued, "So, what I'm thinking is that I front you the money you need to open an office here and hang out your shingle. What do you think about that?"

"It's a long commute from London."

"Hey, fuck London. You belong here. You could be in Teddy Roosevelt's old office, and do your tax law stuff here. Hire a few secretaries, and before you know it, you're raking in big bucks."

"And I wonder who my first client will be."

"Wrong. See? You're wrong on that. You and me have no connection."

"Except the money you loan me."

"I'm not *loaning* you the money. I'm *fronting* it. I'm *investing* in you. And if it doesn't work out for you, then I lose my investment, and I just kick your ass out of the office. You have no downside."

"I don't get my legs broken or anything like that?"

"Whaddaya talking about?"

"And what have I done to deserve this opportunity?"

"You know. For all that you did for my father. For saving his life. For being the one guy who never wanted anything from him, and for not wanting any harm to come to him."

Actually, I did want something from him—a little excitement in my life, and I got that. As for the other thing, after I realized he was having an affair with my wife, I wished him great harm, and I got that, too. But I wasn't about to tell Anthony that Pop and I were even on that score. Instead, I said to him with impatience in my voice, "Tell me exactly what the hell you want from me. And no bullshit about you investing in my future with no strings attached."

We were attracting a little attention, and Anthony glanced around and said in a quiet voice, "Come upstairs and we can talk about that."

He added, "The apartment is empty. The realtor is coming in half an hour. I got the key."

"Tell me here and now."

He ignored me, turned toward the door, and unlocked it, revealing a small foyer and a long, steep staircase. He said, "I'll be upstairs."

"I won't."

He stepped into the foyer, looked back at me, and said, "You want to hear what I have to say."

He turned and climbed the stairs.

I turned and walked away.

As I moved along Main Street, thinking about a taxi or running the five or six miles home, another thought, which I'd been avoiding, intruded into my head.

If I *really* thought about this, and let my mind come to an inevitable conclusion, then I knew that Anthony Bellarosa, despite what he'd told me, was not going to allow Susan, his father's murderer, to live down the street. Or live at all. He just couldn't do that. And there were undoubtedly people waiting for him to take care of it. And if he didn't take care of it, then his *paesanos*—including probably his brothers—would wonder what kind of don this was.

And yet Anthony wanted me to work for him, and the unspoken understanding was that if I did this, then Susan was safe. For the time being.

So . . . I needed to at least go along with this, until I could speak to Susan. It really is all about keeping your friends close, and your enemies closer.

I turned and walked back to the building.

CHAPTER SIXTEEN

The door was still ajar, and I climbed the stairs.

There was a landing at the top, and I opened the only door, which revealed the living room of an empty apartment. The carpet was worn, the beige paint was dingy, and the high plaster ceiling looked like it was ready to fall. An altogether depressing place, except that it had big windows and it was very sunny.

Another good feature was that the Mafia don seemed to have left. Then I heard a toilet flush, and a door at the far end of the room opened, and Anthony said, as if I'd been there the whole time, "The plumbing seems okay." He looked around and announced, "All this shit needs to be ripped out. But I own a construction company—hey, you remember Dominic? He did the horse stable at your place." He further informed me, "Sometime back in the thirties, they turned these offices into apartments. So, I get rid of the tenants, and I can get double the rent as office space. Right?"

I didn't reply.

"I see big, fancy moldings, thick carpets, and mahogany doors. And you know what I see on that door? I see gold letters that say, 'John Whitman Sutter, Attorney-at-Law.' Can you see that?"

"Maybe."

He didn't seem to react to this hint of capitulation, figuring, correctly, that if I'd climbed the stairs, then I was ready to listen.

He said, "Let's look at the other rooms." He walked through a door, and I followed into a large corner bedroom from which I could see the streets below. The walls were painted white over peeling wallpaper, and the carpet looked like Astroturf. Anthony said to me, "The realtor said this was Roosevelt's office."

Actually, the realtor was mistaken, or more likely, lying. Roosevelt, as I said, kept his office at Sagamore Hill, and this was probably his secretary's office. Anthony was being sold a bill of goods by a sharp realtor, who wanted to increase the value of the property. More interestingly, Anthony was totally buying it, the way people do who are more enthused than smart. If Frank was here, he'd smack his son on the head and say, "I got a bridge in Brooklyn I'll sell you."

Anthony went on, "Roosevelt could look out these windows and check out the broads." He laughed, then speculated, "Hey, do you think he had a *comare*?"

I recalled that Frank used this word, and when I asked Susan, who spoke passable college Italian, what it meant, she said, "Godmother," but that didn't seem like the context in which Frank was using it. So I asked Jack Weinstein, Frank's Jewish *consigliere* and my Mafia interpreter, and Jack said, with a smile, "It means, literally, 'godmother,' but it's the married boys' slang for their girlfriend or mistress. Like, 'I'm going to see my godmother tonight.' Funny."

Hilarious. Here's another example of how to use the word in a sentence: Frank had a *comare* named Susan.

Anthony asked, "Whaddaya think? You think he got blow jobs under his desk here?"

"I think the history books are silent on that."

"Too bad. Anyway, I'll get somebody to check with the local historical society about pictures of how this place looked when Roosevelt was here. We're gonna reproduce that."

Whether or not I wanted to work in a museum—I mean, whose office was this, anyway? In any case, a check with the Oyster Bay Historical Society would reveal to Anthony that Roosevelt didn't actually work here. Following that, a check of the *Oyster Bay Enterprise-Pilot* obituaries would show a dead realtor.

He suggested, "We need a moose head on this wall." He laughed, then led me into a smaller room, which looked the same as the bedroom, except it was even shabbier.

He said, "This is where your private secretary sits." He further shared his vision with me and said, "You put a pull-out couch in here and get a little *fica*. Capisce?" He laughed.

How could this deal get any better? Sex, money, power, and even history.

There was a desk and file cabinet in this room, and I asked Anthony, "Who lived here?"

"A literary agent." He added, "He got evicted, but the other tenants have leases, and I need to get them out."

"Make them a fair offer." Like, leave or die.

"Right. A good offer." He led me into the small kitchen at the back of the apartment, and said, "We rip this out and make it the coffee room with a bar. So? What do you think?"

"I think this restoration will attract a lot of local press. Do you want that?"

"Good press for you. I'm a silent partner."

"Not for long."

"I know how to do this so my name never comes up. You don't have to worry about that."

"You've already spoken to the realtor, Anthony."

"No. Anthony Stephano spoke to the realtor on the phone. And when the realtor gets here, my name is Anthony Stephano. Capisce?"

"People know your face."

"Not like they knew my father's face. I keep a low profile. The problem is the name, so we don't use that name. And if anyone thinks my name is not Stephano, they're not going to say shit. Right?"

I suggested to him, "If you used your real name, you could get the seller down to two million."

He smiled. "Yeah? Why is that, John?"

"Oh, I don't know." I took a wild guess and said, "Maybe he'd be nervous."

He smiled again. Clearly he enjoyed the power and the glory of being don Bellarosa, and the notion that men would quake in their boots while talking business with him.

On the other hand, I detected, or imagined, that there had been a subtle shift in the business practices of this organization in the last decade—or maybe it was Anthony's style that seemed different from what I remembered when I was an honorary mobster.

In any case, what remained the same was me; these people did not intimidate me. I was, after all, John Whitman Sutter, and even the dumbest goombah knew that there was a class of people who they weren't supposed to whack, which was why, for instance, U.S. Attorney Alphonse Ferragamo was still alive. The Mafia had rules, and they did not like bad press, or any press at all.

But even if there was no danger of getting whacked, there was always the danger of getting seduced, corrupted, or manipulated. I think that's where I was now. But, I reminded myself, I was here not because of any moral failing on my part, or any further need to screw up my life for kicks—I'd already done that. It was because of Susan.

This lady, of course, would normally be at the very top of any Do Not Hit list, except for the fact that she clipped a Mafia don. *Whoops*.

So, what I needed to do was . . . what?

Anthony returned to the subject and said, "I'm a legitimate businessman. Bell Enterprises. What maybe happened in the past is over. But if people want to think—"

"Anthony. Please. You're insulting my intelligence."

He didn't seem happy that I interrupted his nonsense, but he said, "I'm telling you what you want to hear."

"I don't want to hear bullshit. The best thing I can hear from you on that subject is nothing."

He lit a cigarette, then said to me, "Okay."

"What do you want from me? And why?"

He sat on the windowsill, took a drag, and said, "Okay, here's the real deal—I spoke to Jack Weinstein, my father's old attorney. You remember him. He likes you. And he tells me that I need to speak to you, which I did. He says you are the smartest, most honest, most stand-up guy he's ever dealt with. And this coming from a smart Jew who stood up to my father when he had to. But always in my father's best interest. And Jack tells me I need a guy like you. Just to talk to. Just to get some advice. Like Jack did for my father. Somebody who is not a paesano. Understand?"

"You mean, like a consigliere?"

"Yeah . . . that only means counselor. People think it means . . . like something to do with the . . . people in organized crime. It's Italian for counselor. Lawyers are called counselor. Right?"

"So, this is Jack Weinstein's old job?"

"Yeah. And Jack says I also need somebody like the guys who used to follow the Caesars around and whisper in their ears, 'You're only a mortal man.'"

"Is that a full-time job?"

He forced a smile and said, "It was then. This guy reminded Caesar that he was a man, not a god. In other words, even Caesar has to take a shit like everybody else."

"And you feel you need to be reminded of this?"

Again, he forced a smile and said, "Everybody does. Everybody who's successful. And Jack thinks maybe I need this. Hey, everybody in Washington should have somebody like that following them around. Right?"

"It might help."

As best I could figure, Jack Weinstein, a smart man, easily recognized that young Anthony was in over his head. But Jack saw the potential, and if he could keep Anthony alive long enough, then the young tiger would grow up big, strong, and hopefully smart enough to rule, kill, and scare the crap out of his enemies. And Jack, perceptive man that he was, thought of John Sutter to take the job that he once had with Frank, and maybe, too, to take the place of Anthony's deceased father. I mean, was I flattered to be thought of as a possible father substitute to a young man whose ambition it was to grow up to be as dangerous and deceitful as his real father? And if I succeeded at this, maybe someday Anthony would want to fuck my wife if I had one.

This whole situation had a touch of irony and maybe farce to it—but it wasn't funny. It *would* have been funny if Susan wasn't in this room, but she was, and both Anthony and I knew that.

I said to him, "So, that's what Jack thinks you need. A counselor and someone to tell you when your head is getting too big. What do *you* think you need from me?"

"I need someone I can trust, someone with no connections to my business. Someone who can't gain by my loss. I need your brains and your no-bullshit advice."

His father had additionally been impressed with my pedigree, my respectability, and my white-shoe law firm. The pedigree was still there, but Anthony wasn't interested in that; he was buying brains and balls today. I asked him, "Advice on what?"

"On whatever I need advice on."

"But then I'd hear things I don't want to hear."

"That won't happen." He added, "And even if it did, we have a lawyer-client relationship."

"We do?"

"That's up to you, Counselor."

"What's the pay?"

"Two hundred a year. That's the annual retainer. And you can do whatever else you want to make a buck. Like work on getting my father's assets back. Or tax law. In fact, I need a tax lawyer."

I had the thought that he had more need for a priest and a smack in the ass from his mother than a *consigliere* or someone to tell him to get over himself. And maybe that should be my first piece of advice to him. Meanwhile, I asked, "Is that it?"

"Pretty much. You get this office, too."

"Can I say no to the moose head?"

He smiled, stood, and threw his cigarette in the sink. "Sure. So?"

"Well . . . let me think about it."

"That's all I want you to do." He added, "I know you'll come to the right decision."

"You can be sure of that."

"And call Jack Weinstein. He wants to say hello. He's in Florida. Maybe you want to go down there for a visit."

I didn't respond to that, and said, "I've got a busy day. Thank you for the ride."

"Yeah. Go find Tony. He'll take you home."

"I need the exercise."

We both walked into the living room, and I moved toward the exit door. I said to him, "If I take this office, the bookstore downstairs stays. Same rent."

He didn't reply.

I asked him, "Did you apologize to that waitress?"

"No."

"Are you capable of taking *any* advice?"

"Yeah. When I trust and respect the person giving it."

"I hope you find that person."

"I did. Jack Weinstein. And my father. One is dying, and the other is dead. They referred me to you."

"Okay. And don't seem too anxious with this realtor. People sense when you want something so badly that you'll pay anything for it. Make sure this is what you want. And check out his story about the building. Capisce?"

"Capisco."

I left.

CHAPTER SEVENTEEN

Well, if my arithmetic was correct, I could be a millionaire if I brokered the house deal between Susan and Amir Nasim, then recovered the Bellarosa assets that had been seized by the government.

Neither of these goals seemed attainable, but I did have a solid job offer in hand—*consigliere* to don Anthony Bellarosa. How would that look on my résumé? Would my law school classmates be impressed at my next reunion?

I've known people—like myself—who've played by the rules most of their lives, then something awful happened that made them lose faith in the system, or in God or country. These people are then open to temptation and become prime candidates for a fall from grace.

Well, I could justify any behavior or any bad decision, but at the end of the day, I needed to decide who John Sutter was.

But first, I needed to clean the bathroom. Elizabeth Allard would be here soon.

I didn't grow up cleaning anything—not even in the Army, where I was an officer. I did clean my boat, however, so I was no stranger to Mr. Clean.

I finished the upstairs bathroom, then straightened out my bedroom in case Elizabeth really did want to see her old room.

Assuming we were going to move some items out, I was dressed in jeans, running shoes, and a polo shirt.

The cuckoo clock in the kitchen chimed 4:00, then 4:15. I kept busy by reviewing the pertinent paperwork in the dining room, which kept my mind off . . . well, Elizabeth.

A few minutes later, the doorbell rang. If my bad luck had returned, it was Susan. If not, it was Elizabeth. *Really* bad luck would be both of them.

I went to the door, but didn't look through the peephole to see whom Fate had brought to my doorstep.

I opened the door to—Elizabeth. She smiled and said, "Let's cut to the chase and have sex."

Or did she say, "Sorry I'm late, traffic's a mess"?

Assuming the latter, I replied, "Saturday traffic is always a mess," then we hugged and air-kissed, and she entered.

She was also wearing jeans and running shoes, and a blue T-shirt that said "Smith," which I assumed was not her alias, but rather her daughter's alma mater. She said, "I'm dressed to work."

"Good. Me, too."

Then she said, "But I brought a change of clothes if you'll let me buy you dinner later."

A kaleidoscope of images raced through my mind—clothes on the floor, the bathroom, the shower, the bedroom, the bed—

"Unless you're busy."

"Busy? No. I'm free." I reminded her, "I just got here."

She smiled, then glanced around and observed, "Nothing changes here."

"No. But I was happy to see that." I said, "I made coffee."

"Good."

She put her large canvas handbag on the floor, and I led her into the kitchen. She asked, "How are you getting on here?"

"Fine." I added, "It was good of your mother to extend an open invitation."

"She likes you."

"I'm not sure about that."

Elizabeth smiled again and replied, "She doesn't always show her feelings."

"I have a mother like that."

I poured coffee into two mugs, and asked, "Cream? Sugar?"

"Black." She inquired, "How is your mother?"

"We've spoken twice since I've been back, but I haven't actually seen her yet."

"Really? I can't imagine not seeing either of my children the minute they return from a trip."

I thought about that and replied, "I haven't seen Carolyn yet, and she's a fifty-minute train ride away in Brooklyn."

"Well, you've only been back . . . how long?"

"About two weeks." I suggested, "Why don't we sit on the patio?"

We went out the back door and sat in two cast-iron chairs that had survived the scrap-metal drives of 1942–45. The table was of the same vintage, and I recalled that George used to scrape and paint the furniture every spring.

Elizabeth commented, "Mom and Dad had morning coffee out here nearly every day."

"That's very nice." I asked her, "How is she doing?"

"She looked well this morning. Better than usual."

In my experience, that's not always a good sign with the terminally ill, but I said, "I'm glad to hear that." I added, "I was going to stop by to see her today, but . . . I had an appointment in Oyster Bay."

Elizabeth nodded, then looked around and remarked, "It's so peaceful here." She informed me, "I enjoyed growing up here. It was like . . . this secluded place with a wall around it . . . it kept the outside world away."

"I guess that's the point."

She asked me, "Did you like living in the guest cottage?"

"I did after the Stanhopes moved to South Carolina."

She smiled, but didn't say anything like, "What assholes they were." I suppose after years of living here as the child of estate workers, she'd been conditioned not to say anything derogatory about the lord and lady of the manor. Nevertheless, I continued, "If William hadn't hit the lucky gene pool, he'd be cleaning toilets in Penn Station."

"Now, now, John."

"Sorry. Was that unkind?"

"You're a bigger person than that."

"Right. And Charlotte would be turning tricks on Eighth Avenue."

She suppressed a smile, then changed the subject and said, "The crabapple trees look good."

"I think Nasim has them pruned, sprayed, and fertilized."

"I remember picking crabapples for weeks so Mom could make her jelly."

I actually remembered Elizabeth as a young teenager climbing the trees that summer when Susan and I got married and moved into the guest cottage. I recalled, too, that Elizabeth went to boarding school, so I didn't see much of her. As for Elizabeth's tuition at boarding school— as with her college tuition—Ethel was still collecting on her special relationship with Augustus long past the time when the old gent even remembered getting laid.

Anyway, I said, "That reminds me—there are cases of crabapple jelly in the basement for you."

"I know. I actually don't *like* the stuff." She laughed and continued, "After years of picking, washing, boiling, canning . . . well, but I'll take it."

"I took a jar."

"Take another. Take a case."

I smiled.

We sat there for a minute, surveying the grounds, then Elizabeth said, "Mom made me promise to harvest her garden." She added, "But . . . she may be gone before it's ready." She asked me, "Did you speak to . . . what's his name?"

"Amir Nasim. Yes, I did." I continued, "He seems a decent enough man, and he has no problem with me staying on through the summer, but . . . he'd like to have his property back by September the first, unless Ethel is still . . . with us."

She nodded, then asked me, "Did you ask him if he wanted to sell the gatehouse?"

"I did. He wants to use it himself."

"Well, that's too bad. I mean, sitting here, I'm getting nostalgic . . . I really loved this place." She asked, "Do you think he'd change his mind?"

I saw no reason to keep Nasim's concerns in confidence, so I replied, "He has some security issues."

"What does that mean?"

"I think it means he believes that people from the old country may want to harm him."

"My goodness . . . where's he from? Iran?"

"Yes." I offered my thoughts and said, "He may be paranoid. Or, if he's correct, then the gatehouse may become available when he's assassinated and they settle his estate." I smiled to show I was joking.

Elizabeth pondered all that, then said, "That's unbelievable . . ."

"I think so, too. But in any case, I believe he wants to put his security people in the gatehouse." I thought about telling her of Nasim's desire to buy Susan's guest cottage, but I decided not to bring up Susan's name at all. Instead, I kept it light and asked, "Isn't there a local ordinance against political assassination?"

She forced a smile, but clearly she was disturbed by this news, and disappointed that the gatehouse was not for sale.

I stood and said, "Wait here." I went into the overgrown kitchen garden and came back with the wooden sign and held it up by its half-rotted stake. I asked, "Do you remember this?"

She smiled and said, "I do. Can I have that?"

"Absolutely." I laid the sign on the table, and we both looked at the faded and peeling paint. The black lettering had nearly disappeared, but it had left its outline on the white background and you could make out the words "Victory Garden."

Elizabeth asked me, "Do you think I should put this on Mom's grave?"

"Why not?"

She nodded and said, "That entire World War Two generation will be gone soon."

"True." I was especially anxious for William Stanhope to be gone. I mean, I didn't wish him any harm, but the old bastard was in his late seventies, and he'd outlived whatever small usefulness he might have had.

On that subject, William had actually shown up for World War II, making him a member of the Greatest Generation, though barely. He didn't talk much about his wartime experiences, but not because he'd been traumatized by the war. In fact, as I'd learned from Ethel Allard, William Stanhope had a rather easy war.

As Ethel related the story to me once, her employer and benefactor Augustus Stanhope had sold his seventy-five-foot motor yacht, *The Sea Urchin*, to the government for a dollar, as did many of the rich along the East Coast during this national emergency—you couldn't get fuel anyway—and *The Sea Urchin* was refitted by the Coast Guard as an anti-submarine patrol boat. Then Augustus' dilettante son, William, joined the Coast Guard, and in what could be described as a startling coincidence, Lieutenant (j.g.) William Stanhope was assigned to duty aboard the former Stanhope yacht. In another stroke of good fortune, *The Sea Urchin* was berthed at the Seawanhaka Corinthian Yacht Club, and William, not wanting to use up scarce government housing, patriotically billeted himself at Stanhope Hall. William did go out on anti-submarine patrols and, depending on whom you speak to—William the Fearless, or Ethel the Red—he did or did not encounter German U-boats. Most likely not, and most probably he spent a good deal of shore time on Martha's Vineyard and the Hamptons.

Meanwhile, George was fighting the more dangerous war in the Pacific, and William's father, Augustus, took the opportunity to shag Ethel, who helped the war effort by growing her own vegetables in the Victory Garden.

And here we are now.

In some ways, we *are* coming to the end of an era, but these old dramas do not really end, because as someone wisely said, the past is prologue to the future, and short of a meteor strike and mass extinction, the dramas of each generation roll on into the next.

Elizabeth asked me, "What are you thinking about?"

"About . . . the generations who've lived here, in war and peace."

She nodded and commented, "Who would have thought, in 1945, that we'd be surrounded by subdivisions, and that an Iranian would be living in Stanhope Hall?"

I didn't reply.

She asked me, "Did you see what happened to Alhambra?"

"I caught a peek of it."

"It's awful." She asked, "Do you remember the estate—? Oh, I forgot . . . sorry."

"It really doesn't bother me."

"Good." She looked at me, hesitated, then said, "I think it does."

"Maybe because I'm back."

"Are you staying?"

Again, the threshold question, and as with Anthony Bellarosa, the answer would partly determine whether Elizabeth and I had any serious business to discuss. I replied, "I'm going to give it a few months, then I can make a more informed decision."

"And what do you think is going to happen in a few months to help you with this *informed* decision?"

"Are you making fun of me?"

She smiled. "No, but that's so typically male. Informed decision. How do you *feel*? Right now."

"I have to go to the bathroom."

She laughed. "All right. I don't mean to pry."

"Good." I stood and asked, "Ready to wade through paperwork?"

She stood also, and as we moved toward the kitchen door, she asked, "How long will this take?"

"Less than an hour. Then maybe an hour to pack your car with any personal items you may want to take now."

She glanced at her watch and said, "I'd like to have a drink in my hand by six o'clock."

"That's part of my service."

I opened the screen door for her and she went inside.

As I followed, it occurred to me that we both had so many memories of Stanhope Hall—good and bad—that whatever happened today—good or bad—would be emotional and partly influenced by other people, living and dead, who were still here, in one form or another.

CHAPTER EIGHTEEN

We sat side by side at the dining room table, and I, in my organized and professional manner, identified documents, presented them to Elizabeth for reading, and explained the obtuse language when necessary. She was wearing a nice lilac scent.

She said to me, "I'm happy that it's you who are doing this, John."

"I'm glad I'm able to do it."

"Did you come back just for this?"

"Well, I came to see your mother, of course." I added, "And I need to move my things out of here."

Without hesitation, she offered, "You can move your things into my house. I have plenty of room."

"Thank you. I may take you up on that."

She hesitated, then said, "I'd offer you a room, but my divorce settlement makes my alimony dependent on me not cohabitating."

I joked, "Let me see that divorce settlement."

She smiled, then clarified, "I mean, we wouldn't be cohabitating— I'd just make a room available to you . . . the way Mom did. But Tom would jump on that as soon as he found out."

"You could tell Tom that I'm on his team."

She laughed and said, "You have a reputation as a notorious heterosexual."

I smiled.

She stayed silent awhile before thinking out loud, "Well . . . it's a measly alimony, for only a few years . . ." She said to me, "If you really need a place, you're welcome to use my guest room."

"Thank you." I added, "I would insist on paying you a rent equal to your measly alimony." I reminded her, "I have this place for a while, then I need to return to London to tidy up things there."

She nodded, and we went back to the paperwork.

I came across a deed dated August 23, 1943, conveying a life tenancy from Mr. Augustus Phillip Stanhope, property owner, to Mrs. Ethel Hope Allard, domestic servant, and her husband, Mr. George Henry Allard, then serving overseas with the Armed Forces of the United States.

So I could make the assumption that Mr. Stanhope and Mrs. Allard had, prior to this date, entered into their intimate relationship that led to this generous conveyance. In legal terms, this conveyance was obviously supported by the repeated receipt of sufficient consideration—meaning here, multiple sex acts—though these particular considerations from Mrs. Allard to Mr. Stanhope could not be candidly described in this document.

Regarding that, did anyone question Augustus Stanhope's generosity at the time? Even today, bells would go off. Unless, of course, this was kept secret until Augustus popped off, and Ethel dragged it out to show William Stanhope before he got any ideas about getting rid of the Allards, or before he demanded rent from their meager pay.

Also, I wondered, when did George Allard learn that he was living rent-free, for life, in the Stanhope gatehouse? And how did Ethel explain this to her new husband when he returned from the war? "George, I have some good news, and some bad news."

In any case, William, at some point, knew about the life tenancy in his newly inherited property, and it was a constant thorn in his side, especially when he put the estate up for sale and had to reveal the existence of this encumbrance of unknown duration. I recalled that Frank Bellarosa, when he bought Stanhope Hall, was not thrilled with having Ethel—George was deceased by then—living on his property. But Frank had said to me philosophically, "Maybe she's good luck. And how long can she live?" Answer: ten years longer than you, Frank.

In any case, this document wasn't relevant to the business at hand, so I casually slid it back into its folder. But Elizabeth asked, "What was that?"

"Oh, just the life tenancy grant to your parents. It needs to stay here until the time comes when it's moot."

"Can I see it?"

"Well . . . sure." I placed it in front of her, and she read the single-page document, then passed it back to me. I said, "Next, we have—"

"Why do you think Augustus Stanhope gave my parents a life tenancy in this house?"

"As it says, for devoted and faithful service."

"They were in their twenties then."

"Right. He doesn't say long service."

"What am I not understanding?"

Oh, you don't want to know that, Elizabeth. I suggested, "You should ask your mother." I shuffled through a few papers. "Okay, so here we have your mother's last three Federal tax returns—"

"Mom said it was a reward for *long* service."

Faced with having to respond with the simple truth or a thin lie, I chose neither and continued, "You need to contact your mother's accountant . . ." I glanced at her and saw she was looking above the fireplace at the large framed photo portrait of her parents on their wedding day.

I continued, "Your mother has a paid-up life insurance policy with a death benefit of ten thousand dollars. Here is the actual policy, and you should put it in a safe place."

Elizabeth looked away from the photograph and said, "She was very beautiful."

"Indeed, she was. Still is."

"My father looked so handsome in that white uniform."

I looked at the colored photo portrait and agreed, "They were a handsome couple."

She didn't reply, and when I glanced at her again, I saw she had tears in her eyes. John Whitman Sutter, Esq., who'd done this sort of work before, was prepared, and I took a clean handkerchief from my pocket and put it in her hand.

She dabbed at her eyes and said, "Sorry."

"That's all right. Let me get you some water." I stood and went into the kitchen.

As I said, I did this for a living once. Most of the time, I was a hotshot Wall Street tax lawyer in the city, but in my Locust Valley office I did wills, trusts, health care proxies, and that sort of thing. Half my clients were wealthy old dowagers and grumpy old men who spent a lot of time thinking of people to put in their wills before disinheriting them a week later.

Also, the last will and testament, along with related papers, sometimes revealed a family secret or two—an institutionalized sibling, an illegitimate child, two mistresses in Manhattan, and so forth. I'd learned how to handle this with professional stoicism, though now and then, even I had been shocked, surprised, saddened, and often amused.

Ethel Allard's adultery was no big deal in the grand scheme of things, especially given the passage of half a century. But it's always a bit of a jolt to the adult child when he or she discovers that Mommy had a lover, and Daddy was diving into the steno pool.

In any case, Elizabeth, divorced, with two grown children, a deceased father, and a dying mother, was maybe lonely, and surely emotionally distraught, and thus vulnerable.

So . . . I filled a glass with tap water. So, nothing should or would happen tonight that we'd regret, or feel guilty about in the morning. Right?

I returned to the dining room and saw that Elizabeth had composed herself. I handed her the water and suggested, "Let's take a break. Would you like to walk?"

"I want to finish this." She promised, "I'll be fine."

"Okay."

We cleared up the peripheral paperwork, and I opened the envelope that held Ethel's last will and testament. I said, "I drew up this will after your father died, and I see that it's held up pretty well over the years." Continuing in my official tone of voice, I asked her, "Have you read this will?"

"I have."

"Do you want to review this will with her?"

"I don't want to read her will to her on her deathbed."

"I understand." And I wouldn't want Ethel to increase her five-hundred-dollar bequest to St. Mark's. I said, "I'll keep this copy here for when the time comes."

Elizabeth nodded, then said, "She didn't leave you anything."

"Why should she?"

"For all you've done for her and for Dad."

I replied, "What little I've done was done in friendship. And your mother reciprocated by letting me use this house for storage." Though she did charge me rent when I lived here ten years ago, and she just reinstated the rent.

Elizabeth said, "I understand. But I'd feel better if her estate . . . I'm the executor . . . paid you a fee."

I wondered if Elizabeth thought I needed the money. I did, but I wasn't destitute. In fact, I was making a good living in London, but unfortunately I'd brought with me to London the American habit of living beyond my means. And now I was on an extended, unpaid sabbatical.

But things were looking up. I had an offer from an old, established Italian-American firm. La Cosa Nostra.

Elizabeth said again, "I'd really feel better if you were paid for your professional services."

I replied, "All right, but I'll take my fee in crabapple jelly."

She smiled and said, "And dinner is on me tonight."

"Deal." I stacked a dozen folders in front of her and said, "Take these with you and put them in a safe place. I'll try to visit Ethel tomorrow or Monday."

She asked me, "Is that it?"

"That's it for the paperwork, except for this inventory I've made of personal property, including your father's." I slid three sheets of paper toward her, on which I'd handwritten the inventory, and asked, "Do you want to go through this?"

"Not really."

"Well, look it over later. Meanwhile, item four is sixty-two dollars in cash that I found in the cookie jar when I was looking for cookies." I put an envelope in front of her and said, "If you count that and initial item four, you can have the cash now."

She dropped the envelope in her canvas bag without counting the money, initialed where indicated, and said, "This will buy us a nice bottle of wine."

"Don't drink up your whole inheritance."

"Why not?" She asked again, "Is that it?"

"We're getting close."

I handed her another envelope and said, "These are your mother's funeral instructions."

Elizabeth informed me, "I already have a photocopy of this with up-to-the-minute changes."

I sensed that Elizabeth had become a little impatient with her mother's precise preparations for the big event. I said, "Well, take this anyway."

She threw the envelope in her canvas bag and said, "I love her, but she drives me nuts—right to the end."

I replied, "I'm sure our children say the same about us."

She smiled, then said, "This reminds me—that envelope that my mother wanted me to give you—I spoke to her and apparently she wants me to wait until she's gone."

I nodded, thinking it was probably a bill for the rent. Or instructions on what to wear to her funeral.

Elizabeth inquired, "So, are we done here?"

I stood and said, "We're done here. But you need to find the dress your mother wants to wear. Meanwhile, I'll put that garden sign in your car, and I'd like you to take that photo portrait, and whatever else you'd like to take with you tonight."

She stood also, and we looked at each other, then she asked me, "Will you come up with me?"

"No. You should go to her room by yourself." I added, "And you can take a look at your old room."

She nodded, then said, "The car's unlocked." She left the dining room, and I could hear her making her way up the steep, narrow staircase to the two bedrooms above.

I don't normally talk myself out of sex, but there is a time and place for everything. Even sex. But maybe I was reading Elizabeth wrong, and she was not actually in the mood for love with a handsome stranger from across the sea.

"Dear Ms. Post, I am the attorney of record for an elderly lady who is dying—I wrote to you about her—and her beautiful daughter is the executrix of her estate, so we are working closely together on this. My question is, Should I have sex with her? (Signed) Confused on Long Island (again)."

I think I know what Ms. Post would say: "Dear COLI, No. P.S. What happened to the ex-wife down the road? P.P.S. You are headed for trouble, buddy."

Anyway, I took the framed photo portrait off the wall above the fireplace and noticed how dingy the wallpaper around it was. A new decorating project for Mrs. Nasim.

I carried the portrait outside to where Elizabeth had parked her SUV next to my Taurus, and I saw that it was a BMW, which suggested some degree of business success, or a good divorce attorney. I also saw a garment bag hanging in the rear, and I guessed that was Elizabeth's dinner clothing for tonight.

I opened the cargo compartment and set the portrait facedown, noticing on the paper backing some handwriting. I pulled the portrait toward me and read the words, written with a fountain pen, in what looked like Ethel's hand: *George Henry Allard and Ethel Hope Purvis, married June 13, 1942, St. Mark's, Locust Valley, Long Island.*

And under that, in the same feminine hand, *Come home safe, my darling.*

And beneath that, in George's hand, which I also recognized, *My sweet wife, I will count the days until we are together again.*

I slid the portrait forward and closed the tailgate. Well, I thought, hopefully, they'll be together again soon.

I thought, too, perhaps cynically, that all marriages start with hope and optimism, love and yearning, but the years take their toll. And in this case, by August of 1943, fourteen months after these words of love and devotion were written, Ethel had succumbed to loneliness, or lust, or had been seduced by money and power—or, recalling that scene ten years ago at the cemetery when Ethel had disappeared from George's grave and I'd found her at Augustus' grave—quite possibly she'd actually fallen in love with Augustus Stanhope. Or all of the above.

In any case, Ethel and George had worked it out and spent the next half century together, happily, I think, living in this little house together, raising their daughter, and doing increasingly lighter work on the grand estate whose walls and lonely acres kept the encroaching world away, and kept them, in some mysterious way, a forever-young estate couple who'd met here, fallen in love, married, and never left home.

As I was walking toward the garden path that ran between the gate-house and the wall, I heard a vehicle crunching the gravel behind me. I turned to see a white Lexus SUV heading toward the open gates, driven by Susan Stanhope Sutter.

The Lexus slowed, and we made eye contact. She'd seen the BMW, of course, and may have known to whom it belonged, but even if she didn't, she knew I had company of some sort.

It's awkward making eye contact with the former love of your life, into whose eyes you no longer wish to look, and I didn't know what to do. Wave? Blow a kiss? Flip the bird? Ms. Post? Help me.

It was Susan who waved, almost perfunctorily, then she acceler-ated through the gates, making a hard, tire-screeching right onto Grace Lane.

I noticed that my mood had darkened. Why does Susan Sutter still have the power to affect my frame of mind?

I needed to answer that question honestly, before I could move on.

CHAPTER NINETEEN

Elizabeth and I filled her BMW with her parents' personal items that she wanted to take that night, such as photo albums, the family Bible, and other odds and ends that were priceless and irreplaceable. We piled the rest of the personal property, including George's naval uniforms and Ethel's wedding gown, into the foyer to be moved another day.

It was very sad for Elizabeth, of course, and I, too, found myself thinking about life and death, and the things we leave behind.

On one of our trips to her vehicle, she retrieved her garment bag and a makeup case and took them up to her mother's room.

By the time the cuckoo clock struck six, Elizabeth was sitting in her mother's rocker in the living room, and I was sitting in George's wingback chair across from her. On the coffee table was the three-page inventory list, most of the items now checked. Also on the table were two mismatched wineglasses that I'd filled from a bottle of Banfi Brunello, one of three Tuscan reds I'd bought in Locust Valley after my Oyster Bay adventure with Anthony. I'd also picked up some cheese and crackers at a food shop and a plastic tray of pre-cut vegetables. I stuck to the Brie.

Elizabeth dipped a carrot and said to me, "You should have some vegetables."

"Vegetables are a choking hazard."

She smiled, nibbled at the carrot, then sipped her wine.

We were both tired, and a little sweaty and dusty from the trips to the basement and the attic, and we needed a shower.

She said to me, "I made a seven-thirty reservation at The Creek. Is that all right?"

I informed her, "I think I'm persona non grata there."

"Really? Why . . . ? Oh . . . I guess when Susan . . ."

I finished her sentence: ". . . shot her Mafia lover." I smiled and added, "They're very stuffy there."

Elizabeth forced a smile, then informed me, "Actually, Susan has rejoined the club. We had lunch there. So maybe it's not a problem. But we can go to a restaurant."

I finished my wine and poured another. So let me get this straight— I had been on thin ice at The Creek because I'd brought Mr. Frank Bellarosa, a Mafia gentleman, and his gaudily dressed wife, Anna, to the club for dinner; but it was Susan's murder of said Mafia gentleman that actually got us booted. And now, Susan Stanhope Sutter—Stanhope is the operative word here—had the nerve to apply for membership and was readmitted. Meanwhile, if I reapplied, I'm sure I'd discover that I was still blackballed.

Nevertheless, I said, "The Creek is fine if you don't mind a disciplinary letter to you from the Board of Governors."

She thought about that, smiled, and replied, "That could be fun."

As I refilled her glass, I also thought about running into everyone I used to know there, including Susan. But what the hell. It *could* be fun.

Elizabeth suggested, "Or we could stay here."

I looked at her in the dim light, and as I said, I'm not good at reading a woman's signals, but Elizabeth's signal was loud and clear. I replied, "Let's think about that."

"Thinking is not what we want to do."

I nodded, then changed the subject. "I have something for you." I stood, went into the dining room, and found Susan's photographs of the Allards.

I knelt beside Elizabeth's chair and said, "Susan took most of these, and I want you to have them, though I'd like to make a few copies for myself."

She took the stack of photos and went through them, making appropriate remarks about each one, such as, "I can't believe how many times we were all together . . . I barely remember these . . . Oh, look, here's my college graduation . . . and there's you, John, with your arm around me and Dad . . . oh, God, was I a dork, or what?"

"No, you were not. I'll take a copy of that one."

"No, no."

"You look great with straight black hair."

"Oh my God—what was I thinking?"

We came across a posed photograph taken on the rear terrace of Stanhope Hall, occasion unknown or forgotten. Standing in the photo is Ethel, still attractive in late middle age, and George, his hair still brown, and Augustus Stanhope, late into his dotage, sitting in a rocker with a blanket on his lap. Also, on his lap is a girl of about six or seven, and I realized it was Elizabeth.

She joked, "That's not me."

"It looks like you."

She stared at the photograph, then said, "My mother took care of him before they had to hire around-the-clock nurses." Elizabeth put the photo on the table with the others and added, "Mom was very fond of him."

I replied, "He was a gentleman." I added, of course, "Very unlike his son."

We dropped that subject and continued on through the stack of photos.

Elizabeth commented at one point, "I can't believe how many of these people are dead."

I nodded.

She asked me, "Were you happy then?"

"I was. But I didn't always know it. How about you?"

"I think I was happy." She changed the subject. "Oh, here are Edward and Carolyn. They're so cute."

And so we continued through the photographic time trip, both of us, I think, realizing how much our lives had intersected, and yet how little we knew each other.

Because Susan had taken most of these pictures, she wasn't in many of them, but we came across a photo of Susan and Elizabeth together, taken at the Stanhope annual Christmas party in the mansion. Elizabeth stared at it and said, "She is a beautiful woman."

I didn't comment.

Elizabeth continued, "She was very nice at lunch."

I had no intention of asking about the lunch, so I stood and poured the remainder of the wine into our glasses.

Elizabeth finished with the photos and said, "I'll have them all copied for you."

"Thank you."

She sat silently for a while, sipping her wine, then informed me, "I've heard that . . . Bellarosa's son has moved into one of the Alhambra houses."

I nodded.

She remained silent again, then asked me, "Do you think . . . ? I mean, could that be a problem for Susan?"

I asked, "What did Susan think?"

Elizabeth glanced at me, then replied, "She didn't think so," then added, "She seemed not at all concerned."

"Good."

"But . . . well, I would be."

I didn't reply and opened the second bottle of Tuscan red, a Cabreo Il Borgo, and we sat silently, drinking wine and getting a little tipsy.

We seemed to have run out of things to talk about; or, to put it another way, someone needed to address the subject of sex or supper. Elizabeth had already broached that subject, and I'd let it pass, but she tried another approach and announced, "I'm too drunk to drive." She asked, "Can you drive?"

"No."

"Then let's stay here."

I could, of course, call a taxi for her, and that's what a real gentleman would do—or a limp-dicked, half-wit poor excuse of a man. So I said, "Let's stay here."

"That's a good idea." She finished her wine, stood, and said, "I need to shower."

I, too, stood and watched her walk, a little unsteadily, into the foyer.

I wasn't sure if I was supposed to follow. "Dear Ms. Post—"

"Dear COLI, Just fuck her already."

"Right." I moved toward the foyer, then hesitated. I seemed to recall that I'd already decided that Elizabeth was emotionally distraught and vulnerable, and I should not take advantage of that. On a more selfish level, I didn't want to complicate my life at this time. And Elizabeth Allard Corbet would be a major complication.

On the other hand . . . I mean, this was *her* idea.

My head said no, my heart said maybe, and my dick was pointing toward the staircase. Dick wins every time.

But first, I uncorked the third bottle of wine, took the two glasses, and went to the foot of the stairs, where I heard a door close on the second floor.

I made my way up the steps to the small hallway. The bathroom was straight ahead, her mother's room was to the left, and my room— her old room—was to the right. All three doors were closed, so I opened mine and saw she wasn't there. I set the bottle and glasses on the nightstand. I could now hear the shower running in the bathroom.

I've been here before, on the outside of a closed bathroom door while the lady inside was showering, and I had no clear, verbal invitation to share the shower. "Dear Ms. Post—"

"Hey, stupid, see if the door is unlocked."

"Right." I went back to the bathroom door and gently tried the knob. Locked.

I went back to my bedroom, leaving the door open, and I poured two glasses of wine and sat in the armchair.

The shower stopped. I opened a copy of *Time* magazine, sipped my wine, and read.

A few minutes later, while I was reading a fascinating article about something or other, I heard the bathroom door open, and Elizabeth poked her head through my door, wrapped in a large bath towel, and drying her hair with another towel. She said to me, "Shower's free."

"Good." I stood and asked, "Feel better?"

"Terrific." Then she turned and walked into her mother's room and closed the door. I could hear the hair dryer running.

First-time sex is like a first dance. Who's leading whom? Am I dancing too close, or too far? Do I need a shower? Yes.

I went into the bathroom, leaving the door unlocked, stripped and threw my clothes in the corner on top of hers, then got in the shower, still not absolutely certain where this was going.

After I finished, I dried off with the last towel, wrapped it around my waist, and exited into the hallway. Her bedroom door was still closed, but it was quiet in there. I entered my room and found her in my chair, her legs crossed, sipping wine, reading my magazine, and wearing my Yale Crew T-shirt, and not much else, except a little makeup.

I said, "That shirt looks good on you."

"I hope you don't mind."

I think I knew where this was going.

I took my wine, sat on the bed opposite her chair, and we clinked glasses and sipped without talking.

She looked around at the small room, the old furniture, the faded wallpaper, the worn carpet, and the sun-bleached drapes, then said, "I spent most of my first twenty-one years here."

I didn't respond.

"I always came home on school breaks," she continued, and I could hear that her voice was a little tired and slurred. "It always felt like home . . . it was always here . . . and now, it's time to move on."

I nodded.

She announced, "I'd like to sleep here tonight."

"Of course."

She stretched out her legs and put her feet on my lap. She said, "My feet are sore from all that moving."

I put down my wine and rubbed her feet.

She put her head back, closed her eyes and murmured, "Oooh . . . that feels sooo good."

Her T-shirt—my T-shirt—had ridden north, and I could see that the carpet matched the drapes.

I've been here before, too, and I never felt comfortable dipping my pen in a client's inkwell. But Elizabeth was also a social acquaintance, and not really a client, and . . . well, the line was already crossed. So . . . I mean, not to proceed at this point would be rude.

She held out her empty glass, and I refilled it.

It was past 7:00 P.M., still light outside, and the open window let in a nice breeze and the sounds of birds chirping. Now and then I could hear a vehicle passing on Grace Lane, but no one drove into the gravel driveway.

She finished her wine, put her feet on the floor, and raised herself up from the armchair.

I, too, stood, and she put her arms around my shoulders and buried her face in my bare chest.

I put my arms around her, and I could feel she was limp and barely standing—as opposed to Bad John who was not limp and standing fully erect. I lifted her and laid her down on the sheets with her head on the pillow.

She stared up at the ceiling, then tears welled up in her eyes.

I took some tissues from a box on the nightstand and put them in her hand, and Good John suggested, "Why don't you get some sleep?"

She nodded, and I got the quilt from the foot of the bed and laid it over her.

She said, "I'm sorry."

"Don't be."

"I want to . . . but it's just . . . too much. Everything. I'm too sad."

"I understand." I also understood that Elizabeth was possibly considering her relationship with Susan, and that made two of us.

"Maybe later," she said.

I didn't reply.

"I like you."

"I like *you*."

I opened the small closet, found a pair of khakis and a golf shirt, and got a pair of shorts from the dresser. I took off my towel, and I saw she was watching me. She asked, "Where are you going?"

"Downstairs." I pulled on my shorts, pants, and shirt and asked her, "Do you need anything?"

She shook her head.

"See you later." I headed toward the door.

She said, "Kiss me good night."

I went back to the bed, gave her a kiss on the cheek, then on the lips, and wiped her eyes with a tissue, then left the room and closed the door.

I went downstairs, got a beer from the refrigerator, and sat out on the back patio.

The night was getting cool, and the setting sun cast long shadows across the lawn. In the distance, if I cared to look, was Susan's house, and I understood that it was Susan's proximity and her literal and figurative presence that was causing me the same conflict that Elizabeth probably felt.

And my conflicts and indecisions went beyond the issue of women; my dealings with Anthony Bellarosa, for instance, were affected by Susan's presence, as was my uncertainty about staying here, or returning to London, or going someplace new.

So, I needed to speak to Susan to put these issues to rest, to find out how much—or how little—she actually mattered.

I finished my beer, put my feet on the table, and looked up at the darkening sky. The light pollution from the encroaching subdivisions cast an artificial glow on the horizon, but overhead it was as I remembered it; a beautiful watercolor blue and pink twilight, and in the east the stars were starting to blink on in the purple sky.

The sound of a vehicle on the gravel broke into my stargazing, and I turned as the vehicle passed the gatehouse and saw that it was a white Lexus SUV. It stopped, then moved on slowly toward the guest cottage.

We had been separated for a decade by oceans and continents, and now we were a few minutes' walk from each other, but still separated by anger, pride, and history, which was harder to overcome than continents and oceans.

I'd always felt that we'd parted in haste, without a full accounting of why we were going our separate ways, and as a result, neither of us, I think, was really able to move on. We needed to revisit the past, no matter how painful that would be. And the time to do that was now.

CHAPTER TWENTY

As the sun came over the estate wall and through the kitchen window, I brewed a pot of coffee and took a mug out onto the patio, where I counted four empty beer bottles on the table.

I'd slept in my clothes on the couch, and my only trip up the stairs was to use the bathroom. To the best of my knowledge, Elizabeth never came downstairs.

I sipped coffee from my steaming mug and watched the morning mist rise from the lawn and garden.

As we used to say in college, "Getting laid is no big deal, but not getting laid is a *very* big deal."

On a more positive note, that was the right move. No involvement, no complications.

On the other hand, sex or no sex, Elizabeth and I had connected on some level. I liked her, and she was part of my past, and therefore possibly part of my future. I'd spent ten years sleeping with strangers; it might be nice to sleep with someone I knew. If nothing else, I now had a place to store my property, and a guest room if I needed one. And, hopefully, I had a friend.

I heard the screen door squeak open, and I turned to see Elizabeth walking barefoot across the dewy patio, wrapped in my old bathrobe and carrying a mug of coffee.

She gave me a peck on the cheek and said, "Good morning."

"Good morning."

She asked, "Did you sleep well?"

"I did. How about you?"

"I . . . it was strange sleeping in my old room." She added, "I had sad dreams . . . about being a young girl again . . . and Mom and Dad . . . I woke up a few times, crying."

I nodded and looked at her, then we held hands. She still looked very sad, then seemed to shake it off and said, "Do you know this poem? 'Backward, turn backward, O Time in your flight; Make me a child again just for tonight.'"

"I've heard it."

"That's what I was thinking last night."

I nodded and squeezed her hand.

She said to me, "I thought you'd come up."

"Believe me, I thought about it."

She smiled, then said, "Well, I don't think I was in a very romantic mood."

"No. You wanted to be a child again, just for one night."

She looked at me, nodded, then said, "But . . . I wanted your company. So I came downstairs. You were snoring on the couch."

"Do I snore?"

"God, I thought you were running the vacuum cleaner."

I smiled and said, "Red wine makes me snore."

"No more red wine for you." She looked at the empty beer bottles and asked, "Did you have people over?"

I smiled again and replied, "I was killing garden slugs."

We sat down at the table, still holding hands, sipping coffee. The sun was well above the wall now, and sunlight streamed through the trees into the garden and patio, burning through the ground mist. It was quiet except for the morning birds chirping away, and the occasional vehicle on Grace Lane beyond the wall.

Elizabeth said, "I love this time of day."

"Me, too."

We stayed silent awhile, appreciating the dawn of a beautiful summer day.

Finally, she asked me, "Can I tell you a secret?"

"Of course."

"Well . . . you might think this is silly . . . and I'm almost embarrassed . . . but when I was about . . . maybe sixteen, I developed a major crush on you."

I smiled. "Did you?"

She laughed, then continued, "Even though you were married . . . I thought about you sometimes when I was in college, and whenever I came home and saw you . . . but then I grew up and got over it."

"That's good." I added, "I had no idea."

"Of course you didn't. I never flirted, did I?"

I thought about that, and replied "No, you didn't."

"I was a good girl."

"Still are."

"Well . . . let's not go there."

I smiled.

Elizabeth continued, "And then, when all that happened with Susan and Frank Bellarosa, I couldn't believe what I'd heard from Mom when you moved in here . . . then, after Susan shot him . . . I wanted to call you or come by. Actually, I dropped in to see Mom a few times, but you weren't here . . . and then Mom said that you were leaving."

I didn't know quite what to say, but I replied, "That's very nice. I could have used someone to talk to."

"I know. Mom said you were . . . withdrawn. But I was married, and I wasn't sure in my own mind if I was concerned as a friend, or . . . something else."

"I understand." I added, "I'm very flattered."

"Are you? Well, you're too modest, John. I think you left here because the women were all over you as soon as you were separated, and you fled for your life."

"This is true."

She smiled, then went on, "And here's the rest of my secret—when I heard that you were about to begin a sail around the world, I wished that you would take me with you."

I looked at her and our eyes met. I said, not altogether insincerely, "I wish I'd known."

"That's very nice of you to say."

"Well, I'm not just saying it."

"I know. Anyway, it was just a silly fantasy. I had a husband and two children. Even if you'd asked, I would have had to say no. Because of the children." She added, "Not to mention Mom. I think she was on to me, and *not* happy."

I thought about all of that and about how the course of our lives can change so quickly if something is said, or not said. We feel one thing, and we say another, because that's how we're brought up. We have our dreams and our fantasies, though we rarely act on them. We all are, I think, more frightened than hopeful, and more self-sacrificing—the children, the spouse, the job, the community—than selfish. And that, I suppose, is good in the larger sense of maintaining a civilized society. I mean, if everyone acted like Susan Sutter, we'd all be shooting our lovers or our spouses, or both, or just running off to find love, happiness, and a life without responsibilities.

In some odd way, as angry as I was at Susan for her behavior, I almost envied her for her passion, her ability to break with her rigid upbringing and with her stifling social class. Or she was just nuts.

And while she was breaking the rules, she'd also broken the law. Murder. She'd gotten a Get-Out-of-Jail-Free card on that, but Mr. Anthony Bellarosa was holding a past-due bill that he might decide to collect.

Elizabeth asked me, "What are you thinking about?"

"About not following the rules. And taking chances. And using more heart and less brain."

She nodded and said, somewhat astutely, "Susan did that. And so did Tom. I never did, but you did when you sailed around the world."

"Well, I was put in that enviable position of having nothing left to lose. The only wrong move I could have made was to stay here and go to marriage counseling."

She smiled, and again with some insight pointed out, "You should try to figure out how your marriage got to that point. And you should make sure you don't go there again. Assuming you remarry."

The word "marry," and all its derivations and synonyms, upsets my stomach, so I changed the subject and asked, "Can I get you more coffee?"

"No, thanks. But let me make you breakfast."

"That's all right."

"I insist. Compensation for last night."

I didn't know if she meant compensation for not buying me dinner or for not having sex. I said, "Well, there's not much in the refrigerator."

"I saw that. But we can split that English muffin, and there's crabapple jelly, club soda, and two beers left."

"How did that English muffin get in there?"

She stood and said, "I see you didn't plan on me staying the night."

"No . . ." Actually, I did plan on it, but I didn't plan *for* it. I said, "We can go to a coffee shop."

"No. Just relax. I'll be right back."

"Thanks." So I sat there, thinking about our post-non-coital conversation, which was not much different than if we'd done it.

Bottom line on this was that I really liked Elizabeth, and I'd really wanted to sleep with her, but now I was glad I didn't, and I'd make sure it didn't happen and we could be just friends.

Maybe I should try that again. I'd have sex with her in a heartbeat. Why is this so complicated?

She reappeared with the coffee pot, refilled my cup, and said, "Breakfast will be served shortly, Mr. Sutter."

"Thank you, Elizabeth. I like my muffins well done and my crabapple jelly on the side."

"Very good, sir." She bent over, tousled my hair, kissed my lips, then went inside.

I could feel Little John waking up and stretching. Maybe I needed a cold shower.

I sipped my coffee and tried to think about things other than sex, or Elizabeth's perfect body, or my T-shirt riding up to her smooth, creamy white inner thighs, and her breasts nearly popping out of that bath towel last night, and how they almost fell out of my bathrobe when she bent over just now. Instead, I thought about . . . well, sex was all I could think about.

Elizabeth returned with a tray on which was the toasted English muffin split in two, an open jar of the jelly, a bottle of my Hildon sparkling water, the coffee pot, and the leftover cheese, crackers, and vegetables from last night. She set the tray on the table and said, "Breakfast is served."

"Thank you. Will you join me?"

"Oh, sir, that is not permitted. But if you insist." She sat and poured water into two glasses, saying, "Your breakfast beer is being chilled, sir."

"Thank you." I mean, this was a little funny, but hanging over the humor was the not-so-distant past when the Allards waited on the Stanhopes. I was rarely included in this arrangement, but there were a few times, years ago, when I dined with the Stanhopes in the great house, and Ethel, George, and a few of the other remaining servants would cook and serve a formal dinner to the Stanhope clan and their stuffed-shirt guests. In fact, I remembered now at least one occasion when Elizabeth, home from boarding school or college, cleared the table. I wondered if Lord William the Cheap paid her. Anyway, yes, Elizabeth was being funny, and this was a parody, but it made me a little uncomfortable.

Elizabeth spooned some jelly on my muffin and said, "We make this here on the estate."

I didn't come back with anything witty.

She placed some cheese on my plate and said, "This has been aged on the coffee table for twelve hours."

I smiled.

So we had breakfast, made some small talk about her clothing boutiques, and about the changes that had taken place on the Gold Coast in the last decade. She commented on that subject, "It's more subtle than dramatic. And not as bad as it could be. The nouveaux riches seem happy enough with their five acres and their semi-custom-built tract mansions." She smiled and said, "Some of the women even dress well."

I smiled in return.

She continued, "Well, listen to me—the daughter of estate workers. But, you know . . . I was brought up around the gentry, and I had a very good education, and I feel like part of the old, vanished world."

"You are."

"Yes, but I'm from the other part of that world, and now I'm a shopkeeper."

"Shop owner."

"Thank you, sir. In fact, three successful shops. And I did marry well. I mean, socially. Next time, I'll marry for love."

"Don't do anything silly."

She smiled, then said, "Well, at least my children are Corbets, and they've been well educated."

I said to her, "You know, I lived in England for seven years, and I saw the best and worst of the old class system. In the end, what matters is character."

"That, Mr. Sutter, sounds like bullshit."

I smiled. "Well, it is. But it sounds good."

"And easy for you to say."

"I wasn't born rich," I said.

"But you were born into two illustrious old families. Whitmans and Sutters. All or most of whom were college educated, and none of whom were gatekeepers, shopkeepers, or servants."

That was true, but as far as I knew, none of them had been filthy rich like the Stanhopes. Great Uncle Walt was famous, but poetry didn't pay that well.

As for the Sutters, they'd come over on the ship after the *Mayflower*, and they'd been missing the boat ever since, at least in regard to money.

Regarding the Stanhopes, Susan's great-great-grandfather, Cyrus, had made the family fortune in coal mines and built Stanhope Hall at the turn of the last century. The Whitmans and Sutters, however, would consider the Stanhopes to be ostentatious, mercenary, and perhaps not very intellectual. And as my mother liked to point out, the Stanhopes were totally devoid of social conscience.

Balzac said, "Behind every great fortune is a crime." But in the case of the Stanhopes, what was behind their fortune was dumb luck. And they'd kept most of it through greed, stinginess, and tax loopholes. And on that subject, although I did a lot of free legal work for cheap Willie, I never did tax work for him, or I'd probably be in jail now.

Nevertheless, in Elizabeth's eyes, we were all lumped together, and we'd all been highborn and blessed by fate and fortune.

To try to set the record straight, I informed her, "I happen to know that my distant ancestors were farmers and fishermen, and one of them, Elijah Sutter, was hanged for horse stealing."

"I won't tell."

I further informed her, "By the way, I'm broke."

She said, "Well, it's been nice knowing you."

I smiled, then suggested, "Can we change the subject?"

"Good idea. But let me just say, John, that I think you'd still be happy here if you stayed."

"I can be happy anywhere where there's a country club, a polo field, a yacht club, and two-hundred-acre zoning."

She smiled and observed, "You can take the boy out of the Gold Coast, but you can't take the Gold Coast out of the boy."

"Well said." I tried a piece of Gouda. "Tastes better this morning."

She said to me, "Tell me about your sail around the world."

"There's a lot to tell."

"Did you have a woman in every port?"

"No. Only in Western Europe, Southeast Asia, the Caribbean, and French Polynesia."

"Very funny. Well, tell me another time."

"How about you?"

"Me? Well . . . I've been dating for the last two years." She added, "Nothing serious, and I'm not seeing anyone at the moment."

Dating. Seeing. Women, I've discovered, have more euphemisms for fucking than Eskimos have words for snow. And they rarely use a masculine noun or pronoun when describing their love life. I'm dating someone, I'm seeing someone, I've met someone, I'm involved with someone, I'm serious about someone, I'm not serious about the person I'm seeing, and I date other people, and on and on. Whereas a guy will just ask another guy, "You fuckin' anybody?"

Elizabeth interrupted my mental riff and asked, "Are we supposed to have this conversation before or after sex?"

"Before is good. So there aren't any misunderstandings." I added, "I'm . . . seeing someone in London."

She didn't say anything for a while, then asked, "Is it serious?"

Serious to me usually describes a medical condition, like a brain tumor, but I think I know what serious means in this context, so I answered, honestly, "She thinks so. I do not."

"All right."

So we left it there.

To be truthful, this breakfast conversation was not going as well as I thought it would, and just as I was starting to have second thoughts about Elizabeth, she displayed the astuteness that I'd noticed before and said, "By now, you are subtracting points. First, I raise the class issue, and you think I've inherited the Red gene from my mother, then I pry into your love life, and we haven't even had sex, and . . . what else?"

"Breakfast sucks."

"That's your fault, not mine."

"True. Look—"

"Do you know how to shop for food?"

"Of course I do. I've provisioned my ship from native food stalls all over the world."

"What did you do in London?"

"In London, I called Curry in a Hurry. Or ate out."

"I'll do some food shopping for you."

"I'll go with you."

"That would be nice." She stayed silent awhile, then said to me, "I think Susan wants you back."

I didn't reply.

Elizabeth pushed on. "I think she wanted me to tell you that. So, I'm telling you."

"Thank you."

"Would you like my opinion on that?"

"No. I have my own opinion."

"All right." She stood and said, "I'm going home, then to church, then to visit Mom. Church is at eleven, if you'd like to meet me there. Or you can meet me at Fair Haven. And if you're not busy this afternoon, I'll buy you brunch."

I stood and said, "I'd like to spend the day with you, but . . . I don't want to run into Susan at church, or at Fair Haven."

"I understand."

As for the brunch invitation, I surprised myself by saying, "I have a

Sunday dinner date at four." I thought I owed Elizabeth an explanation and I said, "The same business guy I had dinner with last week, and his family."

"All right . . . I hope it works out."

"Can I meet you at about seven?"

"Call me."

"I will." I smiled and asked, "Can I help you get dressed?"

She smiled in return and said, "You didn't even help me get undressed." She said, "I want you to stay right here and not tempt me now. I'll let myself out."

"Are you sure?"

"I am." We embraced and kissed, and one thing led to another, and somehow her robe got undone, and we were about two seconds from doing it on the table, but she backed off, took a breath, and said, "Later. Tonight."

"Okay . . . tonight."

She tied her robe, turned and walked toward the door, then looked back at me and said, "You need to resolve things with Susan, sooner rather than later."

"I know that."

She went through the screen door, and I stood there, wanting to follow, but knowing I shouldn't.

I poured another cup of coffee and took a walk through Ethel's garden, which was overgrown with weeds that were choking out the vegetables. Why don't vegetables choke out weeds?

Anyway, I did some mental weeding. First, I liked Elizabeth Allard. Second, I had to take charge of events before they took charge of me. And that meant seeing Susan—not tomorrow, or the next day, but this morning. Then the visit to the Bellarosa house would have some purpose, and some resolution.

And then, tonight, I could sleep with Elizabeth—or sleep alone, but very soundly for the first time in two weeks.

━PART II━

Down the passage which we did not take
Towards the door we never opened
Into the rose garden.

—T. S. Eliot
"Burnt Norton," from *Four Quartets*

CHAPTER TWENTY-ONE

A vintage radio sat atop the refrigerator, and Patti Page was sing-ing "Old Cape Cod," which reminded me of a few sails I'd made there with my family. The station was playing a medley of Ameri-can geography–inspired songs, and the next one was "Moonlight in Ver-mont." I was sure that Ethel hadn't moved that dial in two decades.

Time had stood still here in this gatehouse as the changing world encroached on the walls of Stanhope Hall. In fact, life within the walls had changed, too, and time was about to catch up to this place, and to the people who lived here, past and present.

It was not yet 9:00 A.M., and I'd already showered and changed into tan trousers and my last clean button-down shirt. A Savile Row custom-made blue blazer hung over the back of the kitchen chair. I was dressed to call on Susan, or I was all dressed up with no place to go until dinner with the Mafia at four.

But maybe before I phoned Susan, I should first make my Sunday call to Carolyn and Edward. Carolyn, however, slept late on Sunday, and it was 6:00 A.M. in Los Angeles, so maybe I should call my mother, but I usually have a stiff drink in my hand when I speak to Harriet, and it was a bit early for that.

At quarter past nine, Ray Charles was singing "Georgia," and I was still standing in the kitchen with a cup of coffee in my hand.

It was odd, I thought, that I could tell a Mafia don to basically go fuck himself, but I couldn't get up the courage to make the phone call to Susan.

The last mournful notes of "Georgia" died away, and the mellow-voiced DJ said, "That was beautiful. You're listening to WLIG, broadcasting to the land of the free and the home of the brave."

Well, on that inspirational note, I shut off the radio, picked up the kitchen phone, and dialed the guest cottage number that Carolyn had given me. I listened to the phone ring three times and hoped for the answering machine.

Susan must have Caller ID, which showed Ethel's phone number, because she answered, "Hello, John."

I felt my heart give a thump at the sound of her voice saying my name, and I almost hung up, but obviously I couldn't—though maybe I could imitate Ethel's high-pitched voice and say, "Hello, Mrs. Sutter, I just wanted you to know I'm back from hospice, goodbye," then hang up.

"John?"

"Hello, Susan."

Silence.

I inquired, "How are you?"

"I'm fine. How are *you*?"

"Fine. Good. How are you doing?"

"Still fine."

"Right . . . me, too."

She observed, "You didn't rehearse this call very well."

I was a little annoyed at that and said, "I just thought about calling you, and I didn't have time to make notes."

"And to what do I owe the great pleasure of this phone call?"

My goodness. I hadn't expected her to be overjoyed or emotional to hear my voice, but she was distinctly frigid. I had to remind myself that Ethel and Elizabeth had indicated that Susan would welcome a call from me. And Mr. Nasim said that Susan spoke well of me. Even Edward and Carolyn had hinted that Mom wanted to hear from me. So what was this all about?

And the answer was, Susan asking me, "Has your houseguest left already?"

Ah. Before I could reply, she further inquired, "That *was* Elizabeth Allard's car there overnight, was it not?"

"Yes, it was. But . . ." I didn't fuck her. Honest.

"And how is Elizabeth?"

I really didn't owe Susan any explanation, but to set the record straight, I thought I should say something—but this had caught me off guard, and I blurted, "She had too much to drink, and she wanted to see her old room, and we had a lot of estate work to do, and I'm the attorney, so she just stayed over, and—"

Before I became even more unintelligible, Susan interrupted and said, "Well, I don't care. So, what can I do for you?"

"I didn't sleep with her."

Silence, then, "I *really* don't care, John." She informed me, "I need to get ready for church."

Well, having taken the initiative by making this call, I wasn't going to be blown off that easily, so I said, "I'm coming by now with an envelope for you. I'll ring the bell. If you don't answer, I'll leave the envelope at the door."

Silence.

I said, "Goodbye," and hung up.

I put on my blazer, grabbed the manila envelope from the dining room table, and went out the door.

It was a beautiful, sunny day, birds sang, locusts chirped, bees buzzed, and my heart was pounding as I walked up the main drive toward the guest cottage.

I couldn't understand why I was feeling so tense. I mean, if anyone should be feeling tense or awkward—or guilty—it should be Susan. It wasn't *me* who had an affair, then shot my lover.

By the time I covered the three hundred yards to the guest cottage, I was in better control of myself.

As I approached the house, I noticed that the previous owners, to whom Susan had sold the house, had marked the boundaries of their property by planting lines of hedgerows around the ten-acre enclave. When William and Charlotte still lived in the mansion, I'd suggested to Susan that we erect a twenty-foot stone wall with guard towers to cut down on her parents' unannounced visits, but Susan didn't want to block her views, so now I wondered if she was going to have these hedges ripped out. I was certain that Amir Nasim was concerned about these thick growths providing cover and concealment for Iranian snipers.

But back to more immediate concerns. I half wanted Susan not to answer the door; then I could get on with my life with no further thought about Susan Stanhope Sutter. On the other hand, I did feel obligated to pass on Nasim's concerns as well as my concerns about Anthony Bellarosa. Of course, all this could be done in a phone call or a letter, and if she didn't answer the door, that's what I'd do.

The other half of me, to be honest, wanted her to open the door and invite me in. If nothing else, I needed to explain Elizabeth's sleepover—not because it mattered to me, but it might matter to Elizabeth, so I wanted to clear up that misunderstanding so Susan and I could get on to other misunderstandings.

I walked up the slate path to the large stone guest cottage, and noticed that the ivy hadn't been cut and was climbing over the windowsills. Also, the gravel driveway and the forecourt in front of the house were in need of maintenance. These used to be my jobs, to do or to hire out. I did notice that the flowerbeds, Susan's area of responsibility, were picture-perfect. Why was I noticing this?

I stepped up to the front door, and without hesitation, I rang the bell.

I had time for one quick thought before the door opened, or before I left, so I thought back to Susan and Frank screwing their brains out all summer while I was off breaking my butt in the city, while also trying to fight an IRS income tax evasion charge, and in my spare time trying to defend my wife's boyfriend on a murder charge. All of those happy memories put me in the right frame of mind.

I waited about ten seconds, then put the envelope against the door, turned, and walked away.

About five seconds later, I heard the door open, and Susan's voice called, "Thank you."

I looked over my shoulder and saw her standing at the door holding the envelope, dressed in jeans and a pink polo shirt. I said, "You're welcome," and kept walking.

"John."

I stopped and turned around. "Yes?"

"Would you like to come in for a minute? I have something for you."

I glanced at my watch, then with a show of great reluctance, I said, "Well . . . all right."

I walked back to the house, and she disappeared inside, leaving the door open. I entered and shut the door.

She was standing at the far end of the large foyer, near the kitchen, and she asked, "Would you like some coffee?"

"Thank you."

She disappeared into the kitchen and I followed. The house, from what I could see, looked very much like it did ten years before, furnished mostly with Stanhope family antiques, which I called junk and which she must have taken with her to Hilton Head or put into storage.

The big country kitchen, too, looked very much the same, including the old regulator clock on the wall, and I had that *Twilight Zone* feeling that I'd just left to get the Sunday newspapers and returned to discover that I'd been divorced for ten years.

Susan, standing with her back to me at the coffee pot, asked, "Still black?"

"Yes."

She poured coffee into two mugs, turned, and I met her halfway. She handed me the mug, and we looked at each other. She really hadn't aged, as I'd noticed when I'd seen her from a distance a few days ago, and she hadn't gained an ounce of weight in ten years, but neither had I. So with obviously the same thoughts in our minds, we said, simultaneously, "You're looking"—we both smiled involuntarily, then said— "well."

The pleasantries over, I said to her, "I need to speak to you."

She replied, "If you've come here because you're feeling guilty—"

"I'm not *guilty* of anything."

"You can sleep with whomever you wish, but try to stay away from my friends, please."

"Well, then, give me a list of your friends."

"And you do the same, if you have any."

Bitch. I put my coffee mug on the table and said, "Before I go, you need to understand that I did not have sex with Elizabeth Allard."

"I don't care if you did or didn't."

"But you just said—"

"Are you playing lawyer with me?"

Some things never change. Susan is very bright, but no one has ever accused her of being logical or rational. I mean, she *can* be, but when she's stressed, she takes refuge in the nutty part of her brain. It's the red hair. I said, "Look me in the eye."

"Which one?"

"Look at me."

She looked at me, and I said, "I did *not* have sex with Elizabeth."

She kept staring at me, and we held eye contact. I suggested, "Speak to Elizabeth."

She nodded, then said, "All right. I believe you."

So we stood there, and the regulator clock on the wall ticked away, as it did many times when Susan and I passed these deadly silent minutes in the kitchen after a fight. Those fights were usually cathartic, a good sign that we still cared enough to go a few rounds, and more often than not, we kissed and made up, then sprinted upstairs into the bedroom. I was sure she was remembering that, too, but we were not going to the bedroom this time. In fact, I said, "I can come back another time."

She asked me, "What's in the envelope?"

I replied, "Some photos, and some papers that you should have, such as Carolyn and Edward's birth records, which wound up in my storage."

She nodded, then said to me, "If you have a few minutes, I need to discuss some things with you, and I have a few things to give you."

"All right."

She suggested, "Why don't we sit in the rose garden?"

"Okay."

"I'll be right out."

I took my coffee and went out the rear kitchen door into the English rose garden, which was surrounded by a low stone wall, and looked basically the same as I remembered it, except that the cast-iron furniture had been replaced with wicker, which looked not much more comfortable. Women can sit on anything.

The roses were starting to bloom, and I couldn't remember if this was early or late for the blooms—it depended, I guess, on what kind of spring there had been here on Long Island.

So here I was, home but not home. It all looked familiar, but the slight changes were disorienting. Same with the people. I'd feel more comfortable in a native hut on a Pacific island, where nothing reminded me of my past life.

I recalled something my father had said to me when I was in the Army and about to begin an assignment in Germany. He'd said of his four years away at war, "When I returned, I felt so out of place that I wished I was back with my buddies in a foxhole." Considering that he'd later met and married my mother, I was sure that was a recurring wish. More to the point, I now understood what he meant.

Anyway, I sat in a chair at a round wicker table and watched the fountain bubbling in the rear of the neat, symmetrical garden with the sundial in the center.

There were a few garden statues scattered around the rose beds, mostly classical figures, and this reminded me of Alhambra's classical gardens, the reflecting pool, and, of course, my dream. Probably I would never ask her how, when, and where she'd begun her affair with Frank Bellarosa, but if I *did* ask how it happened, she'd say, "How did *what* happen? Oh, *that*. That was so long ago, John. Why are you bringing that up?" And so forth. She's an accomplished amnesiac, and I was certain that she had no more memory of screwing Frank Bellarosa than she had of shooting him. Well, of course she remembered, but only if someone like me was uncouth enough to mention it.

I recalled the last time I saw her, which was about four years ago at my aunt Cornelia's funeral. I don't know why she was there, but because of our children, she was still part of the family in some way. She'd left her new husband back in Hilton Head, so I didn't have a chance to meet the lucky man, or the opportunity to comment on how old he looked, or how fat he was, or whatever. If she'd married a young stud, you can be sure he'd have been there in a black Armani suit.

Anyway, Susan and I had spoken then, but it had been mostly small talk about Aunt Cornelia, and Cornelia's deceased husband, Arthur, and their two brainless sons. We spoke, too, about my father, whom Susan had been fond of, but she didn't mention his funeral that I had missed. I recalled congratulating Susan on her marriage, and I wished her happiness. I think I even meant it.

She'd told me that her husband was a very good man, meaning, I think, that he was not the love of her life.

She hadn't asked me anything personal, and I didn't offer any news on my love life.

Also not on the agenda were the last words we'd spoken to each other before we parted, six years before. I had attended her hearing in Federal court in Manhattan to offer testimony as a witness in the death of Frank Bellarosa. As her husband and onetime lawyer, I didn't have to take the stand, but I wanted to offer some extenuating and mitigating circumstances on her behalf, mostly having to do with her state of mind on the night of the murder, such as, "Your Honor, my wife is nuts. Look at that red hair." Also I informed the court that I wanted to speak for the record about the FBI pimping my wife for the Mafia don while he was in their protective custody in his mansion, and I definitely wanted to say a few words about the questionable actions of the U.S. Attorney, Alphonse Ferragamo.

Well, as it turned out, the judge and Mr. Ferragamo didn't want to hear any of that from me, and the closed-door session had ended with the Justice Department concluding that this case would not be presented to a grand jury. A total victory for Susan, and a reaffirmation of the government's right to cover its ass. As for me, this was the only time I'd ever influenced the outcome of a case by sitting in the hallway with my mouth shut.

I was relieved that Susan had walked, of course, but to be honest, I was also a little disappointed—as a lawyer and as a citizen—that the Justice Department had let her off so easily, without even a slap on the wrist. And as a betrayed husband, I'd wished that Susan had at least been ordered to wear a scarlet A on her prim dress, but then, by extension, I guess I'd be wearing a sign that said CUCKOLD.

Anyway, after the hearing, I had made a point of running into her on the steps of the courthouse in Foley Square, and she'd been surrounded by her happy parents, three relieved lawyers, and two family-retained psychiatrists, which were barely enough for any member of the Stanhope family.

I'd gotten Susan separated from her retinue, and we'd spoken briefly, and I congratulated her on the outcome of the hearing, though I was not entirely happy with that outcome. Nevertheless, I said to her, "I still love you, you know."

And she'd replied, "You'd better. Forever."

And my last words to her were, "Yes, forever."

And her last words to me were, "Me, too."

So we parted there on the courthouse steps and didn't see each other for almost four years, when Edward graduated from Sarah Lawrence.

And the last time we'd spoken, at Cornelia's funeral, the final thing she'd said to me was, "I'll wish you happiness, John, but before that, I wish you peace."

I didn't know why she'd thought I wasn't at peace—that was *my* secret—but I replied, "Thank you. Same to you."

We had parted at the cemetery, and I'd returned to London. Now, four years later, we were about to bury another lady from our past, and if I were in a joking mood I'd say to her, "We have to stop meeting like this." But maybe, I thought, one or both of our children would finally decide to get married, and Susan and I would meet on happier occasions, such as births and christenings and grandchildren's birthdays.

Until then, it was funerals, which reminded me of a line from Longfellow—*Let the dead Past bury its dead.*

Yes, indeed.

CHAPTER TWENTY-TWO

S usan came out to the rose garden, and I was observant enough to notice she'd run a brush through her hair, and maybe tweaked the lip gloss.

Gentleman that I am, I stood, and she, recalling a running joke between us, asked me, "Is someone playing the national anthem?"

We both smiled, and she set a stationery box on the table as well as the envelope I'd brought, then she sat opposite me.

As for the envelope, I didn't want her opening it now and seeing the nude photos of herself; that might be awkward, or embarrassing, or it might send the wrong message. Or did she already look in the envelope? In any case, she left it on the table.

We both sat in silence for a few seconds, then I remembered to say, "I was sorry to hear about your husband."

"Thank you."

That seemed to cover the subject, so I asked the grieving widow, "What did you need to speak to me about?"

"You go first."

"Ladies first."

"All right. Well, I have this box for you that contains copies of some photos I thought you'd like to have. Also, I've found a stack of letters to us from Edward and Carolyn when they were at school, and I've made photocopies for you."

"Thank you. Do you also have the canceled checks we sent them?"

She smiled and replied, "No, but I do have the thank-you notes." She observed, "Now they e-mail, but they used to know how to write longhand."

We both smiled.

She asked me, "What's in that envelope?"

"Same thing. Photos, a few letters from the children. Some documents that you may want to keep."

"Thank you." She then informed me, "Edward and Carolyn both told me they'd be here for Ethel's funeral." She added, "Edward needs some lead time. He's very busy at work. So is Carolyn, but she can get here quickly from Brooklyn."

I remarked, "I always wanted to live long enough to see my children juggling work and family responsibilities. I can't wait for them to get married and have kids."

"John, you make work, family, marriage, and children sound like a punishment for something."

"Sorry. That came out wrong. Anyway, you should keep them up to date on Ethel. I don't have e-mail or a cell phone."

"Do you plan to?"

"If I stay."

She didn't pursue that and asked me, "When was the last time you spoke to them?"

"Last Sunday. They sounded well."

"I think they are." She told me, "They're happy you're back." She took the opportunity to inquire, "How long are you staying?"

"At least until the funeral."

She nodded, but did not ask a follow-up question. The subject was family, so she advised me, "You should see your mother—before the funeral."

"Do you mean hers or Ethel's?"

"Please be serious. You should act toward your mother the way you'd want *your* children to act toward you. You need to set an example for them. She *is* their grandmother. You are her son."

"I think I get it."

"You need to be more of an adult."

"I am my mother's son, and I act as I'm treated."

"Ridiculous." She continued on her subject and said, "Your estrangement from your mother affects our children. I'm thinking of them."

It's always the children, of course, but they rarely give a damn. In any case, this was not about Harriet and me, or the children and me; it was about Susan and me.

She continued on to Point B and said, "Edward and Carolyn are also uncomfortable with your attitude toward my parents." She reminded me, in case I missed the connection, "They are the children's *grandparents*."

"How long do you think this lecture is going to last?"

"This is not a *lecture*. These are important issues that need to be addressed for the sake of our children."

I wanted to say, "They are not children any longer, and you should have thought about them ten years ago when you decided to fuck Frank Bellarosa." Instead, I said, "All right, to the extent that I have any involvement in the lives of anyone here, I'll try to be a better son, a better father, and a better ex-husband."

"And hopefully, less sarcastic."

"And for the record, I have *never* said anything unkind about your parents to Edward or Carolyn."

"Maybe not . . . but they *sense* the hostility."

"They're very perceptive." I added, "I don't even *think* about your parents."

She took the opportunity to give me some good news. "They've gotten a lot more mellow over the years."

The only way those two would be mellow is if they had brain transplants. I said, "Then maybe it was me who brought out the worst in them."

She ignored that and got to the conclusion of this lecture, saying, "What happened between us has impacted a lot of people around us whom we care for and who care for us, so I think we should try to be civil to each other and make life easier and less awkward for everyone."

"It may be a little late for that."

"No, it is not."

I didn't respond.

She asked me, "When are you going to let it go?"

"I've done that."

"No, you have not."

"And you have?"

"I was never angry with you, John."

"Right. Why should you be? What did *I* do?"

"You should think about your role in what happened."

"Please."

"Then think about what you've done for the last ten years."

"I haven't *done* anything."

"That is the point. You just ran off."

I didn't reply, but I glanced at my watch, and she saw this and said, "You are not leaving until I finish what I have to say."

"Then finish."

She stayed silent awhile, then said, in a softer voice, "John, we can't undo what happened—"

"Try that again, with a singular pronoun."

She took a deep breath and said, "Okay . . . *I* can't undo what happened . . . what *I* did. But I would like . . . I would like you to forgive me."

I didn't see that coming, and I was momentarily speechless. I thought about what to say, and I almost said, "I forgive you," but instead I looked at her and reminded her, "You never even *apologized*. You never said you were sorry."

She held eye contact with me, then said, "John . . . what I did was too great a sin to apologize for. What do I say? I'm sorry I ruined all our lives? I'm sorry I had an affair? I'm sorry I killed him? I'm sorry I didn't go to jail to pay for what I did? I'm sorry about his wife and children? I'm sorry that it was my fault that our children have suffered, and my fault that they haven't had you around for ten years? I'm sorry it was my fault you weren't here when your father died? How do I apologize for all that?"

I didn't know what to say, and I couldn't look at her any longer, so I turned away, and I heard her say, "Excuse me."

I looked back at her, but she'd stood and was walking quickly back into the house.

I sat there for a minute, feeling pretty miserable, but also feeling that this was finally coming to some sort of end.

There was a gate in the garden wall, and I looked at it, picturing myself walking through it. I could call her later, when we'd both calmed down. Or did she want me to wait here? Or follow her inside?

Women are always hard to figure out, and when they're upset, I don't even try. The best thing for me to do right now was to do what *I* wanted to do, and I wanted to leave. So I stood, took the box she'd given me, and walked toward the gate. But then I hesitated and looked back toward the house, but there was no sign of her. Apparently, the conversation was over. And that was okay, too.

I opened the gate, then I weakened again, and thought of her coming out and finding me gone. I was really torn, and my tougher side was saying, "Leave," and my softer side was saying, "She's hurting."

Sometimes, in moments like this, I ask for divine intervention, so I did that, but the kitchen door stayed closed. "Come on, God."

Pride goeth before a fall.

"Thanks for the tip."

Say it with flowers.

"What . . . ?" Then I suddenly recalled being here before, literally and figuratively, and I remembered how we sometimes made a peace offering without too much loss of pride.

I went back into the garden and found her rose clippers on a potting bench, and cut a dozen red roses, and put them on the round table, then I walked toward the gate and opened it.

"John."

I turned and saw her at the door. She called out, "Are you leaving?"

"I . . . I was . . ."

"How can you just—?" She saw the cut roses and walked to the table. She picked up a stem and looked at it, then looked at me. We stared at each other across the garden, then I walked slowly back toward the house.

She watched me as I approached, and I stopped at that well-defined midpoint where sparring spouses and exes are neither too close nor too far, but just right for comfort.

She asked me, "Why were you leaving?"

"I thought you wanted me to leave." I reminded her, "You got up and left."

"I said, 'Excuse me,' not goodbye."

"Right. Well, I wasn't sure . . . actually, to be truthful, I wanted to leave."

"Why?"

"This is painful."

She nodded.

So we stood there, neither of us knowing what to say next. She'd asked me to forgive her, and after ten years, I should just say, "I forgive you," and move on. But if I said it, I'd have to mean it, and if I didn't mean it, she'd know it.

Susan and I had both grown up in a world and a social class where things like sin, acts of redemption and contrition, and absolution were drummed into us in church, at St. Paul's, at Friends Academy, and even at home. That world may have vanished, and we may both have strayed so far off course that we'd never see land again, but we were still middle-aged products of that world. So, knowing she'd understand what I meant, I said to her, "Susan, I can and do accept your apology for everything. I really do. But it isn't in my heart, or my power, to forgive you."

She nodded, and said, "I understand. Just don't hate me."

"I don't hate you."

"You did."

"I never did. I told you . . . on the courthouse steps . . . remember?"

"I do." She reminded me, "You told your sister you were going to sail to Hilton Head. I waited for you."

This was getting painful again, but it needed to be painful before it finally stopped hurting. I said, "I did sail there . . . but I turned around."

"And sailed off to see the world."

"That's right."

"You could have been lost at sea."

"That wasn't my plan, if that's what you're suggesting."

"You said it, I didn't."

"Subject closed," I said.

"Everyone was worried. Your parents, your children—"

"That wasn't part of the plan, either. It was just an exquisite act of

irresponsibility and self-indulgence. Nothing more." I added, "I deserved it." I reminded her, "Subject closed."

"All right." She picked a lighter subject and said, "Thank you for
the flowers."

"They're actually your flowers," I pointed out.

"I know that. But thank you for the gesture."

"You're welcome."

"I'm touched that you remembered."

I was still bothered by her suggestion that I'd sailed off around the
world because I was a distraught, self-pitying, heartbroken, sympathy-
seeking, suicidal wreck of a man. Women just don't understand irre-
sponsible behavior, so I returned to the closed subject and said, "It was
also a challenge."

"What was?"

"Sailing around the world in a small boat."

"Oh . . . I thought you said the subject—"

"Men enjoy the thrill of danger."

"Well . . . I don't think the people waiting at home enjoy it, but you
did it, and I hope you've gotten it out of your system."

"Maybe." On that note, I decided to quit while we were still speaking, so I said, "I don't want to make you late for church. So, why don't
we meet tomorrow?"

"I don't think I'm in the mood for meeting people at church."

I didn't think the purpose of church was meeting people, and I
don't know what sort of mood you needed to be in to meet them there,
but I said, "You may feel better if you go to church."

She ignored that and asked, "Why don't we take a walk?"

I thought about that, then said, "All right . . ."

I took off my blazer and hung it on the chair, then we headed out
through the garden gate. Susan carried along a rose stem.

It was just like old times, except it wasn't. And it never would be
again. We were not going to get back together, but this time when
we said goodbye, we could also say, "Stay in touch." There would be
more funerals and weddings, births and birthdays, and there would
be new people in our lives, and that would be all right, and we could

be in the same room together, and actually smile; our friends and family would like that.

That was as good as it was going to get, and after ten years, considering all that had happened and could have happened in our lives, it was a small miracle that we were here now, speaking, and taking a walk together.

CHAPTER TWENTY-THREE

W e walked across the rolling lawn toward the hedgerow in the distance.

Susan was barefoot, which was how she liked to walk around the property, and I wondered if Amir Nasim would approve of bare feet. But we were still on Susan's property, so it was moot until we crossed into Iranian territory.

Susan made small talk about the property as we walked and said, "The Ganzes . . . they were the couple I sold the house to . . . Diane and Barry Ganz—did you meet them?"

"Briefly, after you left. They'd call about once a week to ask me questions about how things worked, or why things didn't work."

"Sorry."

"I tried to help, but I reminded them that I did not sell them the house."

She didn't reply to that, then said, "That was an impulsive move. Selling the house. But I was . . . distraught. And my parents were urging me to join them in Hilton Head."

With William and Charlotte, urging meant pressuring, and I wondered if Susan had figured out the difference in the last ten years.

Also, her selling the house and moving basically killed any chance that we would reconcile, which was one reason the Stanhopes wanted her to move.

Plus, of course, Susan had whacked a Mafia don, and it's always best to leave the neighborhood when you do something like that.

Susan, however, had another explanation for me and continued, "The government had taken over Stanhope Hall from . . . well, you know that. And I wasn't sure if I'd be surrounded by a subdivision, as was happening . . . next door . . . so I sold the house."

I didn't reply, but I noted that she avoided uttering the name Frank Bellarosa, or Alhambra. Maybe she couldn't recall her lover's name, or where he'd lived. Or, more likely, Susan thought, correctly, that I did not want to hear the name Frank Bellarosa, or Alhambra. But that was not the last minefield we would encounter on this walk, so to show I couldn't be wounded anymore, I said, "I saw the houses at Alhambra," and in a poor choice of words, I added, "Frank Bellarosa must be rolling over in his grave." I further added, "Sorry."

Susan stayed silent awhile, then returned to the Ganzes and said, "They took good care of the property, but they planted these hedgerows for privacy, and they block my views. But now that Stanhope Hall is occupied, they do give me some privacy. So I don't know if I should take them out. What do you think?"

"Live with them for a year, then decide."

"Good idea." She informed me, "I sunbathe on the lawn, and that could be an issue with the new owner."

"I know that."

"Oh, have you met him?"

"I have."

"And? What did he say?" she asked.

"Dress modestly."

"Yes, I know. What else did you talk about?"

"Well, I have arranged with him for me to stay in the gatehouse after Ethel passes on."

"Did you? For how long?"

"No later than September first. If I stay here that long. Then he wants his property back." I added, "Nasim wants to put . . . someone of his choosing into the gatehouse." I asked her, "Did he tell you that?"

"No. We never spoke of that." She informed me, "He wanted to buy the guest cottage from me. Did he mention that to you?"

"He did."

We continued our walk across the sun-dappled lawn, and she said to me, "He made me a very generous offer for the cottage and the land." She added, "He seemed upset when I turned him down."

I didn't reply, and neither did I make a pitch for her to accept the offer. Also, I decided not to bring up the subject of Amir Nasim's security concerns at this time; that needed to be discussed along with my concerns about Anthony Bellarosa, and I wanted to save that for last.

Susan, of course, had changed, as we all had in ten years, but I know this woman, and I was fairly certain she would think that Amir Nasim's concerns were silly or paranoid, or at worst, real, but of no concern to her. As for Mr. Anthony Bellarosa's possible vendetta . . . well, she'd understand that on one level, but dismiss it on another. Susan was raised in an incredibly sheltered and privileged environment, and I was sure that hadn't changed much in Hilton Head. I used to think of her as having the Marie Antoinette Syndrome—not so much the "let them eat cake" mentality, but rather the mentality of not comprehending why anyone would want to cut off her head, not to mention the good manners to apologize to her executioner when she stepped on his foot near the guillotine.

Well, maybe she *had* changed over the years, but I wasn't seeing much of it. I did notice, however, that she seemed less nutty. Or maybe she was saving that as a special treat for later, after we got comfortable with each other.

I asked her, "Why did you come back?"

She replied, "I was homesick." She asked me, "Were you homesick?"

I thought about that, then replied, "Home isn't a place."

"Then what is it?"

"It's . . . people. Family, friends . . . memories . . . that sort of thing."

"Well? And didn't you miss that?"

"I did at first. But . . . time heals, and memories fade." I added, "Home can also be suffocating. I needed a change."

"I did, too, but I felt drawn back here." She added, "I didn't want to die in Hilton Head."

"No, that would be redundant."

She almost laughed, then said, "It's a nice place. I think you'd like it there."

"I don't think I'll ever find out."

She stayed silent awhile, then said, "I kept my place there . . . so, if you ever want to use it, you're welcome."

"Well . . . thank you."

"It's near the beach, and near two golf courses. Very relaxing."

"Sounds . . . relaxing." So, we'd gone from barely speaking to her offering me her house at the beach to relax. She was trying, and I was not. Maybe, I thought, as Nasim suggested, she was on a major nostalgia trip, which is why she'd moved back here, and somehow I was included in her happy memories of the past. In any case, my life was in flux, or limbo, or whatever, and hers was settling back into a past that no longer existed and could not be resurrected.

She returned to the subject of her place in Hilton Head and said, "I had it completely refurnished, and moved all my things back here."

"I noticed." I then asked her, "So, are you happy being back?"

"I am. You know, sometimes you just feel it in your heart when you've made the right move."

"Good." I couldn't resist getting in a zinger and said, "I'm sure your parents miss you, but are happy for you."

She glanced at me, knowing from long experience that everything I said about her parents was either ironic or a double entendre, or just plain nasty. She informed me, "To be honest, I needed to spend less time with them."

"I can't imagine why."

She ignored that and went on, "After Dan died . . . I realized that I had no reason to stay there . . . I mean, Carolyn is here, Edward comes to New York more often than he comes to Hilton Head, and I still have family and friends here."

And one enemy on the adjoining property. I could see now that Susan could not be persuaded to leave here because of Anthony Bellarosa's proximity. The best I could hope for was to make her acknowledge the problem and the situation she'd gotten herself into. And if I was working for Anthony Bellarosa, that might keep him from his vendetta. But in the end, it didn't really matter if I was working for don Bellarosa or not, and it didn't matter where Susan lived. Anthony Bellarosa smelled blood, and when the time came, he'd follow that blood scent to the ends of the earth.

A few days ago, protecting Susan had been an abstract thought; now, with her walking beside me, it became real.

The obvious thing to do was to notify the local police, and also the FBI. If the law got on Anthony's case regarding Susan Sutter, and told him to not even *think* about settling the score, then that should be all that was necessary to protect Susan.

On the other hand, Susan had murdered Anthony's *father*, and gotten away with it, and I didn't think that Anthony Bellarosa was going to let that stand. Well . . . his father wouldn't be swayed from his ancient duty to avenge the murder of a family member, but maybe Anthony was not made of the same stuff as his father. Quite possibly, I hoped, Anthony valued his freedom more than he valued the concept of family honor and vendetta. I simply didn't have the answer to that question, and I didn't want to guess wrong, or test either assumption. This was a big problem, and it trumped all my smaller problems.

Susan asked me, "What are you thinking about?"

"Oh . . . about . . . what were we talking about?"

"My parents. And that usually puts you in a dark mood."

"Not at all. And how are they?"

"Fine."

"You must miss them."

Silence, then, "To tell you the truth, they drive me a little nuts."

That was a short trip, but I reminded her, "You said they've become more mellow."

"Well, they have, but . . . they like to look after me."

"I remember that." In fact, as I said, William and Charlotte Stanhope were control freaks and manipulators, and he was not only a skinflint, but also an unscrupulous snake. Charlotte, the other half of this dynamically dysfunctional duo, was a smiling backstabber and a two-faced troublemaker. Other than that, they were quite pleasant.

I had this thought that Susan was half trying to repackage Mom and Dad as kindly senior citizens—mellow and all that—who would no longer be a problem between us, if we somehow got back together. Well, the only way that William and Charlotte would cease to annoy me was if they were dead and buried. With that thought in mind, I asked, "How are they feeling? Any health issues?"

She thought about that question, then replied, "Not that I know of." She added, "In fact, they're coming in for Ethel's funeral."

I was afraid of that; I'd hoped they would take a pass on the funeral of an old servant, but as I said, there is this lingering sense of noblesse oblige among the old families, and William and Charlotte would stay true to that, even if it were inconvenient, not to mention the travel expenses. Maybe they'd hitchhike up. I asked, "Are they staying at The Creek?"

"They've dropped their membership."

"I see. Well, club membership can be expensive."

"They just don't come up here much to use the club."

"Right. And with airfare going sky high, pardon the pun—"

"It's not the *money*, John. It's . . . they have fewer reasons to come to New York."

"Well, you're here now. Carolyn has never left, and they have friends here who love them, so I'm sure you'll be seeing a lot more of them than you thought." I was on a nice roll, and it felt good, so I continued, "And I wouldn't want them to spend all that money for a hotel, so they're welcome to use Ethel's room at the gatehouse. I'd enjoy—"

"John. Stop it."

"Sorry. I was just trying to—"

"You're not the forgiving type, are you?"

"What was your first clue?"

She thought about that, then said, "If you won't forgive, and you won't forget, at least take some comfort in the fact that you've won."

"Won? What did I win?"

"You won it all."

"I thought I lost it all."

"You did, but that's how you won."

"Sounds Zen."

"You know what I'm talking about, so let's drop it."

"All right."

She got back to the prior subject and announced, "My parents are staying with me."

I was afraid of that, too. I really didn't want them on the property; my offer to put them up wasn't sincere.

Susan continued, "So are Edward and Carolyn. It will be nice to have them in their old rooms."

I nodded.

She continued, "I'd like to invite you over for dinner or cocktails . . . whatever you'd like."

I didn't respond.

She said, "It would be less awkward, with you here on the property, if you didn't feel you needed to avoid my parents . . . or me. The children would very much like that."

"I know they would, Susan."

"So?"

I thought about this family reunion, compliments of Ethel. I was looking forward to seeing my children, but I could do without my ex-in-laws. The other thing was . . . well, my public humiliation of being cuckolded by my beautiful wife; by divorcing her, and not speaking to her for ten years, I'd felt avenged, and my pride was intact. I was ready, in theory, as I said, to be in the same room with her, smiling and chatting. But the reality of being in the house of my unfaithful ex-wife, sitting around the table with our children and her parents . . . *Susan, darling, could you pass the peas? William, can I pour you more wine?* Well, I didn't think I was ready for *that*.

"John?"

"Well . . . I don't think your parents would want to sit with me—"

"I don't care *what* they want. They can dine out if they don't like it. I'm asking *you* if you'd like to have dinner at home with me, Edward, and Carolyn."

"Yes. I would."

"Good. They'll be very happy when I tell them."

"Can I bring a date?"

She looked at me, saw I was joking, and suppressed a smile, then gave me a playful punch on the arm and said, "Not funny."

We continued to walk around her ten acres, and now and then she'd point out something the Ganzes had done, or something new that she'd done in the few months she'd been back, and she also remarked on how little the property had changed. She said, "The trees are bigger, and every one of them has survived, except for that copper beech that was over there. I'd replace it, but I had an estimate of about thirty thousand dollars."

I wanted to suggest that her parents pay for it as a housewarming gift, and maybe I'd mention it to them if they came to dinner. Charlotte would choke to death on her martini olive, and William would drop dead of a heart attack. Total win-win.

Actually, this might be an opportunity for me to make amends with William by apologizing for calling him, quote, "an unprincipled asshole, an utterly cynical bastard, a monumental prick, and a conniving fuck." I believe that was the last time we spoke. So maybe it was time for me to apologize for my profanity, rephrase the sentence in proper English, and ask him if he'd worked on those problems.

Susan reminded me, "This is where the children used to pitch their tents in the summer. Can you believe we let them sleep outdoors by themselves?"

"They usually had friends. And it's very safe inside the walls." Or it used to be.

Susan said, "My place in Hilton Head is a gated community."

"Is it?" Of course it is.

"It's hard to believe that Carolyn and Edward live in small apartments with no doorman on crowded city streets, and they love it."

"They're young and adventurous."

"And not afraid. I'm glad we didn't overprotect them, or spoil them."

"Well, it's a fine line between protecting and overprotecting, providing and spoiling." Not to mention underprotecting and underparenting, which was my upbringing, but I'd rather have that than what Susan had.

Bottom line on this conversation was Susan reminding me that we'd done something right; we had been good parents, and that remained a source of pride, as well as a bond. Of course, we blew it at the end, but by the time we separated, Edward and Carolyn were on their way into the real world.

Susan said to me, "If I could turn back the clock, I would."

That did sound like she regretted what she'd done, or, like most of us, me included, she regretted getting caught. The affair itself must've been emotionally stimulating and sexually pleasurable, not to mention deliciously taboo. I mean, she wasn't screwing the tennis pro at the club; this was a Mafia don. So I didn't know if she regretted the affair, or the consequences. That would depend on how far back she wanted to set that clock.

To be honest here, during the time that Susan and I had been estranged and sleeping in separate bedrooms, I'd become briefly involved with a TV news reporter named Jenny Alvarez, who was locally well-known at the time. I'd met her because she was covering the murder indictment against Frank Bellarosa, and I was, of course, the don's attorney. I never regretted my involvement with Jenny Alvarez, probably because there were no unpleasant consequences, and of course, I felt justified because my wife was screwing my most famous client. Well, justified or not, I was playing with fire at a time when Susan and I didn't need any more fire. I always felt I should have told Susan about this brief fling—as I called it, to distinguish it from her affair—but I wasn't sure if my motives for confession would be the correct motives of truth, and honesty, and unburdening my soul. Or would I have been bragging, trying to hurt her, or trying to make her jealous? So, since I couldn't decide, I'd kept it to myself.

But now maybe the time had come to tell Susan that she hadn't been the only one committing adultery. I said to her, "Susan . . ."

"Yes?"

"Well . . . do you remember that TV reporter Jenny Alvarez, who was on, I believe, one of the network stations?"

"No . . . I don't think so."

I described Ms. Alvarez to her, but she couldn't recall the lady, and inquired, "Why do you ask?"

"Well . . . I was just wondering if she was still on the air."

"I don't watch much television news."

"Right. So, Nasim tells me that you and his wife . . . Soheila, right—?"

"Yes . . ."

"—have become friendly."

"Well, I suppose . . . but . . ." She seemed confused and asked me, "Why were you asking about that TV reporter?"

I came to my senses and said, "I used to enjoy her reporting, and I can't seem to find her on any of the stations."

Susan shrugged and said, "There are dozens of new cable stations on the air since you've left."

"Right. So, Edward seems happy working for a major film studio."

Susan was happy to get back to the subject of her children and replied, "He likes what he does—the development office, whatever that is. And I'm surprised that he also likes Los Angeles."

"Me, too. Where did we fail?"

She smiled and said, "But I think he misses the East Coast."

"Maybe."

"John, do you think he'll stay there?"

"He might. You have to accept that."

She nodded, then said, "Well . . . it's only a six-hour flight."

"Right."

She reminisced, "I grew up with family close by . . . I thought that was normal."

"Not anymore."

Again, she nodded, then said, "At least Carolyn is close. But I haven't seen much of her. She's very busy."

"Being an assistant district attorney is a lot of hours, and very stressful."

"I know. She tells me." Susan looked at me and asked, "Aren't you proud that she followed in your footsteps?"

Carolyn was not exactly following in my footsteps; I had been a Wall Street attorney and I made a lot of money. Carolyn was working for peanuts, as many trust fund children do, and she was prosecuting criminals, which sort of surprised me because she once held an idealistic view of the rights of criminal defendants. But perhaps three years in the criminal justice system had opened her eyes a bit. Maybe someday she'd be on the prosecution team in the case of *The State v. Anthony Bellarosa.* I said, "I am proud of her."

"Do you think there's any possibility of her joining your old firm?"

There was no possibility of *me* joining my old firm, and I didn't think the remaining partners of Perkins, Perkins, Sutter and Reynolds wanted an actual Sutter to replace the dead one or the disgraced one. They'd kept the name, of course, so as not to incur the expense of changing it, and also my father was legendary on Wall Street. As for me, well . . . my fall from grace had begun with the lady who was now asking me about getting her daughter a job. Ironic. Also silly. Carolyn's next move would not be to an old Wall Street law firm; it would be to some sort of civil liberties group, or some do-gooder firm. And that was okay; someone in this family needed to have a heart. Plus, it would piss off William. But to address Susan's question, I said, "I will make inquiries."

"Thank you." The subject was employment and the law, so she asked me, "How are you doing in London?"

"Fine."

"Can you be absent from your job until September?"

"I'm on sabbatical."

"So you'll return?"

My future plans seemed to interest a lot of people more than they interested me. Maybe, though, it was time to verbalize my thoughts, and to be truthful and unambiguous, so I said, "When I left London, I honestly thought I would return. But now, being here, I've decided to stay in the U.S. Beyond that, I have no definite plans. But I have gotten a job offer."

She stayed silent awhile, then said, "I'm happy to hear that." She asked, "What sort of offer?"

Rather than say, "Consigliere to the new don Bellarosa," I said, "It's bad luck to talk about it before it happens."

She glanced at me, probably wondering when I became superstitious. She said, "Let me know if it happens."

"I will."

She advised me, "But you should take the summer off."

Susan, like most people who are born into old money, was mostly clueless about that subject, so it never occurred to her that I might not be able to afford three months of working on my tan. I mean, if you're a little short on cash, just sell an annuity. What's the problem?

Also, regarding the subject of Stanhopes and money and work ethic, Edward and Carolyn received annual trust fund distributions and really didn't need to work, but they did, to give meaning to their lives, and to do something interesting, or something useful for society.

Susan's brother, Peter, however, was a totally useless human being, who'd spent his life and his trust fund distributions on perfecting the art of indolence, except for tennis, golf, and surfing, which at least kept his body in good shape while his brain atrophied. Peter was not a good role model for his niece and nephew, but thankfully, they knew that.

And then there was William, who'd managed to reach retirement age without working a day in his life, except for managing the family money. Well, to be fair, there *was* his two-year stint in the Coast Guard, which had been mandatory because of that annoying world war.

And let's not forget Charlotte, who had been both a debutante and a dilettante before marrying William and becoming a full-time social-ite. I suppose that could be a lot of work, but Charlotte would be hard-pressed to fill in the "state your occupation" box on an income tax form unless she wrote "Occupied with lazy household staff."

As for Susan, she'd mostly followed in her brother's footsteps, but then she'd embraced the newly enlightened concept of getting a job, and when I'd met her, she was working as the private social secretary for a fabulously wealthy publishing company heiress in Manhattan. This is a very acceptable job for a young lady of Susan's social class, sort of like a lady-in-waiting for royalty.

We'd met, incidentally, at a summer wedding held under the stars at the Seawanhaka Corinthian Yacht Club. The bride was a Guest, or as I said to Susan that night, a Guest at her own wedding. That got a little chuckle out of her, and we danced. The rest, as they say, is history.

The Stanhopes, at first, accepted me because of my lineage, though they had concerns about my net worth. But in their world, it's more about who your parents are, where you went to school, your accent, and your social skills. Money is good, but money without pedigree is too common in America, so if you're William and Charlotte Stanhope, and you're trying to marry off your daughter, you go for the pedigree and punt on the bucks, which was why Mr. and Mrs. Stanhope, Dad and Mom, gave us their blessings. They soon discovered, however, that they didn't actually like me. The feeling was mutual, but it was too late; Susan and I were madly in love.

It had been a very good marriage, by any objective standard, including good sex, so if anyone had asked me what went wrong, I wouldn't be able to answer, except to say, "She was screwing a Mafia don." Of course, she was also a bit off her rocker, and I admit I can be a little sarcastic at times, but mostly we were happy with our lives and our children and each other.

I think, though, that Frank Bellarosa was like a malevolent force that entered Paradise, and no one was prepared for that. To continue the biblical theme, but with a different story line, Eve killed the serpent, but Adam stayed pissed off about her seduction and filed for divorce.

We walked in silence for a while, and I was sure that she, too, was thinking about the past, and I'd have liked to be able to read her mind, to see if her memories and mine had any similarities. Probably not; I was still dwelling on the negatives, and I was sure she was thinking happier thoughts.

I said to her, "Would you like to go back to the house?"

She replied, "No, I'm enjoying this walk." She added, "Like old times, John."

Indeed, if we could erase or forget that half year that ruined all the years before and the decade after, it would be better than old times; it would be just another summer Sunday together.

So we walked on, like old times, except we weren't holding hands any longer.

CHAPTER TWENTY-FOUR

We'd covered most of her ten acres, except for the treed area around her stable, and I thought she might be avoiding that. Why? Because the stable brought back memories of Mr. Bellarosa, our new neighbor, insisting that his construction company do the work of moving the old Stanhope stables and carriage house from William's land, which was for sale, to Susan's property. It had been truly a Herculean task, disassembling the hundred-year-old structure, brick by brick, and reassembling it near the guest cottage. Plus, we needed a variance because the stable would be close to the Alhambra estate, and Frank Bellarosa had to sign off on that, which he was happy to do for us—or for Susan. And then Bellarosa's guy, Dominic, gave us an estimate that looked like Mr. Bellarosa was underwriting most of the cost.

I mean, did I guess that Frank had the hots for Susan? Well, yes. Was I upset? No. Did I think it was amusing? Yes. Did I think Susan Stanhope was actually going to hop into bed with a Mafia guy? Not in a million years. Should I have paid more attention to what was going on? Apparently. Am I stupid? No, but I was preoccupied with my own tax problems, and I was entirely too trusting. Not to mention entirely too egotistical to even contemplate such a thing.

And little did I suspect that my buddy, Frank Bellarosa, had instigated this potentially ruinous and possibly criminal tax evasion charge against me so that he could pull a few strings and get me off the hook, thereby putting me in his debt, instead of the IRS's debt. It was bad enough that a tax attorney had a tax problem, but solving the problem with the help of a Mafia guy was not one of my smarter moves. On the other hand, it worked.

Well, I certainly learned a lesson or two about life, and about myself, and about seduction and survival. Not to mention relearning an old lesson about the power and the mystery of sexual behavior. I mean, who would have thought that don Bellarosa, the head of a Mafia crime family, and Susan Stanhope, from a somewhat more prominent family, would have much to talk about? Actually, they didn't; it was more You Jane, me Tarzan.

I could see the stables now, and I asked her, "Are you still riding?"

She glanced at where I was looking and replied, "Yes, but I don't own a horse. I ride a little at a horse farm in Old Brookville."

I nodded, recalling the night she'd killed Frank Bellarosa. She had saddled her horse, an Arabian stallion named Zanzibar, and announced to me that she was going for a night ride, which I advised her was dangerous, but she'd pointed out that there was a full moon, and the night was bright, and she'd ridden off.

About two hours later, Mr. Felix Mancuso of the FBI rang my doorbell and politely asked me to come with him to Alhambra. I knew in my guts that Susan had murdered her lover.

Mancuso's colleagues had been house-sitting Frank Bellarosa since he'd become a government witness, and they'd done a very nice job of keeping him safe from his former friends and goombahs. Unfortunately, the FBI did not include Mrs. Sutter on their list of people who were not allowed access to don Bellarosa. In fact, Susan was high on the short list of people who had unlimited access to Frank because they'd been instructed, "Frank needs to get laid to keep him happy and talking." Someone, however, should have remembered that (a) the female of the species is more dangerous than the male, and (b) hell hath no fury like a woman scorned.

Well, guys sometimes forget that, even FBI guys, and to be fair, they probably didn't know about (b) until they heard the shots.

Susan, walking beside me now, was apparently thinking of horses, and not Frank Bellarosa or murder, because she said to me, "There are far fewer places where one can ride now. So many of the equestrian rights-of-way have been closed off, and many of the open fields and old estates are now subdivisions."

Such as Alhambra. I said, with forced sincerity, "That's too bad." I recalled that one of Susan's concerns, after she'd shot and killed her lover, was that Zanzibar was still tethered behind Frank's mansion. I had to promise her I'd ride him home that night, which I did. I wasn't overly fond of her high-strung animal, but I did unsaddle him and water him, though I didn't brush him down, and if she'd known that, she would have killed me. Well . . . poor choice of words again.

She said, "The Ganzes turned the carriage house into a garage, and they used the stables to store lawn and gardening equipment, which is what I'm doing."

"Good idea."

"I really miss Zanzibar. I miss having my own horse. Do you miss Yankee?"

Yankee was my horse, and I hated him only slightly less than I hated Zanzibar, but I replied, "I think about him often."

She glanced at me, then said, "Well, I found good homes for them."

I was glad that the horses, at least, had a good home after she left.

It was a perfect morning, weather-wise at least, and I'd forgotten how magnificent these parklike grounds were. The entire three hundred acres of the original Stanhope estate had been planted with exotic and expensive specimen trees from around the world, and many of these trees were over a hundred years old. The estate had been in decline through the past few decades, but Susan—and the Ganzes—had maintained this ten-acre parcel, and I'd noticed that Amir Nasim had been putting some care into his property as well.

Coming back here, after so many years, I was struck by the fact that there could still be so many huge estates left on the Gold Coast, barely thirty miles from Manhattan, surrounded by a suburban county of well over a million people. The pressure to develop the remaining land to provide mini-mansions for newly minted millionaires was intense, but a new breed of multimillionaires, including foreigners like Amir Nasim, and people whose fortunes were of dubious origin such as Frank Bellarosa, had arrived with the resources to buy the old estates from the old families and breathe new life into them.

Before this had happened, however, there were probably a hundred or more magnificent estates whose mansions had been abandoned because of taxes, reversals of fortune, or maintenance costs, and when I was young, these ruins dotted the landscape, giving the appearance, as Anthony Bellarosa would agree, that an army of Vandals had passed through a wide swath of the Empire. Also, when I was a boy, these huge derelict mansions were the ultimate playhouse for games of make-believe. And when I got older, I played a different sort of game, called love among the ruins—some candles, a bottle of wine, a transistor radio, a bedroll, and a newly liberated young lady on birth control pills.

This all reminded me that one of Susan's many talents was oil paintings, and her forte was painting these abandoned mansions. She had been locally famous for her romantic representations of these vegetation-covered ruins, which she painted in the spirit, if not the style, of Piranesi's engravings of Roman ruins. But the architectural diversity of the Gold Coast mansions, as well as their varying states of decay, ranging from salvageable to lost, allowed her more latitude than Piranesi, of course, and she worked in oils and acrylics. If that sounds like I know what I'm talking about, I don't; I got that straight from the artist. In any case, I was curious, so I asked her, "Are you still painting?"

She smiled, then looked wistful, I thought, and replied, "Not anymore. But I might."

"Why did you stop?"

She thought about that, then replied, "I tried painting in Hilton Head . . . I did a few seascapes, and a lot of those palmetto trees . . . but somehow I just lost the . . . talent, I guess."

"I don't think you can lose talent."

"Well . . . maybe the subjects didn't interest me. You know, like when an artist moves from where he or she was inspired to someplace else."

"Right." I thought, too, perhaps her mental state had changed. If good artists are crazy—and she *was* a good artist, and crazy—then a return to some degree of mental health might kill that spark of mad genius. That's good and bad. Mostly, I think, good. I mean, I can live with a bad painting, but it's not easy living with a crazy wife.

Anyway, I wondered if this new, improved tranquil personality I was now witnessing was the happy result of successful therapy or very good meds.

Susan said to me, "Now that I'm back . . . I should see if I'm inspired."

"Right." But don't stop those meds.

Ironically, one of the best paintings she'd ever done, and probably the last, was of the ruins of Alhambra. Mrs. Sutter, on the occasion of our first visit to Alhambra for coffee and cannolis, generously offered to paint the Alhambra palm court as a housewarming gift to our new neighbors. Susan had photographs of the magnificent two-tiered atrium palm court as it existed before the Bellarosas restored the mansion, and she explained to them that she was going to paint it as a ruin. This surprised Mrs. Bellarosa, who wondered why anyone would want to paint what she called "a wreck." But Mr. Bellarosa, recalling some art he'd seen in Rome, thought it was a swell idea. I, too, was surprised at this offer, because this was no small undertaking, and Susan rarely gave away any of her paintings, though she sometimes donated them for charity auctions. Susan had informed the Bellarosas that though she could work mostly from her photographs and from memory, she needed to set up her easel in the palm court, so she could get the right perspective, and take advantage of the shifting sunlight from the glass dome, and so forth. Frank assured her that the door was permanently open to her.

Thinking back on that evening, as I'd done a few dozen times, there was more going on here than a housewarming gift, or coffee and cannolis.

It was hard to believe, but Susan Stanhope Sutter and Frank the Bishop Bellarosa had connected like a plug in a socket, and I should have seen the lights going on in their eyes. But I didn't, and neither did Anna, and we both remained clueless in the dark.

In any case, the relocation of the stable on Susan's property, and the painting of the Alhambra palm court, led to frequent contact between Mrs. Sutter and Mr. Bellarosa.

Meanwhile, I was in the city a lot, and Anna spent a good deal of time being driven back and forth in the black Cadillac to Brooklyn, where she visited her family and stocked up on cannolis and olive oil.

I still don't know who made the first move on whom, or where and how it happened, but I'm sure that Mr. Italian Stud thought *he* was the aggressor.

Susan continued with her last thought and said, "Most of the abandoned houses are either restored or razed now, but I still have a lot of old photographs that I could paint from."

"Or maybe you should paint your parents and call it American Grotesque." Well, I didn't say that—I thought it. I said, "Paint the gatehouse before Nasim puts aluminum siding on it." That may have actually been a Freudian slip—I mean, inviting her to set up her easel outside my house. Amazing how the subconscious mind works.

She replied, "That's a good idea . . . with the wrought-iron gates."

The subject of Susan's artistic periods, past and present, seemed closed, and we continued our walk down memory lane. Then she changed subjects completely and asked me, "John, what are they saying in London about 9/11?"

I recalled my answer to Elizabeth on that question and replied, "They're saying they're next."

She thought about that and observed, "The world has become a frightening place."

I replied, "The world is a fine place, and most of the people in it are good people. I saw that on my sail."

"Did you? That's good." She then said, "But what happened here . . . it has so changed everything for so many people."

"I know."

"Some people we knew were killed."

"I know that."

"Nothing will ever be the same for those families."

"No, it won't be."

"What happened . . . it's made a lot of people I know rethink their lives."

"I understand that."

"It made me appreciate things . . . I was frantic that day because Carolyn was downtown, and I couldn't get a call through to her."

"I know. Neither could I."

She turned toward me as we walked, and said, "I thought you would call me that day."

"I almost did . . . I did speak to Edward, and he said he'd gotten through to Carolyn on her cell phone, and she was all right, and he said he had called you and told you that."

"He did . . . but I thought I'd hear from you."

"I almost called." I added, "I thought you'd call me."

"I did, but when I called, I realized it was three A.M. in London, so I hung up, and the next day . . . I was drained and too . . . I was crying too much . . . so I e-mailed you . . . but I didn't hear back from you."

"Sorry."

"That's all right . . . but that . . . that horror made me think . . . there are terrible things that can happen to us out of the blue . . . for no reason. Just because we're there, and something evil has come our way. It made me put a lot of things into perspective, and it was a wake-up call . . . and that's when I began thinking about moving back here, and being close to people I grew up with, and . . . well, I began thinking about you."

I didn't respond for a while, then I said truthfully, "I had similar thoughts." I mean, how long can we hold a grudge? Well, in my case, a long time. But 9/11 did get me thinking and possibly started me on the road that led me here, as it had led Susan here.

Susan continued her thought and asked, "How long can we stay angry at people we once loved in the face of such . . . real hatred and evil?"

That sounded like a rhetorical question, but it wasn't, so I answered, "The anger is gone. Even the feeling of betrayal is gone. But what remains is . . . well, a badly wounded ego, and a sense of . . . embarrassment that this happened to me. In public."

"And you haven't gotten over that?"

"No."

"Will you ever?"

"No."

"Is there anything I can do?"

"No."

She took a deep breath and said, "He's *dead*, John. I *killed* him. For us."

The time had come to confront this, so I replied, "That's what you said."

She stopped walking, and I did, too. We faced each other, and she said to me, "I was ready to go to jail for the rest of my life to give you back your pride and your honor. That was my public penance, and my public humiliation, which I did, hoping you would take me back."

I hardly knew what to say, but I tried and said, "Susan . . . murdering a human being is *not*—"

"He was *evil*."

Indeed, he was. But I didn't think she realized that until he scorned her. Right up to that time, I think she was ready to run off with him to Italy, where the government was going to send him under the Witness Protection Program. I said to her, "You need to tell me *why* you killed him."

"I just told you."

I was seeing a little of the old Susan again, the bright green eyes, crazy eyes, and the pouty lips that morphed into a thin, pressed mouth, with her chin thrust forward as if to say, "I dare you to contradict me."

Well, I needed to do that, and I said, "That's what you may believe now, ten years later. But that is *not* why you killed him. Not for me, and not for us."

She stared at me, and I stared back. I had confronted her with this once before, in the palm court of Alhambra, with Frank Bellarosa lying dead on the floor, and a dozen FBI agents and county detectives standing off to the side so that Mrs. Sutter, a homicide suspect, and her husband, who was also her attorney, could converse in private. And when I asked her then why she killed him, she gave me the answer I'd just gotten. I could have accepted that, and from there we could have possibly rebuilt our lives.

But that wasn't the correct answer, and you can't build on lies.

The correct answer, the truth, actually, was something far different than Susan's stated motives for killing her lover. In fact, I have to take some blame for that, or some credit, if you look at it differently.

We continued to stare at each other, and I thought back to my visit to Frank Bellarosa at Alhambra, where he was lying in bed, sick with the flu, not to mention recovering from the after-effects of the shotgun blasts he'd taken some months before at Giulio's restaurant.

This had not been my first visit, but it was to be my last, and a few days later, he'd be dead. He'd said to me, then, apropos of his offer on another occasion to do me any favor I wanted in exchange for me saving his life at Giulio's, "Well, you got me wondering about that favor I owe you."

I had thought long and hard about that favor, so I said to him, "Okay, Frank, I'd like you to tell my wife it's over between you two and that you're not taking her to Italy, which is what I think she believes, and I want you to tell her that you only used her to get to me."

He thought about that, then said, "Done." But added, "I'll tell her I used her, if you want, but that wasn't it. You gotta know that."

I *did* know that. I knew that, as impossible as it was to believe, Frank and Susan were in love, and she was ready to leave me for him. Lust, I understand, from firsthand experience. But the only woman I've ever loved, Susan Stanhope Sutter, who actually still loved me, was madly in love with Frank Bellarosa—and Frank, apparently, was in love with her. *That* was why he'd sold out to the Feds—so he and Susan could be together in Italy, or wherever, and start a new life together. It would probably have lasted a year or two, but people who are obsessed and in high heat don't think that far into the future.

In any case, true to his word, he'd obviously told her what I'd asked him to tell her, on the phone or in person prior to that night, and Susan apparently snapped. Hell hath no fury and all that. Ironically, a few weeks before, he'd given her the gun that killed him, to keep the FBI from finding it. The rest is history, and tragedy, and maybe a little comedy, if you weren't personally involved.

The question, of course, was this: Why did I ask Frank to tell Susan it was over, and that he was not taking her to Italy with him, and that he'd used her to recruit me as his attorney? Obviously, I did that to get Susan back—or to get back at Susan. And, of course, I had no idea that she'd snap and shoot him. Or did I?

I always thought that Frank Bellarosa, who was a great admirer of

Niccolò Machiavelli, would have appreciated my . . . well, Machiavellian solution to this problem. And I still wonder if Frank grasped what he'd done to himself in those last few seconds between him telling Susan it was over and her pulling the gun. If he had any last words, or thoughts, I hoped they were, "John, you son of a bitch!"

Susan and I continued to face each other, and I returned to the present and looked into her eyes. She held my stare, then dropped her eyes and said to me, "I saw him earlier that day, and he told me that he was through with me, and he never loved me, and that his only interest in me was . . . fucking a society bitch . . . and . . . to make me convince you to work for him." She took a breath and continued, "Then he told me to leave and not come back and not call him. But I went back that night . . . and we made love . . . and I thought it was all right again . . . but afterwards, he told me to leave, and I said I wouldn't, so he said he'd call for the FBI to throw me out. I . . . couldn't believe it, and I . . . became angry."

I didn't say anything, and I didn't take my eyes off her. She seemed very calm, the way she is when she's on the verge of an emotional breakdown, or a blow-up. I could never tell which it was going to be. Apparently, neither could Frank, or he'd have been on his guard. He should have at least remembered the gun.

She continued in a barely audible voice, "I told him I loved him, and that I'd given up my life for him. And he told me . . . he said, 'Go back to John. He loves you, and I don't.' He said I'd be lucky if you took me back, and I should thank God if you did. And he called me . . . names . . . and told me to get out . . ."

I stood there, unable to say anything. I did, though, think about Frank Bellarosa, and I wondered how much he had loved her, and how hard it was for him to say what he'd said to her, which, I just discovered, was more than I'd asked of him. But he owed me a very big favor for saving his life at Giulio's, and he wanted to be able to say to me, "We are even on favors, Counselor. Nobody owes anybody anything now." But he didn't live long enough to tell me we were even.

Susan moved a step closer to me, and we were only inches apart. She said, "And that's why I killed him." She asked me, "All right?"

I half expected to see tears running down her cheeks, but Susan is not much of a crier, though I did see her lower lip quiver. I said to her, "All right. He's dead."

We both turned and began our walk back to the house. One of us could have said something, but there was nothing left to say.

CHAPTER TWENTY-FIVE

We walked through the rose garden to the patio. Somewhere along the way, Susan had dropped the rose stem, but the other roses sat on the table and she stared at them.

I was certain that after her confession, she expected me to leave, which I wanted to do, but I still needed to speak to her about Amir Nasim and Anthony Bellarosa, and I wanted to do that now in person, so I said to her, "I have something important to tell you."

She looked at me, but didn't respond.

I continued, "I'm sure you'd rather be alone now, but if you can sit and listen to me for about ten minutes . . ."

She replied, "If it's important."

"It is." I suggested, "Why don't we sit?"

"I need a few minutes. Would you like something?"

"Water."

She went into the house, and I stood at the wicker table and opened the box she'd given me. Inside, as she said, were copies of letters from Edward and Carolyn, and also a stack of family photographs. I flipped through them and noticed a few group shots that included my parents and hers.

I recalled an advertisement I'd once seen for a company that did photo retouching; basically, this Orwellian enterprise could make unwanted people disappear from photographs, then fill in the background where they'd been. I made a mental note to contact these clever people to vaporize William and Charlotte. Unfortunately, altering a photo-graph does not alter a memory or history.

I shuffled through the remaining photographs, and I noted that she had not included any risqué photographs of us. This made me think that despite Emily Post's advice, I should not have put those nude shots of us in her envelope. I looked at the envelope on the table and was about to slip out those photos and put them into my jacket, but the screen door opened, and she came out to the patio carrying a tray with a liter of sparkling water and two glasses.

Susan looked more composed now—and maybe relieved that her belated confession that her adultery wasn't just lust, but also love, hadn't made me walk away. She nodded toward the photos she'd given me and said, "Those are wonderful shots." She added, "I have stacks of them if you'd like to go through them someday."

"Thank you."

She set the tray on the table, sat, and I sat opposite her. She poured water for me and said, "Please get right to the point."

"I will." I drank my water and began, "First, I had tea with Amir Nasim, and he told me that the reason he wants to buy your house is because he wants total privacy. I believe he has issues with the concept of cultural diversity, meaning he doesn't want an attractive unmarried woman living in the middle of his property." I paused, then continued, "But then he told me that he had some security concerns."

I let that sink in, and after a few seconds Susan informed me, "His wife hinted at the same thing."

That surprised me, but then I realized that Nasim would use his wife to pass on that information to Susan. I offered my opinion and said, "I think he's either post-9/11 paranoid, or he's making that up so you'll consider selling him this property."

She thought about that and asked, "What if his security concerns are real?"

"Then he should have gone to the authorities. And he may have, though he never mentioned that to me. But if he had gone to the au-thorities, someone from the FBI or the local police would have called on you." I asked, "Have they?"

"No."

"And I haven't heard from them, either. So I have to conclude that Nasim did not contact the authorities, which makes me wonder about his security concerns."

She considered that, then replied, "Well, you're a lawyer, and you think like a lawyer. But he's from a different culture, and he has a different mind-set about the police."

"That's a valid point. But he's lived here and in London long enough to know that if he goes to the police, they won't shake him down or beat him up for annoying them."

She nodded, then said, "Well, even if his concerns are real, it's his problem, not mine."

I informed her, "Nasim asked me to call him if I noticed anything suspicious."

She nodded and said, "Soheila said the same thing."

I offered, "Or call me."

She looked at me, smiled, but didn't reply.

It occurred to me, of course, that Amir Nasim's concerns about being on a hit list, real or imagined, had the positive effect of raising everyone's alert level on this property, which was a good thing in regard to the more probable threat from Anthony Bellarosa.

Apropos of that, and recalling Ms. Post's advice to me, I wanted to ask Susan if she had a gun. But considering what she'd done the last time she had a gun, that might be a touchy subject with her, especially if I also asked her if she knew how to use it. We actually knew the answer to that. So I'd hold off on that question for now.

I was thinking of Anthony Bellarosa more than Amir Nasim when I said to Susan, "In any case, to play it safe, I'll go to the police, and suggest that they call the FBI. You should do the same."

She didn't respond to that, then looked at me and said, "This is unbelievable . . . that we should even *think* about things like . . . foreign terrorists."

I informed her, in case she forgot, "The world, including this world here, has changed. So we need to think about things like this."

She retreated into a pensive silence, recalling, I'm sure, the world she grew up in, when the biggest outside threat was nuclear Armageddon, which was so unthinkable that no one even thought about it on a day-to-day basis. The only other foreign intrusion into our safe and secure world had been the annual Soviet invasion of the local beaches each summer, launched from the Russian-owned estate in Glen Cove. I was sure that Susan and everyone else around here were nostalgic for those days when our only contact with foreign enemies was a handful of surly Russians leaving empty vodka bottles on the public beach. Now, unfortunately, we were all thinking about 9/11, and waiting for the other shoe to drop.

I further revealed to Susan, "Nasim said he'd pay me a ten percent commission if I could convince you to sell."

That brought her out of her thoughts, and she responded, "That's unethical."

"Actually, it's just good business."

She asked me, "What did you tell him?"

"I told him to make it fifteen percent, and I'd tell you I saw Iranian assassins hiding in your hedgerows."

She smiled, then assured me, "I won't be pressured or intimidated. This is my land, and it's been in my family for over a hundred years. If Nasim is frightened of something here, *he* can move."

"I understand." I also understood that she wasn't going to pack up and leave because of Anthony Bellarosa. Nevertheless, I said, "There's another important matter I need to discuss with you."

She looked at me and said, "Anthony Bellarosa."

This surprised me at first, then it didn't. Susan may be crazy, but she's not stupid. I replied, "Yes. Anthony Bellarosa."

She informed me, "I had heard that he lived on the Alhambra property before I made my offer to buy back my house. He didn't figure into my plans then, and he doesn't figure into them now."

"All right, but . . ." Tolkien's famous line on that subject popped into my head, and I said to her, "It does not do to leave a live dragon out of your calculations, if you live near him."

She shrugged and said to me, "Unless you have something specific to tell me about the dragon, I don't want to discuss this." She added, "I thank you for your concern." Then she smiled and said, "Well, I assume you are expressing concern and not some secret delight."

I wanted her to understand that this was serious, so I didn't return the smile, and I said, "I am *very* concerned."

This seemed to get through to her, and she asked, "How did you find out he lived next door?"

"He stopped by the gatehouse last Monday."

This news, that Anthony Bellarosa had actually been on the property, got her attention, and she asked, "Why?"

I replied, "It was an unannounced social call. He welcomed me back to the neighborhood."

Susan was vacillating between not wanting to discuss this and knowing that she probably needed to hear what I had to say. So while she was trying to decide, I continued, "He wanted to speak to me about his father."

She didn't reply.

I pressed on, "He asked about you."

Susan looked at me, then slipped into her Lady Stanhope mode and said, "If he has anything he wants to know about me, he should ask me, not you."

Susan has a kind of courage, born, as I've indicated, of that upper-class breeding that could best be described as a mixture of haughty indifference toward physical danger, and a naïve belief, bordering on delusion, that she was not a member of the victim class. Another way to understand it is to think of Susan telling a burglar to wipe his feet before he enters. In any case, to get her nose out of the air and her feet on the ground, I said to her, "He's like his father—he doesn't discuss important matters with women."

That had the effect of annoying her, while also reminding her of how she'd created this problem. She said to me, apropos of that, "John, this is not your problem. It's mine. I do appreciate your concern, and I'm touched, really, but unless he's made a specific statement to you that I should know about, then you don't need to involve yourself in—"

"Susan. Get off your high horse."

She leaned back in her chair, crossed her legs, and stared off into the garden.

I said, "To remind you, you killed his father. He will not be discussing that with you. But he did discuss it with me." I didn't mention my subsequent conversations with Anthony at dinner or in Oyster Bay, but I did say, "While he made no specific threats, and never will, I came away with the distinct impression that he's looking for revenge."

She kept staring off at a fixed spot in the garden, probably thinking about rose blight. That's how she handles big problems that she can't deal with; she sublimates and thinks about small problems. That's what she did after she murdered Frank Bellarosa—with his body sprawled out on the floor and a half dozen homicide detectives waiting to take her to jail, she was worried about her horse, and probably worried about how Anna was going to get the bloodstains off the floor.

I decided to end this conversation, knowing that I'd done what I needed to do, and knowing, too, that anything I said after my warning would be conjecture, opinion, and advice which she didn't want. I did say, however, "You should go to the police and give them a sworn statement . . ." In case something does happen. But I didn't say that.

She didn't reply, so we sat there, then finally she asked me, "Is that all?"

"Yes."

"Thank you."

I glanced at my watch and said, "I should be going."

She didn't seem to hear me.

I stood, but she didn't, so I said, "I can let myself out."

Again, no reply.

I understood that it had been an emotionally draining morning for her—and for me. Her confession to me about her real reason for killing the man she loved was enough mental trauma for one day, but then I'd brought up the subject of Amir Nasim and Iranian assassins, and next I reminded her that Frank Bellarosa's son was in the neighborhood and asking about her. I could only imagine what was going through her mind right now.

She helped me understand her mental anguish by asking me, "Have you learned to like lamb in England?"

"Excuse me?"

"I was thinking of lamb for dinner, but if you still won't eat it, then I might do veal."

I cleared my throat and replied, "Lamb would be fine."

"Good." She looked at me, and seemed surprised that I was standing, then asked, "Where are you going?"

"I . . . have a few things to do." I explained, "I wanted to make my Sunday calls to the children."

She thought a second, then suggested, "Why don't we call them together?"

"Well . . ."

"They'd like that."

"Maybe we shouldn't . . . surprise them. And maybe you need some time for yourself now."

She ignored that, poured me the last of the water and asked, "Will you come with me to visit Ethel?"

I assumed I was supposed to sit, so I did, and replied, "I really have a lot to do." And I didn't want to run into Elizabeth at Fair Haven accompanied by Susan, any more than I'd wanted to run into Susan at Fair Haven accompanied by Elizabeth. And then there was my four o'clock dinner with the Bellarosas if I still wanted to show up. I thought about that, and wondered if going there was a good idea. Keep your enemies close and all that.

I looked at Susan and saw now that she'd opened the envelope and was flipping through the photographs I'd given her. They were mostly family shots, and apparently she hadn't come to the adults-only photos, because she said, "I like this one of the four of us loading the boat on the dock at Seawanhaka. Who took that?"

"I don't recall." I suggested, "You can look at those later. I think I should go."

She stopped flipping and focused on a photograph, then flipped slowly through a few more, and she smiled and said, "I *wondered* what happened to these."

I didn't reply.

She seemed to be enjoying the photographs, and she had a sort of naughty grin on her face, then she said, "Oh, my . . ." and pushed a photograph in front of me.

I looked at it and saw it was a timed tripod shot of Susan and me on the rear terrace of Stanhope Hall. The Stanhopes, when they moved, had left behind some outdoor furniture on the terrace, and I remembered that Susan and I sometimes went there for sundown cocktails, and for the view, which was why we'd brought the camera and tripod.

Well, it had been a warm summer day, and after a few cocktails, Susan had suggested a strip version of the game of rock-paper-scissors, with the loser performing oral sex on the other. That seemed like a reasonable suggestion, and a no-lose game, so we began, and Susan had a streak of bad luck and was naked within a few minutes.

The photograph shows me standing against a column with my shorts around my ankles collecting my bet.

Susan observed, "We can't do *that* anymore."

I smiled and replied, "No, I don't think Mr. Nasim would approve of cocktails on his terrace."

She smiled, too, and added, "Or blow jobs."

I realized that Susan was in a different frame of mind than she'd been five minutes before, and I hadn't been paying attention.

She slid a few more photos toward me, and I assured her, "I've seen them."

"Did you make copies for yourself?"

"I did not."

"I can do that for you." She turned her attention back to the photographs and said, "I haven't gained an ounce." She glanced at me and observed, "It doesn't look like you have, either."

My mouth was dry, and I finished my water and again glanced at my watch, but Susan was staring at six or seven photos that she'd spread out on the table. She looked up at me and said, "This brings back some good memories, John."

I nodded.

Then she stood, stared at me, and in a tone of voice that left no doubt about her meaning, said, "I'd like to show you what I've done to the house."

Well . . . why not? I mean, why not? Before I could think of why not, I stood, we reached across the table and held hands, then we walked together into the house.

The tour started and ended in our old bedroom.

CHAPTER TWENTY-SIX

The upstairs master bedroom was warm, and Susan lay naked on her back atop the sheets with her legs parted and her hands behind her head. She was awake, but her eyes were closed.

The window and the drapes were open, and daylight lit the room. An oscillating floor fan swept over the bed, and the breeze cooled the sweat from our bodies and stirred her long red hair.

I sat up and looked at her lying beside me. Her skin had a nice early summer tan, including her breasts, but she was milky white where she'd worn a bikini bottom that barely covered her bright red pubic hair.

With her eyes still closed, she asked, "Are you looking at me?"

"I am."

"How do I look?"

"Like you did the day I first made love to you." Which was true.

"Thank you. I have good genes."

Indeed, William and Charlotte were a handsome couple; unfortunately, their brains were scrambled.

Susan opened her eyes, turned toward me, and said, "I haven't had anyone up here."

I replied, "That's your business."

Still looking at me, she said, "I wanted you to know." She smiled and added, "It's been so long since I've had sex, I forgot who ties who up."

I smiled, too, but I didn't offer any help on that subject, so she asked me, "And you?"

"Well . . ."

"That's all right. I don't want to know."

Of course she did, so to get it out of the way, I said, "There's a woman in London." I remembered to add, "But it's not serious."

"What's her name?"

"Samantha."

"Nice name." She suggested, "Get rid of her."

"Well . . . all right. But . . ."

Susan sat up, took my hand, looked at me and said, "We've wasted ten years, John. I don't want to waste another minute."

"I know . . . but . . ."

"Is this too fast for you?"

"Well, it is rather sudden."

"Do you love me?"

"I do. Always have."

"Me, too. Forever. So?"

I asked, "Are you sure about this?"

"I am. And so are you."

Apparently, this was a done deal. But, to be honest, I think I knew that two minutes after walking into this house. I mean, putting aside all my negative thoughts about her, and despite everything that happened this morning, the minute we laid eyes on each other I felt that extraordinary sexual energy that we used to have, and I knew that she did, too. Sex isn't love, of course, though it will do in a pinch, but in this case the love was already there, and always had been, so all we needed to do was do it. And we did.

It could have been awkward after ten years, but it wasn't; we were at ease with each other, which is the good part of being with a partner whom you've had a lot of practice with. Also, of course, there was an element of newness after all these years, and maybe a slight feeling that this was somehow taboo. You can't beat that combination.

I said to Susan, "I've thought about this."

"Me, too. Often." She asked me, "Why did you take so long to call me?"

"I was . . . well, afraid."

"Of?"

"Of . . . well, afraid this would happen, and afraid it wouldn't."

"Me, too. Now we don't have to be afraid."

"No." I said to her, "I thought you would call me."

"I was playing hard to get." She added, "I was going to give it an-other forty-eight hours before I called you. Then I saw Elizabeth's car there overnight, and I was . . . what's a good word?"

"Destroyed? Devastated? Pissed off?"

"That's it. But I was ready to forgive you."

"There's nothing to forgive."

"Do you like her?"

"I do."

She didn't respond for a few seconds, then said, "She likes you. She told me that when we had lunch. Well, she was coy about it, consider-ing the circumstances, but I could tell."

"She's a nice lady."

"I think so, too. So, we can all be friends."

"Great." A lot seemed to have been decided in the last thirty min-utes that I wasn't aware of, but that's what sometimes happens after you have sex with someone. I mean, you go from a polite "hello" to naked in bed, engaged in the most intimate acts with a person you may or may not know that well, and then—if you're not pressed for time—you need to engage in pillow talk. And talking is where you usually get into trouble, sometimes without even knowing it.

In this case, however, with Susan, Fate had long ago decided that I'd be here, so I might as well get with the program. I said to her, "I never thought we'd be apart for the rest of our lives."

"I *knew* we would not be."

I confessed to her, "I saw you on Tuesday in Locust Valley."

"You did? Where?"

"At that food place, a few doors from Rolf's."

"Oh, right. I was having lunch with Charlie Frick."

"It looked like a woman."

"*Charlene*. Charlie Frick. She's one of the Fricks."

"Apparently, if that's her name."

"John, you just got laid. Can you tone down your sarcasm?"

I didn't see the connection, but I was certain there'd be more of these post-coital non sequiturs. I said, "Sorry."

She asked me, "Where were you? I hope you weren't getting one of your awful sandwiches at Rolf's."

And then there's post-coital criticism of my life. I replied, "Actually, I just got a coffee at Rolf's, and I came out and saw you and Mitzi."

"Charlie. Why didn't you say hello?"

"Because that wasn't how I wanted to meet you for the first time after four years."

She squeezed my hand and said, "Me neither." She asked me, "How did you feel? What were you thinking?"

"I felt . . . I think, sad. And I thought you never looked so beautiful."

She snuggled up to me and put her arms around me. She said, "I love you, and we'll never be apart again, and never be sad again." She kissed me and said, "Can you believe this? Can you believe we're together again?"

"It is hard to believe."

"Will you marry me again?"

I was actually prepared for that question, so I replied, without hesitation, "If that's what you want."

That must not have been the correct answer because she moved away from me and asked, "What do *you* want?"

I tried again and asked her, "Will you marry me?"

"Let me think about it. Okay, I'll marry you."

"You've made me the happiest man in the world."

"I know I have. But let's live together for a year, to make sure."

"All right. No, I mean, let's get married as soon as possible."

"If that's what you want. What are you doing tomorrow?"

Clearly, Susan was happy, and when she's happy, she's funny. I was happy, too, but this was a little sudden, and I wasn't processing it at the speed it was happening, and I really wanted at least ten minutes to think about completely changing my life. But then I remembered what I'd said to Elizabeth about using more heart and less brain, and about taking chances. At this point in my life, I didn't have much to lose by marrying my ex-wife. I suppose I could do worse. On a more positive note, I was in love with her, and I was being given a second chance to be happy.

Susan, who knows me, asked, "Are you talking yourself into or out of marrying me?"

I replied, "I would like nothing more than for us to be married again, and to be a family again."

She sat back against the headboard, and I saw tears welling up in her eyes. She said, "I am so sorry, John, for what happened."

"I know. Me, too."

We sat there for a while, and I watched the fan sweeping the room and felt the breeze on my body. Being here, in our old bedroom, with our old furniture, brought back good memories of making love, lazy Sunday mornings, the children when they were young coming in to snuggle with us, Mother's Day and Father's Day breakfast in bed, and staying up and talking late into the night. I remembered the anniversary card she'd written me: *John, You don't know how many times I wake up in the morning and just stare at you lying beside me, and I will do this for the rest of my life.*

I could dwell on the past, and on the ten-year gap between now and the last time we'd made love here, but I'd done that, and it had gotten me nothing but anger, resentment, and a troubled soul. So I took her hand, looked at her, and said, "I forgive you."

She nodded her head and said, "I knew you would."

So did I.

She moved closer to me and put her head on my shoulder, and we both sat there, enjoying the moment and thinking ahead into the future.

It was, indeed, time to move forward.

Unfortunately, the past was not really dead and buried; it was alive, and it lived at Alhambra, and it was about to catch up with us.

CHAPTER TWENTY-SEVEN

Sex in the shower is my kind of multitasking.

Afterwards, we dressed and went downstairs into the kitchen, and Susan asked me, "Are you hungry?"

I looked at the regulator clock and saw it was a little after 1:00 P.M., and I remembered my Sunday spaghetti and meatballs at the Bellarosas'.

I also remembered I was supposed to call Elizabeth for a possible 7:00 P.M. rendezvous. A lot had been set in motion before this unexpected turn of events, and I wished now that I'd called Susan last week. But who knows what would have happened last week if we'd met? I wasn't really ready then for what just happened, and in fact, I wasn't sure I was ready now for what was happening. But clever people, like me, can change plans as the situation changes. As for my plans with Elizabeth, for instance, people who are getting married should cut down on their dating. As for dinner with the Bellarosa family, that decision wasn't as simple.

"John? Hello?"

I looked at Susan and said, "You know, I could go for a Bloody Mary."

"I don't think I have tomato juice."

"Even better. Vodka on the rocks."

She opened the freezer, retrieved a bottle of Grey Goose and poured it in a glass, then added ice and filled the glass with orange juice, saying, "You can't drink straight vodka this early in the day."

I thought I could. I was starting to remember things from my first marriage, which was also my last.

Susan poured herself an orange juice and handed me my drink. We clinked glasses, and I said, "Here's to us."

"To us."

I sipped my drink and couldn't taste the vodka.

She asked again, "Would you like something to eat?"

"No, this is fine."

"What did you have for breakfast?"

"Uh . . . let me think . . ." I almost had Elizabeth on the patio table, but I shouldn't mention that. I said, "An English muffin."

"Is that all?"

"Crabapple jelly. Coffee."

"And did you dine alone?"

"I did not."

She inquired, "How is it that you and she slept in the same house overnight, and nothing happened?"

I was getting a little impatient with the Elizabeth questions, and I said, "It doesn't matter how or why nothing happened. What matters is that nothing happened."

She sensed I was annoyed and said, "I'm sorry. I can't believe how jealous I am. I won't mention it again."

"Thank you."

"Maybe you're losing your touch."

"Susan—"

"Or were you being faithful to Samantha?"

That sounded like a loaded question, so I explained, "Elizabeth, as you might imagine, is very upset about her mother. We spent the whole day going through Ethel's papers and personal property, and by the end of the day she was emotionally drained, and she drank too much wine and went to bed early. I slept on the couch. End of story."

"All right. I'm sorry." She inquired, "Do you have any third-party witnesses to those events?"

I was about to lose my patience, but when I looked at her, I saw she was smiling, so I, too, smiled, and she put down her glass and hugged me. She said, "I don't want to be jealous."

Could've fooled me. I put my glass on the counter, and we hugged and kissed.

She said, "Let's call Edward and Carolyn."

She seemed excited about that, and I realized that I was, too. I said, "You make the call."

She went to the wall phone, dialed, and said, "I'm trying Carolyn on her cell phone first."

Carolyn answered, and they chatted for a few seconds, and from what I could gather, Carolyn was at Sunday brunch with friends. Susan said to her, "I'd like to speak to you in private for a moment. Yes, all right." Susan covered the phone and said to me, "I want you to tell her." Carolyn came back on the line, and Susan said, "Your father wants to speak to you."

That must have confused Carolyn because Susan added, "No, he's right here." She handed me the phone, and I said to my daughter, "How are you, sweetheart?"

She replied, "Great. So . . . how are *you*?"

"Also great." I could hear street noises in the background, and I asked, "Where are you?"

"In front of Petrossian." She added, "I'm with friends here."

I didn't think assistant district attorneys made that much money, so maybe the Stanhope trust was paying for the champagne and caviar. I joked, "I hope this is an expense account brunch."

"I have a *date*, Dad."

"Oh . . ." I still couldn't think of my little girl with a man, especially one who plied her with caviar and champagne. I joked again, "Then get seconds on the Beluga."

She ignored that and asked, "So . . . what's happening?"

Good question. I glanced at Susan, who decided to put the phone on speaker, and I said, "Well . . . I'm here at your mother's house . . ."

"I know."

"And . . . well, Cari, we've decided to get back together—" I heard a squeal, and I thought she'd gotten hit by a bus or something, then she squealed again and said, "Oh my God! Oh, Dad, that's wonderful! Oh, I'm *sooo* happy. Mom! Mom!"

Susan took the phone from me, turned it off speaker, and began a rapid-fire conversation with her daughter, punctuated by unintelligible squeaks and squeals.

I figured my speaking part was finished, so I moved off and freshened my orange juice with vodka. I heard Susan say, "John, that's enough," then she turned her attention back to Carolyn.

After a few minutes of coded girl talk, Susan put the phone back on speaker and said, "We'll let you get back to your friends. Call me when you have a moment. Your father wants to say goodbye."

I called across the kitchen, "Bye, Cari! Love you!"

"Bye, Dad! I love you!"

Susan signed off and said to me, "She's so happy for us, John. Isn't this wonderful?"

"It is." I said, "She has a date."

"I told her we were going to call Edward now, and she said she'll call him tonight."

"Who is this guy?"

"He's our son. Edward."

"No, I mean her date."

"Oh . . . I don't know. She broke up with Cliff, and now she's dating again. But she's not serious about anyone."

"Petrossian for a two-hundred-dollar brunch sounds serious." I speculated, "Maybe this has something to do with her concern about world hunger."

Susan ignored me and suggested, "You call Edward."

I glanced at the clock and observed, "It's only ten A.M. in L.A. He's probably sleeping."

She took the phone, dialed, and said, "I'm trying his apartment." After a few rings, someone answered, and Susan said, "Hello, this is Mrs. Sutter, Edward's mother. Is he there?" She listened again and said, "Tell him it's important. I'll hold. Thank you." She informed me, "He's in the shower."

"Who was that?"

"A young lady without the good manners to give me her name, nor the social skills to say that Edward was indisposed."

"Maybe that's what she said. Indisposed. And you heard 'in de shower.'"

"Very funny."

Susan, I recalled, had always been a little more critical of her son's choice of girlfriends than she'd been of Carolyn's choice of boyfriends. I usually had the opposite reaction to their significant others. I'm sure Freud could explain that if I wrote to him. *Dear Sigmund—*

Susan said to me, "I hope I didn't alarm him."

I replied, "You probably sent that girl bursting into the shower."

"John, please." Susan put the phone close to her ear and said, "Good morning, sweetheart. No, everything is fine. I just wanted to share some good news with you. Hold on. Someone wants to say hello."

She handed me the phone, and I, using his old nickname, said, "Hello, Skipper."

"Dad!"

"Sorry to pull you out of the shower—"

"No problem. What's up?"

"Who answered the phone?"

"Oh . . . that was Stacy. She's . . . we're going to the beach."

"Terrific. Which one?"

"Probably Malibu. Hey, Dad, you have to come out here."

"I plan to. But I guess I'll see you here soon for a less happy occasion."

"Yeah . . . how's she doing?"

"Not too well. I saw her a few days ago, and I think it will be soon."

"That's really sad." He asked me, "So, how are you doing back in New York?"

"Terrific. Good to be back."

"How's the weather there?"

"Perfect." It didn't seem to occur to Edward that there was anything unusual about his mother and me calling him together, and he seemed to have forgotten that it was about something important. Edward actually has a genius IQ, though most people wouldn't guess that, and he's been a little spacey since I can remember, so I couldn't blame that on California, much as I'd like to.

I could see that Susan was getting a bit impatient, so I said to Edward, "Well, Skipper, you're probably wondering why we called."

"Yeah . . . is everything okay?"

Susan put the phone on speaker and said, "I'm on the line, sweetheart. Your father and I have some very good news."

"Great."

I guess it was my turn to speak, so I said in a happy tone, "Your mother and I are getting married."

"Huh?"

"Married. Again. Remarried."

There was a silence, then Edward asked, "You mean . . . ? To each other?"

Susan chirped in, "Isn't that wonderful?"

"Oh . . . yeah. Wow. Awesome." Then I think he got it, and said, "Oh, wow." He expounded on that. "Hey, are you kidding?"

Susan and I replied in unison, "No," and Susan said to him, "We called Cari and she's just thrilled. She'll call you tonight."

"Great. Hey. I'm . . ." And then something odd happened, and I could actually hear that he was choking up. I had a little lump in my throat, too, and I saw that Susan had tears in her eyes.

I said to him, "We're going to let you get going, Skipper. Have fun at the beach. See you soon."

"Yeah . . . see you . . ."

Susan was dabbing her eyes with a tissue, and suggested to Edward, "Don't make too many plans for when you get in. This is family time. We're having dinner together."

"Yeah? Oh. Okay. Sure. Good."

Susan continued her briefing. "I'll call and e-mail you as soon as we know something. You need to take the first available flight to New York. It doesn't have to be direct or nonstop. And don't forget to ask about first or business class if coach is sold out. Edward? Are you listening?"

Edward had actually stopped listening about ten years ago, but he replied, "Okay, Mom."

"I love you."

"You, too."

I said, "Love you."

Susan hung up and said to me, "They were absolutely thrilled. They really were, John. Could you tell?"

"I could."

Susan dabbed her eyes again and said, "We have a lot of time to make up for as a family."

"We do, and I have a lot of catching up to do with them, but this will all be very positive now."

"It will be." She thought a moment, then said, "Edward still needs a good, strong male figure in his life. He's . . . immature."

I didn't think so, and I should have let it drop, but my sarcastic side said, "He's twenty-seven years old. He can be his own male role model."

She seemed a little annoyed, then embarrassed, and reminded me, "You know how Edward is."

"Yes, he's like me."

"You're slightly more organized. And I emphasize slightly."

Susan had actually been one of the most scatterbrained women I'd ever known, but apparently she'd become more organized since I left. Or at least less scatterbrained.

The problem was, we'd both changed, but the memories had not, or the memories had changed, and we had not. It was going to take a lot of work for both of us to see each other as we were now, not as we were then.

On a more optimistic note, Susan felt so immediately comfortable with me that she didn't hesitate to point out my flaws and make constructive criticisms when necessary. That was a very short courtship.

She obviously sensed what I was thinking, or she was following up on her last comment, and she informed me, "I love you anyway. I love your boyish charm, your sarcastic wit, your very annoying habits, and even your stubborn, unforgiving nature. I love you unconditionally, and I always have. And I'll even tell you why—you tell the truth, and you have character, which I don't see too much of these days, and you have guts, John." She added, "I'm never afraid when I'm with you."

I hardly knew what to say, but I could have followed her lead and replied, "You're spoiled, totally out of touch with reality, slightly bitchy, passive-aggressive, and crazy, but I love you anyway." That was the truth, but I was afraid it might not come out right, so I said, "Thank you." I took her in my arms and said, "I love *you* unconditionally. I always have, and I always will."

"I know." She put her head on my shoulder and said, "This is like a dream."

I could feel her tears on my neck, and we held on to each other.

I don't know what she was thinking, but I was thinking of dinner with Anthony Bellarosa.

CHAPTER TWENTY-EIGHT

Susan had taken on the formidable task of perfecting me before remarrying me. One of my imperfections was my pale skin, which she'd remarked on in the bedroom, and I agreed that I needed a little color. So we moved two chaise lounges into the sunlight on the patio, took off our clothes, and lay side by side holding hands, I in my boxer briefs and Susan in her bikini panties. The radio in the kitchen was tuned to a classical station, and the Chicago Symphony Orchestra, led by Sir Georg Solti, was playing the *Flying Dutchman* Overture.

The sun felt good on my skin, which hadn't seen much sun in London for seven years.

On the side table between us was a liter of San Pellegrino, which reminded me of the first time I'd had this sparkling water, with Susan, on our first visit to the Bellarosa house. The second time was a celebratory lunch with Frank Bellarosa at Giulio's in Little Italy, after our court appearance at which I'd gotten Frank sprung on bail. Perhaps my last bottle of Pellegrino water was also at Giulio's, some months later. This was a social occasion with our wives, and by that time I was more familiar with Italian cuisine, and I was also fairly certain that my wife, lying now beside me, was having an affair with our host, who was practically ignoring her and being very solicitous of me. What more proof did I need?

So, on that occasion, I was not in the jolliest of moods—I mean, as a lawyer, I'm supposed to screw the client; the client is not supposed to screw my wife—and thinking back on it, I should have said to Anna Bellarosa, as she was eating her cannoli, "Your husband here is fucking my wife."

And Anna would have turned to Susan and said, "Susan, I *have* to . . . but *you* . . . ?"

Just kidding. In any case, I've often wondered how the evening would have turned out if I had confronted them in Giulio's. Would Frank and I have gone out to the street to see if his limousine was waiting for us? Probably not. I'm certain I'd have been looking for a taxi to take me to the Long Island Railroad station, alone. And would my abrupt departure have thrown off the timing of the planned hit? I don't know, but I'm sure I wouldn't have been standing next to Frank when he took two shotgun blasts in his Kevlar vest, and I wouldn't have been there to stop him from bleeding to death, and he wouldn't have lived so that Susan could kill him later.

If we are being stalked by Fate, there's no escape, but even Fate has to have a Plan B to allow for human nature, and Kevlar vests.

Susan said to me, "You're very quiet."

"I'm enjoying the moment."

"Talk to me."

"Okay . . . you have beautiful breasts."

"Thank you. Would you like to see my ass?"

I smiled. "Sure."

She pulled off her panties and turned on her stomach. "How's that?"

I turned on my side toward her and replied, "Perfect."

She suggested, "Take off your shorts. Get some sun on that pale butt."

I slipped off my shorts, turned on my stomach, and we faced each other.

She asked me, "Can you do it again?"

"Turn again?"

"No, John, make love again."

"Why would you even ask?"

She smiled, reached over, and pinched my butt cheek. I felt a stirring in my loins, as they say, and the chaise cushion didn't have much give in it, so to avoid a serious injury I flipped again on my back, and Susan exclaimed, "Oh, my goodness! Hold it right there."

She scrambled out of her chaise and positioned herself on top of me with her legs and knees straddling my hips, then lowered herself and I slid right in.

We'd done this here before, on the patio, though I think the chaise lounges were different, and we'd only been caught twice—once by the gardener, who never seemed the same to me again, and once by Judy Remsen, a friend of Susan's who'd stopped by to deliver a potted plant, which she dropped. Our next dinner date with the Remsens had been interesting.

Susan began a slow, rhythmic up-and-down movement, then increased her tempo. Her body arched back, and her face was lifted toward the sun.

Time, which is relative, seemed to stand still, then speed up, then slowed for a very long second as we both reached orgasm together.

Susan rolled forward and fell on my chest, and I could hear her heavy breathing over my own. She slid her hands and arms under my back and squeezed me tightly as she bit gently into my shoulder. She began gyrating her hips, and within seconds she had another orgasm.

I thought she might go for a hat trick, but she stretched out her legs, put her head on my shoulder, and within a minute she was asleep. I can only imagine what my suntan was going to look like. I, too, was sex-and-sun drowsy, and I drifted off, listening to birds singing and Wagner on the radio.

I had a pleasant dream about lying naked on a sunny beach, and when I awoke, I had this good idea that Susan and I should go to the nude beach in St. Martin where I'd spent a few happy days ten years ago.

But as my head cleared, I rethought that and considered the possible pitfalls of suggesting a trip to a place where I'd been during my self-exile. Especially a nude beach. So maybe Susan and I should travel back to Hilton Head with her parents after Ethel's funeral, and we

could begin the process of healing and bonding as a family. The Stanhopes would be delighted that we were together again, and William
would grab my shoulders and say, "John, you silly rascal, it's good to
have you back." And Charlotte would chirp, "My favorite son-in-law is
with us again!"

Actually, they were going to have a monumental fit. I gave this subject some deep thought, realizing I needed to discuss this with Susan.

Susan stirred, yawned, stretched, then gave me a peck on the cheek
and rolled off. She stood beside the chaise facing into the sunlight with
her eyes closed, and she asked me, "Do you remember the time Judy
Remsen dropped by?"

"I do."

She laughed and said, "I felt so bad for her."

"Don't feel too bad. She rushed off to call everyone she knew." I sat
up, drank some Pellegrino water, and watched Susan standing naked in
the sunlight.

She said to me, "Stand here, facing me, and we'll do stretching
exercises."

"I'm sorry. I pulled my groin. You go ahead."

"John, you need to stay in shape."

"I run."

"You need to stretch and work your muscles." She informed me,
"There's a new Pilates studio in Locust Valley."

"A what?"

She explained, but I didn't get it.

Susan began a series of stretching and bending exercises, and it was
so sexy that I asked, "When does this class start?"

"Anytime you're ready."

She continued her gyrations, and I asked, "Is everyone naked?"

"No, John."

"Oh . . ."

Susan slipped on her panties, spread her beach towel on the patio,
then lay on her back and began doing floor exercises that didn't seem
humanly possible.

I glanced at the sun and guessed it was close to 3:00 P.M. I said to
her, "Susan, I need to speak to you about a few matters."

Without interrupting her routine, she replied, "Later. Let's go out to dinner tonight."

I didn't reply.

She continued, "I'd like you to move your things here this afternoon. I'll help you."

I reminded her, "Your parents will be staying here."

"Oh . . . we'll work it out."

I pulled on my shorts, stood, and said, "Let's go inside."

She stopped her leg lifts, sat up, looked at me, and asked, "What else do you need to speak to me about?" She pointed out, "We've discussed what needed to be discussed."

I gathered my clothes and replied, "Some logistical things."

She didn't reply for a few seconds, then stood and gathered her clothes, and we went inside. As we got dressed in the kitchen, she suggested, "Let's sit in my office."

It used to be my den and home office, so I knew the way, and we went into the big front room where I'd seen her through the window a few days ago.

I expected to see that my masculine décor—leather, brass, mahogany, and hunting prints—had been replaced with something softer, but the furnishings and their arrangement looked the same as when I'd left ten years ago, and the only thing missing, aside from me, was some Army memorabilia. I noticed that she even had a framed photograph of my parents on a bookshelf.

Susan commented first. "I kept everything, except what you took."

I didn't reply.

She moved to the small bar and announced, "It's time for a drink."

"I'll stick to vodka."

She poured me a vodka with ice from the bar refrigerator and made herself a vodka and tonic.

We sat together on the leather couch, and Susan put her bare feet on the coffee table. As I'd learned from many years of law practice, I should make my points in ascending order of importance, starting with the least important, which was her parents. Also, start with a question. I asked, "How do you think your parents are going to react to our good news?"

She answered, without hesitation, "They're going to have a shit fit."

I smiled at the unexpected profanity, but to show this was a serious subject, I asked, "And how are you going to react to their shit fit?"

She shrugged, then replied, "It's my life."

"But it's their money."

"I have money of my own." She added, "But not that much after I overpaid for this house."

"All right. So—"

"And that's something I wanted to discuss with you."

"The answer is, I'm broke."

She waved her hand in dismissal and informed me, "Oh, I guessed that. But you can earn a good living and you're good in bed."

I smiled and said, "All right, but—"

"No, what I wanted to tell you is, I don't want us to have a prenuptial agreement this time."

That was a bit of a shock, but she explained, "My only real assets are this house, and the house in Hilton Head, both of which are mortgage-free, and I want you to own half of both of them—and pay most of the bills."

I replied, "That's very generous, but—"

She continued, "As you've already figured out, when we announce our remarriage, my parents will threaten to cut me out of their will, and end their financial support."

I saw that she'd thought about this in the last few hours, or maybe the last few weeks, or years. Apparently, while I was wondering if we could establish some civility toward each other, she was thinking about how much a remarriage to John Sutter was going to cost her. I was very touched that she decided that I was worth more than her parents' money. Nevertheless, what was abstract and noble now was going to be a hard reality for her in a few days when she called Mom and Pop. I said to her, "They are not going to *threaten* to cut off your allowance and disinherit you. They *will*. In a heartbeat."

Again, she shrugged and replied, "You, Mr. Sutter, are my last chance at happiness. And my happiness is all that counts." She smiled and added, "Well, yours, too."

"I don't know what to say."

"Say something nice."

"I'll say something realistic, and that's the nicest thing I can say to you—life is not easy without money."

"I wouldn't know."

"That's the point, Susan."

"Are you trying to worm your way out of this marriage just because I'm down to my last few million dollars?"

I forced a smile and joked, "Don't forget your dowry and the big wedding gift from your parents."

She replied, "You can be sure they'll offer me five million *not* to marry you."

I stayed silent for a while, sipping my drink. Finally, I said, "All right . . . we could do very well on what you have left, stay in this house if you'd like, maybe keep the house in Hilton Head, and I can certainly earn a good living." Which was true, even if I didn't work for Murder, Inc., and I was fairly certain I wouldn't be doing that after this turn of events in my love life.

Susan, picking up on my last statement, reminded me, "You have a job offer."

"I do . . . and we'll get to that shortly. But, money aside, have you considered the emotional cost of an estrangement from your parents?"

"They'll get over it." She added, "But I want you to promise not to throw fuel on the fire."

I considered that and replied, "I'll certainly let them know that I'm a very different man than the person they knew ten years ago."

Susan observed, "You're not. But you can *say* you are." She reminded me, "You called my father a fuckhead."

"No, I didn't. I called him a—"

"I don't need to hear that again." She looked at me and said, "He probably deserved all that, but if you love me, you'll apologize to him."

"All right. I love you, so I'll apologize."

"Thank you."

"And I'm very glad to hear that they've mellowed."

She informed me, "Actually, they haven't. I lied about that." She smiled and winked.

I smiled, too, and admitted, "I didn't believe you."

She got serious and said, "We'll do the best we can, John. It's not going to be easy, but I promise you this—this time, I will always put you ahead of my parents."

That was the first admission I'd ever heard from her that she'd had her priorities reversed when we were married. I understand the power of money, especially when it's in the hands of people like William and Charlotte Stanhope, but ultimately, if you confront that sort of bullying and manipulation, everyone will benefit, even people like those two. I said, with far more optimism than I felt, "Well, we may be surprised at how they react when we tell them."

"*We?* I'm not telling them. *You* are." She laughed.

I smiled and said, "I will ask your father for your hand in marriage, as I did the last time."

"That's very nice. And don't forget to tell them that *you* insisted we not have a prenup." She suggested, "Bring a video camera. I want to see their reaction."

Clearly, Susan was at some point in her life and her emotional development that was causing a belated rebellion against parental authority. This was a few decades late, but I could see that the rebellion was complete in her mind; all she had to do now was follow through.

I thought, too, of her marrying her father's older friend, Dan Hannon, and it didn't take too much analysis to figure out that that was an arranged marriage, and she'd gone through with it to please Daddy. Now she was going to show Daddy a thing or two. I had no doubt she loved me, and that she'd give up her parents and their money for me, but this was also a little bit of payback for Dad.

Susan had some good news for me. "I don't want to sound cold, but they don't have many years left."

I let that alone and raised a related topic. I said to her, "I'm also wondering if our remarriage will affect the children's trusts or their inheritance."

Susan seemed surprised and replied without enough thought, "They would never do that to their grandchildren."

I didn't respond, and I wanted to believe that, but I knew the Stanhopes well enough to answer my own question; William, at least, was so vindictive that if he had a family crest, it would say, "I will cut off my nose to spite my face," and emblazoned on the crest would be the profile of a man without a nose.

Susan reminded me, "The children's money is in *trust*."

I didn't want to upset her, so I said, "That's true." But I'd seen the trust documents, and without getting into legalities, I knew that what Grandpa giveth, Grandpa could taketh away. In addition, her useless brother, Peter, was the trust administrator, and William, through Peter, could manipulate the trusts, and basically stop the monthly payments to the children, plus, he'd make sure that Edward and Carolyn didn't see a nickel of the principle until they were fifty. And of course, he could disinherit his grandchildren anytime.

I really felt duty-bound to tell her all this because even if she was prepared to give up *her* inheritance and allowance, she wasn't prepared to do that to Edward and Carolyn. If it came down to that, then maybe John Sutter would have to go. And I would understand that.

In the meantime, I'd hope that William loved his grandchildren enough that he would not punish them because of the sins of his daughter, so I said, "All right, but you *do* understand that you, Susan, may lose your allowance, and you could be disinherited from an estate worth millions of dollars?"

"Yes, John, I understand that."

I asked, not altogether jokingly, "And you still want to marry me?"

She replied, "Not anymore. You cost too much."

I assumed she was being funny, so I said, "Be serious."

"I can't believe you would ask me that question."

"I apologize."

"But wait . . . tell me again what's in this for me?"

"Just me."

"That's it? Prince Charming with no job and no money?"

"I have a law degree."

"Can I see it?"

We both smiled, sat back, and sipped our drinks. Okay, if that had gone any differently, I'd have been surprised. Susan Stanhope Sutter was in love and wanted me back, and whatever Susan wants, Susan gets. I was in love, too, and had never stopped loving her, so this should work, theoretically.

Susan crossed her legs, stared out the window, and said as if to herself, "Love conquers all."

"Right." As Virgil said it, *omnia vincit amor*, which reminded me of my next subject, if I needed reminding.

CHAPTER TWENTY-NINE

With the Stanhope family issues out of the way, or at least out in the open, I was now ready to discuss with Susan the subject of Anthony Bellarosa, past, present, and future. But Susan wanted to take a stroll to the gatehouse, perhaps to see if there were panties on the floor, so we walked down the long drive from the guest cottage to my temporary quarters.

When I had walked up this drive, six hours earlier, my life was in limbo, and my future plans were uncertain; now . . . well, now I was engaged to be married.

Susan said to me, "When I grew up here, I never would have imagined that this estate would be sold and divided, surrounded by subdivisions, and I'd be living alone in the guest cottage." She added to that, "I never really forgave my father for putting the estate up for sale."

William didn't really need to sell Stanhope Hall, but the upkeep and taxes cost more than I made in a year and more than he wanted to spend to preserve the family estate for his heirs and their progeny. He couldn't take it with him, but he hated spending it before he left. So he moved to Hilton Head and eventually found a buyer in the person of Mr. Frank Bellarosa, whom I'm certain was influenced in his decision to own a second estate by the lady walking beside me.

Now Stanhope Hall—minus Susan's ten-acre enclave and the developed back sixty acres where Susan used to ride—was in the hands of

Mr. Amir Nasim, a man who was not in the Social Register, but who might be on the mullah's hit list. And Alhambra was subdivided, and its former owner, Frank Bellarosa, was dead. A lot of these changes, if you thought about it, were a result of the actions of Susan Stanhope Sutter, who didn't like change.

In any case, we need to live in the world as it is, not as it was. But first, we all needed to tidy up the past a bit.

Susan, however, was momentarily in the present, and she asked me, "Am I going to find something in the gatehouse that I don't want to see?"

"Well . . . did I tell you that I wear silk bikini shorts?"

"Very funny." She picked up the pace and said, "I'll bet you never thought you'd be walking me to the gatehouse when you called on me this morning."

"No, I didn't." But the house held no incriminating evidence— only exculpatory evidence—and more importantly, I had a clear conscience.

We reached the gatehouse, and Susan said to me, "You have no idea how upset I was when I saw Elizabeth Allard's car here all day and all night."

I thought, by now, I did have some idea, but I said, "Not everything is as it seems."

"We're about to find out."

She preceded me into the gatehouse, and in the foyer she saw the Allards' personal property that Elizabeth and I had stacked there. Susan commented, "I see you did something other than drink."

"There was a lot of work to do here."

"What did you do for dinner?"

"Cheese and crackers."

She moved into the sitting room and saw my pillow and blanket on the couch, which I was happy I'd left there. But Susan didn't comment on this evidence that I'd slept alone, so I did. "See?"

She ignored me and looked around the room, then asked, "Does Elizabeth want this old stuff?"

"I don't know, but I inventoried everything, and she signed for it."

We moved into the dining room, where the table and floor were still stacked with storage and file boxes. She asked, "What is all this?"

I replied, "Mostly the contents of my law office and my former home office, which I stored here when I left."

"You can have your old home office back."

"That is very generous of you."

"What were you going to do with all this?"

I was going to store it in Elizabeth Allard's house, but I replied, "Public storage." I added, "But you've solved my storage problem." I further added, "And my housing problem. And all my other problems."

She agreed, "I have." She advised me, "After you resign from your job, you'll need to get rid of your London flat."

"Of course, darling. I'll fly to London right after Ethel's funeral."

"And get rid of your London girlfriend. Before you go there."

"I will, sweetheart." Unless she flies in unexpectedly before then. I needed to make that phone call soon.

Susan announced, "I'll fly to London with you."

"Great. We'll stay at the Berkeley."

"We'll stay in your flat."

I was afraid of that. I keep a nice, neat place for a bachelor, and Samantha doesn't have a key, but there might be a few things in the flat, including some of Samantha's odds and ends, which would annoy Susan.

She had raised the subject of personal space and privacy, so I said, "Before I move in with you, I'll give you all the time you need to clear out anything that you don't want me to—"

"You can and will move in this afternoon, and you can snoop all you want. I have nothing to hide from you." She rethought that and said, "Well, maybe I need an hour."

I smiled and said, "That's all I need in London."

"I'll give you ten minutes while I wait in the taxi."

I had visions of stuffing a pillowcase with letters, Rolodex cards, interesting photos from my three-year sail, and Samantha's underwear—the equivalent of an embassy burn-bag, frantically being filled as the rioting mob broke through the compound gates. But I couldn't burn it, so I'd have to drop it out the window and hope for the best.

"John?"

I replied, "Deal."

I sensed that I was losing some control of the agenda, and my life. Susan had been far from a jealous or controlling woman, except, as I recalled, in the early days of our courtship and marriage. So this was just a phase. It would pass.

She looked around the room and noticed that the photo portrait of Ethel and George was not hanging above the fireplace, and she said, "It's hard to believe . . . they were here before I was born."

I replied, "You know, Susan, this estate was one of the last that had been in the same family from the beginning, and there aren't that many left, so if you think about it, that era had ended even before you were born." I added, "We were all on borrowed time here."

She thought about that, nodded, and said, "Nostalgia is not what it used to be."

Susan moved through the dining room into the kitchen and looked around, commenting, "When I was a little girl, George would drive me here after school, and Ethel would give me fresh-baked cookies and hot chocolate."

I was sure she didn't get that at Stanhope Hall, but if she did, it wasn't her mother who baked the cookies, made the chocolate, or even served it to her. Susan, from what I could gather from Ethel, George, and the servants who were still here when I came on the scene, had been the classic lonely little rich girl. Her parents, I suspect, took not much interest in her until her debutante party, at which time they probably began thinking about a suitable education, and a suitable marriage—they screwed up there—and also began thinking about how their daughter's social success, or lack thereof, would reflect on them.

I suppose I could be more charitable about how I thought of William and Charlotte, and I could blame some of their many faults and failures on their own upbringing—but I've known a lot of the old gentry, and many of them were fine, decent people who loved their children, and were generous with their friends and those less fortunate than themselves. A few were total swine, but if the Four Hundred Families in the Social Register got together to award a prize for the biggest swine, William Stanhope would win the Blue Ribbon, and Charlotte would get an Honorable Mention.

Susan opened the refrigerator and observed, "There's nothing in here."

"Less to move."

Susan suggested, "We should take some photographs before everything is cleaned out."

"Good idea."

I glanced at the cuckoo clock, which showed it was 3:30, and I said, "How about tomorrow morning?"

"All right."

I thought the house tour was over, so I said, "Let's sit on the patio."

"Let's see the second floor."

I followed her into the foyer and up the stairs. She opened the door to Ethel's bedroom and entered.

The drapes were pulled, and the room was dark and had a musty smell to it. The doors of the armoire and closet were open, as were the dresser drawers, and most of the clothing was lying on the bare mattress. It was an altogether depressing scene, reminding me of what the priest at Frank Bellarosa's funeral had said at the grave, quoting from Timothy: *We brought nothing into this world, and it is certain we can carry nothing out.*

Susan did not comment on Ethel's bedroom, and we left, closing the door.

She glanced into the bathroom, and seeing the piles of towels on the floor asked, "Is the washing machine broken?"

"I don't know. Where is it?"

"I'll have my cleaning lady come here and get this place tidied up for Elizabeth tomorrow."

"That's very nice." How could I forget that a cleaning lady came along with my new house and bride?

Susan asked me, "Did she shower here?"

"The cleaning lady?"

"John."

"I believe so. Yes."

Susan went into my bedroom, formerly and lately Elizabeth's bedroom, and looked around without haste. She stared at the bed, then noticed the empty bottle of wine on the nightstand, and focused on the two wineglasses, which I should have gotten rid of. She inquired, "Why are there two glasses here?"

I thought of several replies, including telling Susan about Elizabeth's imaginary childhood friend who drank wine, but to keep it simple and close to the truth, I said, "Elizabeth wanted to sleep in her old room, so we had a nightcap before she retired."

"That is *so* lame."

I took a deep breath, and, remembering that the truth is the last defense of the trapped, I said, "All right . . . so, we . . . had too much wine, and we thought about it, but decided we'd be making a big mistake."

No reply.

So I went on, "Your name came up, and Elizabeth felt . . . uncomfortable about, you know, and to tell you the truth, so did I."

Again, no reply.

You should quit while you're ahead, but I didn't know if I was ahead. To play it safe, I concluded, "That is the whole truth."

"That's not quite what you told me earlier."

"Right. Well, now you have the details." I was a bit annoyed at myself for being so defensive, and remembering, too, that the best defense is a good offense, I pointed out, "I was a free man last night, Susan, and even if I'd slept with her, it would be no business of yours."

She turned and left the bedroom, then started down the stairs. With Susan, it's hard to tell if she's angry, indifferent, or if the trolley has jumped the tracks. Sometimes she needs a few minutes to figure it out herself, so I took the opportunity to tidy up the room.

I heard her call up the stairs, "I'll be on the patio."

I gave it another minute, then came down the stairs with the two glasses and the empty wine bottle, which I deposited in the trash under the sink.

I went out to the patio and saw that Susan was walking through the vegetable garden.

I called out to her, "I have to be someplace at four."

She didn't reply.

I continued, "But I need to speak to you first."

She looked at me and asked, "About what?"

"Sit here, Susan. This won't take long."

She walked back to the patio and inquired, "Where do you have to be at four?"

"That's what I want to speak to you about. Have a seat."

She hesitated, then sat at the table, and I took the chair beside her. I began, "This is going to sound . . . well, a little unbelievable, but, as I told you—"

"So, you didn't sleep with her because you were thinking of me?"

Apparently, we hadn't finished with that subject, so I replied, "That's correct." I expanded on this and said, "It didn't feel right. Especially after I saw you in your car. I can't explain it, but even without knowing how you felt about me, I just couldn't do anything like that before I spoke to you."

I thought that should put this to rest, but women examine these things on levels that men don't even think about, and Susan said to me, "So, you were attracted to her?"

"Not at all." I explained to her, "Men don't need a reason—they just need a place."

"Believe me, I understand that. But she is obviously attracted to you."

"Everyone is."

"You're a total idiot."

"I know that. Can we—?"

"Well, maybe she was so drunk that you looked good to her."

"I'm sure of that. So—"

"I thought she was my friend."

"She is, Susan. That's why she—"

"And I suppose she was feeling very lonely and needy with her mother dying."

"Exactly."

I waited for further analysis, but Susan took my hand and said, "All right. Subject closed."

I doubted that, so I waited a few seconds, then began, "As I told you—"

"I love you."

"And I love you."

"I know you were faithful to me all during our marriage, and I wish I could say the same."

Me, too.

"I just want you to know, John, that he was the only one."

"I know that."

"So many women were chasing after you, and I was never jealous. I totally trusted you."

"I know you did, and you can still trust me."

"But if you'd had an affair while I was . . . while we were estranged, I would understand."

"Good. I mean—"

"Did you?"

"Of course not." I had a brief fling. "I was too distraught to even think about that."

"I'm sorry I betrayed your trust."

"It's behind us." A trite but appropriate expression came to mind, and I said, "Today is the first day of the rest of our lives together."

She smiled, leaned over, kissed me, then sat back and asked, "Did you want to speak to me about something?"

"Yes. And please listen without comment." I began, again, "As I told you, Anthony Bellarosa stopped by here last Monday." I gave her a very brief outline of the visit, mentioning again Anthony's inquiry about her, and Susan listened without comment. I concluded with, "He asked me to have dinner with him."

"And did you?"

"I did."

"Why?"

"I'm not sure. Except that I was concerned about you."

She didn't reply, so I continued, "And I suppose I had a perverse curiosity—"

"I understand. Go on."

"All right. So I met him at Wong Lee's in Glen Cove." I couldn't help myself from saying, "I thought it best to avoid an Italian restaurant, considering what happened . . . well, anyway, Anthony is not as charming as his father, or as bright, but—"

"John, I really don't want to hear anything about his father. Good or bad. Just tell me what happened with Anthony."

"All right." I mentioned Tony, the driver, who inquired about her, then I related the pertinent parts of the dinner conversation with Anthony Bellarosa, and I briefly mentioned my phone conversation with Anna Bellarosa. I concluded with, "I got up and left."

Susan thought about all that and said, "I hope this isn't the job offer you mentioned."

"Well . . . let me continue." I told her about my chance meeting with Tony and Anthony on Grace Lane, and how I went for a one-way ride to Oyster Bay. I gave her an idea of what was said in Teddy Roosevelt's former office, trying to make her understand not only what *was* said, but also what was *not* said about her. I mentioned, too, the black Cadillac Escalade, and suggested she keep an eye out for it. I downplayed a lot of what was discussed, and what I thought, because I didn't want to alarm her; but neither did I want her to think this was something that would go away by itself, or that she should treat the situation with her usual indifference. I finished by saying, "So we sort of left this job offer up in the air."

She looked at me and replied, "It doesn't sound that way to me." She asked me, "Are you *crazy?*"

"Susan, you need to understand—"

"I do understand, John. You believe that you're considering this so-called job offer to try to protect me, but—"

"Why else would I even be speaking to this man?"

"You should ask yourself that question, not me."

"Susan, let's not get into amateur analysis. If I didn't think that Anthony Bellarosa was looking for revenge for what happened . . . all right, I may have also thought that I could work for him in a legitimate capacity—"

"He's a *Mafia* don."

"I don't *know* that."

"John, you *know* that. And I'll tell you something else you know. He appealed to your ego, and you were flattered. And he sensed, too, that you were vulnerable to his advances because of what happened in the past, and because you were not completely satisfied with your life. You are *not* going to repeat that mistake—"

"Hold on. Do I have to remind you who encouraged that relationship with you-know-who, and *why* you encouraged it?"

"Stop it!" She took a deep breath, then got herself under control and said, "You don't have to remind me. I should remind myself."

Neither of us spoke for a while, then she said, "He may be brighter than you give him credit for."

"I know that."

"But you're much brighter than that."

"I know that, too."

"So what are you going to do, John?"

I thought about that and replied, "Well, my situation has obviously changed." I forced a smile and said, "I'm in love and engaged to be married, as of a few hours ago, so I don't have any need to be flattered by anyone else, and all my ego needs have been met, and I'm no longer vulnerable to the temptations of the devil."

Susan looked at me again and said, "Tell the devil to go to hell."

"I will . . . but I'm still concerned about you."

"Don't be." She took my hand again and said, "I am so touched that you were thinking about protecting me when you hated me."

"I never hated you. I loved you."

"I see that." She found a tissue in her pocket, dabbed her eyes, and said, "I do see that."

We sat quietly for a while, then Susan asked me, "Do you have any plans to see or speak to him again?"

I glanced at my watch and replied, "Yes, in about five minutes."

"Where?"

"At his house. I'm invited for Sunday dinner."

"Don't go."

"My instincts say to go. And you need to trust me on this."

She stayed silent for some time, then asked, "What is the *purpose* of going?"

I replied, "I feel if I don't go, I might miss a last opportunity to learn something . . . to get a better understanding of the man, and of his thinking about . . . well, you." I explained, "If I can get him to make a threatening remark, then when I go to the police, I'm sure they'll take it seriously because of what Anthony Bellarosa has said, and also because of what happened ten years ago."

Susan stayed silent a long time, then said, "If I had that moment to live over again, I would not pull the trigger."

Three times, actually. And that reminded me to ask, "Do you own a gun?"

She looked at me and replied, "I did skeet and duck shooting in Hilton Head. I have a shotgun."

I was happy to hear that she owned and knew how to use a shotgun, but recalling Emily Post's advice on the subject of guns, and considering that I was about to move in with her . . . but, well, I'd take her at her word that she regretted her moment of explosive rage against her lover, and I would also assume that she'd developed better coping skills when angry. I asked, "Where do you keep the shotgun?"

"I don't know . . . I think it's in the basement."

"You need to look for it." I stood and said, "I should be going."

She stood and asked me, "Who will be there?"

"Anthony, of course, his wife, Megan, probably their two children, and I suppose, Anna. I don't know who else."

"All right . . . I'll trust your judgment on this."

We walked back into the kitchen, and I said to her, "I'm not actually staying for dinner, of course."

I took my car keys from the key peg, and Susan reminded me, "You should actually bring a hostess gift for his wife."

There was something almost comical about Susan's suggestion that I not forget social etiquette, even when dining with a man who quite possibly wanted her dead. Well, in Susan's world, one thing had nothing to do with the other.

I opened the pantry, but I was out of wine, so I took a jar of Ethel's crabapple jelly that had her personal label on it with the date it was made. I said, "This is a 1999. It will go well with lasagna."

Susan had no comment, then said to me, "While you're gone, I'm going to pack your things and take them to our house."

"Thank you." I reminded her, "But I'm moving back here when your parents arrive."

"It would be nice if we could all stay under the same roof."

"There isn't a roof big enough for that."

"Let's see how it goes when they arrive."

I didn't want to discuss this now, so I said, "Well, ciao."

"When you leave, tell him, 'Va al inferno.'"

"I will do that."

We kissed, and she said, "Good luck."

I left the gatehouse, got into my car, and headed out through the open gates of Stanhope Hall, turning left onto Grace Lane for the short trip to Alhambra.

My first visit to Alhambra, ten years ago, had been a monumental mistake; this visit was a chance to correct that mistake.

CHAPTER THIRTY

And so, to Sunday dinner at the Bellarosas'.

The distance between the gatehouse of Stanhope Hall and the gatehouse of Alhambra is about a quarter of a mile, and for the first half of that distance Grace Lane is bordered by the gray stone wall of the Stanhope estate, which ends where the Alhambra wall of brick and stucco begins.

The Gold Coast, at the height of its wealth and power, which was the day before the stock market crash of '29, boasted over two hundred grand estates and an equal number of smaller manor houses and country homes.

A gentleman and his family living in a Fifth Avenue mansion could be here, at his country estate, in an hour, traveling by private railway car, or he could take a leisurely two-hour cruise in his motor yacht. The gentleman also had the option to travel here in his chauffeured limousine via the Vanderbilt Toll Road, which Mr. William K. Vanderbilt Jr. constructed for himself and his friends, and which he allowed others to use for a fee. Those were the good old days, as they say.

Most of the estates are fronted by walls or wrought-iron fences, punctuated by gates and gatehouses, and many of these structures have survived and are reminders of a past that had flourished briefly, but which nonetheless still loomed large in the consciousness of those who now lived here. The problem with living in a place like this, I think, is the physical evidence around us that said maybe there really *was* a golden age that was better than now.

So to return to Mr. Anthony Bellarosa's analogies to the fall of the Roman Empire, I'd once read that during the Dark Ages, the last few thousand benighted inhabitants of Rome, awestruck by the magnificent ruins around them, believed that the ancient city must have been built by giants or gods.

I had no such belief here, though I think that archaeologists digging on the Gold Coast a thousand years from now might possibly conclude that stockbrokers and lawyers were barbarian tribes who cooked the landed gentry in something called Weber grills.

And while I was in this mind-set, I recalled, too, the story of the Roman Senate who continued to meet long after the fall of the Empire, and who became, in effect, no more than a tourist attraction for curious citizens and barbarians who wandered down to the Forum to see these living ghosts in their quaint togas.

I was never a full-fledged member of the senatorial class, being more of the equestrian class, but whenever I put on my blue blazer, tan pants, and Docksiders, and go into town with my preppie accent, I sometimes feel I am one of the Gold Coast tourist attractions, along with the walls, and the ruins, and the estates now open to the public. "Look, Mommy, there's one of them!"

I slowed down as I approached the former gatehouse of Alhambra, which now served as the guard booth for the gated community.

A sign read ALHAMBRA ESTATES—PRIVATE—STOP AT SECURITY.

I turned left into the driveway. The large wrought-iron gates were open, and I saw that a speed bump and a yellow stop line had been added to the cobblestone allée, which was still lined with stately Lombardy poplars.

I drove through the gates, then stopped as instructed at the old gatehouse.

On the door of the house, I could see a small sign that said ALHAMBRA ESTATES—SALES & MANAGEMENT. I noticed, too, that a big window had been cut into the side of the gatehouse, and behind the open window appeared a man dressed in a khaki military-style shirt. He greeted me with an insincere smile and asked, "How can I help you?"

A metal sign read BELL SECURITY SERVICE, which I remembered was a division of Anthony Bellarosa's Bell Enterprises, which conveniently had the contract for Alhambra Estates. So, since I was an F.O.B.—friend of the boss—and not in the best of moods, anyway, I indulged myself in a little petulance and replied, "I don't know how you can help me. What are my choices?"

"Sir?"

I was briefly nostalgic for Frank Bellarosa's goons—Lenny and Vinnie, both now deceased, and Anthony, now known as Tony. I said, "I'm here to see"—I was feeling reckless—"don Bellarosa."

The guard looked at me closely, then informed me, "Mr. *Anthony* Bellarosa."

"Right. And his brother, Don."

He seemed not amused, but since I was apparently a guest of the boss, he played it safe and inquired, "Your name, sir?"

I replied, "John Whitman Sutter."

Without consulting the list of invitees in his hand, he said, "Right," then gave me directions and remembered to say, "Have a nice day."

As I pulled away, I could see in my side-view mirror that the guard was on the phone, calling, I assumed, the Bellarosa house; so there was no turning back now.

I continued up the straight cobblestone drive that had once ended in the courtyard of the villa called Alhambra. But now I could see that the road continued on in blacktop, running over the site where the mansion once stood. Branching off the main road were smaller roads, which ran to the five-acre parcels and the faux villas. Some of the old trees had survived the construction of houses, roads, swimming pools, and underground infrastructure, but mostly the terrain was bare between the newly landscaped houses.

I suppose it could have been worse—but not much worse. I hadn't been too thrilled when I discovered that Frank the Bishop Bellarosa had bought Alhambra—I mean, we've all had bad neighbors, but this was a bit much—though looking back, I realized that one Mafia don and his family was actually better than a hundred over-mortgaged stockbrokers, or whoever these people were.

In any case, it was not my problem. I recalled that a good deal of my time here had been spent engaged in cocktail-party and country-club chatter about how our world was changing around us, and I'd belonged to too many committees that were involved in legal actions to hold the line against the developers—in essence, trying to freeze some moment in time that had already passed. I'm sure they were still at it.

I stopped the car at the place where the old cobblestone and the poplars ended and the blacktop began. Here Alhambra had stood, and I got out of the car and looked around. This was the highest point of land, and from here I could see a dozen mini-villas sitting on their manicured acres with their three-car garages and their driveways and patios. There was a lot of barbecuing going on, and blue smoke rose into the cloudless sky, like the campfires of a bivouacked army. Other than that, there didn't seem to be much human activity on God's little five-acre parcels.

Beyond the acres of what had been Alhambra, I could see the golf course of The Creek Club, and I recalled that after Susan and I had taken Mr. and Mrs. Bellarosa to The Creek for dinner, Mr. Bellarosa had asked me to sponsor him for membership. Well, that's always a problem when you take a marginal couple to the club for dinner; the next thing you know, they want you to get them in. I was fairly certain that the club membership committee would not approve of the application of a Mafia don, so, without wasting too much tact, I explained to Frank that even Jesus Christ, who was half Jewish on his mother's side, couldn't get into The Creek.

I have to admit, at least to myself, that despite all that happened that spring, summer, and fall, and despite the tragic end of a life and a marriage, I did have some fun with all this—which, I suppose, is like Mrs. Lincoln answering the question of, "Other than that, Mrs. Lincoln, how did you like the play?" with the honest reply, "It was a funny comedy, and I was laughing until the shot rang out."

I looked to where the reflecting pool and the classical Roman garden had once been, but the landscape was so different now that I couldn't be sure exactly where it was, though I thought it may have sat in a low piece of land where a house now stood.

The disturbing images from my dream took form in my mind, but I didn't want to see them any longer, so I wished them away and they were gone.

I looked back down the long sloping allée toward the gatehouse and the road. On the other side of Grace Lane was a big colonial-style house set back about a hundred yards on a hill. This house was owned by the DePauws, though I didn't know if they were still there. But ten years ago the FBI had used their property as an observation post to see and photograph anyone coming and going at Alhambra.

On the night of the failed hit outside of Giulio's restaurant in Little Italy, I'd been escorted to the police station at Midtown South, where I had the opportunity to see many of these photos taken with a telescopic lens, and the police and the FBI asked me to try to identify if any of Frank Bellarosa's photographed visitors were the same two men that I'd seen outside of Giulio's.

Among the photographs of Mr. Bellarosa's friends, family, and business associates were a few nice shots of Susan and me on the occasion of our first visit to the Bellarosas' for coffee and cannolis. It occurred to me then that the FBI knew, long before I did, that Susan and Frank were going at it. I now wondered if the FBI already knew that Anthony Bellarosa and I were on our fourth tête-à-tête. I also wondered what had happened to Special Agent Felix Mancuso who'd tried so earnestly to save me from myself. Maybe I needed to call him.

I got back into my car and proceeded to a small road on the left called Pine Lane, which led me into a large cul-de-sac where three stucco villas with red-tiled roofs stood a hundred yards apart.

I realized that I was now close to the property line of Stanhope Hall, and in fact, I could see, behind the three villas, the line of towering white pines that separated the two estates. So, as the crow flies, or as the horse trots, Susan's guest cottage and Anthony's villa were only about five hundred yards apart.

The three villas on the cul-de-sac were slightly different in style and color, and the security guard said it was the yellow house, so I steered toward the last house on the left and stopped in front of the neat lawn of Casa Bellarosa. I got out, remembering the crabapple jelly.

The wide driveway held the black Cadillac Escalade and a white minivan, which I assumed belonged to Megan Bellarosa, and a yellow Corvette, which I guessed was Anthony's getaway car. Above the garage doors was a basketball hoop mounted on a backboard.

I noticed, too, parked in front of me, a standard black Mafioso-model Cadillac with tinted windows.

I walked up the driveway and turned onto a concrete path that took me to the front portico.

I checked my watch, and saw it was 4:15. I was late, but not fashionably so.

I noticed there was a security camera above the door, so I smiled for the camera and rang the bell.

CHAPTER THIRTY-ONE

Bellarosa had been notified by Bell Security that I was on my way, and he'd also seen me on his security monitor, so he didn't feign any surprise when he opened the door and greeted me by saying, "Hey, glad you could make it. Come on in."

Anthony was wearing a shiny black shirt with the sleeves rolled up, and the shirt was tucked into a pair of charcoal gray pleated pants held up by a pencil-thin belt. His loafers, I noticed, were made of some sort of reptilian leather. I didn't think anyone from the *New York Times* Style section would be calling soon.

Anyway, I said, "Thank you for inviting me."

"Yeah. And you're not gonna run off this time."

Wanna bet?

I thought, out of habit, he was going to ask me if I wanted to check my gun, but instead, he asked, "Any problem at the guard booth?"

I assumed the guard had ratted me out about the don Bellarosa thing, and Anthony wanted me to know he wasn't amused. I replied, "He seemed hard of hearing."

"Yeah? Hard to get good help."

And speaking of hard of hearing, an Italian male vocalist was belting out a lively song, which was booming out of the wall speakers, and Anthony announced my arrival by shouting over the music, "Hey, Megan! We got company!"

Anthony went to a control panel on the wall, turned down the music, and said to me, "Great album. It's called Mob Hits." He laughed. "Get it?"

I smiled.

While we waited for Megan, and while Anthony played with the bass and treble knobs, I looked around the big foyer and into the living and dining rooms. To be honest, it wasn't all that bad. I'd expected an ornate Italian version of Mr. Nasim's horrid faux French, but Megan, and probably a decorator, had played it safe with Chairman-of-the-Board contemporary in muted tones. There were, however, a lot of paint-by-number oils of sunny Italy on the walls, and I spotted two crucifixes.

Megan Bellarosa entered the foyer, and I was pleasantly surprised. She was in her late twenties, tall and thin, and she had a pretty freckled Irish face and blue eyes. Also, she had what looked like natural red hair, so from personal experience I knew she was either bitchy, high-strung, or just plain crazy.

She gave me a sort of tentative smile, wondering, I'm sure, what the hell her husband was thinking when he invited me to a family dinner. I said to her, "It was very nice of you to invite me."

She replied, "I'm glad you could make it. We have lots of food," which removed any concern I may have had about eating the last of the family rations. She asked, "Can I take your coat?"

I didn't have a coat—only a blue blazer—and I don't part with it very easily, so I said, "I'll just wear it." I remembered to say, "You have a beautiful home."

She replied, "Thanks. Anthony can show you around later."

Her accent was distinctly low-class, as was her pink polyester tunic and her black polyester stretch pants. Considering, though, her good features, Professor Higgins could do wonders with her.

I handed her the jar of crabapple jelly and said, "This is homemade."

She took the jar, looked at the label, smiled and exclaimed, "Oh, geez—my grandmother used to make this."

So we were really off to a good start. In fact, Megan gave me a nice big smile, and for a second she reminded me of Susan. The swarthy Bellarosa men, apparently, liked the northern European, fair-skinned type. *Dear Sigmund—*

Before I could analyze this further, Anthony said, "Hey, my mother is excited to see you. Come on."

I followed Anthony and Megan through the foyer into a big sunny kitchen, and standing at the center island, cutting cheese on a board, was Anna Bellarosa. She saw me, dropped her knife, wiped her hands on her apron, and charged toward me exclaiming, "John! Oh my God!"

I braced myself right before impact, put out my arms, and we collided. BAM! She hugged me tight, and I was able to get my arms around her and managed to wheeze, "Anna . . . you look great . . ."

In fact, before impact, I'd seen that she'd put on a few pounds, and I was feeling them now as she squeezed the air out of my lungs. To add to my breathing problem, she was wearing a floral scent that overpowered whatever was cooking.

We unclenched, and I held her hands so she couldn't get her arms around me again, and I looked at her. Her face was still cherub-like and made more so by too much red lipstick and rouge, but under the paint, her skin looked young. Mediterranean diet?

I caught my breath and said, "It's so good to—"

She interrupted, "John, you look *great*. I'm so happy you came." She went on awhile, asking about my children, but not about my evil seductress man-killing wife, and quizzed me on what I was up to.

Anna used to wear enough jewelry to interfere with radio transmissions, but today all she had on was a pair of gold earrings and her wedding band. Plus, she wore a black pantsuit, to denote her widowed status, and I noticed a gold crucifix nestled in her cleavage, which reminded me now, as it did when we first met, of Christ of the Andes.

Anna went on, and I replied as best I could before she interrupted each reply. I noticed that Megan had left the kitchen, and I recalled that the two Mrs. Bellarosas were not on good culinary terms, or any terms at all.

Finally, Anthony interrupted his mother's interruptions and said, "Okay, let him catch his breath, Ma. Hey, John, wine, beer, or hard stuff?"

I needed a triple Scotch, but I asked for a white wine.

Anthony opened the refrigerator and retrieved an uncorked bottle of something and poured two wines into cut crystal glasses.

Anna informed me, "John, I made lasagna for you. Anthony said you liked my lasagna."

"I do." It had been my favorite from Anna's takeout kitchen at Alhambra, and Susan, too, liked her lasagna, though I shouldn't mention that.

Anna continued, "We got hot and cold antipasto, we got stracciatelle, we got a beautiful bronzini that I got in Brooklyn, we got veal—"

"Ma, he doesn't need—"

"Anthony, sta' zitto."

I think that means shut up. I have to remember that.

Anna recited her menu as though reciting the Rosary. I never completely understood why she liked me—except that I'm charming—but when men and women are friends, there's almost always a sexual element present. Not romantic sex, perhaps, but a sort of Freudian concept of sex that acknowledges the attraction as more than platonic, but not quite rising to the level of "let's fuck." With Susan and Frank, however, it was libido from the get-go, and maybe, later, they fell in love. Interestingly, Anna never caught on to this, and she remained very fond of Susan until Susan whacked her dear husband.

Anyway, as far as why Anna liked me, I also knew from what she'd said once that she believed that John Whitman Sutter would be a good influence on Frank, who was being influenced by bad people. That would have been funny if it weren't so sad. In any case, I'm sure Anna had similar thoughts about her son's budding friendship with me.

As Anna prattled on, and as Anthony tried to get a word in edgewise, and I made an appropriate sound now and then, I realized that when I informed Anthony that Susan and I were together again, that would put Anthony in an awkward position in regard to Mom, who understandably was no longer so fond of Susan—and that might just end Anthony's interest in making me his trusted advisor. In fact, I was sure of it.

As I was thinking about this, Anna was thinking that I looked not so great after all, and she pushed a platter of cheese and salami across the counter and informed me, "You look too skinny. Eat."

Anthony laughed and mimicked Mom. "Mangia! Mangia! You're too skinny."

Anna turned her attention to her son and said, "You, too. You're too skinny, Anthony."

Anthony laughed again and poured his mother a glass of red wine, saying, "You don't drink enough vino. Beva, beva."

Anna ignored the wine, but did sample most of the cheese and salami. Atkins diet?

Anthony and I took some cheese, which to me smelled like the Bay of Naples, but it tasted good. So, if I had my choice between an Italian mother and a WASP mother, I'd pick orphan.

Anna was examining the jar of jelly that Megan had left on the counter, and she asked her son, "What's this?"

Anthony explained, "John brought it over."

That seemed to make it okay, but she asked me, apropos of the label, "How's she doing? The old lady."

"Not too well."

Anna seemed to be thinking, then said, "I remember the husband. He used to come over, looking for . . . your wife." I didn't respond, and Anna added, "I don't remember the old lady too much. But we had a nice chat once."

"I'll pass on your regards."

"Yeah. I hope she gets better." She asked me, "So, you're living there?"

"I am." I was.

I had no doubt that Anna was on the verge of warning me that the killer had returned to the guest cottage, and Anthony, perhaps also sensing that Mom was starting to relive bad memories, said to me, "Hey, let's go outside. I want to check on the kids."

Anna instructed him, "Tell them it's almost time to eat."

We went through a sliding glass door onto a huge slate patio that was large enough to accommodate an emergency space shuttle landing, and beyond the patio, surrounded by a six-foot-high metal picket fence, was a swimming pool whose dimensions qualified it as an inland sea.

Beyond the pool, I could see a long wire dog run, and tethered to the wire was a big German shepherd, who even at this distance noticed me, stopped pacing, and began pulling at his leash and barking at me.

Anthony shouted, "Sta' zitto!" and the dog, who was apparently bilingual, stopped barking. I walked with Anthony to the pool, and he opened the gate and called out to the two children, who were paddling around with water wings, "Hey, kids! Say hello to Mr. Sutter."

They looked at me, waved, and said simultaneously, "Hi," then went back to their paddling.

The boy, I recalled, was Frank, age five, and the girl was Kelly Ann, and she looked a year or so older. They were good-looking kids, and under their tans probably fair-skinned like their mother. They reminded me of Edward and Carolyn when they were that age, enjoying the summer in comfortable surroundings and enjoying the world without a care.

I noticed now a middle-aged lady sitting in a lawn chair under the shade of an umbrella, and she was watching the two children like a hawk. Anthony called to her, "Eva, get the kids ready for dinner!"

Anthony turned and we walked back to the patio, and I thought we were going back inside, but Anthony moved toward a striped pavilion on the patio, and I now noticed a man and a woman sitting there.

We walked into the shade of the pavilion, and Anthony said to me, "You remember my uncle Sal."

This sort of took me by surprise, and I was momentarily speechless.

Sitting in a cushioned chair, holding a cocktail glass and smoking a cigarette, was none other than Salvatore D'Alessio, a.k.a. Sally Da-da. I mean, it's nice to have family over for dinner, but it could be awkward if the invited family member once tried to have your father killed. Maybe, though, I was being ethnocentric, and I was making too much of that.

Uncle Sal stayed seated, looked at me, and gave a half nod, mumbling, "How ya doin'?"

I replied, "Hangin' in."

I thought that our reunion after ten years should have caused him more joy, but he just sat there with his cigarette and cocktail and looked off into space.

The first time I'd seen Sally Da-da was at the Plaza Hotel, where Frank had invited half the Mafia in New York to his suite to celebrate his being sprung on bail. It was more than a celebration, however, it was also a show of force, where the don's capos and lesser henchmen came to kiss his ring, and where his affiliated partners and even his rivals had come, by command, to witness this great outpouring of support for the *capo di tutti capi*.

I had been accosted in the room by a man who I classified as Cro-Magnon and who asked me some questions that made little sense to me. I later learned that this man was Salvatore D'Alessio, brother-in-law to don Bellarosa. Much later, I learned that Mr. D'Alessio, who was the don's underboss, wanted to be *capo di tutti capi*, so Frank had to go.

Anyway, Mr. D'Alessio, sitting now a few feet from me, was a big, powerfully built man with thick dyed black hair and thick eyebrows that met in the middle, like you see in the Prehistoric Man dioramas at the Museum of Natural History. He could have been wearing an animal skin, and no one would have commented, but he was in fact wearing baggy black dress pants and a white dress shirt half unbuttoned, with the sleeves rolled up, exposing lots of hair. I didn't think he'd be carrying a gun to a family dinner, but if he was, it might be concealed in his chest hair.

Anthony asked me, "Did you ever meet my aunt Marie?"

I turned my attention to Aunt Marie, who looked like a thinner and older version of her sister Anna. I said to her, "I believe we've met."

She nodded, but didn't say anything.

In fact, I'd met Marie D'Alessio at Frank Bellarosa's funeral Mass, and she'd sat next to Anna, and they took turns crying. It was at this funeral Mass where I'd seen Uncle Sal for the second time, then again at graveside where he kept staring at the coffin, avoiding eye contact with young Anthony Bellarosa.

Marie didn't seem to have anything to say to the ex-husband of Susan Sutter, so I turned my attention back to Uncle Sal, and I noticed now that he was giving me an appraising look. We made eye contact, and he said to me, "Long time."

I guess that meant "Long time no see," which actually means "It's been ages, John, since we've seen each other." I replied, "Long time."

I understood why Uncle Sal wanted to clip his brother-in-law, but I was annoyed that he'd picked the night I was having dinner with Frank and our wives. Though, as Felix Mancuso explained to me later, Sally Da-da probably knew that Frank Bellarosa would never think anyone would break the strict rule of not whacking someone in the presence of their family or in the company of upstanding citizens, which I guess included John and Susan Sutter. So Salvatore D'Alessio had calendared in "Whack Frank" on the same night that my calendar showed "Dinner with Bellarosas/NYC/limo." I would have written in the name of the restaurant, Giulio's, but with Frank, you never knew your exact destination until you got there. Someone else, however, probably Frank's driver, Lenny the Snake, knew the name of the restaurant and passed it on to Sally Da-da, who couldn't resist the opportunity.

I looked again at Salvatore D'Alessio, who was still looking at me, and I had to wonder about a man who would arrange to have his brother-in-law killed in front of his own wife's sister.

Regarding the timing of the whack, Frank Bellarosa never had a day in his life when he wasn't on his guard, and he'd been wearing a bulletproof vest under his tailored suit, so aside from some broken ribs and a severed carotid artery that was not protected by the Kevlar, he'd survived, with a little help from me.

Anthony broke the silence with some good news and announced, "My aunt and uncle just dropped by to say hello."

Uncle Sal stood, and I was struck at how huge this guy was. I mean, even if you shaved off all his hair, he was still pretty big. He said, "Yeah. We're goin'."

Aunt Marie also stood, and said to her nephew, "Anthony, take care of your mother."

"I do."

"You gotta call her."

"I do."

"Have her over more. Not just Sundays, Anthony."

"My *brothers* come in from Jersey and see her all the time."

She ignored this and further advised Anthony, "Since your father died"—she glanced at me for some reason—"since he's been gone, she's all alone."

"She's got fifty cousins and sisters in Brooklyn."

"They got their own lives."

"Okay, okay. Thanks, Aunt Marie."

While this was going on, Uncle Sal just stood there, expressionless, but perhaps thinking that his wife was wasting her time talking to a dead man. Well, I didn't know that, of course, and certainly Uncle Sal had already had ample time and opportunity to put Anthony on the permanently dead list. So maybe they'd worked out some sort of power-sharing arrangement, like, "Anthony, you get the drugs, prostitution, and loan-sharking, and I take the gambling, extortion, and stealing from the docks and airports." That's what I would recommend.

Anthony said to his uncle, "Thanks for stopping by."

Uncle Sal dropped his cigarette on the patio, stepped on it, and said, "Your mother looks good."

Anthony glanced at the cigarette butt on his nice slate patio, but he didn't say anything. So maybe he was thinking, "Why bother? He's dead anyway."

Wouldn't it be nice if Anthony Bellarosa and Salvatore D'Alessio somehow managed to have each other whacked?

I hope I didn't say that out loud, and I guess I didn't because Uncle Sal turned to me and asked, "So, whaddaya up to?"

"Same old shit."

"Yeah? Like?"

Anthony interrupted this windy conversation and said, "John's my tax guy."

"Yeah?" Uncle Sal looked at me for a long time, as if to say, "Sorry my boys missed you at Giulio's." Well, maybe I was imagining that.

Aunt Marie announced, "I'm going in," but before she left, she reminded Anthony, "Your mother needs you." She should remind her husband of that, too.

So I stood there with Anthony and Salvatore in manly silence, then I realized I was supposed to leave them alone. But I didn't want to go back in the kitchen with the women—only faggots would do that—so I said, "I'm going to take a walk." I addressed Uncle Sal. "Well, great seeing you again."

"Yeah."

"Do you have a card?"

"*What?*"

"Ciao." I walked out toward the pool, well out of earshot and gunshot range. I looked at the shimmering pool, then out to where the

German shepherd was glaring at me, which for some reason reminded me of Salvatore D'Alessio.

Salvatore D'Alessio—Sally Da-da to his friends, and Uncle Sal to his nephew—was the real thing. I mean, this guy was not playacting the part of a Mafia boss like so many of these characters did. This was one mean and dangerous man. If I had to put money on who would whack whom first, I'd bet on Uncle Sal being at Anthony's funeral, and not the other way around.

And yet Anthony had the major motivation—personal vendetta—and also he seemed to have more brains, which I know is not saying too much.

Bottom line here was this: Anthony wanted to kill Uncle Sal; Uncle Sal wanted to kill Anthony; Uncle Sal might still be annoyed at me for saving Frank's life and making him look incompetent; Anthony wanted to kill Susan; I wanted Anthony Bellarosa and Salvatore D'Alessio dead.

Who said that Sunday family dinners were boring?

CHAPTER THIRTY-TWO

I saw that Uncle Sal had left, and Anthony was now sitting in a chair under the pavilion. I took the chair across from him, and I noticed that the cigarette butt was gone.

Neither of us spoke, but I thought Anthony was going to put me at ease about Uncle Sal by saying something like, "Under all that hair is a big heart," but he acted as though Uncle Sal hadn't been there, and commented instead on Aunt Marie, saying, "She's a ballbuster."

I wasn't sure if I needed to respond, but Anthony was still chafing at Aunt Marie's public lecture, and he wanted me to know what he thought of her. I said, "Well, I think she's fond of you, and she loves her sister."

"Yeah. Right." He informed me, "She's got two boys. Both in Florida. Nobody ever sees them."

I thought maybe their father ate them, but Anthony let me know, "They're fucking beach bums."

I didn't respond.

He sat back, smoking, and I could see that Uncle Sal's visit had put him in a bad mood, so possibly he was thinking about the best way to end these visits forever, which was why he'd thought about Uncle Sal's wife and sons. His aunt was a ballbuster, and he'd like to make her a widow, like his mother, and his cousins were not a threat if by some chance something happened to their father.

But maybe I was being too clever. Maybe he was thinking about his mother's lasagna. I said to him, "Your uncle looked good."

He came out of his thoughts and replied, "Yeah. He uses the same polish on his hair and his shoes." He looked at me, smiled, and said, "You asked him for his card."

"I wondered what sort of business he was in."

Anthony smiled again, then replied, "The family business." He then assured me, "He didn't know you were jerking him around."

That's good.

Anthony said to me, "You got balls."

I didn't reply, but the subject of balls was out there, so Anthony felt he needed to tell me, "I should've shoved that cigarette butt up his ass, but every time I get pissed off at him, everybody thinks *I'm* the bad guy."

"I think you handled it quite well." I reminded him, "He *is* your uncle."

"Yeah. By marriage. But still, you got to show respect. Right?"

"Right." Right up until the time you kill him.

"But he's got to show respect, too."

"I agree." I had no doubt that men in Anthony's world had been killed for far less than throwing a cigarette butt on their host's patio. It was all about respect, and not embarrassing a goombah in public, but it was also about family ties, the pecking order, and ultimately about the balance of power that needed to be preserved. And maybe that was why neither of these two had made a move on the other yet. Meanwhile, they'd go on pissing each other off until one or the other snapped.

Anthony gave me some good advice and said, "Don't fuck with him. He can't take a joke."

I doubted if Uncle Sal even understood a joke.

Then Anthony said, "I think this is going to be a busy week."

That seemed to come out of nowhere, but it was apparently a preface to something rather than an offhand remark, so I went along with it and asked, "Why?"

"Well, from what I hear, John Gotti has only a few days left."

I didn't respond.

Anthony continued, "There'll be a three-day wake and a big funeral. You know?"

Again, I didn't respond.

Anthony went on, "So, I got to be there." He explained, "I mean, I don't have any business with him, but I know the family, so you have to show your respect. Even if by being there, some people get the wrong idea."

Right. Like, the police and the press might mistake you for a mobster.

He looked at me and said, "You went to my father's funeral. Out of respect."

I wasn't sure *why* I'd gone to his father's funeral, except maybe I felt some . . . guilt, I guess, that it was my wife who'd killed him. I didn't respect Frank Bellarosa, but, I guess, despite all that had happened, I liked him. So I said to Anthony, "I liked your father." I added, "And your mother."

He looked at me and nodded, then said, "Afterwards, like years later, I realized what a ballsy move that was. I mean, to go to my father's funeral when it was your wife who killed him."

I had no reply to that.

He continued, "I'll bet you got a lot of shit about that from your friends and family."

In fact, I hadn't. And that was because no one was speaking to me after that. My father, however, did comment, "That showed poor judgment, John." Even my mother, who loves all things multicultural, said, "What were you thinking?" My sister, Emily, had also called me and said, "I saw you on TV at Bellarosa's funeral. You stood out like a sore thumb, John. We need to get you a black shirt and a white tie." She'd added, "That took guts."

Anthony said to me, "You probably got some shit in the press, too."

I did get a few mentions, but nothing that was really critical or judgmental; mostly the media was happy to report on the irony of the alleged killer's husband being at the funeral. Well, maybe the media doesn't understand irony, but they do understand entertainment value.

My good friend Jenny Alvarez had helped set the tone by reporting on TV that "unnamed sources have described John Sutter as a man who puts his professional responsibilities above his personal feelings, and as the attorney of record for Frank Bellarosa, he felt he should be there for his deceased client's family."

That was a bit of a stretch, not to mention a contradiction, but Jenny liked me, and when a reporter likes you, they'll find, or make up, unnamed sources to say nice things about you. If she was a *really* honest journalist, she'd have added, "In the interests of full disclosure, I need to report that I slept with Mr. Sutter."

Anthony said to me, "Hey, if you want to go with me, that would be good."

I felt that one Mafioso funeral in a lifetime was already one too many, so I said to him, "I, too, have a busy week. But thank you."

"Let me know if you change your mind."

Neither of us spoke for a minute as Anthony smoked and stared off at his swimming pool.

I'm not a Mafia buff, but I'm an attorney with a good brain who once worked for Frank Bellarosa, so I started putting some things together, to wit: John Gotti's death might cause some uncertainty among his business associates, and maybe some opportunities. And if I thought about Anthony and Sally Da-da coexisting in an uneasy truce for all these years, I might conclude that the only way this had been possible was if this truce had been mandated by someone like John Gotti—and he was not long for this world. Therefore, if my deductions were correct, Anthony and his uncle Sal would soon be free to kill each other. And that, perhaps, was why Anthony was in full security mode.

I had another thought that maybe Susan had also been included in this Do-Not-Whack arrangement—the Mafia was all about making money, and avoiding bad press for killing civilians—but maybe after John Gotti's funeral, Anthony might feel free to deal with Susan.

The other possibility was that I was spending too much time with Anthony, and I was starting to think the way I imagined he and his goombahs thought.

The subject of Gotti's imminent death seemed to be closed, and dinner hadn't been announced, so I thought this was the time to give

Anthony my good news about Susan and me, but before I could do that, he asked me, "What are your kids doing?"

I had learned, long before the Bellarosas came into my life, to be circumspect with strangers regarding the location and activities of my children. I mean, neither the Sutters nor the Stanhopes were celebrities, like the Bellarosas, but the Stanhopes were rich, and there were people who knew this name. My great hope in this regard was that a kidnapper would snatch William, ask for a million-dollar ransom, and be turned down by Charlotte. Anyway, to answer Anthony's question, I said, "My son is living on the West Coast, and my daughter is an ADA in Brooklyn."

This information got his attention, and he said, "Yeah? She works for Joe Hynes?"

The legendary Brooklyn District Attorney is named Charles J. Hynes, but his friends call him Joe. I didn't think that Mr. Hynes and Mr. Bellarosa were friends, but I was certain they knew each other, professionally. I replied, "She works with the Feds on organized crime murders," which was not true—but how could I resist saying that?

Anthony thought about this awhile, then looked at me and said, "I never heard of her."

I replied, innocently, "Why would you?"

"I mean . . . yeah. Right." He observed, "There's not much money in that."

"It's not about the money."

He laughed. "Yeah? I guess if you already have money, then nothing is about the money."

"*You* have money. Is that how you think?"

He looked at me, then replied, "Sometimes. Sometimes it's about the power."

"Really?"

"Yeah, really." He lit another cigarette and looked out over his five acres and the adjoining properties, and said to me, "This all belonged to my father."

I didn't reply.

He continued, "You're going to get me compensated for this."

I was tired of this subject, so again, I didn't reply. Also, it was now time to tell him that Susan and I were back together, and that I was not going to work for him. I began by asking him, "Why did you tell your uncle that I was doing tax work for you?"

"Because you are."

"Anthony, we didn't shake hands on that."

"You having second thoughts?"

"I'm past second thoughts."

"You trying to shake me down for more money?"

"The money is fine—the job sucks."

"How do you know until you try?"

I ignored the question, and asked him again, "Why did you tell your uncle I was working for you?"

He replied, "He thinks you have some power. Some connections. And that's good for me."

"Why would he think that?"

"Because he's stupid."

"I see." The king hires a sorcerer who has no magical powers, but everyone thinks he does, which is the same thing as far as the king and his enemies are concerned. Maybe I *should* ask for more money. Or, at least a bulletproof vest in case Sally Da-da wanted me whacked for working for Anthony.

Anthony further informed me, "When you work for me, you don't need to have anything to do with my uncle."

"That's a disappointment."

Anthony got the sarcasm and chuckled.

I raised a new issue, known as a strawdog, and said, "With my daughter working for the Brooklyn DA, you might not want me working for you."

"You're not going to be involved with anything that ever has to do with what your daughter does."

I had this funny thought of Carolyn working on the case of *The State v. John Sutter.* "Sorry, Dad. It's business, not personal." I said to Anthony, "Maybe not, but it could be embarrassing to my daughter if the press ever made the connection between me, you, and her."

"Why?"

"Anthony, you may be shocked to hear this, but some people think you are involved in organized crime."

He didn't seem shocked to hear that, and neither did he seem annoyed that I'd brought it up. He said to me, "John, I have five legitimate companies that I own or run. One of them, Bell Security Service, is landing big contracts all over since 9/11. That's where the money comes from." He leaned toward me and said, "That's all you got to know, and that's all there is to know." He sat back and said, "I can't help what my family name is. And if some asshole in the newspaper says anything about me, I'll sue his ass off."

This sounded so convincing that I was ready to send a contribution to the Italian-American Anti-Defamation League. But before I did that, I should speak to Felix Mancuso about Anthony Bellarosa.

Anthony reached into his pocket and said, "You want a card? Here's my card."

I took it and saw it was a business card that said, "Bell Enterprises, Inc.," and there was an address in the Rego Park section of Queens, and a 718 area code phone number, which is also the borough of Queens.

Anthony said, "See? I'm a legitimate businessman."

"I see that. The proof is right here."

He didn't think that was too funny, but he said, "I wrote my cell and home number on the back." He added, "Keep that to yourself."

There was little more to say on this subject, and dinner still hadn't been announced, so I began, "Anthony . . ." I have some good news and some bad news. "I want you to know that—"

Kelly Ann ran out of the house and announced, "Dinner in ten minutes—" Then she saw the cigarette in the ashtray and shouted, "Daddy! You're smoking! You're going to die!"

Personally, I didn't think Daddy was going to live long enough to die from smoking, but I didn't share that with Kelly Ann.

Anthony's response to being busted was to throw me under the bus by saying, "Mr. Sutter smokes, sweetheart. That's not Daddy's cigarette. Right, John?"

"Right." I reached over and took the cigarette, but Kelly Ann was no dummy and shouted, "Liar, liar! Pants on fire!" Then she turned and ran into the house, and I could hear her shouting, "Mommy! Daddy is smoking!"

Anthony took the cigarette from me, drew on it, then snuffed it out and explained, "Those fucking teachers. They tell them that drugs, alcohol, and smoking are the same thing. They're fucking up the kids' heads."

I didn't respond, but I did think about poor Anthony, surrounded by controlling, ball-busting females. His mother, his aunt, his wife, his daughter, and maybe even his mistress. It was a wonder he hadn't turned gay. More importantly, he seemed to have little control over his domestic life, unlike his father who was the undisputed *padrone* of Alhambra. Plus, Anthony didn't have the *testicoli* to tell his six-year-old daughter to *sta' zitto*. Well, that's my observation, and about half of my Italian. My other thought was that maybe he *was* a lightweight, and I shouldn't worry too much about Susan.

I stood and said, "I'd like to use your phone."

"Sure." Anthony walked me toward another set of double doors at the far end of the house and advised me, "You got to get a cell phone."

"I'll leave a quarter next to the phone."

"You've been gone too long. Leave a buck." He opened one of the doors and said, "That's my den. You can find your way to the dining room."

I entered the dark, air-conditioned room, and he closed the door behind me.

Anthony's den was very masculine—mahogany, brass, leather, a wet bar, and a big television—and I guessed he took refuge in here whenever the estrogen levels got too high in the rest of the house.

The walls were lined with bookshelves, and I spotted his father's collection of books from La Salle Military Academy. Frank, as I said, was a big fan of Machiavelli, but he also read St. Augustine and St. Ambrose so he could argue theology with priests. I wondered where he was now, and whom he was arguing with.

Anthony, on the other hand, favored the pagans, and I saw shelves lined with books about the Roman Empire, and I knew that Anthony wasn't the first Mafia don to be impressed with how the Romans ran things, and how they settled their problems by whacking entire nations. Unfortunately, people like Anthony become educated beyond their intelligence, and they become more dangerous than, say, Uncle Sal.

Anyway, I found the phone on his desk and dialed Elizabeth's cell phone. As the phone rang, I had two thoughts: One was that there was nothing in or on this desk that Anthony wouldn't want me, his wife, or the FBI to see; the other was that his phone was probably tapped by one or more law enforcement agencies, or maybe even by Anthony's business competitors, and perhaps by Anthony himself so he could check up on Megan. But now, with cell phones, the taps on landline phones would not be so interesting, so maybe no one was bothering with a phone tap. Nevertheless, I'd watch what I said.

Elizabeth's voice mail informed me that she couldn't take the call and invited me to leave a message at the beep. I said, "Elizabeth, this is John. Sorry I won't be able to meet you at seven." I hesitated, then said, "Susan and I are meeting." I added, "Hope your mother is resting comfortably. I'll speak to you tomorrow."

I hung up and dialed Susan's cell phone. She answered, and I said, "Hi, it's me."

"John, I'm glad you called. How is it going?"

"All right—"

"Did you tell him—?"

"Not yet, and I can't speak freely."

She probably thought that I was in earshot of Anthony, and not thinking about a phone tap. She said, "Well, let me tell you what's happening. The phone rang in the gatehouse while I was packing your things, and I answered it."

"All right . . ." Samantha? Elizabeth? Iranian terrorists?

Susan continued, "It was Elizabeth, looking for you."

"Right. I used to live there."

"She said that her mother has taken a turn for the worse and has slipped into a coma."

"I'm sorry to hear that, but we knew—"

"And she won't be able to meet you at seven."

"Oh . . . right. She wanted to take me to dinner to thank me—"

"She told me that. And I took the opportunity to tell her that you and I were back together."

"Great. She was hoping we'd get back together."

"That's not the impression I had from our brief conversation. She seemed surprised."

"Really? Well, I'm surprised, too. All right, let me get Anthony aside—"

"John, just tell him you need to leave *now*. I told Elizabeth we'd meet her at Fair Haven." She added, "You can phone him later and tell him."

"Susan, I need to do this now. In person. I'll be there in about fifteen minutes."

"All right. Good luck. I love you."

"Me, too." I hung up and looked around the den again. Above the fireplace was a reproduction of Rubens' *Rape of the Sabine Women*, which I thought said more about Anthony Bellarosa's head than about his taste in art.

I was about to leave, but then I noticed, sitting on an easel, a familiar painting. It was, in fact, Susan's oil painting of the palm court of Alhambra in ruins. I'd seen this painting for the first and last time in the restored palm court of Alhambra with Frank Bellarosa's body lying a few feet away, and the artist herself being led off in handcuffs.

My judgment of the painting then was that it was one of her best. And I also recalled, looking at it now, that I'd made some sort of analogy between Susan's representation of ruin and decay and her state of mind. Even today, I'm not sure if I wasn't overanalyzing this. But I do remember that I put my fist through the canvas and sent it and the easel flying across the palm court.

I moved closer to the painting, and whoever had restored it had done a perfect job; it would be nice if life restoration was as perfect.

More to the point, I wondered who had it restored, and why, and also why it was here in Anthony Bellarosa's den. I could see Susan's clear signature in the right-hand corner, so Anthony knew who painted it.

I could think about this for a long time, and I could come up with any number of valid and invalid theories about why this painting was here; also, I could just ask him why. But that would only confuse what was simple; it was time to tell Anthony I wasn't working for him, and tell him to stay away from my once and future wife.

When Caesar crossed the Rubicon, he knew there was no going back, so with that in mind, I took a letter opener from Anthony's desk, went to the painting, and slashed the canvas until it was in shreds. Then I left the den and walked down a long corridor toward the sounds of dinner being served.

CHAPTER THIRTY-THREE

The long dining room table was set at one end for six people, and on the table were platters of mixed antipasto, a loaf of Italian bread, and a bottle of red wine.

Anthony was at the head of the table, Megan to his right, and his mother to his left. The kids sat together next to their mother, and Anna was helping herself to salami and cheese. She said to me, "Sit. Here. Next to me."

I announced, "I apologize, but I need to go."

Anna stopped serving herself and asked, "Go? Go where?"

I explained to everyone, "Ethel Allard, the lady who lives in the gatehouse, is in hospice, and she's slipped into a coma."

Anthony said, "That's too bad."

I continued, "I do apologize, but I need to be there in case"—I glanced at the children—"in case she passes tonight."

Anna made the sign of the cross, but no one else did, though I considered it briefly.

Young Frank asked, "What's a coma?"

Anthony was standing now, and he said to me, "Sure. No problem. We'll do this again."

Megan, too, stood, and said, "Let us know what happens."

Kelly Ann inquired, of no one in particular, "What happens when you slip on a coma?"

Anna offered, "Let me pack you some food."

"That's very nice of you, but I need to hurry." I looked at Anthony and nodded toward the door. He said, "I'll walk you out."

I gave Anna a quick hug, wished everyone a good dinner, and followed Anthony into the foyer.

He said to me, "When you know how that's going, let me know. And when Gotti goes, you'll know on the news, so after all this is done, we'll get together."

I said to him, "Let's step outside."

He looked at me, then glanced back toward the dining room and shouted, "Go ahead and start," then he opened the door and we stepped outside and stood under the portico. He took the opportunity to light a cigarette and asked me, "What's up?"

I said to him, "Susan and I have decided to get back together."

"Huh?"

"Susan. My ex-wife. We are getting back together."

He thought about that for a second, then said, "And you're telling me this *now*?"

"When did you want to know?"

"Yesterday."

"I didn't know yesterday. And what difference does it make to you?"

He answered indirectly. "You know, I never understood how a guy could take back a wife who cheated on him. I don't know about a guy like that."

I would have suggested that he go fuck himself, but that would have ended the conversation, and I wasn't finished. But I did say, "I hope you never have to find out what you'd do."

That annoyed him, and he told me, "Hey, I *know* what *I'd* do, but you can do what the hell you want."

"Thank you. I have."

"I thought you were a smart guy, John. A guy who had some self-respect."

I wasn't going to let him bait me, and I didn't need to respond, but I said, "That is none of your business."

He replied, "I think it is. I think maybe this changes things between us."

"There was never anything between us."

"You're full of shit. We had a deal, and you know it."

"We didn't, but if you think we did, the deal is off."

"Yeah. If you go back to her, the deal is definitely off. But . . . if you change your mind about her, then we can talk."

"I won't change my mind about her, but you should."

"What does that mean?"

"You know what I mean."

"Oh, yeah. You still on that? Come on, John. I told you, if that was a problem, it would have been settled long ago. Don't get yourself worked up. Go marry her. Have a happy life."

He knew not to say anything that I could take to the police, and in fact, he reassured me by saying, "Women, children, and retards get a pass. Understand?" He explained, "There are rules."

I reminded him, "Someone tried to kill your father right in front of your mother, who could also have been hurt or killed. Did someone forget the rules?"

He looked at me a long time, then said, "That's none of your business."

"Excuse me, Anthony. I was standing two feet from your father when the shotgun pellets went past my face. That's when it became my business."

He thought about that, then said, "It's still none of your business."

"All right. Don't let me keep you from your dinner. Thank you for your hospitality. You have a nice family. I especially like your uncle Sal. And just so there's no misunderstanding concerning Susan Sutter, I'm informing you now, as her attorney, that I'm going to have Susan swear out a complaint with the police, and go on record as being concerned about her safety regarding your intentions toward her. So, if anything should happen to her, the police will know who to talk to. Capisce?"

I expected him to go totally nuts, but he just stood there, staring past me. So I said, "Good day," and I turned and started walking across his lawn.

"John."

I turned, half expecting to see a gun, but instead he walked toward me, stopped, and in a conciliatory tone of voice said, "Hey, John, you don't have to go complaining to the cops. We're men. We can talk."

"We've talked."

"I thought you understood what I was saying. About what you did for my father. I told you that night I stopped by, I owed you a favor for saving his life. So you mentioned something about your wife. Remember? I wasn't sure what you wanted, but now I understand. There was never a problem there anyway. But if you think there is, and that's the favor you want, then you got it." He added, "I swear this on my father's grave."

That should have been the end of it, but only if I trusted him, and I definitely did not. Given the choice between swearing out a complaint with the police and Anthony Bellarosa's word of honor, I'd put my money and my life and Susan's on the sworn complaint against Anthony. And the shotgun.

Anthony waited for a reply, but when none was forthcoming, he said, "No hard feelings. We go our separate ways, and you stop worrying about whatever you're worried about. We're all even now on favors."

I didn't want Anthony Bellarosa to think he was doing me any favors, even if we both knew he was lying, so I informed him, "Your father already repaid me for saving his life. So you don't owe me anything."

This seemed to surprise him, and he said, "Yeah? He paid you back for saving his life? Good. But *I'll* pay you back again for that."

"I do *not* want any favors from you."

"Yeah?" He was clearly getting angry and impatient with me for not accepting his good wishes for a happy, worry-free life, and his promise not to kill Susan. So he said, "You're an asshole. Get the fuck out of here."

That really pissed me off, so I decided that Anthony now needed to know how his father repaid the favor. I moved closer to him, and we were barely two feet apart.

"Yeah? *What?*"

"Your father, Anthony, was in love with my wife, and she was in love with him, and they were ready to run off together, and leave you, your brothers, and your mother—"

"What the *fuck* are you talking about?"

"But he owed me his life, so—"

"He was *fucking* her. That's all he was doing. Fucking your wife for sport."

"So I asked him to tell her it was over, and that he never loved her—"

"You're full of shit."

"And he did that for me, and unfortunately Susan, who was in love with him, snapped, and—"

"Get the hell out of here."

"Anthony, that's *why* she killed him. She loved him and he loved her, and he broke his promise to take her with him to Italy under the Witness Protection Program."

"How the fuck do you know—?"

"He was a government witness, Anthony, and you know that as well as I do. Look it up online. It's all there." He didn't respond to that, so I concluded, "You asked me for the truth about your father, and I just gave it to you."

He practically put his nose in my face and spoke in a slow, deliberate tone. "None of that changes what your wife did. Just so you know."

I put my hand on his chest and pushed him back, ready for any move he might make, but he just stood there, staring at me. I said to him, "That sounds like a threat. Is that a threat?"

He should have backed off on that, but I'd pressed the right buttons, and he said, "Take it any way you want."

"I take it as a threat. And so will the police."

He didn't reply, and I turned my back on him and walked toward my car.

He called out to me, "You think guys like you don't have to worry about guys like me. Well, Counselor, you're wrong about that."

I was glad he understood the concept, but I wasn't sure he was smart enough or cool enough, like his father, to know when to shut his mouth, take a hit, and move on. Or since he'd threatened Susan in front of me, then threatened me, he might be thinking he needed to get rid of both of us.

I got in my car, and as I pulled away from his house, I saw he was still standing on the lawn watching me.

I headed out of Alhambra Estates.

Now, I thought, I didn't have to protect Susan from afar; we were together, and Anthony and I were also where we belonged: nose to nose with everything out in the open.

I stopped the car where the blacktop ended, and I looked at where Alhambra had stood, remembering the library where Frank Bellarosa and I had sat with cigars and grappa, talking about Machiavelli and about the murder charge he was facing. And before I knew it, I was part of the family. Well, history did not repeat itself this time, but history was still driving the bus.

The last time I saw Bellarosa, as I said, he was lying half-naked and dead on the floor of the palm court, beneath the mezzanine outside his bedroom. I looked to where I thought the palm court had been, where a long blacktop driveway now led to the garage of a small villa, and I could actually picture him lying there.

I took a last look around me, knowing I'd probably never again be on the grounds of Alhambra, then I continued on, past the guard booth, and turned right on Grace Lane for the quarter-mile drive back to the guest cottage of Stanhope Hall.

CHAPTER THIRTY-FOUR

I drove through the open gates of Stanhope Hall, past the gatehouse, and up the tree-lined drive to the guest cottage, where I parked next to Susan's Lexus.

I got out of the car and went to the front door. Susan never used to lock doors, and still didn't, so I opened the door, went into the foyer, and as I used to do, I called out, "Sweetheart, I'm home!"

No reply, so I went into the kitchen, and I could see her on the back patio, sitting in a chaise lounge, reading a magazine.

I opened the door, and she stood quickly, hurried toward me, and wrapped her arms around me, saying, "Oh, I'm so glad you're home." She gave me a kiss and asked, "Did you tell him?"

"I did."

"And?"

"Well, as I expected, he didn't take the news of our reunion very well."

"Why did you even *tell* him that? That is none of his business. All you had to tell him was that you were not going to work for him."

"Right. Normally I wouldn't announce my engagement to a Mafia don, but I wanted him to know we were together, and that you were not alone."

She thought about that, then replied, "All right . . . but I still think you're overreacting."

She wouldn't think that if she'd stood with me and Anthony Bellarosa on his front lawn, but I didn't want to alarm her, so I said, "I don't think there will be any problem . . . but tomorrow, you and I will go to the local precinct and you need to swear out a complaint against Anthony Bellarosa, so that—"

"John, I don't need to do that." She added, "That might actually make him—"

"Susan. We will do this my way, and I don't want any arguments. I want him to know that the police are aware of the situation. Understand?"

She looked at me, and despite my matter-of-fact tone, I could tell that she knew that I was concerned. She said, "All right." Then she changed the subject and asked me, "Did you see Anna?"

"I did."

"How was she? Friendly?"

"She was." But did not send her regards to you.

Susan asked, "How is his wife?"

"She seemed nice enough."

I recalled, from long ago, that whenever I went someplace without Susan, I got a cross-examination that rivaled anything I'd ever done with a witness. I really needed a drink, so I announced, "I think it's cocktail time."

"What did his wife look like?"

"Oh . . . she was actually pretty." I added, "But not very refined."

"Who else was there?"

"Salvatore D'Alessio. Uncle Sal. And his wife, Marie." I asked, "Did you ever meet them?"

"No. How would I . . . ?" Then, apparently recalling that she'd been a frequent visitor at Alhambra, she thought for a moment about things she'd been trying to forget for ten years, and replied, "Actually, yes. I did meet them. When I was at the house." She explained, "I was painting in the palm court." She wanted to end it there, but sensing she should share the entire memory with me, she continued, "They stopped by, and Anna introduced them, but we didn't speak."

She concluded, "He was a frightening-looking man."

"Still is."

Susan said, "I'll get you a drink. What would you like?"

"A pink squirrel."

"How do I make that?"

"You pour four ounces of Scotch in a glass and add ice cubes."

"All right . . . I'll be right back."

She went inside, and I gave some thought to Susan meeting Salvatore D'Alessio at Alhambra, and I wondered if it ever occurred to her that she had entered a world in which she had no control, and where she was not Lady Stanhope. In fact, she was nothing more than the mistress of the don, and that didn't bestow much status. It was incredible if you thought about it—and I had—that Susan Stanhope, who'd led such a sheltered and privileged life, and who was so haughty, had debased herself by becoming the sex toy of a powerful but crude man. I mean, history is full of noble ladies who've done this—the wife of a Roman emperor became a prostitute by night—and I suppose a clinical psychologist would have a field day with this interesting dichotomy. Maybe Susan was trying to pay back Mommy and Daddy. Maybe I forgot to compliment her on a new dress. Or, most likely, she herself had no idea why she took a criminal as a lover. The mind, as they say, is the most powerful aphrodisiac, and no one knows how it works. In any case, I was fairly sure that Susan had gotten this out of her system. Been there, done that.

Susan returned with a tray on which was a glass of white wine and my Scotch. She set the tray on the table, we raised our glasses, clinked, and she said, "To us."

I added, "Together, forever."

I sipped my Scotch, and Susan informed me, "That's your Scotch. I've had it since . . . I moved."

I guess none of her gentlemen friends or her late husband drank Dewar's. Or she was telling me a little white lie to make me feel that the last ten years were just a small pile of crap on the highway to a lifetime of happiness. Nonetheless, I said, "It's improved with age." I was going to add, "and so have you," but with women, you need to be careful with those sorts of compliments.

She asked me, "How does that pink squirrel differ from a Scotch on the rocks?"

"Mostly, it's the spelling."

She smiled and said, "It's going to take me a while to get used to your infantile humor again."

"Infantile? I'll have you know—"

She planted a kiss on my lips and said, "God, I missed you. I missed everything about you."

"Me, too."

So we held hands and stood there, looking out at the sunny garden, sipping our drinks. After a minute or so, she asked me, "How was their house?"

"Not too bad, but I didn't stop at the sales office." I wanted to return to a previous subject, so I asked her, "Did you know that Salvatore D'Alessio was the prime suspect behind what happened at Giulio's?"

She glanced at me and replied, "No. You mean . . . his own brother-in-law?"

"That's right. You never heard that?"

"Where would I hear that?"

Well, from the intended murder victim, your lover, for one. But I replied, "The newspapers."

She didn't respond for a few seconds, then said, "I didn't follow it in the news."

"That's right." In fact, I seem to recall that she hadn't even followed the bigger story, a few weeks later, about Susan Stanhope Sutter killing Frank Bellarosa—and that wasn't because she couldn't bear to read about it; that was more about Susan's deeply ingrained lack of interest in, and disdain for, the news in general. Her motto had been the famous observation that if you've read about one train wreck, you've read about them all. Of course, if you were in the train wreck, you might find it interesting to read about it. In any case, coupled with her lack of interest in the news was her upbringing in a social class that still believed that the only time a woman's name should appear in the newspapers was when she was born, when she married, and when she died. So that didn't leave much room for stories about killing your lover. In any case, I believed her when she said she had no knowledge that Salvatore D'Alessio had been the man who ruined our evening in Little Italy. In fact, I'd never mentioned it to her myself.

She asked me, "Why did you bring that up?"

I replied, "Because I think that . . . Anthony Bellarosa may harbor a grudge against his uncle. Also, his uncle may want to finish with Anthony what he started at Giulio's with Frank."

She didn't reply for a long time, then pointed out, "But they . . . they were having dinner together."

"Well, the D'Alessios didn't stay for dinner, but I'm sure they have all dined together." I explained, using Frank Bellarosa's own words on this same subject, "One's got nothing to do with the other."

"Well, of course, it does, John. If that man tried to kill—"

"Susan, don't even *try* to understand." I thought about using an example of me taking out a contract on her father, but that was more of a fantasy than a good analogy, so I said, "The point is, I think this . . . vendetta has been on hold for ten years, and it may come to a head soon. So Anthony may be very busy for a while, trying to stay alive, and at the same time probably making plans to see that his uncle doesn't." Susan didn't respond, so I concluded, "At least that's what I think."

She stared off into the rose garden, then finally said, "That's unbelievable."

"I just wanted to make you aware of what may happen." And wake you up a little. "But this only concerns us to the extent that Anthony may not be living next door for long." Or living at all. "So, the subject is closed." I asked her, "Any word about Ethel?"

"No . . . John, what exactly did you say to Anthony, and what did he say to you?"

"I'll tell you about it over dinner."

"All right . . ."

"What's for dinner?"

She informed me, "I've made my specialty. Reservations."

"Great. What time?"

"Seven. Did I tell you I canceled your seven o'clock dinner with Elizabeth?"

"Yes, and I already left her a message about that."

"Well, she hadn't gotten it when I spoke to her."

"Right. You spoke to her first. So where are we going?"

"I thought you would like to have dinner at Seawanhaka." She added, "For old time's sake."

I thought about my former yacht club, and to be truthful, I had mixed emotions about seeing it again. On the one hand, there were good memories attached to the club—parties, weddings, the annual Fourth of July barbecue on the lawn overlooking Oyster Bay Harbor, and also the fact that this was where Susan and I had first met at the Guest wedding. Aside from that, my best memories were of the great sailing in my thirty-six-foot Morgan, the original *Paumanok*, which I'd loved so much that I'd scuttled her in the bay rather than let the IRS seize her for back taxes. There were no bad memories attached to my yacht club, other than that final sail on the *Paumanok*. But I didn't know if I wanted to go back there; I wanted to leave it as it was.

"John? Is that all right?"

"Maybe some other time."

"Now is the time. I want to remember this day for the rest of our lives, and I want it to end on the back porch with the sun going down and a drink in our hands."

"All right . . . but if anyone says to me, 'John, I'm surprised to see you here after you ruined your life and ran off,' I'm going to punch him."

Susan laughed and said, "If anyone says that, we'll both beat him up."

"Deal." I said, "Well, I need to freshen up."

"I've unpacked all your things, and I've separated your laundry for the cleaning lady. You need to go to the dry cleaner tomorrow." She then pointed out, "You've hardly brought enough to wear."

"Thank you."

"I'll have Sophie—that's my cleaning lady, she's Polish, but speaks good English—I'll have her press your black suit." She added, unnecessarily, "You'll need it soon."

"Thank you." I was relieved to discover that Susan hadn't learned to wash or iron in the last ten years; that would have destroyed my image of her.

She reminded me, "But first, we need to stop at Fair Haven."

"All right."

"I would invite Elizabeth to join us for dinner—I know she's free because I canceled her dinner date—but I'm sure she wants to maintain her vigil at her mother's bedside, and also this is our first night together."

"Yes, of course."

"I did ask her, quite bluntly, if anything happened between you two last night."

"And now you know that nothing happened. I *am* disappointed that you didn't believe me, and I'm frankly surprised that you'd ask her that question, but—"

"I didn't ask her, John."

"Oh . . ."

"I can't believe you'd even *think* I would ask her."

"What do I know?" Meaning, about women.

Susan said to me, "But she did offer to explain her overnight stay, and I told her you'd already addressed that."

"Good. So that's settled. Again." I glanced at my watch and said, "I won't be long."

"I'll go up with you."

We went back inside, climbed the stairs, and entered our bedroom suite. We brushed our teeth at the same sink, as we'd done so many times, and Susan touched up her makeup while I washed Casa Bellarosa off my hands and face.

I found a reasonably clean shirt hanging in my old closet, and Susan slipped on a nice white summer dress that looked good against her tan.

I used to think that Susan took too much time with her preparations, but after ten years of waiting for other women, I realized that Susan was actually fast. She *is* a natural beauty, and she doesn't spend forever in front of the mirror or in her closet. It occurred to me that this time around, I'd appreciate her more. At least for the first few weeks.

She actually finished first and asked, "Ready?"

"I can't find my comb."

"It's in your jacket, where it always is."

I checked and, sure enough, it was there.

So we went downstairs, left the house, and she gave me a set of keys, saying, "These are yours."

"Thank you."

I locked the front door, and she noticed, but didn't comment.

We used her Lexus, and I drove. As we passed the gatehouse, Susan said to me, "I called Soheila, as a courtesy, and told her you'd moved in with me."

"Did she say you were a fallen woman?"

"No, John. She wished me luck."

"That's nice." I reminded her, "I need to move back into the gatehouse when your parents arrive."

"No. If they don't like the arrangement, *they* can find other accommodations."

I replied, with total insincerity, "I don't want to cause trouble between you and your parents."

She had no response to that, but said, "I e-mailed my parents and the children and told them that Ethel has slipped into a coma."

"All right."

I turned onto Grace Lane and headed toward Fair Haven Hospice House.

Susan hit the CD button and Bobby Darin was singing "Beyond the Sea."

We rode in silence, listening to the music.

It was only eleven days until the summer solstice, the longest day of the year, and the sun was still high on the horizon, and the pleasant landscape was bathed in that special late afternoon summer sunlight, and a nice land breeze blew out to the Sound.

This had been the best of days, and the worst of days. But on balance, it was more good than bad. Unless, of course, you were Ethel Allard, or even Anthony Bellarosa, for that matter. But for Susan and me, it had been a very good day.

CHAPTER THIRTY-FIVE

Susan called ahead to Elizabeth's cell phone, so we knew that Ethel's condition hadn't changed, and when we arrived at Fair Haven, Elizabeth met us in the lobby. She was wearing a nice blue linen outfit, and she may have come here in what she'd worn to church after getting the call about her mother.

We exchanged hugs and kisses, and Susan and I expressed our sorrow at this turn of events. Elizabeth appeared composed and somewhat philosophical about her mother's imminent demise, which, she informed us, Dr. Watral said would likely come within forty-eight hours.

Elizabeth, I thought, seemed friendlier to Susan than to me, and in fact, she barely spoke to me. Well, I understood that; we'd shared some pleasant and even intimate time together, and we were both lonely souls who thought maybe this was the start of something. And then Fate stepped in, as it does, and realigned the triangle.

Elizabeth asked us, "Would you like to see her?"

Susan replied, "Of course."

So we took the elevator up to Ethel's room, where a nurse sat in a chair in the corner, reading a romance novel. Ethel was connected to a few more tubes than the last time I'd seen her, but she seemed peaceful.

The window blinds were pulled this time, and the room was dark, except for the nurse's reading lamp and the indirect cove lighting over Ethel's bed.

Elizabeth said to us, "The doctor assures me she isn't feeling any pain, and she does look so peaceful."

Susan moved to Ethel's bedside, took her hand, and leaned close to her face. She whispered, "God bless you, Ethel, and a safe journey home." She kissed Ethel on the cheek and said, "Thank you for the hot chocolate and cookies."

I took a deep breath, moved to Ethel's bed, took her hand, and said to her, "Tell George I said hello when you see him." And Augustus, too. I let her know, "Susan and I are together again." I knew she was in a deep coma, but I thought I felt her squeeze my hand. I kissed her and said, "Goodbye."

Well, there was little more to say after that, so the three of us went into the hallway and Elizabeth said to us, "Thank you for stopping by."

Susan, feeling some guilt perhaps, or knowing that Elizabeth would not leave her mother's bedside, offered, "We're going to dinner at Seawanhaka. Why don't you join us?"

Elizabeth smiled and replied, "That's very kind of you, but I need to stay here." She explained, "I've called a few people, who said they would come by." She looked at me and let me know, "Your mother is coming soon, if you'd like to wait for her."

I didn't, so I replied, "I would, but my mother often loses track of time." I remembered to say, "Please tell her I'm sorry I missed her."

I thought Susan was going to give me an argument, but she didn't.

I didn't want to stay here any longer and run into Harriet, or the Reverend Hunnings, or anyone else I might not want to see, but I thought I should let Elizabeth know, "I've moved out of the gatehouse."

She nodded and said, "I know."

"So, you have full access to the house, and you can make arrangements to remove the furniture and personal items." I added, "I'll speak to Nasim about a reasonable amount of time to vacate the premises."

She nodded again, looked at me, and said, "Thank you. And thank you also, John, for all you've done."

We made brief eye contact, I nodded and replied, "I'll handle whatever else needs to be done, and if you need anything, call me."

Susan added, "Call my cell phone or the house, and I'll get the message to John. And please let us know when Ethel passes."

"I will." Then she looked at us and said, "I'm very happy for you both."

I was sure she was being as sincere as Susan had been in inviting her to dinner.

Anyway, we all hugged and kissed again, and Elizabeth went back in the room to continue her deathbed vigil, and Susan and I went down to the lobby.

On our way out to the parking lot, Susan asked me, "Are you sure you don't want to wait for your mother?"

I picked up the pace and replied, "We'd be here until sunrise." I added, "I need a drink."

"All right . . . but, I want you to call her and tell her we're together again."

I assured her, "I will, but then she'll call you to try to talk you out of it."

"John—"

I interrupted, "That was nice of you to invite Elizabeth to dinner."

"I do like her."

She wouldn't have liked her if she'd said yes. Nevertheless, it was a nice gesture, and Susan was always kind to her friends.

Susan commented, "Elizabeth is one of the last of the old crowd."

I nodded and thought about all the people we'd known who'd died, and those who'd moved away, and I replied, "Indeed, she is."

Susan added, "There are not too many left, as I'm finding out."

"Well, I'm back, and you're back. We'll make new friends in the subdivisions."

"I think not."

We held hands as we walked to the car. Fortune was with me again because we got to the car before I ran into anyone I didn't want to see. But I knew I'd see them all at Ethel's funeral. Thinking back, one of the people I had not been looking forward to seeing at the funeral was Susan. And now . . . well, it's true—life is just one surprise after another. Some pleasant, and some not so pleasant.

* * *

We drove to Centre Island, which is actually a peninsula, but if you live in a ten- or twenty-million-dollar mansion on Oyster Bay or the Sound, you can call it whatever you want.

We drove into the parking field in front of the Seawanhaka Corinthian Yacht Club, and as I expected, the clubhouse looked the same as the last time I'd seen it, and pretty much the same as when it was built in 1892. William Swan, a close friend of Teddy Roosevelt, had been one of the founders of the club and its first commodore, and if he sailed into the harbor today, he'd easily recognize the big, three-story, gabled and shingled clubhouse, with white trim and black shutters. And unless things had changed in my absence, he'd feel right at home inside, as well. The dress code, of course, had changed, but the gentlemen still wore jackets, though ties were not always required, and as for the ladies, they dressed conservatively, but the old boys would still be shocked at the amount of skin showing.

The club was actually founded in 1871, making it one of the oldest Corinthian yacht clubs in America—Corinthian meaning that the yacht owners sailed and raced their own boats, without professional seamen, and this is in the spirit of the ancient Greek Corinthians, who apparently were the first people who competed in amateur racing for fun. The most sailing fun I've ever had, incidentally, was watching William and Charlotte puke their guts out aboard the *Paumanok* during a gale on the Sound. I remember that day fondly.

Susan asked, "What is making you smile?"

"You, darling."

I parked in the gravel field and noted a lot of vehicles—mostly SUVs—on this pleasant Sunday evening, and Susan informed me, "Tonight is Salty Dog."

Salty Dog is a barbecue on the lawn, and though I'm not sure where the name comes from, I never ate the spareribs, just to play it safe.

She added, "But I've made our reservation for the dining room, so we can be alone."

"Good." As we walked toward the clubhouse, I inquired, "Do we own a yacht?"

She smiled and replied, "No. I just wanted to rejoin the club. For social reasons."

That may have meant meeting people, sometimes known as men. I reminded her, "In the good old days, single women were not admitted as members."

"Well, thank God those days are over. What would you do without us?"

"I can't even imagine."

As we approached the clubhouse, I had second thoughts about coming here. I mean, I'd been asked, nicely, to leave for unspecified reasons, which may have included sinking my own boat, and being publicly identified on TV as a Mafia lawyer, not to mention my wife shooting and killing my Mafia client who was also her lover. On the other hand, Susan had been readmitted, and she had no hesitation about coming here. So maybe everyone had forgotten about all of that unpleasantness. What, then, was I concerned about?

"Dear Ms. Post, Well, I'm back with my ex-wife—the one who killed her Mafia lover—and she wants to take me to dinner at our former yacht club. Considering that we were kicked out for bad behavior (she committed adultery and murder, and I became a mob lawyer, and also sunk my yacht so the government couldn't seize it for back taxes), do you think the club members will accept us? (Signed) Still Confused on Long Island."

"Dear . . . Whatever, I assume one or both of you have been reinstated as members, so if you dress and act appropriately, and your dues and charges are paid up, the other members will be delighted to have such interesting people to speak to. Two caveats: One, do not initiate conversations about the murder, adultery, or being a mob lawyer or sinking the boat; wait for others to bring it up. Two, try to avoid repeating any of the criminal and socially unacceptable acts that got you blacklisted in the first place. Good luck. (Signed) Emily Post. P.S. You two have a set of balls."

Susan may have sensed my hesitation because she took my hand and said, "I've been here twice since I've been back, and I haven't had a problem." She reminded me, "The membership committee had no problem here, or at The Creek."

I remarked, "Standards have certainly slipped." In fact, maybe now I could get Frank Bellarosa into The Creek—if he wasn't dead.

We entered the clubhouse, turned right into the bar room as we'd done so many times, and went up to the bar.

I was not surprised to see that nothing had changed, including the bartender, a cheerful bald-headed gent named Bennett, who said to Susan, "Good evening, Mrs. Sutter." He looked at me and, without missing a beat, said, "Good evening, Mr. Sutter."

"Hello, Bennett." We both hesitated for a second, then reached out our hands, and he said, "It's good to see you again."

"Same here. Good to be back."

He inquired, "Dark and stormy?"

"Please."

He moved off to make two dark and stormies, which I actually don't like, but it's the club drink, and . . . well, why upset the universe?

I put my back to the bar and looked around. I recognized an older couple at one of the tables and noted some young couples who seemed to fit in well, though not all the men were wearing blue blazers and tan pants. Also, I couldn't imagine that some of them knew port from starboard, but, I recalled, that was me once.

Susan asked me, "How does it feel?"

"Good."

Bennett put the drinks on the bar, and Susan signed the chit.

I surveyed the room again, this time noting the Race Committee pewter mugs lined up in a niche on the wall, one of which had my name engraved on it. Another wall was covered with half-hull models, and there were old pictures on the other walls of people who were long dead and forgotten, but were immortalized here until the end of time, or at least until the female members got their way and redecorated.

Susan handed me my drink, we touched glasses, and she said, "Welcome back."

The dark and stormy wasn't too bad if you like dark rum and ginger beer in the same glass, which I don't.

We took our drinks and moved into the big main room, which hadn't changed too much and still looked very nautical with all the club members' private flags hanging from the ceiling molding surrounding the room, and the cabinet full of racing trophies, a few of which I'd won.

There were a number of people sitting or standing in the main room having cocktails, and a few of them looked at us and did double takes, and some waved and we returned the greeting, though none got up from their seats to chat. I guessed they were surprised to see me, and to see Susan and me together, and no one wanted to be the first to come over and ask, "So, what is *this* all about?" I knew that after we'd passed through the room, tongues would wag, and possibly someone would be deputized to approach the formerly married Sutters and get the scoop.

In fact, before we got to the double doors that went out to the porch, a woman appeared in front of us, and it took me a second to recognize Mrs. Althea Gwynn, one of the grand dames of the old order, who, as I recalled, fancied herself the arbiter of good manners and acceptable behavior. Her husband, Dwight, I also recalled, was a decent man, who'd either suffered a stroke or was faking it so he didn't have to speak to her.

Anyway, Mrs. Gwynn smiled tightly at me and Susan, and said to me, "I had heard that you were back, John."

"I am."

"How wonderful. And where are you living?"

"At home."

"I see . . ."

Susan informed her, "John and I are back together."

"That's wonderful. I'm so happy for you both."

I really didn't think so, but I replied, "Thank you."

Mrs. Gwynn looked at me and said, "The last time I saw you, John—it has to be ten years now—you and Susan were dining at The Creek with . . . another couple who I believe were new to the area."

"Oh, yes, I remember that. I believe that was Mr. Frank Bellarosa and his wife, Anna, formerly of Brooklyn."

Mrs. Gwynn seemed a little surprised that I'd be so blunt—I was supposed to just say, "Has it been that long?"

Susan said to me, "It *was* Frank and Anna, darling. I remember that."

I replied to Susan, "That's right. We were welcoming them to the neighborhood." I added, "But they didn't stay long."

Mrs. Gwynn didn't know quite what to say, so she said, "Excuse me," and walked off.

Susan put her arm through mine, and we continued through the room. She said to me, "That was very nice of Althea to greet us."

"She's a wonderful woman," I agreed, "to get up off her fat ass to pry."

"Now, now, John. She was just remarking that it's been ten years since she's seen you."

"Right. We were dining at The Creek with . . . who was that?"

"The *Bellarosas*, darling. Formerly of Brooklyn."

We both laughed.

Well, it *was* a little funny, and Mrs. Gwynn was one of a dying breed, and not as important as she thought she was. But in her world, she'd done what she was put on this earth to do. And I was in awe of her steadfast snootiness and snobbery, especially since Susan was a Stanhope.

Anyway, Susan changed the subject and said, "I have your flag, and when we buy a boat, we'll have it rehung."

I wondered what had become of my boat flag; I know what became of my boat, so I said, "I'm not sure of my status here."

She thought about that and replied, "You're allowed to sink one boat every ten years."

I smiled, but wondered how many lovers you were allowed to kill before you were banished forever. I gave myself a mental slap on the face for that.

Susan added, "When we're married, you'll be a member, and I will buy us a nice forty-footer that we'll take down to the Caribbean for our honeymoon."

I commented, "This deal is getting much better," but I wondered if she understood that her six-figure-a-year allowance was at serious risk as a result of that honeymoon.

We walked out to the long, wrap-around covered porch, found two chairs, and sat facing the bay.

It was just 7:00 P.M., and the sun was sinking over the land to the southwest. Out on the lawn, which swept down to the water, the American flag billowed in a soft southerly breeze atop a tall flagpole, and the barbecue was in full swing. I noticed a lot of young couples and kids—more than I remembered in the past. The McMansion People.

Susan and I, as children and teenagers, came here with our parents, who were members, but the Stanhopes and the Sutters did not know one another, and neither Susan nor I could recall ever meeting, and if we did, it was not memorable.

My father had owned a beautiful seventeen-foot Thistle, and he'd taught me how to sail, which is one of my fondest memories of him.

William, my once and future father-in-law, a.k.a. Commodore Vomit, had not actually owned a sailboat; he didn't know how to sail, but he had owned a number of power yachts, though large power craft are not encouraged to be kept here at the club. William and Charlotte's membership at Seawanhaka Corinthian was mostly social, which was another skill he wasn't good at.

I looked out at the three club docks, which jutted about a hundred feet into the bay. The Junior Club dock was crowded with adolescents, male and female, who were happy to be away from their parents, and who seemed to be engaged in pre-mating rituals. I recalled doing the same thing when I was young, and I also recalled that the boys, and even some of the girls, used to horse around a lot on the dock, and someone usually wound up in the water. I asked Susan, "Did you ever get thrown in the water?"

"At least once a week." She reminisced, "This beastly boy, James Nelson, used to show his adolescent affection for me by throwing me off the dock."

"You should have married him."

"I would have, but I suspected he wasn't going to grow out of it." She asked me, "Did you throw girls off the dock?"

"I may have."

"Did anyone throw you off the dock?" she asked.

"Only my mother, and only when she could find an anchor to tie around my ankle."

"John. Don't be awful."

We held hands, and I looked south across the water. I could see the lights of the village of Oyster Bay, where I nearly had a new career, and I wondered if Anthony was still going to buy that building. It annoyed me, of course, that this man, whose fortune was so closely tied to criminal activity, had so much money. I'd felt the same way about his father. But I reminded myself, people like that don't sleep well at night. Or if they did, their waking hours must be filled with dread and anxiety. And usually, the law, or a bullet, caught up with them. In fact, I hoped the bullet would catch up to Anthony, soon.

Susan said, "It's so beautiful here."

"It is." The sunlight was sparkling on the water, and a few dozen sailboats and power boats were out on the bay, and fair-weather clouds moved slowly across the blue sky. I looked to the southeast toward Cove Neck, where Teddy Roosevelt's house, Sagamore Hill, was now a National Historical Site, and where a few Roosevelts still lived, including old friends of ours, so I asked Susan, "Have you stayed in touch with Jim and Sally?"

She replied, "I did for some years, but they've moved to San Diego."

"What are they doing in Mexico?"

"Southern California." She suggested, "Stop being an East Coast snob."

"Look who's talking."

"I have an excuse—I was *born* a snob. You had to take lessons."

"Point made."

She said, "We should go in."

"Let's cancel dinner and sit here."

"All right. I'll be right back."

Susan stood and disappeared into the clubhouse. I watched a forty-foot yawl coming in, its sails full with the southerly breeze, and I could almost feel the helm in my hands and the heeling deck beneath my feet.

Susan returned and said, "The Sutters are only drinking tonight."

"The Sutters are my kind of people."

We sat gazing at the sparkling water and the land across the bay, and the sky, and the boats, now with their running lights on, headed for their moorings as the sky darkened.

I looked out on the east lawn, and I said to her, "That's where we met. Right where the wedding tent was pitched."

"That's so sweet of you to remember," she said, but then suggested, "I think, though, it was closer to the porch here. I was coming out of the clubhouse and you were going in."

"That's right. I had to go to the bathroom."

"That's so romantic."

"Well . . . anyway, I saw you—actually, I'd seen you earlier and tried to find out if you were with anyone, or if anyone knew who you were." I added, "Well, I guess I've told you this."

"Tell me again."

So I related the story of my stalking, and my discovery that she wasn't with a date, and that she was a Stanhope, and fabulously wealthy, which of course meant nothing at all to me because I was so captivated by her beauty and her self-assured manner, and so forth. Someone should have tipped me off that her parents were dreadful people, but I wasn't looking to get married; I was looking to get . . . well, laid.

Anyway, I got that, plus got married, and also got her parents as a punishment for my original dishonorable intentions.

I said to Susan, "Thinking back on it, that line I used was divine inspiration."

"And what line was that, John?"

"You remember. I said, regarding the bride . . . what was her first name . . . ? Anyway, I said she was a Guest at her own wedding. Remember?"

Susan sat quietly for a second, then informed me, "That was the third time I'd heard that line that night."

"No."

"And I swore that the next man who said that to me, I would tell him he was an idiot."

"Really?"

"Really. And that was you."

"Well . . . I thought it was funny. And you laughed."

"I did laugh. And that's how I knew you were special."

"I'm glad you laughed." I added, "You were the first woman that night who did."

The waitress came by with two more dark and stormies, and also a platter of crudités, and a platter of shrimp, which I guess Susan had ordered.

So we sat there, drank, talked, and watched the sun go down.

At sunset, colors were sounded and the cannon on the lawn boomed, and everyone stood silently and faced the flag as it was lowered.

The color guard folded the flag and carried it away, and Susan said to me, "Remember this day."

"Until I die."

"Me, too."

CHAPTER THIRTY-SIX

Susan and I woke up in the same bed, and it took us a few minutes to adjust to this sleeping arrangement after ten years. Thankfully, I didn't call her by another woman's name, and she got my name right on the first try, but it *was* a little disorienting at 6:00 A.M.

Within half an hour, however, we'd slipped back into our old morning routines and dressed and went downstairs.

After a hearty lumberjack breakfast of yogurt, granola, and fish oil capsules, I announced to her, "We are going to the police station, and you are going to file a complaint."

She didn't respond, so I stood and said, "Let's do that now."

She remained seated and replied, "He hasn't actually threatened me."

"He has."

She glanced at me, then stood and got her handbag. I put on my blue blazer, and we left the house and got into her Lexus.

I headed south toward the Second Precinct of the Nassau County Police Department, which was about a half-hour drive from Stanhope Hall, and half a world away.

It had been the detectives from this precinct who'd initially responded to the FBI's report, ten years ago, of a shooting at Alhambra, and I assumed there might still be people there who remembered the incident. How could they forget it? So we'd get the attention we needed, though perhaps not the attention we wanted, considering that the FBI hijacked the case from the state, and the U.S. Justice Department gave Susan a pass on the murder.

Well, maybe the county police were over it by now, and this complaint would give them an opportunity to ask questions of Mr. Anthony Bellarosa, heir to his father's evil empire.

Anyway, it was another beautiful, sunny day, and if it wasn't for this cloud hanging over us, our future would be as bright as the sky.

I glanced at Susan and saw she seemed withdrawn. I said to her, "This won't be pleasant, but as your attorney and future husband, I feel this is a necessary precaution."

She didn't reply. Maybe she thought that I was pushing the past in her face, but I wasn't. I was, however, addressing the consequence of what she'd done ten years ago, and she, too, needed to address that.

I gave her a short briefing on what to expect, and what to say, but she didn't seem to be listening. I myself had little experience with making a complaint to the police, and I really wasn't certain exactly what would happen, but as an attorney, I could figure it out when I got there.

Susan slid a CD into the player, and we drove on, listening to Wagner blasting out of a dozen speakers.

We approached the village of Woodbury, and I spotted the sign for the Second Precinct station house. I turned right off Jericho Turnpike, then left into a side parking lot marked for visitors, popped Richard Wagner out of the CD player, and said to Susan, "This may take an hour or more. Then we're done."

She asked me, "Will the police go to see him?"

I replied, "Yes, they will."

She didn't seem happy about that, so I said, "It's just standard procedure. To get his side of it." But in truth, the detectives who followed up on this complaint were, as I said, going to take the opportunity to give Anthony Bellarosa a hard time and, more importantly, to deliver an unambiguous warning to him and tell him he was under the eye. And if luck was really with us, he'd say something incriminating, and they'd have cause to arrest him. But even if they didn't arrest him, Anthony would be one pissed-off *paesano*, which was probably Susan's concern. Well, he was already pissed off, and now he needed to be put on notice.

We got out of the car and walked around to the front. The precinct house was a one-story brick colonial-style structure with white trim and shutters, and it reminded me of the Friendly's ice cream restaurant that we had just passed. We walked through the front door into a vestibule that led into a public reception area.

There was a long counter on the far side of the room, manned by two uniformed officers. As we approached, the younger of the two officers, whose name tag read Anderson, eyeballed Susan, then turned his attention to me and asked, "How can I help you?"

I said, "We're here to file a complaint."

"Okay. What kind of complaint?"

I replied, "A physical threat directed at this woman."

He looked at Susan again and asked her, "Who made this threat?"

She replied, "A neighbor."

I expanded on that and said, "The neighbor is a man named Anthony Bellarosa, who may be involved in organized crime."

"Yeah? How do you know that?"

Apparently Officer Anderson wasn't familiar with that name, and I knew that Anthony Bellarosa kept a very low profile, so I replied, "He is the son of Frank Bellarosa."

The young officer still didn't seem to know the name and said, "Okay. And who are you?"

"I am this lady's attorney."

That seemed to get his attention, and he sized up the situation, noting, I'm sure, our clothing and prep school accents, and he probably concluded that this could be something interesting. Interesting was not his department, so he turned around and asked the higher-ranking officer at the desk behind him, "Hey, Lieutenant—you ever hear of a wiseguy named Anthony Bellarosa?"

The lieutenant looked up from his computer, looked at Susan and me, and replied to Anderson, "Yeah. Why?"

Officer Anderson informed him, "This woman is a neighbor of his, and she says he made threats against her."

The lieutenant stood and came over to the counter and asked me, "Is this your wife, sir?"

"Soon to be. My name is John Sutter, and this is Susan Sutter, and I am her attorney." And so he didn't think I was marrying my sister, I explained, "We have been previously married to each other."

"Okay." He said to Officer Anderson, "Show them into the interview room and take a case report."

Officer Anderson found some forms behind the counter, then came around and escorted us into a small room off to the right. He said, "Have a seat, and let's talk about what happened."

He began by filling out a police form, apparently used to initiate reporting of any type of occurrence that could possibly come to the attention of a law enforcement agency. Officer Anderson asked for our names, address, and related information to identify Susan as the complainant in this report, and then requested a brief description of what had occurred, including the identity of the parties involved in the incident. I did most, if not all, of the talking on behalf of my client.

After completing this report, Officer Anderson began to take a full statement from us on another police form as to the extent of our complaint against Anthony Bellarosa and the specific details involved. Again, I was Susan's mouthpiece, and I outlined the conversations that I had with Anthony Bellarosa, and in particular the statements he made as they related to Susan's well-being. When Officer Anderson finished writing, he handed me the form, PDCN Form 32A, which I read, and then gave to Susan along with my pen and said, "Sign here."

She signed it without looking at it, which is what she always does. She hadn't even read the prenuptial agreement that her father's attorneys had drawn up. And why should she bother after the opening line, which said, "The husband gets to keep nothing beyond the pen he used to sign this document"?

Officer Anderson took the forms and stood, telling us to wait in the room while he inquired if a detective was available to follow up on any related investigation and take a more extensive statement if required. When he left the room, I advised Susan, "If someone else interviews you, please try to show some interest in this."

She shrugged.

A few minutes later, a man in civilian clothes carrying the report entered the room and introduced himself as Detective A. J. Nastasi, and we all shook hands.

Detective Nastasi was an intelligent-looking man and he was in his forties, so he was old enough to remember the original incident that had brought us here. He was dressed in a very dapper pinstripe suit that would blend in nicely at my old law firm. He seemed to be a man of few words—the thoughtful, silent detective type—and I'm sure he'd heard it all by now.

Detective Nastasi glanced at the report and said to Susan, "So, Anthony Bellarosa has threatened you."

She replied, "No."

"Okay . . . but you think he may pose a threat to you."

She replied, "I'm not sure."

Detective Nastasi wasn't sure either, so I said, "Detective, I'm the one who has heard what I believe are threats made by Anthony Bellarosa and directed toward Mrs. Sutter, and I'm prepared to provide you with a statement to that effect."

"Good." He said, "Please follow me."

Susan and I followed Detective Nastasi back through the open area, then down a flight of stairs into the detective squad room, which was buzzing with activity—civilians being questioned or making statements to detectives, and phones ringing.

We passed through the busy squad room, and Detective Nastasi opened a door marked DETECTIVE LIEUTENANT PATRICK CONWAY— COMMANDING OFFICER.

Detective Nastasi ushered us into the quiet office, which was unoccupied. He said, "We can use this room." He added, "More private."

Apparently, we'd gotten someone's attention, or Anthony Bellarosa had.

Detective Nastasi sat behind his commanding officer's desk, and we sat in the two facing chairs. He played with the computer awhile, reading the screen, then said, "Just so you know, Anthony Bellarosa has never been charged with a crime, and there have been no complaints of any type lodged against him." He looked at us and said,

"But to be real, he's not the kind of man anyone would complain about." He looked at Susan and added, "So, if you begin this, then you should understand that we will pay him a visit, and discuss with him what you've alleged. Okay?"

I replied, "That's why we're here."

He kept looking at Susan and asked, "Okay?"

She didn't reply, and Nastasi leaned back in his chair and asked, "You want to withdraw this sworn complaint?"

I replied, "Speaking as her attorney, she does not."

He continued to look at Susan, sizing up the situation, but, getting no response, he went back to his computer and began typing on the keyboard.

I was becoming a little annoyed with her. I mean, all I was trying to do was to save her life, and the least she could do was to cooperate.

As Detective Nastasi kept typing, I wondered if the police had taken her here ten years ago after they'd led her off from Alhambra in handcuffs. But most likely they'd have taken her directly to the Homicide Squad at police headquarters in Mineola, which is the county seat. Though when you've seen the inside of one police station, you've seen them all, so I wanted to be sensitive to what she was feeling now, and sensitive to the bad memories that she was reliving. But I needed to be tough with her so that this potential threat did not become a reality. Unfortunately, reality was, and had always been, a problem with Susan. So, to wake her up, I said to her, "All right. Let's go." I stood and said to Detective Nastasi, "We need to think about this. In the meantime, we want to withdraw the complaint." I turned to Susan and said again, "Let's go."

She started to rise, glanced at me, then sat back in her chair and said, "Let's finish this."

That seemed to make Detective Nastasi happy, and I thought he understood and appreciated my bluff. He said to Susan, "I think you're making the right decision, Mrs. Sutter." He assured her, "Let us worry about this, so you don't have to."

She informed him, "I am not worried."

"Okay." He looked at me and said, "But *you're* worried."

"I am."

"Right. Tell me why you're worried."

I replied, "Detective, as I said, I'm the one who actually heard what I believe are credible threats made by Anthony Bellarosa and directed toward Mrs. Sutter." I continued, "Mrs. Sutter is my former wife, and to give you some background about why I think these threats are credible—"

"Right. I know all that." He informed us, "I was there that night."

I looked at him, and he did seem familiar, but there had been a lot of county detectives, FBI agents, and forensic people at Alhambra that night. However, in the interest of bonding with Detective Nastasi, I said, "Yes, I remember you."

He informed me, "And I remember you." He looked at Susan and said, "You, too." He asked her, "Didn't you leave this state?"

She replied, "I did."

"And you are back now"—he tapped the complaint form—"at this address?"

"I am."

He said, "And Bellarosa's at his father's old address."

I replied, "In a manner of speaking." I explained about the subdivision without sounding judgmental about multimillion-dollar McMansions.

Detective Nastasi consulted his computer monitor as I spoke. Then he said to me, "That case was never resolved in state court."

I assumed he was speaking of the homicide charge against Susan Sutter, so I replied, "It was resolved in Federal court." I added, "The . . . the murder victim was a government witness."

Detective Nastasi nodded, then looked at Susan, and said to me, "Off the record, I wasn't too happy about that. But, okay, it's done, and we need to talk about what's happening now because of what happened then."

I glanced at Susan, who had withdrawn into a place I call Susan-Land, and she didn't seem annoyed or upset about Detective Nastasi's off-the-record statement, nor did she seem contrite about the murder, or sheepish about beating the rap.

To get this back on track, I said again to Detective Nastasi, "I'm prepared to give you a statement now."

He said to me, "Usually, we hear from the complainant first, but . . . I'll take your statement first." He swiveled his chair back to the keyboard and said, "I type fast, but take a breather now and then."

I reminded him, "I'm an attorney."

"Okay, Counselor. Ready when you are."

After the preliminaries of who I was, where I lived, and so forth, I began my statement by mentioning the murder of Frank Bellarosa ten years ago, then I stated that I had been living in London for the past seven years, but that I was still admitted to the New York State Bar. Detective A. J. Nastasi typed as I spoke.

I then recounted the night that Mr. Anthony Bellarosa paid me an unannounced visit at the gatehouse where I was temporarily living, and without getting into everything that was said that night, I got to the crux of the matter and recounted my conversation with Mr. Bellarosa regarding my former wife, Susan Sutter.

Detective Nastasi continued to type, appreciating, I hope, my clear, factual narrative as well as my good grammar and diction.

Susan, who was hearing some of this for the first time, didn't react, but just sat there staring into space.

I then told of my dinner with Mr. Bellarosa at Wong Lee's restaurant, and I mentioned his offer to hire me as one of his attorneys.

Detective Nastasi glanced at me for the first time, then continued to type.

I'm obviously good at sworn testimony, despite what two of my incarcerated tax clients may think, and I stuck to the pertinent facts of the complaint—omitting any facts that might be misconstrued as me and Anthony negotiating a job offer.

I then went on to the chance meeting I had with Bellarosa when I had been jogging on Grace Lane, and my car ride with him and his driver to Oyster Bay, and our visit to the building that Mr. Bellarosa was thinking of buying, and his further attempts to convince me to work for him.

Some of this wasn't relevant to the issue of the threats, but I could tell that Detective Nastasi was intrigued by all of this. Susan, however, seemed to be getting a bit annoyed, perhaps about my flirting with her dead lover's son. I could almost hear her say, "Are you *insane?*"

I explained, for the record, that I had negative feelings about Mr. Bellarosa's interest in me, but I was concerned about Susan's safety, so I thought it might be a good idea to continue to engage in these conversations with Mr. Bellarosa so that I could better determine the threat level, and also determine my next course of action.

Detective Nastasi interrupted me for the first time. "You and Mrs. Sutter had at this time decided to remarry."

I replied, "No."

"Okay. But you were speaking about it?"

I replied, "We were not speaking at all." I added, "We hadn't spoken in about three years."

Susan said, "Four."

"Right, four." I was glad she'd been listening.

Detective Nastasi nodded, then asked me, "So why were you bothering to go through this trouble?"

I glanced at Susan and replied to Detective Nastasi, "I . . . I still had positive feelings toward her, and she is the mother of our children." Plus, I wasn't paying alimony, so there was no good reason for me to want her dead.

There was a silence in the room, so I continued, "Because we weren't romantically involved, my growing concern about Bellarosa's intentions toward Mrs. Sutter was not colored by emotion." I added, "Now the situation between Mrs. Sutter and me has changed, so I was able to discuss this with her, and we decided to come here as a precaution."

Nastasi nodded, probably wondering how much spin I was putting on this for him and for Susan. He said to me, "I think I understand why you were speaking to Bellarosa, Mr. Sutter." He then editorialized, "But it's not a good idea to talk about business opportunities with a man who may be involved in organized crime."

"Thank you for the advice, Detective. But as you say, his rap sheet is as clean as I assume yours is."

Detective Nastasi smiled for the first time, then turned back to his keyboard and said, "Please continue."

I concluded with my visit to the Bellarosa home for Sunday dinner, mentioning that by this time, Mrs. Sutter and I had reunited, and that she had advised against this. I also mentioned that Mr. Salvatore D'Alessio, a.k.a. Sally Da-da, had been there briefly.

Detective Nastasi asked me, "And you'd met him before?"

"Yes. Ten years ago when I was doing some legal work for Frank Bellarosa."

"Right." He commented, "These are very bad guys you were having Sunday dinner with, Mr. Sutter."

"I didn't actually stay for dinner."

"Good." He stopped typing, and I could tell he was thinking about something, and he said to me, "Hey, you were at that failed hit in Little Italy."

Apparently, he'd made a word association between Salvatore D'Alessio, Frank Bellarosa, and the attempted whack. I replied, "That's correct."

"You saved Bellarosa's life."

"I stopped the bleeding." I added, "Good Samaritan."

He glanced at Susan, probably thinking about the irony of me saving the life of my wife's lover, and the further irony of her later killing the man whose life I'd saved. But if Detective Nastasi had anything to say about that, or about us, he kept it to himself and continued, "Okay, so on this occasion—at Anthony Bellarosa's house yesterday, did Anthony Bellarosa make any threats against Mrs. Sutter?"

"He did." I related some of our conversation out on the front lawn and quoted Anthony directly. "He said, apropos of something I said, 'None of that changes what your wife did. Just so you know.'"

Detective Nastasi asked me, "And that was a direct quote?"

"Word for word."

"Okay. And you said?"

"I asked him if that was a threat, and he replied, quote, 'Take it any way you want.'" I added, "The last thing he said to me was, 'You think guys like you don't have to worry about guys like me. Well, Counselor, you're wrong about that.'"

Detective Nastasi finished typing that, then asked me, "Did you take that as a personal threat?"

"I did."

"Okay. Anything else to add?"

I replied, "Just that I take these threats against Mrs. Sutter—and me—seriously, based on what I heard and based on the fact that Mrs. Sutter killed Anthony Bellarosa's father."

Detective Nastasi duly recorded that on his keyboard, and looked at Susan and asked, "Do you want to add anything to Mr. Sutter's statement?"

"No."

"Do you want to say something about how you feel about this possible threat on your life?"

Susan thought a moment, then replied, "Well . . . having heard all of this—some of it for the first time—I believe the threat may exist."

Detective Nastasi typed that without comment, then swiveled around and said to us, "Usually, these guys never threaten. They just do. So maybe this is all talk."

I responded, "I know that. But this guy is young. He's not his father." I added, "I think he's a hothead." I didn't tell him that I'd said a few things that made Anthony very angry, hoping he'd make an actual, quotable threat. And neither did I tell Detective Nastasi that I'd had a minor meltdown and slashed a painting in Anthony Bellarosa's office— that was irrelevant except to Anthony, who would have a shit fit when he discovered it. I did tell Nastasi, however, "The threat may or may not be real, but it was made, so that in itself could be considered harassment and threatening under the law."

"Right. I got that, Counselor." He added, "Let's see what he says when I talk to him."

"All right. So, what's next?"

Detective Nastasi hit the print button and said, "You read this and sign it." As the pages printed out, he further informed us, "This will be part of the case report. We take threats seriously, and we will follow up with the party named. Meanwhile, I advise you both to avoid all contact with this man."

"Goes without saying."

"Right. But I have to say it." He added, "I'd advise you also to take some normal precautions, but I'll leave that to you to decide what kind of precautions." He looked at us and said, "After I speak to him, I'll get back to you and advise you further."

I asked, "When will you speak to him?"

"Very soon."

My statement was hot out of the printer, and Detective Nastasi handed it to me and said, "Look it over, then if everything is in order, I'd like you to sign it."

I scanned the pages, then took my pen and signed where my name was printed.

Detective Nastasi gave each of us his card and said, "Call me if you think of anything else, or if you see him around, or if you see anything that arouses your suspicion." He added, "Or call 9-1-1."

I nodded and asked him, "Do you intend to put him under surveillance?"

He replied, "I'll take that up with my supervisors after we speak to Bellarosa."

That seemed to be about it for now, so Detective Nastasi walked us back through the squad room and up the stairs and into the big reception room. I said to him, "Thank you for your time and your attention to this matter."

He didn't reply to that, but said to us, "If you intend to leave the area for any reason, please let us know." Then he assured us, "You did the right thing by coming in."

We shook hands, and Susan and I left the station house and walked toward the car. I said to her, "We *did* do the right thing, and this is going to be all right."

She asked me, "Can we change the subject now?"

"Sure. What would you like to talk about?"

"Anything."

We got in the car and I headed home. We drove in silence awhile, then Susan said, "Thank you."

"You're welcome."

"Do you care about me, or my money?"

"Your money."

She pointed out, "But you were worried about me even before you proposed to me."

Did I propose? Anyway, I replied, "I've always cared about you, Susan, even when I wanted to break your neck."

"That's very sweet." She thought a moment, then said, "This is all my fault."

I assured her, "It is. But it's *our* problem."

She thought about that, then said, "I didn't know he threatened you."

I didn't respond.

She asked me, "What did you say to him that made him say that to you?"

I told him that his father was going to abandon his whole family for Susan Sutter, and it felt good saying it.

"John? What did you say to him?"

"I just turned down his job offer without showing the proper respect."

"That hardly warrants the kind of threat he made."

I changed the subject and said, "I think we should take a vacation right after Ethel's funeral."

"I'll think about it." She said, "Meanwhile, it's a beautiful day, and I need a break, so why don't we drive out to the Hamptons for the day?"

If she meant a mental health break, we'd be gone a few months, but I replied, "Good idea. We'll stop and get our bathing suits."

"There's that beach in Southampton where we don't need bathing suits."

"Okay." I made a course correction, and within ten minutes we were on the Long Island Expressway heading east to the Hamptons for a skinny-dip in the ocean.

I had once owned a summer house in East Hampton, and so had my parents, and the Sutter family would spend as much of the summer as possible out east. When my children were young, and when I was still on speaking terms with my parents, those had been magical, barefoot summers, filled with awe and wonder for the kids, and with peace and love for Susan and me.

I had sold the house because of my tax problems, and I hadn't been back to the Hamptons in the last decade, so I was looking forward to spending the day out east, and not thinking about this morning, or tomorrow.

Susan said, "This will be like old times."

"Even better."

"And the best is yet to come."

"It is."

CHAPTER THIRTY-SEVEN

There are no officially sanctioned nude beaches in the Hamptons, but we found the secluded ocean beach in Southampton that was unofficially clothes-optional.

I parked the car in the small windswept lot and we got out. The beach was nearly deserted on this Monday in early June, but there were two couples in the water, and when the surf ran out, we confirmed that they were skinny-dippers.

Susan and I ran down to the wide, white-sand beach, shucked our clothes, and dove in the chilly water. Susan exclaimed, "Holy shit."

It *was* a bit cool, but we stayed in for about half an hour, and before hypothermia set in, we ran back to the beach. As we pulled on our clothes over our wet bodies, Susan said, "I remember the first time we did this together, when we were dating." She reminded me, "I'd never done this before, and I thought you were crazy."

"Crazy in love." In fact, there were a lot of things that Susan Stanhope hadn't done before she met me, and maybe I was attracted to that sheltered rich girl who was gamely going along with my silly antics. I was trying to impress her, of course, and she was trying to show me she was just like everyone else. Eventually we both started being ourselves, and it was a relief to discover that we still liked each other.

We jogged back to the car and drove into the formerly quaint, now boutiquified village of Southampton, and had a late lunch at one of our old haunts, a pub called the Drivers Seat. At Susan's strong suggestion, I ordered a grilled chicken salad and sparkling water, but when I got up to go to the men's room, I changed it to a bacon cheeseburger with fries and a beer. Susan apparently remembered this trick, and when she went to the ladies' room, she reinstated the original order. A good friend once said to me, "Never date or remarry your ex-wife." Now I get it.

After our salads, we took a walk along Job's Lane, which, according to a marker, was laid out in 1664, and was now filled with trendy shops, restaurants, and adventurous settlers from Manhattan Island.

Susan said, "Let's buy you some clothes."

"I have some clothes."

"Come on, John. Just a few shirts."

So we stopped in a few shops and bought a few dress shirts, and a few sports shirts, a few ties, and a few jeans, and a few other things I didn't know I needed. She bought a few things for herself as well.

We decided to stay overnight, so we also bought workout clothes and bathing suits, and Susan called Gurney's Inn, out near Montauk Point, which has spa facilities, and she booked a room with an ocean view. We then drove east, through the remaining villages of the Hamptons, including East Hampton, where we'd once had our summer house, and I asked her, "Do you want to drive past our old house?"

She shook her head and replied, "Too sad." She reminded me, "The children really loved that house, and loved being here." Then she brightened and said, "Let's buy it back."

I replied, "You can't buy back all your old houses."

"Why not?"

"Well, money, for one thing."

She informed me, "I don't want to sound crass, John, but someday I'll inherit my share of a hundred million dollars."

That was the first time I'd ever heard what the Stanhopes were actually worth, and I almost drove off the road. I mean, the Stanhope fortune, when it was mentioned at all, was always preceded by the adjectives "diminished" or "dwindling," which made me feel sorry for William and Charlotte. Not really, but I always pegged their net worth at about ten or maybe twenty million, so this number came as a surprise. Now I was *really* in love. Just kidding.

Anyway, I knew that Edward and Carolyn, the only grandchildren, would be in William's will, and then there was Susan's brother, Peter, the Lotus Eater, and, of course, Charlotte, if she survived William. Charlotte, however, was not a Stanhope, so in the world of old money, the bulk of the Stanhope estate would bypass her—who, in any case, had her own family money—and through some clever tax and estate planning, and complicated trusts, most of the Stanhope fortune would pass to William's lineal descendents. That was how William got it from Augustus, and how Augustus got it from Cyrus.

So some quick math would reveal that Susan Stanhope should pop a bottle of champagne at William's funeral.

Unless, of course, she married me, so I reminded her, "Your share may be closer to zero."

She had no reply to that, but I could tell reality was setting in.

We continued on, past the villages and through a stretch of desolate dunes. Farther on was the Montauk Point Lighthouse, on the eastern-most tip of Long Island. The last time I'd seen the lighthouse, it was from the water, ten years ago, when I'd rounded the point on my sail to Hilton Head, and I've wondered about a million times what would have happened if I'd actually stopped there and seen her.

I still don't think either of us would have been ready for a recon-ciliation, but if we'd spoken, I don't believe I would have stayed away ten years. But who knows?

Before we reached the point, Gurney's Inn came up on the ocean side of the road, and I pulled in and parked at reception.

We checked into the ocean-view room, then we changed into our newly purchased workout clothes and spent a few hours using the spa and exercise facilities.

Susan had scheduled a beauty treatment of some sort, so I took the opportunity to go back to our room, and I called the general number of the Federal Bureau of Investigation in Manhattan.

After a bit of a bureaucratic runaround, I got someone in the Orga-nized Crime Task Force, and said to him, "My name is John Sutter, and I am looking for Special Agent Felix Mancuso."

"And what is this in reference to, sir?"

I replied, "He handled a case that I was involved in ten years ago. I would like to speak to him about a new development, if he's there, please."

"And he'll know what this is about?"

"He will."

"All right. I can't confirm that he's here, sir, but if you leave your contact information, I will have him, or someone, get back to you."

"Fine." I gave him the number of Gurney's Inn, which I said would be good until morning, then I gave him the number of the guest cottage as my home phone.

He asked, "Is there a cell number we can reach you at?"

I replied, "I don't have a cell phone."

He didn't respond for a second, and I thought I'd committed some sort of criminal offense, so I explained, "I've just transferred here from London." I added, "I'll have one soon."

"All right, so someone can leave you a message at these numbers?"

"Correct." I added, "Please tell Special Agent Mancuso that it's important."

"Will do."

I hung up and went back to the spa for our scheduled couples' massage.

Susan had booked a masseuse for herself, a tiny East Asian lady, and a masseur for me, who may have once been convicted of torture.

As we were lying side by side on the tables, Susan said to me, "I went to the business office and e-mailed the children and my parents to update them on Ethel's condition, and told them they should think about getting here soon."

"Did you tell your parents our good news?"

"No, and in my e-mail to the children, I told them not to say anything to anyone until you made the announcement."

"Right." I hoped when I told Mom and Dad the good news, they'd drop dead before they disinherited their daughter. *A hundred million?* Maybe I should have been nicer to them. Or maybe I should call Sally Da-da and work out a deal.

Actually, I used to know people on the Gold Coast and here in the Hamptons who were worth hundreds of millions, so that number didn't completely stun me. What stunned me was that William, who always acted as though he was a paycheck away from being homeless, actually had that kind of money. This really annoyed me. I mean, that cheap, tightwad bastard . . . but maybe Susan had the number wrong. It wouldn't be the first time. Actually, I thought, it could be *more*.

Susan asked, "What are you thinking about?"

"Oh . . . I'm thinking about getting your oiled-up body back to the room."

The masseuse tittered, and the masseur chuckled, and Susan said, "John."

We finished our massages in silence, then took our oiled-up bodies back to our room. The message light wasn't on, and we made love, napped, then dressed and went down to the cocktail lounge and watched the ocean and the darkening sky.

We had a dinner reservation at the hotel, and we got to the restaurant late and tipsy as the last of the sun faded from the sky.

Susan looked at me across the candlelit table and said, "I never thought I'd see you again sitting across from me in a restaurant."

I took her hand and said, "We have many good years ahead of us."

"I know we do."

Her cell phone rang, and she looked at it, and said to me, "I don't need to take it."

She shut off the phone and slipped it back into her purse.

I wasn't sure if I should ask who'd called—it could be her parents, or our children responding to her e-mail, or Elizabeth with some bad news. Or it could be a man. And if she wanted me to know who it was, she'd have told me.

However, she seemed suddenly less cheerful, so I did ask, "Who was that?"

She replied, "Nassau County Police Department."

I said, "Play the message."

"Later."

"Now."

She retrieved her cell phone, turned it on and punched in her password, then handed it to me.

I put the phone to my ear and heard, "Hello, Mrs. Sutter, this is Detective Nastasi, Nassau County PD. I just want you to know that I called on the subject tonight, at his home, and his wife informed me that he was out of town for an unspecified period of time. Call me back at your convenience." He added, "Please pass this on to Mr. Sutter."

I hit the replay button and handed her the phone. As she listened, I thought about Anthony Bellarosa being out of town. That didn't comport with him needing to stay close to home for John Gotti's imminent death and funeral. Maybe, though, Uncle Sal had jumped the gun—pardon the pun—and Anthony was somewhere out there in the ocean, feeding the fishes as they say. Wouldn't that be nice? But if not, then Anthony's sudden disappearance was more worrisome than it was comforting.

Susan shut off her phone again and put it back in her purse.

I said, "We'll call him tomorrow."

She changed the subject and said, "I want you to order from the spa menu."

"Why? What did I do wrong?"

She informed me, "You are what you eat."

"Well, then, I need to change my name to Prime Rib."

"I recommend the steamed halibut."

"I had fish oil for breakfast."

"I want you around for a long time."

"Well, it's going to seem like a long time if I have to eat that crap."

"Go ahead, then, order your steak, and kill yourself."

"Thank you."

The waitress came and we ordered.

The halibut wasn't that bad with a bottle of local chardonnay.

When we got back to the room, I saw that the message light still wasn't lit.

I didn't *need* to speak to Felix Mancuso, but if there was one person in law enforcement who understood this case—not only the facts and the history, but also the human element of what had happened ten years ago—it was this man, who'd not only tried to save my soul from a great evil, but who also had been troubled by his colleagues acting as pimps for don Bellarosa.

Well, for all I knew, Mancuso was retired, transferred, or dead, but if he wasn't any of those things, then I knew I'd hear from him.

Susan and I went out on the balcony and looked at the ocean. On the distant horizon I could see the lights of great ocean liners and cargo ships, and overhead, aircraft were beginning their descent into Kennedy Airport, or climbing out on their way to Europe, or the world.

Susan asked me, "Do you think you want to sail again?"

I replied, "Well, what good is a yacht club without a yacht?"

She smiled, then said, seriously, "I never want you to sail alone again."

I hadn't been completely alone, but I understood what she meant and replied, "I won't sail without you."

She stayed quiet awhile, and we listened to the surf washing against the shore, and I stared, transfixed by the night sky and the black ocean.

She asked me, "How was it?"

I continued to look out into the dark, starry night, and replied, "Lonely." I thought a moment, then said, "It's easy to imagine out there, at night, that you are the last man left alive on earth."

"It sounds awful."

"Sometimes. But most of the time I felt . . . as though it was just me and God. I mean, you can go a little crazy out there, but it's not necessarily a bad kind of crazy." I added, "You have a lot of time to think, and you get to know yourself."

"And did you think about me?"

"I did. I honestly did. Every day, and every night."

"So what stopped you from setting a course for home?"

There were a lot of answers to that question—anger, pride, spite, and the total freedom of being a self-exiled man without a country or a job. But, to Susan, I said, "When I know, I'll let you know."

We stretched out in the lounge chairs and watched the sky, then fell asleep under the stars.

Through my sleep, I heard the ocean, felt the sea breeze, and smelled the salt air, and I dreamed I was back at sea. But this time, Susan was with me.

━━ PART III ━━

The Present is the living sum-total of the Past.

—Thomas Carlyle
"Characteristics"

CHAPTER THIRTY-EIGHT

The next morning, Tuesday, was partly cloudy, and after a run on the beach and a soul-nourishing spa breakfast, we headed home to Lattingtown and Stanhope Hall. This is a drive of about two hours, and during that time we spoke a little about the last ten years, trying to fill in some of what Susan referred to as "the lost years." Also lost and missing was any mention of significant or insignificant others, so there were some gaps in the historical record. Sort of like black holes. She did remind me, however, "Call Samantha."

I thought about asking her when, where, and how she and Frank Bellarosa first hooked up, but she wouldn't like that question. Also, I realized that this was not bothering me any longer, so maybe I was really getting over it, and getting on with it.

I pulled into the gates of Stanhope Hall, and we noticed a moving van parked to the side of the gatehouse. I also saw Elizabeth's SUV, so I pulled over, and Susan and I got out and went inside the gatehouse.

Elizabeth, in jeans and a T-shirt, was in the foyer, supervising the move. She saw us and said, "Good morning. I stopped by the guest cottage to tell you I was going to clean out the house, but you weren't home." She added, "I thought it would be a good idea to just get this done, so we don't have to negotiate for time with Nasim after the funeral." She then looked at me and said, "John, I hope I'm not kicking you out."

Well, no, but you *are* burning my bridges, and now I can't come back here when the Stanhopes arrive.

"John?"

"No. I'm finished with the house."

"That's what you said." Elizabeth offered, "The movers will take all your boxes and files to the guest cottage, if you'd like."

"Thank you," I said before she mentioned her previous offer to store me and my files in her house.

Susan asked Elizabeth, "How is your mother doing?"

Elizabeth shrugged. "The same." She added, "I know the end is near, and I can't believe it . . . but I've accepted it." She looked around the gatehouse and said, "They were here for over sixty years . . . and now . . . well, life goes on." She said to Susan, "I asked John if Nasim would consider selling the house, but Nasim wants it for himself." She pointed out, "We could have been neighbors again."

Susan replied, in what sounded like a sincere tone, "That would have been wonderful." She informed Elizabeth, "I was going to have my cleaning lady do some work, and I'm sorry if John left a mess."

John wanted to say that Elizabeth left more of a mess than John left, but John knows when to keep his mouth shut.

Elizabeth assured Susan, "Oh, don't worry about it. I'm out of here, and Nasim can do what he wants." She informed us, "He drove by before, and I told him that he could have the house as of now." She looked at her lawyer and asked, "All right?"

I replied, "You're the executrix."

She continued, "He knew from his wife's conversation with Susan that you'd reunited and were living together in the guest cottage." She added, "He wishes you both luck and happiness."

Susan said, "That's very nice."

Well, Mr. Nasim could now put security people in the gatehouse, though I would advise him not to use Bell Security. Also, he was probably wondering how this new development would impact on his goal of getting Susan to sell. Maybe I should tell Nasim that we, too, had security problems, and I had a shotgun, so we could join forces and provide supporting fire in case of an attack.

Susan interrupted my strategic thinking and said to Elizabeth, "By the way, we haven't told my parents yet that we've reunited. So, if you communicate with them, please don't mention it."

Elizabeth replied, "I understand."

Susan added, "Same with John's mother, and Father Hunnings."

"I won't mention it to a soul."

"Thank you." Susan asked, "Do you mind if I go get my camera and take some photos before everything is moved out?"

Elizabeth informed her, "I've already done that, and I'll send you copies." She said, "This was the only home I ever knew growing up, and I'm going to miss all the memories that used to come back when I visited Mom." She glanced at me and smiled, and I thought she was going to tell Susan about her memory of having an adolescent crush on me. But Elizabeth is not a troublemaker, and she concluded, "They were good times when we were all here at Stanhope Hall."

Susan, who is a sensitive soul, gave Elizabeth a big hug, and they both got misty-eyed.

I never know what to do when women get emotional—do I join in?

The ladies got themselves back together, and Susan said to Elizabeth, "If we're not home, the movers can leave the boxes in my office. John's office." She added, "The door is unlocked."

Elizabeth replied, "I'll supervise that." She reminded me, "I still have that letter that Mom wrote to you, but I don't feel right about giving it to you until she passes."

I assured her, "That's the right thing to do," though I didn't think Ethel was going to rally, sit up in bed, and ask, "Can I see that letter again?"

We chatted for a few more minutes, then Susan and I got back in her Lexus, and Susan asked me, "What letter?"

"Ethel wrote me a letter, to be delivered upon her death."

"Really? What do you think is in the letter?"

"Her recipe for crabapple jelly."

"Be serious."

I continued up the tree-lined drive toward the guest cottage and replied, "I don't know, but we don't have long to find out."

Back at the guest cottage, we unloaded our new clothes and spent half an hour getting me more settled in than I'd been. I was actually starting to feel like I was home again, and it was a good feeling.

I asked Susan for the pass code to the house phone, and I went into the office, but there were no messages for me, only a few from her girl-friends.

Susan joined me in the office and asked me, "Are you expecting a call?"

"I am."

"Who knows that you're here?"

"The police, our children, Elizabeth, Mr. and Mrs. Nasim, Anthony Bellarosa, and Felix Mancuso."

"Who is Felix . . . oh, yes. I remember him." She asked me, "Why did you call him?"

"Because of Anthony Bellarosa."

She shrugged and said, "Do it your way."

"With your help and cooperation." I said to her, "I want us to have a security alarm system installed here."

She let me know, "This house has been standing here for one hundred years without an alarm system, and I don't intend to put one in now."

"Well, let's start locking the doors and windows for a change."

"I lock them at night."

My late aunt Cornelia, who lived in a big Victorian house in Locust Valley, never locked doors or windows, except at night, when she re-membered. It was a generational thing to some extent, and a statement, which was, "I am not afraid, and I will not let others change the way I have always lived." I liked that, but it was not reality. We've all changed how we live since 9/11, for instance, and we don't need to like it; we need to do it.

Susan, however, was on this nostalgia trip, trying to re-create her life as it was ten years ago. She'd gotten back her old house, and her old husband, rejoined her clubs, and was thinking about buying our former summer house in East Hampton. You can do a lot with money, but one thing you can't do is turn back the clock. And if you try, the results are often disappointing, disastrous, or, in this case, dangerous.

With that in mind, I asked her, "Where do you think the shotgun is?"

"I *think* it's in the basement, John. I don't know. I haven't unpacked all the boxes since I moved."

"I'll look later."

"Don't open the box marked, 'Boyfriends.'"

"Do you keep old boyfriends in a box?"

"Just their ashes." She promised, "I'll look later."

She sat down at the desk, accessed her e-mail, and said, "Here are replies from Edward, Carolyn, and my mother." She read them and said, "Just confirming . . . and saying let them know . . ."

I reminded her, "Your parents think they're sleeping here."

"Let's see how that goes."

"Susan, they are going to show up in a rental car on your doorstep—"

"*Our* doorstep, darling."

"And they will not be happy."

"Then they can turn around and go somewhere else."

"I think you should tip them off . . . maybe a hint. Like, 'I'm living with a man who I used to be married to.'"

She began hitting the keys and said, "Dear Mom and Dad . . . I have a boyfriend who looks a lot like . . . no, how about . . . For reasons I can't explain now, I've booked you a room at . . . where?"

"Motel Six in Juneau, Alaska."

"Help me, John."

"See if there's a cottage available at The Creek. You can get them in on your membership. Same with the guest rooms at Seawanhaka."

She finished the e-mail and said to me, "If I send this, they'll call and ask why they can't stay here."

"Tell them your allowance isn't covering expenses, and you've taken in boarders."

She shut down the computer without sending the e-mail and said to me, "Let them come here, and we'll deal with it then."

"That's a great idea." And to get into the proper spirit of this reunion, I said to her, "I've rehearsed a happy and upbeat line for when they show up." I took her by the hand and led her to the front door, opened it, and said, "Here they come, and they're out of their car."

"John—"

I stepped outside, threw my arms in the air, and shouted, "Mom! Dad! I'm baaack!"

Susan thought that was funny, but she reminded me, "You're an idiot."

We went back to the office, and I found in my wallet the card of Detective Nastasi, and I said to Susan, "I'll call him." I dialed his office number, got through to him, and I said, "Detective, this is John Sutter, returning your call." I hit the speaker button so Susan could listen.

Detective Nastasi said, "Right. Well, you got my message. His wife said he's out of town."

I informed him, "Bellarosa said to me on Sunday that he had a busy week because John Gotti was expected to die very soon, and he needed to go to the wake and the funeral."

"Yeah? Well, Gotti died yesterday afternoon at the prison hospital in the Federal penitentiary in Springfield, Missouri." He added, "It was in the papers and on the news."

I replied, "I've been out of touch." I thought about asking him if Jenny Alvarez was still covering the Mafia beat—she might have some inside information—but I thought better of that and said, "Maybe Bellarosa went to Springfield, Missouri."

"Maybe." He reported, "I checked with the security guy at the booth there at Alhambra, and the guy says he hasn't seen Bellarosa since he left yesterday morning, and I just called the booth again and another guy said the same thing."

"Well, you should know that Bell Security is a wholly owned subsidiary of Bell Enterprises, Inc., whose president, CEO, and principal stockholder is Anthony Bellarosa."

"No kidding? How about that?" He asked me, "You think that's a coincidence?"

"Uh . . . no."

He laughed, then said, "Actually, I had a friend of mine in the District Attorney's Squad run a check on Anthony Bellarosa. The file shows Bell Enterprises as his legit company in Rego Park—linen service, restaurant supply, trash carting, limousine service—usual wiseguy stuff."

I hoped there wasn't anything there about my new law firm of Sutter, Bellarosa and Roosevelt.

Detective Nastasi assured me, "So, we understand about Bell Security." He asked me, "How did you know about that?"

"He told me."

Detective Nastasi had no comment on that and said, "You know, when I spoke to his wife, I got the impression that he really was gone, and I didn't see the Escalade that's registered to him. So maybe he did fly to Springfield to be with the family."

"Maybe you can check on that."

"Maybe. All right, Mr. Sutter, we'll keep on this, and as soon as I speak to Bellarosa, I will get back to you. Meantime, since you're a neighbor, if you see him or hear anything about his whereabouts, give me a call, but don't go looking for him."

"I don't intend to."

"Good." He then said, "They tore the mansion down."

"They did."

"That was some place. They don't build them like that anymore."

"No, they don't."

"What do you think those houses go for?"

"I don't know . . ." I glanced at Susan, who held up three fingers, and I replied, "About three."

"No kidding?"

I suggested, "Maybe crime pays."

He reminded me, "We don't have a thing on him."

I was a little annoyed now, so I said, "You need to look harder."

"Well, that's the DA's job, and the Feds."

Regarding that, I said to him, "As an attorney, I know that the FBI has no jurisdiction in a case of threatening or harassment, but I'm wondering if you should call the Organized Crime Task Force to see if they're tracking his movements for other reasons."

He informed me, "The FBI wouldn't tell me if my ass was on fire."

"All right . . . but if they're watching him for other things, they should know about this, just in case . . ."

"Okay. I'll take care of that."

"Good."

"Any more suggestions?"

Oddly, I didn't think he was being sarcastic. I think he was covering his aforementioned ass in case Susan Stanhope Sutter got whacked on his watch. I replied, "I'm sure you're doing all you can, but I'd appreciate knowing that all the area patrol cars are aware of my complaint."

"They have been notified." He added, "When I speak to Bellarosa, I'll reevaluate the situation and the response."

"All right. Thank you for staying on this."

"You have a good day, and regards to Mrs. Sutter."

"Thank you."

I hung up and looked at Susan, who was sitting now in a club chair perusing a magazine, and she said, "I think he's in Missouri with the Gotti family, so we don't need to think about this for a while."

"Right." Unfortunately, that's not the way it worked. Sally Da-da was out of the state when he'd tried to have Frank whacked. This was not the kind of work that a don or a capo did himself; that's why it was called a contract. And that's why when the contract was fulfilled, the guy who put it out was on the beach in Florida.

And *that* was why you needed to keep your enemies close; because when you didn't know where they were, they became more dangerous.

Susan said to me, "Come with me to Locust Valley. I need some wine and liquor, and I want to do some food shopping. I'll let you pick out a granola you like."

I actually wanted to wait for Mancuso's call, and to look for the shotgun, but I thought I should go with her, so I said, "All right. Sounds like fun."

"Shopping for anything with you is far from fun."

On the subject of dating or remarrying your ex-wife, my friend also said, "They've got your name, rank, and serial number from the last time they captured you."

Well, that was very cynical, but the upside was that the reunited couple could dispense with the long, stressful, best-behavior courtship.

We got into the Lexus, and Susan wanted to drive. She said to me, "We should get rid of your rental car."

"I need a car."

"Buy one."

"Susan, sweetheart, I have no money and no credit in this country."

"Really? Well, I do."

"How much do you think your father would give me to go back to England?"

"One hundred thousand. That's his standard offer for unacceptable men."

"I wish I'd known that when we were dating."

"In your case, he'd double that."

"I'll split it with you."

As we approached the gatehouse, we saw Elizabeth outside, so Susan stopped, and Elizabeth came over to the car and leaned in my window. She was wearing the same lilac scent as the other night. Susan said to her, "Why don't you join us for dinner tonight? That will help get your mind off things."

Elizabeth replied, "Thank you, but I want to get back to Fair Haven."

Susan said, "I understand. But if you change your mind, we'll be at The Creek about seven P.M."

That was the first I knew that Susan wasn't cooking, and that was a relief, though maybe in the last ten years she'd learned what all those things were for in the kitchen. On the other hand, I was not happy to hear that we were going to The Creek.

Elizabeth turned to me and said, "I have a case of crabapple jelly for you."

"Thank you."

She said to Susan, "That's John's fee for handling the estate."

I thought Susan was going to say, "No wonder he's broke." But instead, she said to Elizabeth, "If you just want to come by the club for a quick drink, call."

"Thank you."

And off we went to Locust Valley. I said to Susan, "I don't really want to go to The Creek."

She replied, "Let's get it over with."

"How can I refuse an invitation like that?"

"You know what I mean."

I thought about it, then replied, "All right. It could be fun. Maybe Althea Gwynn will be there."

We drove into Locust Valley and stopped first at the wine and liquor store, then at the supermarket, where we ran into a few women Susan knew, and even a few I knew. We did the supermarket-aisle chat each time, and only one woman, Beatrice Browne, a.k.a. "Bee-bee," said something provocative. She said to me, "I'm surprised you're back, John."

To which I replied, "I'm surprised you're still here."

Bee-bee didn't know quite how to take that, so she put her cart into gear and moved off.

Susan advised me, "You're just supposed to say, 'It's wonderful to be back.'"

"It's wonderful to be back."

"Don't respond directly to a goading statement or a loaded question."

"It's wonderful to be back."

Susan moved on to fruits and vegetables, and within thirty minutes we were back in the car. As we loaded the cargo space, she asked me, "Is there anything else you need? Toiletries? Pharmacy?"

"It's wonderful to be back."

She let out a sigh, got behind the wheel, and we headed home.

On the way, she said to me, "I'd like you to call your mother today."

"If I call her, I can't tell her we're together because she may call your parents."

"Ask her not to." She continued, "She needs to know that her son is now living with his ex-wife. And she needs to know that before my parents know it, and before the funeral."

"Where do these rules come from?"

"Common sense and common courtesy."

"What would Emily Post say?"

"She'd say to do what your prospective bride tells you to do."

"It's wonderful to be back."

Susan reached out, pinched my cheek, and said, "It's wonderful to have you back."

CHAPTER THIRTY-NINE

Back at the guest cottage, we unloaded the Lexus, then Susan suggested, "Let's take a run up to the Sound."

I replied, "I have a lot of things to do here in my new office, and I need to organize my sock drawer."

"Good idea. I'll only be about an hour."

I said to her, "I don't want you running on Grace Lane or anywhere off the property."

"John—"

"Run on the estate property." I reminded her, "Not everyone has a two-hundred-acre estate to run on. Maybe I'll join you later."

She seemed a little annoyed and said, "I didn't realize I was going to be bossed around so much."

That made two of us, but I replied, "Just humor me."

"I always do. All right, I'll see you in about an hour."

"Take your cell phone and call me, or I'll call you."

"Yes, sir."

"And no shorts."

She smiled, went upstairs to change, and I went into my office and saw that the file and storage boxes were now stacked against a wall, along with a case of crabapple jelly.

I also saw that the message light on the phone was blinking, and I retrieved the only message, which said, "John Sutter, this is Felix Mancuso returning your call." He gave me a cell phone number, which I wrote on the back of Detective Nastasi's card, then I erased the message.

To kill some time until Susan left, I looked around my old office, recalling too many late nights spent here at the desk, trying to solve other people's tax or estate problems, most of which they'd created themselves.

Hanging above the couch was a new addition to the office—three of Susan's oil paintings of locally famous ruins: the chapel of Laurelton Hall, Louis C. Tiffany's art nouveau mansion; some stone pillars of what remained of Meudon, an eighty-room palace that had been a replica of Meudon Palace outside of Paris; and the colonnade of a place called Knollwood, which had once been the home of a fellow named Zog, the last king of Albania, reminding me that Mr. Nasim was not the first foreigner who'd bought a piece of the Gold Coast, nor would he be the last.

As I looked at the paintings, I was reminded that Susan truly had some talent, and I wondered why she'd stopped painting. Maybe, I thought, it had something to do with her last effort, Alhambra, and all the bad memories associated with that housewarming gift to the Bellarosas. And this, of course, reminded me of my vandalism in Anthony's den. I'll bet that pissed him off when he saw it. And I'll bet Sigmund Freud would have fun explaining to me my destructive behavior—and he might conclude that, aside from my own unhappy associations with that painting, I was also subconsciously trying to draw Anthony's attention and wrath away from Susan and toward myself. Well, Sigmund, it wasn't so subconscious.

Susan called out, "See you later."

I sat at the desk and looked at the phone, but hesitated. My instinct had been to call Felix Mancuso, but my understanding of how the police worked told me that this was a break with protocol and would not make Detective Nastasi happy. As he said, the FBI wouldn't tell him if his ass was on fire, and I was sure he'd withhold the same urgent information from them. Also, he said *he* would contact the FBI.

On the other hand, I once had a personal relationship with Felix Mancuso and he was a smart and decent man, and I trusted him. I'd nicknamed him, in my mind, St. Felix, but beyond his do-gooder personality was a tough man who seemed to take personally the criminal activities of the Mafia, La Cosa Nostra, as a result, I was sure, of his own Italian heritage—i.e., his *paesanos* embarrassed him and pissed him off.

So, if nothing else, I just needed to speak with him, and to be certain I was covering all bases. Because if something happened, and I hadn't done everything I could have because of the pecking order, then . . . well, it was moot, because I would do everything and anything I could to protect Susan. One of us needed to do that.

I dialed Felix Mancuso's cell phone, and he answered, "Mancuso."

I said, "Hello, Mr. Mancuso, this is John Sutter."

"Well, hello, Mr. Sutter. And to what do I owe the pleasure of your call?"

I remembered that Felix Mancuso was a rather formal man, in his manner and his speech, and as a special agent he was also an attorney, like myself, though that did not make him a bad guy. I replied, "I'm calling you, unfortunately, about pretty much the same thing as the last time we spoke."

"Really? How can that be?"

"Well, it's a long story. But to begin, I've been out of the country for the last ten years, and as of about two weeks ago, I'm back on Long Island to stay."

"Welcome home."

"Thank you. And I've reunited with my ex-wife."

There was a pause, then, "Congratulations. And how is Mrs. Sutter?"

"Not too bad, considering I'm back in her life."

He chuckled and said, "Don't sell yourself short, Mr. Sutter. She's a lucky woman to have you back."

He may have been alluding to the fact that Susan Sutter, aside from committing adultery with a Mafia don, also murdered said don who was the FBI's star government witness against his own criminal empire. And to add insult to injury, Susan had walked free. Other than that, I hoped Felix Mancuso didn't harbor any resentment toward Susan.

He asked me, "So, how can I help you, Mr. Sutter?"

I said, "I'm not sure if you can, but a situation has developed here that actually has its origins in what happened ten years ago."

"I see. And what is that situation?"

I replied, "Frank Bellarosa's son, Anthony, is living at Alhambra—in one of those houses that were built there—"

"I know that. Ironic, isn't it?"

"Yes, but irony is not the problem. The problem is that Susan has moved back from Hilton Head, and she's bought back her house on the Stanhope estate, and—"

"I understand."

"I thought you would." I also informed him, "She's been back about two months, and I've just moved in with her."

"All right. Has Anthony Bellarosa made any specific threats or statements to her that would cause her to believe he harbors a grudge, or intends to . . . let's say, avenge his father's death?"

"You mean vendetta."

Mr. Mancuso knew that vendetta was not the name of an Italian motor scooter, and he replied, "That's a good word. And?"

"Actually, he has not spoken to her. But he has spoken to me, and I came away with the impression that he might be looking to even the score."

"I see." He asked me, "How did you and Anthony Bellarosa have occasion to speak?"

This was not the question I was looking forward to, considering that Felix Mancuso had spent so much time and energy trying to save me from myself in regard to Frank Bellarosa. So I wasn't keen to tell him that I'd been speaking to the don's son about job opportunities.

"Mr. Sutter?"

"Well, Anthony had this idea that I might want to resume my association with the Bellarosa family."

"Really? And where did he get that idea?"

I explained, "I believe from Jack Weinstein. You remember him."

"Indeed, I do." He added, "Another very bright attorney who lost his way."

I really didn't need a lecture, but I needed a favor, so I sucked that up and continued, "And Anthony himself has this idea, based partially on what he recalls his father telling him, that I would be a trusted and valuable member of his organization." I added, as an example of why this was so, "Frank Bellarosa told Anthony that John Sutter had the best combination of brains and balls he'd ever seen."

The phone went quiet for a few seconds, then Mr. Mancuso asked me, "And?"

I really didn't want to pursue this subject, so I reminded him, "I'm only relating this in the context of your question regarding how Anthony and I came to speak. The real issue is that Anthony has made statements to me that I construed as threatening toward Susan."

"Such as?"

"Well, first, understand that my conversations with Anthony took place before Mrs. Sutter and I reunited. That reconciliation occurred only two days ago. So, Anthony, I think, felt free to make these remarks about Susan, thinking that, like most ex-spouses, I prayed daily for the demise of my former spouse."

Mr. Mancuso chuckled politely, then asked again, "What did he actually say?"

I filled him in on some of what Anthony Bellarosa had said about Susan, and he interrupted me by asking, "How many occasions did you have to speak with him?"

I replied, "Four separate occasions."

"Really?"

I thought he was going to say, "That was four too many," but he said nothing further, so I explained about keeping your friends close and your enemies closer.

He informed me, "I think some author or screenwriter made that up."

That was a disappointment—it sounded like real Italian folk wisdom. Anyway, I continued, "My last interaction with him was Sunday . . . at his house."

"Really?"

"He invited me to dinner."

"Did he?"

"I didn't stay for dinner, of course, but I took the opportunity to tell him to go to hell and stop bothering me and my future wife."

"And how did he react to that?"

"Not too well." I told him a bit about my visit to Anthony's house, my happy reunion with his mother, and meeting my old pal, Sally Da-da. I concluded, "Anthony's last remark to me, regarding something I'd said, was, quote, 'None of that changes what your wife did. Just so you know.'"

Mr. Mancuso stayed silent a moment, then asked me, "Have you gone to the police?"

"Yes. Yesterday. We filed a formal complaint."

"May I have the details of your visit to . . . that would be the Second Precinct—correct?"

"Correct." I filled him in on the details, gave him the contact name of Detective A. J. Nastasi, and mentioned that Detective Nastasi had gone to Anthony Bellarosa's house yesterday, but that Anthony seemed to be out of town. I would have mentioned my thought that Anthony was with the Gotti family in Springfield, Missouri, but I didn't want to sound like a Mafia groupie. I did mention, however, that Detective Nastasi had responded to the shooting at Alhambra ten years ago, so that he had, in my opinion, good background knowledge and good interest in this case.

Mr. Mancuso commented, "There is a lot of unfinished business from that evening."

I didn't respond to that, but said, "I'm not sure how Detective Nastasi will react to my calling the FBI."

"Don't worry about that, Mr. Sutter. Since 9/11, we're all on the same team, and we've learned to share information and to cooperate on many levels of law enforcement."

That didn't quite square with what Detective Nastasi told me, but I replied, "Well, that's one good thing that's come out of that tragedy. So, I'll let him know—"

"Don't do that. Let us do that for you."

"I see . . . well, Detective Nastasi, at my suggestion, said this morning that he would contact the FBI Organized Crime Task Force to alert them to this problem. Do you know of any such call?"

"No, I don't. But I'll make some calls and get back to you."

I said, "I thought we could meet."

He reminded me, "As an attorney, you know that the FBI has no direct jurisdiction in a case of what appears to be a personal threat that is not related to Anthony Bellarosa's possible connection to organized crime." He added, "That is a matter for the local police."

"I understand that. But—"

"But we may be able to assist the local police. And we may be able to determine if some Federal law pertains to this."

"Good."

He then informed me, "I'm no longer with the Organized Crime Task Force. But . . . because I worked on the original case, and because you've called me directly, I can make a request that I meet with you. Then I can put you together with the right people here, if appropriate." He added, "I still have a personal interest in the case."

"Do you?"

"I always have, Mr. Sutter."

I understood that he'd taken a personal interest in me, perhaps as part of a continuing education study of how attorneys of high moral integrity become Mafia lawyers. Or maybe he just liked me. His other interest in the case, personal or professional, had to do with the general suspicion that U.S. Attorney Alphonse Ferragamo, who few people seemed to like, had framed Frank Bellarosa for a murder he did not commit. And finally, Mr. Mancuso could not have been happy when the Justice Department—the great wheel of slow but fine-grinding justice, of which Mr. Mancuso was a small cog—told Susan to go home and sin no more.

Mr. Mancuso mused, "That case has always bothered me."

"Me, too." I informed him, "I don't need my soul saved this time."

He chuckled and reminded me, "I didn't do a very good job of that last time."

"Better than you know."

"Good. And I hope you've learned something from that."

"We all have, Mr. Mancuso. Yourself included."

He thought about that, then replied, "Yes, we all learned something about ourselves and about how justice works, or does not work, Mr. Sutter. But all's well that ends well, and I'm happy to hear that you and Mrs. Sutter have reunited."

Actually, he wanted Mrs. Sutter in jail—nothing personal, just business—but I replied, "Thank you." In the interests of re-bonding, I asked him, "And how are you doing?"

"Very well, thank you." He added, "I was about two weeks from retiring when the planes hit the Towers. Now I'm with the Joint Terrorist Task Force."

"I see. Well, I suppose that's where the action is these days."

"Unfortunately, it is." He let me know, "Organized crime is far from a thing of the past, but it's not the problem it once was."

"It is for me, Mr. Mancuso."

He agreed, "Position determines perspective."

"Right. Well, I appreciate you calling me back, and your interest in this."

"And I appreciate you thinking of me, Mr. Sutter, and I thank you for your confidence in me."

"Well, I'm about to be a taxpayer again, Mr. Mancuso, so I thought I'd take advantage of some government service."

Again he chuckled, recalling, I'm sure, how entertaining I could be. He asked me, "Is there a cell phone number where I can reach you?"

I replied, "I'm embarrassed to say no. I need to set up credit and all that. But I'll give you Mrs. Sutter's cell number." I gave it to him and said, "I've mentioned to her that I called you, and I'll tell her we spoke, so she won't be surprised at your call, though you may find her . . ."

"Distraught?"

"What's the opposite of distraught?"

"Well . . . you mean to say that she is not distraught about Anthony Bellarosa's proximity and his statements to you?"

"That's what I mean to say. But *I* am concerned."

"Rightfully so. In fact . . . well, I don't need to add to your concern, but I spent twenty years dealing with these people, and I think I know them better than they know themselves. So, yes, Anthony Bellarosa needs to do something, whether or not he wants to risk that. He needs to live up to the old code, or else he will lose respect and his position will be weakened." He added, "It's about personal vendetta, but it's also about Anthony's leadership position."

"I understand. And I'd like you to make Mrs. Sutter understand. Without frightening her."

"She needs to be frightened."

I didn't reply to that, and hearing it from Special Agent Mancuso was a jolt.

He continued, "But stay calm, and take some precautions, and keep in touch with the local police." He added, "I believe there is a danger, but I don't believe it is imminent."

"Why not?"

"We can discuss that when I see you." He concluded, "All right, I'll make every effort to come out to you tomorrow. Are you free?"

"Yes, I'm unemployed, and so is Mrs. Sutter."

He didn't respond to that and said, "Please give her my regards."

"I will . . ." I was about to sign off, then I had a thought and said, "I may have more work for you, Mr. Mancuso."

"Maybe I should have retired."

I laughed politely, then said, "Something to do with your current assignment on the Terrorist Task Force." He didn't respond, so I continued, "The person who bought Stanhope Hall, Mr. Amir Nasim, is an Iranian-born gentleman, and in a conversation with him last week, he indicated to me that he believes he may be the target of a political assassination plot, originated, I believe, in his homeland."

"I see."

He didn't seem overly interested in this for some reason, so I said, "Well, we can discuss that when you get here if you'd like."

"Please go on."

"All right . . ." So I gave him a short briefing and concluded, "Nasim could be paranoid, or he could have other motives for sharing his concerns with me. But I'm just passing it on to you."

Mr. Mancuso said, "Thank you. I'll look into it." He added, "As we say now to the public, 'If you see something, say something.'"

I assumed that also pertained to law enforcement agencies, so I reminded him, "Please call Detective Nastasi."

Mr. Mancuso wished me a good day, and I did the same.

Well, I felt that I was covering all bases—including reporting on possible terrorist activities in the neighborhood—and that I was being proactive and not reactive, and also that this little corner of the world, at least, was a bit safer than it had been two days ago.

Having said that, I still needed to find the shotgun.

So I went into the basement and spent half an hour among packing boxes, most labeled, but none labeled "Shotgun," or even "Boyfriends, ashes of."

I did, however, find a box marked "John." I assumed that was me, and Emily Post would tell me not to open it. But with the justification that Susan snooped through the gatehouse . . . better yet, the shotgun could be in there, though the box was a bit short. Anyway, I cut open the tape with the box cutter I'd found, and opened the lid.

Inside were stacks of love letters, cards, photos, and some silly souvenirs for Susan that I'd brought back from business trips.

There were also a few printed e-mails on top of the older items, and I took one out and saw that it was from Susan to me in London, dated four years ago. It read: *John, I'm sorry to hear about Aunt Cornelia. I will be in N.Y. for the funeral, and Edward says you will be, too. Just wanted you to know. Hope to see you there, and hope you are well. Susan.*

My reply was attached: *I will be there, as per Edward.*

Short and not so sweet.

I had no idea why she printed this out. Well, I did have an idea, and oddly—or maybe not so oddly—seeing this was painful. She'd been trying to reach out to me, and I was unreachable.

But as Mr. Mancuso and William Shakespeare said, all's well that ends well. Even if we all lost some years that didn't need to be lost.

And standing there—with this e-mail in my hand, and the shotgun still not found, and with Felix Mancuso's words of concern on my mind, and the past casting a long shadow over my and Susan's bright future—I suddenly had this thought that I needed to kill Anthony Bellarosa.

CHAPTER FORTY

Susan always returned from her estate runs through the rose garden, so I sat on the patio with a bottle of cold water and a towel, waiting for her. She'd been gone over an hour, and though I wasn't concerned, I wasn't entirely unconcerned. It occurred to me that we could not live like this for any length of time.

I had one of her cordless phones with me, so I dialed her cell phone. It went into voice mail, and I left a message and decided to go look for her.

I took the cordless phone with me, which has a limited range but was better than nothing, and I went to the front of the house and got into my Taurus.

The cordless phone rang, and I answered, "John Sutter."

I was relieved to hear Susan's voice say, "I'm here . . ." She was out of breath and panted, "On the patio."

"I'll be right there."

I returned to the patio, and Susan was standing on the path in the rose garden, bent forward with her hands on her knees, taking deep breaths. Also, except for her running shoes, she was stark naked.

I thought I should inquire, "Where are your clothes?"

She drew in a long breath and replied, "Oh . . . my sweats are in the laundry, and you said not to wear shorts, so this is all I had left." She added, "Good run."

I wasn't totally buying this, but to play along, I said, "Good thinking. Where did you keep your phone?"

She replied, "Don't ask."

I wondered if it was on vibrate.

She came onto the patio, put her cell phone on the table, then wiped her sweaty face and body with the towel. She took a long swig from the bottled water, then said, "I saw Nasim, and he doubled his offer."

I smiled and replied, "If it were me, I'd pay you to stay."

She put her towel and her bare butt on the wicker chair, then put her feet on the table. She asked me to take off her running shoes, which I did along with her socks. She wiggled her toes, meaning I should rub her feet, which I also did as she poured water over her head, then took a long drink. She threw her head back, drew another breath, and asked, "What have you been doing?"

"Pilates."

She smiled, then said, "It's cocktail time, and it's your turn to make them." She ordered, "Grey Goose and cranberry juice."

I inquired, "Can I get you some clothes while I'm inside?"

"No. I really like being naked."

No argument there. I went into the kitchen and made her drink and made a Dewar's and soda for myself. I also emptied a jar of peanuts into a bowl to give the illusion that it wasn't all about the cocktails.

A word about that—this was, and I'm sure still is, a hard-drinking crowd in our perfect Garden of Eden. Most of it is social drinking, not fall-off-the-barstool drinking, though I'm sure there's a good deal of closet drinking at home. In any case, Susan and I had probably been at the low end of the local weekly alcohol consumption, but by the standards of, say, a dry county in the Midwest, we'd be court-ordered into AA and denounced from the pulpit. More to the point, since our local alert level had just risen to Condition Red, we'd be well advised to limit our alcohol intake.

I carried everything outside on a tray, and noticed that Susan had retrieved her workout clothes from somewhere and thrown them on a chair, which she also used to elevate her legs. The towel was draped around her shoulders and hung over her breasts for modesty.

I gave her her drink, we clinked glasses, and I said, "To summer."

I sat, and we both sipped our drinks and ate peanuts, enjoying the quiet, and the soft breeze that moved through the towering trees beyond the rose garden.

I let her know, "I was a little concerned."

She didn't reply for a few seconds, then said, "You worry too much."

I knew that was coming, so I replied, "There is actually something to worry about."

"I know, but . . . what else can we do?"

There were a number of things we could do, but she didn't want to do them. I said to her, "I looked in the basement for the shotgun, but I couldn't find it."

"Maybe it's somewhere else."

"If we can't find it by tomorrow, I'm going to buy one, or buy a rifle."

She reminded me, "I'm good with a shotgun."

Not too bad with a pistol, either, but that was a sore subject. I informed her, "While you were out, I spoke to Felix Mancuso."

She nodded, and I continued, "He wants to arrange a meeting with us, maybe tomorrow, and I gave him your cell phone number."

"I think it's time you got your own cell phone."

"That's not the point."

"You're running up my bill."

"Susan . . . I really want you to get your head out of the sand and start helping me."

She replied, "All right. I will do whatever you tell me to do."

That, of course, is wife-talk for, "You are a bully, and a complete shithead, and I am the unwilling victim of your domineering personality, but I'll do whatever you tell me to do, darling."

She asked, "Didn't I follow your instructions about running on the property, and taking my cell phone, and not wearing shorts?" She added, "Look at me. I had to run around the estate naked because of you."

It's difficult to get angry at a beautiful naked woman, but I suggested, "When following my instructions, don't be too literal-minded."

She stayed quiet for a moment, then said, more seriously, "No one likes the bearer of bad news. You are only the messenger, and I get the message."

"I know you do."

"And I love you for being worried about me."

I wanted to tell her that Felix Mancuso shared my concern, but that would be better coming from him.

We went upstairs to our bedroom, and Susan informed me, "Running naked makes me hot."

So we took care of that, then showered together. As we were getting dressed for dinner at The Creek, Susan's cell phone rang, and she looked at the display and said, "I think this is your call."

I took the phone and Felix Mancuso said, "How about ten A.M. tomorrow?"

"Fine. You know where we are."

"I do."

In fact, he'd been here twice on business—once to drive me home from Manhattan after the Bellarosa rubout attempt, and once to tell me that my wife had just murdered Frank Bellarosa next door. I said, "See you then," and hung up. I said to her, "Tomorrow, ten A.M." I added, "I want you to be available."

"Of course, darling."

I drove Susan's Lexus down the long drive and past the gatehouse, which now looked dark and forlorn. In a day or so, Nasim might have his own people in there, unless, of course, he decided that no one was really trying to assassinate him. My concerns were more verifiable, so I really didn't mind if I had to go through Checkpoint Nasim to get to my house. Every bit of security helped, though I reminded myself that Anthony Bellarosa's hit men could strike anywhere.

Of more immediate concern was my reentry into The Creek Country Club. On the positive side, no one had ever been whacked there at dinner, though I'd thought about it myself when my dinner companions were boring me to death. I said to Susan, "For the record, I'm not thrilled about going to The Creek."

She replied, "It will be fine. You're with me."

"Right." I still couldn't understand why Susan got a pass on murder, and I was blackballed for bringing a Mafia don to The Creek for dinner. Well, I did understand—she'd only broken the law; I had broken the unwritten club rules. Plus, she was a Stanhope. Regarding her affair with the Don Who Came to Dinner, as I said, that was just too juicy to get her blackballed. In fact, they should give her a year of free membership.

The Creek is a short ten-minute drive from Stanhope Hall, and before I could think of a good reason to turn around, we were headed up the long, tree-lined drive to the clubhouse.

The Creek Country Club is a very pleasant place with a golf course, a beach with a cabana on the Sound, tennis courts, and guest cottages where either the Stanhopes or I would be staying shortly. The clubhouse is an old mansion that still exudes charm and grace, and the food is good after a few cocktails, and gets better after a bottle or two of wine. The service is sometimes off, but that's part of the charm, which I'd tried to explain to Mr. Frank Bellarosa when he and Anna had been our guests here. Frank hadn't quite understood the old tradition of so-so club food and quirky service, which marked him as an unsophisticated lout. There were other problems with his visit here that night, of course, including his and his wife's attire, his snapping at Richard, the old waiter who'd been here forever, and, as I mentioned, his unrealistic and incomprehensible desire to be a member of this club. But thank God I'd avoided that awkward situation when Susan shot him.

I parked in the small lot and we went inside. Susan checked in, and we skipped the bar and lounge, which was crowded and fraught with unpleasant possibilities. The hostess showed us directly to the dining room, seated us at a table for two in the corner, then took our drink orders.

There weren't many people dining this evening, but I saw a few familiar faces, though no former friends or former clients.

Susan asked me, "Are you happy to be here?"

I replied, "When I am with you, darling, I can be happy anywhere."

"Good. We'll take my parents here one night."

I assured her, "If they are comfortable with that, then I look forward to it."

She seemed a bit skeptical, but said, "They love me and want me to be happy."

"Then we all have something in common."

She suggested, "Maybe we'll have our wedding reception here."

"I wouldn't want to put your father through that expense again. I mean, same husband and all that."

She informed me, "This one is on us."

I wondered who paid for Susan's wedding to Dan what's-his-name. I suggested, "Let's keep it small."

"Maybe we could do it outdoors at the guest cottage."

"Don't forget to invite the Nasims. They love a party."

She reminisced, "Our reception at Stanhope Hall was the highlight of the summer season."

Susan had apparently forgotten that it was a theme party, and the theme, set by her father, was "Let's relive World War II"—with food rationing, liquor shortages, and blackout conditions after 10:00 P.M. I said, "It was a night to remember."

She had a good idea and exclaimed, "John, let's do it at Seawanhaka!" She looked at me and continued, "That's where we met, and you're a sailor, so that would be perfect."

All this wedding talk was making me jumpy, so to move on, I agreed. "Perfect."

"Wonderful. I'll call tomorrow and see what's available."

"Call me, too, and see if I'm available."

She took that well and smiled.

Our waitress came with our drinks—two wimpy white wines—and delivered the menus.

Susan and I clinked glasses, and I said, "Lovelier the second time around."

"You're so sweet."

I scanned the menu to see if they'd added an Italian dish since the celebrity Mafia don had dined here. Veal Bellarosa? The Don's Famous Machine Gun Meatballs? Shotgun Pasta Made with Real Shells?

Susan said, "Order sensibly."

"I was thinking of the Chicken Kevlar."

"Where do you see that?"

"Entrées, third down."

She looked and said, "That's Chicken *Kiev*."

"Oh . . . right. Kiev." I put down my menu and said, "It's hard to read in this light. You order for me."

The waitress returned, and Susan ordered chopped salad for two and two poached scrod, which made my mouth water just thinking about it.

Anyway, it was a pleasant and uneventful dinner at The Creek, uninterrupted by anyone we knew, and I was thankful that it was a quiet night in the dining room.

On our way out, however, I caught a glimpse of the bar and lounge and saw a number of people I knew, and a few of them spotted Susan and me. In fact, I saw a lady at one of the tables who reminded me of my mother. Actually, it *was* my mother, sitting with four ladies of her age.

She hadn't seen me, so I continued on toward the front door.

I had not seen my mother since Aunt Cornelia's funeral four years ago, though we'd spoken on the phone about once a month and exchanged appropriate greeting cards. I'd invited her to London, but like many active senior citizens these days, she was too busy. In fact, she was traveling a lot with Elderhostel—not to London, but to exotic places where she could commune with nature and bond with indigenous people who were wise, noble, unmaterialistic, and probably unhygienic. So she was not tempted by my offer to take her to the Imperial War Museum.

Harriet had been a founding member of the Conflicted Socialist Party, refusing, on principle, to join a private club, but not hesitating to be my or someone else's guest. And now, since my father died, it appeared that she'd become a guest of what some members called the

Widows' Wine and Whine Club. I used to spot these ladies in the cocktail lounge here, sipping their wine or sherry, and speaking of their dearly departed husbands with far more affection than they actually had for them when those pains in the asses were alive.

I continued with Susan out the front door. But then I stopped and said, "The time has come to meet the beast."

"What do you mean?"

"My mother is in the lounge."

"John, that's awful." She added, "Let's go say hello."

We retraced our steps and entered the lounge.

Harriet spotted us as we entered, stood, and let out a screech of joy. "John! John!" She said to her friends, "Girls! It's my son, John! Oh, what good and blessed fortune has smiled on me tonight."

Those were not her exact words. In fact, she had no words, so overcome was she with emotion.

I walked to the table with Susan, who took the lead and bent over and exchanged a hug and kiss with her once and future mother-in-law. I did the same.

Harriet introduced us to her friends by saying, "Ladies, this is my son, John, whom I think some of you may remember, and this is his former wife, Susan Stanhope, whom I think you all know, or you know her parents." She then introduced the four ladies to us, and indeed I remembered the Merry Widows or their late husbands, some of whom appeared to be alive the last time I saw them.

Harriet was dressed chicly in her 1970s peasant outfit, and probably wore the same sandals she'd worn at her first anti-war demonstration. That was before Vietnam, so it was another war, though which one remains a mystery to this day. Harriet has long gray hair that I think she was born with, and the only jewelry she wears is made by indigenous people who've been screwed by Western Civilization, and are now returning the favor.

We made idle chatter with the ladies for about one minute, and I could sense that some people at the bar and tables were talking about us. I haven't had so much attention in a bar since cocktails here with the Bellarosas ten years ago.

Harriet did not invite us to sit, so Susan took the opportunity to say to my mother and her friends, "I'm going to steal Harriet away for a minute, if that's all right."

Harriet excused herself, and we went to the lobby. If my mother was wondering why Susan and I were together, she wasn't bursting at the seams to know, and she just looked at Susan.

Susan said to her, "John wants to tell you something."

Indeed, I had many things I wanted to tell Harriet, but I resisted the impulse and said, "Susan and I have reconciled."

Harriet nodded.

I continued, "And we are going to remarry." I gave her more good news and said, "I'm moving back from London."

Again she nodded, then looked at Susan as though she wanted her to confirm this nonsense.

Susan said to her, simply and plainly, "We have never stopped loving each other, and John has forgiven me."

Harriet replied as though, somehow, she knew all of this and had rehearsed a good response. She asked, "Have you forgiven *him*?"

That was a loaded and snotty question, but Susan replied, "We've discussed all the hurt we've caused each other, and we've put it behind us and are ready to move on."

Harriet looked at both of us, then said, "Well, children"—that's what she called us—"I must say this is very sudden, and I'm not sure what to say."

Come on, Harriet, just say, "Fuck you," and get back to your friends.

Susan said to her, "I want you to be happy for us."

Harriet sidestepped that and asked, "Have you spoken to William and Charlotte?"

Susan replied, "We wanted you to be the first to know, though we did call Edward and Carolyn, and they are delighted."

"I'm sure they are."

Susan continued, "We would appreciate it if you didn't mention this to anyone until we have the chance to do that."

Harriet nodded again, then said to Susan, "I don't believe your parents will approve of this, Susan."

Susan replied, "We would like their approval, but we are prepared to proceed without it."

"Are you?"

That meant, of course, that Harriet hoped we understood that the word "approval" in this context meant money.

Susan informed Harriet, "John and I have discussed all of that."

"All right. But I hope your remarriage does not alienate your parents from their grandchildren."

Definition of "alienate": *to be cut out of the will; to have your allowance cut off; to have Grandpa screw around with your trust fund.* And this from a woman who didn't believe in inherited wealth, unless, of course, the dirty old robber baron money was going to her grandchildren. Harriet was a case study in contradictions and hypocrisy.

Susan replied, "I don't see how our remarriage would affect my parents' relationship with their adult grandchildren."

"I hope it doesn't."

I get a little impatient with this kind of polite and evasive talk, so I said to my mother, "You don't need to be happy for us, or to give us your blessing, or even come to our wedding, for that matter. But you do need to mind your own business."

Harriet looked at me as though trying to figure out who I was or how I got there. She said to me, "John, you're being rude."

I continued to be rude and said, "For God's sake, Harriet, life is too damned short for you to just stand there without a smile, or a hug, or a single nice word for us."

Susan said softly, "John . . ."

I announced, "We're leaving. Good evening, Mother."

I walked to the door, and Harriet said, "John."

I turned, and she came toward me, stopped, and looked up at me. We held eye contact for a moment, then she said, "I, too, would like a smile, a hug, or a nice word from you."

Harriet is *very* good at going from aggressor to victim, persecutor to mommy martyr, and ice queen to huggy bear in the blink of an eye. So I responded the way I'd always done since I first figured her out when I was a child, and I gave her a big hug, and we kissed and made up until the next time she took it to the brink.

Susan was smiling, and we did a nice warm and fuzzy group squeeze. I would have given two years of my life for a triple Scotch just then, and so would Harriet.

Anyway, we held on to our smiles, and Harriet said to us, "Your news took me by surprise, and of course I'm happy for you."

"I know you are," said Susan. "John is the most wonderful man in the world, and the only man I've ever loved."

I wasn't too sure about that last part, and Harriet wasn't too sure about the first part, but she said, "That's wonderful."

I said, "It's wonderful to be back."

Susan shot me an annoyed look, then said to Harriet, "We'll let you get back to your friends."

Harriet replied, "I suppose we'll all be together soon at the funeral parlor."

Susan said, "I don't know if you've heard, but Ethel has slipped into a coma."

Harriet nodded. "Yes, I've heard." She prognosticated, "I'm afraid the end is near." Then she eulogized, "Ethel Allard is a great lady."

Well, Harriet Sutter would think so.

We said good night, and Susan and I walked to the car. Susan said, "I'm glad we got that over with."

I wasn't sure if she meant my coming out to dinner at the club or my reunion with Lady Macbeth.

Susan had a perceptive glimpse into the future and said, "This is not going to be easy, is it?"

I used that opening to say, "I think we should move away."

"We did that. Now we are back." She added, "Together."

I assured her, "It's wonderful to be back."

"Your mother looked well."

"She makes her own makeup from recycled medical waste. Mostly blood and bile."

"John."

"Do you think we were both adopted?"

She assured me, "For all their faults, they do love us."

"Well, you got a preview of that strange love two minutes ago. I can't wait to see how your parents are going to top that."

Susan thought a moment, smiled, then said, "Maybe it's us."

"You may be on to something."

We got in the car and headed back to Stanhope Hall. After speaking to Felix Mancuso, I wasn't looking forward to entering the guest cottage at night, but this was not on Susan's mind, and she chatted about our future while I was thinking about the next ten minutes.

CHAPTER FORTY-ONE

It was a dark night, the moon hidden by gathering rain clouds. I'd asked Susan to drive, and as she pulled up to the closed gates of Stanhope Hall, I pressed the remote control button and the gates swung slowly inward.

We proceeded past the gatehouse, and the gates automatically closed behind us.

The three-hundred-yard driveway that led to the guest cottage was narrow, curving, dark, and lined with huge trees, but Susan always saw this as more of a challenge than a hazard, and she began picking up speed.

"Slow down."

"John—"

"Stop!"

She hit the brakes and asked, "What—?"

I reached over and shut off the headlights, then said, "Go on. Slowly."

She looked at me, then understood and began driving slowly up the drive, which was paved with gravel that crunched under the tires. She said, softly, "I can't believe we have to do this."

To lighten the moment, I joked, "Nasim does this every night."

We continued on, and I asked for her cell phone, which she gave me, and I punched in 9-1-1, but not send.

The guest cottage came into view to our left, about a hundred yards away, and I could also see the lights from Stanhope Hall, which lay about a quarter of a mile beyond the guest cottage. If Nasim were watching through binoculars, he might think the assassins were coming for him.

As we drew closer to the cottage, I saw a few lights on inside the house and two exterior lights—one above the front door and one on a stone pillar to mark the turnoff from the driveway that led up to Stanhope Hall. Susan turned left from the main drive into the cottage driveway, and I said to her, "Turn around in the forecourt."

As we reached the forecourt in front of the cottage, Susan swung around so the SUV pointed back to the driveway.

I gave her the cell phone and said, "I'll check out the house, and you will stay here, ready to drive off quickly and call 9-1-1." I added, "And push the panic button on your key fob."

"John, if you think there's a danger, let's just go to a hotel tonight."

I replied, "I don't think there's a danger, but I think we should take normal precautions."

"This is not normal."

"It is now." Then I smiled and said, "Stay here, and stay awake."

"John—"

I got out of the SUV, walked to the front door and checked that it was locked, then I walked to the side path that led to the rose garden to see if any windows were open or broken.

I went around to the back patio and checked the windows and doors, and peered inside. Then I moved to the other side of the house, and as I rounded the corner, something moved in the dark, and I froze.

I'd left a lamp on in the living room, and the light from the window illuminated a patch of the side lawn, and someone came into the light. It was Susan. She spotted me and said, "Everything looks good here."

"I *told* you to stay in the car."

"I stayed in the car. Then I got out of the car." She added, "You were taking too long."

I was very angry with her, but at the same time I was impressed with her courage. Susan is not timid, does not take orders well, and doesn't have much patience with men who want to protect her. I'd seen that dozens of times at sea, and many times when we'd taken cross-country horseback rides. So I said calmly, "I learned in the Army that we all need to follow orders, and do only what we've been told to do, so that no one is taken by surprise." I pointed out, "If I'd had a gun, I might have shot you."

"Wait until we're married."

I wasn't getting anywhere with logic, so I gave up, walked to the kitchen door, and unlocked it. I said, "Wait here."

I went directly to the foyer to assure myself that the basement door was locked, then I did a quick walk-through of the ground floor, turning on the lights in each room. As I said, it's a big house, and I had no intention of securing it room by room every time we came home. But for now—until the police spoke to Anthony Bellarosa and until I spoke to Felix Mancuso, and until we had a gun—that's what I'd do, at least at night. This security check also showed Susan that this was real.

Susan did not wait outside, and she was in the foyer now, so I said, "Stay *here*," and I went upstairs and checked out the five bedrooms, then came down and found her in the office. Apparently we were having a problem with the word "here."

She was accessing her e-mail, and said to me, "My parents are flying in tomorrow . . ." She gave me the details of William and Charlotte's broom ride, then said, "Edward will be in Thursday night, and Carolyn says to let her know when Ethel passes, and she'll take the train in for the wake."

"All right." I noticed the message light on the phone was blinking, so I put it on speaker and retrieved the message. Elizabeth's voice, sounding tired and strained, said, "I just wanted you to know that Mom passed away at eight-fifteen this evening." There was a pause, then she said, "I'll call you tomorrow with the arrangements. Thanks again for being such good friends."

Neither Susan nor I said anything, then Susan dialed the phone, and I heard Elizabeth's voice mail. Susan said, "Elizabeth, we are so sorry. But know that she's at peace now, with God. If there is anything we can do to help with the arrangements, please call us."

I said into the speaker, "Let me know if you'd like us to meet you

at the funeral home. Don't try to handle this all yourself. We want you
to let us help."

Susan hung up and said to me, "I remember when George died,
and how I thought that an era was coming to an end . . . and that a
little piece of my childhood went with him."

I walked to the bar and asked, "Drink?"

"Please. Anything."

I poured two brandies while Susan sent out e-mails, notifying the
appropriate people of Ethel's death.

So, I thought, Ethel Allard was dead. And, I recalled, so was John
Gotti, and they'd died within a day of each other. Aside from that fact,
I'm sure they had very little in common. And yet these two deaths had
impacted my life; Ethel's death had brought me home, and Gotti's death
might unleash a danger that had been on hold for the last ten years.

I gave Susan her brandy, we touched glasses, and Susan said, "To
Ethel."

I shared my thought with Susan and said, "She brought me home."

Susan nodded and confessed, "I asked her to speak to you about
me."

"I know, and she did."

"That was very selfish of me to ask that of a dying woman."

I assured her, "I think she was happy to do it."

Susan agreed, "I think she was."

We took our drinks upstairs, undressed, and got into bed.

We talked and read for a while, then Susan fell asleep. I got out of
bed and went into the basement to take another look for the shotgun.
I still couldn't find it, so I went to the kitchen and got a long carving
knife, then returned to the bedroom, locked the door, and pushed my
dresser in front of it.

I sat up in bed, thinking about all the events that had to happen, in
a certain sequence, to get me here in this bedroom with a carving knife
on my night table.

Well, it could have been worse; I could have been lost at sea. Or,
even worse, married. Or it could have been better; Frank Bellarosa
could have found the restaurant in Glen Cove ten years ago and never
laid eyes on Alhambra, or Susan Sutter.

But things happened and didn't happen, people lived and people died, and at the end of the day, you had to stop wondering why, and you had to start thinking at least one move ahead of anyone who had a fatal move planned for you.

I turned off the lamp, but kept myself half awake through the night.

CHAPTER FORTY-TWO

I t rained through the night, which made it difficult to hear if anyone was trying to get into the house.

I sat up in bed and looked at Susan sleeping beside me; this was still hard to believe. Even harder to believe was that Susan was a marked woman. Well, I'd lost her to Frank Bellarosa, but I was not going to lose her to Anthony Bellarosa.

It had been a long night, and I think I'd gotten myself worked up because of what Felix Mancuso had said—*She needs to be frightened*—and I was glad Mancuso was coming so I could tell him he'd kept me up all night. Susan had no such complaint.

I'm not the paranoid type, and when I'd made my sail around the world, I was one of the few skippers I met who did not keep a rifle on board, even though a few men had refused to crew for me because of that.

There was one time, however, off the Somali coast, when I did need a weapon, and I had to settle for a flare gun. It turned out all right, but barely. After that, I gave in to reality and picked up an AK-47 in Aden, which was easier to buy there than a bottle of Scotch, and cheaper.

With the AK-47 on board, I realized that I slept better at night, and I wondered how I'd gone so long without it. Reality sucks, but having your head in the clouds or up your butt can be fatal.

It was a gray, rainy dawn, but it was a welcome dawn. Of course, people can be murdered at any hour, but we have a primal instinct that tells us to stay alert when we're supposed to be sleeping; there are night predators out there, and they hunt when we sleep.

I got out of bed, put on my robe, and went down to the basement again. After fifteen minutes of searching, I became convinced that the shotgun was back in Hilton Head, or that the movers had stolen it. Well, it was easy enough to buy any shotgun or rifle I wanted at a local sporting goods store. God bless the Second Amendment, and privately owned gun shops. It couldn't be any easier if I was in a souk in Aden.

Here, however, despite my constitutional right to bear arms it was very difficult to obtain a license to own a concealed weapon—a handgun in this area—which is what I actually needed when Susan and I were out of the house. And I was fairly sure that Anthony Bellarosa and La Cosa Nostra did not have that same problem.

I went upstairs and found Susan sitting at the kitchen table in her white teddy that accentuated her tan. She was reading a women's fitness magazine while absently popping vitamins into her mouth and washing them down with carrot juice, which matched her hair.

She looked up from her magazine and said, "Good morning."

I was a little sleep-deprived, and annoyed about the shotgun, and not in the best of moods on this gray morning, so I didn't reply.

She asked, "What were you doing in the basement?"

"I was trying on your winter dresses."

"John, it's too early."

I noticed a pot of coffee brewing, so I poured myself a cup.

Susan suggested, "Have some carrot juice."

"Thanks, but I already had an injection of pomegranate juice."

"It's *really* too early for that."

I asked her, "Are you sure you took the shotgun from Hilton Head?"

"Yes, and I remembered where I put it."

"Good. And where is that?"

"In the attic."

"You said it was in the basement, Susan."

"Basement, attic. Same thing."

"Really? Okay . . . so, if I go up to the attic—"

"I've already done that." She pointed to the broom closet and said, "It's in there."

"Of course." I opened the broom closet, and leaning against the wall between a sponge mop and a broom—where long things are kept—was a gun case.

I took the case out of the closet and removed the shotgun, then ·made certain it was on safety before I examined it.

It was a twelve-gauge, double-barreled, side-by-side, Italian-made Beretta. On the walnut stock was a brass plate on which was engraved *Susan Stanhope Sutter*, and the nickel finish on the receiver was engraved and gold-inlaid with an elaborate floral design. If I had to guess how much this model sold for, I'd say about ten thousand dollars. Maybe it was a wedding gift from Sally Da-da, with thanks to Susan for clipping Frank Bellarosa.

Susan straightened me out on that and said, "Dan gave that to me when I joined a local shooting club."

Apparently Dan didn't know what happened to her last boyfriend.

She suggested, "You can sell it, and get another one if you want."

I guess I had to decide if the shotgun had any sentimental value for her—fond memories of her and Dan blasting clay pigeons out of the sky, or vaporizing ducks in a swamp.

She set me straight on that, too, and said, "He didn't shoot. I did." She added, "He golfed. And golfed."

I assured her, "We can keep this. It has your name on it."

She shrugged and went back to her magazine.

I broke open the gun to be sure she hadn't left shells in the chambers, and peered down the barrels, which were clean enough, but probably the whole gun could use a cleaning and oiling. I asked her, "When was the last time you fired this?"

Without looking up from her magazine, she replied, "About two years ago."

I commented, "It would have been nice to have this last night."

She had no reply.

I asked her, "Do you have a cleaning kit?"

"I couldn't find it."

"Shells?"

"I'll look for them."

Well, the shotgun wouldn't have done much good last night. I said, "I'll just go to a sporting goods store today."

She didn't respond.

I put the shotgun back in its case and said, "I think we should get a dog."

"I had a dog."

"Is he in the attic?"

She ignored that and said, "Dogs are a lot of work. Why do you want a dog?"

Apparently we weren't on the same page. I said, "For security."

"Oh . . . well . . . all right. But let's wait until after the funeral, and after everyone has left." She added, "My parents don't like dogs."

I was sure their pet rats didn't either. I reminded her, "They're probably not staying here."

"Would you mind if they did?"

"I'd be surprised if they did."

She threw her magazine aside and said, "John, I don't think they will react as negatively as you think they will."

"I will be happy to be proven wrong."

"Did I hear that right?"

I had this horrifying thought that today was the first day of the rest of my life. I suggested to her, "Cut down on your Vitamin Bitch pills."

I walked to the refrigerator to see about breakfast, but before I opened the door she said, "For *that* remark, you have to eat *this* for breakfast."

I looked back over my shoulder, and Susan was lying on the table with her spread legs dangling over the edge and her teddy pulled up to her breasts. My goodness.

Well . . . I was thinking about an English muffin, but . . .

After my breakfast of champions, Susan, I, and the shotgun went upstairs to the bedroom, and Susan informed me, "Sophie is coming today. So why don't we put that in your closet?"

"All right." I put the shotgun in my walk-in closet, resting it against the wall behind the open door. I told her where it was, then I got in the shower.

She opened the shower door and joined me, and I scrubbed her back with a loofah sponge, then as she scrubbed my back, I said to her, "Using sex as a means of controlling me or modifying my behavior is not fair."

"All's fair in love and war, John."

"All right. Remember you said that."

"Plus, it works." She put her hand between my legs, gave John a little tweak, and got out of the shower.

As we got dressed, she asked me, "What is the purpose of Felix Mancuso's visit?"

I replied, "To see if the FBI has any interest or jurisdiction in this matter."

She stayed silent for a moment, then said, "He doesn't like me."

"It's not personal. It's professional."

She replied, "I think it's personal."

It was time to dig up the dirty past, because Felix Mancuso would do that anyway, and Susan needed to be prepped for this, so I reminded her, "You killed his star witness in the FBI's case against organized crime, and it's not often that the FBI gets a man like Frank Bellarosa to sing." She didn't respond, so I continued, "Losing a witness to murder, on his watch, did not help Special Agent Mancuso's career."

She stayed silent awhile, then informed me, "He was very much against allowing me to visit."

I knew that, but I was surprised she knew it, or that she was willing to discuss any of this. But I guess the time had come for her to unblock it. As for Felix Mancuso's disapproval of letting Frank and Susan go at it, this was because of his own professional standards, as well as his sense of morality and propriety, and maybe his positive feelings for me, which not everyone around him shared.

And so, to that extent, Susan was correct; it was personal. In any case, what happened was certainly not Mancuso's fault—no one could have foreseen Susan shooting don Bellarosa—but I'd had the impression at the time that Mancuso was the fall guy. Why? Because when the shit hits the fan, the guy who said "I told you so" is usually the guy everyone else pushes in front of the shit stream.

But rather than tell Susan that St. Felix basically thought she was a Mafia groupie and a tramp, I brought the discussion back to the professional issues and said, "Mancuso was also not thrilled that you walked free on the murder charge."

She surprised me by saying, "That was more the fault of his superiors." She added, "I was ready to pay the price."

I looked at her, and I was certain she meant that. And she was right—it wasn't her fault that the government took a dive on the case; the scales of justice are always tipped toward the best interests of the government, and sometimes that means burying inconvenient or embarrassing facts, and letting the guilty go free. It occurred to me that if she'd been indicted and took a plea for maybe manslaughter, she'd be getting out about now. And I'm pretty sure I wouldn't have divorced her, and that I'd have waited for her. Though I may have still taken that sail around the world.

I finished dressing and switched to another unpleasant subject, reminding her, "The next few days are going to be stressful," meaning not only Ethel's wake and funeral, plus trying to avoid our own funerals, but also her parents being somewhere in this zip code. I added, "We need to . . . communicate with each other."

Susan nodded, then said, "I had a very sad dream about Ethel . . . she was sitting alone, crying . . . and I asked her why she was sad. And she said to me, 'Everyone is dead.' So I tried to comfort her . . . but she kept crying, and I was crying, and I had this . . . overwhelming sense of being alone . . . then I said, 'I'll call John.'"

She looked at me, and I could see she was on the verge of tears, so I took her in my arms and we hugged. I said to her, "You're not alone."

"I know. But I was for so many years, and it didn't feel good."

We went downstairs and sat in the kitchen, reading the *Times* and having coffee, waiting for Sophie, for Felix Mancuso, William and Charlotte Stanhope, and whomever and whatever else the day had in store for us.

CHAPTER FORTY-THREE

Sophie, the cleaning lady, came at 8:00 A.M., and Susan's personal trainer, an androgynous chap named Chip, arrived at 8:30. The gardeners showed up to work in the rain, UPS delivered something at 9:00, the mailman came at 9:15, and the dry cleaner came by to drop off and pick up at 9:30. It occurred to me that a Mafia hit man would have to wait his turn in the foyer.

The phone rang all morning, and after Susan finished with her trainer, she spent some time in the office making and taking phone calls and e-mailing. A lot of this communication had to do with Ethel's wake and funeral, and Susan spoke to Elizabeth a few times and also spoke to the funeral home, the florist, and a few limousine companies—do *not* use Bell Car Service—and she also got hold of the caretakers for the Stanhope cemetery. I wanted to suggest that she get two more holes dug for William and Charlotte while she was at it—but she might take that the wrong way. On that subject, I had a question for her. "What do you do when you miss your in-laws? You reload and fire again."

I didn't actually ask her that question, but that did remind me to buy shotgun shells, and further reminded me to tell her, "Reserve a cottage for your parents at The Creek."

She replied, "Let's first see if they want to stay with us."

"What time are they arriving?"

"I told you five times—they arrive at LaGuardia at three-fifteen, and they should be here about five." She added, "We'll have cocktails and discuss . . . things."

"All right." Where do you keep the rat poison? "What time is the viewing tonight?"

"I also told you that. Seven to nine." She filled me in on the daily viewing schedule, and apparently Ethel had left instructions for an extended engagement at the funeral home, so that no one had an excuse to miss her final act. Susan concluded, "The funeral Mass is Saturday at ten A.M. Do you want me to write this down?"

"No. I have you, darling."

She further informed me, "This Sunday is Father's Day. In my e-mail exchanges with my parents and the children, it appears that we'll all be here on Sunday, so I've suggested dinner at home to mark the occasion."

Susan seemed more optimistic than I was about this reunion, but I said, "That's very thoughtful of you." I inquired, "Do your parents know that I'm here?"

"They know from the children that you are back for the funeral, and that you are living in the gatehouse."

"Actually, I'm not."

"They haven't been updated on that."

"Right. And they have no problem with me being here for a Father's Day dinner?"

"They understand that Edward and Carolyn want you to join us for Father's Day." She added, "I told them I was fine with that."

"I see. So when do we tell your parents that I'm living here and sleeping with you?"

"When they arrive." She explained, "It's better to present them with a fait accompli."

Which, hopefully, would lead to them having a grand mal seizure, followed by me administering a coup de grace with the shotgun. "All right. Do it your way."

She changed the subject and inquired, "Do you think I should invite your mother, or will that be sad for her with your father gone?"

I replied with overdone enthusiasm, "Harriet would be *delighted* to be included, and I look forward to having dinner with her *and* your parents."

Susan looked at me closely and asked, "Can you handle all that?"

I replied, "The answer is martinis."

She had no comment on that, except to say, "I'm counting on you, John, to set a good example for Edward and Carolyn."

"You can count on me, sweetheart." I honestly intended to do my best to put the fun back into dysfunctional, and I suggested, "Your father and I will sit at the opposite heads of the table and sing a duet of 'Oh, My Papa.'"

She still seemed skeptical for some reason, so I added, "I will honor your father on that special day, Susan, because he gave me you."

"That's very sweet of you, John." She reminded me, "We're really doing this for Edward and Carolyn, so if you have to bite your tongue a few times, the children will respect you even more for being a big man. And if my father is not pleasant, then that is his problem."

"Always has been."

"And please do not sit there like you did at the last dinner we had together, simmering until you exploded and called him . . . whatever."

"An unprincipled asshole, a—"

"All right, John. And you promised to apologize for that."

"I'm anxious to do that."

She looked at me closely and said, "John . . . it's for the children . . . and I don't mean their emotional well-being—I mean their financial well-being."

"I know exactly what you mean." I did remind her, however, "You didn't think your parents would financially punish their grandchildren because of us." I couldn't resist adding, "No one would be so vindictive."

She replied, "Let's not test that assumption."

"I hear you." I asked her, "Will we have the pleasure of your brother's company for these sad and happy occasions?"

She replied, "Peter will not be in for Ethel's funeral. But he'll try to make it in for Father's Day."

"Wonderful. And where is Peter working these days?"

"The Bahamas."

"Doing what?"

"Surfing."

"Right. Well, if he starts now and catches a few good waves, he can be here by Sunday."

I thought that would make her angry, but she smiled and said, "The Stanhopes bring out the best of your wit."

You ain't seen nothing yet, lady. I changed the subject and reminded her, "Felix Mancuso will be here shortly. I'm counting on *you*, Susan, to put aside any negative feelings you may have toward him, and to be helpful and pleasant." I added, "Just as I will do with your parents."

"All right. Point made." She thought for a moment, then said to me, "This is everyone's chance to make up for the past. Or at least, let go of the past."

"Indeed, it is."

I thought about my deathbed conversation with Ethel, who I sincerely hoped had had similar conversations with everyone who visited her. We don't all have the certainty of a long goodbye, so we often miss the chance to set things right before we stop breathing and talking.

Alternately, we can leave letters behind for everyone, in case we didn't get a chance to say, "Sorry I was such an asshole," and I suspected that Ethel's letter to me was along those lines. And if the truth be known, there were three such letters from me, sitting with my solicitor in London; one each to Edward and Carolyn, and one to Susan. The easiest letter to write is the one that begins, "If you're reading this, it means that I am dead . . ." Maybe I should also write one to William and Charlotte: *Dear Assholes* . . .

Susan asked me, "What are you thinking about?"

"About . . . how lucky we are . . . you and I . . . and how lucky I am that you made this happen . . . and that no matter what happens next, we've had this time together."

The doorbell rang at 10:00 A.M., and I opened the door to Special Agent Felix Mancuso.

We shook hands and exchanged greetings, and as I showed him into the foyer, he took off his rain hat, and I saw that his baldness hadn't progressed much in ten years, but what was left of his hair had gone from black to salt-and-pepper. When his beat had been La Cosa Nostra, Special Agent Mancuso's Italian-made suits were always better than theirs; but now, I noticed, his gray suit and his shirt and tie were nothing special, and he'd blend in nicely on the streets of New York as he followed terrorists around the city—or whatever he did with the Terrorist Task Force. I noticed, too, he was wearing a flag pin on his lapel, the better to blend in with everyone else in New York.

Susan was in the kitchen, and I'd asked her to give me ten minutes with Mancuso, so I showed him into my new old office and invited him to sit in my old leather club chair. He did a quick scan of the room as I sat at my desk chair and shut off the phone ringer.

He said to me, "This is a very nice place you have here." He asked, "And this was your wife's family estate?"

"We like to say ancestral home."

He saw I was being droll, so he smiled.

I informed him, "She owns only this guest cottage and ten acres. Most of the remaining acreage and the main house are now owned by Mr. Amir Nasim, who, as I mentioned, has a few problems of his own that may interest you."

Mr. Mancuso did not reply to that. He said, instead, "I wish you luck here. It must be nice to be home."

"It is, except for my Alhambra neighbor."

He nodded.

As I said, he'd been here twice before—once when he'd offered me a ride home from the city after Frank Bellarosa survived the Giulio's shooting, and once when he'd given me a ride to Alhambra to show me the result of Susan's better aim in ending Frank's life.

On that subject, I needed to clear some of the air from the last time we'd spoken, and I began, "Mrs. Sutter told me that she believes you may harbor some negative feelings toward her."

He replied, frankly, "I did. But I've become more realistic since we last had occasion to interact."

And, I thought, probably less idealistic. Especially after he'd taken a career hit for something that was not his fault. In the end, Susan had gotten off easier than Special Agent Mancuso, proving once again that life is not fair. I said to him, "I think Mrs. Sutter can be more helpful this time."

He probably wondered how she could be any less helpful than last time, but he replied, "I'm glad to hear that." He informed me, "My personal feelings, Mr. Sutter, have never interfered with my professional conduct."

To keep it honest, I said, "You know that's not true." I pointed out, "But that could be a positive thing. For instance, I appreciated your personal concern about my involvement with Frank Bellarosa." I suggested, "Mrs. Sutter could also have benefited from your advice."

He thought about that, then replied, "You make a good point. But quite frankly . . . well, that was *your* job."

"Also a good point. And I'll go you one better—she should have insisted that I not get involved with Frank Bellarosa, but instead she encouraged me to do so."

He did not seem surprised at that revelation, probably having long ago deduced the dynamics of the John-Susan-Frank triangle. He did say, however, "There was a point when . . . well, when it was no longer simply some taboo fun or whatever it was for the both of you. It was at that point when you both needed to save each other, and your marriage."

"And don't forget our souls. But by the time we realized that, Mr. Mancuso, it was far too late."

"It usually is."

I gave him some good news. "Mrs. Sutter was *vehemently* opposed to my even speaking to Anthony Bellarosa."

He responded, as I knew he would, "I'm glad someone learned their lesson." He smiled, and I was treated to that row of white Chiclets that I remembered.

I reminded him, "We've *all* learned our lessons."

The intercom on the phone buzzed, and I picked it up. Susan asked, "Shall I make my grand entrance?"

I was glad I hadn't hit the speaker button, nor would I ever with Susan on the line. I replied, "Yes, and please have one of the servants bring coffee."

"The last servant left thirty years ago, but I'll see what I can do."

"Thank you. About five minutes." I hung up and said to Mr. Mancuso, "We're out of servants at the moment, but Mrs. Sutter will bring coffee."

Again he smiled, then took the opportunity to say, "I never understood how two people from your world could have gotten involved in Frank Bellarosa's world."

I thought about that and replied, "Well, if that's a question, I don't have an answer."

He suggested, "Part of the answer may be that evil is seductive. I think I told you that."

"You did. Add to that a little restless boredom, and you have at least part of the answer to your question." I added, "I'm speaking for myself. I'm not entirely sure what motivated Mrs. Sutter to do what she did."

"Did you ask?"

"Not directly. But you can ask her if it's bothering you." I added, "It might possibly have to do with sex."

He didn't seem shocked by that, though he would have been shocked if I'd told him it was also about love. But that was none of his business.

He thought a moment, then replied, "Adultery is a symptom of a larger problem."

"Sometimes. But to paraphrase Freud, sometimes adultery is just adultery." I asked, "And what difference does it make now?"

"Because, Mr. Sutter, to know and to understand is the first step toward real reconciliation. More importantly, it is absolutely critical that you know who you are, who she is, and what you are forgiving."

I could see that Mr. Mancuso was still practicing psychology and still giving spiritual advice. Plus, he'd added marriage counseling to his repertoire. I asked him, "I don't mean to be . . . disrespectful, but do you have any professional training outside of the law and law enforcement?"

He didn't seem insulted by the question, and responded, "As a matter of fact, I spent two years in the seminary before deciding that wasn't my calling."

I was not completely surprised. I'd actually known a number of

Catholic lawyers and judges and a few men in law enforcement who'd once been seminarians. There seemed to be some connection there, though what it was, was only partially clear to me. I asked him, "What made you decide that the priesthood was not your calling?"

He replied, without embarrassment, "The temptations of the flesh were too great."

"Well, I can relate to that." I thought about suggesting that he become an Episcopalian and give the priesthood another try, but he changed the subject and said, "If I may make a final observation about what happened ten years ago . . . in all my years of dealing with crime, organized and otherwise, I have rarely come across a man with the sociopathic charm and charisma of Frank Bellarosa. So, if it makes you feel any better, Mr. Sutter, you, and your wife, were seduced by a master manipulator."

"That makes me feel much better."

"Well, I offer it for what it's worth."

Felix Mancuso seemed to believe that the history of the human race could best be understood as a struggle between good and evil, with Frank Bellarosa being Satan incarnate. But that did not explain Frank Bellarosa's all too human feelings of love for Susan Sutter, and his final good and honorable deed toward me that caused his death.

To move on to the present problem, I let him know, "Anthony Bellarosa is not as complex or as charming, or even as intelligent, as his father."

Mr. Mancuso replied, "No, he's not. And that's why he's far more likely to resort to violence whenever he's frustrated or when anyone challenges him."

"Right. He is not Machiavellian. He's more like Caligula."

Mr. Mancuso smiled and nodded. He informed me, "His unofficial nickname is—not to his face—Little Caesar." He speculated, "I think it's the word 'little' that would set him off. Not the word 'Caesar.'"

I confessed, "Anthony and I had a few conversations about the decline and fall of the Roman Empire."

He had no comment on that, which I thought was a little odd, so I continued, "Over dinner at a Chinese restaurant in Glen Cove."

Again, he had no comment, so I inquired, "Did we have company there?"

He informed me, "I had the opportunity to read the statement you gave to the police."

"I see." But I never mentioned that detail in the statement.

Well, it must have been the waitress. Only a government worker could have been so incompetent. Joking aside, I wasn't thrilled to think that there may have been a bug in my wonton soup. But Mr. Mancuso wasn't confirming or denying—he was taking the Fifth.

So I changed the subject and said, "Your remark to me that Susan should be frightened caused me to have a sleepless night."

"Well, I didn't want you to take this lightly." He added, "I hope I didn't upset Mrs. Sutter."

"She's blissfully unaware that Anthony Bellarosa is, or may be, a psychopath. I'd like *you* to raise her level of concern . . . without over-doing it."

"I understand." He added, "What I don't understand is why she's not properly concerned now."

I replied, "It's her nature, and also her upbringing."

"What does that mean?"

"It's a bit complex, but basically, she's led a sheltered and privi-leged life—sort of like . . . well, a dodo bird on an isolated island—and therefore she doesn't know what danger looks like, sounds like, or smells like."

He thought about that, processed it, then observed, "We had a whole country like that until September of last year."

"Interesting analogy."

Mr. Mancuso informed me, "I actually had the opportunity to read the Justice Department's psychiatric report on Mrs. Sutter as well as the analysis offered by her family-retained psychiatrists, and it's . . . interesting."

I was sure of that, though I knew he wasn't able to elaborate. I did say, however, "Her mental state ten years ago is not my concern. My concern is her present attitude toward the obvious danger she is in— and the problem there, I believe, is more her personality than any psychological conflicts or subconscious . . . whatever. And what I'd like you to do is to wake her up."

He nodded and replied, "I'll give her the facts and also my opinion on the threat level."

"Good. Give it to me now." I suggested, "Use our new color-code system if that's easier for you."

He forced a smile, then said, "I'll need to hear what you and Mrs. Sutter have to say before I come up with a color."

Susan hadn't made her entrance yet, so Mr. Mancuso confided in me, "You may be interested to know that I've lectured on this case at the Academy."

"Really? I hope you weren't too hard on the Sutters."

He didn't respond directly, but said, "The audience always had more questions than I had answers."

"Me, too."

He looked at me and said, "I welcome this opportunity to revisit some of these issues and questions."

"Well, Mr. Mancuso, I don't, but that's what's happened."

He agreed, "The chickens are coming home to roost."

Before I could reply to that statement, Susan opened the door and said, "One more chicken."

CHAPTER FORTY-FOUR

Felix Mancuso and I stood, and I said, "Susan, you remember Special Agent Mancuso."

She smiled pleasantly, offered her hand, and said, "Of course I do. Thank you for coming."

He replied, "I'm glad to be of service again."

I didn't think Susan was so happy with his service last time, and they both knew that.

The pleasantries out of the way, Susan motioned to Sophie, who was at the door with a serving cart, which she wheeled in, then left and shut the door.

Susan invited us to help ourselves, which we did, then she sat on the couch, and Mr. Mancuso and I returned to our seats.

Susan was dressed modestly in a traditional native outfit of tan slacks and a white blouse, over which she wore a tailored blue blazer. I would have liked to see a cross around her neck, but that might be overkill.

I mean, maybe we were both overreacting to Felix Mancuso's middle-class, Catholic morality, and his opinion of Susan's past adultery, and murder, and me working for the mob; but Felix Mancuso seemed to be genuine in his beliefs, and I was certain that Susan and I shared many of his moral convictions, as well as his low opinion of our past behavior. But it was time to move on to new problems.

Susan inquired, "Did I miss anything important?"

I replied, "Not really. We were just rehashing the subject of how you and I screwed up our lives."

She replied, "Well, I'm glad I didn't miss anything too important." We all smiled.

Mr. Mancuso said to her, "I wish you and Mr. Sutter good luck and happiness in your future marriage."

Susan replied, "Thank you. That's very kind of you."

Susan, I could tell, was in her full Lady Stanhope mode, which may or may not have been the right thing to do with Felix Mancuso. Susan, however, could have been reacting to the last time she'd seen Special Agent Mancuso—she'd been wearing a nice riding outfit, but also wearing handcuffs, which seriously diminished her stature. Not to mention she'd been crying, and a female police officer was bossing her around, and her lover's body was splattered on the floor in full sight of everyone. So, yes, this reunion with Special Agent Mancuso was difficult or embarrassing for her, which was probably why she'd showed up as Lady Stanhope.

Felix Mancuso said to Susan, "As I explained to Mr. Sutter on the phone, I am no longer with the Organized Crime Task Force, but because of my prior involvement with the case that has led to this possible threat, and because Mr. Sutter called me directly, I have been assigned to evaluate this matter and make a recommendation regarding how the Bureau will proceed." He added, "This appears to be a state matter—a personal threat with no direct link to organized crime, other than Mr. Bellarosa's alleged involvement in organized crime—but rest assured, the Bureau will offer the local authorities any support or information they need or ask for."

I thought I should tell him, "Someone from the county police told me that the FBI wouldn't tell him if his ass was on fire."

Mr. Mancuso actually smiled, then reassured me, "Regardless of that perspective, we've opened up many lines of communication since 9/11." He further assured me, "We all have the same goal here, which is to put Anthony Bellarosa behind bars for the rest of his life, and personally, I don't care if he spends his life in a Federal or a state prison."

But, of course, a Federal prison would be Mr. Mancuso's first choice. *My* first choice was to see Anthony dead. I reminded him, "Our primary goal is to ensure that nothing happens to Mrs. Sutter."

"That goes without saying."

Susan, the subject of this conversation, said, "For the record, I'm concerned, but not paranoid." She added, "My goal, if you're interested, is to live a normal life." She said to Mr. Mancuso, "As with terrorism, if you're frightened, and if you change the way you live, then the terrorists win. Well, they're not going to win. *He* is not going to win."

Felix Mancuso looked at Susan Sutter appraisingly, then said to her, "I admire your courage."

Susan didn't reply, so Mancuso moved on to another subject and said to us, "As I've mentioned to Mr. Sutter, I've had the opportunity to review the statements you've made to the police, so I have a general idea of what's transpired in the last few weeks, and I have an understanding of why you are both concerned."

I reminded him, "You yourself seemed concerned."

He nodded, and replied, "I have done some investigative work on Anthony Bellarosa's criminal enterprises over the years, and while I've never had direct contact with him, I have had direct contact with a number of his associates, and also a number of people who I believe were victimized by him and his organization." He added, "And I've spoken to a number of my colleagues who have had direct contact with Bellarosa, and the picture that emerges is of a man who is violent, but careful."

I offered my opinion and said, "I think he's a hothead, so he won't always be so careful about what he does."

He nodded, then informed us, "Anthony Bellarosa represents the new, middle-class, suburban Mafia. These men are third- and fourth-generation Italian-Americans, and some of them are not even a hundred percent Italian, and many of them are marrying non-Italians, as did Anthony Bellarosa. So, what I'm saying is that the stereotype does not always fit, and the level of violence is down, but it's there under the surface, and it's always an option with these people." He added, "Especially when it's personal."

I understood all of that, and I thought again of Anthony as a young tiger cub, three or four generations removed from the wild, apparently domesticated, but still reacting to some primitive instincts when he smelled blood. I said to Mancuso, "The police said they don't have a rap sheet on him."

Mr. Mancuso replied, "We think he's had at least fourteen people beaten, but we can't connect him, directly or through contract, to any homicides."

Recalling some Mafia lore, I inquired, "So, he hasn't made his bones?"

Mr. Mancuso replied, "I'm sure he has, or he wouldn't be where he is in the organization, but it's never come to our attention, and he doesn't make a habit of it."

Susan said, "I think I missed something. About the bones."

I left it to Mr. Mancuso to explain, "That means to personally commit a murder. As opposed to contracting for a murder."

Susan said, "Sorry I asked."

Felix Mancuso drew a notebook out of his pocket and said to us, "I'd like each of you, in any order you wish, to tell me anything you may not have said in your statement to the police." He instructed us, "What you tell me can be opinions, impressions, and feelings, in addition to observations and details that may not have seemed important to you, but which may mean something to me in a larger context, or could become important later."

That seemed to give me a lot more latitude than I'd had with the police, and it opened the possibilities of having a little fun with my descriptions of Sunday at the Bellarosas'. On the other hand, this was a serious matter, plus I didn't want Mr. Mancuso to get the idea that I thought his *paesanos* were unintentionally funny. Susan suggested that I go first, so I began at the beginning with the knock on my door, and Mr. Anthony Bellarosa crossing my threshold.

I concluded with, "Anthony was on a mission, which was to recruit me, so he brought up the subject of Susan to use later as a bargaining chip." I added, "The deal was always going to be that she stayed alive as long as I worked for him."

Mr. Mancuso didn't comment on that and said, "Please proceed."

So I poured more coffee and continued the story of John and Anthony, going next to the dinner at Wong Lee's, meeting Tony, formerly known as Anthony, and relating my phone conversation with Anna, and even repeating Anthony's jokes about Mom, which caused Mr. Mancuso to smile, perhaps remembering his own mother.

I went on to Anthony's rudeness to the Chinese waitress, to give everyone a less amusing image of Anthony Bellarosa. I continued on to the rest of the conversation with Anthony, about his father, and related matters, and I concluded with my abrupt and angry departure. I asked Mr. Mancuso, "Am I giving you too much information?"

He assured me, "There is no such thing as too much information when you're in the information business." He further informed me, "We build personality profiles on these people, and anyone, like yourself, who has had intimate contact with a person such as this can provide valuable insight into how they think, act, talk, and react."

"Okay." So, I told him Anthony's jokes about Chinese women, but he didn't smile. Neither did Susan, who said, "Disgusting."

That may have crossed the too-much-information line, so I moved on to the details of my chance encounter with Anthony on Grace Lane, and my ride to Oyster Bay. I kept the narrative honest, and as Mancuso had suggested, I editorialized now and then.

Mr. Mancuso nodded a few times and raised his eyebrows at appropriate points in my story to show me he disapproved of my possible interest in being Anthony's *consigliere*, notwithstanding my prior explanation about my concern for Susan. Now and then, he jotted a note.

When I finished with the Oyster Bay episode, Susan commented, "Well, he certainly picked the right person to tell him when his head was getting too big."

That was supposed to be funny, so I chuckled, and even Mr. Mancuso smiled. I suggested, however, "Why don't we leave the opinions to me, darling, until it's your turn?"

Mr. Mancuso urged me to continue, and I picked up the narrative on Sunday morning, and my visit to Susan, to establish the time frame when we'd reconciled. I laid it on a little thick here, mentioning Susan's remorse for what she'd done, and assuring Mr. Mancuso that Susan, like Mary Magdalene, had achieved an understanding of her sins, leading to her full redemption and possible sainthood.

Well, I didn't really go that far, but I wanted Mr. Mancuso to understand that Susan Sutter, sitting here now, was not the same fallen woman she'd been ten years ago, and that she was worth saving. Felix Mancuso needed to put aside any subconscious thoughts he might be harboring about the wages of sin being death, or that if something happened to Susan, she had it coming. Special Agent Mancuso was a professional, but he was also a man who had been deeply shocked and professionally wounded by what happened ten years ago. Nevertheless, he'd do his job, but he'd do it even better if he believed he was on the side of the angels.

He interrupted my canonization of Susan and said, "If I may be personal . . . I'm not following how you reconciled so quickly after a ten-year separation."

Well, Susan Stanhope Sutter is one of the great lays of my life. No—the *greatest.*

"Mr. Sutter?"

"Well . . . it was as though this dam had burst, letting loose a decade of anger, hurt, disappointment, betrayal, and stubbornness. And after that flood subsided, what was left was a deep, placid lake of . . . well, love."

I thought I heard Susan groan, but Mr. Mancuso nodded and said, "Please continue."

I recounted my drive to Alhambra, including Bell Security Service at the gate, and my meeting Megan Bellarosa, and my reunion with Anna. It was here that I could get into trouble with Mr. Mancuso if I made fun of an Italian mother, so I downplayed Anna's bossiness toward her son, and I emphasized her positive qualities of love, warmth, hospitality, and good cheer. I concluded that segment of the story with, "I wish I had a mother like that." I realized that I wasn't being totally insincere, so it came out all right, and Mr. Mancuso smiled.

I was doing pretty good so far, having gotten past the tricky stuff about Anthony and me talking about a new career for me, and from here on, the story put me in a favorable light, but more importantly, I was leading up to the barely concealed threats on Susan's life.

I informed Mr. Mancuso, "Salvatore D'Alessio, a.k.a Sally Da-da, was on the back patio with his wife, Marie."

Mr. Mancuso didn't seem to react to that, so I inquired, "Are you watching his house?"

Mancuso said, "That was in your statement to the police. Please continue."

"All right." I related the details of my chance reunion with Uncle Sal, and shared with Mr. Mancuso my thoughts and observations regarding the relationship between Sal and Anthony, then I moved on to my continuing employment interview with the CEO of Bell Enterprises, emphasizing here that Anthony was too dense to understand that I wasn't leaping at his offer. I also mentioned my thought that the women in Anthony's life did not treat him like the *padrone*. Mr. Mancuso smiled at my use of the Italian word, and nodded. I mentioned, too, about telling Anthony that my daughter was an assistant district attorney in Brooklyn.

Mr. Mancuso commented, "So, you have a member of the family in law enforcement."

Susan, proud mom, chimed in, "She loves her job, and she works twelve-hour days." She added, "I'm very proud of her."

Mr. Mancuso smiled, probably thinking, *At least one member of this family has gone straight.*

We were all bonding now, and I was in the home stretch and way ahead, so I moved on to Anthony's den and my phone call to Elizabeth and Susan. I would not have even mentioned the phone call to Elizabeth, except that Mr. Mancuso had probably already listened to the tape recording of that call, along with mine to Susan. And, as a lawyer, I know that when you leave something out, or lie to the law, even about a small thing, it calls into question your veracity about other things.

Mr. Mancuso seemed interested that I was in Anthony Bellarosa's private den, and he asked me to describe it.

So to add a few details to Anthony Bellarosa's personality profile, and to further justify my social call on him, I said that Anthony kept his father's books from La Salle Military Academy on his shelves, and that Anthony had a collection of books written by, or about, the Romans.

Mancuso nodded and said, "As I mentioned before Mrs. Sutter joined us, Anthony Bellarosa may have a Caesar complex." He smiled and added, "Many of them do." He said to me, "Please continue."

I was going to move on from the subject of the Romans, but I found it interesting that a man who was basically uninteresting and uncomplicated had this other side to him, and I suggested, "Some of his admiration for the Romans may have to do with what I mentioned before—Anthony is henpecked, and . . . well, the Romans were macho."

Mr. Mancuso nodded politely, but I had the feeling he thought I was getting carried away with myself, so to make my point and also to continue my description of the den, I said, "Over the fireplace, he has a reproduction of Rubens' Rape of the Sabine Women." I added, in case Mr. Mancuso wasn't familiar with the classical tale, "The Romans raped the women of the Sabine tribe."

Mr. Mancuso nodded, and Susan assured me, "I think we understand. Can we move on?"

"All right." I finished my description of the den, and I was now at the point in my story where I had to tell about seeing Susan's oil painting of Alhambra in Anthony's den, and slashing it to ribbons. I hadn't put this in my statement to the police, and Susan didn't know about this, and I couldn't guess at what she'd think or say. Also, I couldn't determine if this destructive act made me a tough guy or a nut job. So, without putting any spin on it, I simply said, "There was an oil painting on an easel in Anthony's den, and I recognized it as the painting Susan had done of the palm court at Alhambra—"

Mr. Mancuso interrupted and said to me, "You put your fist through it that night."

"I did." I added, "Someone had it restored."

Susan, who never knew I'd smashed her painting, looked at me, but said nothing.

I got to the point and said, "I took a letter opener and slashed the painting to shreds."

No one had anything to say about that, so I poured another cup of coffee for myself.

Finally, Mr. Mancuso asked, "Why?"

Good question. I replied, "It was a symbolic act with deep psychological overtones, coupled with a primal belief that my enemy should not possess anything that was associated with, created by, or even touched by my once and future wife."

Mr. Mancuso seemed deep in thought, as though he were making mental notes for a psychological profile on me.

Susan, I sensed, was looking at me, so I made eye contact with her.

I realized my explanation was a little weird, so I tried a simpler explanation and said, "I was just pissed off at him, and I guess I wanted to leave him a message."

Felix Mancuso said to me, "Well, I'm sure he got the message, Mr. Sutter. And knowing his type, I'm also sure he has a return message for you."

"I'm sure he does."

I concluded my account of Sunday with Anthony by relating, almost word for word, as I'd done with Detective Nastasi, our confrontation on his front lawn, and my telling him that his father was a stool pigeon and was selling out his friends and family in exchange for immunity from prosecution. I did not, however, reveal to Mr. Mancuso, or to Susan, that I'd told Anthony that his father and my wife were in love, and were prepared to run off together—and would have, if Frank hadn't owed me a favor.

I ended with something I hadn't said to Detective Nastasi, and hadn't really focused on before. I said to Felix Mancuso, "Anthony Bellarosa's eyes, his face, and his tone of voice . . . If we weren't standing on his own front lawn, and if he'd had a gun, I think he would have killed me."

Susan stood, came up beside me, and took my hand.

Mr. Mancuso had no comment, but he also stood and said, "I think it's time for a break."

CHAPTER FORTY-FIVE

Felix Mancuso remained in my office, and Susan and I took our break in the upstairs parlor, long ago converted to a family room, where we would gather to watch television when Edward and Carolyn were young. I don't know what the prior owners had done with this room, but Susan had faithfully reproduced the feel, if not the actual furnishings, of the room, including some old movie posters that I remembered, though *The Godfather* seemed to be missing.

Susan opened two bottles of spring water and gave one to me. We remained standing, and I looked out the window at the rain.

Susan said to me, "I have a much clearer picture now of what happened between you and Anthony Bellarosa."

I replied, "More importantly, I hope you have a clearer understanding of the threat he may pose to you."

"And to you."

I replied, "He's angry at me, and maybe disappointed. But he'll get over it. This is about you."

She said to me, "He *threatened* you, John."

I didn't reply.

She asked me, "Why in the world did you slash that painting?"

"I told you."

"But . . . why would you want to make him even more angry?"

I looked away from the window and replied, "If you really want to know, Susan, that fucking painting brought back to me your time spent at Alhambra, your affair with—"

"All right. I think you overreacted, but—"

"That was why I put my fist through it ten years ago, and this time, no one is going to have it restored."

She stayed silent for a moment, then said, "I understand."

Neither of us spoke for a while, then Susan said, "But what I don't understand is . . . I'm not understanding what caused Anthony Bellarosa's explosive rage . . . he apparently liked you, and thought highly of you . . . and then he turned on you and threatened you." She asked, "Why?"

I finished my water and replied, "As I said to Detective Nastasi, and as I just said to Mancuso—I told Anthony that you and I were back together, and that he and I were through." I added, "Think of it as . . . well, a romantic triangle." I wanted to say, "You know about that," but I said instead, "He's not used to being scorned." I added, "And what really set him off was me telling him that his father was singing his heart out to the FBI."

She nodded, but I could see that she still seemed unsatisfied with my explanation. Susan, for all her aloofness and intermittent nuttiness, had an uncanny ability to spot bullshit. Especially when it came from me.

She looked at me and asked, "Are you telling me everything?"

I turned the question around and asked her, "Are you telling *me* everything? About you and Frank?"

She looked me in the eye and replied, "I did. I told you I loved him, and that I killed him because he told me it was over, and told me that he used me, and never loved me, and that he was going to Italy with Anna. And I also told you that I didn't kill him for us—that was a lie. What more can I tell you?"

I took a deep breath and replied, "Nothing."

She asked me again, "Are you telling *me* everything?"

We both stayed silent for a while, and I realized that the time had come—actually, I never intended for this time to come, but this was still bothering me more than I realized, and she'd been honest with me, so I needed to do the same, and if she reacted badly, then we'd both learn something new about each other.

I suggested we sit, but she remained standing, so I did, too. I said, "All right . . . here's the missing piece—here's why Anthony lost control of himself." I let her know, "I told Anthony that you and his father were in love, and that you were both planning to abandon your families and go to Italy together." I added, "He didn't believe me, and insisted that his father was just—quote, sport fucking. But I convinced him that his father was ready to say arrivederci to his wife and sons."

She nodded, and I could have left it there because that explained Anthony's sudden change of heart toward John Sutter, the messenger of this unwanted news. But having begun, I needed to finish, so I said to her, "There's more. And it's not something you want to hear."

"I'm used to that by now."

"All right." So I began by telling her what I'd already told Anthony—that Frank Bellarosa offered me any favor that it was in his power to do, in exchange for me having saved his life. Then I told her, "The favor I asked him was . . . to tell you it was over, Susan, and that he never loved you, and that he was using you to get to me, and that he was not taking you to Italy with him." I added, "And, obviously, he did that. For me."

I looked at her, and we made eye contact. I could see she was having trouble grasping this, but then she understood that everything that Frank Bellarosa had said to her that night came from my mouth, not his heart. And so she'd shot the man she loved, and who still loved her.

Susan sat on the couch and stared blankly at the wall.

I said to her, "I told all this to Anthony—that his father would have abandoned him, his mother, and his brothers, and the only reason he didn't was because his father owed me his life." I added, "I didn't need to tell Anthony that, but . . . I was angry at him, and I wanted him to know that his sainted father was not only a government stool pigeon, but also not such a good father and husband." I was also trying to divert some of Anthony's attention away from Susan, and toward me, but if I said that, it would sound self-serving, so I concluded, "*That* is why Anthony went into a rage and threatened me."

Susan kept staring at the wall, and I couldn't read anything in her face.

I now needed to tell her something I hadn't told Anthony, and something I'd never really come to terms with in my own mind. I said to her, "When I asked Frank to tell you it was over, I thought, or hoped, that you would get over him . . . but maybe subconsciously I thought you would get even with him." I took a deep breath and continued, "But maybe that occurred to me afterwards because . . . well, when you killed him, I couldn't be sure in my own mind if that was something I wanted or hoped for when I set this in motion . . . I wasn't sure if I should be taking credit for his death, or if I felt guilty and was taking some of the blame . . . and even today, I'm not sure about that."

Susan looked at me, and there was still no expression on her face.

Then I said to her, "I wanted you back, and I wanted you not to love him . . . though I'm not sure I wanted him dead. But if I did, then you were right about that—I should have killed him myself."

She remained seated, and I could see she was past the shock, and I was sure she was thinking about her killing a man who still loved her, and who did not really betray her, but who was just following my off-stage direction—as a matter of honor—to repay a favor.

I couldn't even begin to guess how she felt now about what she did, or how she felt about me.

There wasn't much left to add, but I did say, "I'm not sure I need to apologize to you for asking him to lie to you—you both lied to me often enough—and I'm certainly not asking you to forgive me. But I do want you to know that I take some of the blame for what happened."

She spoke for the first time and said, "I killed him. Not you."

"All right. But . . . when you think about all of this—"

She said, "I think he loved you more than he loved me."

"He owed me a favor."

She took a deep breath and continued, "He was always talking about you, and that made me uncomfortable, and . . . angry . . . and—"

"All right. I don't need to hear that." I said to her, "You have a lot of thinking to do before you decide . . . how you feel. I'm going to finish up with Mancuso. You don't need to join us."

I turned and headed toward the door.

"John."

I looked back at her, and she asked me, "Did you really want me back?"

"I did."

"Then why didn't you take me back after he was dead?"

"I changed my mind."

"Why?"

"Because . . . I realized afterwards that . . . I wanted you to leave him because you *wanted* to leave him—I wanted you to come back to me because you loved me more than him . . . so, him leaving you, and him being dead, was not quite what I wanted."

She didn't reply.

I was about to turn and leave, but she again said, "John."

"I need to go."

"You need to tell me why we didn't get back together after I killed him."

"I just told you."

"No you didn't."

As I said, Susan knows me, and I can run, but I can't hide. So I said, "All right. I was . . . humiliated. In public. When your affair with him was just between the three of us—and, of course, the FBI—I could have forgiven you. But when it became national news, and the subject of tabloid humor and locker-room jokes, then . . ." I looked at her and said, "And you wonder why I got in my boat and got the hell out of here?" I asked her, "What kind of man do you think I am?"

She put her hands over her face, and I could see she was crying. I wasn't sure *what* she was crying about—her murder of Frank Bellarosa, which she'd just discovered was less justified than she'd thought, or maybe she was crying because she finally understood the havoc she'd unleashed on everyone around her. Or possibly she realized that I was having second thoughts about us being together again.

I turned and left the room.

CHAPTER FORTY-SIX

Felix Mancuso was still in my office, and he was on his cell phone. I remained standing until he finished, and I said, "Mrs. Sutter is not feeling well, so we should reschedule this." I offered, "I can come to your office tomorrow, if that's convenient."

He looked at me, then asked, "Is everything all right?"

I replied, "She's upset."

He nodded and said, "This is very stressful for her. But I do need ten more minutes of your time." He added, "And I'll need to speak to her when she's ready."

I replied, "I don't think there's much more she can add to what I've said, or to what you already know, but that's your decision." I suggested, "You can phone her." I sat at my desk and said, "Please continue."

He looked at me again, then began, "First, you should know that Anthony Bellarosa seems to have disappeared." He explained, "We're not sure if that has anything to do with this problem or problems of his own, or with John Gotti's death, or if it's just one of his normal disappearances." He explained, "Many of these people just disappear for a time. Sometimes it's business, but more often it's pleasure."

I wasn't fully attentive to Felix Mancuso, because my mind was still on Susan, but I did manage to ask, "Could he be dead?"

Mr. Mancuso replied, "He could be. But we're not hearing that, and according to Detective Nastasi, Bellarosa's wife, Megan, didn't seem to be particularly upset that he left with no explanation other than business."

I suggested, only half jokingly, "Maybe she also wants him dead."

Mancuso did not respond to that, but said, "The police would have liked to speak to him, to put him on notice that you'd made a complaint, and to let him know he was being watched. And of course, they'd have liked him to make an incriminating statement so they could place him under arrest. But unfortunately, for reasons unknown, he has disappeared."

Ironically, if I had been his *consigliere*, I'd have advised him to make himself available to the police, and politely tell them that he refused to answer any questions without his attorney present. In my world, this is what you do—but in his world, you didn't play along with the cops. So, yes, disappearing, before the police instructed you to keep them informed of your whereabouts, was a very street-smart move. Plus, it's not illegal to leave home. I did ask, however, "Can you or the police get a warrant for his arrest?"

He replied, "We're working on several ways to present this to a state or Federal judge, but other than the fact that he is wanted for questioning, based solely on your complaint, we don't have a lot to convince a judge." He added, "But we'll give it a try." He further informed me, "I'm discovering, since 9/11, that my new job with the Terrorist Task Force is easier in regard to what the courts and the law allow, but Anthony Bellarosa is not a suspected terrorist. He's an old-fashioned mobster, with all his civil liberties intact."

I said to Mr. Mancuso, "Did I mention that I saw a signed photograph of Osama bin Laden in his den?"

Mr. Mancuso smiled and continued, "In any case, Anthony Bellarosa's disappearance, while not unusual, is troubling in regard to this problem, and perhaps interesting in regard to his problems in the organization."

I asked, "Do you mean problems with Salvatore D'Alessio?"

"Perhaps." He said, "We'll see if Anthony Bellarosa surfaces for John Gotti's funeral."

"Well," I said, "I hope someone finds his body so I can get a good night's sleep."

Mancuso asked me, on that subject, "Do you own a gun?"

I replied, "We have a shotgun."

"Do you know how to use it?"

I replied, a bit curtly, "You put a shell in each chamber, take it off safety, aim, and pull the trigger." I added, "I was in the Army, and Mrs. Sutter was a skeet and bird shooter. It's her shotgun."

"All right." He advised me, "Neither the FBI nor the police encourage civilians to confront an intruder, or to own or buy a weapon for the purpose of—"

"Mr. Mancuso, I understand. Rest assured that neither I nor Mrs. Sutter is going to ambush Anthony Bellarosa on his front lawn, but if anyone enters this house with intent to do bodily harm, then we will take appropriate action." I reminded him, "I know the law."

"I know you do." He continued, "If Anthony Bellarosa returns to his house, or if we discover his whereabouts, then someone from the Bureau or the local police will advise you of that."

"I hope so."

He went on, "I've confirmed with the Second Precinct that their patrol vehicles have been alerted regarding this situation." He further informed me, "The Bureau may also have a presence in the area."

I nodded, and he continued on to a few more points, and also asked me to clarify or expand on a few of my previous statements. He seemed to have good short-term recall for everything I'd said, and I already knew that he had a good long-term memory for events that happened ten years ago. In that respect, we had something in common.

I was still not quite myself after what happened with Susan, and though I was relieved that I'd finally gotten that off my chest, I realized that digging it all up, yet again, had put me in a bad mood. And in addition to my full confession to Susan, I had to revisit my humiliation at being America's Number One Cuckold of the Week.

"Mr. Sutter?"

I looked at Mancuso.

"I asked, is anyone else living in this house?"

"No . . . well, an old family friend has just passed away—Mrs. Allard—and we're expecting house company for the funeral."

He inquired, "And who will that be?"

I replied, "Our children, Edward and Carolyn." I gave him their ages, and he made a note of that. I continued, "And possibly Mrs. Sutter's parents, William and Charlotte Stanhope, though they may stay elsewhere." I added, "Also, Mrs. Sutter's brother, Peter, may be here for Father's Day."

He nodded, and said, "That's right. It's this Sunday. Hard to believe the month is going so quickly."

"It's not for me."

He didn't respond to that and continued, "Is anyone living in that small house I saw near the gates?"

I explained, "That is the gatehouse, where the recently deceased lady, Mrs. Allard, lived, and where I was living until Sunday."

"I see. Is anyone there now?"

"The gatehouse has passed into the possession of Amir Nasim on the death of Ethel Allard."

"She left it to Amir Nasim?"

It would have taken too long to explain to Mancuso about Ethel Allard fucking Augustus Stanhope, and life tenancy, and all that, though as a lawyer himself, Mr. Mancuso would understand the legal concept; but as an ex-seminarian, he wouldn't be happy to hear that the wages of sin were sixty years of free rent. In any case, I said to him, "Mrs. Allard was a life tenant." I added, "It's my understanding that Nasim wants to beef up his security, so he may put some people in there."

Mr. Mancuso nodded and inquired, "Do you know anything about the situation in Nasim's house?"

I replied, "I know the house has fifty rooms, and it would take an assassin a week to check them all out." To be less flippant, I added, "As far as I know, he lives there alone with his wife, but there could be live-in help. I saw one female servant." I advised him, "You can ask Mrs. Sutter. She's more familiar with the domestic situation at Stanhope Hall."

Mr. Mancuso noted that, then asked me a few questions about our living habits, our travel plans, if any, and so forth. He suggested, "You might consider an alarm system and a dog."

"We're working on that."

He also advised, "If you have the resources, you should seriously consider engaging the services of a personal security company."

I suggested, "How about Bell Security?"

He forced a smile and replied, "That might be counterproductive."

I said to him, "It sounds to me as though we may be in great danger."

He thought about that and replied, "At this point, I'd say the danger level is yellow, and moving toward orange."

"But not red?"

He replied, "Let's not become too focused on threat levels." He added, "There is a threat, and I will speak to the police again, and to the appropriate people in the Bureau, and we will evaluate the situation and keep you posted."

I nodded, then asked him, "Why did you say to me on the phone that you thought the threat was not imminent?"

He didn't reply for a few seconds, then said, "It's a bit complicated, but it has to do with John Gotti's death, and with Salvatore D'Alessio, and with some changes that may occur in the next few weeks."

"In other words, Anthony Bellarosa is occupied with other things."

"Basically, that's the situation." Mancuso further explained, "Anthony Bellarosa has some security concerns of his own, and that may be the primary reason for his disappearance." He let me know, "The word is that one of them—Bellarosa or D'Alessio—will be retired within a few weeks. Traditionally, there is a moratorium on vendetta during the period of a wake and funeral."

"That's a very civilized custom." I asked, "Does that include any vendettas against the Sutters?"

"No. But it does give Anthony and Sal a quiet week in regard to each other."

"I'm glad to hear that." I asked, "Why wasn't this settled ten years ago?"

He replied, "Again, it has to do with Gotti's death, and the truce that was brokered by him after the incident at Giulio's." He further explained, "Organized crime is about making money—it's not about gang wars or making headlines and color photos on television that upset the public. And that is why Anthony and his uncle have coexisted in an uneasy truce for all these years. But now . . . well, as with your situation, Mr. Sutter, the chickens are coming home to roost."

I didn't reply.

Mr. Mancuso added another, agricultural image to his explanation. "What we sow, we reap."

That wasn't exactly what I wanted to hear from Felix Mancuso, who I thought of as a white knight, not the Grim Reaper. But maybe he was referring to only Anthony and Uncle Sal, not Susan and me.

Mancuso concluded his explanation of the present state of affairs by saying, "You and Mrs. Sutter are not Anthony's first priority, and maybe not even his second. But after he takes care of his other business with his friends and family—or they take care of their business with him—then he has to settle the score with Mrs. Sutter. That's personal, but it's also business in regard to his image." I thought he was going to ask, "Capisce?" but he said, "That's the situation as we believe it stands now."

"I see." I thought a moment, then said, "But you could be wrong."

"Possibly, so you should not relax your guard."

"I had no intention of doing that."

"Good. And I'll say this . . . if Salvatore D'Alessio disappears, or is murdered, then that should be a signal to all of us that Anthony Bellarosa is alive and settling some scores." He added, "And if it's Anthony who is found dead, then you, and Salvatore D'Alessio, and some others, can breathe easier."

"I understand." I told him, "I'm rooting for Sally Da-da."

Mr. Mancuso did not comment.

I thought about all of this and said, "Well, as a practical matter, we need to be here this week, but—"

"I would advise you to go about your normal business this week." He added, "You'll have company, and you'll be around people for this wake and funeral, and as I said, Anthony Bellarosa and his uncle need to settle their differences first. That's the only strategy that makes sense."

"Right." But I was sure no one ever accused Anthony of being as logical or intelligent as his father. I asked Mancuso, "So, you don't think there is any danger to my houseguests . . . my children?"

"I can't say that with a hundred percent certainty, but I seriously doubt if Anthony Bellarosa would do anything that would shock the public consciousness, or bring down the full weight of the law on his head, or most importantly, anger his friends and associates to the point where they'd turn on him." He added, "And your daughter is an assistant district attorney. That makes her bulletproof." He reminded me, "It's Mrs. Sutter that he wants, and possibly you as well, and that's the license he has gotten from his organization." He reminded me, "Whoever put out the contract on Frank Bellarosa—let's say it was his brother-in-law—did not want you, or Mrs. Sutter, or Mrs. Bellarosa harmed, which is why you're here now." He concluded, "These are professionals—not street gangs."

"I'm glad to hear that." So maybe I should offer William and Charlotte our bedroom, and I'd loan William my raincoat and hat.

I said to Mr. Mancuso, "Mrs. Sutter and I may leave the area next week, after our guests depart."

He replied, "That's your decision. But if you do leave, keep your destination to yourselves." He added, "Don't even tell friends or family, and don't write postcards home until you've moved on to a new destination."

"Understood." But, as of fifteen minutes ago, I wasn't sure if Susan and I were going anywhere together.

Mr. Mancuso concluded his briefing by saying, "I know that you, and I'm sure Mrs. Sutter, as good, law-abiding citizens, can't quite believe this is happening to you, and you may be thinking that the forces of law and order should be doing more to protect you, but rest assured, we are doing everything we can to see that no harm comes to you, and that we are treating this very seriously, and also know that your problem is being addressed as part of our larger issues with organized crime."

I could have commented on several points in Mr. Mancuso's standard speech, but I said only, "Thank you."

We both stood, and I walked him to the front door. I asked him, "Are you going to call on Amir Nasim?"

He replied, "That would make sense while I'm here."

I said, "I don't know if he's in, but he usually is."

Mr. Mancuso informed me, "He's in."

I didn't ask him how he knew that, because he certainly wasn't going to tell me. He did say, however, "I'm going to inform Nasim that you and Mrs. Sutter have some security issues, as he does, and I'll ask him to contact the local police if he sees anything unusual or suspicious."

"He asked me to do the same for him."

"Good. This should be a very safe compound."

I never thought of Stanhope Hall as a fortified compound, but I replied, "We can provide mutual security. Maybe we should sign a treaty."

Mr. Mancuso smiled and said, "Just be good neighbors."

I asked him, "Do you have anything in your files on Amir Nasim?"

"I can't comment on that."

"I know, but you can tell me, as his neighbor, if there is any credible threat against him."

Mr. Mancuso thought a moment, then said to me, "In confidence, I will tell you that Amir Nasim plays a dangerous but lucrative game of providing information and logistical resources to anyone who can afford his services. So he's made a lot of friends, but also a lot of enemies, and his problem is he can't tell one from the other."

I inquired, "Why don't you arrest him?"

Mr. Mancuso did not reply, but he gave me a final heads-up. "When you leave this estate, be extra cautious and do not hesitate to call 9-1-1 if you feel you're being watched, followed, or stalked."

I nodded, and thought about buying a personal defense weapon for the road.

Mr. Mancuso further briefed me, "It won't be Anthony Bellarosa— you understand that."

"I understand, but . . . in this case, it's so personal that I wonder if he wouldn't—"

"Not in a million years. And if something happens to his uncle, Anthony won't be within a thousand miles of the hit, even though that, too, is personal."

I asked, "Whatever happened to personal vendetta and family honor?"

He replied, "It exists, but now it's outsourced."

He gave me two of his cards, and we shook hands and I thanked him for coming. He asked me to say goodbye to Mrs. Sutter, and asked, too, that she call him when she was up to it.

I watched him get into his gray government sedan, and continued to watch as he went down the connecting driveway to the main drive and turned toward Stanhope Hall.

Well, I had a few balls up in the air—wake, funeral, in-laws and children coming, an Iranian double-dealer in the main house, the police, the FBI, and last but not least, Anthony Bellarosa, who was negotiating a contract on me and Susan. All things considered, the pirates off the Somali coast were a lot less of a problem.

And then, of course, there was Susan. I was feeling more protective toward her, and that made me realize that I was in this for the long haul. But I had no idea what *she* was feeling at this moment, so I should go upstairs and find out, or I should get in my car and take a drive to clear my head and stock up on armaments.

I went back into the house and climbed the stairs to the second floor. The door to the family room was closed, and I hesitated, then opened it.

Susan was still sitting on the couch, but she was now curled up in the corner of the couch, surrounded by throw pillows. I know what that position and that body language means, and it doesn't mean "Come here and give me a big hug and a kiss."

I said to her, "I'm going to the sporting goods store."

She didn't reply.

"Is that store in Glen Cove still there?"

No reply.

I was instantly annoyed, which is one of my many personality flaws, and I said to her, "I'm staying in the house, but if you'd like, you can move my things into a guest room, or I'll do it myself."

She looked at me, but didn't respond.

I left the family room, went downstairs, and checked the phone book in the office and discovered that the sporting goods store was still where it had been ten years ago.

I went out into the rain, got into my car, and drove down the long drive and onto Grace Lane.

Not one of my better days, but on the bright side, maybe I didn't have to be nice now to William and Charlotte.

I took my time driving to Glen Cove, and I used the time to think about today, tomorrow, and the days ahead. It occurred to me that there was nothing here for me, except unhappiness and bad memories. So as soon as I was through here with whatever I needed to do, I'd go back to London. Susan, who was quite capable, would have to make her own decisions and take care of herself. I'd advise her to return to Hilton Head, but beyond that, I felt no further obligation toward her, and no desire to be part of her life.

That wasn't true, of course, but that would have to be my exit line as I packed my bags—then maybe we could try again, ten years from now.

CHAPTER FORTY-SEVEN

I remembered the sporting goods store owner, a Mr. Roger Bahnik, who had always been helpful and patient when I'd brought Edward or Carolyn in for various camping and sporting items. I'd also come here myself for deep-sea fishing gear as well as some nautical odds and ends, so I considered reintroducing myself, but Mr. Bahnik could possibly remember Susan's misuse of a firearm, and since my purpose here was to buy a weapon and ammunition, I thought it best to remain anonymous until I had to show my ID.

I stated my purpose, feigning little knowledge of firearms or ammunition, though I'm sure I was being unnecessarily devious. Mr. Bahnik showed me to the big boys' gun shop in the rear of the store, and he asked me if I was shooting skeet or birds, and if birds, what kind.

I replied, "Very big birds."

Mr. Bahnik suggested an appropriate heavy game load, and I also bought a box of rifled deer slugs, which can put a very big hole in a person.

Mr. Bahnik was wearing a holster with a handgun, as is required when you sell guns, and I would have liked to buy two of Mr. Bahnik's handguns—one for me, and one for Susan's purse—but as I said, I'd need a special permit to carry a concealed weapon; I could possibly obtain this permit, but it would take about six months, and that would be six months too late. Susan, unfortunately, had that prior problem with a handgun, and I doubted if the authorities would look favorably on her gun permit application.

But I still needed a personal defense weapon for the road, so I asked to see some carbines, which Mr. Bahnik was happy to show me.

He unlocked the gun case and laid out a few small carbines on the counter. I examined an old World War II Winchester .30 caliber M-1 carbine, which I'd fired in the Army. These rifles are only about three feet long and fit nicely under a car seat, and maybe even into one of those big handbags I see the ladies carrying.

Mr. Bahnik briefed me, "The M-1 will be accurate to about three hundred yards, and it will bring down a deer, but mostly it's used for small game, and also as a personal defense weapon." He inquired, "What are you using it for?"

I didn't want to tell him I was going to carry it in the car because the Mafia were after me, so I replied, "Home security."

"Ah. Excellent. The missus will like this—lightweight, about five pounds, semi-automatic, and a soft recoil."

"She'll love it." I confessed, "It's an anniversary gift."

Mr. Bahnik knew I was joking—or hoped I was—and laughed.

I got a box of .30 caliber carbine rounds, and a cleaning kit for the carbine and one for the shotgun, and Mr. Bahnik threw in an American flag patch that I could sew onto my hunting jacket, or pajamas.

I noticed an orange hazmat suit hanging on a wall, along with a nice selection of gas masks. These items seemed to be a new addition since my last visit, and I asked him, "Are you selling many gas masks and hazmat suits?"

He glanced at his display on the wall and replied, "I sell a few gas masks . . . but no takers for the hazmat suits." He informed me, "I am, however, selling a lot of freeze-dried rations and jerry cans for water." He added, "And a few radiation detectors."

"And weapons?"

"Business has picked up." He added, "And candles, Coleman lanterns, flashlights . . . that sort of thing." He joked, "We don't do this well even during the hurricane season."

I didn't respond, but I was happy to learn that Mr. Bahnik was doing well and that the Gold Coast was prepared. Life in the USA had certainly changed.

Mr. Bahnik tallied up my purchases as I completed some paperwork for the carbine and ammunition. The government forms didn't ask too many silly questions, and I used my passport for photo ID. My American Express card was still working, though I don't recall having paid the bill for a while, and we completed our transaction.

Mr. Bahnik wrapped my M-1 carbine in plain brown paper so that I could carry it to the car without upsetting shoppers or law enforcement people, and he put my other purchases in a big shopping bag that said "Sporting Goods—Camping Equipment—Guns." No mention of gas masks.

My name, and maybe my address on the paperwork as well as my face seemed to be registering now with Mr. Bahnik, and I could see that he was recalling something—perhaps my happy visits to his store with my children. Or, more likely, he was recalling something he'd read or seen on TV about ten years ago. He looked at me and said, as if to himself, "Oh . . . yes."

I thanked him for his help, and as I walked toward the door, I could see he was looking at me, perhaps concerned that he'd see me and Mrs. Sutter on the evening news again. Well, he might.

The rain had stopped, but the sky was dark, and I could hear thunder in the distance, and I knew it would start again.

Back at Stanhope Hall, I had the good fortune of running into Amir Nasim, who was standing outside his newly acquired gatehouse, speaking to two men in suits. Decorators? I thought not. I stopped and got out of my Taurus, and Mr. Nasim excused himself from his company and approached me.

We exchanged greetings, and he was a bit cool to me, which could have been because I'd refused his suggestion that I convince Susan to sell her house to him. Also, he realized that my status on the property was apparently permanent. On the other hand, he'd gotten his gatehouse back sooner than either of us could have foreseen.

Perhaps, too, he was upset about Felix Mancuso's visit. And there were two reasons he'd be upset about the FBI calling: one, he just didn't want the FBI to come calling; and two, Mancuso had told him about the Sutters' problems with the Mafia. Or all of the above.

But Mr. Nasim is a polite chap, and he kept his forced smile as he said to me, "So, I understand that congratulations are in order for you and Mrs. Sutter."

I didn't want to spoil his good wishes by giving him the update that Mrs. Sutter and I were not speaking at the moment, so I replied, "Thank you."

He inquired, "Is it your plan to continue living here?"

I actually didn't know if I'd be living here until I got back to the guest cottage to see if my bags were packed. Also, if I expressed any thought about us leaving, then his offering price would go down, and I'd also lose my ten percent commission. But seriously, I replied, "We love our home."

"Well . . . you will let me know if your plans change."

"You'll be the first to know."

Mr. Mancuso's visit did not seem to be on Nasim's agenda, and he said to me, apropos of the two gentlemen walking around the gatehouse, "I have engaged the services of a private security firm to analyze my needs and to make recommendations for enhancing my security here."

I assured him, "Good idea." Then I advised, "Don't use Bell Security." I explained, "That's a Mafia company."

I couldn't tell if he thought I was being funny or serious, but he assured me, "It is not that company."

"Good. And on that subject, I assume that you spoke to Special Agent Felix Mancuso of the FBI this morning."

He nodded and replied, "Yes, I did." He informed me, "He spoke of your and Mrs. Sutter's concerns about a possible problem regarding events that took place some years ago and which may now be resurfacing."

"Correct. So we all seem to have some security issues, and I would be very happy if we could coordinate our efforts in that regard."

He thought about that and probably concluded that I was trying to get some free security service. He replied, "Of course, we can do that." He observed, "As a practical matter, this is the same property, and your egress and mine are the same, so we do need to discuss the issue of authorized visitors." He added, "Just as they do next door at Alhambra Estates."

Poor comparison, but I replied, "Correct."

He further informed me, "The first thing I am doing, as of now, is having this gatehouse occupied by two uniformed guards who will arrive shortly." He continued, "I am having the remote control frequency changed, as well as the pass code, and I will have the gates closed more often than they are now open." He assured me, "But, of course, I will give you and Mrs. Sutter the new codes and new remote controls."

"Thank you." Mr. Nasim was certainly making life a bit more secure for the Sutters, but he was also happy to make our coming and going a little more inconvenient. Well, that was his right—the guest cottage was smack in the middle of his property, and while the deed for the guest cottage included a right-of-way up the main drive, it was now Amir Nasim who controlled the gates, and thus the access to that right-of-way. If we all didn't have similar security concerns (people who were trying to kill us), I was sure I'd be in court with Mr. Nasim within a month. But for now, everyone's concerns and needs coincided, so it was serendipitous for the Sutters that Amir Nasim believed that people were trying to whack him. Talk about luck.

On the subject of visitors, he asked me, "Are you expecting any company, Mr. Sutter?" He added, "Or anyone who you do not want to have access?"

I replied, "Well, I'm not receiving any calls from the Mafia today."

He seemed taken aback at my direct response, or perhaps he was surprised at my making a little joke of something he probably didn't find too funny. Along the lines of unwanted visitors, I thought about giving him the description of William and Charlotte and telling him to have them stopped and strip-searched in the gatehouse. But that would get back to Susan, and she wouldn't understand that this was just a joke that Mr. Nasim didn't get.

I did say, however, "With Mrs. Allard's death, we are expecting some company." I briefed him on the Stanhope arrival at about 5:00

P.M., and the arrival of Edward and Carolyn tomorrow evening, either by car or by taxi. It slipped my mind to mention Peter's possible arrival on Saturday or Sunday, and with any luck, the guards would imprison the wastrel in the gatehouse basement. I did mention, though, Elizabeth Allard, whom he knew, and my mother, whom I described as a sweet old lady. I also mentioned the small army of service people and tradesmen that Susan engaged.

Mr. Nasim nodded as I briefed him, and he said, "Yes, perhaps then you can deliver to me a list of these people, and I will be certain to inform the security guards."

I said to him, "We will need to work out some system that is not inconvenient for me or for Mrs. Sutter."

"Of course."

"I need to be in contact with your security people, and they need to be in contact with us. Also, Mrs. Sutter and I need to be authorized to give them instructions."

He didn't seem to like any of that, but he replied, "I am sure we can coordinate all of that, Mr. Sutter."

"Swell." I advised him, "That ten-foot wall that runs for over a quarter of a mile along Grace Lane will not keep any motivated trespassers out. Also, the remainder of the perimeter is basically wide open, except for a stockade fence in the rear of your property and tree lines on either side, so while the gate may be secure, you have close to a mile of unsecured perimeter around the property."

He informed me, "We are discussing sensor devices, and I should tell you that there will be an all-terrain vehicle with a security person and a dog patrolling the property during the evening hours. I will keep you informed."

"Please do." I inquired, "Will those security people be armed?"

"Of course."

Most of these guys were moonlighting or retired cops, or former military, and they could be trusted with a weapon. But I had the impression—from Anthony Bellarosa, actually—that security was now a growth industry in America, and that always meant hiring marginal people to fill the ranks, just as the FAA did at the airports. I advised Mr. Nasim, "Be certain that all these security guards have had background checks, and that they are licensed to carry a handgun, and that there are at least two active or retired law officers on each and every shift." I added, "Get this in writing."

He remarked, "I am glad I spoke to you, Mr. Sutter."

"Likewise." And to be an even better neighbor, and to acknowledge my benefits from Mr. Nasim's fortification of Stanhope Hall, I offered, "I would be happy to contribute a fair share toward your costs." Actually, Susan would.

He assured me, "I am not incurring any extra cost as a result of your presence here, and I am happy to include the guest cottage and your acreage in my security arrangement."

"Thank you, but, as we say, you get what you pay for, so I need to insist that I be a party to your contract, and that I pay, directly to your security company, my share, pro rata, based on my ten acres."

He smiled and said, "Ah, you are ever the lawyer, Mr. Sutter, and a man who knows his numbers."

"Is that agreeable—or should I get my own security service here, which may be inconvenient and confusing?"

He understood my concerns, as well as my power play, and he nodded and agreed, "All right." He suggested, "Perhaps you can give me some legal advice about the contract."

"You can be sure that *our* contract with the security company will be up to my standards."

It was his turn to make a power play, and he said to me, "Those hedges which encircle your ten acres are a possible problem in regard to my security, and yours as well. So perhaps you will consider removing those."

"I would, but Mrs. Sutter likes to sunbathe in the nude, and I assume you wouldn't want to see that."

Mr. Nasim may have thought I was being provocative, or that I was baiting him, and he replied tersely, "I should think that security would take precedence, so perhaps you can ask Mrs. Sutter if she would perhaps consider removing the hedges and constructing a small enclosure for her . . . nature hours."

Good one, Amir. And actually quite reasonable. I replied, "I'll discuss that with her."

"Thank you." He thought a moment, then said to me, "If you and Mrs. Sutter find this situation not to your liking, perhaps you will reconsider my offer to purchase your property."

Actually, I might. But it wasn't my property. I realized, too, that Susan's house and property—surrounded by foreign-held territory, whose paranoid or justifiably frightened owner was hiring armed guards with dogs—was no longer prime real estate. Even the local realtors, who could sell a toxic waste dump to a couple with children, would find this one a challenge. *And this beautiful English cottage is situated in the middle of a grand estate owned by a wonderful Iranian couple who are under a death threat, so you may see some dogs and armed men around the well-manicured grounds, but the dogs are friendly, and the men will not shoot during the daylight hours. Offered at three million.*

"Mr. Sutter?"

"Well . . . that is Mrs. Sutter's decision, and I believe you already have her decision. But, I will . . ." I thought if I could get William and Charlotte shot, or eaten by the dogs, then Susan might be able to buy back the whole estate with her inheritance. But the maintenance costs . . . I crunched some numbers as Mr. Nasim waited patiently for me to finish my thought. I said to him, "I will raise the question again, but only because you asked."

"That is all I want you to do. And you might mention to Mrs. Sutter that I am happy to be able to provide some measure of safety for her during this time of . . . uncertainty in her life, but that unfortunately this security comes with some inconvenience." He gave me another example of the inconvenience by saying, "I'm afraid, for instance, that I need to limit your use of my grounds—on the advice of my security advisor."

More bullshit, but he was making a good case for us selling to him at a reduced price.

He continued, "As an example of my concerns, I saw Mrs. Sutter running yesterday, and I am not sure that would be a good thing with the dogs and the patrols."

I asked, "Are you sure that was she? What was she wearing?"

"Well . . . she was dressed modestly, but that is not the issue."

"Right. I get it." I *knew* she wasn't running naked.

He concluded his pitch, "And while it is my sincere hope that Mrs.

Sutter's situation is resolved quickly and happily, my situation is, unhappily, of long duration. So I don't believe that these acres will return to peace and tranquility at any time in the near future."

"Loud and clear, Mr. Nasim."

"Yes? Good. Well, then, please pass on my condolences to Mrs. Allard's family, and perhaps I will have the pleasure of meeting your family in the next few days."

I thought about asking him if he had an extra bedroom for William and Charlotte—actually, he had about twenty—but I wasn't sure if the Stanhopes and the Nasims would get along. I mean, they might— William could give Amir the history of the house, and explain the significance of the blackamoors, and Charlotte could show Soheila how to shake a mean martini.

Anyway, I said to Mr. Nasim, "Perhaps we can all get together for tea."

"Let me know."

"I will. And in the meantime, please keep me fully apprised of your security arrangements, and have the contract drawn up in both our names."

We parted without a handshake, and I got back in the car and continued on to the guest cottage.

I didn't see my luggage on the lawn, and that was a good sign, but I didn't know what awaited me inside.

I mean, there were two ways to look at what I had done ten years ago to break up Frank and Susan's happy affair: one, I did it to get Susan back because I loved her; and two, I did it out of spite and anger because I hated both of them. Maybe it was the usual combination of both those things, and I'm sure Susan understood that, but she loved me, so she was inclined to think I did it more for love than for hate. And she was right.

And bottom line on her shooting Frank—I'm sure all three of us wished it hadn't happened, especially Frank, and especially now that, as Mr. Mancuso was kind enough to point out, twice, the chickens were coming home to roost.

CHAPTER FORTY-EIGHT

I carried my purchases into my home office, and Susan was there, multitasking on the phone and the computer, while scribbling notes on a pad.

She gave me a distracted smile, then continued her phone call and her e-mail.

I unwrapped my carbine and put it on the coffee table, then I began feeding rounds into the magazine.

Susan ended her phone call and asked, "What is that rifle for?"

"For the car."

She didn't reply.

I laid the loaded magazine on the coffee table and got right to the point, asking, "Where am I sleeping?"

"In the master bedroom."

"Good."

"*I'm* sleeping in the guest room."

I saw that she was joking, so I said, "I wouldn't blame you if you wanted some time to think about . . . what I said, and what I did."

"I thought about it."

"And?"

"And . . . I understand why you did it, and I truly don't believe that you meant for . . . what happened to have happened." She restated the obvious and said, "I had the affair, and I killed him. Not you."

"All right."

She continued, "I know that all you were trying to do was to get me to come back."

"Right." I reminded her, "All's fair in love and war."

She recalled where she'd heard that, and said, "That's . . . true." She continued, "It's impossible for us, now, to really understand what we were thinking and feeling ten years ago, so neither of us should judge the other for what happened then."

"I agree."

She concluded, "You realized, before I did, the problem with Anthony Bellarosa, and you could have cut and run, but instead you tried to help me, even before we were together, and now you've made my problem your problem, and put your own life in danger."

I couldn't have put it better, and if I'd just met John Sutter and heard that, I'd say he was a hell of a guy. Or an idiot. I said to her, "I love you."

She stood and we embraced, and I could feel her tears on my neck.

She said, "I love *you*. And I need you."

"We're good together."

"We are."

She composed herself, looked me in the eye, and she said, "This is the end of it. I never again want to talk about what happened then. Ever."

"I agree. There's nothing more to say."

"That's right." She took a deep breath and said, "So, I see you found the sporting goods store."

"I did, and the proprietor remembered me, and he also remembered that we have an anniversary coming up at the end of the month, so he suggested I buy you this small rifle, which is called a carbine, so we could go down to the dump and shoot rats together."

She played along with my silliness and said, "How sweet." She looked at the rifle and exclaimed, "You didn't have to be so extravagant, John."

"Ah, it's nothing."

I picked up the carbine and explained its operation and its many fine points, then I handed it to her and said, "Feel how light this is."

She took the rifle, hefted it, and agreed. "I could carry this into Locust Valley and walk around with it all day."

"And it fits nicely under a car seat."

"I can see that."

I took the rifle from her, slapped in the magazine, checked the safety, and chambered a round. I said, "You just click it off safety, aim, and pull the trigger. It's semi-automatic, so it will fire each time you pull the trigger—fifteen rounds. Okay?"

She nodded.

I then demonstrated how to get off a hip shot for close targets, then I raised the rifle to my shoulder and said, "For a shot of let's say, over twenty feet, aim it as you would aim a shotgun for skeet, but you don't have to lead the target, and—"

Unfortunately, Sophie appeared at the door just then, screamed, and fled.

I thought I should go after her—without the rifle in my hands—but Susan said, "I'll be right back," and left to track down Sophie.

I used the time to make us two light vodka and tonics. I was feeling good that Susan and I had finally and completely put the past behind us, and also I was feeling good about buying the rifle and the shotgun ammunition, and good, too, that Felix Mancuso was on the case.

What was also good was that Amir Nasim had decided to put in a full security system, which, if he was really concerned, he should have done some time ago. Then, I had this thought that Felix Mancuso had taken the opportunity to scare the hell out of Nasim, telling him perhaps that it had come to the attention of the FBI that the threat to his life was real and imminent. Condition Red, Amir.

But would Mancuso have done that to Nasim just to get him to pay for the Sutters' round-the-clock security service? Or was it just a coincidence that Nasim was talking to those security advisors after Mancuso's visit? Possibly Nasim had called them as soon as he discovered that the gatehouse was in his possession. In any case, I had the feeling that Felix Mancuso had given Nasim the same advice he'd given me: Hire some guns.

Susan returned and told me, "I gave her a raise."

"Will she clean my guns?"

"No, John, but I assured her that you're fairly normal, and I gave her the raise because there's an extra person in the house now."

"Good. Did you tell her that the Mafia is after us?"

"No, I did not. But I will brief her again about answering the door to strangers."

I informed Susan, "There won't be many strangers calling. Nasim has instituted a new regime for Stanhope Hall."

"What do you mean?"

I handed her her vodka and tonic and said, "I just ran into him, and he was talking to some security advisors." I toasted, "To a new Iranian-American mutual defense treaty."

I briefed Susan on my conversation with Nasim, and she commented, "This is going to be very inconvenient . . . and it affects my quality of life."

I pointed out, "So does getting killed."

She thought about that and said, "This is not what I hoped for when I returned."

"I'm sure not. But . . . well, we all have to give up some freedom for security."

"No we don't."

I'd had this argument in London, and here in New York with Susan. It was a matter of degree—how much personal freedom do we want to give up and how much freedom from fear are we getting in return? I said to Susan, "Let's see how it works. Meanwhile, no more running around the property naked."

She smiled.

I also told her, "He'd like us to take out our hedges for our mutual security." I added, "I told him, however, we like our privacy."

Susan thought about that and said, "If he didn't have such a problem with the dress code . . . or the undress code . . . well, I think Nasim is just putting the pressure on me to sell."

"That is certainly part of it." I looked at her and said, "You should think about that."

"I will not."

"Then buy the estate back from him."

"And where would I get that kind of money?"

My eyes drifted, unconsciously, to the carbine on the coffee table.

She made a few mental connections, looked at me, and said, "That's not funny."

"What?" I asked, innocently.

She changed the subject and asked, "What did you and Mancuso talk about?"

I briefed her on our conversation about Anthony Bellarosa's disappearance, and the possible scenarios that might play out in the next week or two. I also discussed with her Felix Mancuso's reassurances concerning our houseguests and our children.

On this subject, she asked me a lot of questions, so I gave her Mancuso's card and said to her, "He wants you to call him, and you should ask him all your questions, and mention any concerns you have."

"All right. I'll do that today."

"Good. Also, you should know that Special Agent Mancuso paid a visit to Mr. Nasim, and that may have prompted the fortification of Stanhope Hall."

Susan thought about that and asked, "How did we get involved with all of this? All these people . . . ?"

I hoped that was a rhetorical question, because if I had to answer it, I'd have to begin by bringing up things we'd just agreed not to speak about ever again. Of course, the Nasim problem was not of Susan's making, but if Susan had not urged Frank Bellarosa to buy Stanhope Hall, then the estate would not have been seized by the government, and quite possibly it would now be owned by a nice family who didn't know anyone who wanted to kill them, and so forth. And if Susan hadn't had an affair with and murdered Frank Bellarosa, then Susan and John would have been living here in marital bliss for the last decade, without worrying about being the object of a Mafia vendetta. And so forth.

But rather than mention any of that, I replied, "This will pass."

She looked at me, and asked, "What would I have done without you?"

I had a similar question, but . . . well, I'd made this decision with my heart, not my head, so . . . I shouldn't ask myself too many questions.

Susan moved on to more important subjects. "I have a caterer coming to help me shop and cook for the week, and I have Sophie all week, and I think we have enough wine, beer, mixers, vodka, Scotch, and everything, but Mom and Dad drink gin martinis and we don't have any gin. They drink Boodles. So, would you mind running out for gin?"

"I just went out for guns."

"Please, John."

"Okay. I'll see if I can get a pass to leave the compound."

She ignored that and asked, "Should I call my parents and tell them about the new security at the gate?"

"That might be a good idea." I suggested, "Tell them it has to do with Nasim, not us."

"Of course. And I'll let Edward and Carolyn know. Peter, too."

"And Nasim wants the names of our guests in writing. So please take care of that."

"I will."

"Don't forget our household staff, tradespeople, and delivery people."

"I'll take care of it." She commented, "This sucks."

"Right. Okay, I'll be back within the hour. Meanwhile, take the shotgun shells upstairs and put the carbine in the hall closet."

"Don't you want to take the carbine?"

"No, I'll take the Taurus."

"I mean . . . do you believe we're having this conversation?"

I didn't reply to that, and said, "I'll see you later."

She decided to walk me out to the car, and before I got in the Taurus, she gave me her cell phone and said, "Call me." Then she gave me a big hug and a kiss, and said, "Be careful."

I got in the car and headed down the long drive toward the gatehouse.

The gates were still open and unmanned, and I turned right onto Grace Lane.

After about a minute, I saw a black Escalade coming toward me, and it slowed as it got closer.

I couldn't see through the tinted windows, and it was too far to see the license plate, but obviously the Escalade was slowing for a reason. I was now sorry I hadn't taken the carbine.

The Escalade stopped in the middle of the road, about thirty feet from me, and as I got closer, I could see the American flag decal on the side window, and I could also see that it was Anthony's license plate.

But was Anthony in the car? And would he use his own car to whack John Sutter? He was stupid, but this was like Mafia Hit 101—don't use your own car or your own people, and don't whack anyone in your own neighborhood.

I could speed past the Escalade, or make a U-turn, but for the above reasons, and because I was curious about who wanted to speak to me, I drew abreast of the Escalade and stopped.

The driver's window went down, revealing Tony.

I lowered my window, and he said to me, "Hey, Mr. Sutta. I thought that was you. How ya doin'?"

"I'm doing very well. And how are you doing?"

"Great."

I could see movement in the back seat, and I had the Taurus in drive and my foot ready to hit the accelerator. And if I had the carbine across my lap, I'd really feel better about this conversation.

He asked me, "Whaddaya up to?"

This idiot always asked the same stupid questions, and I replied, "Same old shit."

"Yeah? How's Mrs. Sutta?"

I almost said, "Fuck you," but instead I asked, "Where's your boss?"

He smiled, and if we'd been closer, I'd have buried my fist in his face. He kept smiling and replied, "I don't know. Why do you want to know?"

I divided my attention between Tony and the movement in the back seat. I said to Tony, "Tell him I'm looking for him."

"Yeah? Why ya lookin' for him?"

I recalled that these conversations with Tony, even when he was doing business as Anthony, were not very enlightening or meaningful. I replied, "I remembered some other stuff about his father that I wanted to tell him."

"Yeah? He likes to hear that stuff. Me, too. Tell me."

Well, he asked, so I said, "If Frank had lived a little longer, he would have given you up to the Feds, and you'd still be in jail."

"Hey, fuck you."

"No, fuck *you*, Tony. And fuck your boss, and fuck—"

The tinted rear window went down, and I was ready to cut the wheel and ram the Escalade, but Kelly Ann said, "You're cursing! No cursing!"

I took a deep breath, and said to her, "Sorry, sweetheart." I said to Tony, "Tell your boss to stop hiding and act like a man."

Tony would have said, "Fuck you," but Kelly Ann was waiting to pounce, and I could hear Frankie, sitting next to her, mimicking his older sister, "No cursing, no cursing."

Tony said to me, "I'll let him know what you said."

"That's very kind of you. But I'd like to tell him in person."

"Yeah. We're workin' on that."

"Good. And my regards to his future widow."

That seemed to confuse him, then he got it, and said to me, "Yeah, you too," which wasn't exactly the correct reply, but I got it.

We rolled up our windows and continued on our ways.

The question would be, "Why are you making things worse?" And the answer is, "Things could not be any worse, so there's no downside to pissing off the guy who already wants to kill you." In fact, it makes me feel better, and it might cause him to make a mistake. And that's all I wanted—one mistake on his part, so I could kill him myself.

——PART IV——

Honor thy father and thy mother.

—Exodus 20:12

*I tell you there's a wall ten feet thick
and ten miles high between parent and child.*

—George Bernard Shaw
Misalliance

CHAPTER FORTY-NINE

I t was ten minutes past five, and the rain had arrived, though the Stanhopes had not. But Susan assured me, "They called ten minutes ago, and they just got off the Expressway." She gave me an ETA of fifteen minutes, which was more than enough time for my second Dewar's and soda.

Susan and I were in the kitchen, and Sophie had laid out hors d'oeuvres on the center island, which I wasn't allowed to touch. Also, the caterer had arrived, and she and Susan had planned a few menus for the week. Plus, Sophie was going to live in the downstairs maid's room for the next five days. This was a convenience for Susan, of course, but it also gave William and Charlotte someone to boss around besides their daughter, and it might even ensure that we'd keep our voices down if we all got into a screaming match.

The phone rang, and Susan spoke to someone and said, "Yes, we're expecting them." Susan hung up and said to me, "It's the florist, finally." She informed me, "There are guards now at the gates."

I didn't comment on that, though I did note all this preparation for the arrival of Mom and Dad. But I recalled, from my last life here, that William and Charlotte never seemed to notice or appreciate all that Susan did for them when they came to visit. Well, they were demanding parents, but yet they spoke of Peter as if *he* were the perfect child. In fact, he was a useless turd, but he knew how to butter up Mom and Dad, and he knew where his bread came from.

My other thought was that Susan was far too optimistic about her parents actually staying here. She'd had their old guest room cleaned and stocked with bottled water and snacks, and I was sure there were flowers for their room. I looked at Susan, and though I didn't want her parents here, neither did I want her to be disappointed or hurt. I said to her, "Look, Susan, why don't I go to a hotel—?"

"No. You are my future husband and the father of our children. You are staying here with me, Edward, and Carolyn."

"But—"

"But I do want you to disappear until I get a drink into their hands." She suggested, "Wait in the office with the door closed, and I'll buzz you on the intercom. About fifteen or twenty minutes after they arrive."

"They'll see my car when they pull up."

"I'll tell them it's my second car."

"They'll see that there are guards in the gatehouse and that I couldn't be living there."

"All right, do you want to greet them with me?"

"No, Susan, I want to *leave*. I'll be back—"

"You are *not* leaving." She explained, "You're just hiding for a while."

"All right." So I grabbed a napkinful of hors d'oeuvres and my Scotch, then I looked at her and said, "Good luck."

"John, just remember one thing."

"What's that?"

"Half of a hundred million dollars."

I smiled, and carried my hideout rations into the office and closed the door. The blinds were open, and I could see the florist van pull up. I watched as two men unloaded enough flower arrangements to bury an Italian funeral home.

I lowered the blinds so that William and Charlotte didn't get a peek at their future son-in-law, and sat at the desk and checked my e-mail, ate hors d'oeuvres, and sipped my Scotch.

Susan had called Mr. Mancuso, and she told me that he'd given her some assurances, some advice, and also some of the same information about Anthony's disappearance that he'd given me. He'd also told her that he was impressed with her courage, but that she needed to balance that with some extra vigilance, and so forth. Apparently, according to Susan, they were now good buddies, which made me happy.

I had not told Susan about running into Tony because she had enough on her mind, but right after the incident I had called Felix Mancuso using Susan's cell phone, and I left him a message on his voice mail relating my intemperate remarks to Anthony's driver. I suggested that he or someone from his office might want to question Tony regarding his boss's whereabouts, if they hadn't done so already. I had also informed Mancuso that Amir Nasim was in the process of installing a full security system at Stanhope Hall that would rival whatever they had in place at 26 Federal Plaza, which was the address on Special Agent Mancuso's card. I suggested, too, that he might consider updating Detective Nastasi, or I'd do that if the FBI and the local police were not sharing information this week.

I'm good at covering all my bases, and my ass, and my brain works well when my life is in danger.

Anyway, I checked through almost two weeks of e-mail, most of it from clients in London who couldn't seem to grasp the fact that I was on an extended sabbatical, which reminded me that I needed to inform my firm of my decision to resign. And I also needed to inform Samantha of my decision to resign from her.

I should phone, but it was past 11:00 P.M. in London, so maybe I should just e-mail and get that over with, but that wasn't the right thing to do . . . and, I thought, maybe I should wait to see what happened in the next thirty minutes. I mean, it could get ugly, but I knew that Susan would, as she said, put her priorities in order. The problem was, she had several priorities: me, the children, and the money, and they might be mutually exclusive.

So it might have to be me who needed to put the priorities in order, and by that I meant I might bow out if it came down to John or half the hundred million. Not to mention the children's trust funds and Susan's allowance.

While I was thinking about being noble and selfless, I could hear the florists going in and out the front door, and Susan giving them instructions in that upper-class tone of voice that was polite but unquestionably authoritative.

How, I wondered, was this woman going to live without money? I mean, those fucking flowers cost more than most people made in a month. Not to mention the stupid froufrou hors d'oeuvres, and the caterer, and Sophie . . . well, why think about that now? We had more serious problems, like staying alive.

I sent a few e-mails to friends in London, but I didn't mention anything about quitting my job, relocating to New York, marrying my ex-wife, or the Mafia trying to kill me. Some of that could get back to my firm, or to Samantha. I mean, I was ready to burn my bridges, but if I somehow found that I needed to re-cross the pond, then I'd need that bridge.

I had e-mailed my sister, Emily, who was still living on some beach in Texas with boyfriend number four or five. Emily and I are close, despite our long geographic separations for the last dozen years. I'd told her about Ethel's passing, and then gave her the good news about Susan and me.

I pulled up her reply, which said: *Wonderful. Love, Emily P.S. Wonderful. P.P.S. I'll miss Ethel's funeral, but I will not miss John and Susan's wedding. Let's speak when you get a chance.*

I replied: *You are wonderful. Life is wonderful. Will call you when I can. Love, John P.S. The Stanhopes will arrive momentarily. Not so wonderful. But maybe good for a few laughs.*

Regarding that, the doorbell rang. I peeked out the blinds and saw next to my blue Taurus another blue Taurus that I was certain was the Stanhopes' rental car. I had this *wonderful* vision of William and Charlotte driving their blue Taurus through the gates onto Grace Lane and being met by a stream of machine-gun fire.

I could hear Susan exclaim, "Welcome!"

William the Terrible said, "Damned traffic in New York—how can you live here?"

Charlotte chirped, "It's so *wonderful* to see you, darling!"

And so forth.

The happy voices disappeared down the corridor, and I turned back to the keyboard and began typing an e-mail to Edward and Carolyn:

Hi! Your grandparents have unfortunately arrived safely . . . delete that . . . Grandma and Grandpa have just arrived, and I'm hiding . . . delete . . . G and G just got here, and I haven't yet said hello, so I'll keep this short. Remember, when you get here, that your mother and I love you very much, and we love each other, and we will all try to make Grandpa and Grandma feel welcome and loved, and even Uncle Peter, that useless . . . delete . . . who may be joining us. Your mother and I will try to call you tomorrow, and let you know how things are going, or call us. Edward, if we don't speak, have a safe flight. Carolyn, let us know what train you're taking. Love, Dad. P.S. Your grandparents are worth a hundred million dollars dead . . . delete.

I read the e-mail, not sure if I should send it. I mean, Edward and Carolyn knew there would be some friction between me and their grandparents, and the children were adults, so I needed to treat them as such and give them a heads-up. My letter seemed positive, but they'd understand the subtle hint that there could be a problem when they got here. I had no idea what Susan had told them on this subject, if anything, but I needed to be proactive, so I pushed the send button and off it went into cyberspace.

To kill time, I went online and typed in *in-laws, perfect murders of,* and actually got a few hits.

Next I went onto a Web site that an American client had told me about, which showed aerial views of homes and commercial properties around the country. I'd actually used this site once in my work for an American client, and I'd even checked out Stanhope Hall and Alhambra a few months ago during a nostalgia attack.

Within a minute I had an aerial view of Stanhope Hall taken this past winter, which showed me just how huge the main house was. I could also see the hedge maze, the love temple, the tennis court, the plum orchard, and even the overgrown burned-out ruins of Susan's childhood playhouse, which was about half the size of a real cottage.

I zoomed in on the gatehouse, then moved to the guest cottage and the nearby stables. Then I shifted the view toward Alhambra, and I could see the long, straight line of white pines that separated the estates, and I thought of Susan's horseback rides from Stanhope Hall to the Alhambra villa.

This photograph, of recent vintage, did not show Bellarosa's razed villa, of course, or the mock Roman ruins, or the reflecting pool; it showed the red-tiled roofs of the new mini-villas and their landscaping, and the roads that connected them.

I zoomed in on Anthony's house with the big patio and the over-sized pool, then I moved the view back toward the pine trees and the Stanhope estate, and the guest cottage.

On the ground, it was a circuitous route from Susan's cottage to Anthony's villa, but from the air, as I suspected, it was only about five or six hundred yards—a third of a mile—between the two houses.

Note to self: If I was jogging cross-country to Anthony Bellarosa's house, I could be there in less than five minutes; and it was the same traveling time if Anthony Bellarosa was coming this way.

CHAPTER FIFTY

T he intercom buzzed, and I picked up the phone and asked, "Did they faint or leave?"

"Neither. But they're over their initial shock."

"Are they ready for another shock when I tell them we're not entering into a prenuptial agreement?"

"Let's limit it to one shock a day. It's your turn tomorrow."

"All right. Where are you?"

"I'm in the kitchen, making them martini number two, but I'll be in the living room in a minute." She said, "I've made you a stiff drink."

"Good. See you there."

I walked out of the office into the foyer. I took a minute to recall twenty years of their bullshit, then I entered the living room.

William and Charlotte were sitting near the fireplace in side-by-side chairs, and Susan was sitting on a love seat across from them. Between them was a coffee table covered with plates of hors d'oeuvres, and I could see that William and Charlotte had fresh martinis in front of them, and Susan had a white wine.

I considered running toward them with my arms out, yelling, "Mom! Dad!" but instead I said simply, "Hello," and walked toward them.

Susan stood, then William and Charlotte rose without enthusiasm.

I first kissed Susan, to piss them off, then I extended my hand to

Charlotte, who gave me a wet noodle, then to William, who gave me a cold tuna. I asked, "So, did you have a good flight?"

William replied, "Good enough."

Susan said, "Sit here, John, next to me. I've made you a vodka and tonic."

"Thank you." I sat next to Susan on the love seat, and she took my hand, which came to Mom and Dad's immediate notice and made them wince.

Schubert was playing softly in the background, and the room was lit with candles and adorned with flowers. Sort of like a funeral home.

I sipped my drink and discovered it was pure tonic.

William the Color Blind was wearing silly green trousers, an awful yellow golf shirt, and a shocking pink linen sports jacket. Charlotte had on pale pink pants and a puke green blouse, and they both wore these horrid white orthopedic walking shoes. I'm surprised they were allowed to board the aircraft.

William, I noticed, really hadn't aged much in ten years, and he had a full head of hair and was still using the same hair coloring. Charlotte's face had aged a lot, with a network of deep wrinkles that looked like cracked house paint. She'd let her hair go naturally bright red, and she was wearing earrings, a necklace, and a bracelet all made of coral and seashells, giving her the appearance of a dry aquarium. Neither one of them had gained much weight, and both of them were amazingly pasty-faced for golfers, as though they used whitewash for sunblock.

I said to them, "You're both looking very well."

William did not return the compliment but said, "Thank you. We feel well."

It's here where the senior citizen usually gives you a complete medical report, and while this usually bores me senseless, in this case I was anxious to hear about any ailments, no matter how small or insignificant; you never know what could develop into something fatal at that age. But they weren't sharing their medical history with me, except that Charlotte said, "Our internist said we could live to be a hundred."

That bastard.

Susan addressed the big subject and said, "John, I've told Mom and

Dad that we are getting remarried, and I also told them how happy Edward and Carolyn are for us."

I said to Mom and Dad, "My mother, too, is delighted. And Ethel, right before she passed away said to us, 'Now, I can go in peace, knowing—'" I felt Susan's nails dig into my hand, so I cooled that, and said, "Susan and I have thought long and hard about this"—since we had sex on Sunday—"and we've discussed all aspects of our remarriage, and we are certain this is what we want to do."

Susan reminded me, "And we're in love, John."

I said, "And we're in love."

Neither Mom nor Dad had anything to say about any of that, so Susan continued, "As I said to you before John joined us, I understand that this comes as a surprise to you, and I understand why you have some doubts and reservations, but we are certain about our love for each other."

William and Charlotte sat there as though their hearing aids had died, and they simultaneously reached for their martinis and took a good slug.

Susan continued, "John and I have discussed all that happened in the past, and we've put that behind us, and we hope that we can all move forward. We feel that the past has taught us what is important, and whatever mistakes we've made have taught us invaluable lessons, which we'll use to strengthen our love and our family."

William and Charlotte finished their martinis.

I guess it was my turn, so I said, "I'm sure you want Susan to be happy, and I believe I can make her happy." It was time for my mea culpa, and I said, "I made many mistakes during our marriage, and I take most of the blame for what happened between us, but I want you to know, I've grown as a person, and I've become more sensitive to Susan's needs and wants, and I've strengthened my coping skills, and learned how to manage my anger, and—" Again, the nails in my hand. So I concluded, "I could give you a *hundred million* reasons"—or half of that—"why I think I can be a good husband to Susan, and a hundred million reasons why—"

"John."

"What?"

"I think Mom and Dad may want you to address what happened the last time we were all together."

"Right. I was getting to that." As I recalled, we were in an Italian restaurant in Locust Valley, and William had just sold Stanhope Hall to Frank Bellarosa, and William was asking me to draw up the contract of sale, for free, and then he was going to stick me with the restaurant bill, as he always did, and I'd had about all the crap I was going to take from him, so I called him—

"John."

"Right." I looked at William, then at Charlotte, and said, "One of the major regrets of my life has been my words to you, William, when we last had dinner together. My outburst was totally unacceptable and unprovoked. My words, which spewed forth from my mouth, like . . . well, that bad fra diavolo . . . anyway, if I could take those words back—or eat them—I would. But I can't, so I can only offer my most sincere and abject apology to you and to Charlotte for you having to hear that stream of vile obscenities, and to Susan, too, for having to witness the three people she loved most . . ." I was losing the sentence structure, so I concluded, "Please accept my apology."

There were a few seconds of silence, then William said, "I have never been spoken to like that in all my life."

Really?

Charlotte said, "That was so hurtful."

Maybe they needed another martini. Well, I'd promised Susan I'd apologize, and I did, but these two shitheads were having none of it. Nevertheless, I gave it the old Yale try and said, "You don't know how many times I sat down to write you a letter of apology, but I could never form the words on paper that were in my heart. But now that I can deliver these words of apology to you—from the same mouth that disgorged those coarse, vulgar, crude, and profane words . . . now, I hope that you can see and hear that my apology is from my heart." I pointed to my heart.

I could see that William, even with two martinis in his dim brain, was sensing that I was having a little fun with this. Charlotte, who is truly dim, takes everything literally.

Finally, William said, "I was stunned, John, that a son-in-law of mine, a man whose parents I respect, would use that kind of language—in a public place, or anywhere for that matter, and to use it in the presence of ladies." And so forth.

I hung my head and listened to him go on. Obviously, William had hoped for this day, and he was going to squeeze every ounce of petty pleasure out of it.

Finally, Susan interrupted him and said, "Dad, John has asked you to accept his apology."

William looked at her and then at me and said, "Charlotte and I will discuss this. And be aware, John, that we don't dispense forgiveness as easily and as lightly as do so many young people today." He let me know, "Forgiveness can be asked for, but it has to be earned."

I took a deep breath and replied, "I hope I can earn your forgiveness."

"It's not a matter of *hope*, John, it's a matter of working at it."

All right, fuckhead. "That's what I meant."

Susan said, "Let me freshen your drinks." She took their glasses and said to me, "Give me a hand, John."

I stood and followed her into the kitchen.

She said to me, "Thank you."

I didn't reply.

"I know that was difficult, but you did it."

"It came from my heart." I pointed to my heart.

"I think it came from your spleen."

"I thought you said they mellowed."

"No, I *told* you I lied about that."

"Right."

Susan took the Boodles out of the freezer and said, "This stuff isn't working."

"It will. One martini, two martini, three martini, floor." I said, "There's no vodka in my tonic."

"You will thank me for that."

"I just need one more to get through this."

"You're doing great."

"Really?"

"Yes. But don't overdo it. You're borderline sarcastic."

"Me?" I asked her, "Would we be going through this if they weren't rich?"

She poured the gin into both glasses and replied, "If they weren't rich, they wouldn't be so difficult."

"We'll never know."

"And please do not use the words 'a hundred million' again."

"I was just trying to quantify—"

"Remember the children. I don't care about us, but I do care about them."

I thought a moment and said, "I don't want our children to lose their self-respect or their souls for a pot of gold."

"No. That's our job."

I asked her, "Where are Mom and Dad sleeping tonight?"

"It hasn't come up."

"Do they know I'm sleeping here with you?"

"Well . . . Dad commented on the guards in the gatehouse, but I don't think he's put two and two together yet." She added, "When the time comes, we should all just say good night and not make a big thing of it."

"All right. And what are our dinner plans?"

"Well, we all go to the funeral home, then I'll suggest we come back here for a light supper. Unless they'd rather go to a restaurant."

"How about that Italian restaurant in Locust Valley where we had the last supper?"

She laughed and said, "Okay, but don't skip out on the bill this time."

"Ah! *That's* why he's still pissed off."

Susan poured a touch of dry vermouth in each glass, added an olive, and said, "Let's get back so they don't think we're talking about them."

"They're talking about us."

She put both glasses on a silver tray, handed it to me, and said, "You do the honors."

I started for the door, then stopped and said to her, "If this doesn't work out by Sunday, I never want to see those two again. Understand?"

"It will work. *You* will make it work."

I continued on, back through the foyer and into the living room, where I said, cheerfully, "Here we go! And there's more where that came from."

They took their glasses, tasted their martinis, and William said, "Susan makes a perfect martini."

"And I didn't spill a drop," I said proudly.

Susan raised her glass of wine and said, "Let me again say how happy I am that you're here, where we all once lived in beautiful Stanhope Hall, and even though it's a sad occasion, I know that Ethel is looking down on us, smiling as she sees us all together again."

That almost brought a tear to my eye, and I said, "Hear, hear."

We didn't touch glasses, but we did raise them and everyone drank.

I had the feeling that William and Charlotte had spent the last five minutes congratulating each other for being such assholes, and also coordinating an attack on John.

Along those lines, William said to his daughter, "I saw Dan's son, Bob, the other day at the club, and he passes on his regards."

Susan replied, "That's nice."

"He told me again how happy you'd made his father in his last years."

Susan did not reply.

It was Charlotte's turn, and she said, "We all miss Dan so much. He was always the life of the party."

William chuckled and added, "And did he ever love to golf. And he made you love the game, Susan. You were getting quite good." He inquired, "Are you golfing here?"

"No."

"Well, once it's in your blood—I'll bet Dan is up there golfing twice a day."

Charlotte said to Susan, "You left those beautiful clubs he bought you. Would you like us to send them?"

"No, thank you."

I wanted to snap their scrawny necks, of course, but I just sat there, listening to them updating Susan on all the news from Hilton Head, and continuing to drop Dan's name whenever possible.

Susan should have suggested to them that I might not want to hear about her dearly departed husband, but these two were so off the chart that I suppose it didn't matter. Also, of course, they'd be in a better mood if I ate all the shit they were shoveling.

Meanwhile, my only past sin had been not putting up with their crap, but their daughter had committed adultery and murder, and it was I who had to apologize to them for calling William an unprincipled asshole, an utterly cynical bastard, a conniving fuck, and a monumental prick. Or was it prick, then fuck? Whatever, it was all true.

Susan could sense I was simmering and about to boil over, as I'd done ten years ago in the restaurant, so she interrupted her father and said, "Edward and Carolyn will be here tomorrow night, and they're so excited to see you."

Charlotte said, "We're so looking forward to seeing them." She remembered to ask, "How are they doing?"

Do you really give a damn? I mean, I had assumed they'd already had this conversation, but I saw now that they hadn't even asked about their only grandchildren. What swine.

Susan filled them in on Edward and Carolyn, but I could see that Grandma and Grandpa were only mildly interested, as though Susan were talking about someone else's grandchildren.

We exhausted that topic, so William turned to me and inquired, "How about you, John? How are you doing in London?"

He really didn't give a rat's ass about how I was doing in London, and I recognized the question—from long experience—as a prelude to something less solicitous.

I replied, "London is fine."

"Are you working?" he asked.

I replied, "I've always worked."

He reminded me, "You took a three-year sail around the world," then he generously conceded, "Well, I suppose that's a lot of work."

I wanted to invite him to take a long sail with me, but he'd figure out that he wasn't coming back. I said, "It was challenging."

"I'm sure it was." He smiled and inquired, "So, did you have a woman in every port?"

I replied, "That is an improper question to ask me in front of your daughter."

Well, that sort of stopped the show, but Susan jumped in and said, "Dad, the past is behind us."

William, like all cowards, backed off and said, "Well, I didn't mean to touch on a sore subject."

Susan assured him, "It is not a sore subject. It is a closed subject."

"Of course," said Mr. Sensitive. Then he had the gall to ask me, "How is it that you haven't remarried after all these years, John?"

"I dated only married women."

William didn't think that was so funny, but Charlotte seemed satisfied with my explanation, though she commented, "It sounds like you wasted all those years on women who were not eligible."

Susan asked, "Can I get you both another drink?"

Mom and Dad shook their heads, and William informed us, "We limit ourselves to three martinis."

A minute? I pointed out, "You've only had two."

"We had one before you got here."

"That doesn't count." I added, "I hate to drink alone."

"Well . . . all right," he acquiesced.

I stood to run off and make two more, but Sophie poked her head in and asked Susan, "Do you need anything?"

William, who treats household help like indentured servants, replied, "Two more martinis and clear some of these plates and bring fresh ones and clean napkins." Then, to Susan, he said, "Show her how to make a martini."

Susan stood, Sophie cleared the plates, and they left. Then Charlotte excused herself to use the facilities, and I found myself alone with William.

We looked at each other, and I could see his yellow eyes narrowing and the horns peeking through his hair. Smoke came out of his nostrils, and his orthopedic shoes split open, revealing cloven hoofs, and then he reached down the back of his pants and played with his spaded tail.

Or maybe I was imagining that. His eyes, however, *did* narrow.

Neither of us spoke, then finally he said to me, "This does not make us happy, John."

"Well, I'm sorry to hear that. But your daughter is happy."

"She may *think* she's happy." He let me know, "Susan was lonely after Dan died, and she became quite upset after the terrorist attacks, and for the last several months she's been dwelling on the past."

I didn't reply.

He continued, "So, what I'm saying to you, John, is that she's not herself, and what you're seeing now is not what you might be seeing a few months from now."

I replied, "I appreciate your not wanting me to make a mistake, and I'm touched by your concern for my future."

His eyes narrowed again, and he said, "We actually don't care for you."

"Was it something I said?"

"And we don't think that Susan does either." He explained, "She's confused." He further explained, "We know our daughter, and we think she's just going through a stage of life, which will pass."

"Then you should tell her what you think of her mental state. Or I will."

He leaned toward me, and in a quiet voice said, "We will need to discuss this, John, man to man."

"I'm happy to do that." But bring your own man, shithead; I'm not hiring one for you.

William got to the crux of the matter and said, "People in our position—I mean, Charlotte and I—have to be very careful in regard to acceptable suitors for our daughter." He asked, "Are you following me?"

"Of course. You want her to be happy."

"No— Well, yes, of course we do. But I'm speaking about . . . well, money."

"Money? What does this have to do with money?" I assured him, "We'll pay for our own wedding."

He seemed frustrated with my dullness, but continued patiently, "I have no idea how you're doing financially, but I'm sure that Susan's annual allowance, and her future inheritance, has influenced your thinking. Now, don't take that the wrong way, John. I'm sure you think you're fond of her, but quite frankly, I think you both divorced for the right reasons—you were unsuitable for each other—and you stayed away from each other for ten years because of that. So now the question is, why are you courting her again, and why have you proposed marriage?"

It was more the other way around, but I was gentleman enough not to say that. I said, "William, if you're suggesting that I'm a gold digger, I am truly offended."

"John, I'm not saying that. I'm just saying that your thinking and your feelings may be influenced by those considerations—subconsciously, of course."

"Well, you raise an interesting point . . . so, you think that, subconsciously . . . well, I guess I need to think about that." I admitted, "I wouldn't want to *think* I was marrying for love, when deep down inside it was for money."

I may have crossed the sarcasm line, but William gave me a pass and leaned even closer to me, and said bluntly, "Perhaps we can discuss some financial arrangement that would induce you to move back to London."

If he was talking about the measly one hundred thousand dollars that he offered to all Susan's suitors, then I was insulted. Even two hundred thousand dollars was an insult. It would have to be seven figures.

"John?"

I looked at him, and I realized that if I told him to go fuck himself, the rest of the week could be a bit rocky. But if I played along, that would make him a happy houseguest, and after we'd finished our Father's Day dinner, I could then tell him to go fuck himself. Or maybe I should wait until Edward left on Monday morning. Go fuck yourself has to be timed just right.

He said, "I hope you will think about this."

"I will. I mean, not about the financial . . . But about what you said regarding Susan's being confused and not herself." I feigned deep thought, then nodded to myself and came to a reluctant conclusion. I said, "I wouldn't want her to make a mistake about us remarrying . . . and then be unhappy."

"No, John, we don't want that."

"So . . . well, then maybe we should"—bright idea—"live together."

Poor William. He thought that my spinning wheels were going to stop at three lemons, and I'd get up and go home. He cleared his throat and said, "I was speaking of a financial inducement for you to return to London."

"Oh . . . right. Well . . . I don't want to hurt Susan by leaving . . . but I also don't want to hurt her by entering into a doomed marriage . . ."

William assured me, "You would both be much happier in the long term if you separated now." He advised me, "It needs to be quick, merciful, and final."

This sort of reminded me of the deal I made with Frank Bellarosa. Anyway, I took a deep breath—actually, it was a sigh, and said, "I need to think about this."

William smelled a deal and said, "I'd like your answer by Sunday, or Monday morning before we leave, at the latest."

"All right." I inquired sheepishly, "About that financial inducement . . ."

"We can discuss that when we speak."

"Well . . . it would help me now to know how much I'm being induced."

William himself didn't know how much he wanted to spend to ensure his only daughter's happiness. And he didn't know what my price was to tear myself away from the love of my life. He *did* know, however, that I was very aware that he could cut off Susan's allowance and disinherit her. So that lowered her value, and lowered my price to dump a Stanhope.

I could see him struggling with this, pissed off beyond belief that Susan was going to cost him a wad of cash. And of course he was pissed off at me for lots of reasons, including my getting any of his money. Maybe he'd reduce her allowance to amortize the payoff.

Finally, he asked, "What do *you* have in mind?"

"How does two million sound?"

I thought he was going to fall face first into the baked brie, but he caught his breath and mumbled, "Perhaps we can agree on half of that—but paid in ten annual installments, so that your inducement is ongoing."

"Ah, I see what you're getting at. But if I got it all up front, I wouldn't renege on the deal. I give you my word on that."

"I would want a written contract."

"Right. Like a non-nuptial agreement."

"And non-cohabitation."

"Of course." I love to do deals, so I said, "But if I got it all up front, I'd discount the two million."

"I think we need to discuss that number, and the terms. Later."

"What are you doing after dinner?"

But before he could respond, Susan and Sophie returned, and William, gentleman that he is, stood and, while he was up anyway, grabbed a martini off Susan's tray.

Sophie rearranged the coffee table and left. Susan sat and asked, "Where's Mom?"

William said, "Freshening up."

Susan took stock of the situation and inquired, with a smile, "Have you had a good man-to-man talk?"

William replied, "We were just discussing what's going on here at Stanhope Hall."

I looked at William, and I could see that he was a bit more relaxed now, maybe even hopeful that his worst nightmare might be ending before it began. I considered winking at him and flashing two fingers—Victory—and not at any price; only two million.

Charlotte returned, took her seat, and scooped up her martini.

Susan, thinking that she was continuing with our subject of Stanhope Hall, said, "As I mentioned in my e-mail, the owner, Amir Nasim, has some security concerns, so he's hired a security firm to advise him of what needs to be done."

William inquired, "What sort of security concerns?"

Susan explained, "He's originally from Iran, and his wife told me that he has enemies in that country, who may want to harm him."

Charlotte was now licking the bottom of her martini glass, and she stopped in mid-lick and said, "Oh, my."

William, always thinking of himself, asked me, "Do you think there's any danger to us?" Meaning him.

I replied, "No one is likely to mistake the guest cottage for Stanhope Hall, or mistake Mr. and Mrs. Nasim for any of us."

William agreed, and said, stupidly, "Well, maybe we'll have a little excitement here."

No one laughed or slapped their knees, but I did say, "If you'd feel more comfortable elsewhere, Susan can inquire about the cottages at The Creek."

Susan chimed in, "I don't think we should overreact, John."

I didn't reply, but I did note that neither William nor Charlotte expressed any concern about their daughter and their grandchildren.

William did say, however, "When we lived in Stanhope Hall, we never even locked our doors." He looked at his zoned-out wife and asked, "Did we, darling?"

"We did," Charlotte agreed, or disagreed, depending on what she thought he said.

I was actually glad I was drinking hundred-proof tonic because I was better able to appreciate William and Charlotte with a clear head.

Susan reminded them of why they were in New York, and said, "I am feeling so sad about Ethel. It's hard to believe that she's gone."

Charlotte remarked, "The poor dear. I hope she didn't suffer at the end."

And so we spoke about the departed Ethel for a few minutes, recalling many happy memories, and, of course, not recalling that Ethel was a pain in the ass. Charlotte did say, however, with a smile, "She was a stubborn woman." Still smiling, she remarked, "Sometimes I wondered who was mistress and who was servant."

Susan reminded her, "We don't use those words any longer, Mother."

"Oh, Susan. No one minds."

I noticed that William had nothing to say about Ethel, good or bad, and he just sat there, perhaps thinking about his father fucking Ethel, then Ethel fucking his father.

I thought this might be a good time to straighten out the mistress thing—about Ethel being Augustus' mistress; so of course Ethel was *a* mistress, but not *the* mistress of Stanhope Hall. I mean, she was dead, and so was Augustus, so to liven up the conversation, I said to Charlotte and William, "I was going through Ethel's paperwork, and I found the life tenancy conveyance among her papers, and that got me wondering why Augustus conveyed such a valuable consideration to two young employees, who—"

"John," said Susan, "I think we should get ready." She looked at her watch and said, "I'd like to be at the funeral home at seven." She stood.

Well, I should save this for when there were more people around to appreciate it, so I stood, and so did Mom and Dad, who swayed a bit.

Susan said to me, "Mom and Dad's luggage is still in their car. Would you mind getting it?"

"Not at all, darling."

William already had his keys in his hand, which he gave to me, and said, "Thank you, John." I guess that meant he wasn't going to help. Well, then, I wasn't going to discount the two million.

I went out into the rain, retrieved their cheap luggage, which looked like a bank giveaway, and hauled it up the stairs to their room.

They weren't in their room yet, so I didn't get a tip, and I left the luggage on two racks that Susan had set up. Then I went to the master bedroom, where Susan was getting undressed, and I inquired, "Do we have time for a quickie?"

She smiled, and asked, "Is that the alcohol talking?"

"Very funny." I commented, "Those two put away half a bottle of gin."

"They were very tense, and I think upset." She observed, "But Dad seemed much less upset after the third one got to him."

"He did, didn't he?"

She inquired, "What did you two talk about?"

I considered telling her that her father had tried to buy me off, and I *would* tell her . . . but if I did that now, *she* might be upset. It was better, I thought, to have her think that her father's better mood was alcohol-induced. And tomorrow, when she saw that Dad and I were getting along tolerably well—without the martinis—she'd be happy, and her happiness would spread like sunshine over all of us, including Edward and Carolyn.

And then, Sunday after dinner, or Monday morning, after the children were gone, and before Scrooge McDuck headed south, I'd ask Susan what she thought was a fair price for me to accept from Dad for going back to London. Well, I might present it differently, such as, "Your father had the *nerve* to offer me a bribe to leave you. I have *never* in my life been so insulted." And so on.

After she got over her shock, I'd tell her he offered me two million dollars, but that I wouldn't leave her for less than five. I mean, *that's* serious money. I could actually live off the interest, as the Stanhopes did.

Susan sat at her makeup table and did some touch-ups. She said to me, "That actually went better than I expected. And I thank you again for being . . . nice."

"It's easy to be nice to nice people."

She thought that was funny, but then advised me, "Cool the borderline sarcasm. They're not that dense."

"You think?"

"And do *not* bring up Ethel Allard's life tenancy in the gatehouse." She asked, "Why did you do that?"

"I didn't realize it was a sore subject."

"You know it is." She further advised, "You need to find less obnoxious ways to amuse yourself."

"Okay. How about a quickie?"

"John, we're going to a wake." She glanced at her watch and asked, "How quick?"

CHAPTER FIFTY-ONE

William and Charlotte would have blown the needle off a Breathalyzer, so I drove. I'd left the carbine home so the Stanhopes wouldn't see it, and also so I wouldn't be tempted to shoot them.

Susan, sitting next to me, was looking good in black, but she was in a quiet, post-coital, pre–funeral home mood.

The Stanhopes, in the rear seat of the Lexus, had changed out of their tropical bird costumes and were also wearing black, which made them look like buzzards. The car, by the way, smelled of gin, and I was getting a little tipsy.

I had no doubt that William had told his wife about our private discussion, putting his own spin on it, and now they were turning this over in their tiny, alcohol-soaked brains.

Well, three of us knew that we were negotiating for Susan Stanhope Sutter, who didn't even know she was for sale.

Anyway, despite a long and draining day, and what promised to be a long evening, I was in a chipper mood. Maybe I thrive on danger, conflict, and bullshit. Plus, of course, I just got laid. And I didn't get laid with just *anyone*—no, I had sex with Mr. and Mrs. Stanhope's daughter, which made it so much more enjoyable. That's a little perverse, I know, but at least I'm aware of that, and it's really low on the kinky scale, and not worth examining too much.

And of course, if Mom and Dad were paying attention, they realized I was sharing their daughter's bedroom. And if they had been lingering outside our door, they also knew why we were fifteen minutes late.

No one seemed to have much to say as I drove up to Locust Valley, so to liven up the mood, I said, "Let me buy dinner tonight. There's a nice Italian place in Locust Valley that I haven't been to in ten years."

"John."

"Yes, darling?"

Susan informed me, "Mom and Dad have had a long day, so we're having a quiet supper at home."

"Excellent idea, sweetheart. I'm sorry I missed that memo."

"Now you know."

William and Charlotte seemed unusually quiet, so I glanced in my rearview mirror and saw they'd both nodded off and missed my generous offer to buy dinner at our favorite Italian restaurant. I asked Susan, "What was the name of that place? Vaffanculo?"

She leaned toward me and whispered, "Behave. This is too important for you to screw it up with your childish humor."

"Sorry."

"You were doing so well. Can't you control yourself?"

"I try, but sometimes I can't resist—"

"This is not about *you*. It's about Edward and Carolyn. And *us*."

Susan, of course, didn't know that I had some power over dear Dad now, but that power would disappear the minute I told William to take his offer and shove it up his *culo*. So I was looking forward to tweaking him for a few days, but I'd have to do it when Susan wasn't around.

"John? Do you understand?"

I held up two fingers, which she took to mean "Peace," and she said, "Thank you." On Monday, I'd explain that it meant two million dollars.

To be a little objective here, I understood that William, as a father, thought he was trying to do the best for his daughter. But he was also a control freak, and he had no clue about what was really best for Susan. Plus, of course, he hated me without justification. Well . . . we just never clicked. So this was about him. And instead of him talking to Susan, then to me, he got right down to offering me money to take a hike. And why would he think that John Whitman Sutter would take his money? Even after all these years, he had no idea who I was.

And on that subject, I would *insist* on a prenuptial agreement that gave me nothing more than what I came into the marriage with, meaning nothing. That should make the old bastard happy, but more importantly, it made me happy to know that I was going to remarry Susan for the right reason. Love. Well . . . maybe a new boat. In case I had to leave again.

Anyway, I was feeling like I was standing on the pinnacle of the moral high ground; my heart was pure, and my wallet was empty. So I should at least be allowed to have a little fun with the Stanhopes before they left.

I looked at both of them in the rearview mirror. Maybe they were dead. Well, we were going to the right place.

As we approached the funeral home, Susan said, "I know you don't like wakes. No one does, but—"

"Depends on who's in the coffin."

"But try not to show how bored you are, and try to act appropriately."

"I've grown up a lot in the last ten years."

"Then this is a good time to demonstrate that."

"I'll make you proud to be with me."

She smiled, took my hand, and said, "I was always proud of you, even when you acted like an idiot."

"That's very sweet."

She leaned toward me, kissed my cheek, and said, "You look so handsome in that black suit."

I pulled into the parking lot of the funeral home and said, "Thank you. Maybe I can get a job here."

I realized that the Stanhopes were awake, and I wondered how much of our conversation they'd heard. They weren't exactly hopeless romantics, but clearly they could see and hear that Susan and I were in love—despite her criticisms of my core personality. Well, Willie, if you don't get it, then I feel sorry for you, and for Charlotte. They could really make life easier for themselves, and for us, if they'd just say, "We're happy for you. Have a wonderful life."

But they, like me, carried around too many grudges and griev-ances—but unlike me, they were deep down mean-spirited. And at the end of the day, this is where it all ends—at the funeral home.

The Walton Funeral Home in tony Locust Valley is like the Campbell Funeral Home on Manhattan's Upper East Side—a very good last ad-dress.

This was where George Allard had been waked ten years ago, and also my aunt Cornelia, and my father, and too many other family and friends since I was a child.

Walton's is situated in a nice old Victorian house, similar to and not far from my former office, and I suppose if I stayed in New York, then someday this is where I'd wind up because these places never seem to go out of business. People are dying to get in and all that. I like Par-lor B.

Ethel, however, was in Parlor A, which is small and usually reserved for the elderly who have outlived most potential mourners, or for the truly unpopular. Like the Stanhopes.

I could barely hear the piped-in organ music as I signed the guest book, so I asked a guy in black to turn it up a bit and check the treble. Then we entered Parlor A.

There were a lot of flower arrangements along the walls, but not many people in the seats. The Allard family occupied most of the front row, but we went first to the coffin, and the four of us stood there look-ing at Ethel Allard.

She seemed peaceful—I mean, she wasn't moving or anything—and the undertakers had done a good job with her hair and makeup. She wore a very nice lavender-and-white lace dress that looked like it was from another era. Good choice, Ethel.

Susan whispered, "She's so beautiful."

I agreed, "She looks good." For someone who's old and dead.

William and Charlotte commented that Ethel hadn't aged much in ten years. In fact, she looked better than Charlotte, who was alive.

I said a silent prayer for Ethel, then I took the lead in getting us away from the coffin, and I turned and walked to Elizabeth, who stood, and was looking very good in black. We kissed, and she said, "Thank you for coming."

I said, "She was a remarkable woman, and I will miss her."

Susan came up beside me, and she and Elizabeth exchanged kisses and appropriate remarks. Susan asked her, "How are you doing?"

Elizabeth nodded and replied, "I'm happy that she's with Dad now."

Well . . . who knows where she is or whom she's with.

Next, the Stanhopes greeted Elizabeth, and I could sense that there was some distance there on both sides. The Stanhopes were ostensibly there out of a sense of noblesse oblige, but really they'd come to see their daughter, and their few friends in New York, and I hoped their grandchildren. My being in New York was a bonus for them.

In truth, William and Charlotte had some issues with Ethel, mostly having to do with Ethel's life tenancy in what had once been their property, and also having to do with the reason for that life tenancy. Not to mention Ethel not knowing her place, which Charlotte actually did mention, and which in turn went back again to Ethel screwing Augustus. Well, I guess William was happy that his father's mistress was dead.

Elizabeth, for her part, I'm sure, never cared for William and Charlotte—who did?—but she'd been programmed over the years to be nice to them, and of course, she was very nice now and thanked them for coming all the way from Hilton Head.

Then Elizabeth, perhaps not recalling or not fully appreciating the Stanhopes' feelings toward their once and future son-in-law, said to them, "Isn't this wonderful about Susan and John?"

Well, you wouldn't think that faces could freeze and twitch at the same time, but theirs did. Elizabeth got it right away and said, "Let me introduce you to my children."

She introduced us to Tom Junior and Betsy, who we all remembered as little tykes, and they were good-looking young adults, and very well dressed and well mannered. Maybe I should try to match them up with Edward and Carolyn. We could start a dynasty. But for now, we all expressed our sorrow about Grandma's passing.

Then Elizabeth introduced us to some other family members in Row A, and finally at the end of the row was Elizabeth's ex, Tom Corbet, whom I remembered. Tom then introduced us to a good-looking man named Laurence, who Tom said was his partner.

Well, what can I say? These things are always awkward when exes are in the same room with their new loves, and it doesn't matter much if the new love is of the same or the opposite sex. It occurred to me, too, that if things had gone differently Saturday night and Sunday morning, I might be sitting next to Elizabeth now, and I'd be greeting Susan, William, and Charlotte with cool indifference bordering on hostility. Goes to show you.

Anyway, because Tom had introduced Laurence as his partner, this quite naturally prompted William to inquire, "What business are you two in?"

Tom replied, "Wall Street," and Laurence replied, "CBS News."

This seemed to confuse William, who pressed on. "I thought you were partners."

Elizabeth was all too happy to clear that up, and everyone had a little chuckle, except William, who'd just learned a new meaning to an old word that he didn't want to know. Charlotte, even sober, never knows what anyone is talking about anyway.

Then Susan, saint that she is, told Elizabeth we'd be there until closing time, and to please let her know if there was anything that she or John could do. John seconded that, but John had no idea how he could help out in a funeral home. Water the flowers? Turn up the organ music? Hopefully, William and Charlotte would tire before 9:00 P.M. That was one good thing they could do for me.

Elizabeth thanked us for all we'd done already and added, "I love you both."

That was sweet. And to continue the love fest, I said, "It's too bad that it took a funeral to bring us all together—you, and Susan and me, and William and Charlotte, who I've missed terribly all these years."

I thought I heard a little squeaky sound come from Charlotte, who didn't miss *that*, and I definitely heard a snort from William. Come on, guys. Loosen up and let the love in.

Susan suggested we sit, so we took seats behind Elizabeth and her two children.

Some wakes are better than others, partly depending, as I said, on who's lying in the coffin. Also, you do get to see people you haven't seen in a while, and you can promise to get together for happier occasions. This wake, however, promised to be deadly. All right, all right.

I mean, I didn't seem to know anyone who was there, or anyone who was drifting in. Maybe I should go over to Parlor B and see what was going on there.

Susan did know some people, however, and she stood a few times and said hello to arriving mourners, and now and then she'd drag someone over to say hello to me and her parents.

William and Charlotte, too, knew a few of the older crowd, and they got up and greeted some of them, then they drifted off to the back of the parlor where the senior citizens had gathered, away from the coffin, which probably upset them.

I recalled that at George's wake ten years ago, the old servants' network, or what was left of it then, had gathered in good numbers at Walton's to pay their final respects to one of their own. I recalled, too, that even a few of the old gentry and their ladies had made an appearance. But now I didn't see anyone who could be from either of those opposite but joined classes, and this more than anything else I'd seen here made me realize that the old world that had been dying when I was born was truly dead and buried.

And then, coming through the door, appeared an old lady in a wheelchair pushed by a nurse in a white uniform. Susan saw her and said to me, "That's Mrs. Cotter, who was our head housekeeper. Do you remember her?"

I didn't recall having a housekeeper, head or otherwise, so I assumed she meant at Stanhope Hall. I replied, "I think I do."

Mrs. Cotter was wheeled up to the coffin by the nurse, and they remained there for some time, then they did a one-eighty and moved toward Elizabeth.

Susan stood and took my hand, and we went to where Elizabeth and Mrs. Cotter were now sitting face-to-face, and Elizabeth held the old lady's hands in hers. They were both crying and speaking through their tears.

Mrs. Cotter was infirm, but she seemed sharp enough, and she recognized Susan right away. Susan knelt beside her, and more tears started to flow as all three women reminisced about Ethel, and George, and about the past, and caught up on life.

This seemed to be all that was left of the glory days of Stanhope Hall—the former master and mistress burping martinis in the rear of Parlor A; their daughter trying to re-create at least some parts of those better days; Mrs. Cotter, whom I did remember presiding over a diminished staff in a house that was being closed up, room by room; Elizabeth, the estate brat; and Ethel, who was in the enviable position of not having to attend any more funerals.

Susan said to Mrs. Cotter, "You remember my husband, John Sutter."

Mrs. Cotter adjusted her bifocals and said, "I thought you ran off with another woman."

The elderly, God bless them, can and do say whatever they want, even if they don't get it quite right. I replied, politely, "I'm back."

"Well, you never should have left in the first place. Miss Stanhope had all the suitors she wanted, and from some of the best families."

Everyone was suppressing smiles, and Mrs. Cotter, happy for the opportunity to speak up for Miss Stanhope, continued, "This is a fine young lady, and I hope you appreciate her."

"I do."

Mrs. Cotter seemed content to leave it at that, and Susan said to her, "My parents are here, Mrs. Cotter, and I know they would want to say hello."

And then something strange happened. Mrs. Cotter said to Susan, "Thank you, but I have no wish to speak to Mr. Stanhope."

Well, that stopped the show. Then Mrs. Cotter said to her nurse, "We can leave now."

Elizabeth walked with them to the lobby, and Susan and I went back to our seats.

I didn't know what to say, so I didn't say anything. But, I thought, William must have been a particularly difficult employer, tight as a drum, and not overly generous with the severance pay. I was happy to have my very low opinion of William validated by Mrs. Cotter in front of his daughter.

Susan did comment, "I seem to remember some friction between Dad and Mrs. Cotter."

To lighten the moment, I said, "She certainly put me in my place."

Susan smiled and said, "She doesn't remember, but she liked you. She said I should marry you."

We left it there, and I went back to dividing my attention between my watch and the arriving mourners. I noticed now some people who were obviously friends of Elizabeth, male and female, and also a few women who were so badly dressed that they could have been her customers. I suppose I've been conditioned since childhood to look down on the nouveaux riches, but they themselves make it easy for people like me to make fun of them. I mean, they are a bad combination of money without taste, and conspicuous consumption without restraint. And they seemed to be taking over this part of the planet.

After about half an hour, I was bored senseless, so I didn't notice that my mother had arrived until I realized that Susan was speaking to Harriet, who was standing with Elizabeth in the first row.

Harriet looked at me and asked, "Aren't you going to say hello, John?"

Bitch. I stood and apologized. "I'm sorry, Mother. I was deep in prayer."

She actually smiled at that, then she, Susan, and Elizabeth continued chatting.

Harriet, by the way, was wearing a coarse cotton dress of multi-colors, and I was certain that it was the mourning dress of some fucked-up tribe that lived in some fucked-up jungle in some fucked-up country somewhere. Harriet was multicultural before it became fashionable, and any culture would do, as long as it wasn't her own.

So, before she started dancing around the coffin throwing burning bananas into the air or something, I excused myself and escaped to the sitting room. Tom and Laurence were taking a break, and I sat with them. I said, "Explain to me again how you can be partners and be in different businesses."

We all got a good chuckle out of that, and Tom confessed, "I thought I had a mother-in-law from hell, God rest her soul, but your two are straight from the inferno."

I replied, "Oh, they're not so bad."

Tom said, "Well, I'm only going by what Elizabeth used to tell me, and she got most of that from Ethel. So I'm sorry if I misspoke."

I conceded, "They're not the most likable people. But they do have some good qualities." I was in a don't-give-a-shit mood, so I explained, "They're rich and old."

That got a good laugh, and Tom said, "Well, *big* congratulations on your coming marriage."

So I sat there awhile making small talk with Tom and Laurence, glad for the company. Then William walked into the big sitting room with an older gent, and he saw me, but he didn't acknowledge me. Well, that wasn't going to stop *me* from being polite and respectful to my future father-in-law, so I held up my hand and flashed two fingers.

William turned away and sat with his friend.

Tom asked me, "Are you leaving?"

"No."

"Oh, I thought you just gave William the two-minute warning."

"No, I was giving him the Peace sign." I explained, "Sometimes I just give him the middle finger."

Tom and Laurence thought that was funny, so I expounded on that and said, "When I was dating Susan, William and I used to argue about the Vietnam War, and I'd flash the Peace sign, and he'd flash the Victory sign, which is the same thing. Right? Well, we got some laughs out of that, and then I started giving him the middle finger, which he didn't think was so funny, so he started to shake his index finger at me as a warning that I was pissing him off, and then I would wiggle my pinky— like this—to make fun of his small dick."

Tom and Laurence were laughing, and people were starting to notice, including William, and also the Reverend James Hunnings, whom I just noticed, and who was giving me a look like he was about to shake his finger at me. Anyway, I thought I should leave, and I excused myself.

Back in Parlor A, I sat in the rear and watched the comings and go-ings, and basically zoned out. The smell of the flowers was overwhelming, and the wall sconces had these stupid flickering lights that could bring on a seizure.

My mind drifted back to George's funeral again, and I recalled that Frank Bellarosa had actually shown up, which caused a little stir in the crowd. I mean, it's not every day you get a Mafia don at Walton's, and I wondered if the mourners knew he was there because of me. And for Susan, of course. I hoped everyone just thought that Bellarosa had come because he lived in the neighboring estate.

In any case, Frank arrived with Anna and they knelt at the coffin, Catholic-style, crossed themselves, and bowed their heads in prayer. I swore I saw George trying to roll over. After paying their respects to the deceased, the Bellarosas turned and shook hands with everyone in the first row, expressed their condolences, and, thankfully, left.

I had no idea why he'd shown up in the first place, except that it was my understanding that the Italians never missed a funeral, no matter how remote their relationship might be with the deceased. They must scan the obituaries every morning, then call around to see if anyone knew Angelo Cacciatore, or whomever, and then make a decision about going to the wake based mostly on not wanting to insult the family. Even if it wasn't their family.

Anyway, Frank Bellarosa had other motives for taking a half hour out of his busy criminal life to come to George Allard's wake, and to send a huge flower arrangement; he wanted to ingratiate himself into my and Susan's life. Actually, he was already screwing one of us, and at that point, it wasn't me.

But I promised Susan I wouldn't think about those things, so instead I thought about happy things, like seeing Edward and Carolyn, being with Susan again, and the slippery bathtub in the Stanhopes' guest bathroom.

After about twenty minutes, I got up and checked out the floral arrangements along the walls. I knew a lot of the senders, including my old pals Jim and Sally Roosevelt, who I understood would not be coming to New York for Ethel Allard's funeral, though they knew the Allards for forty years. Also in that category was my sister, Emily, who I wished had come in, just for the family reunion, but Emily has as little as possible to do with this world, having long ago decided that our mother is crazy, and that everyone else who lived here was stuck in the unhealthy past.

And speaking of Harriet, I figured out right away that the potted geranium sitting on a stand had come from her. Harriet is very green, so no one gets cut flowers from her. Usually, for an occasion, she brings or sends something like potted parsley or dill, or whatever. I mean, she's nuts, but at least she didn't bring a tomato bush to Walton's Funeral Home.

I saw a very big arrangement whose card said it was from John, Susan, Carolyn, Edward, William, Charlotte, and Peter. I knew why the first four names were on the card, but I didn't know why Cheap Willie, Airhead Charlotte, and Useless Peter couldn't send their own flowers. Just being on the same card with them gave me stomach cramps. How was I going to spend the rest of William's life being nice to him?

I looked at the other flower arrangements, and it was nice to see so many names from the old days, people who may have moved on, but who had gotten word of the death of Ethel Allard, who, for all her faults, was a good church lady, a good friend to a select few, and one of the last links to the days of the grand estates and the ladies and gentlemen who once lived in them—a world that she detested, but which, ironically, she was more a part of than she understood.

I glanced at the cards on a few other flower arrangements, then found myself staring at a small card pinned to a very large spray of white lilies. It said, *Deepest Condolences*, and it was signed, *Anthony, Megan, Anna, and family.*

CHAPTER FIFTY-TWO

We stayed until the only one left in Parlor A was Ethel.

We saw Elizabeth to her car, along with her son and daughter, and Susan asked her, "Would you like to join us at home for a late supper?"

Elizabeth declined, but I pressed her, wanting company so I wouldn't have to speak to the Stanhopes.

Elizabeth sensed this, but told us that Tom and Laurence were going to stop by her house, which I thought was very civilized, so we invited them as well, and Elizabeth called Tom on his cell phone, and he and Laurence were happy to join us. I love spontaneous parties, and I suggested to Elizabeth, "Let's invite Uncle . . . what was your uncle's name?"

Susan cautioned me, "We don't want to overwhelm Sophie."

The Stanhopes didn't seem too happy about the company, and that made me happy.

So we all got on the road, and at about 9:30, I approached the gates of Stanhope Hall.

My remote still worked, but as I drove through the opening gates, a young man in a silly sky blue uniform stepped out of the gatehouse—now the guard house—and held up his hand.

I stopped, and he asked me, "Who are you here to see?"

I replied, "Me. Who are *you* here to see?"

I straightened him out and told him to leave the gates open for the next two vehicles, then I proceeded up the dark drive.

William commented, "Well, that's a fine thing. Can't even get into your own property. In our community, Palmetto Shores, every security person knows every resident or their cars. Isn't that right, Susan?"

Susan replied, "Mr. Nasim just began this service, Dad."

But William went on, singing the praises of his and Charlotte's, and I guess Susan's, gated paradise. I really needed a drink. More importantly, I think Susan was already tired of Mom and Dad, and they'd been here only four hours.

But to be nice, I said to everyone, "I'm really looking forward to Susan and me coming to Hilton Head. Palmetto Shores sounds great."

The back of the car fell silent, and I continued on, parked the car, and we all went inside.

Susan had called ahead to Sophie, who was in the kitchen trying to rustle up enough grub for nine people—ten, if we could get ahold of Uncle What's-his-name.

I did my guy thing and set up a nice bar on the kitchen island, and Susan helped Sophie. But William and Charlotte, as always, were useless, and they sat in the living room with martini number five.

Elizabeth arrived with Tom Junior and Betsy, and Elizabeth asked, "What is going on at the gatehouse?"

Susan explained as I made drinks for everyone, and Elizabeth commented, "That's sad . . . but I still have good memories of living there." Elizabeth then asked if I had a Tuscan red, which reminded me of our first and last date. I asked her kids to raise their right hands and swear that they were twenty-one, which made them and their mother smile.

I had a great idea, and went into the living room and got a framed photo of Carolyn and Edward and said, "They'll be here tomorrow night. Maybe the four of you can go out."

Susan said, "John."

That means something different every time, but it usually means, "Shut up."

Elizabeth, however, said, "That would be nice."

Tom and Laurence showed up, and I had to explain about the

guards and the paranoid Iranian. They both thought that was exciting, but I could see that Elizabeth was starting to think there was more to this, and she glanced at Susan, then at me, and I nodded.

This gave me another great idea, and I said to Susan, "Let's call the Nasims and ask them to come over."

"I'm not sure what they can eat or drink."

"I'll tell them to bring their own food." I added, "Mr. Nasim would love to speak to your father about Stanhope Hall."

"I don't think my parents are up for much more company."

That was why I wanted to invite the Nasims. I said, "Amir and Soheila might be hurt or insulted if we didn't include them in our funeral rituals." I asked Elizabeth, "Would you mind?"

She replied, "Not at all." She added, "They knew Mom for nine years, and they were always very nice to her."

"Good."

Laurence was following the conversation and inquired, "Can we ask him who wants to kill him and why?"

I replied, "Of course. He's very open about that."

I felt the balance tipping in my favor, but then Susan said, "No. Some other time."

So the Stanhopes would have to forgo a multicultural experience. Maybe I'd invite the Nasims over for dinner and include my mother. She slobbers over third world people, and she'd be proud of me for having Iranian friends.

Anyway, by 10:30, we were all a little lubricated, and we sat in the dining room and passed around platters of hot and cold salads, which I was afraid might agree with William and Charlotte. I'd insisted that they sit at opposite heads of the table, and to make sure they had no one to talk to, I placed Susan, me, and Elizabeth in the middle, and I placed Tom and Laurence on either side of William, and Tom Junior and Betsy on either side of Charlotte. I'm good at this.

William and Charlotte excused themselves early, as I knew they would, and by midnight everyone left, and Susan, Sophie, and I were cleaning up.

I said to Susan, "That was nice. It looked like everyone was having a good time."

Susan agreed, "That *was* very nice."

"Your parents seemed a bit quiet."

"They were tired."

"I think we're out of gin."

"I'll get some tomorrow." She looked at me, smiled, and said, "This is like old times."

"It is." But it wasn't.

We hugged and kissed, which made Sophie smile, and Susan said to me, "I'm so happy, John, but also sad."

"I know."

"But I know we can make up for all the lost years."

"We'll stay up two hours later every night."

"And never take each other for granted, and call twice a day, and not work late at the office, and no more stupid nights out with the girls—"

"Do you mean me or you?"

"Be serious. And we're going to have your mother for dinner once a week—"

"Hold on."

"And meet Carolyn in the city for dinner and a show, and fly to L.A. once a month to see Edward."

"You forgot Hilton Head."

"And we'll do that, too. And you'll see, John, that my parents will accept you. They'll never love you the way I love you, but they will come to respect you, and when they see how happy I am, they'll be fine."

I didn't reply.

She said, "Admit that tonight wasn't as bad as you predicted."

"It got a little rocky there over cocktails, and maybe we didn't have to hear about Dan so much, and I could have done without the prying questions, or the lecture on working hard for forgiveness . . . but other than that, it was a pleasant reunion."

"But it could have been worse." She predicted, "Tomorrow will be better."

"And Monday will be even better than that."

She kissed me and said, "I'm going up."

"I'll check the doors."

Susan went upstairs, and I checked all the doors and windows and made sure the outdoor lights were on. Then I said good night to Sophie, got the carbine out of the hall closet, and went up to the master bedroom.

Susan was reading in bed, and she glanced at the rifle, but didn't comment.

I'd loaded the shotgun earlier with the heavy game buckshot in one barrel and a deer slug in the other, and I took the gun from my closet, and with a weapon in each hand I asked Susan, "Would you rather sleep with Mr. Beretta or Mr. Winchester?"

She continued reading her magazine and said, "I don't care."

I leaned the carbine against her nightstand and rested the shotgun against my side of the bed. I said to her, "A full-perimeter security system will be in place in a week or so."

She didn't reply, so I changed the subject and asked her, "Did you have a chance to look at the floral arrangements?"

"I did."

"Okay. So?"

"I saw it."

I said, "I wouldn't read too much into it." I explained, "I mentioned Ethel's illness when I was there Sunday, and Anna remembered her. And Anthony isn't even home. So I think that was just a nice gesture from Anna and Megan."

"Or maybe a thank-you for slashing the painting."

I thought about that and said, "I'm sure Anthony saw that first and got rid of it."

Again, she didn't reply. So I got undressed and slipped on my Yale T-shirt.

Susan inquired, "Am I going to have to see that every night?"

"It's who I am."

"God help you."

I guess that was a joke. But it was close to blasphemy.

I got into bed and read one of the city tabloids that Sophie brought with her every morning to improve her English, which I think explained some of her problems with the language.

Anyway, I was specifically looking for an article about John Gotti, and I found a small piece that reported that Mr. Gotti's body had arrived from Missouri and was lying inside a closed coffin at the Papavero Funeral Home in the Maspeth section of Queens. The article seemed to suggest that there was no public viewing of the body, and that funeral plans were indefinite because the Diocese of Brooklyn had denied Mr. Gotti a public funeral Mass.

That seemed a little inconsistent with the forgiving message of Christ, but, hey, it was their church and they could do what they wanted. Still, it struck me as a badly thought-out public relations move, and likely to backfire and cause some public sympathy for John Gotti.

More importantly to me, it seemed as though there wasn't going to be a long wake and a Mass, so Anthony Bellarosa might not feel the need to surface in public this week. Maybe I should send an e-mail to the Brooklyn Diocese explaining that I, the FBI, and the NYPD really wanted to see all the *paesanos* who showed up at the wake and the funeral Mass. What's wrong with this cardinal? Didn't he see *The Godfather?*

Anyway, future plans for Mr. Gotti's mortal remains and his immortal soul were on hold, awaiting, I guess, further negotiations. Maybe somebody should offer a big contribution to the diocese. Maybe somebody did, and the cardinal was holding out for more.

Frank Bellarosa, incidentally, had no such problems. I was sure that his soul had as many black spots on it as Mr. Gotti's did, but Frank thought ahead. And I think, too, he had a premonition of his approaching death, though not the way it actually happened.

I recalled very clearly that the day after our Mafia theme party at the Plaza, Frank and I, with Lenny and Vinnie and a big black Cadillac, crossed the East River into the Williamsburg section of Brooklyn, where Frank had grown up. We went to his boyhood church, Santa Lucia, and had coffee with three elderly Italian priests who told us how difficult it was to maintain the old church in a changing neighborhood, and so forth. Bottom line on that, Frank wrote a check for fifty large, and I guess the check cleared because when Frank's time came—I glanced at Susan—a few months later, there was no problem having his funeral Mass at Santa Lucia.

But times change, and the Catholic Church had apparently gotten tired of providing funeral Masses for the less desirable sheep in its flock, who were, of course, the people who most needed the sacrament.

I thought, too, of Ethel's wake at Walton's, and her upcoming Saturday funeral service at St. Mark's, presided over by the Reverend Hunnings, and then her interment in the Stanhopes' private cemetery. Ethel Allard's death was not going to make national news the way John Gotti's had, or Frank Bellarosa's before him.

This makes sense, of course, even if it doesn't seem fair; if you live large, you die large. But if there *is* a higher authority, who asks questions at the gate, and examines your press clippings, then that's where things are sorted out.

Susan said, "Good night," and turned off her bedside lamp.

I read the tabloids for a while longer, then kissed my sleeping beauty, patted my shotgun, and turned off my light.

CHAPTER FIFTY-THREE

Thursday morning dawned gray and drizzly. I was hoping for good weather so the Stanhopes could go out and play five rounds of golf.

Susan, perfect hostess and loving daughter, was already downstairs, and I noticed that the arsenal had been put away somewhere, so as not to upset any houseguests or staff who might want to make our beds or clean the bathroom. I really needed to make Sophie comfortable with weapons. Maybe I'd teach her the Manual of Arms, and the five basic firing positions.

I showered, dressed, and went down to the kitchen, where Susan had a pot of coffee made and a continental breakfast laid out on the island.

We kissed and hugged, and I inquired, "Are your parents taking a run?"

"They haven't come down yet, but I heard them stirring."

"Should I bring some martinis up to them?"

She ignored that—and I don't blame her—and said, "I checked my e-mail, and Carolyn will be in on the 6:05 train, and she'll take a taxi from the station." She then filled me in on Edward's itinerary and a few other things I needed to know, and I was happy to hear that we were going to skip the afternoon viewing at Walton's. I'm sure Ethel would have liked to skip her entire funeral, but she had to be there, and we didn't, and I knew she wouldn't notice.

Anyway, I poured coffee for myself and for Susan, who urged me to share her vitamins, which I politely declined. I did, however, sink my teeth into a granola muffin.

So we sat at the table, reading the three tabloids that Sophie had gone out to buy, and I saw that Mr. Gotti was still in limbo at Papavero Funeral Home. The coffin was still closed, and only the family was allowed to visit. There was, however, some talk of a *private* funeral Mass in the chapel at the cemetery, by invitation only, date, time, and place to be determined. Well, that was a move in the right direction. Maybe the Brooklyn Diocese caught some flak from La Cosa Nostra Anti-Defamation League. I wondered, too, if Anthony Bellarosa and Salvatore D'Alessio had been invited.

I stood and went to the wall phone, and Susan asked, "Who are you calling?"

"Felix Mancuso."

"Why?"

"To get an update." I dialed Mr. Mancuso's cell phone, and he answered. I said, "Hi, John Sutter."

"Good morning."

"And to you. Look, I don't want to be a pest, but I was wondering if you'd heard anything about Anthony's whereabouts or any news I can use?"

He replied, "I would have called you. But I'm glad you called." He informed me, "I did get your message about your chance encounter with Bellarosa's driver, Tony Rosini—that's his last name—and we're following up on that."

That was about as much as I was going to get out of Felix Mancuso, and I didn't want to pursue this with Susan in the room, so I told him something he didn't know. "I was at the wake last night of Ethel Allard, whom I told you about, and one of the floral arrangements there—a really nice spray of white lilies—had a card signed from Anthony, Megan, Anna, and family."

Mr. Mancuso stayed silent a moment, then said, "His wife and his mother's names are on the card. So I wouldn't read too much into it."

That was my thought, too, and I was glad to have it confirmed. But to fully appreciate the underworld subtlety of this gesture, I asked, "Please explain."

So he explained, "Well, had it been signed with just Anthony's name, then he was sending a message to you, and to your wife."

"It wasn't our wake."

"Well, that's the message."

"Which is . . . ?"

"You know." He advised me, "Put it out of your mind."

"Okay." I was really glad I had Felix Mancuso to do cultural interpretations for me. I asked, "You got my message about Amir Nasim putting in a full security system here?"

"I did. That's good for everyone."

"Well, it's not good for Iranian or Italian hit men."

"No, it's not good for them."

I asked, "Did you urge Nasim to do that?"

Mr. Mancuso replied, "He came to his own conclusions."

"Okay . . . but is this threat to him real?"

"He has enemies."

There was no use pursuing that, so I updated him, "Susan's parents have arrived and are in the house."

"Have you told them about your concerns?"

"No. We're telling them that this security has to do with Nasim."

"All right. No use alarming them."

I said, "So you suggest that they stay elsewhere."

"No. I didn't say that."

"Well, I'll take that up with Mrs. Sutter."

After a few seconds, Mr. Mancuso chuckled and said, "You should work for us."

"Thank you. I'll pass that on."

He informed me, "I had a very nice talk with Mrs. Sutter yesterday."

"She said."

He continued, "I think she understands the situation, and she's alert without being alarmed."

"Good. Did you tell her I want a dog?"

He chuckled again, and replied, "I've been asking my wife to get a dog for twenty years."

"No one is trying to kill you."

"Actually, they are." He added, "But that's part of my job, and not part of yours."

"I hope not."

He said, "I'm impressed with Mrs. Sutter."

"Good. Me, too." I added, "And she with you."

"Good. Well, is there anything else I can do for you?"

"Yes. I was reading in the tabloids about John Gotti and the Brooklyn Diocese and all that. Did you see that?"

"I did."

"So, how does this affect Anthony's possible appearance at the wake and the funeral?"

"Well, there is no public wake, so all of Mr. Gotti's friends and associates got a pass on that. But there will be a small, private funeral Mass at about noon in the chapel at Saint John's Cemetery in Queens—that's sort of the Mafia Valhalla—on this Saturday. So we'll see who surfaces there."

The newspapers hadn't said anything about the time, place, or date, but I guess Special Agent Mancuso had better sources than the *New York Post*. I said, "Coincidentally, I'm going to Mrs. Allard's funeral service and burial on Saturday here in Locust Valley. So I'm afraid I wouldn't be able to make John Gotti's send-off."

"I don't think you'd be invited, Mr. Sutter."

"Actually, I was. By Anthony."

"Really? Well, I'll be there, as an uninvited guest, and if I see anyone there who you know, I'll speak to them on your behalf."

"Thank you. And please call me."

"I will."

I said to him, "Speaking of the dead, Anna Bellarosa told me that she and her three sons visit dead Dad's grave every Father's Day." I glanced at Susan, who had been listening to my conversation, but now went back to the newspaper. I continued, "So that may be a good time and place to look for Anthony."

Mr. Mancuso replied, "Good thought. We'll also double the stake-out at Bellarosa's house and his mother's house in Brooklyn on Father's Day."

It *would* be good, I thought, if Anthony felt he needed to be at his father's grave on Father's Day—maybe to get inspired, or maybe to avoid getting yelled at by Mom. And of course there'd be the dinner at his house, or Mom's house. But Anthony really wasn't stupid enough to go home or to Mom's—but he *might* go to the cemetery. I reminded Mr. Mancuso, "Santa Lucia Cemetery."

"I know. I was there." He stayed silent a moment, then he was thoughtful enough to remind me, "You went to Frank Bellarosa's funeral Mass and burial."

"I did."

"Why?"

"We should have a few beers one night."

"I'd like that."

"Good." I asked him, "Are you and the county police in touch?"

"Detective Nastasi and I spoke last night."

"I'm happy to hear that. And are you still assigned to this case?"

"Until it's resolved."

"Great." I asked him, "How is the war on terrorism going?"

"Pretty good today."

"Well, it's still early."

He informed me, "Every day that nothing happens is a good day."

"I know the feeling."

Our business concluded, we signed off with promises to speak again, and I sat down and contemplated my granola muffin. I said to Susan, "This tastes funny."

"It's made with yogurt. What was he saying on his end?"

I filled her in, but decided not to mention Mr. Mancuso's suggestion that her parents get out of our house. Or was that my idea? Anyway, I thought I should hold on to that and use it if the Stanhopes became insufferable. Also of course, I really didn't want to alarm everyone, especially Edward and Carolyn.

But Susan asked me, "What was he saying about my parents?"

"Oh, he said if he heard anything that would change our alert level here, then he'd advise us, and we should ask your parents to find other accommodations."

She thought about that, then said, "I would be very upset if I had to tell Edward and Carolyn about our problem and ask them to sleep elsewhere."

"Not a problem. Mancuso said the children will be fine here. It's only your parents who would have to leave."

"I don't understand . . ." Then she understood and said to me, "John, that's not funny, and not nice."

"Sorry. It's my ace in the hole." I suggested, "Think about it. Less chance of friction. More chance of bonding."

She actually seemed to be thinking about it, and said, "Let's see how it goes today."

"Okay." I pointed out, "*You* seemed a bit impatient with them last night."

"It was a long, tense, and emotional day."

I didn't reply, which was good because I heard Them on the stairs.

William and Charlotte came into the kitchen, and Susan kissed her parents, and I satisfied myself with "Good morning."

William, I recalled, liked his cold cereal in the morning, and Susan had lined up six boxes on the counter of these godawful sugar concoctions, and William picked something with cocoa in it that I wouldn't feed to the pigs.

Charlotte doesn't eat breakfast and doesn't drink coffee, so Susan had set out a chest of herbal teas, and Susan boiled water for the old bat.

I mean, it wasn't even 8:00 A.M., and I was already strung out.

I was impressed, however, that to look at them, you would never know that they had consumed enough gin and wine last night to float a small boat. Amazing. Maybe they had annual liver transplants.

Anyway, the four of us sat around the kitchen table and made small talk.

Then William said to me offhandedly, "I didn't realize from Susan's e-mail and phone calls that you were actually staying here."

I replied, "Well, I moved in only a day or so ago." I explained,

"Upon Ethel's death, Mr. Nasim, as you know, was able to reclaim the gatehouse, and he wanted to install his security people there—as you saw—so that left me homeless in New York, and Susan was kind enough to let me use my old bedroom here."

He thought about that, then pointed out, quite correctly, "That's also her bedroom."

Susan explained, unnecessarily, "We're sleeping together."

William, of course, knew that by now. Hello? William? But I guess he wanted to hear it from the sinners' own mouths. Meanwhile, I was sure he and Charlotte had not been too judgmental of Susan when she lived and dated in Hilton Head. I mean, really, Susan is an adult, and I have adult tendencies, and it's none of their business what we do behind closed doors. Not to mention we'd already been married to each other, and we had two children, for God's sake. But, as I say, William is a control freak, plus, of course, this really had to do with John Sutter, not propriety.

Anyway, we dropped that subject, and William shoveled spoonfuls of milk-sodden Cocoa Puffs into his mouth, and Charlotte sipped tea made out of Himalayan stinkweed or something.

I was thinking of an excuse to excuse myself, but then William said to Susan, "Your mother and I were thinking that you have enough company with Edward and Carolyn coming—and John here—so we've decided to stay at The Creek."

Thank you, God.

Susan objected, and I did my part by saying, "Won't you reconsider?" Maybe you should go home.

Anyway, we went back and forth, and when I was sure they were adamant, I said, "Maybe you can stay just one more night."

"Well . . ."

Oh my God. What did I do?

Then William stuck to his guns and said to Susan, "Please call The Creek and see if a cottage is available."

Charlotte chirped in, "We've always enjoyed staying there, and it's no reflection on your wonderful hospitality, dear."

I replied, "I understand that."

Charlotte looked at me and said, "I was speaking to Susan."

"Of course."

Susan went to the phone, called The Creek, and secured a cottage for Mr. and Mrs. Stanhope, her parents, and instructed the club to put all charges on her bill, including food, beverage, and incidentals. William was happy. I was giddy.

I said to Susan, "See if you can get Mom and Dad golf privileges. And don't forget the cabana. And maybe tennis lessons."

Susan ignored me, finalized the arrangements, then hung up and said, "You're booked until Monday."

So it was settled. I guess the Stanhopes didn't want to share a house with me, and probably they were afraid of another spontaneous or planned house gathering, and I'm sure they found the guards at the gate to be inconvenient. Not to mention the possibility of Iranian assassins hiding in the bushes.

But for the record, everyone agreed that it might work out better if Mom and Dad had their own space, close to here, but not too close, though we were all a little disappointed, of course.

I inquired, "Can I help you pack?"

William assured me that they could do that themselves, but he asked if I'd carry their luggage to the car.

I replied, "Whenever you're ready."

Charlotte slipped up and said, "We're packed."

"Well, then"—I stood and said—"I'll just go and get your things."

And off I went, taking the steps four at a time.

So, within half an hour, William, Charlotte, John, and Susan were outside saying ciao, but not arrivederci.

William announced that he and Charlotte had some old friends they wanted to see, and maybe they'd play golf with them and have lunch and also dinner, and unfortunately wouldn't be at Ethel's wake today or tonight, and they were sorry to miss Edward and Carolyn this evening, and so forth.

But we'd all get together Friday night at the funeral home, then play it by ear—whatever that meant. I hoped it meant we wouldn't see them until the funeral service Saturday morning, if then. But we were all on for Father's Day, and I reminded William, sotto voce, that we'd speak no later than Monday morning. I winked, but he didn't return the wink.

Susan and I stood in the forecourt and waved as they drove off. I flashed William the V-sign, but I don't think he saw it.

Susan and I walked back to the house, and she said, "Well, I'm a little disappointed, but a little relieved."

"I know exactly how you feel."

"Come on, John. You practically pushed them out the door."

"I did not. He stumbled."

We returned to the kitchen, and I tried another muffin. "This smells and tastes like manure."

"It's bran." She said to me, "Well, you tried, and I tried, but I don't think they were comfortable with this situation."

"What was your first clue?"

She thought a moment, then said, "Well, it's *their* problem."

"It is. And don't let them make you feel guilty. You're a good daughter, but they're manipulative, narcissistic, and self-centered." Plus, they're assholes. I added, "And they don't care about seeing their grandchildren."

Susan sat at the table, and she looked sad. So I said, "We'll have a nice Father's Day together. I promise."

She forced a smile.

I hesitated, then took her hand and said, "If me leaving . . . I mean, leaving for good, will—"

"If you say that one more time, I'll kick you out."

I stood and gave her a big hug, then said, "Your father and I have a date to discuss business, Sunday night or Monday morning."

She thought about that and said, "I don't like being discussed as though I was a blushing virgin."

"You're not a virgin?"

"What are you going to talk about?"

"Well, the deal." I let her know, "We need a prenuptial agreement. That's what will make the deal work."

"This is not a *deal*. It's a marriage."

"Not when you're a Stanhope. And that's your problem, not mine."

"All right. Talk to him. Try not to screw up my allowance and my inheritance."

"Do you care?"

"No. But take care of the children."

"I will." I added, "Whatever it takes."

Then she said something that did not shock me. She said, "God forgive me, I hate them."

She was a little weepy, so I put my arms around her and said, "We've moved on from the past, and now you have to move on from your parents."

"I know." She said, "I feel sorry for them."

It's hard for me to feel sorry for anyone worth one hundred million dollars, especially if they're assholes, but to be nice, I said, "I know what you mean . . . I feel sorry for Harriet, and I felt sorry for my father . . . and I think he died feeling sorry for himself. But . . . we are not going to become them."

She nodded, stood, and said, "Let's do something fun today."

Well, I just pushed the Stanhopes out the door, and it doesn't get more fun than that. I asked, "What would you like to do?"

"Let's go to the city and have lunch, then go to a museum, or shop."

"Shop?"

"When was the last time you were in Manhattan?"

I replied, "September of last year."

She looked at me, nodded, and said, "I've never been to Ground Zero." She thought a moment, then asked, "Is that something we should do . . . ?"

"It's not exactly a fun day in the city."

"I know . . . but you were there . . . can we do that today?"

"You can let me know how you feel when we're driving in."

"All right . . ." She took my hand and said, "I feel safe when I'm standing next to you."

"That's very nice." I said to her, "I never felt so alone and so depressed in my life as I did when I came back to New York last September."

She said, "Carolyn came to Hilton Head, and she said to me, 'Mom, I wish Dad was here.' And I said to her, 'Me, too.'"

I replied, "Well, I'm here."

CHAPTER FIFTY-FOUR

As we drove toward Manhattan, Susan looked at the skyline and observed, "It's so strange not seeing the Towers there . . ." Then she said, "Let's go to Ground Zero."

I glanced at her and replied, "All right."

So we drove the Taurus into Lower Manhattan, and spent some quiet time on the observation platform overlooking the excavated ruins. It was hard to comprehend this tragedy, and harder to understand the senseless deaths of so many human beings, including people we knew. The gray, drizzly day added to our somber mood.

We took a walk through the streets of Lower Manhattan. When I worked here, this was a very busy and bustling part of the city, but now the streets and sidewalks look emptier than I remembered, and I knew that had to do with September 11. Maybe I'd be working down here again, but with a new firm, of course—one that valued my brash career decisions, my sailing adventures, and my past association with organized crime. In fact, getting a good job was not going to be that easy—Anthony Bellarosa's generous offer notwithstanding—so, since I might be the only person who would hire me at my required salary, I should work for myself. My future father-in-law would be delighted to finance my new firm, and Carolyn could work with me, and we'd be Sutter & Sutter: tax law, environmental specialists, and women's legal rights.

Susan asked, "What are you thinking about?"

I told her, and she smiled and asked, "Which of those areas would you feel comfortable working in?"

We walked up to Chambers Street and entered Ecco restaurant, where I used to bring clients. After we were seated, I looked at the lunch crowd, which was mostly Wall Street types who are easy for me to spot, though I didn't see a single face I knew. Ecco's clientele also included high-priced defense attorneys who had business in the nearby courts, plus a few high-ranking law enforcement people from nearby Police Plaza and Federal Plaza. I looked around for Mr. Mancuso, but I didn't think he'd splurge on a sixty-dollar lunch, though maybe this is where we'd have our beers one night after work.

Susan asked, "See anyone you know?"

"No, I don't. And it's only been ten years."

She commented, "Ten years can be a long time."

"It can be."

We had a good lunch, with a good bottle of red wine to take the chill out of our bones, and we held hands and talked.

After lunch, we took a walk to my old office building at 23 Wall Street, and as I always do with visitors, I pointed out to Susan the scars in the stone that were caused by the Anarchists' bomb at the turn of the last century. She was sweet enough not to remind me that I'd shown this to her about twenty times.

I was going to enter the big, ornate lobby to look around, but I noticed that there was now a security point right near the door, complete with metal detectors and tables where you needed to empty your pockets. This was a little jarring, and also depressing, so we moved on—not that I wanted to take the elevator up to Perkins, Perkins, Sutter and Reynolds to hug and kiss my former partners.

Well, I was ready to leave Memory Lane and take a subway or taxi up to Midtown for some really great shopping, but Susan said to me, "Let's walk to Little Italy."

I didn't reply.

She said, "We *need* to go there as well."

I thought about that, then agreed, "All right."

So we walked in the drizzle up to Little Italy and found ourselves on Mott Street, which hadn't changed much in ten years, nor had it changed much in the last hundred years.

A minute later, we were in front of Giulio's Ristorante. Not much had changed here either in the last hundred years, though I know for a fact that the plate-glass window and the red café curtains had been replaced ten years ago—right after Frank Bellarosa caught a double-barreled shotgun blast in his Kevlar vest, and sailed backwards from the sidewalk, then reentered Giulio's through the window.

I looked down at the sidewalk where Vinnie had fallen after he took a single shotgun blast full in the face from less than six feet away. The shooters, two of them, had been crouched on the far side of Frank's limo, which was parked at the curb . . . then I saw both men stand and rest their arms and shotguns on the roof of the car . . . then they fired . . . two for Frank, and one for Vinnie, and the sound of the blasts was deafening.

Then the guy who had fired only one shot and I made eye contact.

Susan said to me, "John . . . what happened?"

I looked at her. She'd been inside the restaurant, still at the table with Anna, and I realized I'd never told her exactly what had gone on out here.

I hesitated, then related what happened to Frank and Vinnie, and continued, "So the shooter looks away from me, then looks back at Frank, who's half in and half out of the window . . . Vinnie is definitely not a problem anymore . . . so I guess the guy decides that Frank is taken care of too, and he doesn't have a good shot at him anyway . . . only his legs . . . so he looks back at me—like . . . he's not sure what to do about me."

Susan said, in a barely audible voice, "Oh my God." She asked me, "Why didn't you run?"

"Well, it happened so fast . . . ten seconds maybe. But . . . I wasn't sure why he was hesitating . . . then I thought, I guess I'm not on his list . . . but he was looking at me, and the shotgun was still in his hands . . . and I'm thinking I'm a witness, so maybe I shouldn't be looking at his face."

Susan took my arm and said, "Let's go."

I remained in the spot where I'd stood ten years before, and continued, "So I decided I didn't want to wait for the shot—so I gave him the finger, and he smiled, then swung the gun back toward Frank and fired his final shot into Frank's legs."

She stayed silent a moment, then asked, "You did what?"

"I gave him the finger. Like this—" I raised my middle finger in a passable Italian salute.

Susan remained silent, then said to me, "That was insane."

"Well . . . maybe. But here I am."

She pulled on my arm and said again, "Let's go."

"No . . . let's go inside."

"No, John."

"Come on. We're here, it's raining, and I need a cup of coffee."

She seemed hesitant, then nodded and said, "All right."

So we entered Giulio's Ristorante.

It was exactly as I remembered it, with a high tin ceiling, three paddle fans, a white ceramic tile floor, checkered tablecloths, and cheap prints of sunny Italy on the white plaster walls. The place wasn't much to look at, but it was spotless, and it was authentic—a throwback to the Italian immigrant culture of the last century. Also, I recalled, the food was authentic Italian—not American Italian—so you had to be careful what you ordered, unless you liked *trippa*, for instance, which I found out the hard way is diced pig's stomach, and the sheep's head—*capozella*—is no treat either.

Also authentic, I recalled, was the clientele, who were mostly locals from the shrinking Italian neighborhood, as well as recently arrived Italian immigrants, who were looking for real home cooking.

And then there was another sort of clientele—gentlemen who wore expensive suits and pinky rings and who did not smile much. I remembered these men quite clearly from when I'd had lunch here with Frank. And I also recalled that Frank, who'd been a happy guy after I'd sprung him on bail, had put on his Mafioso face as soon as we walked in.

Anyway, it was well after lunch now, but there was a smattering of older men at the tables having coffee, pastry, and conversation. I didn't see anyone who might be friends of Anthony, or of Sally Da-da, and this was a good thing.

A middle-aged waiter in an apron came over to us, smiled, and said, "Buon giorno."

Susan replied, "Buon giorno."

I said, "Good afternoon." I added, in case he thought we were there to extort money, "Table, please."

"Yes, yes. You coma sitta here, nice a table by the window."

That was the table that Frank landed on when he came in through the window. That didn't bother me, but I had another idea and pointed toward a rear table where the Bellarosas and the Sutters had had their last supper together. I said, "We'll take that table."

"You wanna that table?"

Susan explained, "We sat there a long time ago."

He shrugged, "Okay. Thasa nice a table, too."

So we sat at the nice a table, and we ordered cappuccino, a bottle of San Pellegrino water, and a plate of mixed pastry.

The waiter took an immediate liking to Susan—they all do—and said to her, "I'm a gonna bringa you some beautiful dolce, and some nice a chocolate for you."

How about me?

Susan said, "Grazie," then said something else to him in Italian, and he smiled and replied. I think this is how she got into trouble the last time.

Anyway, we sat there, with our backs to the wall, which is how I'd sat here with Frank at our post-courthouse lunch, and Susan and I held hands, and stared at nothing in particular.

Finally, Susan said, "This is good."

I replied, "I wasn't sure."

It did occur to me that we were in the belly of the beast, so to speak, though I didn't really expect Anthony Bellarosa to walk through the door. Or the ghost of Frank Bellarosa for that matter. No, I felt we were chasing away the ghosts, and making new memories, rather than burying them, or letting them consume us.

The cappuccino came, and the bottled water, and a huge plate of Italian pastry, along with a dish of chocolates—for Susan—and also a bottle of Sambuca and two liqueur glasses, which were *in omaggio*—on the house.

We sat there, talking and drinking coffee, and eating too much pastry, and sipping Sambuca, killing the afternoon Italian-style. This was a lot less stressful than shopping, and more companionable than a museum. Good date.

At about four o'clock, Susan said, "We should go so we can get ready for Edward and Carolyn."

I got the bill and overtipped the waiter, and we left Giulio's, took a taxi back to our car, and began the drive home.

Not a bad day, so far. I got rid of the Stanhopes and got rid of Frank Bellarosa's ghost. Anthony next.

CHAPTER FIFTY-FIVE

I had decided to surprise Carolyn at the station, and I parked the Taurus near the taxi stand and waited for the 6:05 to pull in.

I'd left the carbine home again, not thinking I'd get into a shoot-out with the Mafia in broad daylight at a crowded commuter station. And yet every time I left the rifle home, I was angry at myself for not having it with me. So, like Susan, I needed to face reality.

The 6:05 blasted its whistle and came to a hissing stop at the station. The rush-hour train disgorged dozens of commuters onto the platform, and I had a flashback to my former life. Could I do this again?

I got out of the car and scanned the passengers, then spotted Carolyn as she made her way toward the waiting taxis. I called out, "Hey, beautiful! Need a lift?"

She was apparently used to this and kept walking, head and eyes straight ahead. Then she stopped in her tracks and turned in my direction.

I waved, and she yelled, "Dad!" and hurried toward me.

We hugged and kissed, and she said, "Dad, it's so good to see you."

"It's good to see you, sweetheart." I said, "You're looking more beautiful than ever."

Carolyn ignores compliments, but she did smile and said, "This is so . . . I am so happy for you."

"Me, too." She was carrying only a handbag and a lawyerly brief-case, so I asked her, "Where's your luggage?"

"Oh, I have a set of clothes at Mom's."

"Good." Exactly how much *were* they paying these ADAs in Brooklyn? Surely, my socially sensitive daughter wasn't spending her annual trust fund distribution on clothes and baubles for herself.

Anyway, we got in the car, and I noticed that she was wearing all black, which apparently was the new "in" non-color, suitable for work, after-work cocktails, weddings, and funerals.

Also, incidentally, her hair is black, like my mother's was before she went gray, and there had never been a hint of Susan's red hair, so there was hope that Carolyn wasn't cuckoo.

I drove out of the small parking lot and noticed the expensive cars driven by wives who'd come to pick up their hardworking husbands. There were young children in some of the vehicles—the nanny left early today—and if I looked at these couples, I could see immediately which ones were happy to see each other, and which ones wished they'd taken another train ten or twenty years ago.

I had no doubt that each couple had a story, but I didn't think any of them could top mine and Susan's.

I drove through the village and headed toward Stanhope Hall.

Carolyn asked me, "Are you happy, Dad?"

"What man wouldn't be happy about getting married?"

Carolyn is not into my humor and asked again, "Are *you* happy?"

I glanced at her and said, "I wouldn't be here if I wasn't happy to be here."

"I know."

I said to her, "Your mother, too, is very happy."

"I know that. We speak or e-mail twice a day."

Of course.

To put the ball in her court, I said, "Well, I'm getting married for the second time, and you haven't been married even once."

"Dad."

We chatted about her job and caught up on other subjects.

Carolyn, as she did every summer, had spent a week in London in August, and this was our time together each year, except for when I came to New York for funerals, weddings, and business trips. So she said to me, "I guess I'm not visiting you in London this year."

I smiled and replied, "No. But your mother and I are going to London, maybe very soon, to move me out." Carolyn likes London, so I asked, "Why don't you come with us?"

She replied, "I don't think I can get away on short notice, but thanks." Then she suggested, "Why don't you keep your London flat?"

I thought about that, and it wasn't a bad idea, depending on future finances. But I wasn't sure if Susan would be in favor of that. In any case, I might be using the flat myself if the Stanhopes got their daughter back. I said to *my* daughter, "That's an idea."

As we approached Stanhope Hall, Carolyn asked me, "How are Grandpa and Grandma?"

"They're wonderful."

"I got your e-mail."

"Good."

"So? How are you getting along with them?"

"Not bad, actually."

"Are they happy for you and Mom?"

"I thought you were in daily contact with your mother."

"We haven't spoken much about that."

"Well, let's save that for when Edward gets in."

I'd gotten my new remote control from one of the security men—the company was called All-Safe Security, which seemed redundant—and he'd also given me the new pass code, with the wise advice that I shouldn't be giving it out to a lot of people I didn't know. I love dealing with overtrained underachievers. Yes, I am a snob.

Also, of course, in situations such as this, the line between the guards and the guarded becomes blurred, and the distinction between being protected and being a prisoner with a pass is very subtle.

As the gates swung open, the All-Safe Security guard (ASS guy) stepped out of the gatehouse-guardhouse, and he actually recognized me from thirty minutes ago and waved me through. It helped, too, that I had the remote control and the same car I'd left in.

Carolyn remarked, "Mom mentioned about the guys at the gates."

"No big deal."

She dropped that and asked, "Are Grandpa and Grandma home?"

I wish they were. I said, "They've decided to stay in a cottage at The Creek."

"Why?"

They're assholes. I replied, "They thought they'd be more comfortable there, and they wanted to take some work off your mother."

Carolyn didn't respond.

I really needed Carolyn and Edward to have positive feelings toward Gramps and Granny. I mean, these kids are amazingly non-judgmental about those two, and as far as I knew, Edward and Carolyn actually liked Count Dracula and his wife. But we were at a critical juncture here, and we were all sharing the same zip code, if not the same house, so we needed to remind the children of how much they loved G&G. Plus, someone needed to brief Edward and Carolyn on the financial facts of life. And that was really a job for Susan. I suppose I could be present at this talk, but it wasn't my money. Plus, I might say something that could be misconstrued, such as, "Your grandparents are scum-sucking pigs."

Anyway, I said to Carolyn, "We'll see Grandma and Grandpa tomorrow night at the funeral home."

Carolyn asked about another one of my favorite people. "How's Grandma Harriet?"

"She's very well and is looking forward to seeing you and Edward." And, hopefully, you're both in *her* will.

To say something nice about Harriet, she *is* fond of her only two grandchildren. She's not huggy-kissy, but she keeps in close contact with them, and she's sort of a mentor to Carolyn, instructing her granddaughter on the finer points, for instance, of recycling the kitchen garbage into tasty snacks for illegal immigrants from San Picador, or wherever they come from. Edward is a bit of a challenge for her, but if she can get him to start shutting off the lights, then she's done a good thing for Edward and the environment.

But beyond the brainwashing, I think she sees Edward and Carolyn as her opportunity to make up for her failures with John and Emily. And that, too, is a good thing.

As I continued up the tree-lined drive, I asked Carolyn, "Does it feel good to be home?"

She replied, without inflection, "Yes."

Carolyn actually never cared much for God's Heaven on Earth, or its inhabitants, or its country clubs, cocktail parties, lifestyles, reactionary politics, or anything about it. Susan and I did, however, make her go to the Debutantes Ball under threat of being grounded for the rest of her life.

She asked me, "Are *you* happy to be home?"

"It's good."

I parked the car in the forecourt, and we went to the front door, which I unlocked. Carolyn, perhaps putting this together with the guards at the gate, asked, "Why are you locking the door now?"

I replied, "Republican fundraisers have been walking into people's houses and writing big contribution checks to the GOP."

Although Carolyn doesn't get or appreciate my humor, she did laugh at that.

Susan was upstairs, but she heard us coming in, and she hurried down the steps. Mother and daughter embraced and kissed, and I was smiling.

We went into the kitchen, where Sophie was laying out some fruit, cut vegetables, and to-die-for yogurt dip.

Susan had a bottle of champagne on ice in a bucket, and I popped the cork and poured three flutes of bubbly. I actually don't like the stuff, but Susan and Carolyn have champagne taste, and I filled my glass and toasted, "To the Sutters."

We touched glasses and drank.

The weather had cleared a bit, so we went out to the patio and sat at the table.

Susan and Carolyn were current with each other on all the news and happenings, and I realized I was a few months behind Carolyn's life. I did know that Cliff got dumped, and now I heard about Stuart, her Petrossian date, who also had champagne taste and hopefully the money to afford it.

I wasn't exactly bored, but I did change the subject to work, and

Carolyn said, "Dad, you can't believe the things I see, read, and hear every day."

I thought I could. Well, Carolyn was seeing some of the dark side of American society, and this was good for a young lady raised at Stanhope Hall. Susan had never had much exposure to the underbelly of life, but Carolyn had, and with any luck, she knew better than to have an affair with a married Mafia don.

We avoided the subject of G&G, knowing we should save that until Edward showed up.

The portable phone rang, and I took it. It was the ASS guy asking if we were expecting an Edward Sutter, who had arrived by taxi.

I replied, "I believe that's our son."

"Just checking."

We went out to the forecourt and waited for Edward.

A few minutes later, a yellow cab pulled up, and Edward jumped out with a big smile on his face.

Susan ran over to him, and they hugged and kissed. Then it was Carolyn's turn—ladies first—then my turn. Edward gave me a tight hug and said, "Dad, this is really great."

"You look terrific, Skipper. Good tan."

So we all stood there, together as a family for the first time in ten years. I could see that Susan appreciated the moment, and I was sure she thought about her role in why it had taken us ten years to be standing here together, as well as why this moment was close to a miracle. In fact, I could see she was getting emotional, and I put my arm around her and showed the kids what a great and sensitive guy I am.

I was not raised in such a warm and demonstrative family, and neither was Susan, nor anyone we knew. Family relationships, in general, were cooler when we were growing up, and here, in our lofty strata of society, they were closer to freezing.

But the world had changed, and Susan and I had probably overcompensated for our affection-starved childhoods. I hoped that Edward and Carolyn, when they married and had children, would hug and kiss a lot, and not have affairs or kill their lovers.

I asked Edward if he had luggage, and he replied as Carolyn had that he had another wardrobe here, though he didn't call it a wardrobe. It was stuff.

Unfortunately, he didn't have enough stuff on him to pay the cab, as usual, so I took care of it with a big tip. The driver said to me, "Thanks. Hey, this is some mansion."

I didn't want to tell him that the mansion was up the road, so I said, "Have a nice day."

Edward remembered his overnight bag in the back seat and stopped the driver and retrieved it. Was I this spacey? I didn't think so. I should ask Harriet. She'd be honest with me. Brutally honest.

We sat on the back patio, Susan and I holding hands on the table, and we had another champagne toast to the Sutters and ate the fruit and vegetables that Sophie had carried out for us. How did I do without a Sophie for seven years in London?

Edward and Carolyn, I should mention, who were raised with household help, never got comfortable with the concept, and always seemed awkward around domestic staff. Susan, on the other hand, had grown up thinking that everyone, including probably the homeless, had at least a maid to clean the refrigerator box they lived in.

I asked Edward, "How was your flight?"

"Okay. But this airport stuff sucks. I got pulled over."

"Why?"

"I don't know."

Edward didn't look like a terrorist, but I took the occasion to remark on his black jeans and black skintight T-shirt. I informed him, "If you put on good trousers and a real shirt and a sports jacket, preferably a blue blazer such as I am wearing, everyone will see you as a person of substance and importance, and they will treat you with courtesy and respect." I reminded him, "Clothes make the man."

He replied, "Dad."

Susan said, "John."

Carolyn just rolled her eyes.

Then we all laughed.

Edward asked me, "What's with the guys at the gatehouse?"

I replied, "As your mother e-mailed you, Mr. Nasim has become concerned—perhaps because of 9/11—that there may be people who want to harm him."

Edward asked, "Who?"

"I think his fellow countrymen."

"Wow. Can they do that? I mean, like, here?"

"Well . . . times have changed." I rehashed my joke and said, "I checked the town ordinances, and it says that no political assassinations are allowed Monday to Saturday before eight A.M. or after six P.M. And none on Sunday."

Edward, at least, thought that was funny. I moved on to the purpose of their visit, and Susan and I told them about the wake the previous night, and she also announced, "We'll all go tonight for only half an hour, then I hope we can all go to dinner together."

Everyone seemed agreeable to that, and Susan suggested, "Why don't we go to Seawanhaka for old time's sake?"

Carolyn feigned some enthusiasm, and Edward truly didn't care, so it was settled.

Susan needed to talk about Grandpa and Grandma, and we'd prearranged this, so I poured the last of the champagne into everyone else's glass and said, "I need to make an important phone call. About fifteen minutes."

I went inside and made myself an important vodka and tonic, then went to my office.

As I said, this was a Stanhope family matter, and I would leave it to Susan to tell Edward and Carolyn as much or as little as she thought they needed to know.

If she was honest with them, she'd tell them that Gramps and Granny were not thrilled that I was back, and that their kindly old grandparents might threaten to lock Mommy out of the vault if we remarried. Or cohabitated, or if I came within a thousand miles of my ex-wife. And if Susan was completely honest with them, and with herself, she'd alert them that their trust funds and their inheritance were also at risk.

As I said, neither Edward nor Carolyn seem that interested in money, and I think they'd be more hurt about their grandparents' attitude than about the millions.

Eventually, though, we'd all feel the financial squeeze, but hopefully that would bring us closer together as a family. We could all move into Carolyn's one-bedroom apartment in Brooklyn and sit around the table eating Hamburger Helper while badmouthing Grandpa and Grandma: "I told you he was a scum-sucking pig, kids. Pass the Kool-Aid."

I checked our telephone messages, and there was one from Mr. Mancuso, who said, "Still no sign of him. I'll call Mrs. Sutter's cell phone if that changes. And I'll call either way Saturday from the cemetery. Also, we spoke to Tony Rosini, and he don't know nothing. But we'll keep on that. Also, FYI, Sally Da-da is going about his normal routine—but with extra bodyguards. Call me if you need anything."

Well, I hope Uncle Sal didn't take advantage of the family discount and hire Bell Security Service. I'd recommend the ASS men to him, if I saw him.

Regarding Anthony—where the hell *was* this guy? He must know by now, from his friends and employees, that the Feds and the police had been asking about him. Not to mention Uncle Sal, who surely wanted to know where his nephew was. And me, too. The only one who probably didn't care was his wife.

Anyway, I accessed my e-mail and saw a message from Samantha: *You haven't called this week and you haven't e-mailed. What am I to assume from that?*

Well, you should assume that this is not a good sign.

Or you could assume that I'm dead. But you would never guess that Bachelor John is engaged to be married.

I really liked Samantha, and I wanted to be totally honest with her, but the problem was that she knew people in my office. And if I told her that I was never coming back, then that would get back to my employers, who promised, in writing, that my position in the firm was secure until September 1.

Meanwhile, back at the estate, it appeared that my job offer with La Cosa Nostra was off the table, my first clue being that the CEO who interviewed me now wanted to kill me. Plus, Mr. Nasim's offer to me of a ten percent commission if I could facilitate the sale of the guest cottage to him might also be off the table, as a result of my marrying the property owner. I could see why he'd think there was a conflict of interest there, and why he'd just wait until Susan and I had more security hassles than we wanted.

The bright spot here was William's offer to buy me out. So, to crunch some numbers, I had the impression from Susan that her allowance was about two hundred and fifty thousand dollars a year—which was considerably more than the five bucks a week that I used to get from my parents. But the cost of living has gone up, so maybe Susan's five thousand dollars a week is a reasonable allowance. Plus, if William gave me a million, paid in ten annual installments, he'd have to clip one hundred thousand dollars off Susan's allowance every year to make it up, and to teach her a lesson. But if he didn't want to do that, then it came out of his own pocket. Ouch!

Also, I didn't think he'd be around for ten years, unless he cut back on the martinis. Or was that what was keeping him alive?

Actually, this was all moot. I really wasn't going to take his money. I was going to take his daughter. And I didn't care if he cut her off. I didn't want *his* or *her* money. But what about Edward and Carolyn?

And for that matter, what about Susan? Was she *really* ready to stand shoulder to shoulder with me, raise her middle finger to Mom and Dad, and join me in yelling, *"Vaffanculo!"*?

And was I ready to let her do that?

Those were the questions of the moment, so I didn't know if I needed a return ticket to London.

I e-mailed Samantha: *I apologise (with an s), and I have no explanation for my lack of communication. We do need to speak, and I will call you Monday, latest.* I left it unsigned, and without a closing sentiment, as she had done.

Well, that was a step in the right direction. I was never sure about Samantha anyway—I date women I couldn't possibly marry, or who announced early that they wouldn't marry me if their lives depended on it. It's worked well so far.

The intercom buzzed, and I picked it up. Susan said, "I'm still on the patio with Edward and Carolyn, if you'd like to join us."

"Be right there."

I left my vodka in the office, went back to the patio, and took a seat.

Susan said, "I think I've explained the situation correctly and clearly to Edward and Carolyn, and we've agreed that us being a family again is our only consideration."

I looked at Edward, then at Carolyn, and back to Susan. I really did hope that she explained the situation correctly and clearly. And I'm sure she did, in regard to her own possible financial punishment for remarrying Dad. But I wasn't certain that she'd taken the next step and explained that Grandpa might extend the punishment of their mother on to them.

I said, "All right." I added, "Subject closed. Who wants more champagne?"

Susan and Carolyn did, and Edward and I opted for Irish champagne—beer.

Susan and Carolyn volunteered to get drinks, and Edward and I sat there.

He looked at me and said, "I can't believe Grandpa would do that."

I replied, "We don't know *what* he's going to do." I added, "His bark is worse than his bite." Which was totally not true; the old bastard bit hard.

Edward, sensitive soul that he is, said, "He should be happy that Mom is happy."

"He might be. We don't know." I suggested, "Why don't we all put this out of our minds and just have a nice family reunion?" I added, bluntly, "Be nice to Grandpa."

"Okay."

I still didn't know if Susan had told the children that they might have to live on their salaries for the rest of their lives. That didn't bother me as much as the thought of Peter Stanhope, useless turd and soon-to-be brother-in-law, getting it all. Well, if the time came, I might be able to scare him into handing over some bucks to his niece and nephew, which was better for him than John Sutter holding him up in court for ten years.

Edward said, "Mom really loves you."

"That's why I'm here, Skipper." I added, of course, "I love her."

The object of my affection came out carrying an ice bucket with a bottle of bubbly, and Carolyn had the beer and glasses on a tray.

We sat there, talking under the gray sky, and now and then the clouds would break, and sunshine covered the patio and the Sutters.

CHAPTER FIFTY-SIX

We arrived at Walton's Funeral Home at about 7:30 P.M., and we all signed the visitors' book, which fortunately didn't have Time In and Time Out columns.

This, the second night of the wake, would usually be the last viewing, but Ethel, God rest her soul, wanted to make sure that no one else rested, so—Held Over by Popular Demand, Ethel Allard, Appearing Friday Night for the Last Time Anywhere.

The Sutters went to the coffin, and we paid our respects to the deceased and said our silent prayers. Carolyn and Edward have not seen much death in their young lives, and they were clearly uncomfortable in the presence of mortality. Carolyn was actually crying, and Edward looked very sad. They both liked Ethel, and the feeling had been mutual, and I was happy that they were able to feel grief and loss.

Once more, I took the lead and moved us away from the coffin.

We greeted Elizabeth and her family again, and I took the opportunity to reintroduce Edward and Carolyn to Tom Junior and Betsy, whom they'd both not seen in at least ten years. I noticed now that there was an age difference of six or seven years between Elizabeth's children and mine, which was significant at that age, but not an insurmountable obstacle if they liked each other. But perhaps the timing and the setting were wrong for me to try to fan the flames of passion. In fact, I didn't even see a spark. Oh well.

Tom Corbet and Laurence were there again, and I gave Tom credit for being a good ex-husband and an involved father. My own performance as an ex-husband, I thought, had been appropriate for the circumstances, and I would have been a better divorced father if I hadn't left town for a decade. But that was water under the bridge, over the dam, under my hull, and an ocean away.

I suggested that we move around, so we worked Parlor A a bit, then moved into the sitting room to see if there was anyone there that we needed to greet. You get points and give points for going to a wake, and everyone wanted their visit noted. We all get a turn in the coffin, so you have to do some advance work if you want a good crowd when it's your turn.

Susan, Edward, and Carolyn spoke to some people they knew, and it seemed to be a different crowd tonight, so I knew a few people as well, including Beryl Carlisle, a married lady who used to flirt with me whenever possible, and who was now divorced, as I was—so what was I doing tonight?

Well, Susan and I were back together. Isn't that great? And, in fact, there she is. Susan, come over and say hello to Beryl. Excuse me.

When I lived here, the bane of my existence had been weddings and funerals—too many of both—not to mention christenings, engagement parties, birthdays, and retirement parties. I mean, if we have to celebrate people's life transitions, why not a divorce party? I'm in.

I checked my watch and saw that only twenty minutes had passed, though it seemed much longer. I made my way back to the lobby, where the exit sign beckoned.

Susan was supposed to be rounding up the troops, but she was taking her time, and I waited, staring intently at one of those quasi-spiritual paintings—this one had sunlight streaming through the clouds into a forest, where little sylvan creatures lived in peace and harmony. Dreadful. But better than making more deadly conversation with my fellow mourners.

Susan came up behind me and said, "We're ready."

I turned and saw that our group had grown. Susan announced, "Tom and Betsy would like to join us."

That was a hopeful sign. But for some reason, my mother was also standing there, and she informed me, "Susan has also invited me to join you."

How did she get here? I recovered nicely and said, "Grandma never needs an invitation."

So off we went, with Edward and Carolyn bravely volunteering to ride with Grandma, who is new to driving, and has been for fifty years. Tom Junior and Betsy came with us, and they were happy to get sprung early from Walton's, and they were chatty. Nice kids. I wondered if Betsy would like L.A. Tom told me he wanted to move to Manhattan. Or if he couldn't afford Manhattan, then Brooklyn. Great idea.

We were shown to a round table in the dining room at Seawanhaka, and I made sure the kids sat together, and that Susan sat between me and Harriet.

The waitress took drink orders, but Harriet wasn't drinking because she had to drive, though she drove the same, drunk or sober. I decided that Susan was the designated driver, so that left me to have a double Scotch on the rocks. The kids shared a bottle of white wine.

They all seemed to be getting along well, and we didn't intrude on their conversation, except that I mentioned how much I loved Los Angeles. I think I also said that Brooklyn was becoming the Left Bank of New York. Susan gave me a little kick under the table.

Harriet was actually quite pleasant, but that had more to do with Susan than with me. She liked Susan, and always had, despite the fact that Susan had made a poor marital choice.

A few other refugees from Parlor A drifted in, and Harriet and Susan worked the room a little, and I took the opportunity to go out on the back porch with my drink and look at the sailboats swaying at their moorings.

Despite the money, and the relatively large population, this place sometimes has the feel of small-town America. That's the nice part of living here. But it's also the drawback. You can isolate yourself, especially if you have enough land and money—but you can't really be anonymous.

I liked London because in London I had no past, and as in any big city, you could keep to yourself, or you could find company, anytime and anyplace, on any day you wished. Here you were part of a community, whether you liked it or not.

I could see why young people—like the four sitting at the table— would want to live in L.A., or New York, or anyplace where they could do what they wanted, when they wanted, and do it with whomever they wanted.

I didn't know if my London days were over for sure, or if I'd wind up in Manhattan, or here, or in Walton's. It was hard to believe that two idiots—Anthony Bellarosa and William Stanhope—could alter my future, and Susan's future, and our future together.

Harriet drove the Corbet kids back to their mother's house, and the Sutters headed back to Stanhope Hall.

I said to Edward and Carolyn, "I'm glad you were able to spend some time with Grandma Harriet."

They agreed, and Carolyn said, "She's really neat."

Maybe it *is* me. I said, "Make sure you keep in touch with her." Aside from a few thousand sea otters, she's got only four likely human heirs, and she's not fond of two of them.

I asked, offhandedly, "How did you guys get along with Tom and Betsy?"

No reply.

I said, "You seemed to be having a good time."

Edward said, "They're nice."

I pressed on, "They seem like great kids."

No reply.

Susan said, "John."

I didn't reply.

Before we got to Grace Lane, Susan called Sophie on the house phone and chatted a moment, before asking her, "Do we have onions for tomorrow?"

Sophie replied, "We got no onions here."

"Okay, I'll get some tomorrow. See you in a few minutes." She glanced at me, and I nodded, happy that Sophie didn't have a gun to her head, which was what "no onions" meant.

We hadn't actually told Sophie about the little Mafia problem, of course, or even about the Iranian assassin problem. We just told her that we'd put in some security in case of trespassers or maybe burglars. She didn't seem too happy about that, but she understood the concept of coded passwords: onions or no onions. We'd actually gone through tomatoes, garlic, and cucumbers before we settled on onions. She liked onions.

When we got to Grace Lane, I used Susan's cell phone to call the gatehouse and announce our imminent arrival. So when we got to the gates, they were already open, and the ASS guy waved us through. Maybe this would work out.

Back in the guest cottage, the four of us sat in the upstairs family room and talked, as we'd done so many nights, so many years ago. And it was almost like old times. Better yet, it was like we'd been doing this for the last ten years.

I looked at Susan and saw she was as happy as I'd ever seen her. Well, it's true; we don't know what we have until we lose it. And if we can get it back, it's better than it was the first time.

At about midnight, we all hugged, kissed, and said good night.

I said to Edward and Carolyn, "Try to be down for breakfast at nine."

Susan said, "Sleep as late as you want."

Who's in charge here?

Susan and I got ready for bed, which included breaking out the arsenal. She said to me, "I want the shotgun tonight."

"You had the shotgun last night."

"No, I had the carbine."

"Why do you always do this?"

She laughed, then gave me a big hug and said, "John, I'm so happy. But I'm also frightened."

"Are you?"

"A little. Sometimes."

"That's okay." I let her know, "Mancuso left a message. Anthony is still missing."

"Good."

Not good. I said, "He may show up Saturday at Gotti's funeral, and Mancuso will be there."

"He should arrest him."

I'd rather have Uncle Sal whack him, which would solve a lot of people's problems. But for now, Uncle Sal was a bit jittery, too.

I said to her, "I promise you, this will all be over very soon."

She didn't want to know how I knew that, and she moved on to another problem and informed me, "Edward and Carolyn understand that their grandfather disapproves of our marriage, and that he may end my allowance, and possibly disinherit me."

"Okay. And do they understand that the same thing may happen to them?"

"I didn't raise that issue."

"Well, you should have."

"John, that will *not* happen."

"All right." I asked, "Did you tell them to be extra sweet to Grandma and Grandpa?"

"I did not." She assured me, "They love their grandparents and don't need to be told to be nice to them."

Unlike, for instance, John Sutter. I said, "All right." No use speculating; we'd see who was right about that. I moved on to another important question and asked, "Where's my Yale T-shirt?"

"In the wash."

"How long will it be in the wash?"

"For a long time."

This sounded to me like it might be in heaven. I like to sleep au naturel, anyway, so I got undressed and got into bed.

Susan got undressed, too, and said, "You were very nice to your mother tonight."

"She's a lovely woman."

"She loves you, John."

"I can tell."

"And I want to do something nice for you for being so good with my parents, your mother, and for behaving in the funeral home."

"What sort of positive reinforcement did you have in mind?"

"I was thinking of a blow job."

"That's just what I was thinking."

CHAPTER FIFTY-SEVEN

C arolyn made it down for breakfast at 9:00 A.M., but Edward did not. Susan reminded me, "It's six A.M. in Los Angeles."

I replied, "We're in New York. And six A.M. anywhere in the world is a good time to rise and shine."

Mother and daughter rolled their eyes and went back to their granola and newspapers.

It was a rainy day, so our options were limited, but we decided to go into the city and hit a museum, then, of course, Susan wanted to shop for clothes with Carolyn. My mission was to bully Edward into buying a suit and some new sports jackets.

While we were waiting for Prince Edward to arise, I scanned the tabloids and found a piece about John Gotti. The latest in the ongoing saga of Mr. Gotti's inconvenient body was that it was still resting comfortably at the Papavero Funeral Home, but as Mancuso already knew, it would be moved to a chapel at St. John's Cemetery in Queens on Saturday morning, which was tomorrow. The public was not invited.

On that subject, there was still no word from Mr. Mancuso regarding Anthony Bellarosa's whereabouts, but Mr. Mancuso did say he'd call us either way from the cemetery to let us know whether or not Anthony was among the select group of invited friends and family. My hunch was still that Anthony Bellarosa's next public appearance would be at Uncle Sal's funeral, or his own. As long as it wasn't my or Susan's funeral.

Anyway, the article in the tabloid went into some background about Mr. Gotti's career, including people he personally murdered, and people whom he had ordered to be murdered, including his boss, Paul Castellano, who'd been shot in front of Sparks, one of my favorite steakhouses. Give that place another bullet. It occurred to me that if I'd had my partners whacked ten years ago, I'd still be at 23 Wall Street, and the only name on the door would be mine.

Well, that would be an extreme management style, and probably not appropriate for a white-shoe law firm. But still . . .

On the personal front, the article mentioned the tragic death of Mr. Gotti's twelve-year-old son Frank, who had been killed in the street in front of the Gotti home in Howard Beach, Queens, as a result of a neighbor, named John Favara, running over the boy while he was riding his minibike. The death was ruled an accident, but accident or not, four months later, Mr. Favara disappeared, never to be seen again. I recalled when this tragedy happened, and when I read of Mr. Favara's disappearance four months later, I wondered if anyone had suggested to him that he might have a better and longer life if he moved out of the neighborhood.

But you should never criticize other people's bad decisions. I mean, as unlikely as it seems, anyone could find himself living next door to a Mafia don who has a personal vendetta against him. In fact, I knew of one such couple. Maybe they should move.

Another personal bit of information about the late John Gotti was that he, like Frank Bellarosa, was a big fan of Niccolò Machiavelli. Well, it's good to see tough guys trying to improve their minds by reading the Renaissance masters. You're never too old to learn something new about human nature, how to win friends and influence people, and running a principality or a criminal empire.

On that subject, the article also mentioned that Mr. Gotti saw himself as a Caesar. So apparently he tried to combine these two different management styles—dictatorial and cunning. Apparently, too, he'd succeeded to some extent, just as had Frank Bellarosa, who, in addition to being Machiavellian, was also a big fan of Benito Mussolini.

People like this—Italian or otherwise—love power, and they love to wield power. And you can tell where they're coming from by the role models they choose. Anthony Bellarosa—Little Caesar—however, was, I thought, basically a man with delusions of grandeur, and he was a failed successor to his father's empire. But this was not my problem— my problem was that he was a dangerous thug who acted on impulse. His instincts, like his father's, may have been good, because it certainly wasn't his brains that had kept him alive so long. I recalled that out-thinking Frank Bellarosa was like matching wits with a worthy oppos-ing general; outthinking Anthony was like trying to outthink a predatory animal, who has no intellect—just an empty stomach that needs to be filled.

Well, back to John Gotti. The article also mentioned Mr. Gotti's penchant for two-thousand-dollar Brioni suits. I said to Susan, "I'm going to buy Edward a Brioni suit."

"Are they good suits?"

"Excellent. About two thousand dollars." I added, "Handmade in Italy."

"You should buy one for yourself."

"Why not? Maybe we'll get a deal."

Edward appeared around 10:00 A.M., and while he was having coffee, Susan made him his favorite breakfast of fried eggs, sausage, and heavily buttered biscuits. This is also my favorite breakfast so I said, "I'll have the same."

"No you won't."

I mean, someone was trying to kill us, so what difference did it make to my longevity if I ate unhealthy foods? What am I missing here?

Susan had decided to get a car and driver for our city adventure—no waiting in the rain for taxis and no parking hassles—and the car showed up at eleven. It's true—rich or poor, it's nice to have money.

Our first stop in Manhattan was the Frick Museum on Fifth Avenue, and I asked Susan if her friend Charlie Frick worked there. She didn't reply, so I don't know, and I didn't see her there.

We sucked up one hour and twenty-seven minutes of art, then had a great lunch at La Goulue, one of my favorite restaurants on the Upper East Side.

Edward, deep down inside, is a New Yorker, and most of his friends live in this city, but he's chosen a career and maybe a life that will keep him on the West Coast. Susan can't come to grips with this, but if she had the Stanhope fortune, she'd find a way to get Edward back. Ironically, for an investment of only about fifty thousand dollars, I could have asked Anthony to think of a way to speed up her inheritance. That's really not a nice thought. It's moot, anyway; I had my chance, but the timing was wrong.

After lunch, the car dropped Edward and me off at Brioni's on East 52nd, and the ladies stayed with the car to sack and pillage along Madison and Fifth Avenues.

Edward is as fond of shopping as I am, but we did get him a Brioni suit with matching accessories. Edward really didn't want a two-thousand-dollar suit, but I told him it would make his mother happy, and it was her Amex card, so all it was costing him was some time and a little boredom. The suit would be ready in eight weeks and sent to Los Angeles. In my next life, I want to be Susan Stanhope's son. Actually, she did tell me to get one for myself, but we needed to start economizing, though Susan hadn't come to grips with that yet.

Edward and I decided that was enough shopping for one day, and Edward called the car on his cell phone, and we were picked up and delivered to the Yale Club on Vanderbilt Avenue.

We sat in the big main lounge, read the newspapers, talked, and had a few glasses of tomato juice into which, I believe, someone had added vodka.

Susan called Edward's cell at five, and he said we were having afternoon tea at the Yale Club. He's a good boy. Chip off the old block.

Rush-hour traffic in the rain on a Friday was a mess, so we didn't get home until after 7:00 P.M.

I was shocked to discover that the trunk of the car was filled with boxes and bags, and it took the four of us, plus the driver, to carry them into the house. But before I could make a sarcastic remark, Susan announced, "Carolyn and I bought you a tie."

Well, I felt just awful about what I almost said, so I did say, "Thank you. I hope you didn't spend too much."

I thought I should tell Susan, privately, that she should be storing her acorns for what might be a money famine, but she had as much information as I did on that subject, so maybe that's what she was doing—storing Armani, Escada, Prada, and Gucci for lean times. Good thinking. Plus, with the Brioni suit, we'd kept the Italian economy in good shape.

I checked for phone messages, and there were several, but none from Mr. Mancuso, who in any case would have called Susan's cell phone if he had anything important to tell us.

I also checked my e-mail, and there was a message from Samantha that said, *Flying to New York tomorrow. Arriving late afternoon. Meet me at The Mark at seven.*

Good hotel, but I didn't think that was going to work out, so I quickly typed, *The Mafia is trying to kill me, and I'm engaged to be married. Hard to believe, but . . .* There had to be a better way to say that. I deleted and typed, *Dear Samantha, My ex-wife and I have reunited and—*

Susan walked in and asked me, "Who are you e-mailing?"

I pushed delete and said, "My office."

"Why?"

"I'm resigning."

"Good." She pulled up a chair and sat beside me. "Let me help," she offered.

"Well . . ." I looked at my watch. "This could take a while, and we should get to the funeral home."

"This will take a few minutes."

I guess the time had come to burn a bridge that I'd intended to leave standing. So, with Susan's help, I crafted a very nice, thoughtful, and positive letter to my firm, letting them know what a difficult decision this was for me, and expressing my hope that this did not cause them any inconvenience, and so forth, assuring them that I would be in London in a few weeks to gather my personal items, and brief my replacement, and sign whatever paperwork was necessary for my separation from the firm.

Susan suggested, "Tell them you're getting married."

"Why?"

"So they understand why you're not returning."

"That's not necessary."

"They'll be happy for you."

"They don't care. They're British."

"Nonsense. Tell them."

So I announced my good news, which would get to Samantha, via phone or e-mail, within nanoseconds. Well, it was 2:00 A.M. in London so I had some time tonight to e-mail her.

I pressed the send button, and off it went to London. These things should have a one-minute delay so you can reconsider, or at least get your wife or girlfriend out of the room.

Bottom line here was that I had been trying to cover all my bases and play all the angles. But in the final analysis, I needed to take a leap of faith and hope for the best.

If I had to leave Susan, it would not be because I wanted to leave her. It would be because I had to leave her to ensure her future, and the future of our children. It's a far, far better thing I do, and all that.

Or, quite possibly, she'd make the hard decision for those same reasons. A mother's instinct is to protect her children, and I understood that.

Susan asked me, "What are you sitting there thinking about?"

"I'm thinking about you and Edward and Carolyn . . . and how good it is that we have this time together."

"We have the rest of our lives together."

And that was the other problem.

CHAPTER FIFTY-EIGHT

We arrived at Walton's at 8:15, and as always, on the last night of the viewing, everyone who'd put it off was there, plus there was a large contingent of church ladies from St. Mark's in attendance.

We went through the usual routine at the coffin—Ethel still looked good—then said hello to the front-row ticket holders, then worked Parlor A again, then checked out the lobby and the sitting room. I had a strong sense of déjà vu.

William and Charlotte were there, though I didn't get the opportunity to speak to them. Actually, we avoided one another. My mother, too, was there, and I made sure to say hello.

Also there was Diane Knight, Ethel's hospice nurse, which was nice, but I noticed that I never see the deceased's attending physician at the funeral home. I guess that could be awkward.

I also spotted Ethel's accountant, Matthew Miller, and I spoke to him for a minute about getting together for Ethel's final accounting. I mean, you should not actually do business at the funeral home, but you can make appointments.

Susan's luncheon companion, Charlie Frick, was also there, and I introduced myself and told her I'd gone to her museum earlier in the day. I let her know, "Nice place. Lots of artwork." Then I drew her attention to the dreadful inspirational painting in the lobby, and said, "That would look good in the Frick."

She excused herself and moved off, probably to speak to Susan about me.

I also ran into Judy Remsen, who'd been a good friend of ours in the old days, and she seemed delighted to see me. She already knew our good news and was very happy for us. This is the lady who had caught us in flagrante delicto patio, and I'm sure she remembered that every time she saw me. I didn't mention the incident of course, but I did say, "Stop by next week and join us for sundowners on the patio."

"I . . . yes, that sounds wonderful."

"Call ahead." I smiled.

She excused herself.

Then I ran into Lester Remsen, Judy's husband, who had also been a friend as well as my stockbroker. Lester and I had had a falling-out over my bringing Frank and Anna Bellarosa to The Creek for dinner. Susan had also been at the dinner, of course, but she got a pass on that, as she gets a pass on nearly everything. I'm always the bad guy. But, hey, I just suck it up.

Lester offered his professional services if I should need them again. Defense stocks and electronic security were hot at the moment. I said, "Hazmat suits. That's going to be big."

I also saw the DePauws, the couple who lived in the house on the hill across from the gates of Alhambra, where the FBI had set up their observation post to photograph cars and guests arriving at Frank's estate—myself and Susan included—and I asked him if he was still doing that for the FBI.

He said no, and the DePauws excused themselves.

Beryl Carlisle avoided me, and Althea Gwynn snubbed me.

It's wonderful to be back.

In the lobby, I spotted the Reverend James Hunnings. This is a man who, as I've mentioned, is not my favorite man of the cloth, though he seems to be everyone else's. So maybe it's me. But I think it's him.

Anyway, he spotted me, walked over, and said in his pulpit voice, "Good evening!"

"Good evening!" I replied, without, I hope, mimicking him.

"And how have you been, John?" "

"Great." Until five seconds ago. I inquired, "How have you been?"

"I have been well. Thank you for asking."

"And Mrs. Hunnings? How has she been?"

"She is well, and I will tell her you asked about her."

I never understood why his wife hadn't had an affair. She was actually quite attractive, and she had a little sparkle in her eye.

He asked me, "Do you have a moment?"

"Uh . . . well . . ."

"I would like to speak to you in private."

Well, I was a little curious, but I also wanted to get to my cocktail. Decisions, decisions. I said, "All right."

He led me up the stairs of the old Victorian house to a door with a cross on it, which I assumed was reserved for clergy of the Christian faith.

The room had a desk and a grouping of chairs around a table, and we sat at the table.

He began, "First, I want to welcome you home."

"Thank you."

"I hope you will be rejoining the Saint Mark's family."

I guess he meant the congregation. It was hard to follow the newspeak after you'd been gone awhile. Anyway, this was my chance to tell him I'd become a Buddhist, but instead I replied, "I am sure I will."

He continued, "I've heard, of course, that you and Susan have reunited."

"Good news travels fast."

"Indeed, it does." He went on, "I assume you and Susan plan to remarry at Saint Mark's."

"That would be fitting." Do we get the repeat discount?

"Well, then, I hope you and Susan will consider prenuptial counseling."

I'd already gotten that from William, but I replied, "Well, we've been married. To each other."

"I know that, John, but, if I may be candid, the circumstances of your separation and divorce should be addressed in a pastoral counseling context, which I am happy to provide."

"Well . . . you know, Father, it's been so long since we divorced, that I can barely remember what led us to that decision."

He found that a little hard to believe—and so did I—but he advised, "Speak to Susan about counseling, and please get back to me on that."

"Will do."

He made a final pitch and said, "You want to build on a solid foundation, so your house will not crumble again."

"Good analogy." I had the uncharitable thought that Father Hunnings just wanted to learn all the inside juicy details of Susan's affair, her murder of Frank Bellarosa, and maybe even our sex lives since then. I gave myself a sharp mental slap on the face and said, "I appreciate your concern."

He replied, "I am just doing my job, John, and trying to do God's work."

"Right. Well . . . yeah. Good." I glanced at my watch.

He continued, "And speaking of houses, I understand that you and Susan are living together."

Who ratted? Well, I knew where this was going, so I replied, "I'm sleeping in a guest room."

"Are you?"

"Of course." This was really unbelievable, but you had to put yourself in his shoes, I guess. He had to be able to say he'd brought this up with one of the sinners, and that he'd made his disapproval known. I could almost hear him at the dinner table tonight with his wife—What was her name? Sarah? Really attractive.

"John? I said, This would not be a God-pleasing relationship if you were sharing the same bed."

I was starting to feel like I was eighteen, which was kind of fun. I replied, "I understand."

"Good." He then said, "I imagine that Edward and Carolyn are happy for you."

"They're thrilled."

He then made some sort of mental leap and said, "Your mother has asked me to speak to you."

"About what?"

He replied, "She mentioned to me that you and she had become estranged." He added, "She was very upset that you were not here for your father's funeral."

"No more upset than I was when I found out he died." I added, "I was at sea."

"Yes, I know." He changed the subject and inquired, "If I may ask, how have Mr. and Mrs. Stanhope received this news?"

That sounded like a question to which he already knew the answer. I replied, "They're here for the funeral, so you should ask them directly, if you haven't already."

"I saw them here this evening. But we spoke only for a moment."

Really? I informed him, "They're in a cottage at The Creek, if you want to call them."

Father Hunnings said, "They were always active and generous members of Saint Mark's, and I respect them both greatly, and I know that Susan loves them both, so I am concerned for all of you if they have not given you their blessing."

I took a deep breath and said to him, "I don't care about their blessing—or their money. And neither should my mother, if that's her concern. And if William and Charlotte are still making contributions to Saint Mark's, then Susan and I can get married elsewhere, if that's *your* concern."

He held up his hand—Peace? Shut up? He said, "My concern, John, is that your marriage to Susan is not ill-advised, and that it fulfills your expectations and hers, and that you enter into the sacrament of Holy Matrimony with full knowledge of your duties and obligations."

There was more going on here, but I wasn't sure what it was. Though, if I took a wild guess, I'd say that William had already spoken to Father Hunnings, and told him that he and Mrs. Stanhope were vehemently opposed to this marriage, and would Father Hunnings be so kind as to speak to John and to Susan in a counseling session, and then, of course, separately. Divide and conquer. William would undoubtedly tell Father Hunnings that he thought John Sutter was a gold digger. And William might even tell Father Hunnings that John solicited a bribe from him to break off the impending engagement and marriage. And, of course, William would mention offhandedly a generous contribution to St. Mark's.

I wouldn't put any of this past Wily Willie. But I really didn't think Father Hunnings would go along for the whole ride; he'd just take it as far as he could, and maybe see if William Stanhope had legitimate concerns. Or he'd take it to the next level and ask me about soliciting money from William. And maybe he'd even plant some seeds of doubt in Susan's head.

William was a ruthless, Machiavellian prick, but rather than point that out to Father Hunnings, who thought well of William, I said, "Susan and I have decided to remarry, and that should not be anyone else's business."

"Of course," he allowed, but then continued, "it's just that this is so sudden after all these years of being apart, and you've only been together for . . . what? A week?"

"Since Sunday." I added, "About noon."

"Well, I am sure you will not rush into marriage without allowing some time to get to know each other again."

"Good advice." At least he could tell William he gave it a good shot. I stood and said, "Well, Susan and the children are probably wondering where I am."

He stood too, but he was not finished. He said to me, "I visited with Mrs. Allard often while she was in hospice." He let me know, "She was a lady of great faith and spirit."

"She was one of a kind," I agreed.

"She was. And she mentioned that you'd had a good visit at Fair Haven."

"I'm sorry I missed you there."

He continued, "She confided in me, as her priest, that she'd written you a letter."

I looked at him, but did not respond.

He went on, "She told me in very general terms of the contents of that letter and asked if I thought she should give it to you."

Again, I didn't respond, so he said, "I believe Elizabeth was to give you the letter on Ethel's death." He asked, "Did she?"

I said, "I'd rather not discuss this."

He nodded and said, "As you wish." He glanced at his watch and said, "Oh. It's almost time for prayers."

We walked to the door together, and he said, "I hope you will be staying to pray with us."

"I wish I could."

We walked down the stairs, and I took the opportunity to tell him, "I am the attorney for Mrs. Allard's estate, as you know, and while the will has not been admitted into probate as yet, I think I can reveal to you that Mrs. Allard has made a generous contribution to Saint Mark's."

We reached the bottom of the stairs, and Father Hunnings nodded and said, with a good show of disinterest, "That was very beneficent of her."

What was that word? I assured him, "The bequests should be distributed within eight weeks. If you'd like to be at the reading of the will, I'll notify you of the time and place." Or I'll just put the five-hundred-dollar check in the mail, minus the postage.

Father Hunnings was trying to figure out how much money Ethel Allard could possibly have, and also if her beneficence to the church would significantly cut into her family's share of the loot. He wouldn't want to be sitting with them if he was going to be hauling away a good part of their inheritance. I'd seen this before.

Finally, he replied, "It's not necessary that I be there."

"If you change your mind, let me know." I inquired, "Do you like cats?"

"Uh . . . not actually. Why?"

"Well . . . Mrs. Allard . . . but we can discuss that another time."

We bid each other good evening.

I saw Susan in the lobby, and she informed me that her parents had left to have dinner with friends. This surprised me—not that they weren't going to join the Sutters for dinner, but that they had friends.

Nevertheless, I said, "I'm surprised and annoyed that they passed up an opportunity to be with their grandchildren."

Susan replied, "Well, they did speak to Edward and Carolyn."

"And was it a happy reunion?"

"It seemed to be."

That didn't sound real positive. I said, "Your parents are avoiding me, and are sulking. And they know that Edward and Carolyn are very happy for us. Therefore, your parents are not happy with Edward and Carolyn."

"John, let's not overanalyze this."

"All right. What are we doing now?"

"Do you want to stay for prayers?"

"I thought we could pray privately at a local bar."

She smiled and said, "Let's go to McGlade's. We haven't been there in a while."

About ten years, actually. I said, "Sounds good."

We rounded up the kids, and Susan passed on our destination to a number of people. Funeral customs vary widely in America, but around here, some people like to hit a bar after the last evening viewing of the body—especially if it's a Friday night. What better place to deal with your grief?

So the Sutters made the two-minute trip to McGlade's Pub in Station Plaza, where there was a lively Friday night crowd.

We gave the hostess our name and bellied up to the bar.

Susan and I chatted with some patrons, a few of them from Walton's, Parlor A and Parlor B, and I was nice to almost everyone.

Edward and Carolyn spotted a few people their own age whom they knew, and they all gathered in a group at the far end of the bar.

The jukebox was playing sixties stuff, and the place was lively, and filled with commuters, townies, and assorted others of all social classes, which is the mark of a good pub. In fact, on the menu, as I recalled, it said, "McGlade's—Where Debutantes and Mountain Men Meet." Susan used to say that was us.

As the designated driver, I stuck to my light beer while Susan morphed from Lady Stanhope to Suzie, and banged down a few vodka and tonics. I could see that she was very popular, and it occurred to me that if I hadn't come along when I did, she wouldn't have been a widow for long.

After about forty-five minutes, the hostess had a table for us, and we decided to leave Edward and Carolyn at the bar with their friends, and we sat alone, which was nice. There was not a single healthy thing on the menu, so I had a great American pub-food dinner. Love those Buffalo wings.

It did seem like old times, except that at ten o'clock Susan called home before Sophie went to bed, and Sophie confirmed that as of that time, there were no Mafia hit men waiting in the kitchen for us. No onions.

At a little before midnight, we convinced the kids that they needed to leave with us, and a few minutes before we got to Stanhope Hall, Susan called the gatehouse, so when we got there the gates were open, and the guard waved us through. I stopped, however, got out, and explained to him, out of earshot of the children, about my problem with my Mafia neighbor, and he already knew a little about that. I said to him, "I'm going to call you from the house in about ten minutes. If I don't, you call the police, and if you'd like, come to the guest cottage." I added, "Gun drawn."

I didn't know how he was going to react to that, but he said, "Wait here and I'll wake my relief guy, and I'll come with you."

I didn't want to make a big thing of this in front of Edward and Carolyn, so I said, "That's all right. Just wait for my call."

He then informed me, "I'm an off-duty Nassau cop." He introduced himself as Officer Dave Corroon and even flashed his creds in case I thought he was just a rent-a-cop with megalomania, like so many of these private security guys. He said, "My advice is to wait for me if you think there's a potential problem at your house."

I explained about not wanting to trouble my children. Then I gave him what we called in the Army the sign and countersign. Onions, no onions.

He thought that was clever.

I got back in the Lexus, but no one asked me what I was talking about to the guard, and I proceeded to the guest cottage.

Susan tried Sophie's cell phone, then the house phone, but no one answered, and I assumed she was asleep.

As we all got out of the car, I said, "I need some fresh air. Let's sit on the patio a minute and talk about tomorrow."

Susan thought that was a good idea, and if Edward and Carolyn didn't, they didn't say anything.

Susan led them to the path on the side of the house, and I said, "I'll be right there."

I unlocked the front door and opened the foyer closet where I'd left the carbine, and it was still there. So I took it out and did a fast check of the first floor, then the second floor. In the master bedroom, I dialed the gatehouse, and Officer Corroon answered and asked, "Everything okay? You got onions?"

"No onions here."

"Okay. Call if you think you see or hear onions."

"Thanks." I hung up, went downstairs, and put the carbine in the broom closet, then went out to the patio.

Susan and Carolyn were sitting at the table talking, and Edward was snoozing in a lounge chair.

We let him sleep, and we went through the itinerary for tomorrow. Depart here no later than 9:30 for the funeral Mass at St. Mark's at 10:00 A.M. Then to the Stanhope cemetery for burial, and if Father Hunnings didn't go on too long at graveside—pray for rain—we'd be out of the cemetery before noon, then back to St. Mark's for a post-burial gathering in the basement fellowship room. Not my idea of a fun Saturday, but every day is not a beach day.

Carolyn inquired, "Should we synchronize our watches now?"

Susan thought that was funny. But if I'd said it . . .

Susan informed us, "Elizabeth is having friends and family to her house Saturday night, seven P.M., and I think we should go."

I'd never actually been inside Elizabeth's house, and I thought I should go see the guest room and check out the storage space in the basement. Just in case. I replied, "Fine. Okay—dismissed."

Not even a smile.

Carolyn woke her brother, and they excused themselves and retired for the evening.

I needed a little nightcap after all that near-beer, so we went into the office and I poured myself a brandy.

I said to Susan, "Father Hunnings asked to speak to me privately in his branch office at the funeral home."

"About what?"

I told her, and she thought about the conversation. She said, "I certainly don't need prenuptial counseling, and I am very annoyed that my parents have spoken to him about us."

I replied, "Their only concern is your happiness."

"Then they should have no concerns. *I'm* happy. They are not." She added, "*They* need the counseling."

"They'd be so much happier if they gave us all their money."

She smiled, then thought of something else and said, "I can't believe Father Hunnings mentioned that we are living together."

"Well, I think your parents brought that up, so he has to address it."

"Why don't they all mind their own business?"

"You know the answer to that."

She didn't respond and asked, "What do you think is in that letter?"

"Maybe something more important than I'd thought."

"And Elizabeth has the letter?"

"She did have it."

"You should ask her for it tomorrow night."

"I will."

She asked me what was going on at the gatehouse, and I told her, and said, "This guy, Officer Corroon, seems sharp." I advised, "Get to know who the off-duty police are. The rest of them could have a second job with Bell Security for all I know."

She nodded.

I asked, "Do you think the kids are getting wise to something?"

She replied, "They were very quiet in the car when you were talking to Officer Corroon . . . but I don't know what they're thinking."

I said, "If they ask, we stick to the Nasim story."

She thought about that, then said, "Sometimes I think we should tell them. For their own safety."

"No. They're already on the lookout for Iranian hit men. We don't need to tell them that we really meant Italian hit men." I added, "Carolyn will be gone Sunday night and Edward Monday morning, and I don't want them worrying about us after they've left."

She nodded, then switched to a happier subject and said, "That was fun at McGlade's."

"It was. Where debutantes and mountain men meet. Which reminds me, who was that mountain man who was hitting on you?"

"Are you jealous?"

"Have I ever been?"

"No. Well . . . when we were first dating."

"I don't remember that."

"I can refresh your memory if you'd like."

"You make this stuff up." I said, "Okay, we have a long day ahead of us, so we should get to bed, and not have sex."

"Thank God."

"I'll check the doors and windows and be right up."

She went upstairs, and I sat at the computer. It was almost 7:00 A.M. in London, so Samantha should get my e-mail before she had her first cup of coffee—assuming she checked her e-mail regularly, which she didn't. I *really* didn't want her to get on a plane to New York. I mean, I had enough problems here, and though Susan is not the jealous type, I was quite sure she didn't want to have drinks at the Mark with Samantha.

So I began typing a very nice Dear Samantha letter, which I'd already composed in my mind, explaining the situation with honesty and regret. I didn't mention the Mafia problem because she'd worry—though maybe me getting whacked would please her. You never know with women who have been scorned. Just look at Susan with Frank—whoops. Delete that.

I reread the letter, tweaked it, then pushed the send button, feeling as though I'd just pushed the detonate button to blow up my last bridge to London.

Well . . . there was no going back now. Actually, since last Sunday, there never was. Done.

I retrieved the rifle from the broom closet, checked all the windows and doors, then went up to the master bedroom.

Susan was lying in bed, naked, with a pillow under her butt. Bad back? Yoga? Ah! I get it.

CHAPTER FIFTY-NINE

S aturday morning was rainy. Good funeral weather.

The Sutters, all dressed in black and carrying black umbrellas, piled into the Lexus. I drove, and within fifteen minutes we were parked near St. Mark's Episcopal Church in Locust Valley.

The small but handsome Gothic structure had been built at the turn of the last century with money that had been confiscated from a poker game being played by six millionaires in a Gold Coast mansion.

And who, you might ask, would confiscate money from millionaires enjoying a high-stakes poker game? Well, socialists would, or government tax men—but not to build a church. Actually, it was the men's own wives, good Christian ladies, who were being playful, but who had probably been incited to rob from the rich—themselves—by the parish priest, who thought he needed a new church, and knew how to get it.

Hunnings, I'm sure, would do the same thing if given half a chance. In any case, it was a nice church, despite the sinful origins of the funding—gambling and robbery.

Susan, I, and the children did the meet-and-greet in the narthex, then we found a pew close to the front.

The church was about half full, which was not bad for the funeral service of an elderly woman on a rainy Saturday morning. I didn't see William's chestnut locks as we moved down the center aisle, or Charlotte's emergency-exit red hair, which is hard to miss. So they weren't here yet. Maybe they had too many martinis at dinner last night, got nasty, and their friends beat them up.

Ethel's closed coffin was sitting on a bier near the altar rail, covered with a white pall. Some of the flower arrangements from the funeral home had been placed along the rail to brighten things up, and the organist was providing background music. The rain splashed against the stained glass windows, and the air was moist and heavy and reeked of wet clothing and candle wax.

I'd been here at St. Mark's for many happy occasions—weddings and christenings—and sad occasions—weddings and funerals—and, of course, for Easter Sunday and midnight services at Christmas as well as regular Sunday service now and then. In fact, if I closed my eyes, I could see Carolyn's and Edward's christenings, and I could even picture Susan walking up the aisle in her wedding gown.

This place had many memories, and many ghosts, but maybe the saddest memory was of a boy named John Sutter sitting in a pew with Harriet and Joseph and Emily . . . thinking that he had normal parents, and that the world was a very good and safe place.

And speaking of the devil, Harriet sidled into the pew and squeezed herself in next to Carolyn. We all said hello, and Harriet whispered to me, "I'd like to ride with you to the cemetery."

"Of course." If Harriet drove herself, there would be a few more bodies along the way for the hearse to collect.

The Reverend James Hunnings approached in his appropriate ecclesiastic garb, bowed toward the altar, then walked somberly to center stage. He extended his hands and proclaimed, "I am the resurrection and the life, saith the Lord." I hoped he wasn't speaking about himself.

Ethel, if she could hear, would be pleased with Father Hunnings' performance as well as that of the organist. The hymns had been chosen by Ethel, and the choir and the congregation were in fine voice.

Elizabeth delivered a beautiful eulogy about her mother, followed by Tom Junior and Betsy. You do learn a few things about the deceased during these eulogies, and Ethel sounded like a nice lady. Maybe she was.

Father Hunnings, too, spoke well of the deceased, saying that she was a lady of great faith and spirit, words that he'd tried out on me last night.

The service continued, including Holy Communion, which meant we could skip Sunday service. I took the opportunity of time and place to say a prayer for my father.

Finally, Father Hunnings invited us to give the sign of peace, and the Sutters kissed; I even kissed Harriet. Then we shook hands with the people around us, and I turned toward the pew behind me and extended my hand to . . . William Stanhope. When did he sneak in?

Carolyn, Edward, and Susan kissed Charlotte and William, then it was my turn with Charlotte, and there was no way out of it for either of us, unless I faked a heart attack. So in keeping with the wonderful message of peace, I planted a quick one on her wrinkly cheek and mumbled, "Peas be with you."

The funeral home had provided professional pallbearers, and the Allard family followed the coffin, and then Father Hunnings, then the acolytes picked up the rear, followed by the mourners.

It was still raining, so there were umbrellas being popped open, which added to the usual confusion about who's riding in whose car to the cemetery and who goes in which limousine. Ethel, for sure, was going in the hearse.

Susan insisted that my mother ride in front with me, so I had the pleasure of listening to Harriet giving me driving advice. This is a joke—right?

I maneuvered my way into the line of cars in the funeral procession with Ethel in the lead, followed by three stretch limousines for the family, and about twenty other cars, with a police escort, and we made our way across town to Locust Valley Cemetery. A corner of this nondenominational cemetery is actually the Stanhope family burial ground, which ensured them maximum privacy and a comfortable separation from the less important stiffs.

I parked as close to the gravesite as possible, and we walked with the crowd through the rain toward the open grave.

The funeral home had delivered the flower arrangements and placed them away from the grave, forming a circle, within which we all assembled, and someone handed out roses. There were about fifty mourners gathered around the coffin, which was sitting on a bier next to the hole that was covered with some sort of Astroturf. I noticed that at the head of Ethel's grave was the old sign that said "Victory Garden."

George Allard's tombstone lay next to Ethel's final resting place, and Elizabeth went over and put her hand on George's name. That was very nice.

I looked around and noted the other gravestones, most of which had Stanhope as the last or middle name. One of the perks of marrying a Stanhope is that you get a free plot here, and I was really looking forward to that.

William and Charlotte were standing on the other side of the coffin, facing me, and I looked at them. Surely, standing here among all his deceased forebearers, William must be thinking about his own mortality, and about his immortal soul, and his deeds here on earth, which would determine if he was going to be told to take the Up elevator or the Down elevator. He should be thinking, too, about the only immortality we can be sure of—his children and his grandchildren, and the generations that would come after him. Maybe, I thought, or prayed, today William would have an epiphany, and bless our marriage, and embrace our children.

I looked at him closely to see if the Holy Spirit was moving him. But he just looked hungover. Then he sneezed. Pneumonia? Maybe I'd be back here next week.

And speaking of dead Stanhopes, somewhere, maybe fifty yards from here, was the headstone of Augustus Stanhope, and I recalled Ethel's visit to her lover's grave on the occasion of George's interment here. I'd never told anyone about that, except for Susan, and thinking about it now, I wondered if Ethel had taken any other secrets with her to the grave—and this reminded me of the letter. There had to be something in that letter, or Father Hunnings wouldn't have mentioned it. But what? Possibly a secret will to trump the will we all had been looking at, or some deed, or some other inter vivos transfer from Augustus that gave Ethel or her heirs a claim on the Stanhope fortune? Or maybe the letter revealed a paternity that no one knew about. Maybe William Stanhope was the illegitimate son of the Italian gardener. Who knows? But if you live long enough, as Ethel had, you know a few things.

An acolyte held an umbrella over Father Hunnings' head, and when everyone was assembled, Father Hunnings began, "In the midst of life we are in death."

And fifteen minutes later, he ended, "In sure and certain hope of the resurrection to eternal life through Our Lord Jesus Christ, we commend to Almighty God our sister Ethel; and we commit her body to its resting place; earth to earth, ashes to ashes, dust to dust . . ."

Susan, I, Edward, Carolyn, and Harriet threw our roses on the coffin. "Rest in peace."

Harriet walked with Edward and Carolyn, and as we moved from the grave, Susan took my hand and said, "Do you remember, at George's funeral, we promised that we'd come to each other's funeral, even if we were divorced?"

"I remember that." Or something like that. "Why do you ask?"

"Because . . . those three years you were at sea . . . I kept thinking . . . what if he's lost at sea? How can I . . . ?" Then she broke down and started crying.

I put my arm around her, and we walked with the somber, black-clad mourners with our black umbrellas through the rain past the black limousines.

We all gathered in the basement fellowship room of St. Mark's Church, and I could see that there were more people here than had been at the cemetery. The cemetery no-shows, however, seemed to consist mostly of the elderly and the very young, plus the church ladies who'd set up the punch bowls and the food, so these people got a pass on the burial in the rain.

The punch seemed to be alcohol-free, but I was hoping that someone had spiked at least one punch bowl, and all I had to do was find it.

I'm not a big fan of Episcopal cake and cookies, and my stomach was growling for a liverwurst sandwich on rye with deli mustard. But I settled for some potato salad that had little specks of mystery meat in it.

These post-burial gatherings are sort of awkward—I'm just not sure if we're supposed to continue the mourning, or yuck it up with the family and friends of the deceased. I asked Susan about this—Emily Post had been a little sarcastic the last few times—and Susan said that we're just supposed to exchange good memories of the deceased, and prop up the bereaved family for a little while longer. I guess I knew this, but having been gone for ten years, I felt like a foreigner sometimes, and I had been noticing that I'd missed or misunderstood some of the subtle changes that had occurred here in the last decade. Or maybe I'd changed more than the culture had.

Harriet seemed to be more popular than I'd realized, which was surprising, but good. Also good was that her car was here, and I didn't need to drive her home.

I spotted William and Charlotte standing by themselves, sipping the awful punch. I watched carefully to see if William sneezed or coughed, but he seemed more bored than terminally ill. Damn it. Also, I was annoyed that Susan hadn't dragged Edward and Carolyn over to keep them company and suck up to them. There weren't that many opportunities left, and Susan was letting one get by. I looked around for the kids, but I didn't see them, though I did see the Corbet kids.

Maybe I should give up my matchmaking and also my attempt to get the kids to hang around with their grandparents. Susan was no help in either case, so why should I worry about it? Love? To hell with it. Money? Who cares? Leave it to Fate.

I love to mingle in a crowd of people I don't know, especially if most of them are elderly; you can really get into some interesting conversations. The punch helps, of course. I did see Tom Corbet and Laurence, so the three of us stood in the outcast corner and chatted.

I spotted the Reverend James Hunnings, and his wife had joined him, so I went over to say hello to her—and him—and I noticed that Mrs. Hunnings had aged in the last ten years. This was a big disappointment; I hate it when my fantasy women get old. Nevertheless, she still had a sparkle in her eye and she was charming. Her name, I recalled now, was Rebecca, and she said to me, "Jim tells me that you're back, and that you and Susan have reunited."

Who's Jim? Oh, James Hunnings. Her husband. I replied, "God works in mysterious ways."

Hunnings butted in, as I'm sure he does often, and said, "Indeed, He does. And wondrous ways."

Right. Take, for example, your wife not leaving you. I said, "That was a beautiful church service and a touching eulogy."

"Thank you, John. It's not difficult to eulogize Ethel Allard. She was a lady of great faith and spirit."

Rebecca Hunnings smiled at me, then excused herself, leaving me alone with Jim, who said to me, "I hope you've given some thought to what we discussed."

"I've spoken to Susan, and she agrees with me that we would not benefit from premarital counseling."

"Well, with your permission, John, I'd like to speak to her about that."

"You don't need my permission."

"Fine." He informed me, "I just spoke to William and Charlotte, and we have an appointment in my office this afternoon to discuss . . . well, their concerns."

"Good. But keep in mind that they hate me."

That took him aback, but he recovered and said, "Their concern is for their daughter's happiness."

"Mine, too."

"I know that, which is why this is so troubling."

"Right." I asked him, "Did William seem under the weather?"

"I don't think so. Why do you ask?"

"Oh, he looked a bit unwell at graveside, and I was concerned."

"He looked fine."

"No cough or anything?"

"Uh . . . no. Oh, by the way, I did take the liberty of speaking to Elizabeth about that letter, and she informs me that it's in her possession and she has not yet given it to you."

"That's correct."

"Well, I must be frank with you, John—I've advised her to examine the contents herself, then discuss it with me before she delivers it to you."

"Really? And why did you do that, if I may ask?"

"Well, as I said, Ethel discussed with me—in general terms—the contents of the letter, and Ethel herself was unsure if you should see it."

"Well, the last I heard from Elizabeth, her mother had instructed her to give it to me after her death."

"I see . . . well, there seems to be some confusion then."

"Not in my mind. But I'll take it up with Elizabeth."

He seemed to be struggling with something, then he said, "This letter . . . may contain what could be construed as gossip . . . or scandal." He looked at me and continued, "Not the sort of thing a Christian lady such as Ethel Allard should concern herself with, or perpetuate."

Why not? I love gossip and scandal. Where's my letter? I pointed out, "Ethel is dead."

He explained, "Neither Elizabeth nor I want her mother's memory to be . . . let's say, sullied, in any way. So, of course, Elizabeth wants to see the letter first."

I wonder who put that idea in her head? Well, if Father Hunnings wasn't blowing smoke, then the letter wasn't about money. I like gossip better. Scandal is good, too. It was time to go, so I asked him, "Will I see you—and Mrs. Hunnings—tonight at Elizabeth's house?"

"Rebecca and I will try to be there."

"Good." I moved off and found Susan, but I didn't tell her what Father Hunnings and I had just discussed. Instead, I asked her, "Were the kids sucking up to their grandparents?"

"John, that's awful."

"I meant to say, are Edward and Carolyn interacting in a loving way with Grandma and Grandpa?"

She replied, "They spoke briefly, but Mom and Dad have left."

"Already? Are they feeling all right?"

"Yes, but . . . this is not really their crowd."

"Ah. So, Lord and Lady Stanhope just popped in to say hello to the peasants."

"Please." She added, "It was good of them to come."

"I think they actually came to see Father Hunnings for a moment." I informed her, "Your parents have an appointment with him this afternoon."

"Really?" She thought about that, then said, "That's really annoying."

"Your parents are only concerned about your happiness." I announced, "Prince John is ready to leave."

She ignored that and asked me, "Have you seen Elizabeth?"

"No, but we'll see her tonight and that would be an appropriate time for me to ask her about the letter." I added, "I hope she's invited a better class of funeral mourners." I asked her, "Did Edward and Carolyn spend any time with Betsy and Tom?"

"I don't know. Why are you pushing that?"

"I think it would be great if they married people from their hometown. Like we did."

"No one does that anymore."

"Too bad. Ready? Let's collect the kids."

"They left."

"They don't have a car."

"They had a ride to the train station, and they needed to leave quickly to catch a train, so they asked me to say goodbye to you." She added, "They're going to the city to meet friends."

"Did you tell them to be home in time to go with us to Elizabeth's house?"

"They're staying at Carolyn's apartment tonight."

"All right . . . well, they've been good troupers. They should spend some time with their friends."

Susan pointed out, "One less night for them to be in the house."

I looked at her and nodded.

CHAPTER SIXTY

Susan had turned off her cell phone ringer on the way to St. Mark's, and she'd left it off during the burial service—phone calls at graveside are not good—and then she and I forgot it was off.

So it wasn't until we got home at about 2:00 P.M. and went to our office to check e-mails and phone messages that she remembered to look at her cell phone display. She said, "I have four calls from Felix Mancuso . . . the first at ten forty-seven." She put the phone on speaker and played the first message. Mancuso said, "All right, to keep you informed regarding Anthony Bellarosa—I arrived at the Papavero Funeral Home early, and there was no one there except John Gotti. There was a big floral display from Anthony Bellarosa and family, and also from Salvatore D'Alessio and family. Anthony's flower display, for your amusement, was shaped like a Cuban cigar, and D'Alessio's was a royal flush—in hearts—and there were some others shaped like racehorses and martini glasses."

I hadn't seen anything that creative at Walton's for Ethel. WASPs are boring.

Mr. Mancuso continued, "Stretch limos arrived all morning, but most of the mourners were hiding their faces with umbrellas on their way in and out. And the police and media are definitely not invited inside. All right, they're carrying the coffin to the hearse and it looks like the cortège is ready to roll, so I'm going to join the procession. Bottom line here, we can't determine if Bellarosa or D'Alessio are here, but we'll see at Saint John's."

Susan and I looked at each other, and I said, "We need to be more creative with the flowers for the next funeral."

Susan ignored that and played the next message, which came at 11:36: "Mancuso. Okay, quick update—I'm still in the funeral procession, and we're now in Ozone Park, where he had his headquarters at the Bergin Hunt and Fish Club . . . which I'm now passing . . . there are hundreds of people standing in the rain and waving. I'm waving back. FYI, there are four or five news helicopters overhead, so you can see this on television if you want. I'm in the gray car waving. Call me when you get this."

Susan said, "Next message came at twelve thirty-three." She played message three: "Mancuso. I am now at Resurrection Mausoleum, at Saint John's Cemetery. About a hundred people from the limos filed into the chapel, but again they were all holding umbrellas in front of their faces, but I did see Salvatore D'Alessio—he's easy to spot—and his wife. But no Anthony Bellarosa, which doesn't mean he's not here. The press and the police are not invited inside the chapel. All right, next stop is the gravesite. I'll call you after that."

Susan said, "Last call from him—came in at one thirty-seven." She played the message: "Mancuso. Here is the bottom line—to the best of our knowledge, Anthony Bellarosa was not at the burial. During and after the graveside service, the Bureau and the NYPD got a good look at every man's face, and we conducted some informal interviews with the usual suspects regarding Anthony Bellarosa's whereabouts. No one was very cooperative and nobody knows nothing. I did pull D'Alessio aside, and I'll fill you in on that when we speak. Call me."

I thought about Anthony not being at Gotti's funeral, and I hoped that meant he really was at the bottom of the East River.

Susan dialed Felix Mancuso's cell from the house phone, and put it on speaker.

He answered, "Mancuso."

"Sutter. Susan is here with me on speaker."

They exchanged greetings, and Susan said to him, "I had my cell off for the funeral, and forgot to turn it on. Sorry."

"No problem." He said to us, "So Anthony did not show up, which is significant."

"I guess so." Italians show up at anyone's funeral.

He explained, "That means that he's either dead, or he's in hiding."

"Dead sounds good."

He didn't comment on that directly, but further explained, "If Anthony Bellarosa is not dead, then he thinks he will be if his uncle can find him." He added, "That is the working theory."

"Good theory." I asked Mr. Mancuso, "What did Uncle Sal say to you?"

"He said that he thinks his nephew is dead."

Susan and I exchanged glances, and I asked Mancuso, "He actually said that?"

"He did. And he told me who probably killed Anthony."

"Who?"

"John Sutter."

That took me by surprise, but I'm quick and replied, "I have an alibi."

Mr. Mancuso allowed himself a small chuckle, then said, "D'Alessio told me to pull you in for questioning."

I remarked, "I didn't think Uncle Sal had a sense of humor."

"Apparently he thinks this is a funny subject."

I glanced at Susan, who was not smiling. She just doesn't get sick humor. I asked Mancuso, "What do *you* think? Is Anthony dead or alive?"

Mancuso replied, "Well, D'Alessio has had extra bodyguards with him for the last week—three or four men, though not today at the funeral, of course—so if D'Alessio has that many men with him tonight and tomorrow and so forth, then we have to assume that Anthony is alive and that he has a contract out on his uncle."

Susan asked him, "What contract?"

Mr. Mancuso explained, "A . . . call it a death warrant."

"Oh."

"Signed by Anthony Bellarosa." Mr. Mancuso further explained to her, "It's not actually in writing." He added, "And Salvatore D'Alessio most probably has a contract out on Bellarosa's life."

Susan had no comment. But certainly she had a flashback to her lover, who not incidentally had the same last name.

Felix Mancuso recapped for us, "So, it appears that Anthony Bellarosa has chosen to go into deep hiding rather than go about his business surrounded by bodyguards, as his uncle is doing." He added, "I think we'll know within a week or two who made the right move."

I inquired, "Why do you think it will be that soon?"

He replied, "Every day that Anthony is not around to run his half of the business is a day that his uncle gets more control and more power." He informed us, "I did this for . . . well, a very long time. So I've seen this, and I know how they think and how they act."

I thought about that, then asked him, "If you had to make a bet—and if you were looking at the odds—which one of them would you bet on to be alive next week?"

He hesitated, then replied, "Actually . . . well, I hate to say this, but we have a . . . a sort of pool here."

"Can I get in on it?"

He forced a chuckle and replied, "Sure."

Susan said, "Please."

Mr. Mancuso got professional again and said, "The odds are really fifty-fifty. D'Alessio is not overly bright, but most of the underbosses and the old Mafiosi are with him, so that gives him an advantage in regard to getting to Anthony and having the job done professionally. Anthony's strong points are that he's young, energetic, and ruthless, and he has a lot of young talent around him. He's also cautious, as I said, but he's a hothead, as you said, and he'll forget about caution for this job, which may be his downfall—or may lead to a surprise win."

I thought about all that, and my instincts and my intellect said to go with the old guy—Uncle Sal, who was also my sentimental pick. I inquired, "So, you're giving even odds?"

"That is correct."

"What's the maximum bet?"

"Fifty."

"John."

That was Susan, and I motioned for her to be quiet. I said to Mr. Mancuso, "Could you front me fifty on Uncle Sal?"

"Done."

"I'll give it to you when I see you." I added, "Let me know if the odds change."

"I certainly will do that."

I would have asked him how I'd know if I won, but that was a silly question. I did ask, however, "Why did hundreds of people line the funeral route of a Mafia don?"

He replied, "Probably thousands, actually. And I don't have a single answer for that. Maybe curiosity . . . maybe just the herd instinct . . ." He added, "Some people thought Gotti was a hero, so maybe that's something we need to think about."

I glanced at Susan, then I said to Mr. Mancuso, "Well, we went to the funeral of a lady who lived quietly, died peacefully, and was buried without a lot of fuss. And I'm sure she's with the angels now."

Mr. Mancuso replied, "I'm sure she is." He then said, "Well, I have nothing further. Any questions?"

I looked at Susan, who shook her head, and I said, "Not at this time."

He said, "Have a happy Father's Day."

Actually, I would if William was sick with pneumonia. I replied, "You, too."

I hit the disconnect button and said to Susan, "I feel good that Felix Mancuso is on top of this."

She nodded.

"And the FBI, and the county police, and Detective Nastasi."

Again, she nodded, but she knew I was just trying to make things sound better than they were. We were both disappointed that Anthony Bellarosa hadn't shown his face and hadn't given the FBI and NYPD a crack at him. Usually, if the police or the FBI could question a suspect or a person of interest, they could, at the very least, instruct him to keep them informed of his whereabouts. And they could follow him. But Anthony had done a disappearing act, which made everyone nervous.

Mr. Mancuso's odds of fifty-fifty were either too optimistic, or he was trying to make us feel better. The odds were really in favor of Anthony killing Uncle Sal before Uncle Sal killed Anthony. But that wasn't a bet I wanted to make.

And then, when Anthony took care of Uncle Sal, he'd turn his attention to the Sutters. That was my bet.

CHAPTER SIXTY-ONE

We spent a few lazy hours of a rainy Saturday afternoon in the upstairs family room, reading and listening to music.

I went downstairs at 4:00 P.M. to ask Sophie to bring us coffee and pastry, then I went into the office to check my e-mail.

There was no reply from my law firm to my Friday night resignation letter, but I knew I'd hear from them Monday.

There was, however, a reply to my letter to Samantha. Bottom line, she was not happy. In fact, she was pissed.

She pointed out, quite correctly, that I'd not called, not written, and had generally left her in the dark until I dropped the bombshell. She also said she was hurt, devastated, and deeply wounded. It was a really well-written letter for an e-mail, and she's very much a lady and didn't use words like "shithead," "asshole," or even "fuck you." I mean, that was what she was saying, but she said it in a more genteel way.

Well, I felt awful, and I wished I could have delivered my bad news to her in person or at least by phone—she deserved better than an e-mail—but the situation had gotten away from me, and I'd done the best I could, considering her imminent arrival and what was going on here.

I wasn't going to respond to her letter now, but I would speak to her by phone, or maybe even in London, and if she really wanted an explanation, I'd give her the whole story. Most likely, however, she never wanted to hear from me again. I wondered if she'd know if I got whacked. I guess she would from my firm, who'd be annoyed that I hadn't come in to take care of my out-processing.

Anyway, I deleted the letter in case the FBI went through my e-mail posthumously. I wouldn't want Felix Mancuso to think I'd been a cad.

I went back to the family room, and Sophie brought up coffee and pastry.

Susan said to me, "You're very quiet."

I replied, truthfully, "I took care of that business in London."

"About time," she said, and went back to her magazine.

At 6:00 P.M., I turned on the TV and found a local news station that was leading off with the John Gotti funeral.

Susan looked up from her magazine and asked, "Do we have to watch that?"

"Why don't you get ready for Elizabeth's open house?"

Susan stood and said, "If you hurry, we can keep our six-game winning streak going."

So, sex or another funeral? I said, "Five minutes."

She left, and I turned my attention to the television, which showed an aerial view of the Gotti funeral procession, taken earlier in the day from a hovering helicopter.

The female helicopter reporter was saying, "The procession is slowing down in front of the Gotti home in Howard Beach, a middle-class Queens neighborhood, with John Gotti's modest home in such contrast to the man himself, who was far from modest."

Not a bad observation—a little hokey, but point made.

She continued her spontaneous reporting over the sound of the helicopter blades, "John Gotti was a man who, to many, was larger than life. The Teflon Don, who no charges could stick to."

To whom no charges could stick. This was *not* BBC.

She continued, "You can see the hundreds of people who've come out on this rainy day—friends and neighbors, maybe out of curiosity, maybe to pay their respects to their neighbor . . ."

Well, at least one neighbor wasn't there to pay his respects; he was dead.

She went on, returning to the subject of Mr. Gotti as a bon vivant, and said, "He was also called the Dapper Don because of his Italian, handmade thousand-dollar suits."

A thousand? Did I get taken on that Brioni at two thousand? No. That's what they cost. Maybe Gotti got the celebrity gangster discount. I should have mentioned Anthony's name at Brioni's.

The lady in the helicopter said, "The procession is picking up speed now, and they will be heading to Ozone Park, where John Gotti had his headquarters—the Bergin Hunt and Fish Club, but really the headquarters of his criminal empire."

Really?

The aerial view pulled away to show the long line of vehicles moving through the gray drizzle—the hearse, the twenty or so flower cars piled with floral arrangements, and the twenty or more black stretch limousines, in one of which was Salvatore D'Alessio, though apparently not Anthony Bellarosa.

I looked for Mr. Mancuso's gray car among the dozens that were following the black limousines, and I actually saw a gray sedan with all its windows open, and arms waving to the crowd. I guess that's FBI humor.

I heard Susan call, "John!"

I called back, "This is important."

"You're going to miss something more important if you don't get in here."

"Coming!"

I was about to turn off the TV, but then the scene switched back to the studio, and the news anchor guy said, "Thank you, Sharon, reporting earlier today from our Eye in the Sky helicopter. We'll have more footage of the John Gotti funeral after we hear this report on the life of John Gotti from our city news reporter, Jenny Alvarez."

Who?

And then there she was on the screen. My old . . . fling. She looked great with TV makeup . . . maybe a little orange . . . but still very pretty, with a nice big smile.

Jenny said, "Thank you, Scott. Those were amazing shots of the funeral cortège, taken earlier today, as the body of John Gotti was laid to rest at Saint John's—"

"John Sutter!"

"Be right there."

Jenny was saying, "One of the pallbearers today was Mr. Gotti's lawyer, Carmine Caputo, who we interviewed after the burial."

Mr. Caputo's face appeared on the screen, and he took a few questions from a reporter who looked like he was about sixteen years old. Mr. Caputo, old pro that he was, did not answer a single question, but used the opportunity to eulogize his client—family man, father, husband, good neighbor—well, except that one time—good friend—except when he had Paul Castellano whacked—and a generous contributor to many worthwhile causes, including, I hoped, Mr. Caputo's law firm. I hate it when clients die without paying their bills, as Frank had done to me. But Mr. Caputo seemed sincere in his affection for Mr. Gotti, so he'd been paid.

Jenny came back on the screen, and I thought for sure she was going to make the segue to the last big Mafioso funeral she'd covered—that of don Frank Bellarosa—and mention Mr. Bellarosa's upper-crust lawyer, John Sutter. This was her opportunity to defend me again and say, "If Carmine Caputo could be at John Gotti's funeral, why was everyone so fucking bent up that John Sutter went to Frank Bellarosa's funeral? Huh? And John didn't carry the coffin, for God's sake." Then film footage of me would come on the screen, and when the camera returned to Jenny, she'd be wiping her eyes and saying, "John? Are you out there?"

"John!"

"Coming!"

Jenny, however, did not mention any of that, and I was . . . well, hurt.

I was also sad that she'd gone from network news to this rinky-dink local cable show. Maybe she took to drink after we broke up.

Jenny, who knew her Mafia lore, was saying, "Saint John's Cemetery is known as the Mafia Valhalla and holds the remains of such underworld luminaries as Lucky Luciano, Carlo Gambino, and Aniello

Dellacroce, the Gambino family underboss—and now John Gotti, the boss of bosses . . ."

I watched her as she looked straight into the camera, as though she were looking at me, and I *knew* she was thinking about me. I also noticed a wedding ring on her left hand. Oh well.

I turned off the TV and nearly ran into the bedroom.

Susan was at her makeup table and said, "You're too late."

I got undressed, fell into bed, and put a pillow under my butt.

She glanced at me and commented, "Well . . ."

Elizabeth Allard Corbet's house was a big old rambling colonial located in the hills of Mill Neck, near Oyster Bay.

We parked on the heavily treed street and walked toward the house. The sky was clearing, and it looked as though tomorrow was going to be a good day, at least weather-wise.

A small card on Elizabeth's door said, *Enter*, so we did.

It was about 7:30, and the large foyer was already filled with people. As is my custom, I said hello to the first guy I saw and asked, "Where's the bar?"

He pointed. "Sunroom."

I took Susan in tow, and we made our way through the living room into a sunroom on the side of the house where two bartenders were helping people deal with their grief.

Drinks in hand—vodka tonics—Susan and I waded into the maelstrom.

I spotted a few people I recognized from the funeral home or the burial service, but mostly the crowd seemed to be made up of couples who were younger than us, probably friends and neighbors of the Corbets—as opposed to friends of the deceased. I didn't see the Stanhopes and didn't expect to. Neither did I see Father Hunnings. Maybe they were all still in Father Hunnings' office discussing me and Susan. These people should get a life.

I didn't see my mother either. Maybe she was in on the meeting. In fact, maybe they'd asked other people to come and give testimony against me—like Amir Nasim (Mr. Sutter is a bigot), Charlie Frick

(He's a philistine), Judy Remsen (He's a pervert), Althea Gwynn (He's a boor), Beryl Carlisle (He's impotent) . . . maybe even Samantha (He's a scoundrel) flew in from London. Possibly, they were now forming a lynch mob. But my mother would tip me off. She loved me, unconditionally.

Susan announced, "There's no one here whom we know."

"They're all plotting against me in Hunnings' office."

"I think you need another drink."

"One drink, then we're leaving."

"Fine. But you should speak to Elizabeth if possible."

We wandered through the living room and into the dining room, where there was a buffet laid out, and I noted a huge liver pâté, oozing fat.

Susan said, "You don't want that. Have some cut vegetables."

"Choking hazard."

We moved into a large family room at the rear of the house, but other than Tom Junior and Betsy, there was no one there that we recognized.

Susan said, "This is a big house for Elizabeth and two kids who don't live here."

I thought it best not to mention my guest room, but I did say, "Must be lots of storage space in the basement."

"What made you think of that?"

"Well . . . most of that stuff from the gatehouse was brought here."

She nodded absently, thinking about something else.

Meanwhile, I was thinking that I could have been very comfortable here. I mean, I was happy beyond belief that I was with Susan again, but that was not a done deal—though in her mind it was. But in the days and weeks ahead, she'd have to face some hard realities, and harder choices when Mom and Pop laid it on the line for her.

She would, I was certain, choose me over them and their money, and if the children's money was also at stake, we'd have a family council, and I would still be the winner over Grandpa and Grandma.

But I wasn't going to let that happen. And I wouldn't make a big deal of it; I'd just disappear. Well, first I'd kick William in the nuts. That's the least I should get out of this.

Susan asked me, "Could you live here?"

"Live . . . where?"

"I'm wondering if we shouldn't move from Stanhope Hall and get away from the memories, from Nasim, from . . . everything there."

I didn't reply immediately, then I said, "That is totally your decision."

"I want you to tell me how you feel."

Why is it always *feel* with women? How about, "Tell me what you *think*"?

"John?"

"I'm not completely in touch with my feelings on that subject. I'll get back to you on that."

"Elizabeth wants to sell, so let's think about it."

That was a step in the right direction away from Stanhope Hall. I agreed, "Let's see how we feel."

She nodded and observed, "There are people on the patio. Let's go outside."

So we walked through the family room, and stopped to say hello to Tom Junior and Betsy, and we discovered that their father and Laurence had gone back to the city, but the kids were joining them tomorrow for Sunday brunch in SoHo. That's what I'd be doing if I moved into the city by myself.

I said, "There's Elizabeth. We'll say hello, then you need to excuse yourself, so I can speak to her about that letter if I think it's appropriate."

She nodded, and we walked over to Elizabeth, who was standing with a group of people in the center of the large patio.

We all kissed, and Elizabeth introduced us to her friends, one of whom was a younger guy who I immediately sensed was single, horny, and sniffing around our friend and hostess. His name was Mitch, and he looked a little slick to me—trendy clothes, coiffed hair, buffed nails, and a phony smile. Capped teeth, too. I did not approve of Mitch, and I hoped that Elizabeth didn't either.

Susan said to Elizabeth, "That was a beautiful funeral service and a moving burial rite."

Elizabeth replied, "Thank you both so much for all you've done."

And so forth.

Then Susan excused herself, and I hesitated, then said to Elizabeth, "This may not be a good time, but I need about five minutes to discuss something that's come up."

She looked at me, and she knew what this was about. She could have put it off, but she said to her guests, "John is the attorney for Mom's estate. He wants to tell me where she buried the cash."

Everyone got a chuckle out of that, and Elizabeth and I went into the house and she led me to a small library and closed the door.

I said to her, "This is a very nice house."

"Too big, too old, too much upkeep." She added with a smile, "Tom did all the decorating." She opened a liquor cabinet and said, "Let me freshen your drink."

"I'm all right."

"Well, I need one." She poured gin or vodka from a decanter into her glass.

I asked her, "How are you holding up?"

She stirred her drink with her finger, shrugged, and said, "All right. Tomorrow won't be so good."

"No. But time does heal."

"I know. She had a good life."

I could have slid right from that to the letter, but I sensed that we needed another minute of small talk, and I said, "I really enjoyed Tom's company."

"I do, too. We're friends. I like Laurence, too, and I'm happy for both of them."

"Good. Your kids are great. I love them."

"They're good kids. It's been hard for them, but at least all this happened when they were old enough to understand."

I nodded and said, "Same with my two."

"Your kids are terrific, John."

"I wish I'd been around for them more in the last ten years."

"That wasn't all your fault. And you have a long time to get to know them again."

"I hope so." I smiled and said, "My matchmaking seems to have fizzled."

She, too, smiled and replied, "You never know." She added, "Wouldn't that be nice?"

Then, on the subject of mating, she asked me, "Did you like Mitch?"

"No."

She laughed and said, "You're too subtle, John."

"You can do much better."

She didn't respond to that, and we stood there a moment, neither of us coming up with a new subject for small talk.

So I said, "I spoke to Father Hunnings, and he said he spoke to you about the letter that your mother wrote to me."

She nodded.

I continued, "He told me that your mother discussed with him—in general terms—the contents of that letter, and that Ethel asked him if she should give it to me."

"I know that."

"And Father Hunnings, as you know, wants to see the letter to determine if he thinks I should see it."

She didn't reply, and I could see that this was not going to be a slam dunk for me. I said to her, "I have no objection to sharing this letter with you—you are Ethel's daughter. But I do have an objection to Father Hunnings seeing it before I do. Or seeing it at all."

She nodded, and I could tell she was wavering.

So we both stood there. As an attorney, I know when to rest my case.

Finally, Elizabeth said, "I have the letter . . . unopened—it's addressed to you . . . but . . . if you don't mind, I'd like to think about it . . . maybe speak to Father Hunnings one more time."

I reopened my case and said, "I think this is between me and you."

"But Mom spoke to him . . . and now I'm in the middle."

"What was the last thing she said to you about the letter?"

"You know . . . that I should give it to you after her death. But . . . what if it *is* scandalous? Or . . . who knows what?" She looked at me and asked, "What if it has something to do with Susan?"

I'd already thought about that, as Elizabeth obviously had. Elizabeth and Susan were friends, but somewhere in the back of Elizabeth's otherwise beautiful mind was the selfish thought that if Susan were gone, then John was free. That's egotistical, I know. But true. In any case, I didn't think that Ethel, even if she knew some scandal about Susan, would be writing to me about it. In fact, she'd wanted Susan and me to reconcile. And even if the letter *was* about Susan, I couldn't think of many things that would change my mind or my heart regarding how I felt about her. Well, I suppose I could think of a few things.

I said to Elizabeth, "This is something your mother wanted me to know. But I understand your concern about preserving her good reputation and her memory. So, may I suggest that we look at the letter now, together? And if it's something like that, then you can keep it and destroy it."

She shook her head. "I can't do that now."

"All right. When you're ready."

She nodded. "Maybe Monday. When this is all behind me. I'll call you."

"Thank you." I smiled and said, "Maybe your mother was just telling me what an idiot I am."

She smiled in return and said, "She actually liked you." Elizabeth confessed, "But she never liked me liking you. She liked Tom. And Susan."

"I like Tom and Susan, too. But Tom likes Laurence now."

She smiled again and said, "It's all about timing."

"It is." I opened my arms, and she stepped forward and we hugged.

She said, "Let's speak Monday."

"Fine."

We walked together back to the patio, where Susan was speaking to Mitch and the other guests in Elizabeth's little group.

Mitch said to Elizabeth and me, "Hey, let's get the shovels and go digging for the money."

Asshole.

Elizabeth ignored him—I'd given Mitch a thumbs-down, and he was finished—and said to Susan, "Sorry. John had to show me where to sign some papers."

Susan smiled and said, "Make him earn his crabapple jelly."

We chatted for a minute, then I said, "Unfortunately, we need to go."

Susan and I thanked Elizabeth for her hospitality, and told her to call us if she needed anything. We wished everyone a good evening, and I said to Mitch, "Don't wear those sandals if you go digging."

Mitch did not reply.

Susan and I walked around the side of the house to avoid the people inside, and she informed me, "You were almost rude to Mitch."

"I didn't like him."

"You don't even know him."

"There's nothing to know."

"Well, I think he and Elizabeth are . . ."

"Not anymore."

"What do you mean?"

"I gave him an unsatisfactory rating."

She thought about that, then asked, "You said that to Elizabeth?"

"I did."

She stayed silent awhile, then inquired, "When did you become Elizabeth's mentor and confidant?"

Whoops. I wasn't following Susan's thought process. I replied, "She *asked* me what I thought of him. So I told her."

"You should learn not to answer so bluntly. And you should also learn not to meddle in people's affairs."

"All right." I added, "It's wonderful to be back."

She didn't respond to that and we walked in silence. Clearly, Susan still harbored a wee bit of jealousy. Good. To change the subject, I asked her, "Don't you want to know about the letter?"

"Yes, I do."

So I explained to her how Elizabeth and I had left it, and I added, "I just don't see what could be in that letter that has any importance or relevance to me. So we shouldn't worry about it." I continued, "Ethel is—was—an old woman with some typical hang-ups of that generation, and a lot of old-fashioned ideas about what is important."

Susan pointed out, "Father Hunnings was also concerned—or worried."

"Well, talk about hang-ups. Did I tell you that I swore to him we were sleeping in separate bedrooms?"

"John, you shouldn't have lied to a priest."

"I was protecting your honor."

"Let me do that." She thought a moment, then said, "I think we need to give Father Hunnings the benefit of the doubt about this letter. He's trying to do the right thing."

I suggested, "Let's see if I get to read the letter that was addressed to me, and let's see what it says. Then I'll let you know if I think he's trying to do the right thing."

We drove back to Stanhope Hall, and when we got to Grace Lane, Susan called the gatehouse to open up, then called Sophie, who assured us that there were still no onions in the house.

Sophie wasn't expecting us for dinner, but she quickly threw together a platter of bean sprouts and tofu. It's hard to choose a wine for that.

Susan and I had a quiet, candlelit dinner on the patio. The sky had cleared and the stars were out, and a nice breeze blew in from the Sound.

Susan said, "This has been one of the best and one of the worst weeks of my life."

I assured her, "It will only get better from here."

"I think it will."

Well, I didn't. But what else was I going to say?

She said, "I'll miss Edward and Carolyn being here."

"And I'll miss your parents being close by."

"I won't." She switched to a happier subject and asked me, "What would you like for your Father's Day breakfast?"

"I was thinking of leftover bean sprouts, but maybe I'll have fried eggs and sausage." I added, "Buttered toast, home-fried potatoes, coffee, and orange juice. Make that a screwdriver."

"And would you like that served in bed?"

"Of course."

"Edward and Carolyn said they were sorry they couldn't be home for breakfast."

"No problem."

"They'll be here in time for dinner."

"Good."

She suggested, "We should have a word with them about their grandparents."

I didn't reply.

"John?"

I poured myself another glass of wine and said to her, "I'm not getting involved with that. If you think they need another reminder about the financial facts of life, then *you* give it to them." I reminded her, "I already kissed William and Charlotte's asses. My job is done."

"All right . . . I sense that you're frustrated, and upset—"

"Not at all. I did what I had to do, and I'm done doing it. I will be more than cordial tomorrow at dinner, and I will speak to your father privately tomorrow night, or Monday morning—about you. But only because that's what *he* wants. Though I can tell you, nothing is going to change his mind about this marriage, and I will not even try to change his mind. So, you, Susan, need to face some realities, and make some decisions."

"I've already done that."

"That's what you think. Look, I came here with nothing, and I am prepared to leave here with nothing."

"You're not leaving here without me. Not again."

"I won't hold you to that."

She took my hand and said, "Look at me."

I looked at her in the candlelight, with the breeze blowing through her hair, and she never looked more beautiful.

She said, slowly and deliberately, "I understand what you're saying and why you're saying it. But you can forget it. You're not getting away so easily this time. Even if you think you're doing it for me and for our children."

I looked into her eyes, and I could see they were getting misty. I said, "I love you."

"And I love you."

She said to me, "I'm tired of them controlling me with their money. So if I lose the money, and I lose them, then I'm free."

"I understand." I asked, "And the children?"

"He won't do that—my mother would not let him do that."

Wanna bet? I said, "Okay. That's good. Then it's settled." I said to her, "I almost didn't come in for the funeral."

She replied, "I knew you were coming in, even if you didn't." She pointed to the sky and said, "This was in our stars, John. This is the way it was meant to happen."

Oddly enough, I felt the same thing, as all lovers do. But the question now was, What did the stars have in store for us next?

CHAPTER SIXTY-TWO

Susan served me breakfast in bed, though I think Sophie cooked it—which was much better than the other way around.

It was a beautiful June day, and sunlight shone on my tray of sizzling fat. I hardly knew where to begin.

Susan, in her nightie, sat crossed-legged next to me and sipped a cup of coffee. I inquired, "Do you want a sausage?"

"No, thank you."

I dug into the sausages and eggs.

She said, "This is your special day. What would you like to do on Father's Day?"

Shoot your father. I replied, "It's such a beautiful day. Let's go to the beach."

"I thought we could go shopping."

"Uh . . . I thought . . ."

She had a shopping bag next to her, and she gave it to me. "Here's your Father's Day present, and we need to buy you something to go with it." She informed me, "That's from me, Carolyn, and Edward. Carolyn and I bought it for you when we were in the city."

"Great. You shouldn't have."

"Open it."

I reached into the bag for my horrid, two-hundred-dollar tie, which now needed a new suit to match. But it didn't feel like a tie box. It felt like underwear, or maybe a new Yale T-shirt. But when I pulled it out, it was a white yachting cap, with a black shiny bill, and gold braid on the crown. I stared at it. The last time I wore one of these was when I was on the Race Committee at Seawanhaka—a lifetime ago.

Susan said, "Happy Father's Day."

I looked at her, still not quite sure that I was understanding this.

She said, "Try it on."

So I put it on and it fit. I said, "This is very . . . thoughtful." Should I look out the window for the yacht?

Susan explained, "I've gone through some yachting magazines, and chosen five boats that we can look at today."

I really didn't know what to say, but I said, "This is . . . really too extravagant."

"Not at all."

I turned toward her—without upsetting my breakfast tray—and gave her a big kiss. I said, "Thank you, but—"

"No buts. We are going to sail again."

I nodded.

"One condition."

"Never by myself."

"That's right."

"Agreed."

So we sat there awhile holding hands—my eggs were getting cold— and finally I asked, "Can we afford this?"

"We're all chipping in. Edward and Carolyn want to do this for you."

That still didn't answer the question, but I was very moved by the thought.

Susan produced some magazine pages and gave them to me. I looked at a few classified ads that were circled in pen, and I saw that we were in the right class—forty to fifty-footers—an Alden, two Hinckleys, a C&C, and a forty-five-foot Morgan. The prices, I noticed, were a bit steeper than a mainmast—but, as they say, if you have to ask how much a yacht costs, you can't afford it. Still, I said, "These are a lot of money."

"Think of all the hours of enjoyment we'll all get out of it."

"Right." I remembered all the good times we'd had as a family sailing up and down the East Coast. Then I thought about my sail around the world, which was something far different. I said, "We have to get the kids to take some time this summer to sail with us."

"They promised. Two weeks in August."

"Good." And then I thought about everything that could and would happen between now and August—the Stanhopes, Susan and me, and Anthony Bellarosa. Well, I'm too pessimistic. Or realistic. But I didn't want to spoil the moment, so I said, "This was really a great idea. How did you think of this?"

"It was easy. Carolyn, Edward, and I sat down to discuss your Father's Day gift, and we each wrote a suggestion on a piece of paper, and we all wrote the same thing. Sailboat."

I guess that was quicker than doing pantomime. I said, "They're great kids."

"They were so happy they were able to do this for their father."

I was getting a little emotional, so I joked, "Where's my tie?"

"Oh, it didn't look as good here as it did in the store. I'll bring it back."

I wonder why things look different in the store for the ladies. Lighting? Well, it must have been really awful. I said, "I'll take the boat. Give the tie to your father."

"Good idea. As soon as the kids get here, we'll go out and see these boats." She added, "They want to help."

Well, it was their money. Actually, it was William's money, which made this a really great gift. I couldn't wait to tell Cheap Willie that he'd helped out with my two-hundred-thousand-dollar Father's Day present—at least with the down payment. We'd need to finance the rest, and I wasn't sure if everyone's allowance and the trust fund distributions would be rolling in after today. This was a very appropriate and heartwarming gift to me, but it was also pure folly. Nevertheless, it's the thought that counts.

Susan said, suggestively, "Finish your breakfast, and I'll give you another gift."

The hell with breakfast. Well . . . maybe one more sausage.

She hopped out of bed and said, "You have to keep your hat on."

She explained, "You're a sailor who's washed ashore in a storm, and I'm the lonely wife of a seaman whom I haven't seen in years. And I'm nursing you back to health, and I just came in to take your breakfast tray."

"Okay." Don't take it too far.

She moved to the side of the bed and asked, "Is there anything else I can get for you, sir?"

"Well—"

"Oh, sir, how is that tray rising by itself?"

I smiled. "Well . . ."

"Let me take that, sir, before it topples."

She put the tray on the dresser, then came back to the bed and said, "With your permission, sir, I will massage ointment on your injured private parts."

I tipped my hat and said, "Permission granted."

So I didn't get much breakfast, but I don't have a lot of trouble choosing between sex and food.

Carolyn and Edward came in on the 9:28 train, and Susan picked them up at the station.

They gave me a kiss and hug for Father's Day, and a nice card that had a picture of a sailboat on it. I thanked them for the real sailboat, and they were beaming with the pure joy of giving.

Edward said, "Welcome home, Dad."

Carolyn said, "You are *our* Father's Day present."

Susan got weepy, and so did Sophie, and even Carolyn, usually tough as nails, wiped her eyes. Edward and I, real men, just cleared our throats.

I didn't share with the children my thoughts that their funds to pay for this could soon dry up. Realistically, we'd have the answer to that before anyone wrote out a check, so I wasn't too concerned. The worst scenario was that they'd be disappointed that they couldn't follow through with their gift. And they'd know whom to blame for that. On that subject, I did *not* remind them, "Be very nice to

Grandpa and Grandma." I said, however, "Let's sail to Hilton Head in August."

Susan advised me, "Let's not mention this to my parents today."

"Right. We'll surprise them in August." Susan did not second that. Bottom line here, it was still the Stanhope money that colored what we did and said. Well, hopefully, that would end soon.

Anyway, we got into the Lexus and went out to look at a few boats.

The first two, an Alden forty-seven-footer and a Hinckley forty-three-footer, were in public marinas, and we inspected them from the dock.

The next one, an old forty-one-foot Hinckley, was docked at a private house on Manhasset Bay, and we called ahead, and the owner showed it to us. The fourth boat, a forty-five-foot Morgan 454, was moored at Seawanhaka, and we had a club launch take us out to it, but we didn't go aboard. The fifth, a 44 C&C, was also at Seawanhaka, but the launch pilot said the family had taken it out for the day. He did tell us it was a beautiful boat.

Back at the club, there was a barbecue being set up on the lawn for Father's Day, and I suggested to Susan, out of earshot of the children, "Why don't we take your parents here instead of having dinner at home? Then your father and I can take that Morgan out later and see how it handles."

She reminded me, "We don't want to mention this to him."

"I think he and I can have a very productive man-to-man talk in the middle of the Sound."

She must have misunderstood me, because she said, "John, threatening to drown my father on Father's Day is not nice."

"*What* are you talking about?" I wondered if he was still a good swimmer.

We all sat on the back porch and had Bloody Marys. Susan asked me, "So, did you see anything you liked?"

I replied, "They were all great boats. We need to make some dates to take them out and see how they handle." I added, "And I want to see that C&C that was out."

Edward said, "I liked the Morgan. It reminds me of the one we had."

Carolyn agreed, "That would be big enough for Dad and Mom to take to Europe."

So the Sutters sat there on the porch, sipping Bloody Marys and watching the sunlight sparkle on the bay, and the sailboats at their moorings, their bows pointed at the incoming tide, talking about which yacht we liked best. It really doesn't get much better than this, which was probably what the passengers on the *Titanic* were thinking before they hit the iceberg.

Before we went home to get ready for the Stanhopes and my mother, we stopped at Locust Valley Cemetery.

Susan, Edward, and Carolyn had been here for my father's burial, but maybe not since then, so I checked at the office for the location of the grave of Joseph Sutter, while Susan bought flowers from a vendor who had set up shop near the gate.

We walked on a winding, tree-lined road through the parklike cemetery. The headstones here were no more than a foot high, and not visible among all the plantings, which created the illusion that this was a nature preserve or a botanical garden.

The Stanhope cemetery off in the distance was sectioned off by a hedge and a wrought-iron fence, and the tombstones and mausoleums in there were more grandiose, of course—unless you had been a servant—and there was no mistaking that you were walking among the dead. Here, I felt, you had been returned to nature. This is where I wanted to be—at least five hundred yards from the closest Stanhope. Maybe I could talk Susan into breaking a family tradition—or maybe we'd all be banished to a public cemetery anyway.

There were a number of people in the cemetery on this sunny Father's Day, and I could see bouquets of flowers on many of the graves, as well as small American flags stuck into the earth beside the headstones of those who'd been veterans.

Susan said, "We need to come back here next week with a flag for your father's grave."

I hoped we weren't back here next week for eternity. But maybe I should stop at the sales office just in case.

We found the grave of Joseph Whitman Sutter. Like most of the others, it was a small white granite slab, about a foot high, and except for the engraved lettering, it looked more like a low bench than a gravestone.

In addition to his name and dates of birth and death, it also said, *Husband and Father*, along with the words, *In Our Hearts, You Live Forever.*

To the right of Joseph's grave was an empty plot, no doubt reserved for Harriet.

There was already a bouquet of flowers resting on my father's stone, and I assumed that was from my mother, notwithstanding her aversion to cut flowers—though maybe it was from a secret girlfriend. That would be nice. I had to ask Harriet if she'd been here today.

As I looked at my father's grave, I had mixed memories of this man. He was gentle—too gentle—a loving husband—bordering on uxorious—and a decent, though somewhat distant father. In that respect, he was a product of his generation and his class, so no blame was attached—though I'd have liked him to have been more affectionate toward Emily. As for me, well, we worked together, father and son, and it wasn't easy for either of us. I would have left Perkins, Perkins, Sutter and Reynolds, but he'd really wanted me to stay and carry on the family name in this old, established practice. If that was meant to be his immortality, then I'm sure he was disappointed when the other partners forced me out. He'd been in semi-retirement by then, but after I left he returned full-time, and died one night in his office.

Anyway, my brief criminal defense career was behind me—unless I gave Carmine Caputo or Jack Weinstein a call—and more to the point, Joseph Sutter's whole life was behind him. And basically, it had been a good life, partly because he and my mother had had an oddly good marriage. They never should have had children, but they had sex before birth control pills, and things happen when you've had one cocktail too many. That was probably how half my generation was born.

One time, when Joseph was in an unusually reflective and candid mood, he'd said to me, "I should have been killed in France about ten times—so every day is a gift." Indeed. I felt the same way after three years at sea.

Susan had her arm around me, and Edward and Carolyn stood off to the side, staring quietly at Grandpa's grave.

I placed the bouquet of flowers beside the other bouquet and said to him, "I'm home, Dad."

CHAPTER SIXTY-THREE

My mother arrived first, and I could see that she and her grand-children were honestly fond of one another. Too bad it wasn't Harriet who had the hundred million.

We sat on the patio with a pitcher of sangria, which was as close to a third world drink as I could come up with for Harriet. I said to her, "For every bottle of wine we drink, a rice farmer in Bangladesh gets a Scotch and soda."

Susan and Harriet are on the same page when it comes to organic food, so we snacked on bowls of bat shit or something, and chatted pleasantly.

I was actually starting to like my mother, which was easy to do if I blotted out everything from my birth until about ten minutes ago. But seriously, she was a person who, if nothing else, cared; she cared about the wrong things, or cared about the right things in the wrong way, but at least she was engaged in life.

On that subject, I wondered what she had spoken to Father Hunnings about. And who actually approached whom? Harriet, like Ethel, seemed to care more about the oppressed people of the world, whom she'd never met, and about animals and trees that never hugged *her*, than about the people around her, such as her son and daughter. But there seemed to be a new Harriet taking form—one who cared about her grandchildren, and who also spoke to her priest about her estrangement from her son. What was she up to? Well, maybe with Ethel's death, Harriet had caught a glimpse of her own mortality, and she'd realized that the route to heaven began at home.

Harriet was asking Carolyn and Edward about their jobs, and she seemed genuinely interested, though with Carolyn she had some problems with the criminal justice system. And on the subject of criminals, I wondered if Anthony Bellarosa had come out of hiding to be with his family for Father's Day. Most probably not, but if he had, I'd know about it because, as per my suggestion to Felix Mancuso, the FBI or the NYPD were staking out the Santa Lucia church cemetery in Brooklyn where Frank Bellarosa had been laid to rest.

Anna would be at the cemetery, and as per Anna, so would Frank's other two sons, Frankie and Tommy, and maybe Megan and her kids as well. Although Megan never knew her father-in-law, one of the conditions of marrying into an Italian family was the requirement to visit the graves of every family member who'd died in the last century.

According to Mancuso, Mom's house in Brooklyn and Alhambra Estates were being watched all day. Personally, I didn't think Anthony would come out of his hole, especially today when he knew the FBI would be watching his and his mother's house. But Anthony *might* visit his father's grave. And if Uncle Sal had the same thought, Anthony might be dead in the cemetery before he got arrested.

Anyway, Harriet and Carolyn had exhausted the subject of a bachelor of arts degree in humanities for serial killers, and Harriet asked me, "Why are there armed guards at the gate?"

I explained, "Mr. Nasim thinks the ayatollahs are after him." I concluded, "I blame our government for that."

Harriet knows when I'm being provocative, and she never rises to the bait. More importantly, according to Susan, Harriet didn't know about Anthony Bellarosa living next door; if she had, she'd insist that we share that disturbing fact with Edward and Carolyn. When we were young, Harriet used to say things to me and to Emily like, "Your father has a bad heart, and he may die at any time, so you should be prepared for that." I think, perhaps, she'd gotten hold of a very strange book on how to raise children.

In any case, Edward and Carolyn and everyone else just assumed that the armed guards had been hired by Nasim for his stated reasons;

no one, so far, had thought there might be a second explanation for the security.

Nevertheless, I changed the subject to Ethel's wake and burial, which led me into telling Harriet, "We all went to visit Dad's grave today."

My mother looked at me, but did not reply. Well, this was still a sore subject with her. I'd missed the funeral, and my reason for that—I was at sea and didn't know my father had died—was not cutting it. As far as she was concerned, this was just another example of her son never missing a chance to cause his mother hurt and pain.

I asked her, "Were you there today?" Say no. Please say no.

She replied, "I left a bouquet on the headstone. Didn't you see it?"

"We did. But I know how you feel about cut flowers." So I thought Dad had a girlfriend. "So I wasn't sure that was you."

"Who else would leave flowers on his grave?"

Maybe Lola, the receptionist with the big jugs, or Jackie, the hot office manager. I replied, "I don't know. I'm just pointing out that you don't approve of cut flowers."

"That was all they had for sale."

"Right. Anyway, it's a very beautiful spot, and I'm sorry we didn't coordinate going together."

"Well, I'm glad you went."

Meaning, I'm surprised you bothered. Some people spread sunshine and warmth; Harriet spreads guilt. Did I say I was starting to like my mother?

On the subject of cemeteries and funerals, Carolyn commented that she had watched a few minutes of the Gotti funeral on a TV in the bar where she'd met her friends last night. She commented, "I understand the family, friends, and so-called business associates turning out, but those people on the street—waving and cheering, and making the sign of the cross—that was . . . depressing. And then they interviewed some people who were saying that Gotti was a hero, a man who cared about them, and who gave back to the community—like he was Robin Hood." She asked, rhetorically, "What is wrong with those people?"

Harriet had an answer. "People feel alienated from the traditional

forms of governmental power, and they are looking for heroes who . . ."
And so forth.

Carolyn, a recent convert to law and order, wasn't buying her grandmother's explanation of why the downtrodden citizens of Queens, New
York, gave John Gotti a hero's send-off.

Anyway, this subject was uncomfortably close to the subject of
Frank Bellarosa's life, death, and funeral. I was afraid Harriet was going
to say something like, "John, you went to Frank Bellarosa's funeral,
after Susan killed him. Don't you think that the common person felt
that they had lost a hero?" I'd have to turn that question over to Susan.
Whoops. Slap.

I asked, "Did anyone see the Yankee-Mets game yesterday?"

Well, before we could analyze the game, William and Charlotte arrived, punctually at 4:00 P.M., and fired up the party. Charlotte practically ran to Edward and Carolyn and smothered them with kisses. And
Crazy William shouted to Carolyn, "You get more beautiful every time
I see you, young lady!" Then he boxed playfully with Edward, and he
gave me a manly swat on the ass and shouted, "Hey, big guy! Let's crack
open some brewskis!"

Well, not quite. But William did accept everyone's wishes for a
happy Father's Day with a forced smile. He even mumbled to me,
"Happy Father's Day."

William and Charlotte passed on the sangria and turned down my
offer of martinis, but they each had a glass of white wine, which to them
was like drinking tap water. We sat around the table and made small talk,
which consisted mostly of Charlotte telling everyone what she and William had been doing for the last few days. I was surprised she remembered, and no one gave a rat's ass anyway. William was mostly quiet,
thinking, I'm sure, about our past and future negotiations.

I was actually glad that Harriet was there, because it forced the
Stanhopes to act like normal people.

I watched William closely for any signs that his sneeze had turned
to a cough. You need to be careful at that age. But he seemed all
right—maybe a little pale. Was that an age spot on his forehead or
melanoma?

I thought, too, about William and Charlotte's meeting yesterday with Father Hunnings. The good pastor, I hoped, had told them to mind their own business, and to be generous with their wedding gift, pay for the reception, increase Susan's allowance, and take up skydiving.

Or William had successfully recruited Father Hunnings into the anti-John faction, and William had convinced Hunnings to intercede and counsel Susan about marrying a man who might be a gold digger, and was for sure mentally unbalanced and a wiseass. Hunnings and I never cared for each other, of course, and I hadn't made any points with him the other night, so this would be a labor of love for him— Father Hunnings' Revenge. Well, what you sow, you reap. Maybe I should learn to be nicer to people who could possibly screw me up. Maybe not.

Susan had instructed Sophie to announce dinner no later than 4:45—how much of this could we take?—and Sophie appeared on the patio at the appointed time and said, "Dinner is served."

So we went into the dining room, and Susan seated us—the two dads in the places of honor at opposite heads of the table, so we had to look at each other. Susan sat my mommy to my left, and sat Charlotte to William's right. We'd agreed to put the kids strategically to the left of Grandpa, and across from Grandma Charlotte. Susan sat to my right, and I announced, "The first course is a Polish dish called Trust Fund Salad." Of course, I didn't say that. But I did have a repertoire of money slang that I could work in during dinner to make the kids giggle, such as "green stuff," "gravy," "bread," "dough," and "liquid assets." Well, I don't know about that last one.

Susan proposed a toast to the Greatest Dads in the World, and William somehow thought that included him and said, "Thank you." Susan also said, "And to Joseph."

That brought a tear to my mother's eye. And this is the lady who'd succeeded in crushing any paternal instincts that Joseph Sutter might have had. But as I said, she was becoming a good grandma, and I hoped that this grandmotherly love was reflected in her will. The whales don't need the money.

I took the opportunity to say, "I'm sorry Peter couldn't be here." I inquired of the Stanhopes, "Where is he working now?"

William replied, "He's in Miami, and he handles most of the family business from there."

I didn't want to be the one to point out that there was no family business—only old money that was in the care of professionals—but I wanted some of that money for my wife and children, so I resisted saying, "Peter is a beach bum who couldn't make change for a dollar bill without consulting a financial planner." Instead, I said, "Please pass on my regards to him." And tell him I'll see him in court.

On the subject of the Stanhope fortune, if William had worked for this money, I would not be so covetous of it; people can do whatever they want with the money they've earned. But this was *inherited* money, acquired solely through genetic succession, and not through toil, brains, or even luck. Therefore, it was my belief that Shithead needed to pass it on to his progeny—even to Peter the Useless—just as it had been passed on to William's worthless self. This money should not be used as a weapon or as a Pavlovian doggy treat.

Anyway, dinner proceeded well enough, and as I said, with Harriet there, the Stanhopes were not able to be complete assholes. For instance, they never brought up Susan's deceased husband, who had also been my children's stepfather. If they had brought up his name in front of my children, I know I'd have snapped and said, "Edward and Carolyn thought he was a boring old fart, just like you two," and then dinner would be over.

Ditsy Charlotte, however, did say, "We're very anxious to get home."

We all felt the same way, but I replied, "I can't wait to see your place in Hilton Head."

And they said . . . nothing. But William looked at me down the length of the table, and smoke shot out of his nostrils.

Susan kept the conversation going whenever it sagged, but I didn't like it when she said to the children, "Tell your grandparents about . . ." whatever. I mean, it was a little forced, though to be objective here, Grandma and Grandpa Stanhope weren't eliciting much from their grandchildren, and I had the distinct impression that they'd put Edward and Carolyn on hold until the question of Mom and Dad was resolved.

Susan had asked me to be cordial and not to sulk. I went her one better. I'm very good at theatrical good cheer (bordering on parody), and I really let it fly. I said to William, for instance, "I'm not going to have a happy Father's Day until you let me make you and Charlotte a martini." And at one point I addressed him as "Dad," which made him twitch. Better yet, my expansive table chatter drove them both deeper into themselves.

Harriet, I think, noticed that the Stanhopes did not like her son. She didn't either, but I could tell she didn't like it when it came from them. I was *her* idiot son, not theirs. That's my mom.

I was trying to decide if I should begin a chorus of "Oh, My Papa," but we could do that later in the living room, where there was a piano—Susan and Charlotte both played, and they could do a duet while the rest of us stood with our arms around one another and sang.

Well, dinner was finished by 6:30, which was the way Susan had planned it, and I'm sure no one felt that the time had just flown by.

But we needed the Father's Day cake, so we retired to the living room and sat around the coffee table. Sophie wheeled in the cart and served coffee, tea, and after-dinner cordials.

Sophie also brought in a big cake that she'd made herself and decorated with the inscription, "Happy Father's Day." Unfortunately, it actually read, "Happy Fathers Pay." We got a laugh out of that, and I said to William, "This is *your* cake, Dad."

He didn't think that was so funny.

Susan produced a gift bag with a designer's logo on it and gave it to her father. "Happy Father's Day, Dad."

William smiled, happy to get some of his allowance back. He extracted the card, opened it, and read it to himself without sharing the message, or even saying that it was from all of us. What a swine.

William then took the tie box from the bag, and figured out how to open it. He held up one of the most godawful ties I've ever seen. It was sort of an iridescent pink, and it changed colors like a chameleon as it swung from his fingers.

He actually seemed to like it, and he said, "Thank you, Susan."

Susan said, "It's from all of us, Dad."

I wanted to say, "I got a yacht," but to be nice, I said, "I wish I'd gotten that."

Which caused Harriet to ask, "What did the children get for you, John?"

I already had my answer and replied, "Two plane tickets to Hilton Head," and I smiled at the Stanhopes, who twitched again. Neurological disorder?

Well, the dysfunctional family festivities were nearing an end, unless I asked Susan and Charlotte to play the piano. Carolyn announced that she'd like to catch the 8:25 train so she could get home and do some work before an early morning trial conference. Harriet offered to drive Carolyn to the station, but Carolyn had been traumatized by her last ride with Grandma, and she said that Edward would take her, and see her off. Edward was then going to stop at a friend's house, and he was leaving early in the morning for the airport, so he'd say goodbye now to his grandparents.

We all went out to the forecourt, and everyone hugged and kissed and wished one another a safe trip. This is where the Stanhopes and the Sutters are at their best—goodbye.

Harriet said, "Well, we only seem to get together at weddings and funerals." Then she added, provocatively, "And I hope the next occasion will be John and Susan's wedding."

I hoped the next occasion was William's funeral, but I said, "We're getting married at Seawanhaka before the summer is over."

Harriet seemed genuinely happy, and she smiled at William and Charlotte, who looked like they'd smelled a fart, and asked them, "Isn't that wonderful?"

Well, you could hear their denture glue cracking. Good old Harriet—she came through with a zinger at the end. And it wasn't directed at me for a change.

Anyway, I gave Carolyn a final hug and kiss and said, "I won't be calling you from London anymore."

"I love you, Dad."

William twitched again. Well, if the man had a heart, he'd understand this kind of family love, and he'd take me aside and say, "I bless this marriage, John," then drop dead.

Harriet drove off without killing anyone, then Edward and Carolyn followed in the Lexus.

I looked at William and decided that the time had come. I said to him, "If you're not in a hurry, we can have a drink in my office."

He glanced at his wife, then said to me, "All right."

We went back inside, and Susan said she and her mother were going to help Sophie with the cleanup "while the men relax," which was very old-fashioned and very sweet. It was also bullshit; Charlotte didn't know a dishwasher from a DustBuster. Hopefully, Susan would take this opportunity to work on Mom. As for William and me relaxing over a drink, I thought maybe I should go get the shotgun first.

But I didn't, so I showed him into my office, and I closed the door.

CHAPTER SIXTY-FOUR

I offered William a martini, and he was tempted, but unfortunately declined.

William sat on the couch, and I sat in the armchair.

I had absolutely no intention of opening the discussion, or even engaging in small talk, so I sat there, looking at William as though he'd asked to speak to me.

Finally, he got a little uneasy and asked, "Did you want to discuss something?"

I replied, "I thought *you* wanted to discuss something."

"Well . . . I suppose we need to discuss what we . . . discussed."

"Okay."

He cleared his throat and said, "First, let me say, John, that we— Charlotte and I—don't harbor any personal animosity toward you."

"You told me you and Charlotte didn't care for me."

"Well . . . that's not the issue. The issue is Susan."

"She likes me."

"She *thinks* she does." He reminded me, "We've discussed this, and it really doesn't matter if I like you or you like me. So, let me say that Charlotte and I are convinced that a marriage between you and Susan would lead to unhappiness for both of you, and ultimately another divorce."

I didn't reply.

He continued, "And therefore, to save all of us from future pain and unhappiness, John, I'd like you to reconsider your proposal of marriage."

"I understand that." I reminded him, "You also indicated that you thought my intentions were not completely honorable, and that my love for Susan might be confused with my love for her money."

He cleared his throat again and replied, "I believe I said that might be a subconscious consideration."

"Well, I thought about that, and I've concluded that I love her only for her. And I love my children, and I love us being a family. Did you notice that tonight?"

"I . . . suppose I did. But Edward and Carolyn are adults, and not living here. So, I'm sure you can maintain your relationship with them without remarrying their mother."

"We've been doing that, William, but it's not the same."

He didn't seem to know where to go next, so he cut to the chase and said, "I am prepared to offer you one million dollars, paid in ten equal annual installments, if you will break off this engagement and return to London—or take up legal residence anywhere out of the country."

We looked at each other for a few seconds, then I said, "If your only objection to this marriage is any claim I may have on Susan's money— her allowance and her current assets, and future inheritance—then that could be addressed in a prenuptial agreement."

He didn't reply, so I continued by asking him, "How much did I get when Susan and I divorced? I seem to recall getting nothing. So we can copy that agreement and sign it again." I pointed out, "That would demonstrate to you, I hope, that my intentions are actually honorable."

William realized he'd been sucked into a trap, and he was thinking hard about a way to get out of it. He really is stupid, but when it comes to money, he fires up his remaining brain cells. Finally, he said to me, "The issue is not only money, John. As I said, the issue is Susan's happiness. We do not want to see our daughter as distraught as she was . . . well, the last time."

That was interesting. I'd never really known what Susan was feeling after I'd left. I'd imagined two things—one, she was sad, but had bounced back and was getting on with her life; or two, she was devastated, miserable, guilt-ridden, and considered her life as over. I'm sure it had been all of that, and since we'd reunited, I had a sense of what those years had been like. And now William, her loving father, did not want to see her hurt like that again. Well, if William wasn't such a duplicitous, manipulative, conniving dickhead, I could believe him, and I could feel some empathy for him as a father. But I wasn't going to endow him with any feelings of paternal love, just because he claimed those feelings. Possibly, though, he was also speaking on Charlotte's behalf, and ditsy as she was, I thought she'd probably been very saddened by her daughter's unhappiness.

Finally, I responded, "This may come as a shock to you, William, but Susan and I had a wonderful, loving marriage, and it would have continued that way if"—I really didn't want to get into this, but the time had come—"if she hadn't had an affair with Frank Bellarosa, and then killed him."

William drew a deep breath, then looked at me and said, "Charlotte and I have discussed . . . what happened, and we can only conclude that your marriage was not as wonderful as you thought it was." He pointed out, "If it had been, then what happened would not have happened."

I'd thought the same thing myself, obviously, but looking back on our marriage, even in the most critical light, it had been a very good marriage. Susan herself agreed with that. But even in Paradise, shit happens. Maybe ninety percent of the married people I'd known who'd had affairs were basically happy at home and stayed at home. Now and then, unfortunately, a husband or wife became obsessed with a lover and mistook that for love. And that was a recipe for emotional and marital disaster. Not to mention that sometimes people got shot.

But rather than explain all this to William, even if it was a little bit of his business, I said to him, "Susan has told me, and I'm sure told you and Charlotte at some point in the last ten years, that there was nothing fundamentally wrong between us. What happened was an aberration and not indicative of a deeper problem." I added, "She became . . . sexually obsessed with this man." I pointed out, "Assuming she's learned something from that, it won't happen again."

William seemed uncomfortable at the thought of his daughter being sexually obsessed with a man. He might have thought she was still a virgin. He banished the image of Susan and Frank together and said to me, "I think, perhaps, you are both deluding yourselves, and trying to rewrite some history." He informed me, "You, John, if I may be blunt, have always had a wandering eye."

Well, fuck you, William. True, I flirt—or did—and yes, I like to look at the ladies, but I'd never once had an affair (only that fling with Jenny Alvarez) during my twenty-year marriage. But that was none of his business, so I said, to concede the point and move on, "We've both grown up a lot, and learned not to play with fire."

I thought, perhaps, this had gone over his pointy head, but he understood, and this apparently gave him another thought about how to break up this engagement. He said, "I'm sure you understand that Susan has had a number of suitors over the years."

This was an upper-class, older-generational way of telling me that Susan screwed a bunch of guys. I mean, really, William. Are you going to now make your daughter out to be a slut who I wouldn't want to marry?

Well, yes. He said, "I'm not sure you would accept the fact that Susan has been with a number of men. That would rear its ugly head—it might come up in conversation, or she might get a letter or a phone call from a previous gentleman friend—and that would likely lead to arguments, and eventually . . . well, more unhappiness. For both of you."

I was fairly certain that most fathers didn't advise their prospective son-in-law to reconsider the marriage because their daughter had a sexual history that would fill a small library. But William saw this as a quick and sure way to dampen my ardor for his daughter. Then we could get back to money.

I said to him, "I appreciate your concern and your candor. But you need to understand that Susan and I know that neither of us has been a saint for the last ten years. In fact, William, I *did* have a woman in every port, and even a few inland. Not to mention on board. But my past and her past are totally irrelevant to our future." Unless one of those assholes in Hilton Head called her. "So, we don't need to pursue that." I did add, "I'm frankly surprised that you would raise the subject of your daughter's sex life with me."

That made his face flush, and his eye twitched. He cleared his throat yet again—strep?—and said, "Well, I'm just trying to get you to take off your rose-colored glasses."

William's clichés were old when *he* was a kid. I replied, "I always look before I leap."

"I hope you do. But, I sense that you are planning to go ahead with this marriage, despite my and Charlotte's objections."

I got silly and said, "It is my intention, Mr. Stanhope, to ask you for your daughter's hand in marriage, and also to ask you and Mrs. Stanhope for your blessing."

He may have remembered this from last time around, and sentimental old fool that he was, he was going to get teary-eyed and say, "I am proud and honored to call you my future son-in-law."

Actually, he snorted.

"Sir?"

"*Blessing?*" He snorted again, and said, "We do not and never will bless this marriage."

"Then, I suppose, a generous dowry is out of the question."

"*Dowry?* Surely you jest."

"Well . . . yeah."

While we were on the subject of blessings and the sacrament of Holy Matrimony, I said to him, "I am a little annoyed with you, William, for discussing this with Father Hunnings."

He didn't seem surprised that I knew about that—it's usually part of the deal that when you go to a priest with your problem about a fellow parishioner, the priest then goes to that parishioner. That's the point.

I don't think I'd want to be a priest—all sorts of people unburden themselves to you, and ask for advice, or guidance, or as with William, they're trying to recruit God through you, to do some heavy lifting for them.

In any case, William had given some consideration to my statement, and said, "My going to Father Hunnings should not *annoy* you, John. You should welcome the offer of pastoral counseling."

I replied, "You don't want Susan and me to marry—so what type of pastoral counseling are we actually talking about?"

He explained, "The type that would make you understand that what is best for you is not necessarily best for your bride-to-be."

"I see. Well, I think I've already gotten that opinion from you. So why are you involving Father Hunnings in this?"

"I hope I don't need to explain to you that in our religion, prenuptial counseling is a condition of marriage in the church."

"Well, there is counseling, and then there is counseling. Why do I feel that you've already put the fix in?"

"Are you suggesting that I've . . . influenced Father Hunnings—?"

"I think prejudiced him is a better word. And perhaps offered him an incentive to counsel Susan against this marriage."

"That is an outrageous statement."

"Nevertheless, I stand by it."

"Then I will need to repeat your accusation to Father Hunnings."

"You will if it's not true, but you won't if it is."

He seemed to get his outrage under control and said, "This may be a moot point if we can come to an understanding about this marriage." He reminded me, "I've made you an offer."

"Which I reject."

"All right . . ." William, of course, was not going to fold and leave. He had a few aces up his sleeve—to use a cliché—and he hadn't even played one of them yet. Instead, he reshuffled the cards and redealt. He said, "I'm prepared to increase my offer to you. Two hundred thousand dollars now, and then ten annual payments of one hundred thousand."

Well, front-loading a deal is very good, and usually gets the desired response. Money talks. But I love to negotiate, so I said, "It is my understanding that Susan's annual allowance exceeds even your down payment. So what is my incentive to go back to London with just a percentage of what I would share with Susan if I stayed here?"

Well, now he had to play one ace and explain to me some facts of life in answer to my question. He leaned forward and made eye contact with me, then said slowly, so I'd understand, "John, if you and Susan marry, I can assure you that her allowance will be terminated."

No shit? Wow. I asked him, "You would put your daughter in financial distress?"

He smiled—an evil smile—then inquired, "Are you suggesting, John, that a marriage to you is the same as being in financial distress?"

Good one, William. But I saw that coming and replied, "Well, I'd thought after our marriage, I could fulfill an old dream of becoming a professional surfer . . . but . . . well . . ."

Quite possibly he thought I was making fun of his son, so maybe I should have said, "Professional golfer." Why did I say surfer? Freudian slip? Or did I mean to shove that up his ass?

He looked really annoyed, but did not rise to the bait, as they say, and informed me, "I think you would have to work."

I had some information for him and said, "I have always worked, except for my sabbatical at sea. And I made quite a good living, William, here and in London. Unfortunately, my professional standing here was compromised as a result of what happened ten years ago. I take full responsibility for my actions, but I do need to remind you that your daughter was complicit in the events that led to my leaving my family firm. I have forgiven her, unconditionally, and forgiven myself while I was at it, but it will take me some time to regain my professional standing here in New York and to achieve an income that will provide your daughter with a lifestyle to which she has become accustomed." I added, "And let me remind you, William, that it was you and Charlotte who always insisted that Susan not work, and you induced her not to work by giving her an allowance, and I'm sorry I acquiesced to that. And as a result of her being kept by you all her life, she is not presently employable in any financially rewarding job—and *you* are partly to blame for that, so *you* need to take some responsibility."

William apparently didn't want to be confused or influenced by inconvenient facts, so he replied simply, "I say again, if she marries you, her allowance is terminated."

"Fine. Susan and I discussed this possibility, and it does not affect our decision to marry."

This time he smirked, and said, "Susan may want to rethink that."

Fuck you. I said, "*You* may want to rethink being so petty, manipulative, and spiteful."

"I will not be spoken to in that manner."

"William, every word of that is true."

He looked like he was about to take his cards and leave, but he had another ace to play, and he said, "Also, if you marry, I will remove Susan as a beneficiary of my and Charlotte's wills."

Now we're talking real money. I mean, both of them dying *and* leaving Susan close to fifty million were key ingredients to a blissful marriage. Especially him dying. I let him know, "If you do that, I will tie up the estate in litigation for at least ten years." I added, "Peter may find that inconvenient."

He was really hot now, and his face reddened again. High blood pressure?

My future father-in-law said to me, "That is the most outrageous thing you have ever said."

"No it's not. Come on. Think."

"You . . ." He stood, and I waited for him to topple over, but he didn't, so I, too, stood and said, "You've insulted me with your offer to buy me. I am not for sale." I informed him, "I don't give a damn about your money, and neither does Susan. And you don't give a damn about your daughter. This is about me and you, and not her happiness. You know damned well that we are happy to be together again, and our children are happy for us. You, William, are very unhappy that I'm back in your life, and you'd rather lose your daughter than gain a son-in-law who doesn't put up with your bullshit. So, sir, you've made your decision, and Susan and I have made ours."

He didn't seem to react much to my harangue—he just stood there and looked off into space. But then he turned to me and said, "We will see what Susan's decision is."

"Indeed, we will. But you and your wife will leave this house now and make an appointment to speak to your daughter another time." I went to the door, opened it, and said, "Good evening." I added, "Happy Father's Day."

He stepped quickly out the door, then stopped, turned, and in a quiet voice said, "Think, too, of your children."

That was his last ace, and he'd played it, so I had to reply, "Have your trust attorney call me on that."

He went off to find Charlotte, who was definitely not in the kitchen scrubbing pots.

I closed the door, and a few minutes later I heard Susan, Charlotte, and William speaking softly in the foyer. Then the front door opened and closed.

A few seconds later, the office door opened and Susan stepped inside. She said, "Should I even ask how it went?"

I looked at her, and I really wanted to tell her that her father was everything I'd always said he was, and more, but that was not really the issue. I said to her, "Well, some good news and some bad news."

"What is the good news?"

"The good news is that your father offered me one million two hundred thousand dollars to go back to London."

"What? He did *what*?"

"I just told you."

She stood there, stunned, I think. Then she looked at me and asked, "What did you tell—? Well, I don't have to ask that."

"Of course not. I told him no. I want two million. And that's the bad news. He won't budge from a million two hundred thousand."

She realized I was being facetious, though she wasn't sure if this was so funny.

She sat on the couch and stared into space, then finally said, "That is outrageous. That is . . . despicable."

"I thought so, too. I mean, you're worth a quarter million a year— oh, that's the other bad news. If you marry me, you're cut off."

She looked at me, nodded, and said, "I don't care."

"It doesn't matter if you do or don't. You've been a bad girl, and your allowance is cut off. Or will be. Also your inheritance."

Finally, she started to absorb all of this and said to me, "Couldn't you reason with him?"

"No." I asked her, "Do you want a drink?"

"No."

"Well, I do." I poured myself some brandy, and Susan changed her mind, so I made it two.

We didn't have anything to toast, so we sipped.

Finally, she said to me, "My mother was . . . well, telling me why I shouldn't marry you."

"Anything good?"

She forced a smile and said, "She thinks you're not in a position to keep me in the style to which I've become accustomed."

"Did you tell her I was an animal in bed?"

She smiled for real and replied, "I did tell her we've always had a fulfilling sex life."

"Is she jealous?"

"Maybe." Susan also revealed, "She hinted that you drink too much."

We both got a good laugh out of that. I observed, "I only wish I could go one-for-one with either of them."

I sat next to Susan on the couch, and we held hands and didn't speak for a while. Then she said, "My father seemed very angry."

"I was very cordial to him, even after he insulted me with a bribe. I really was, Susan."

"I believe you."

"But at the end, I had to threaten him with litigation if he cut you out of their wills." I added, "The allowance is gone, and even if I had a legal theory to proceed on that, I don't feel I would be morally justified to pursue it. And I hope you agree."

"I agree." She reminded me, "I am now free."

"Right." I suggested, "You might want to cut back on your personal trainer."

"Don't make fun of me."

"Sorry." So now I had to decide if I should mention William's parting shot—the children. But I'd let him do that; Susan needed to hear this from her father. I said to Susan, "I believe he wants to speak to you soon."

She nodded. "We will speak tomorrow morning. Here. On their way to the airport."

"Fine. I'll make myself scarce."

"Thank you." She looked at me and asked, "Did he mention the children?"

"I believe he will mention that to you tomorrow."

She nodded.

Susan did not look happy for someone who'd just gotten her freedom, and to be honest, I couldn't blame her. Freedom is scary.

So, to wrap this up, I said, "Look, if it comes down to me or—"

"John, shut the fuck up."

That took me completely by surprise. Where did she learn to swear like that? It sounded funny with her patrician accent. I asked, "Could you clarify that?"

"Sorry." She laughed. Then she put her head in her hands and tears ran down her cheeks. She said, "Damn it."

I put my arm around her and squeezed her tight. I said, "We will be fine, Susan." I reminded her, "We knew where this was headed."

She wiped her face with her hands and said, "You knew. I didn't believe it."

I gave her my handkerchief and suggested, "You have to be honest with yourself. You *knew*."

She nodded. "Those . . . I just try so hard with them. How can they be so . . . heartless?"

I didn't reply.

She continued, "It's not the money. Really, it's not. I just don't understand how they can be so . . . can't they see how happy we are together?"

I really didn't want to interfere with this cathartic moment, but I had to say, "*That* is what they don't like." I reminded her, "Your father has never liked me, and, to be honest, the feeling is mutual. But unlike me, he's more driven by hate than by love. And there is nothing we can do about that."

She nodded, wiped her eyes with my handkerchief, took a deep breath, and said, "All right. I'll speak to him tomorrow. And I won't give in to him. There's nothing more he can threaten me with . . . except the children's money. So, we need to speak to the children."

"Right."

She asked me, "Do you think I should speak to Peter?"

"I would advise you not to. But that's your decision." I'm going to sue the bastard if I have to.

"All right . . ." She turned and put her head down on the arm of the sofa, and put her feet in my lap. I took off her shoes, and she wiggled her toes. She asked me, "Did you have a good Father's Day, aside from blowing a million-dollar deal?"

"I did. I really did. I'm starting to like my mother."

"Good. She loves you in her own way."

"She certainly does." I suggested, "Maybe we should rethink the yacht."

"I guess we should."

"How about a rowboat?"

"Can't afford it." She stretched, yawned, and said, "This has been an exhausting day. But you know what? I feel like someone has taken a thousand-pound weight off my back."

"Actually, you're about a quarter million dollars a year lighter."

She stayed quiet a moment, then asked, "Were you . . . surprised when he offered you money?"

"To tell you the whole truth, he offered that to me the first night they were here."

"He did? Why didn't you tell me?"

"Well, why ruin the week?"

"You need to tell me everything in a timely manner."

"Can we change the subject?"

"How about sex?"

With that opening, I should have told her that her father tried to save me from marrying a loose woman, who happened to be his daughter. But there are rules, spoken and unspoken, and that would really cross the line and serve no purpose other than making Susan think even less of her father than she already did. And yet I despised him so much, I actually thought about telling her. But that would raise other issues that didn't need to be part of our future.

"John? Hello? Sex?"

"Didn't we do it this morning?"

"No, you had sex with a seaman's wife."

"Right."

I stood, locked the door, and took off my blazer.

Susan slipped off her panties, hiked up her skirt, and whispered, "Hurry, before my father comes home."

So, recalling those half-clothed quickies we used to have in Stanhope Hall before we were married, I stripped from the waist down and lay on top of her, and she rested her legs on my shoulders.

One of the joys of sex with Susan Stanhope was knowing that I was also figuratively fucking her father. But this time, it was just Susan and me in the room, and it was great.

CHAPTER SIXTY-FIVE

Susan and I had fallen asleep on the couch, and I was awakened by the ringing phone. It was dark outside, and the only light in the office was from a floor lamp that had been on when William and I had our talk.

I got up and made my way to the desk. The Caller ID showed Restricted, and the desk clock showed 9:32, though it seemed later.

I picked up the phone and said, "Sutter."

Mr. Mancuso said, "Good evening, Mr. Sutter."

I could hear noise in the background, men and women talking, but I had the feeling he wasn't in his office or at home.

He said, "I have some news for you."

I thought maybe they'd found Anthony eating spaghetti at Mom's, and I said, "Good news, I hope."

"News."

I glanced back at Susan, who was stirring. I said to Mancuso, "Let me get Susan." I put the phone on hold and said to her, "It's Mancuso."

She sat up, and I put the phone on speaker, then said to Mr. Mancuso, "We're here."

He said, "Good evening, Mrs. Sutter."

She stood beside me and replied, "Good evening."

He began by saying, "Just to let you know, Anthony Bellarosa did not show himself at his father's grave, but his wife and kids did, and so did the rest of the family, including Anthony's brothers and their wives and kids. They all had dinner at Anna's house."

Poor Megan. I knew, of course, by the tone of his voice that there was more news.

Mancuso continued, "At about 7:45 this evening, Salvatore D'Alessio was having dinner in a restaurant with his wife, Marie, and his two sons, who had flown in from Florida for Father's Day."

Well, I knew where this was going. I glanced at Susan, and she, too, knew what Mr. Mancuso was going to tell us.

He continued, "It is the D'Alessios' habit, apparently, to dine at this restaurant, Giovanni's, in the Williamsburg section of Brooklyn, near their house." He added, "They always go there on Father's Day."

I observed, "That is not a good habit."

"No," he agreed. He did add, however, "It's a nice old family restaurant. In fact, I'm there now."

I didn't ask him why he was there because I knew why, and I was fairly certain he wasn't having dinner with the D'Alessios.

Mr. Mancuso returned to his subject and said, "So, at about 7:45, as the D'Alessios were having dessert, two men entered the crowded restaurant wearing topcoats, and they walked directly to the D'Alessio table. According to several witnesses, both men raised sawed-off double-barreled shotguns from under their coats, and one of them said, 'Happy Father's Day, Sally,' then fired a single shot at point-blank range into Salvatore D'Alessio's face."

Susan took a step backwards, as though she'd been hit with the blast, and she slumped onto the couch.

I said, "Hold on." I put the phone on hold and asked her, "Are you all right?"

She nodded.

I slipped on my shorts and pants, then took the phone off speaker, sat in the chair, and picked up the receiver. I said to Mancuso, "It's just me now."

"All right . . . so that's the news."

I took a deep breath, then said, "Well . . . I guess I owe you some money."

"I never got around to placing that bet for you, Mr. Sutter."

"Okay . . ." I sat there and glanced again at Susan, who didn't seem to notice or mind that she couldn't hear Mancuso. I asked him, "Anyone else hurt?"

"No. It was professional." He suggested, "You can see it on the news."

I asked, "Can you give me a preview? Or something I won't see on the news?"

"All right . . ." Mr. Mancuso gave me his professional opinion of the hit. "So, it is Sunday. Father's Day. And Salvatore D'Alessio is out to dinner with his family. And D'Alessio is very much old-school, and he thinks there are still some rules that won't be broken. But he's not stupid—well, actually, he is, but anyway, assuming it was D'Alessio who tried to have Frank Bellarosa killed at Giulio's in the presence of Frank's wife and two upstanding citizens, then D'Alessio understands that he himself has broken the rules. And he knows that Anthony does not play by many rules anyway. So, D'Alessio does have one bodyguard with him outside of Giovanni's, and D'Alessio is wearing a Kevlar vest under his Big and Tall Man suit, and he's also carrying a .38 caliber Smith & Wesson, and he's got his family with him so he's not expecting trouble, but he's prepared for it."

I commented, "Well, he should have expected it and been better prepared."

"Correct. The bodyguard, who Marie D'Alessio described to us as their driver—though they walked to the restaurant—took a longer walk, and seems to have disappeared. As for the Kevlar vest, apparently the two shooters knew or anticipated this, so the first blast was aimed at D'Alessio's face." He reminisced, "Frank Bellarosa got very lucky that night, but Mr. D'Alessio's assailants were not going to repeat the mistake of Mr. Bellarosa's assailants."

"No. That would be stupid," I agreed.

Mr. Mancuso continued, "Well, that single blast to D'Alessio's face knocked him onto the floor, whereupon one more shot was fired into his head, though he was undoubtedly already fatally wounded, according to what the medical examiner is telling me." He added, "That second shot was . . . well, a personal message." He explained, "There is no undertaker who could rebuild that head and face for an open casket."

Too much information.

Mr. Mancuso continued, "As these two shots were fired, the second assailant pointed a shotgun at Marie D'Alessio's head and shouted, 'Nobody move or she dies,' so the two sons sat there, frozen, according to witnesses, but Marie was screaming. Then the two men left and got into a waiting car." He concluded, "From the time the two men walked in to the time they walked out was about fifteen seconds." He added, "Marie, when she looked at her husband, fainted. One of the sons threw up, and the other son became hysterical." He said, as if to himself, "Happy Father's Day."

I nodded. Well, that certainly put my stressful day with Harriet and the Stanhopes into perspective.

I tried to picture this scene of a restaurant on Father's Day, filled with families, and two men coming through the door, and before anyone even knows what's happening, one of them blows Salvatore D'Alessio's head off, after wishing him a happy Father's Day. What was the D'Alessio family doing in that few seconds before Sal's head and their world exploded? Talking? Laughing? Passing the pastry? Did Salvatore D'Alessio know, in that second before the blast, that it was over for him?

I remembered how fast it had happened in front of Giulio's—actually, I didn't realize *what* was happening until it was almost over. With no point of reference in my life, my brain did not comprehend what my eyes were seeing. In fact, it didn't even register when Vinnie's face disappeared in a cloud of blood, brains—

"Mr. Sutter?"

"Yes . . ."

"I said, you may not want Mrs. Sutter to see this on TV."

I glanced at Susan, who was curled up on the couch, staring off into space. I replied, "Right."

"And perhaps you should not have any of the tabloids lying around tomorrow."

"Right . . . well, I guess that answers the question of whether or not Anthony Bellarosa is alive."

"Correct. I think we should assume that he ordered the hit." He pointed out, "It seems like the kind of message he would want to send to his uncle's colleagues. Meaning, this is what happened to my father in front of my mother."

"Right . . . well, I wouldn't have given Anthony that much credit for showmanship, or symbolic acts, but maybe he does have a little of his father in him." So maybe he could appreciate my act of slashing his painting; his father would have.

Mr. Mancuso stayed silent a moment, then said, "I, too, was surprised at how the hit went down. I had expected something . . . quieter. A disappearance, so as not to draw the full attention of the law, or too much public attention. Or, if it was going to be violent, then I didn't think Anthony would make it so obvious that he was behind it." He added, "He might as well have had the killer say, 'Happy Father's Day, Uncle Sal.'" He speculated, "This hit may cause him some problems. And that brings us to another subject." I didn't respond, so he went on, "It is possible, as we've discussed, that Anthony will now turn his attention to Mrs. Sutter, and possibly to you."

I glanced again at Susan, who was now looking at me. She needed to hear this, so I hit the speaker button, replaced the receiver, and said to Mancuso, "Susan is back."

He said to us, "Based on the usual modus operandi, I'm fairly certain that Anthony Bellarosa is, and has been, out of town for this last week, and he can document this when we ask him where he was on the night of his uncle's murder. In any case, wherever he is, my guess is that he will stay put for another week or so, or at least until he's certain that he's coming home as the undisputed boss." He concluded, "Probably he'll wait until after his uncle's funeral, though he may actually show up for that."

I pointed out, "Well, he should if he was the cause of the funeral."

He allowed himself a small chuckle, but Susan didn't smile.

He went back to the more immediate subject and informed us, "Anthony's absence, however, does not preclude him from taking care of business here, as Mr. D'Alessio's murder obviously demonstrates. In fact, if there is any more such business, it may be done while Anthony Bellarosa is still out of town."

Susan thought about that, then asked, "So what do you suggest we do?"

"I suggest taking extra precautions, including hiring a personal bodyguard."

I pointed out, "That didn't help Uncle Sal."

"No, it didn't. But hopefully your bodyguard will not be working for the other team as D'Alessio's was. Also, I'd advise you both to stay within your security zone at Stanhope Hall as much as possible. Meanwhile, I'm asking the county police to see if they can assign you a twenty-four-hour protection detail. Also, I've asked if the Bureau can assign one or two agents to you, but quite frankly, we're shorthanded since 9/11."

Susan looked at me, then asked Mancuso, "How long are we supposed to live like this?"

He replied, "I wish I could tell you." He tried out some good news and said, "Bellarosa will surface soon, or we will find him. And when that happens, the NYPD will take him in for questioning regarding the murder of Salvatore D'Alessio, and the FBI will assist if requested. The county police will also speak to him about the threats he's made against both of you. With any luck, as I've said, we can make an arrest. At the least, we can make sure he's on notice and under constant surveillance." He reminded us, "The problem now is that he's missing. And missing people, if they're not dead, are more dangerous than people who are present and accounted for."

Susan had believed that it was good that Anthony Bellarosa was missing, but now she understood the problem with that. She asked, "Why can't you find him?"

Mr. Mancuso, who'd probably answered this question many times, replied, "It's a big country, and a big world." He added, "He has the resources to remain missing indefinitely." He reminded us, "He's not a fugitive from the law, so we're assuming that he'll just appear when he thinks it's best for him to do so."

What Felix Mancuso said sounded logical, of course, and certainly if I were Anthony Bellarosa, I'd be more worried about my *paesanos* and the law than thinking about killing any more people—especially people who, for all he knew, were being protected by the police and the FBI. And yet . . . I knew, deep inside, that this had more to do with revenge than business, and that the revenge murder of Salvatore D'Alessio was just the first of two. Maybe three.

I had a thought, and I said to Mancuso, "I have business in London . . ." I glanced at Susan, who was nodding—"so, I'm thinking that this might be a good time for me and Mrs. Sutter to take a week or so in London, and then maybe a week or two on the Continent." I added, "In other words, we, too, should go missing."

He replied without hesitation, "That would be a very good idea at this time—until the situation here becomes more clear." He added, "If you stay in touch with us, we can keep you up to date on developments."

"We'll certainly be interested in news from home. And please don't hesitate to call us the moment Sally Da-da's friends whack Anthony."

Mr. Mancuso never responded well to my murderous remarks regarding Anthony Bellarosa—he was a professional—but he did say, "We're hoping to locate him first."

"I hope Uncle Sal's friends locate him first."

He ignored that and asked me, "When do you plan on leaving?"

I looked at Susan, and she said, "Tuesday is fine with me."

Mancuso agreed, "That would be good." He reminded us, "Keep the particulars of your itinerary to yourselves."

"We will."

"And enjoy yourselves. You need a break."

Mr. Mancuso seemed happy that we were getting out of his bailiwick. Again, he liked us, and he would be personally saddened if we got whacked. And professionally, of course, he would be more than saddened; he would be in the same embarrassing situation he'd been in when Susan whacked his star witness. He certainly didn't need that aggravation again.

He assured us, "I'm confident that we will catch some breaks while you're gone, and that Anthony Bellarosa will be either in jail, under tight surveillance, killed by his own people, or frightened into permanent retirement and relocated to Florida or Vegas, where many of his colleagues wind up when they need to give up the business."

I wasn't so sure about Anthony retiring and moving away, but I did agree with Felix Mancuso that Anthony's career was at a crossroads. Not my problem, as long as none of those roads led back to Grace Lane.

I thought, too, of Anthony in hiding, or in exile, and I wondered if he had normal human feelings of missing his family, and not know-ing when or if he'd see them again. On the other hand, this was the life he'd chosen. And then, of course, I thought about my own exile. That was not the life I'd chosen—well, maybe it was—but it wasn't my first choice.

Anyway, Anthony Bellarosa didn't even know where London was, and he thought Paris was the name of a Vegas hotel. So this was a good idea, and we'd have fun while Anthony was trying to figure out if he was the boss, or if he was in trouble.

I said to Mr. Mancuso, "We'll call you Tuesday from the airport."

"Please do."

I asked him, "Other than being called to the scene of a murder, did you have a good Father's Day?"

"I did, thank you. And how about you?"

"I had a wonderful day with my children, and my fiancée." I added, "My mother and future in-laws were here, too." I informed him, "Every-one will be out of here by tomorrow morning."

"That's good." He asked us, "Are you being . . . cautious?"

"We are," I assured him. "However, Susan and I did go to Giulio's for coffee and pastry on Thursday."

"Did you? Well . . . that was probably a good thing."

"It was, actually."

He stayed quiet a moment, then said to me, or really to us, "I've often wondered . . . what would have been different in all our lives if you hadn't stopped him from bleeding to death."

"Well . . . you can be sure I've wondered about that myself a few times." I glanced at Susan, who wasn't looking at me, and said, "But I would never have let him bleed to death."

"I know that. And neither would I. But I mean, if you couldn't have saved his life, and he'd died then and there . . . well, we wouldn't be having this conversation."

"We would not." And Susan wouldn't have killed Frank on Felix Mancuso's watch, and I wouldn't have divorced her and been in self-exile for ten years, and Anthony would not now be a threat to our lives. But who knows if something worse might have happened in these last ten years? Like me running off with Beryl Carlisle. I said to Felix Mancuso, but also for Susan, "Well, if we believe in a divine plan, maybe this is going to have a better ending than if Frank Bellarosa had lost one more pint of blood on the floor in Giulio's restaurant."

He stayed quiet a moment, then said to me, and to Susan, "I've thought the same thing. I really believe that . . . well, that there is a purpose to all this, and that part of that purpose is to test us, and to impart some wisdom to us, and to show us what is important, and to make us better people."

Susan said, "I believe that. And I believe that we have a guardian angel who will watch over us."

Well, then, I thought, why bother to go to London? But to be on the team, I said, "Me, too."

Mr. Mancuso said, "Someone here needs to speak to me. Have a good trip, and don't hesitate to call me anytime."

"Thank you," I replied, "and have a good evening."

"Well . . ."

"Right. Then have a good day tomorrow."

"You, too."

Susan said, "And thank you."

I hung up, and we looked at each other.

Finally, Susan said, "I, too, wonder how our lives would have been if I hadn't—"

"Stop. We will never—and I mean *never*—discuss that again."

Susan nodded. "All right. But maybe there really is a purpose to what happened."

"Maybe." And I was sure we didn't have long to find out what it was.

CHAPTER SIXTY-SIX

I suggested to Susan that we go up to the family room and watch a little of *The Godfather, Part IV: Anthony Whacks Uncle Sal.*

She didn't think that was either funny or something she wanted to do.

Susan picked up the phone and dialed.

I asked, "Who are you calling?"

"Edward."

"Why? Oh, okay." A mother's instinct to protect her children is stronger than a man's instinct to watch television.

Edward answered his cell phone for a change, and Susan said to him, "Sweetheart, I'd like you to come home now."

He said something, and she replied, "You have an early morning flight, darling, and your father and I would like to spend a little time with you. Yes, thank you."

She hung up and said to me, "Fifteen minutes."

I nodded. Well, if left to his own devices, Edward would roll in at 3:00 A.M., and we'd be up all night with the shotgun waiting for him. I said to Susan, "At least he'll be out of here tomorrow, and we'll be in London Tuesday."

She asked me, "John, do you think there is any danger to the children? I won't go to London if—"

"They're in no danger." I thought about Anthony's nice, clean hit at Giovanni's Ristorante, and I also recalled what Anthony himself said to me on his front lawn, and I assured her, "Women and children get a pass . . . well, children anyway." I further noted, "Carolyn is a district attorney, and that makes her virtually untouchable."

Susan nodded, "All right . . . then I'm looking forward to London."

"And then Paris."

"Good. I haven't been out of the country since . . . the time we went to Rome."

Cheap boyfriends. Or provincial bumpkins. Meanwhile, I've been out of the country ten years, and I would have liked to stay around here awhile—but back to London.

She asked, "Am I going to enjoy London with you?"

"I hope so. I want to show you the Imperial War Museum."

"I can't wait." She asked me, "Will there be ladies calling and knocking on your door in London?"

"Ladies? No. Of course not. But maybe we should stay in a hotel."

She reminded me, "We can't afford it."

Another new reality.

So we sat in the office and talked a little about what Mancuso had said, and about how we really saw this situation. Susan was optimistic, and I, too, thought that maybe Anthony Bellarosa had more problems with his *paesanos* than we had with Anthony. But I wasn't betting my life, or hers, on that.

We heard Edward pull up, and Susan went to the door and opened it before he unlocked it.

The three of us went up to the family room, and Sophie brought us the leftover cake, then wished us good night.

So we chatted about the day, and about sailboats, and about Susan and me visiting him in Los Angeles, and maybe bringing Grandma Harriet along. Hopefully, she'd like L.A. and stay there. We also told him that we were going to London for a few days, and then someplace else. Edward didn't need to know where until we got there, and maybe not even then. He also didn't need to know right now about the Mafia hit in Brooklyn. If he heard about this when he was in L.A., he'd probably put two and two together and realize why we were going to Europe on short notice. Or Carolyn would do the addition for him.

Apropos of nothing that we were discussing, Edward asked, "How did it go with Grandma and Grandpa after we left?"

I let Susan reply, and she said truthfully, "Not too well. But we'll speak to them again tomorrow."

He asked, "Why don't they want you to get married?"

My turn, so I said, "They don't like me."

He pointed out, "You're not marrying *them*."

"Good point," I agreed, "but they see this in a larger context."

Edward cut through the bullshit, and said, "It's all about their money."

"Unfortunately," I admitted, "it is about their money. But not anymore."

Susan said to her son, "We—all of us—may experience some financial loss as a result of this marriage."

"I know that."

I said to him, "Your mother and I don't care about us, but we do care about you and Carolyn."

He informed us, "I spoke to Carolyn about it. We don't care either."

Susan and I looked at each other, and she said to Edward, "Let's see what they say tomorrow." She reminded him, "You have an early flight."

He stood and said, "See you in the morning." Then he asked, "How did they get like that?"

Well, assholes are born, not made.

Susan replied, "I don't know, but I hope it's not genetic."

We all got a laugh out of that, and Edward said good night.

Susan said to me, "I really don't like discussing this with the children."

"They're not children."

"They are *our* children, John. And I don't like that my parents are making them into pawns."

That was the maternal instinct again. She was worried about what would become of Edward and Carolyn if they were thrown out into the cold cruel world and told to fend for themselves, like the other ninety-nine percent of humanity.

I didn't share Susan's concerns—they'd be fine, and *they* knew they'd be fine, and I believed we raised them to take care of themselves—but I did understand her thinking, which was, "Why should they live without money if millions are available to them?"

In effect, there was a choice here that most people don't have—millions, or monthly paychecks?

Well, I'd pick the millions—especially if I got the money because William Stanhope died—but I damn sure wouldn't kiss anyone's living ass for the money. However, when it's about your children, you do smooch a little butt.

Bottom line here was that I was standing between three of the Stanhopes and the Stanhope millions.

But, yes, we'd see what happened tomorrow. I knew what William was going to say to Susan, but I wasn't absolutely sure what Susan was going to say to William—or what she was going to say to me afterwards.

Susan said, "I'm ready for bed."

"I'm not."

"You're not going to watch the news, are you?"

"I am."

"Why do you want to see that, John?"

"Everyone enjoys seeing the coverage of a Mafia hit." I actually hadn't seen a real mob hit on TV since Sally Tries to Whack Frank, in which I had a supporting role.

Susan announced, "I'm going to bed."

"Good night."

She gave me a quick kiss and left.

It was 11:00 P.M., so I turned on the TV, and found the local cable channel where I'd seen Jenny Alvarez.

And sure enough, there she was, saying, "Our top story tonight is the brazen gangland murder of Salvatore D'Alessio"—a photograph of a Neanderthal came on the screen—"a reputed capo in one of New York's organized crime families—"

The caveman's face was replaced by the lighted exterior of Giovanni's Ristorante, which was not a bad-looking place. Mancuso seemed to like it, so maybe Susan and I should take Carolyn there. The owner was no doubt upset that his patrons had to witness a man's head being blown off at dinner, and upset, too, that everyone had left before he could present them with a bill. But he must know that he would make this up in the weeks ahead. New Yorkers love to go to a restaurant where a mob hit has gone down. Look at Giulio's, for instance, or Sparks, where Paul Castellano had been whacked by Gotti. Still going strong. Free publicity is better than paid advertising, not to mention the restaurant achieving mythic status, and getting an extra bullet or two in the Italian Restaurant Guide.

Well, I'm being silly, so I turned my attention back to the television. There was a lot of police activity out front, and Jenny's voice was saying, ". . . here at this neighborhood Italian restaurant in the Williamsburg section of Brooklyn. Salvatore D'Alessio was once the underboss to the infamous Frank Bellarosa, who was murdered ten years ago at his palatial Long Island mansion by a woman who was reputed to be his mistress."

Reputed? Why didn't Jenny say Susan's name and show a picture of her? Well, maybe they were afraid of a lawsuit. Right. Susan was Frank Bellarosa's *killer*, but only his *reputed* mistress. I might even represent Susan if Jenny mentioned her by name as Frank's mistress or girlfriend. That would be interesting—*Sutter v. Cable News 8, Jenny Alvarez, et al.* John Sutter for the plaintiff. Is it true, Mr. Sutter, that you were screwing Ms. Alvarez, and she dumped you? No, sir, we shook hands and parted as friends.

Oh what tangled webs we weave, when we stick it in and then we leave.

Anyway, Jenny was saying, "Bellarosa himself had been the target of an attempted mob hit, ten years ago, and it is believed that tonight's victim, Salvatore D'Alessio, had been behind that botched attempt on Bellarosa's life. And now, Salvatore D'Alessio—known in the underworld as Sally Da-da—has been murdered, and sources close to the investigation are speculating that the man behind this mob hit is Frank Bellarosa's son, Tony—"

"Anthony! Don't say Tony."

There didn't seem to be a photograph of Anthony available, and Jenny went on a bit as some old footage of Frank Bellarosa came on the screen—Frank on the courthouse steps on the day I'd gotten him sprung on bail—and I actually caught a glimpse of myself. Bad tie.

And at that moment, unfortunately, Susan walked into the family room, looked at Frank Bellarosa on the TV screen, froze, then turned and left without a word.

Well, it *was* a little jarring to see Frank on television, looking good, smoking a cigar, and joking with the press. He hadn't looked as lively the last time I saw him, in his coffin.

I should have shut off the TV and gone to bed, but this was important—not to mention entertaining.

Jenny was now saying, "So, if these rumors are true, then it appears that, after ten years, some chickens have come home to roost among the organized crime families of New York."

Also, don't forget—what you sow, you reap.

She continued, "According to reliable sources in law enforcement, Tony Bellarosa has been missing from his home, his place of business, and his usual haunts for about a week, and he did not attend the Gotti funeral yesterday."

Then she went on about the apparent power struggle that was developing as a result of the vacuum created by Mr. Gotti's death, and so forth, which brought her back to Anthony and Uncle Sal, then to Anthony's father, Frank, and then . . . there I was again, standing next to Frank on the steps of the courthouse. Jenny continued her off-screen reporting, and there was no soundtrack for the film, but I was answering a question that had been asked to me by none other than a younger Jenny Alvarez. I hadn't aged a day. At that point, Jenny and I were not even friends—in fact, she'd been a ballbuster on the courthouse steps, and I'd taken an immediate dislike to her, and her to me. And then . . . well, hate turned to lust, as it often does.

Jenny was back on the screen, and this was another opportunity for her to mention me by name as the handsome and brilliant attorney for the dead don, whom we'd just seen on the screen. But she wasn't giving me an on-air mention—just that few seconds of old news footage. Surely she remembered that night at the Plaza. Instead, she reported, "Another interesting angle to this story is that Tony Bellarosa is the *nephew* of the victim, Salvatore D'Alessio. Bellarosa's mother and D'Alessio's wife—now his widow—are sisters. So, if these rumors about Tony Bellarosa's involvement in this gangland slaying are true, then this gives us a glimpse into the ruthless—" and so forth.

Well, I don't know about ruthless. To be honest, the only difference between me and Anthony in regard to whacking an annoying relative was that Anthony knew who to call to have it done while he was out of town. I wish I knew who to call when I was in London—1–800-MOBCLIP? Just kidding.

Jenny finished her reporting and her commentary, then said to the anchor, "Back to you, Chuck."

A young anchorman came on the screen, and in what was supposed to be a spontaneous question to his reporter, he asked, "Jenny, what are your sources saying about the motive for this killing?"

Jenny replied, as scripted, "Sources tell me that if Tony Bellarosa was behind this hit, then the obvious motive is revenge for what happened ten years ago when his father, mother, and another couple—"

And she still didn't mention me by name. Was she protecting me, or torturing me?

Chuck commented on ten years being a long time to wait for revenge, and Jenny explained to him and her viewers about patience in the world of La Cosa Nostra, long memories, and vendetta.

Chuck inquired, "So, do you think this killing will lead to more killings?"

Jenny replied, "It's quite possible."

I thought so, too.

Well, it seemed to me that Anthony—formerly Tony—had gotten himself in a pickle—or, worse, a jar of hot pepperoni. I mean, did that idiot—that *mamaluca*—think that no one was going to connect him to the murder of his uncle Sal? Well, obviously, that's what he *thought* he wanted, as his message to the mob that he'd carried out a family vendetta—but I'm sure he hadn't wanted to fire up the media and the forces of law and order. Unlike his father, Anthony did not think ahead. Anna said it best. "You don't *think*, Tony. Your father knew how to *think*." *Stonato*. Moms know.

And speaking of Anna, how was Anthony going to explain to Mom about having Uncle Sal clipped? Well, for one thing, Anna wouldn't believe the lies that the police and the news media were making up about her son. She hadn't even believed that her husband, the martyred St. Frank, had been involved with organized crime. And the same denial applied to her brother-in-law, Sal, and so forth.

Of course, Anna knew all this was true, but she could never admit any of this to herself, or she'd lose her jolly disposition, and her sanity. Still, Salvatore D'Alessio's funeral was going to be a tense family affair, especially if Anthony showed up, and Marie didn't play the game that the boys had invented long ago.

Jenny was now talking about Anthony Bellarosa, and it seemed to me that she was winging it. In fact, she said, "Very little is known about Frank Bellarosa's son, and he seems to have kept a low profile since his father's death. But now, with his uncle's death, and his alleged, or rumored, involvement—"

I turned off the television and ate Susan's leftover cake.

Well, I could give Jenny a little more information about Tony, beginning with his name change.

Anyway, I thought, it was looking better for the Sutters. Stupid Anthony had unwittingly—half-wittedly—unleashed a media storm; the Father's Day Rubout—and that was good for Susan and me. Also the TV coverage was nothing compared to tomorrow morning's blood-splattered tabloid photos. Hopefully, before the police arrived at Giovanni's, someone had taken a few pictures of Salvatore D'Alessio lying on the floor with his head in shreds, and those pictures would be worth a lot of money to some lucky people who had taken their cameras to dinner for Father's Day photos. And sometimes, the NYPD themselves leaked some gory photographs to the press to show the public that La Cosa Nostra was not really an Italian fraternal organization. That would be a good public relations counterpoint to John Gotti as a man of the people. I could imagine some photographs of Marie splattered with her husband's blood, brains, and skull. I knew how *that* felt. If nothing else, there'd be some color photos in the tabloids of the post-whack scene—the table, blood on the floor, the vomit. No, no vomit. Blood was okay, but never vomit. Children could see it.

I finished Susan's cake, then went downstairs and rechecked the doors, windows, and exterior lighting, after which I went upstairs to the bedroom.

Susan was still awake, reading.

I said, "You should get some sleep."

She didn't respond. Apparently, she was upset.

I said to her, "Look, there is going to be a lot of TV coverage of this, but I promise you, I won't look at it again, and we won't buy any American newspapers in London."

Again, she didn't respond.

I said, "It's good that we're going to London."

She nodded, then said, "You see why I went to Hilton Head."

Well, no, I didn't, but to validate that, I said, "You see why I spent three years on my boat."

She didn't reply to that.

I got the shotgun and the carbine out of my closet and leaned the shotgun against her nightstand, and the carbine against my nightstand.

As I started to get undressed, she said to me, "I'm sorry you had to see him on TV."

"Don't worry about it. In fact, do not talk about it."

She didn't respond.

To change the mood and the moment, I said to her, "Do you remember that time we went to Paris, and sat in that little café . . . where was that?"

"On the Ile de la Cité. And you were flirting with the waitress."

"Oh, well . . . do you remember that dinner we had in Le Marais, and you were flirting with the sommelier?"

"You're making that up."

I got into bed, kissed her, and said, "This was the best Father's Day I've had in ten years." Not so good for Uncle Sal, or anyone else in Giovanni's, but . . .

"Me, too."

"And thanks for the yacht."

"We *are* going to buy a sailboat." She turned off her lamp and said, "Good night."

I turned off my lamp and said, "Sweet dreams."

Then I lay awake, thinking of this day, and of tomorrow, and of Tuesday in London. Hopefully, when we got back, Anthony Bellarosa would be in jail or dead, and if not, there was nothing keeping us from taking up residence in my London flat until Anthony was no longer a threat. But first, we had to get on that plane.

CHAPTER SIXTY-SEVEN

Monday morning. It was a bright, beautiful day.

We were up early to see Edward off, and Susan made him a hearty breakfast of ham and eggs—which I helped him eat—and at 7:30 A.M., a car and driver came for him. I would have driven him to the airport, but he didn't want to say goodbye at JFK. I remember a time when airports were like train stations or ship piers, and your friends or family walked you to the gate and could practically get on the plane, and could definitely get on the ocean liner to see you off with cocktails. But those days were long gone, and Edward had no memory of that simpler time. It occurred to me that there was a whole generation who accepted this war without end as normal. In fact, it was now normal.

Susan, Edward, and I stood in the forecourt, and I noted that Edward hadn't forgotten his overnight bag. I asked my son with the genius-level IQ, "Do you have money?"

"Mom gave me money."

"Good. Your ticket?"

"Got it."

"Photo ID?"

"Got it."

"Well, I guess you're good to go."

Susan said to him, "Call or e-mail as soon as you get in."

"Okay."

I remembered some trips I'd made when I still lived at home, and my send-offs hadn't been quite as sad or solicitous as the send-offs that Susan and I give to our children. Well, maybe we overdo it as much as my parents underdid it.

Susan said, "We'll call you from London."

"Yeah. Good." He asked, "When are you going to London?"

"Tomorrow." As we told you last night.

"Great. Have a good trip."

I reminded him, "Don't forget, you have a Brioni suit coming in about eight weeks."

"Yeah, thanks."

Susan reminded him, "Write or e-mail your grandparents—all of them—and tell them how much you enjoyed seeing them."

"Okay."

Well, the briefing seemed to be finished, and the driver was waiting, and Edward seemed anxious to get on the road.

We hugged and kissed, and he said to us with a smile, "You look good together."

That sort of caught me off guard, and I didn't reply, but Susan said, "Thank you. We'll see you in L.A. in July, maybe August, then here in August for our sail." She added, "And maybe a wedding in between."

He smiled. "Great."

One more hug and kiss, and Edward was in the car, which moved slowly down the gravel drive. He opened the rear window and waved, and then the car disappeared into the shadows of the tree-lined driveway.

Susan was wiping her eyes with a tissue. It's always sad to see a loved one off, but it's much sadder when you don't know when—or if—you'll ever see them again.

Sophie was staying until the Stanhopes arrived, which was scheduled for about 9:30 A.M., unless I went over to The Creek and cut the brake lines on their car.

Anyway, Sophie wanted to know if she should go out for the newspapers. I really wanted to see the blood-spattered front pages and read the sensational coverage of the Father's Day . . . what? Massacre? No. Only Sally Da-da had been clipped. That wasn't a massacre. How about the Father's Day Pop-Pop?

But I'd promised Susan—and Felix Mancuso—that there would be no newspapers in the house. Maybe I'd go out later, after the Stanhopes left, and read the *Daily News* and the *Post* in a coffee shop.

I replied to Sophie's offer, "No newspapers today." I did say to her, however, "Mrs. Sutter and I may be in the news today."

"Yes? Nice."

"Well . . ." I let her know, "Maybe not so nice. Okay, we'll be gone until . . . sometime in July. Maybe longer." Then we'll be cleaning the toilets ourselves. "You have the key, so please stop by once a week to check the house."

"Okay. You have nice trip. Where you go?"

"A romantic month in Warsaw. Can we pick up anything for you?"

"Yes. I give you food list. Thank you."

"You're very welcome."

She hesitated, then said to me, "Mrs. Sutter so happy now."

"Thank you."

"Mother and father not happy."

What was your first clue? I said to Sophie, "They're going home today."

"Yes? Good." She turned and went back to whatever she'd been doing.

So, to expand on what I was saying to Sophie about our names in the newspapers, I was fairly certain that some of the interesting background of this murder, which hadn't been covered in Jenny's slapdash instant-TV reporting, would come out in the tabloids over the next few days. Specifically, there would be more on Frank Bellarosa's murder ten years ago, including the name of his killer (the blueblood society lady, Susan Stanhope Sutter) along with some nice file photos of her. And another interesting fact in that case was that Susan Sutter's husband, John Sutter—use a good file photo, please—had been the dead don's lawyer, and the Sutters had lived on the magnificent estate called Stanhope Hall, adjoining the don's palatial estate, Alhambra. Plus, of course, there would be lots of speculation about Mrs. Sutter's relationship with her Mafia neighbor. Well, it could have been worse; Susan could have been Frank's lawyer, and I could have been his lover. That's how Hollywood would make the movie.

So this was all going to be dug up again, and I was concerned about Edward and Carolyn seeing it. Thanks, Anthony, you asshole. I hoped that we didn't have to dodge the news media outside the gates as we did last time around. I mean, the story was not about Susan and me, but you never know how these things are going to turn—especially when there's a rich, handsome couple involved in some way. Maybe Jenny would show up, as she had ten years ago—before we became close—and do a background piece standing in front of the gates with the gatehouse behind her: "Here, behind these iron gates and these forbidding walls, live John and Susan Sutter, who ten years ago were immersed . . ." Enmeshed? Entangled? Whatever. Well, if she showed up, I'd go out there and give her a big hug and kiss, and shout into her microphone, "Jenny! Sweetheart! I missed you!"

That's silly. It did occur to me, however, that I should call Mr. Nasim and give him a heads-up about all of this before he read something in the tabloids that mentioned John and Susan Sutter of Stanhope Hall. Maybe he'd double his offer for the house.

On the other hand, Susan and I were leaving tomorrow, so why bother calling anyone? My and Susan's philosophy is: When the shit hits the fan, it's time to hit the road.

Well, maybe one positive thing might come out of all this media coverage—maybe Anthony would have trouble finding a hit man who wanted to take the Sutter job. I mean, hit men are sort of low-profile guys, and they don't like to hit public figures or people who are in the news. Right? That was an encouraging thought.

It was now 9:00 A.M., and Susan, sitting at the patio table with her coffee, her portable phone, and a pad and pencil, dialed her travel agent.

As the phone rang, she asked me, "Do you mind flying economy class?"

"What's that?"

Before she could tell me, her agent answered, and Susan and the agent chatted a minute, then Susan booked us two economy class seats to London on Continental Airlines, departing JFK at 7:30 A.M. She said to the travel agent, "No, we don't need a hotel. My husband has a flat in London."

When did I get married? Did I lose a day somewhere?

Then she booked us on the Chunnel train to Paris, and in Paris, Susan blew it out and booked us for a week at the Ritz, where we'd stayed the last time. Then Air France economy class back to New York, arriving Wednesday afternoon, July 3, so we'd be back in time for the annual Fourth of July barbecue at Seawanhaka—unless we decided to go on the lam in London.

She hung up and said to me, "I'm really excited about this trip."

"Me, too."

"John, when can we get married?"

"We actually don't need to. I can just file a petition in matrimonial court—de lunatico inquirendo—to annul our divorce decree, then we'll be automatically married again."

"You are *so* full of shit."

"Right. How about July Fourth at Seawanhaka? Everyone we know will be there anyway, and it won't cost us anything, except what we spend for ourselves."

She didn't think that was such a good idea—women are not practical—and she called the club manager at Seawanhaka. Happily and luckily, the second Saturday in August was available, so Susan booked it for an outdoor wedding reception—details to be discussed at great length for the next two months.

She hung up and said to me, "This is perfect. We'll spend our wedding night in a guest room at the club, then the next morning, the four of us will sail off in our new yacht for a two-week honeymoon."

"Are your parents coming with us on our honeymoon?"

"No, John. Edward and Carolyn."

"Oh, right." I reminded her, "They didn't come on our last honeymoon."

She ignored that and said, "We'll go to L.A. the week before, spend a few days with Edward, and bring him back with us for the wedding."

"Good plan."

So that sounded like a wonderful summer. Then, if things were resolved here, I'd find a job in September, and we'd live happily ever after—in a smaller house, without the Stanhope paydays every month. In the meantime, all we had to do was not get bumped off.

I was sitting at my desk in my home office with the door closed, composing an e-mail with misinformation to Elizabeth about Susan and me going to Istanbul—we needed to decide where it was that we were supposed to be going—and returning in three or four weeks. At that time, we'd settle Ethel's estate.

I also reminded her, gently, about the letter, and asked her if we could meet today before I left early the next morning. I then called the gatehouse and told them to let Elizabeth Allard pass through.

As I hung up, a blue Ford Taurus pulled into the forecourt, and out stepped Dick-Brain and Ditsy. I should have told the guard to put them in chains, but apparently Susan had pre-cleared them.

I watched them through the window as they walked to the house, and they were speaking to each other as though they were doing a last-minute rehearsal. They looked a little grim, so I assumed they hadn't been visited by an angel in the night who'd told them that God loved all humanity, except them, so they'd better not cut off the bucks to their family or they'd go straight to hell.

The doorbell rang, and I could hear Sophie greeting the Stanhopes. I was surprised that Susan hadn't answered the door herself; in this world, you don't let a household employee greet family or close friends, unless you're truly indisposed. So, Susan was sending them a message— or busy sharpening a meat cleaver.

I heard the door close and the air suddenly became cold, and black flies appeared out of nowhere, then green slime began oozing out of the walls. The Stanhopes had arrived.

CHAPTER SIXTY-EIGHT

Susan and I had decided that she'd meet with Lucifer and the Wicked Witch of the South in the living room, and I would stay behind closed doors in the office so she could consult with me, or call me into the discussion, if appropriate.

I'd negotiated a lot of tax settlements this way, as well as some nasty family disputes about inheritances; different rooms for different people so that the parties could not get ugly or physical with each other. It usually works.

I checked my e-mail, and there were some messages from friends in London, inquiring about what they'd heard, either from Samantha or from my law colleagues. Well, I couldn't reply to any of these e-mails until the jury came in from the living room with the verdict. So I played poker with the computer, and I was on a winning streak—lucky at cards, unlucky at love?

About fifteen minutes after the Stanhopes arrived, there was a knock on my door, and I said, "Come in."

Sophie appeared and informed me, "I go now."

"Well, thank you for all you did."

The door was still open, and I could hear voices in the living room, and the tone and the cadence was distinctly somber and grave.

Sophie handed me a piece of paper, and I thought it was a note from Susan, or Sophie's bill, but a quick glance showed me it was a list, written in Polish.

She said, "You give to food store."

"Huh . . . ? Oh, right." During my romantic month in Warsaw. Why do I have to be such a wiseass? Well, maybe I could pick this stuff up in Glen Cove, or Brooklyn.

Sophie hesitated, then said, "Missus is sad. Maybe you go . . ." She pointed her thumb over her shoulder.

I replied, "All right. Thank you. You're a very nice lady. We'll see you when we return."

"Yes." She left and I closed the door behind her.

I heard her leave through the front door, and saw her get into her car and drive off.

Well, I suppose I could go in and resolve the matter by putting William in a choke hold and making him sign a blank sheet of paper that I'd fill in later. There is a legal basis for that—*necessitas non habet legem*—necessity knows no law.

But I did promise Susan I'd sit tight and not interfere with this family business, and she promised me she'd speak to me before they left.

So, to kill time, I pulled up a few online news sources and read about Salvatore D'Alessio's last supper. Most of the coverage was straight reporting, with not much new that I didn't already know from Jenny Alvarez and Felix Mancuso, my man on the scene. One story, however, did say, "Calls to the Bellarosa residence on Long Island have not been returned, and calls to Mr. Bellarosa's place of business, Bell Enterprises in Ozone Park, Queens, have been met with a recorded message."

Well, I thought, that's no way to run a business. What if someone needed limousines for a funeral? Like the D'Alessio family?

The story went on to say, "Sources close to the investigation say that it is likely that Tony Bellarosa has left the country."

I hope he's not in London or Paris. I mean, I wouldn't want to run into him at the Tate Gallery or the Louvre. I should definitely avoid Madame Tussaud's Wax Museum.

Anyway, I had an idea, and I found Anthony's card in my wallet and dialed his cell phone. After three rings, a recorded message said, "This number has been disconnected at the customer's request. No further information is available."

That didn't sound like Anthony had met with a sudden accident;

it sounded like he didn't want to be tracked through his cell phone signal.

In any case, if I'd reached him, it would be a silly conversation—*Anthony, where are you? John, where are you? I asked first, Anthony.*

I then e-mailed Carolyn regarding the murder of Mr. Salvatore D'Alessio, a fellow resident of the borough of Brooklyn, and a man who I was certain had been well known to the Brooklyn District Attorney's office. I was also certain that Carolyn's office was abuzz with this mob hit, and her colleagues were busy working with the NYPD and the FBI to develop leads regarding the killers, and Uncle Sal's runaway bodyguard—and most importantly the identity of the person who paid for the whack. Well, figuring out that Anthony Bellarosa was the lead suspect was a no-brainer; finding him would not be so easy.

I let Carolyn know, if she didn't already know, that Mom and Dad might be mentioned in the news. I did not say, "I hope this doesn't cause you any embarrassment," but she understood that. She also understood by now—or someone in the office had mentioned to her—that Anthony Bellarosa might be looking to settle the score with Mom. I did not mention this to her, but I did tell her that we were leaving for Europe the next morning and that we'd be in touch by phone before we left. She would understand what that was about.

I recalled that Anthony and Carolyn had met once, at Alhambra, and though I was not present, I was fairly sure that Carolyn had not been taken with the dark, handsome thug next door; in that respect, she had better judgment than her mother.

Anyway, Carolyn Sutter, Brooklyn ADA, might possibly have more information than I had, and I was sure she'd share that with her mother and father if appropriate.

So, having taken care of Bellarosa news and business, I went online and found some good Web sites for Paris, one of which had the name of two restaurants where Americans were welcome.

At about 10:00, Susan opened the door and entered. She looked pale and shaken, but not weepy. I sat her on the couch, then I sat next to her.

She took a deep breath, then said, "Well, their position is clear. If we marry, then my allowance is cut off, and I am disinherited, and disowned. Even if we don't marry, they'll do the same thing unless you leave the country."

I took her hand and said, "We knew that."

"Yes . . . but . . ." She took another breath and continued, "My father also said that he will disinherit the children . . . and stop the disbursements from their trust fund . . . and hold up the disbursement of the principal until they reach the age of fifty." She looked at me and asked, "Can he do that?"

I replied, "As I said, he can disinherit them at any time. As for the trust fund, I would need to see the trust documents. But I did see them once, and I know that Peter is the trustee, and your father, through Peter, can stop the distributions and hold the corpus and appreciation—the whole amount—until Edward and Carolyn reach the age of fifty."

She did some math and said, "That's almost twenty-five years from now."

I tried to show her the bright side of that and said, "Without the distributions, the fund should quadruple by then." Unless the fund administrators made some really bad investment choices.

She said, "I'm worried about *now*. Not twenty-five years from now."

"I know." I tried to get a sense of what she was thinking, and I got a hint when she withdrew her hand from mine.

So this was the moment that I knew would come, and I'd already given her my solution to the problem, which she'd rejected when it was just me laying out the problem and the resolution. But now that she'd gotten the final word from dear old Dad—and I was sure he was *not* bluffing—it had hit her like a judge handing down a life sentence.

Out of curiosity, I asked, "How about your mother?"

She shook her head, then replied, "She said that all I had to do was tell you to leave and everything would be all right again."

That wasn't true, but I didn't respond.

Finally, she asked me, "What should I do, John?"

Well, if you have to ask, Susan, you already know the answer.

"John?"

I took a deep breath and said, "What you have to do is get a lawyer—"

"Why? You are a lawyer—"

"Listen to me. You need to make sure that this sort of thing does not happen again. Your father needs to set up a trust fund for you, and new trusts for the children that will basically transfer to all three of you the portion of his estate that you and the children would receive as an inheritance. And this trust fund needs to be set up so that you and the children will receive annual distributions, free from his control, and his manipulation, and *you* need to pick the fund trustee, and it will *not* be Peter. Do you understand?"

"I . . . why would he do that?"

"Well, for a consideration on your part. In other words, in exchange for something he wants from you."

"What . . . ? Oh . . ."

"You and the children need legal assurances that he can't control your lives with his money, and in return you—and I—give him what he wants—in writing."

"John. No . . ."

"Yes."

She looked at me and I turned toward her and our eyes met. She kept staring at me, then tears ran down her cheeks.

In as firm a voice as I was able to muster, I said to her, "This is the *only* way, Susan, that we—you and I together—can protect the children, and protect your future as well."

She looked away from me and wiped her eyes with her hands.

To bring this home, I stood and said, "Go back in there and tell him I am prepared to return to London—without his million dollars—but not until I have spoken to him about what he has to do for you, Edward, and Carolyn before I leave." I assured her, "He'll understand."

She remained seated, still shaking her head, then she said, "The children say they don't care . . ."

"They don't. But we do." I asked her, "Do you want Peter to be the sole beneficiary of the Stanhope fortune?"

She didn't reply, but she didn't have to.

I took her hand and lifted her to her feet. I suggested, "Go in the kitchen or someplace, get yourself composed, get angry, then go in there and tell him what the deal is."

She didn't respond.

I continued, "If he storms out, then you're free of him and his money. But if he wants to speak to me, then we'll work out an arrangement that loosens his grip on the money bag."

She shook her head again, then said in a barely audible voice, "No . . . John . . . I will not let you go."

"You—we—have no choice. Look, Susan . . . maybe in a year or so, after we've had a chance to think about this, and see how we feel—"

"No!"

"Okay, then *I'll* speak to him now. Send him in here."

"No."

"Then I'll go out there—"

"No . . . no . . . let me . . . I just need a minute . . ." She started to sit again, but I took her arm and moved her toward the door. I said, "It's okay. You're brave and you know what you have to do."

"No . . . I won't . . ."

I got very stern and said, "We will *not* sacrifice our children's future for our own selfish—"

She pulled away from me and said, "I will *not* let you leave again."

I took her by the shoulders and said, "I am leaving. But not until I put things in order here, for the children, which is what I should have done ten or twenty years ago—"

"No. John, please . . ."

"But I promise you, Susan . . . I promise that we will be together again."

She looked at me, and tears were still running down her cheeks. She sobbed, then put her head on my shoulder and asked, "Do you promise . . . ?"

"I do. Okay . . ." I moved her toward the door, and walked her out to the foyer. She turned and looked at me. I smiled and said, "Tell your father that your lawyer wants to speak to him."

She didn't smile, but she nodded, and I went back to the office and closed the door.

I stood there for a full minute, then sat at the desk.

I picked up a pencil and made a few notes about what I needed to cover with William. But my mind, and my heart, was not in it. Basically, I was going to negotiate a deal with him that ensured that Susan and I would never see each other again.

It was possible, I suppose, that William would reject the idea of giving up control of his money, and thus of his daughter—because what was he getting out of the deal? Certainly not Susan's love and companionship, or the love of his grandchildren. All he was getting out of this deal was the guarantee that John and Susan Sutter would never again see each other, and I wondered if that was enough for him. Well, I guess that depended on how honest he was about his motives for ending this engagement. Did he and Charlotte really believe that Susan was making a terrible mistake? Or was this really about William's hate for me?

Surely William realized that if he accepted this deal, then he'd not only be rid of me but also lose his daughter and his grandchildren as soon as they were financially independent. Basically, I'd turned this back on him, and put him in a no-win situation. And yet he might go for it if he were more consumed with hate for me than love for Susan, Edward, and Carolyn. I was sure, too, that Peter would pressure his father into taking the deal if it meant that Peter, too, would get his inheritance now. Then Peter could also tell Daddy to go fuck himself.

The door opened, and Susan stepped into the office. I stood and we faced each other. She said to me, "My father totally rejects your suggestion."

"All right." That answered at least one question.

She seemed drained, I thought, and I don't think I've ever seen her looking so lost and defeated by any situation.

She looked away from me and said, "But . . . his offer to you stands if you will accept it now, and get on the flight to London tomorrow . . . alone."

"All right." I waited for her to say something, but she didn't, so I guess I had my answer to another question. And really, I didn't blame her. Love, unfortunately, does not conquer all. Or, to be more kind, Susan's love for her children—our children—overrode her love for me.

And I felt the same way. Whoever said that children were hostages to fortune must have had a father-in-law like William Stanhope.

I wanted to tell Susan that without any legal guarantees for herself and the children, her father would and could do whatever he wanted with his money, including turning everything over to Peter. But that would sound self-serving, like I was trying to convince her that my leaving did not necessarily guarantee her, or the children, a financially secure life; it guaranteed her that William would continue to control her life, and probably pick her next husband for her. Maybe William wanted her to marry dead Dan's son, Bob.

On that subject, I asked her, "What did he offer *you*?"

She hesitated, then said, truthfully, "A large increase in my allowance if I sold this house and moved back to Hilton Head."

"I see." Well, the reign of William the Dominator continues. As I said, I didn't blame Susan, and I believed that if it was only our lives to consider, then she'd throw her parents out the door. I did not, and would not in the future, think any less of her for making this hard decision. I had already made the same decision. I said to her, "Tell him I'm leaving tomorrow. And tell him, too, that he can take his bribe and shove it up his ass."

Susan just stood there, then dropped her eyes and said, "I'm sorry . . ."

"Don't be. This is *our* decision, not just yours." I said, "Better yet, send him in here and I'll tell him myself."

She shook her head. "He doesn't want to see you . . . he just wants your answer."

"My answer is I'll leave tomorrow if he comes into this office now."

"I'll tell him." She looked at me and said, "I love you."

"I know you do."

"Do you love me?"

"I do." But I can't.

She nodded again and said, "We had this time together . . . and I will never forget this week."

"Neither will I." I suggested, "You need to get on a plane to somewhere tomorrow and get out of here until things settle down."

"I know . . . they want me to come to Hilton Head. But . . ." She asked me, "What am I going to do without you?"

"You'll do fine." I reminded her, "I'll be here waiting for your father."

She took a step toward me, but I said, "Take care of this."

She looked hurt, and she looked so lost. I wanted to take her into my arms, and I would, but not until they were gone.

She stood motionless, then nodded and left.

I stared at the door, hoping she'd turn around and come back, and we'd both go into the living room and throw the Stanhopes out of the house. Our house. I also hoped that she wouldn't make that decision.

I felt . . . a lot of things. Anger, for sure. But mostly I felt that sense of loss that I remembered from ten years ago; that understanding that it was over, and worse, that it should not be this way—that there was too much love between us that was being thrown aside for reasons that might not be good enough to justify the decision to part. And I felt, too, there was something wrong here . . . that Susan had been right and that Fate had brought us together again. So how was this happening?

I remained standing, staring at the door.

The only comfort I could take in this was that Susan, and Edward and Carolyn, could now see William Stanhope for what he was—and that knowledge would do them more good over the years than his money. The other thing that was comforting was my sure belief that William understood that I was waiting in the wings, and that I would reappear if he didn't follow through on his promise to at least maintain the status quo. And surely the bastard would be happy to hear that I didn't want his money; but somewhere in his dim brain he'd eventually understand that I didn't owe him anything either, and that I was a six-hour plane ride away, and free to return if he didn't take care of my children.

I thought about tomorrow—about getting on the flight, alone, and returning to London. Probably, I could get my job back, if I wanted it, and Samantha, too, if I wanted her. But really what I wanted to do was to find a yacht owner who needed an experienced skipper for a long sail. That, I knew from the last time, would remove the temptation—my and Susan's—to make a bad decision based on love.

I heard a car pulling up and looked out the window. Elizabeth's SUV came to a stop, and she got out.

I went to the front door and opened it before she rang the bell.

She smiled and said, "Good morning."

"Good morning. Come in."

"Just for a moment." She let me know, "I got your e-mail."

We entered the house, and I showed her into the office and closed the door.

She looked around, noted Susan's oil paintings on the wall, and commented, "Susan is very talented."

I glanced at the paintings, and a flood of memories came back to me—twenty years of living with a woman who had been delightfully crazy, and who had become, over the last ten years, a little less crazy, though no less delightful. And now, the Susan who had just walked out of here was . . . well, defeated. That, more than anything else, made my heart ache.

Elizabeth asked, "John? Are you all right?"

"Yes. So how are you holding up?"

"I have good and bad moments." She added, "I'll be fine."

"I know you will." I asked her, "Would you like to sit?"

"No. I'm running late for a staff meeting at one of my shops."

"They can't start without you."

She smiled. "I'm afraid they might." She opened her bag and took out a small, stationery-sized envelope. She said to me, "This is yours."

I took the plain white envelope and saw that it was addressed to "Mr. John Sutter," in Ethel's hand. I said to Elizabeth, "Thank you." I took it to the desk, picked up a letter opener, and said, "Let's read it."

"No. You read it. Mom addressed it to you."

"Well, I know, but we agreed—"

"If there is anything in there that you want to share with me, give me a call." She added, "I trust your judgment on this."

"All right . . . but . . ."

"You don't look well."

"Father's Day hangover."

She smiled and said, "You should have seen *me* Sunday morning."

"That was a nice gathering."

"I'd like to have you and Susan over for dinner when you return from your trip."

"That would be nice."

"Tell her I stopped by and said hello and bon voyage."

"I will."

"And get some caffeine and aspirin."

"I will. Thanks."

I walked her out to her car, and she asked me, "Is that the Stanhopes' car?"

"It is."

"Oh, God. I see why you're under the weather."

I forced a smile and said, "They're leaving for the airport soon."

"Let's celebrate. See if Susan wants to come by tonight for drinks."

"Thanks, but we need to pack. Early flight."

"Let me know if you change your mind." She asked, "Why are you going to Istanbul?"

"Just to get away. I spent a week there when I was sailing."

She looked at me and said, "Maybe someday, some handsome man will ask me to sail with him around the world."

Maybe sooner than you think. I said, "If you wish it, it will happen."

She didn't reply.

I said to her, "Tell Mitch I said hello."

"Who?"

Well, that answered that question.

She gave me a peck on the cheek and said, "Send me a postcard."

"I will. We will."

"Bye." She got in her BMW and drove off.

I went back in the house, into the office, and shut the door.

Well . . . I had too much on my mind and too much on my plate to think about Elizabeth. And, in truth, my heart was still here.

I stood at the desk and looked at the envelope on it.

The intercom buzzed, and I picked it up.

Susan said, "I'm in the kitchen. My father will not see you in the office, but he will speak to you on the phone later—or after you return to London."

She sounded more composed now—or maybe shell-shocked. I replied, "All right."

"He's going out to the car so that I can spend a few minutes alone with my mother."

"Fine."

"Please don't go out to speak to him."

"I won't." I said to her, "I'll see you after they leave." I hung up.

I heard the front door open, and I saw William walking to his car.

I'm usually in control of a situation, or if I'm not, I take control. But there are times—like this time—when the best thing to do is nothing. And, really, what did I need to say to William Stanhope? I didn't need to tell him what I thought of him—he already knew that. And I certainly wasn't going to ask him to reconsider his demands, or try to soften his heart. So the only thing I could do now that would be positive and productive would be to go out there and smack his head against the steering wheel until the airbag popped. And I would have if he was younger.

And on top of all this, Anthony Bellarosa was still out there, though after tomorrow, when Susan and I were gone—in opposite directions— that problem would be on hold, and with luck, resolved.

I stared at William, who'd gotten in the car and started it, probably listening to the radio. I wondered how he and Charlotte were going to react when they heard about Salvatore D'Alessio's murder, and Anthony Bellarosa being the prime suspect, and discovered that their daughter was again in the news. Well, I'm sure they'd insist that she return to Hilton Head immediately. I realized that neither one of us was coming back here to live.

I sliced open the envelope, pulled out four folded sheets of plain white stationery, and glanced at Ethel's neat but crabbed handwriting. I read:

Dear Mr. Sutter,

I write this letter to you from what I believe is my death bed, and I write in anticipation of your return from London to settle the affairs of my estate. This letter will be given to you at the time of my death by my daughter, Elizabeth Corbet, on the condition that you do, in fact, return from London for that purpose, and, further, that you and I have spoken, in person, upon your return.

Well, I thought, I'd met both conditions—I flew in from London, and I visited her in hospice. And she met the final condition. She died.

The only certainty there was that she was going to die; my trip to New York had not been so definite. In retrospect, I should have stayed in London and saved everyone a lot of trouble and sorrow.

I watched William Stanhope awhile, trying to decide if I should just go out there and tell him, calmly but firmly, that he was not to screw around with his grandchildren's trust funds or inheritance. I mean, what was he going to do if I walked toward the car? Drive off to the airport and leave his wife here?

I looked back at Ethel's letter to me and read:

I am tired and not feeling well as I write this, so I will get right to my purpose. I know that you and your father-in-law have never cared for each other, and I know, too, that this state of affairs had caused your former wife much grief, and caused trouble between you and her, and I believe, too, that the Stanhopes influenced Mrs. Sutter in her decision to sell her house and join them in Hilton Head.

Well, I could see where this was going—Ethel was playing Cupid at the end, just as she'd done when I'd visited her. Why, I wondered, did she care about Susan and me getting together again? Well, she liked Susan, and I was sure they'd bonded again since Susan had returned, and Ethel knew that Susan wanted to reunite with me. So, Ethel, with not much else to do while waiting for the end, had gotten it into her head to make a final pitch on Susan's behalf.

I put the letter aside for later. Okay, Ethel. But you forgot about William Stanhope. Actually, she hadn't, which was why she'd men-

tioned him. Also, Ethel *never* liked William, and this was her chance to
. . . what?

I picked up the letter again and continued reading:

What I am about to write is very difficult for me to put into words.
Therefore, let me be direct. William Stanhope is a man who has
shown himself to be morally corrupt, depraved, and sinful.

Whoa. I sat down and turned to the next page.

His shameless and dissolute behavior began when he was a college
student, and continued throughout his military service, and beyond, and did not cease even after his marriage. I have difficulty,
even now, so many years later, allowing my mind to return to that
time. I do not wish to be explicit in my descriptions of his behavior, but I will tell you that he forced himself on the youngest and
most innocent of the female staff at Stanhope Hall—

I stopped reading and drew a deep breath. *My God.* I reread the last
line, then continued:

He fancied the foreign born girls, those being the most unlikely
to resist him. Before and during the war, it was the Irish girls
who fell prey to him, and one of them, Bridget Behan by name,
attempted to take her own life after he had his way with her. And
after the war, there were a number of displaced persons, mostly
German and Polish girls who could hardly speak English, and
who were terrified of being deported, and this caused them to
bend to his will. One of these girls, a Polish girl of no more than
sixteen, whose name I am sorry I cannot recall, became pregnant
by him, and he had her returned to her country.

I cannot tell you here all that happened during those years,
but I can tell you that his disgraceful behavior continued, un-
abated, until he and Mrs. Stanhope departed for Hilton Head.

And now, Mr. Sutter, you are thinking to yourself why have
I waited until this moment to reveal this? First, I must tell you

that I, and others at Stanhope Hall, attempted to bring this matter to the attention of Augustus Stanhope while he lived, but to his shame, he would not hear our complaints. And to my everlasting shame, I did not press the matter with him. And to my husband George's shame, *he* would not take the matter to Augustus Stanhope, and told me to be silent. You must understand that in those days, it was not likely that these girls would make a complaint to the authorities, or if they did, would they be believed over the word of William Stanhope? I know, too, that these girls were at times threatened with discharge or deportation, and at times they were paid to keep their silence. I cannot tell you how many young girls fell victim to William Stanhope, but by my reckoning, not a year passed without some incident or complaint that came to my attention. Now, I must say here that some of these girls, perhaps more than I know, were willing participants in these liaisons, and sold themselves for money. But there were at least as many who did not welcome his attentions, but who nonetheless succumbed to his insistent pressure and his physical aggression.

I realize, as I write this, that I have no proof of what I say, except that there is a fine, upstanding lady who is as familiar with these events as I am, and her name is Jenny Cotter, a name which you or Mrs. Sutter may recall from her years as head housekeeper at Stanhope Hall. Mrs. Cotter is alive as I write this, and is in residence at Harbor View Nursing Home in Glen Cove. She can, and is willing to, give you more particulars if you should need or want more than I have written here.

And so, Mr. Sutter, my letter to you is as much my confession as it is my apology for staying silent all these years. Please understand that my only purpose in remaining silent, aside from my husband's insistence that I do so, was so as not to cause young Miss Susan—later Mrs. Sutter (and Mrs. Stanhope, for that matter) any pain or heartbreak. But now that I am about to make my journey into the Kingdom of Heaven, I know that I need to unburden my soul of this, and I know, in my heart, that you are the person I should have gone to with this matter many years ago. And I would have, if not for Mrs. Sutter, and this is now in your hands to decide if she should know. I pray that you read this letter, and pray that you confront Mr. Stanhope with this letter and the word of Mrs. Cotter as proof of his transgressions and offenses against these girls. I know that God will forgive me for my silence, and God will forgive him as well if he is forced to look into his soul and face up to his sins and ask for God's forgiveness.

Sincerely yours,
Ethel Allard

I looked at the four pages in my hand, then looked out the window at William Stanhope, sitting impatiently in his car, waiting for his wife and daughter to finish with their visit.

I opened Susan's phone book and dialed William's cell phone.

I saw him find his phone in his jacket pocket, look at the Caller ID, then answer, "Yes?"

I said to him, "William, this is your future-son-in-law. Come in here. I need to speak to you."

CHAPTER SIXTY-NINE

I still don't understand," Susan said, "how you convinced him to change his mind."

"I can be very persuasive," I replied.

She'd been questioning me about this, on and off, since her parents left an hour ago, but mostly she was just happy and relieved that it had turned out so well. She called it a miracle, and maybe it was. Thank you, Ethel, and tell that angel at the Heavenly Bar to give you another sherry. It's on me.

We were sitting in the shade on the patio, celebrating with a few beers, and Susan asked me, "What can I make you for lunch?" She promised, "Anything you want."

"I was thinking of yogurt. But a pepperoni pizza wouldn't be so bad."

Without comment, she picked up her portable phone, called information, then connected with a local pizza parlor. She'd have to memorize that number.

The protocols involved in ordering a pizza seemed to be a mystery to Susan Stanhope—Sicilian or regular?—but she was making good progress. She said to the pizza man, "Hold on," then said to me, "He wants to know if there is anything else you want on that?"

"Well, how about sausage and meatballs?"

She added that to the toppings, listened to another pizza question, then asked me, "Do you want that cut into eight slices or twelve?"

I remembered a joke that Frank had once told me and I replied, "Twelve—I'm hungry."

She smiled, then gave our phone number and address—Stanhope Hall, Grace Lane, Lattingtown—no, there's no house number, just look for the gatehouse—then she called the gatehouse to clear the deliveryman.

I sat with my bare feet on the table and took another swallow of beer.

Susan returned to the subject of William's apparent capitulation and said to me, "I know my father, and I know that these are going to be tough negotiations."

"I'm a good negotiator." Especially when I have the other guy's balls in my hand, and I'm squeezing. Or should I twist?

"John . . . do you think he was . . . insincere? Or that he'll renege?"

"He will do no such thing."

"But . . . I just *don't* understand—"

"Susan, I believe that your father had . . . well, an epiphany. I think, when he was sitting alone in his car, that it just came to him that he was wrong, and maybe he was moved by the Holy Spirit. I mean, I couldn't believe it myself when I saw him from the window, getting out of the car with this rapturous look on his face, then coming into my office, and saying, 'John, I would like to speak to you.'"

What he actually said was, "How *dare* you insist that I come into your office?"

Well, I apologized to him, of course—or did I tell him to sit down, shut up, and read the letter? In any case, as he read the letter, he went from livid to pale, and it was sort of interesting to see someone's skin color change that quickly. I wish I'd had a video camera. Also, his hands trembled. After that, the negotiations were rather easy. He did bluster now and then, saying things like, "No one will believe the ramblings of an old woman on medication," and so forth. So I suggested we show the letter to his daughter and his wife to see what they thought, then pay a visit to Mrs. Cotter at the nursing home to see if she could clarify any of this. That shut him up, of course, but he did utter the word "Blackmail."

I know this is blackmail, and I'm a lawyer, and this goes against all my beliefs and principles. What William had done—or what he is alleged to have done—was not only despicable, but also a crime, though unfortunately the statutes had run out on his crimes years ago. So if he was to pay for these crimes, then it would have to be in another way. The Bar Association and the courts might have another view of this, but at least Ethel would speak up for me when I stood before the Final Court.

Susan said to me, "He looked . . . pale. Shaken."

"Did he? I didn't notice."

"And my mother seemed confused that he'd had this sudden and complete change of heart."

"Well, she hadn't shared his divine revelation."

"John . . . ?"

"Yes?"

"Did you . . . threaten him with something?"

"What could I threaten him with?"

"I don't know . . . but—"

"Can we change the subject?" I asked, "Whose turn is it to get beer?"

She stood and went into the kitchen.

I finished my beer and thought about Ethel's letter. She'd made her deathbed confession to me, but according to Father Hunnings, Ethel had also spoken to him about the contents of this letter—and Hunnings had advised Ethel not to give it to me, and he'd also put some pressure on Elizabeth to withhold the letter. Why? To protect Ethel's memory, as he said? Or did he want to get ahold of the letter himself, then give it to William in exchange for . . . what? A comfortable retirement?

Susan returned with the beers and said, "John, I think you're too modest. I think that my father's change of heart was because of something you said, not because of some . . . divine message."

I replied, modestly, "Well . . . I did my best, and I *was* persuasive, but I really think I had help from a higher source."

She reminded me, "I *told* you I believe that this was our Fate, and that we have a guardian angel watching over us."

"It seems that way." I took a slug of beer.

She moved on to another subject and asked me, "Do you think we should get married at Saint Mark's?"

"Why not? Father Hunnings gives a discount for the second time."

She laughed, then reminded me, "You don't like him, and I don't think he is particularly fond of you."

"Really? Well, then I'll speak to him and smooth things over." And mention that I read Ethel's letter, and maybe I *would* ask him if he had any knowledge—other than in a general sense—of the contents.

Susan said, "I'd like it if you would do that." She added, "I'd like to get married there again."

"No problem. And I'll even get Father Hunnings to waive the pre-nuptial counseling."

She smiled and said, "I think you're getting all full of yourself after your success with my father."

"I'm on a roll," I agreed. And while I was remaking my world to suit myself, I assured her, "Not only will your parents bless our marriage, they will also pay for it."

"All I want is their blessing."

"*I* want to give them the bill. And don't forget to e-mail them with a Save-the-Date. They'll want to come in early to help out with the arrangements—and discuss your dowry."

She ignored my suggestions and asked me, "John, are you willing to forgive and forget? I mean, about my parents?"

I thought about that and replied, "It's not my nature to hold a grudge."

Susan thought that was funny for some reason, and suggested, "No, it's the central core of your being."

"You know me too well." I replied, seriously, "I can't ever forgive or forget what they've put us through during our marriage, and just recently, but . . ." I can be magnanimous in victory, so I continued, "I will say this: If your father—and your mother, as well—is looking for forgiveness and trying to make amends, then I'm open to that, and I'm certain that your father is going to forgive me for calling him an un-principled asshole, and so forth. But my question to you is: How do *you* feel about them?"

She took a deep breath, then replied, "I'm angry. And I've seen this very unpleasant side of them. But they are my parents, and I love them, and I will forgive them." She added, "We would want that from our children."

"Well, we would, but we don't need their forgiveness for anything."

She stayed silent a few moments, then confessed, "I did. For what I did. And they forgave me, unconditionally. Just as you have."

I nodded and said, "Life is short."

Maybe I could eventually forgive Charlotte and William for what they did to the Sutter family—the best revenge is living well. But I could never forgive William for what he did to those young girls, and that would stay with me, and with him, until the day we both died.

So we sat in the shade of the patio and looked out into the sunny rose garden as we sipped our cold beers. It really was an exquisite day, and nature was in full bloom, and the air was scented with roses and honeysuckle. I watched a big monarch butterfly trying to decide where to land.

Susan broke into my quiet moment and said, "We need to e-mail the children with this good news, and give them some calendar updates, and . . . well, maybe mention that they might see something in the newspapers about . . . us."

"You should e-mail Carolyn about this good news. I've already e-mailed her about our possible mention in the bad news."

Susan nodded, then said, "I'm sorry."

"Subject closed."

"All right. Then I'll e-mail Edward . . ."

"And definitely tell him that Grandpa has blessed our marriage by handing over his trust fund to him. But don't say too much about our possible appearance in the news."

"All right. But you know that he and Carolyn will discuss this."

"Fine. And we'll answer their questions truthfully, but with a little spin." I further suggested, "Call your parents and set up a date when they can visit Edward in L.A. They need to get to know their heirs better."

She smiled, then said, "That's not a bad idea."

Again we sat in silence, enjoying and savoring the moment together. There are not many perfect hours such as this, especially on a day that had begun so badly, which made this moment all the more extraordinary.

Of course, in every Garden of Eden, there is at least one serpent lurking in the flowers, and we actually had two. The first had a name, and it was Anthony Bellarosa. We knew he was here, and we were avoiding him, and we even avoided speaking of him—at least for now.

The second serpent had no name, and it had recently slithered into the garden. But if I had to give it a name, I'd call it Doubt.

So, to kill this, before it killed us, I said to Susan, "What we did was an act of love."

She didn't reply, so I continued, "I never doubted your love, and I know that your heart was breaking."

Again no reply, so I concluded, "And if we had to do it over again, we would do the same thing."

She sat there for a long time, then said, "You didn't even want to take his money. And I . . . I feel so venal, so compromised—"

"No. Remember why we did what we did. It wasn't for us." It was to screw William and Peter. And, of course, to see that Edward and Carolyn got their fair share of the family fortune.

"John, that might be true for you, but I'm not sure about me."

"Don't doubt your motives. Your father created an impossible dilemma."

"I know . . . but, God, I felt that I was selling myself and betraying you, and giving up our love for—"

"Susan, I don't feel that way, so neither should you."

"All right . . . you're a very loving and wise man."

"I am. Have another beer."

She forced a smile, then said, "I hope this never comes back to haunt us."

I pointed out, "If we could work through what happened ten years ago, then this is nothing."

"I love you."

"That's why we're here." I asked, "Where is the pizza guy?"

"I don't know. I've never ordered a pizza in my life."

"Well, we'll fix that in the next twenty years."

We sat and talked about London, and Paris, with maybe a side trip to the Loire Valley, as we'd done many years ago.

Susan's portable phone rang, and it was the guard at the gate announcing the pizza man.

I got up, went through the house, and waited for him outside the front door. But as I stood there, I realized that it was moments like this, when you are least expecting it, that your world could suddenly explode—as it had for Salvatore D'Alessio.

I saw a small van coming up the driveway. I went back into the house, bounded up the stairs, grabbed the carbine, went down into my office, and looked out the window. The van stopped, and a young Hispanic-looking guy got out, retrieved the pizza from the rear, then ambled toward the front door. I mean, I wasn't thinking that the pizza delivery kid could be a hit man, but it was just the act of me standing outside, with no one around, and Alhambra Estates five hundred yards away through the trees, that had spooked me for a moment. Well, that was good. Uncle Sal had been stuffing a cannoli in his mouth, or doing something other than watching the door, and the next thing he knew, he was looking down the barrels of a shotgun. Then, bang, he was in hell.

The doorbell rang, and I went to the front door. I stuck the carbine in the umbrella stand and opened up.

I looked over the pizza guy's shoulder as we exchanged pizza for money, plus a nice tip, and I locked the door.

I can balance a pizza box on one finger, but I used my whole hand, and carried the box and the carbine out to the patio.

Susan couldn't help but notice the carbine, and asked, "Do we really need that out here?"

"I hope not."

I opened the box on the table, and the aroma wafted into my nose and engulfed my soul.

I sat, and Susan went inside, then returned with plates, napkins, knives, and forks. I explained that napkins were optional, and the rest of the stuff was not necessary.

I know that Lady Stanhope has eaten pizza—I've seen her—but she always approaches food like this with some trepidation and perhaps a little disdain.

I showed her how to flip the point back and bite it off, then fold the slice to stabilize it. I said, "It's basic physics."

So we sat there with our beers, and our pizza, and our rifle, and we had a nice lunch.

Susan confessed, "This actually tastes good."

"And it's good for you."

"I don't think so, but we can have this once in a while."

I pointed out, "We could buy the whole pizza parlor."

She laughed, then said, "Well, John, you saved the day, and I guess I owe you something." She asked me, "Aside from the yacht, and unhealthy food, what would you like?"

"Just you, darling."

"You already have me."

"And that's all I want."

"How about a sports car?"

"Okay."

I ate half the pizza—six slices—and Susan had a second piece, and we wrapped the rest for my breakfast.

Then we went to the bedroom to work off the pizza—sort of a victory lap—and pack for our trip. I had a whole wardrobe in London, so I just threw some odds and ends in my suitcase, and Susan saw this as an opportunity to pack more of her clothes in my luggage. She said, "I have some nice things in the basement that I haven't gotten around to unpacking."

Well, we could be gone a lot longer than three weeks, so I didn't object.

After we packed our suitcases, we took a nap, then at about 5:00 P.M., I got up and said to Susan, "I'm going to run into Locust Valley for a few things. Would you like to come?"

"No, I have a lot to do here, but I'll give you a list of what I need."

So I got dressed and said to her, "Keep the doors locked, and don't go outside."

She didn't reply.

I further advised her, "Keep the carbine or the shotgun near you. I'll put the carbine in the umbrella stand near the front door."

"John—"

"Susan, we have about"—I looked at my watch—"less than fifteen hours before we're lifting off the runway. Let's play it safe."

She shrugged, then asked me, "What time do you want the car to pick us up for a seven-thirty A.M. flight?"

We'd have to leave for the airport at about 5:00 A.M. in the dark, so I replied, "We will take my rental car so that I can keep the carbine with us, and we'll park the car in the long-term lot."

"I'd really rather take a car service and avoid the hassle."

"Me, too. But we need to take that final precaution."

She didn't look happy about that and said, "John, we're going on *vacation*—not into battle."

"Don't argue with me, or I'll call your father and tell him to straighten you out."

She smiled and said, "You are going to be insufferable."

"Yes."

I gave her a kiss, and she said, "Don't be too long. Do you want my cell phone?"

"I do." She gave me her cell phone, and I said goodbye, took the carbine, and went downstairs. I placed the rifle in the umbrella stand, then went out the front door, which I locked.

I had the keys for both cars, and I decided to take my Taurus, which would be easier to park downtown.

I got in and drove down the driveway. When I got to the gatehouse, I used the remote and the gates swung inward. I had a thought, and I honked my horn, then got out of the car.

The gatehouse door opened, and a young security guard, whom I didn't know, came out.

I said to him, "I'm Mr. Sutter and I live in the guest cottage."

"Yes, sir."

"Are you alone?"

"I am until eight P.M., then a second man comes on duty."

"All right . . . well, what I need you to do, in about fifteen or twenty minutes, is to drive up to the guest cottage and just walk around to see that everything looks okay."

"Well . . . I'm not supposed to leave my post."

"That is part of your post tonight." I gave him a twenty-dollar bill and said, "Mrs. Sutter is in the house, and we are expecting no visitors, so do not let *anyone* in, unless you call us and get an okay. I will be back in about half an hour." Actually, it could be closer to an hour, but he didn't need to know that.

He seemed happy with his tip and replied, "No problem," whatever that means.

I got back in the car and headed toward Locust Valley.

Aside from Susan's shopping list in my pocket, I had Ethel's letter, which I needed to photocopy. In fact, I'd make twenty copies, and send one to William every month, plus Father's Day, Christmas, and his birthday.

As I got to the edge of the village, I called Susan, and she answered. I said, "Traffic is heavy, and parking will be tight, so I'm not sure how long this will take."

"Take your time."

"Do you need onions?"

"No onions, sweetie."

"Okay." I told her, "I asked the guard at the gate to check out the house in about fifteen minutes." I reminded her, "The carbine is in the umbrella stand in case you need to go downstairs. Leave the shotgun in the bedroom. I'll call you later."

The village was crowded with cars jockeying for parking spaces. I glanced at the dashboard clock: 5:39. Well, with any luck, I could be back within the hour.

What could happen in one hour?

CHAPTER SEVENTY

I bought everything on the list for our trip, and I also made a dozen copies of Ethel's letter at a local print shop in case William needed monthly reminders of why we were negotiating a family financial agreement. I began the fifteen-minute drive back to Stanhope Hall. It was now 6:23 on the dashboard clock.

I used Susan's cell phone to call the house, but she didn't answer, so I left a message. "I'll be home in ten or fifteen minutes. Call me when you get this."

She was probably in the shower, or despite my advice to stay inside, maybe she was on the patio without her portable house phone. Another very likely possibility was that she was in the basement, looking for clothes to pack, and there was no phone down there.

When I was a few minutes from Grace Lane, I called the gatehouse to tell them to open the gates, but no one answered. Maybe the guard was on the other line, or he was outside, or using the bathroom.

I turned onto Grace Lane and pressed on the accelerator. Within three minutes, I was in front of the gates, and I used the remote control to open them.

I drove through the moving gates and glanced at the gatehouse as I passed by. No one stepped out the door, and I continued on faster than I would normally drive up the curving gravel driveway to the guest cottage. I wasn't worried, but neither was I completely unconcerned.

I saw that Susan's Lexus was gone, and I breathed a sigh of relief. At the same time, I was angry at her for not calling to let me know she was going out, and also angry at her for going out at all, especially without her cell phone. The woman just doesn't listen.

I parked the Taurus, retrieved the shopping bags, unlocked the front door, and went inside.

Then I realized that this made no sense. I could imagine her just hopping in her car and running off on an errand, but I couldn't imagine her not having the sense to call me. I took her cell phone out of my pocket to see if I'd missed a call from her, but there was nothing on the display except the time: 6:42.

I glanced back at the umbrella stand and saw that the carbine was missing.

Then I smelled cigarette smoke.

I stood frozen, and my heart started beating quickly. I dropped the shopping bags, then took a step backwards toward the front door and started to dial 9-1-1 on the cell phone.

Anthony Bellarosa stepped out of my office and said, "Drop the fucking phone."

I stared at him. He was wearing the blue uniform of All-Safe Security, and he had my M-1 carbine in his hands—aimed at me.

"Drop the fucking phone, or you're dead."

I couldn't believe that he was actually standing there. Mancuso said he was out of town, and Mancuso also said Anthony would not do this himself. And I believed that . . . except I also believed that this was personal, and that Anthony had more on his mind than murder.

"Drop the *fucking* phone!"

He fired.

I could hear the bullet pass by my left ear and smack into the heavy oak door behind me.

He said, "If I wanted to kill you, you'd already be dead. Like my uncle. But don't *make* me kill you." He pointed the rifle at my chest and said, "Drop it."

I dropped the phone.

He cradled the rifle in his right arm and said, "Yeah, good balls, but not much brains today, John."

"Where is Susan?"

"She's okay. I was saving her for when you got home."

"Anthony—"

"Shut the fuck up." He asked me, "Are you carrying?"

I shook my head.

"Take off your jacket."

I took my jacket off, and he said, "Throw it down."

I dropped it on the floor, and he said, "Okay, strip and let's see what you got."

I didn't move, and he said, "Take your fucking clothes off, or I swear I'll blow out your kneecaps."

"Where is Susan?"

He smiled and said, "She's naked, like you're gonna be. Like we're all gonna be. Come on. Strip."

Again, I didn't move. Anthony was about fifteen feet from me, and I couldn't cover that distance before he got off a shot.

He pointed the rifle toward my legs, then fired two shots. I didn't feel anything, then I realized he'd put both rounds into one of the shopping bags and fluids were leaking onto the floor.

"That was your last fucking warning. Get your clothes off. Slow."

I took off my clothes and dropped them on the floor.

"Turn around."

I turned around.

"Okay, pretty boy. No gun, no wire. You are totally fucked. Turn around."

I turned facing him. My heart was pounding and my mouth was dry. I tried to think. What was he up to? Why wasn't I dead? Was Susan all right? Well . . . I knew the answers to all that.

He was wearing a gun and holster, and he unhooked a pair of handcuffs from his gun belt and said, "Catch," then threw them to me, but I let them hit my chest and fall to the ground.

"Put the cuffs on, asshole, or I blow your legs out from under you." He swung the barrel of the rifle toward my legs again. "Come on, John. I don't have all fucking night. You want to see Susan? Put the cuffs on, and we'll go see Susan. I *want* you to see her."

I lowered myself into a crouch and reached for the cuffs. I could possibly spring off from this position and get to him, but he knew that, so he took a step backwards as he brought the rifle up to his shoulder and aimed it at me. "Now!"

I retrieved the handcuffs and snapped them loosely on my wrists.

"Okay, you're going up the stairs on your hands and knees. Down."

I got on the floor and started crawling toward the stairs. Anthony moved behind me, and I could hear the bolt on the front door slide shut.

I made my way up the stairs on my hands and knees, and Anthony kept his distance as he followed me. He let me know, "I have the rifle pointed right at your naked butt, and my finger is twitching on the trigger."

I weighed my options, but there was nothing to weigh. I just wanted to see that Susan was alive—then I'd think about what to do.

Anthony also let me know, "Tony took your wife's Lexus. I hope you don't mind. So, you're thinking to yourself, 'How did this dumb wop get the drop on me?' Right? Is that what you're thinking, smart guy?"

The thought had crossed my mind, and I was angry at myself for being so damned stupid. But the attacker always has the advantage. His late uncle would agree with that.

"You and your wife think you're so fucking smart. Or maybe you and your stupid wife thought I wasn't coming after you, and you got sloppy."

I reached the top of the stairs, and he said, "Stay on your hands and knees and move toward your bedroom."

Anthony moved quickly past me, keeping the rifle aimed at me as he went toward the bedroom door. He stopped and watched me as I crawled down the hallway toward him.

He said, "Yeah, your dumb wife gets a call from the gatehouse, but it's Tony calling, and he says, 'I got a package for you, Mrs. Sutter. I'll bring it around when I check out the property, like your husband asked me to do.' So, you got to be careful who you talk to, John. Maybe that security guy you talked to was working for me. Right? Hey, say something. Say something smart."

"Fuck you."

"That's not so smart. I can't believe I was going to hire you. Look at you—buck naked on your hands and knees, with cuffs on, and you're crawling where I tell you to crawl. So you're really not that fucking smart. And I'm not as dumb as you thought I was—okay, stop there."

I stopped about ten feet from the bedroom door.

He continued, "Yeah, so Tony rings the bell, she looks through the peephole, sees a guy in an All-Safe uniform, then just opens the door. How fucking dumb is that? And you should've been there, John, when Tony pushes her into the house, and I walk in behind him. I mean, she just stares at me, and right away she knows who I am. And then she remembers Tony from when she was fucking my father. And I say to her, 'You killed my father, you bitch,' and I thought she was going to piss her pants. And then she goes for this rifle in the umbrella stand, and I knock her on her ass."

"You're a real man."

"Shut the *fuck* up." He said, "So you keep a rifle by the door. You expectin' trouble?" He laughed. "Does that rich bitch even know how to use a gun?" He realized that was a stupid question and said, "That bitch shot my father for no reason—"

"I *told* you the reason—"

"You're a lying asshole, but I'll get the truth out of you and her tonight." He threw open the door, stepped aside, and said, "Go see your wife."

I started to stand, but he shouted, "Hands and knees, asshole!"

I crawled through the bedroom doorway.

"Up on your knees."

I got up on my knees.

Susan was lying on the bed, naked, and it took me a moment to realize that her wrists and ankles were tied to the bedposts. Then I noticed white tape over her mouth.

She turned her head toward me, and I could see fear in her eyes. But thank God she was alive.

Anthony shut the door behind me and said, "So there she is, John. You wanted to see her, and now you and me can see *all* of her. And I see she's a real redhead."

I kept staring at Susan, and she was looking at me, tears running down her face.

I stood and took a step toward her, then I felt a blow to the middle of my back, and I fell forward onto the floor. I lay there, less stunned than I pretended to be, and I tried to judge how far he was from me.

He said, "Get up."

I could tell he'd moved away from me, so I lay motionless, hoping he'd come close enough to hit me again with the rifle butt.

Instead, he fired a round into the floor next to my face, which made me jump. He shouted, "Get up, or the next one goes up your ass!"

I lifted myself back to my knees, took a deep breath, and looked at Susan. She was pulling at her bonds, which I saw were nylon ropes, and she was crying and trying to call out. I also saw that there were red marks on her face, where he'd apparently hit her, and I saw a leather belt—one of my belts—lying on the bed.

Anthony said, "I'm going to rape your wife, and you're going to have a front-row seat."

"You're a sick bastard."

"No. I'm a nice guy. I told you, women and children get a pass. So I'm not going to kill her, but when I get through with her, she and you are gonna *wish* you were dead."

I didn't say anything, but I knew I had to make a move, even if it was a bad move. Where was the shotgun? It wasn't where I'd left it propped against the nightstand. Maybe it was in the closet.

Anthony moved around to the far side of the bed, and he put the muzzle of the rifle to Susan's head and said to me, "Crawl over to that radiator. Come on, asshole. Move it."

I knew if I went to the radiator, I'd be cuffed to the pipe, and that would end any chance I had to turn this around.

Anthony picked up the leather belt on the bed, stepped back, and brought it down hard across Susan's thighs. Her body arched, and I could hear a muffled scream through the tape.

He raised the belt again, and I shouted, "No!" I moved on my hands and knees toward the radiator under the window. I looked around the room as I crawled to the radiator and saw Susan's robe and panties on the floor, and I also saw that the two suitcases were knocked off their luggage racks, and the clothes were strewn around the carpet. Where was the shotgun?

"Kneel next to the pipe with your back to the wall. I want you where you can get a good view."

I knelt beside the radiator. He took another pair of handcuffs from his gun belt and flung them at me, hitting me in the face.

"Cuff yourself to the radiator."

I hesitated, and he said, "You're fucking with me, John. I don't want to kill you. I want you to watch. Don't fuck me up, and don't fuck yourself up."

I cuffed my left wrist to the radiator pipe and knelt, staring at him.

Anthony set the rifle on the bureau and looked at me. He said, "Okay, let the fun begin."

He walked to the foot of the bed and looked at Susan. "Well, I can see why my father liked to fuck her. Good tits, nice ass, and great legs."

Anthony had a script, a fantasy, and I knew he'd thought about this. And I hoped, too, that he really didn't intend to commit a double murder.

He lit a cigarette and said to me, "So you were going to London. What's the matter? You don't like it here? Something here scare you?"

He drew on his cigarette and said, "Just so you know what to look forward to, John—you're going to watch her give me a blow job, then I'm going to fuck her so hard she won't be good for you anymore."

When I didn't respond, he said, "And you better watch, asshole. And when this is all over, you two will shut your fucking mouths and thank God you're alive. But if you go to the cops, then I swear on my father's grave, I'll kill her, and I'll kill your kids. No free pass for them if you go to the cops. Understand?"

I nodded.

"Okay. So you understand the rules. No one has to die. You just got to live with this so every time you fuck your wife, you can both think about me. Right?"

Again, I nodded.

"Good. And you don't care, anyway. My father fucked her, I'm gonna fuck her, and maybe we'll let Tony fuck her later. Right?" He looked at me and said, "I don't hear much coming out of your wise-ass mouth now, Counselor."

He pulled the tape off Susan's mouth. "What do *you* have to say, bitch?"

She took a deep breath between her sobs and said, "Please. Just do what you want and leave us alone."

He laughed. "Yeah. I'm gonna do what I want all right."

He threw his cigarette on the rug and ground it out with his heel. He asked me, "Why'd you slash my painting, John?"

I didn't reply, and he said to Susan, "I liked that painting, and your husband here fucked it up. So you're gonna paint me another one. And when you're done, you and John are coming over to the house to give it to me and Megan. Right?"

Susan nodded. "All right."

He smiled, then looked at me. "Okay, John? You and your wife come over for coffee. Just like the old days. And you sit there, like you did ten years ago when you knew my father was fucking your wife, except this time, it's me who fucked your wife. And you won't have shit to say about it."

I nodded. It was possible, I thought, that we'd get out of this alive, and if I ever got close enough to Anthony Bellarosa to have coffee with him, then I would be close enough to put a knife in his heart.

He said, "And you're both gonna be nice to my wife, and bring over a bottle of wine, and say, 'This is a very nice house, Mrs. Bellarosa,' and 'Thank you for inviting us, Mrs. Bellarosa.'"

This was Anthony's revenge fantasy, and he'd obviously thought about this for a long time, and he was going to draw it out, to taunt us, humiliate us, and do everything he could to make sure this stayed with us long past the time he walked out the door.

And then I thought of the other painting in his den—the *Rape of the Sabine Women*. And now I understood—or had I always understood?— why it was there, and why Susan's painting was also in his den.

I realized, too, that this bastard was so sure of himself that he thought he could rape Susan and smirk about it every time he saw us. And I didn't want him to think otherwise. I said, "Just don't hurt her."

He smiled at me and said, "I'm going to make her feel *good*. Like my father did."

Susan said to him, "Please. Just do it and leave. We won't say anything."

"You're fucking right you won't say anything."

I saw Anthony glance at his watch, and I wondered if he was on a schedule, or if he was waiting for Tony to return.

He lit another cigarette and said to me, "When I'm done with your wife, I'm gonna call Tony, and when he gets here, we can have some real fun."

I didn't respond.

"Yeah. This is going to be a *very* long night. But it's better than being dead." He looked at Susan and said, "Okay, sweetheart. You waited long enough. You excited?"

Susan didn't respond.

"Come on, tell me you're excited."

"I'm excited."

He laughed, then went to Susan's bureau and took the camera that she'd put there to pack.

He ground his cigarette out on the bureau, then examined the camera. He took three shots of Susan on the bed, then a shot of me. He threw the camera on the bed and said, "Okay, we'll use up that roll tonight when Tony gets here. Hey, you don't mind if I keep the film? I'll send you copies." He looked at me and said, "If you live. And that depends on how good she is to me. And I want you both on that plane tomorrow. Understand? I want you the fuck out of here. You're gonna need a nice vacation after tonight." He unbuckled his gun belt and threw it on the bureau. He kicked off his shoes, got undressed, and dropped his clothes on the floor.

As he walked toward the bed, I could see that he was aroused. He said to Susan, "How's that look, sweetheart? You think you can take all that?"

She nodded.

I noticed that he had a pocketknife in his hand. He unclasped the knife and cut the nylon cord on Susan's left wrist, then moved around the bed and cut the other three cords.

"Okay, bitch, out of bed." He grabbed her hair and pulled her off the bed, then shoved her onto the floor. "You kneel right here where your husband can see you."

Susan knelt alongside the bed, and we made eye contact. I nodded and said to her, "It's all right."

He smiled at me and said, "Yeah? It's all right? Good. It's all right with me, too."

He put the knife under her chin and told her, "Don't try anything, or I'll kill you both. Understand?"

She nodded.

"All right . . ." He took a step closer to her and said, "Put that in your mouth."

Susan hesitated, so he grabbed her hair again and pulled her face into his groin. He glanced at me and said, "You better fucking watch this, or I'll beat her ass with that belt."

I nodded.

He said to her, "Open up. That's it . . . put it in there, bitch . . . okay . . . ooh, that's nice . . . John? Watch her suck my cock—"

All of a sudden, he let out a scream, dropped the knife, and jumped backwards.

Susan fell face first on the floor and rolled under the bed. Anthony was holding his groin, doubled over and groaning in pain, then he dropped to the floor, stuck his head under the bed skirt, and grabbed for her.

I shouted, "Anthony, you fuck! You dumb piece of shit!" I grabbed the radiator and rocked it, trying to break the connection between the radiator and the pipe, but it held. *Damn it.* "Anthony!"

As I looked up, he was standing and moving quickly to the far side of the bed, screaming, "You fucking bitch! You're dead, you fucking bitch!"

I saw Susan's head and shoulders rising above the bed, then as Anthony came at her, she stood, and slowly and deliberately raised the shotgun to her shoulder. He was less than three feet from her when he stopped dead in his tracks and said, "What the—?"

I heard a loud blast, and I saw Susan's right shoulder lurch back.

Anthony's whole body moved backwards, then he lost his footing and fell.

I saw Susan switch to the other barrel as she took a step toward him. She raised the shotgun to her shoulder again and pointed the barrels at his face.

"Susan!"

She looked at me.

"No. *Don't.*"

She looked back at Anthony, who I could see was still moving, and he raised his right arm in a protective gesture.

"Susan! Find the keys to these cuffs. Quick!"

She took another look at Anthony, then threw the shotgun on the bed and found the keys in Anthony's pants pocket.

She knelt beside me, but we didn't speak as she unlocked the cuffs. I stood quickly and went to the door and locked it. I looked at Anthony again, who was still very much alive, his hands over his chest, and his body rocking from side to side.

I took Susan in my arms. She was trembling, and I said, "Just sit here . . ." I moved her toward a chair and sat her down. "Are you all right?"

She nodded, and stared at Anthony.

I walked across the floor to Anthony and stood over him. Our eyes met. Then I looked at where he was holding both hands over the wound on the right side of his chest, and I saw blood seeping between his fingers. I'd expected to see his chest peppered with buckshot, but Susan had used the barrel with the deer slug. I looked at the wall behind where he had been standing, and I saw the bullet hole in the pale blue wallpaper.

I looked back at Anthony and again our eyes met. I said to him, "You brought this on yourself."

His lips moved and a wheezing sound came out of his mouth. I heard him whisper, "Fuck you."

"No, fuck *you.*"

I could see now that the blood coming through his fingers was mixed with red froth, meaning it was a lung wound. Not good, but he could live . . . if he got to a hospital. I noticed, too, that there was blood on his penis, which was the least of his problems.

I went back to Susan, who was still sitting, staring at Anthony. "Are you all right?"

She nodded, never taking her eyes off Anthony.

I took her robe and panties off the floor and gave them to her. I said, "I'm going to call the police."

She grabbed my arm. "No."

"Susan. He needs an ambulance."

"No! Not this time."

I looked at her, then I said, "All right . . . get dressed."

I helped her up, and she slipped on her robe, then walked toward her closet. On the way, she stopped and looked down at Anthony.

I could hear him try to say something, then Susan knelt beside him and put her head down close to him and listened. She shook her head and said to him, "No ambulance. You're going to die."

He grabbed at her, and she knocked his arm away, then stood and went into the closet.

I walked into my closet and pulled on a pair of jeans and a shirt, then I went back to Anthony and knelt beside him. His breathing was becoming more labored, and I could hear a wheezing sound coming from the hole in his chest. Also, the blood from the exit wound was soaking the carpet around him, and there was dark blood coming out of his mouth, which was not a good sign—at least not for him.

To treat a sucking chest wound you seal the entry and exit holes to keep the air in the lung from escaping, and you wrap the chest wound tightly to slow the bleeding. But did I want to do that?

Susan came out of the closet dressed in jeans and a sweatshirt. She glanced at Anthony and saw he was still breathing.

I took the roll of film out of the camera, then I gathered the carbine, the shotgun, and Anthony's gun belt with the holster and the pistol. I took Susan's arm, unlocked the door, and led her out of the room and down the stairs.

We went into the office, and I threw the weapons on the couch, then I sat her in the club chair. I went to the bar and poured each of us a brandy.

She took a long drink, and I did, too, then I sat at the desk and picked up the phone.

"John. Don't."

I ignored her and dialed 9-1-1. A female operator answered, and I said, "I want to report a home invasion, an attempted rape, and a shooting."

I gave the operator the location, then I gave her some details of the incident as police and emergency service vehicles were being dispatched.

The operator said, "About five minutes."

I told her about the iron gates that might need to be forced open, and she asked me, "Do you think there are any other perpetrators on the premises?"

I replied, "There was, but I think he's gone and waiting for a call from the assailant."

"Okay, sir, you just sit tight there with your wife, and please secure any firearms."

I thanked her and hung up. I said to Susan, "They'll be here in five minutes."

She looked at me and asked, "Will he be dead?"

"I don't know."

"I aimed for his heart. But he moved."

I had no comment on that, but I did say, "You're very brave, and very smart."

She took another sip of brandy and said, "I wasn't too smart when I opened the door."

"I probably would have done the same thing."

She didn't reply, but I saw she was looking at the shotgun on the couch.

She said to me, "We should check on him. Before the police arrive."

I thought, of course, about Frank Bellarosa, lying on the floor in Giulio's, his carotid artery spurting blood. *Stop the bleeding.* That was rule one of basic first aid. So I stopped the bleeding. He lived, and here we were, ten years later, dealing with the consequences.

Susan stood and walked toward the shotgun on the couch.

"Susan."

She looked at me and said, "Before you got here . . . he said to me—you and your husband think you're so fucking smart, so fucking above—"

"I know what he said."

"So fucking high and mighty . . . well, he said, when I get through with you, you're never going to be the same again . . . and your fucking husband is never going to look at you the same again . . . and you can live with that, bitch, the way I live with thinking about you killing my father . . ." She picked up the shotgun and said, "And he told me I might like it so much, I might want to do it with him again."

I stood and moved between her and the door. I said, "You can't do that. I won't let you."

She stared at me, the shotgun cradled in her arm, then said, "I am so sorry, John, for everything that has happened to us."

"That subject is closed."

"Are you sorry you saved Frank's life?"

I was, and I wasn't. I said to her, "I did the right thing."

"It was the *wrong* thing."

I looked at her and asked, "Did you think so at the time?"

She didn't reply for a few seconds, then said, "No. But afterwards . . . I wished you'd let him die. And now . . . we're not going to make that same mistake."

I put out my hand and said, "Give me the gun."

She pushed the shotgun toward me and said, "He threatened our children. So *you* take care of it."

I hesitated, then took the shotgun from her. We made eye contact, and she said, "Do this for Edward and Carolyn."

I'd thought about killing Anthony, and I would have without a second thought when he was a threat to us. But killing a wounded man in cold blood was not the same. And yet . . . if he lived . . . there would be an investigation, a public trial, testimony about what happened here . . . and there'd always be that threat hanging over us . . . but if he was dead . . . well, dead was dead. Dead was simple.

I took a deep breath and said, "I'll check on him."

I carried the shotgun into the foyer and up the staircase, then stopped at our bedroom door. I checked to see that the selector switch was set to the left barrel—the one that held the heavy-load buckshot, then I opened the door.

I could see him on the floor, and his chest was still heaving.

I moved closer, then I knelt beside him.

His arms were at his sides now, and the blood coming out of his wound had slowed and was no longer frothy with air.

I looked at his face, which was so white that the stubble on his cheeks looked like black paint. I felt his pulse, then his heart, which was beating very rapidly to compensate for the loss of blood pressure.

I leaned closer to him and said, "Anthony."

His eyelids fluttered.

"Anthony!" I slapped his face, and his eyes opened.

We looked at each other. His lips moved, but I couldn't hear anything except a gurgling sound.

I said to him, "When you get to hell, and you see your father, tell him how you got there, and tell him who shot you. And ask your father for the truth about him leaving his family for Susan. Anthony?" I slapped him again and said, "Can you hear me?"

His eyes still had some life in them, but I didn't know if he could hear me over the sound of the rushing in his ears, which happens when the heart is trying to pump the last of the blood through the veins and arteries.

I said loudly, "And tell your father thanks for doing me that last favor."

His eyelids fluttered again, and I knew he'd heard me.

I kept staring at him. His eyes were wide open now, and they followed my movements, and I had the thought that he might live.

Susan came into the room, and she looked at me, then at him, but she didn't say anything.

I could hear the sound of police sirens outside, and I said to her, "Go and unbolt the door for them. Quickly."

"John, you have to do it, or *I'll* do it."

"Go. I'll take care of it."

She looked again at me, then at Anthony, then turned and left.

I stared at Anthony, who was showing too many signs of life . . . and it was too late now with the police outside to fire the shotgun.

I noticed that his blood had coagulated over his wound, and it was seeping, rather than flowing freely. *Stop the bleeding . . . Start the bleeding.*

I knelt on his chest, and his eyes opened wide in terror. I stuck my index finger into his wound, pushing down as far as I could into his warm chest cavity, and when I withdrew my finger, his blood gushed up and began flowing again.

I kept my full weight on his chest, which heaved convulsively, then stopped.

I stood, went into the bathroom, washed my hands, and threw the shotgun back on the bed.

When I went downstairs, Susan was standing at the open door. In the forecourt were two police cars and uniformed officers were moving quickly toward the house.

I put my arm around her shoulder and said, "It's finished."

CHAPTER SEVENTY-ONE

The police searched and secured the premises and determined that there were no other perpetrators present.

The EMS people, who carried a stretcher upstairs, didn't carry it downstairs, and a uniformed officer told me, "He's dead." The medical examiner, when he arrived, would make that official.

The police had tagged the weapons as evidence, and the crime scene investigators were on the way to begin the slow, arduous process of turning the scene of a violent personal assault into a neat scientific project.

While this was going on, a homicide detective by the name of Steve Jones had requisitioned our home office to conduct an interview with me while Susan was taken by EMS vehicle to the sexual assault unit at North Shore University Hospital.

I wasn't happy that I hadn't been allowed to accompany Susan to the hospital, but Detective Jones explained that this was standard operating procedure, to wit: In cases involving serious felonies, witnesses are separated. Well, one size does not fit all, and even though we were witnesses, and even though Susan killed the alleged assailant, we were also obviously crime victims, so I said to Detective Jones, "We will, of course, cooperate fully, but I have to insist that I be present when you interview Mrs. Sutter." I further explained, "I am an attorney, and I am also *her* attorney." I suggested, "It might be a good idea to call Detective Nastasi in the Second Precinct, who took our original complaint about threats that the assailant made against us."

Detective Jones considered all that, then left the office to consult with his Homicide Squad supervisor and an assistant district attorney from their Homicide Unit, both of whom had recently arrived. This was, of course, a high-profile case, so Detective Jones, who, I'm certain, usually ran his own investigation, now had to share his duties and power with higher-ups who'd taken over the living room.

Bottom line on this, when a society lady kills a Mafia don—on her estate or his—the case takes on another dimension, and everyone wants in on it. I remembered this from the last time it happened.

Detective Jones returned and informed me, "Detective Nastasi is on the way." In response to my other request, he said, "We have no objection to you being present when I interview Mrs. Sutter."

"Thank you."

Detective Jones then said to me, "As an attorney, you understand that you are a witness to a homicide and possibly more than a witness, so before I take your statement, I need to read you your rights." He added, "As a formality."

I wasn't completely surprised by this, but I *was* getting annoyed. On the other hand, there was a corpse lying in my bedroom, and Detective Jones needed to be sure he was dealing with a justifiable homicide. Actually, he wasn't—I mean, Susan shooting Anthony was borderline justifiable, but me speeding up his death was called murder. I said, "Let me save you the trouble." Then, from memory, I advised myself of my rights.

Detective Jones seemed satisfied with that and didn't ask me if I understood what I just said to myself.

Before I began my statement, I told Detective Jones that the deceased perpetrator, Anthony Bellarosa by name, had identified his accomplice to me as Tony Rosini, a man who I said was known to me.

Detective Jones passed this on to another detective, then informed me, "I was one of the detectives who responded to the other Bellarosa homicide ten years ago."

I wasn't quite sure why he mentioned that, but I was still annoyed that Susan and I had been separated, so I replied, "Has it been ten years between Bellarosa murders?"

He ignored my sarcasm, and I began my statement. Detective Jones wrote it all out longhand on lined paper, though of course I could have typed it on the computer or written it myself. But this is the way it's always been done, so why introduce new technology?

I neglected to mention in my statement that I knelt on the assailant's chest and reopened his wound to make sure he died before the EMS arrived. I mean, Detective Jones didn't ask, so why should I volunteer?

All this took over an hour, and after I read my statement, I signed it, as did Detective Jones and another detective, who witnessed my signature.

I saw a police car pull into the forecourt and a uniformed officer escorted Susan to the front door. Detective Jones went to the door and accompanied Susan into the office.

We hugged, and she said, "I'm all right. They gave me some sedatives and painkillers and asked me to return tomorrow for a follow-up visit—but I think I'll see my own physician instead."

We were joined in the office by Detective Jones's supervisor, Lieutenant Kennedy, and also by an assistant district attorney, a young lady named Christine Donnelly, who reminded me of Carolyn. To help put everyone in the right frame of mind at this critical juncture in the investigation, I said, "Our daughter Carolyn is an ADA in Brooklyn."

Ms. Donnelly smiled at that news and commented, "It's not easy working for Joe Hynes, but she'll learn a lot."

There is, as I knew, an amazing fraternity of law enforcement people, and you should never miss an opportunity to tell a cop or an ADA that your favorite uncle is a cop in the South Bronx—or someplace—and that your daughter, niece, or nephew works for some attorney general somewhere—even if you have to make it up.

Anyway, it was Detective Jones's case—he'd caught the squeal, as they say—and he began by inquiring of Susan if she was feeling well and so forth.

Then he read her her rights and asked her to give a statement regarding what happened this evening. As she began, Detective Jones began writing on his lined paper.

I understood that it was best if I didn't say anything, though of course I could have advised my client if I thought she was making an incriminating statement, such as, "I told John to go back upstairs and take care of him." Then Detective Jones might inquire, "What did you mean by 'take care of him'?"

Of course, we were not officially suspects in a homicide, but someone *was* dead, so Susan and I needed to be careful of what we said.

I'd already told Susan, before the first detective arrived, to state unequivocally that she believed our lives were in danger and that was why she'd shot a man who was not actually armed at the moment she shot him. I further advised her, as her attorney, to state that the perpetrator had ignored her command to stop and put up his hands and that he lunged at her.

This was no small technicality, unfortunately, and I didn't want the grand jury to have any doubts. The reality, of course, was that Susan was aiming for his heart, then wanted to finish off Anthony with a shotgun blast to the face. I certainly understood why she'd want to do that, but I wasn't sure if the police or the district attorney would understand—especially considering her unjustifiable murder of the alleged assailant's father.

Bottom line here was that Susan Stanhope, nice lady that she was, had another side to her personality, which she'd shown ten years ago and which, I hoped, would not show itself again for a while.

As Susan related her story, Ms. Donnelly jotted a few notes and so did the Homicide Squad supervisor, Lieutenant Kennedy, but they let Susan do all the talking.

Susan reached the point in her story when Anthony Bellarosa and Tony Rosini literally dragged her up the stairs and into the bedroom, pulled off her robe and panties, and tied her to the bedposts.

I could see that Ms. Donnelly, too young to be hardened yet by stories of human depravity, was visibly upset. I thought of Carolyn and wondered what a few more years in the Brooklyn DA's office would do to her.

Susan, too, was becoming upset at this point in her story, but she took a deep breath and pushed on. She said, "Bellarosa tied me facedown on the bed, then used a belt—I think John's belt—to beat me on the buttocks . . ."

I stood and said, "I haven't heard this, and I don't need to. Please let me know when Mrs. Sutter comes to the point where I enter the bedroom."

I left the office and went outside for some air. By now, there were a half dozen police cars in the forecourt and a number of crime scene vehicles, but the ambulance was gone, and I assumed that they'd taken Anthony's body to the morgue. Well, I thought, if they didn't take too long with the autopsy, then Anthony and Uncle Sal could be waked together, maybe in the same funeral home in Brooklyn where Frank had reposed. And then—if the Brooklyn Diocese had no objections—they'd have a double funeral Mass at Santa Lucia, and a double burial in the church cemetery. Wouldn't that be ironic? Or at least convenient for friends and family. In any case, I'd skip those funerals.

A uniformed officer found me and escorted me back into the office.

Susan picked up her story by saying, "I was hoping that John figured out that something was wrong and that he'd called the police . . . but then I heard Anthony's voice in the hall and another voice, and when I realized it was John, my heart sank . . ."

I sat and listened to Susan describing from her perspective what happened in the bedroom. Her story and mine differed only in regard to what she was thinking. She stated, for instance, "As I said before, Bellarosa told me that the first thing that would happen when John got there was that he was going to make me kneel on the floor and give him . . . oral sex. So I knew I could . . . bite him and he'd be in such pain that I could roll under the bed and retrieve the shotgun that I'd put there." She let everyone know, "He made John handcuff himself to the radiator, but he didn't think *I* was a threat to him."

Well, I'll bet Anthony rethought that when Susan blew a hole through his chest.

Susan finished her statement by saying, "He said he was going to kill us, and I knew our lives were in danger. So when I retrieved the shotgun and told him to freeze and put his hands up, he yelled at me, 'You're dead, you bitch!' Then he lunged at me and grabbed for the barrel of the shotgun." She remembered to add, "I had no choice except to pull the trigger."

Detective Jones, Lieutenant Kennedy, and Ms. Donnelly glanced at one another, then Detective Jones said to Susan, "Thank you." He asked her to read her statement, which she did, then she signed it as did Detective Jones and Lieutenant Kennedy. Lieutenant Kennedy and Ms. Donnelly then excused themselves, but I stayed with Susan and Detective Jones, who asked Susan a few questions.

As Susan replied, I called her travel agent and left a message canceling our trip. Also, we weren't able to stay in our house, which had become a crime scene, as well as a place that suddenly had bad memories attached, so I called The Creek and booked us a cottage with a late arrival.

Detective Jones then excused himself, leaving us alone in the office.

I asked Susan, "How are you doing?"

She shrugged and replied, "Tired and drained. But . . . I'm feeling this post-traumatic euphoria that the nurse at the hospital said I might experience."

"I understand." I also understood that the euphoria would wear off and that both of us had some tough times ahead. But having to deal with the investigation of what happened was ironically keeping our minds off what happened.

Detective A. J. Nastasi came into the office, and we exchanged greetings. He expressed his regrets, then he said to us, "I've been assigned to assist the Homicide Squad in this case."

I nodded. It was remarkable, I thought, how quickly this case had gone from us swearing out a threat complaint against Anthony Bellarosa to homicide. But if we all really thought about it, it was inevitable that this would end with a death—though I was never sure whose death.

Detective Nastasi said, "I have some information that may interest you, if you're up to it."

We both nodded.

He informed us, "The All-Safe Security guard on duty here has disappeared, so we think he had a part-time job with Bell Security." He added, "This guard probably provided Bellarosa and Rosini with the uniforms and also kept Bellarosa—or someone close to him—informed of your movements."

I nodded. I knew this was an inside job.

Detective Nastasi continued, "Everyone assumed that Bellarosa was out of town, but we found a card key in his wallet from a motel in Queens, and the NYPD checked it out, and he's been there for the last week under an assumed name." He added, "We found a Chevy Capri parked near his house—one of about twenty cars that are leased by Bell Enterprises—and we're assuming this was the car he used this week."

I nodded again. The best place to hide is under everyone's nose. Anthony Bellarosa, as I said, was not the brightest guy on the planet, but like all predators, he could easily adapt his hunting skills to outwit people who were hunting *him*. And then, of course, he turned and became the hunter again.

Detective Nastasi further informed us, "It appears, too, that the Bell Security guard at Alhambra Estates let Bellarosa know that there was no police stakeout at his house, and Anthony drove into Alhambra Estates, parked his car a few hundred yards from his house, then we think he walked through his own property, probably with Tony Rosini, and kept going until he got here."

I recalled the aerial view of the property that I'd seen on the Web site. I'd always known this was a possibility, though I'd hoped that the perimeter security for Stanhope Hall would be in place by the time we returned from Europe. Regardless, Anthony Bellarosa would have found his way to Susan, sometime, someplace.

Detective Nastasi said, "As for Tony Rosini, we picked him up at the Bellarosa residence—he apparently has a room there in the basement—and he said he was there waiting for his boss to call for a pickup. That's all he knows." Nastasi added, "As of now, he's being held as an accessory to a number of felonies." He said to Susan, "Early tomorrow, you'll need to identify him in a lineup as the man who accompanied Anthony Bellarosa. Then we can charge him."

Susan nodded.

Detective Nastasi let us know, "The fact that the alleged perpetrator has died will make this investigation and the resolution of this case a little simpler and faster than if he'd survived."

True. Dead thugs tell no tales, and they can't make statements to the press or to the police that contradicted statements made by their victims. Most importantly, Anthony was not coming back.

Nastasi asked us, "Do you have any questions about what is happening or what will happen with this case?"

Susan asked him, "How long will you need us to be available?"

He replied, "A month or two, although that's not my decision to make."

Susan informed him, "We're getting married the second Saturday in August, then we're going on a honeymoon."

He nodded and said, "Congratulations." He added, "That shouldn't be a problem."

"No, it won't be." Lady Stanhope then inquired, "Where is my car?"

He replied, "It hasn't turned up, but I guess Rosini knows where it is. When we find it, we'll need to hold it until the crime lab is through with it."

She nodded, then asked, "When can we return to our house?"

"In a day or so."

I didn't think Susan actually wanted to return so soon, but if or when we did, we both knew it would be temporary. After we survived the media circus, and got through the criminal investigation, we would sell the guest cottage to Amir Nasim and go someplace else. Where, I didn't know—maybe we'd throw a dart at a map of the world.

Detective Nastasi broke into my thoughts and said to Susan, "I believe that the grand jury will come back with a finding of justifiable homicide. So don't worry about that." He suggested, "Find a place to stay tonight, keep in touch, and tomorrow morning we'll do that lineup." He concluded, "Detective Jones says we don't need you here any longer."

We thanked him, shook hands, and another detective escorted us to our bedroom, which was still filled with crime scene investigators. A photographer was taking pictures of the blood and of Anthony's chalk outline on the carpet.

We packed a few items in overnight bags and went back downstairs.

I was surprised to see FBI Special Agent Felix Mancuso waiting for us in the foyer, and it was an awkward moment. He first inquired of Susan how she was doing, and she replied, "I'm all right."

He got right to the point and said, "Well, I feel as though I'd misled you regarding Anthony Bellarosa's whereabouts and his intentions." He added, "I never believed he'd do this himself."

I replied, "Don't worry about it, Mr. Mancuso. We all made some educated guesses, and some of them were wrong." I added, "We appreciate what you did, and your personal interest in this matter."

"That's very kind of you." But I could see that he was still vexed, and he admitted, "I wasn't understanding Anthony Bellarosa . . . I didn't understand how driven he was by hate . . . and by this ancient concept of blood for blood." He added, "We don't see much of that anymore in our nice, civilized society, but I'm seeing it in my new job."

I could have told Felix Mancuso that the veneer of civilization was, indeed, very thin, but he knew that, and yet, like all of us, he was constantly surprised when the old Beast reared its ugly head. I said to him, "We're staying at Susan's club tonight, and we're exhausted."

"Understandably so. Let me walk you out."

We walked out to the forecourt. The night was clear and balmy, and there were a million stars overhead.

Mr. Mancuso said to Susan, "I hear from Detective Jones that you were very smart and very brave."

Susan, forgetting or ignoring what I told her about justifiable homicide, replied, "I was very stupid. He wasn't going to kill us. He said that about six times. This was not blood for blood. He wanted to humiliate us and to make our lives hell." She took a deep breath and said to him, but really to me, "I could have just let him rape me, and it would have been over. But I risked my life, and John's life, to kill him."

That, as Mr. Mancuso and I both knew, was an incriminating statement, but he liked us and he felt some responsibility for what had happened, so he said, "I'm sure you *did* believe that your life was in danger, Mrs. Sutter, and you did the right thing by shooting him."

Susan, still wanting to get this off her chest, said, "If he'd wanted to kill me for what I did to his father, I would understand that . . . an eye for an eye . . . but . . . he wanted to kill our souls, and I could not allow that."

Mr. Mancuso thought about that, then said, "I understand, but . . . well . . . maybe I would have done the same thing."

He walked us to the Taurus and said, "By the way, the medical examiner told me that Bellarosa was still alive when the EMS arrived, but before they could administer any emergency care, he died."

I exercised my right to remain silent on that subject.

Mr. Mancuso continued, "It appears . . . well, the ME said that it looked like the wound had clotted, but . . . the clot in his chest somehow broke, and he re-bled. Hemorrhaged." He looked at me and asked, "So . . . I was wondering if you'd tried to administer any first aid—as you did with Frank Bellarosa—and if perhaps you'd inadvertently caused a re-bleed?"

Mr. Mancuso, I assumed, was tipping me off that there could be some questions later regarding the medical examiner's report on the cause of death. I mentally thanked him for this and replied, "I did what I had to do." I clarified that and said, "I called 9-1-1."

So we left it there, and if Mr. Mancuso thought I'd intervened to speed up Anthony Bellarosa's death, he didn't say it. I did, however, hope that he understood it.

There didn't seem to be anything more to say on these subjects, so we all shook hands, and Susan and I got into the car and drove down the long, dark driveway.

The gatehouse was lit, and there were police cars outside the door and news vans on the street. The gates were open, and I drove through them, out of Stanhope Hall, and onto Grace Lane.

We did not return to Stanhope Hall, but spent a week in the cottage at The Creek, speaking to friends and family by phone, but not meeting with anyone. We also made ourselves available to Detective Jones for some follow-up questions. Susan had no trouble identifying Tony Rosini, whom she'd known ten years ago, and he was charged with a number of Class A felonies, including kidnapping, that would put him in prison for a period that could be measured in geological time.

Detective Jones had questioned me about the medical examiner's autopsy report—specifically, regarding if I knew how Anthony Bellarosa's wound, which had clotted so nicely, had reopened, leaving pieces of the clot around the wound and other pieces embedded deep in the wound. He said, "As if someone had shoved something into the wound."

I found that hard to believe, or even to understand, and replied, "I have no medical training—except some basic first aid in the Army—so I can't answer that question."

He didn't seem entirely satisfied with my reply, but he did say, "I think the grand jury will return a verdict of justifiable homicide."

To which I replied, "What else could they possibly conclude?"

After a week at The Creek, I booked us at Gurney's Inn in Montauk Point.

On our first night there, we walked along the beach, east toward the Montauk Point Lighthouse in the distance. There weren't many people on the beach at midnight, but a group of young people had built a driftwood fire in the sand, and a few hardy fishermen were out in the surf, casting for bluefish.

The moon was in the southwestern sky, and a wide river of moonlight illuminated the ocean and cast a silvery glow across the beach. There was a nice sea breeze skimming across the water, kicking up whitecaps and carrying with it the smell of salt air and the sound of the surf against the shore.

Susan and I held hands and walked barefoot over the white sand, not saying anything, just listening to the sea.

We climbed a small sand dune and sat facing the ocean. Out on the horizon, I could see the lights of cargo ships and tankers, looking like small cities floating on the water.

We sat there for a long time, then Susan asked me, "Are we still getting married?"

"Am I still getting my yacht?"

She smiled and said, "Of course. After our wedding, we'll sail to England with the children and clean out your flat. Then . . . we'll send Edward and Carolyn home by plane."

"Then what?"

"Can we sail around the world together?"

"We can."

"Is it dangerous?"

"Does it matter?"

"No, it doesn't."

I said to her, "It's a transformative experience."

"Good. I need to be transformed." She put her arm around me and asked, "Where do you want to live for the rest of our lives?"

"I think we'll know the place when we see it."

"You'll love Hilton Head."

I smiled and replied, "I just might." Keep your friends close, and your enemies closer. I asked her, "Will you miss New York? Stanhope Hall?"

"I suppose I will—it's part of me. But we both have good memories of where we grew up, fell in love, got married, raised our children, and . . . our life together. And when we come here to visit, we can think of ourselves as time travelers who've gone back to a wonderful time and place in our lives, and we'll make believe we're young again and that we have our whole lives ahead of us."

"Well, we *are* young, and we do have our whole lives ahead of us."

She hugged me tight and said, "It's wonderful to have you back."

I looked at the Montauk Lighthouse and remembered when I'd sailed away from here ten years ago. I had no idea where I was going, or if I was ever coming back. And it didn't matter—because in my mind, and in my heart, Susan had been with me every day at sea. I spoke to her often, and I believed, wherever she was, she knew I was thinking of her.

I showed her the world, in my mind, and we watched the stars together, weathered bad storms together, and sailed into safe harbors together—we even walked the streets of London together. She'd never really left my side for ten years, so this was not a reunion, because we had never been apart, and this voyage we were about to take would be our second together.

And if Fate had already decided that we would not return from the sea, then that was all right. Every journey has to end, and the end of the journey is always called Home.

Now voyager sail thou forth to seek and find.

—Walt Whitman

ACKNOWLEDGMENTS

As in all my novels, I've called on friends and acquaintances to assist me with technical details, professional jargon, and all the other bits and pieces of information that a novelist needs, but can't get from a book or the Internet.

First, thanks to my *very* old friend U.S. Airways Captain (retired) Thomas Block, contributing editor and columnist for many aviation magazines, and co-author with me of *Mayday*, and author of six other novels; Tom is a great researcher, and as a novelist himself, he understands what's needed to give fiction the ring of truth.

Thanks, too, to Sharon Block for her careful reading of the manuscript, her excellent suggestions, and for giving Tom a reason to get up every morning.

Once again, many thanks to my good and longtime friend, John Kennedy, deputy police commissioner, Nassau County Police Department (retired), labor arbitrator, and member of the New York State Bar. John has given me invaluable advice and information in those areas of *The Gate House* that called for knowledge of law enforcement. I took some literary license, where necessary, and any errors or omissions are mine alone.

Also in the area of the law, I'd like to thank my attorney and good friend, David Westermann, who read (pro bono) the sections of this book having to do with wills, estates, trusts, and related matters. Dave gave it to me straight, but again, I took literary license where necessary, and I made up some law for fun.

Many thanks to Daniel Barbiero, a great friend and a great sailor, who read the sections of the book pertaining to sailing, the Seawanhaka Corinthian Yacht Club, and related subjects. It was fun doing the research at the Seawanhaka bar, the Rex bar in Saigon, and all the other bars over the last half century.

Thanks, too, to John E. Hammond, historian and author of *Oyster Bay Remembered* (Maple Hill Press), for sharing with me his amazing knowledge of Long Island's Gold Coast. Once again, I need to say I exercised my novelist's right of literary license, and any errors or omissions of historical fact are mine alone.

This book truly would not have been possible without the hard work, dedication, and professional craftsmanship of my excellent and very patient assistants, Dianne Francis and Patricia Chichester. I'm going to let them write my next book.

Very special thanks to Jamie Raab, publisher of Grand Central Publishing, editor of Nelson DeMille, and a great friend. Jamie was the biggest fan of *The Gate House* long before I wrote the first word, and she's been there every step of the way. So in many ways, I share the authorship of this book (but not the royalties) with Jamie.

It's always a good idea to thank the CEO, even if you don't mean it, but in this case, my thanks are most sincere to my friend David Young, chairman and CEO of Hachette Book Group. David, like Jamie, believed in a sequel to *The Gold Coast* even when I had doubts—doubts that were dispelled with judicious quantities of single malt Scotch whisky. Cheers, David.

I'd also like to thank my mother-in-law and father-in-law, Joan and Bob Dillingham, for some insightful tips on Episcopalians as well as funerals, weddings, and related church matters; any resemblance in this book to fact is purely coincidental.

And, I have saved the best for last. Every author needs a spouse or a significant other to help prevent the common affliction of writers known as Swollen Head Syndrome, and I have been fortunate to have found such a person: my bride of less than two years, Sandra Dillingham DeMille. Sandy, in addition to editing some of my most annoying traits, is a very good manuscript editor, and also my source of information on the more subtle points of the world of the WASP. For all of this, and for giving me James Nelson DeMille, I thank you, and I love you.

The following people have made generous contributions to charities in return for having their names used for some of the characters in this novel: Diane and Barry Ganz, A. J. Nastasi, and Jake Watral, who all made contributions to the Crohn's & Colitis Foundation of America; Dan Hannon, who contributed to the Diabetes Research Institute; Roger Bahnik, Dave Corroon, and Diane Knight, who all contributed to the Boys & Girls Club of Oyster Bay–East Norwich; Stephen Jones and Matthew Miller, who made contributions to the Fanconi Anemia Research Fund; and Christine Donnelly, who, with her family, contributed to the Mollie Biggane Melanoma Foundation.

Many thanks to those caring and public-spirited men and women. I hope you've enjoyed seeing your names as characters in *The Gate House*.

And finally, I used two additional names in this book—Justin W. Green and Joseph P. Bitet—in honor of their service to the country as soldiers serving in Iraq. Welcome home.